Rebels of Gor

John Norman

OPEN ROAD

INTEGRATED MEDIA

NEW YORK

978-1-4976-4858-6

This edition published in 2014 by Open Road Integrated Media, Inc.
345 Hudson Street
New York, NY 10014
www.openroadmedia.com

Rebels of Gor

Chapter One

The Parapet

It was early, quite early.

It was damp on the parapet, and cold.

The air was thick with fog, and it was difficult to see the encampments in the distance.

I drew my cloak more closely about me.

"Do you think they will advance again?" asked Pertinax.

"Of course," I said.

"Where is Nodachi?" he asked.

"I do not know," I said.

Following the last day of the Ninth Passage Hand, Tor-tu-Gor, Light-Upon-the-Home Stone, had rested.

"The days will now grow longer," had said Lord Nishida.

"It will become more difficult to supply the holding," I had said.

"Very much so," had said Lord Nishida, looking over the parapet.

There were four of us at the wall at this time, myself, lean Lord Nishida, Nishida of Nara, who had commanded at Tarncamp, ponderous Lord Okimoto, Okimoto of Asuka, who had commanded at Shipcamp, and sandy haired Pertinax, once of Earth, student of Nodachi, swordsman. Both Lords Nishida and Okimoto were daimyos of the shogun, Lord Temmu, master of Temmu's fortress, now for several months under siege.

"I should return to the cavalry," I said.

"What there is left of it," said Pertinax, bitterly.

"Perhaps you might find safety there," said Lord Okimoto.

3

I shrugged. "It is my command," I said.

"An urt sold for a silver tarsk yesterday," said Pertinax.

"He who controls the fields controls the islands," said Lord Okimoto.

"I fear," said Lord Nishida, "we lie beneath the shadow of the iron dragon."

"No," said Lord Okimoto, "no!"

"What is this?" I asked.

"A legend," smiled Lord Nishida. "Dismiss it."

The voyage from the Alexandra to the World's End had been long and perilous, beset by trials, those of Thassa, the sea, and those of men, as well. Desertions had occurred, some in the vicinity of the farther islands, particularly Daphna and Thera; later a mutiny had occurred which, though suppressed, had cost men, a mutiny in the wake of which still lay division. Men had been lost, too, in the boarding of an ambush vessel, a bait at sea, and in resisting the attacks of its associated marauders. We had also lost several men following the first landing at the World's End, offshore from the ancestral lands of Lord Temmu. There had been three signals, trails of ascending smoke, red, yellow, and green, red betokening that the shore was held, land having been retaken, yellow that the holding of Lord Temmu still stood, and green that all was safe, and, accordingly, a landing might be effected. We learned from this that secrets had been betrayed. It was with difficulty that we had managed to extricate the remnants of the landing force from the beach. Later we had managed to attain the castle of Lord Temmu which was, indeed, still in his hands. An exploratory force was later launched against the enemy from the holding, but it had been decimated. It seemed that one could make no move of which the enemy was not well apprised. No further excursions in force had been risked against the enemy, the forces of the shogun, Lord Yamada, which had soon invested the holding, even to blockading the wharves below, denying access to the sea. Following the defeat of the exploratory force Lords Nishida and Okimoto had retained some three hundred and fifty Pani warriors, and some eleven hundred mercenaries and mariners, the latter most recruited in, or in the vicinity of, the great port, Brundisium. Lord Temmu had had at his disposal some two thousand warriors, all Pani, which were billeted within what was, in effect, a walled, mountaintop town, dominated by his castle, included here within what we speak of as the "holding." Of fighting men then, discounting the tarnsmen withdrawn into the mountains, at their camp, Lords Nishida, Okimoto, and Temmu had less than thirty-five hundred men. There were, of course, or had been, in his holding, auxiliary personnel, free women, contract women, and slaves. At the time of the debacle of the exploratory force we had had some one hundred and forty tarns in the mountains, not yet committed, with their riders and support personnel. Unfortunately this was no longer the case. Picked units of Yamada's infantry, it was conjectured of some two hundred troops each, undetected, or unreported, by scouts, approaching through four narrow passes, had surprised, and stormed, the cots and ancillary structures of Lord Temmu's tarn cavalry. Had the encampment been one of an infantry, an isolated outpost, this exploitation of the element of surprise, and the precision of the ensuing encirclement, might have resulted, for most practical purposes, in a victory merging on wholesale extermination. Pani seldom give quarter. Many heads would have been gathered. On the other hand, even from Tarncamp in the northern forests, a world away, and from various incidents on the voyage itself, I had had ample reason to respect, and fear, the intelligence of the enemy. At the World's End, these suspicions had not abated but had become darkly coercive. Perhaps one's foe is at one's elbow, uniformed identically, smiling, sharing paga, bearing a concealed knife. One recalled the ambush ship, and its lurking assailants, and the treacherous signals which had lured men ashore to the south, and the fate of the exploratory force, whose march and order, whose route, whose strength and weaponry, may have been as familiar to the enemy as to its own commanders. In any event, given an abundance of evidence which suggested spies amongst us, and ample indications of treachery, and despite the supposedly secret location of the tarn encampment hidden in the mountains, and the supposed security of posted guards, I had ordered that tarns, in shifts of forty each, be kept equipped and saddled, ready for instant flight. Accordingly, despite the undetected, and precipitous attack of Yamada's strike force, several tarns and their riders, vastly outnumbered and unable to offer an effective resistance, comprehending the hopelessness of their situation, had taken flight, making good their escape. I was not present at the time of the attack, having been summoned to the castle of Lord Temmu, that I might report on the readiness of the cavalry. Needless to say, my absence at the time of the attack, despite my having been ordered to the castle, excited speculation, and suspicion. I learned later of the nature of the attack, the silent, signaling smoke arrows coordinating the four prongs of the attack, from four passes, the following blasts of conch horns, and the rolling of drums, the streaming into the valley of armed men, the small, narrow, rectangular banners of Lord Yamada affixed to their backs, the killings, the slayings of caged birds, the burning of buildings, the taking of heads. Several of the cotted birds were freed by our own men, that they might not be killed, and these, unencumbered, might return to the wild. Any who might return to the feeding pans at dusk would presumably be killed at their feeding. Several of the readied tarns, some bearing more than one man, had eventually taken to the air successfully. Several had earlier been slain by glaives, or struck with arrows, even as they prepared to take flight. Some of the birds from the cots were hastily saddled and successfully flown. Although this had occurred weeks ago, as is common in military matters, several birds and riders, and others, were unaccounted for. We presumed the birds dead, or reverted, and the men dead, or, scattered, possibly lost, or hiding, in the mountains, attempting to evade enemy patrols and kill squads. I supposed some might have deserted. "No," had said Pertinax, who had accompanied me to the castle. "Why not?" I had asked him. "You do not know?" he had said. "No," I had said. "Because you are their captain," he had said. "I do not understand," I had said. "They do," he had said. Of the one hundred and forty tarns which we had managed to bring across Thassa to the World's End, we now had fifty one, including the two which Pertinax and I had brought to the castle weeks ago, in reporting to Lord Temmu. We retained seventy tarnsmen and twenty auxiliary personnel. The survivors, naturally, at least those aflight, had made their way to the castle. In the following days I reorganized the much reduced command. I was proud of the cavalry and it had well proven its reliability and formidableness in combat, for it had met and defeated a far larger force in the skies over the northern forests, a force intent on the destruction of Tarncamp, and, later, one supposes, Shipcamp. As a tarn force it was superbly trained and uniquely equipped for aerial combat, far more so than the usual tarn forces of known Gor, which usually consisted, in effect, of mounted infantry, spear bearing, and armed with a saddle-clearing crossbow. We used the supple temwood lance and a bow modeled on the Tuchuk saddle bow, the lance lighter and longer than the spear, exceeding its reach, and the string bow capable, of course, of firing several missiles to one of the traditional crossbow. The great peasant bow was impractical to use on tarnback. At closer quarters one might use quivas, saddle knives, or Anango darts. The large arrow quivers, saddle quivers, one on each side, could carry fifty to a hundred arrows. Tarns were unknown at the World's End and it had been anticipated that their appearance in war would, at least initially, provide the forces of Lord Temmu with a fearsome, unanticipated weapon, the very sight of which might dismay and terrify at least common soldiers, the Ashigaru contingents, commonly raised from impressed peasants. As well, of course, an aerial arm had much to offer from a number of points of view, such as raids, reconnaissance, communication, and, in limited numbers, the rapid and clandestine movement of small groups of armed men. Needless to say, Lord Temmu and his advisors were muchly disconcerted and, apparently, baffled, by the devastating raid on the tarn encampment. He had lost, in an afternoon, something like two-thirds of his aerial command. How had it been that several men, perhaps altogether some eight hundred or so, had managed, by various routes, undetected, to converge simultaneously on a supposedly secret camp? And it seemed that these men must have been especially trained, or warned, about what they would find once the battle was joined or the raid effected. Surely they had not fallen into consternation, nor had they scattered and fled at the first sight of so unfamiliar, obviously dangerous, and mighty a form of life as the tarn. Many, at their first sight of a tarn, particularly at close quarters, are unable to move, so paralyzed with fear they are. Yet these assailants had, at least on the whole, diligently addressed themselves to the destructive, murderous work for which they had obviously been well prepared. It is interesting to wonder whether or not such men might approach tarns as readily in the future. Surely some were seized, some disemboweled by raking talons, some having their heads, or an arm or leg, torn from their bodies. Had they been led to believe that the tarn was no more, I wondered, than a large, harmless feathered creature, something in the nature of a large jard or gull? It was enormous and carnivorous. Its talons were like hooks; its beak like snapping, severing sabers. Its scream could be heard in the mountains for pasangs. The beating of its wings could lash the leaves from trees. Its strike, the sun behind it, could break the back of a running kaiila. No, I thought, they would have been warned. Had they not expected something that terrible they would doubtless have recoiled at the very sight of such a creature. Had they been lied to, they might have been distraught and shocked, confronting reality, and, simple soldiers, might have rebelled, and fled. But it seemed they had not been lied to. They would have realized then that their lives were at stake. Some may have feared that they would not leave the valley alive. With desperate courage they had attacked. Then, I realized, he who had prepared them must himself have known the tarn, and known it well. Who, here, then, at the World's End, I wondered, might have imparted so dire an instruction. Perhaps Tyrtaios, I thought, the deserter.

"See this map," had said Lord Temmu. "You will relocate your camp at this place. There is game, and water. It is a hidden place, a secret place, where the remainder of the cavalry will be safe until needed."

"For most of the enemy," said Lord Nishida, "we may still hope that the very sight of a tarn may have an awesome effect, that it may terrify the ignorant, that it may excite superstitious apprehensions, that it may loosen discipline, disrupt formations, even produce rout."

"That is why," said Lord Temmu, "it is important to keep tarns hidden."

"The effect of exhibiting tarns in battle, dismaying troops, and such," I said, "would presumably be temporary."

"They will be used sparingly, at least at first," said Lord Okimoto. "One wishes them to remain, for a time, mysterious, uncanny, and frightening."

"One cannot well keep them here, in the holding, in any event," said Lord Nishida. "There is not enough food here to sustain such creatures."

"You wish me to relocate the cavalry here?" I had said, indicating the place on the map called to my attention by Lord Temmu.

"Yes," he said.

It was a convergence of two streams. One need only follow one or the other stream.

"We have lost much," I said. "We have little more than was brought from the camp, most on the readied tarns. We will need tents, supplies."

"Of course," said Lord Temmu. "Such things may be carried overland."

"What we need will be carried on tarnback, or in improvised tarn baskets," I said.

"Excellent," said Lord Temmu. "Then porters will not be aware of the camp's location."

"Or others," said Lord Okimoto, "who might follow the porters."

"When can you leave?" asked Lord Temmu.

"Tonight," I said, "under the cover of darkness."

"As the holding is invested, and it seems hazardous to risk more troops below," said Lord Nishida, "it is anticipated that food will grow short."

"We shall supply the holding, as we can," I said, "by air."

"Ichiro, your bannerman," said Lord Temmu, "is familiar with my fields. Confiscate rice, and slay any who might resist, or be unwilling."

"It is for the shogun, Lord Temmu," said Lord Okimoto.

"I fear," said Lord Nishida, "many of our fields have fallen into the hands of the forces of Lord Yamada."

"He who controls the fields, the rice, controls the islands," said Lord Okimoto.

"Here?" I said, placing my finger on the map, where the two streams converged.

"Yes," said Lord Temmu.

"We will depart at the Twentieth Ahn," I said.

"Excellent," he had said.

I would, of course, not place the camp at the position indicated. Several had been present, other than myself, and Lords Temmu, Nishida, and Okimoto, officers, high warriors, and scribes, even a reader of bones and shells. "Where all are to be trusted," had said Nodachi, the swordsman, "trust none."

Only myself, and those of the tarn command, insofar as it could be managed, would know the place of the camp, which I must soon determine. Moreover, the watches would now be kept only by members of the tarn command. I had eventually located a sheltered valley between cliffs, a place difficult to approach save by air, some one hundred and twenty pasangs north from the holding of Lord Temmu. Communication between the camp and the holding would be by tarnsmen, two or more tarns to be housed in the castle area. Those in the castle area, of those supposedly informed, would assume the camp was at the convergence of the two designated streams, at least until there was a reason to believe otherwise, perhaps in virtue of a fruitless raid, loosed upon unoccupied tents, pitched on an empty field. As one cannot trust spies, perhaps it might behoove spies not to trust others, as well.

"It is quiet," said Lord Nishida, peering over the parapet.

"We can see little," said Lord Okimoto.

Surely there had been no signal arrows from the lower posts, no torches, no cries of warning.

"The fog will soon lift," said Lord Nishida.

Several times, at night, enemies from below, dark-clad, agile night fighters, had forced pitons into the cliff, but these had been broken free during the day, by Ashigaru, lowered from the walls above. The situation of the holding of Lord Temmu, surmounting cliffs landward, almost in the clouds as seen from below, rendered siege towers impractical. Trails leading to the valley below were narrow and easily defended. On the seaward side, a single, narrow, walled trail ascended tortuously from the wharves below to the courtyard of the holding. This trail, too, now barricaded, would be easily defended. The site of the holding, atop the cliffs, over the centuries, had apparently been variously fortified and commanded. Doubtless its lines, appointments, battlements, keeps, and structures, in number and nature, over the years, had changed, had come and gone, but the mountain, with its proud, summoning escarpment, had endured. As the remote, precipitous, unapproachable crag might commend itself to the wild tarn so too would this place commend itself to tarns amongst men. Was this not a possible place of wealth, and power? From such a place might not one command, govern, and rule? Might one not find here a suitable aerie for tyranny? From such an ensconcement might one not descend with fire and sword, and to such a place might one not withdraw, with immunity, laden with treasure? In the quiet, on the parapet, in the damp, chill air, standing there in the fog, I wondered on myself. Who knows oneself? Is one not always a stranger to oneself?

"The men are hungry," said Lord Okimoto.

"The edge of hunger can be keener than the blade of a sword," said Lord Nishida.

"It is then a matter of time," said Lord Okimoto.

"Possibly," said Lord Nishida.

I looked down.

The fog was now torn into patches and, below, I could see the ditches, the breastworks, the hurdles, the stakes, and, a half pasang behind, the tents, many tents, near the ashes of what had been one of the environing villages.

It would be difficult for a sortie to reach those tents before alarms could be sounded and resistance mustered. And the distance, too, would serve well to separate the personnel of such an excursion from the shelter of their own walls, enabling their pursuit, interception, or encirclement. The bolt of lightning strikes and vanishes. It is skilled in the lore of the raid. Penned verr may be slaughtered at the discretion of the butcher. They are less skilled.

Men see land differently, the merchant in terms of profitability, the sage in terms of quietude, the poet in terms of mood, the painter in terms of beauty, the peasant in terms of home, in terms of soil, fertility, tillability, and yield. But I feared I saw it differently. I was of the scarlet caste. The military eye does not see land as others see it. It sees it in terms of what might be done, and not done, and how easily, sees it in terms of movement, columns, the marshaling of men, the arrangement of troops, the order of battle, in terms of passage, heights, time, concealment, attack, marches, and tactics. High grass, a wood, may conceal foes. If there is a marsh to the right, would the attack not be likely from the left? Has a frightened animal darted past? What has frightened it? Keep high ground on the shield side.

I looked about myself.

As song to the poet and gold to the merchant would not this place, so lofty and beautiful, with its aspects and promises, call to the ruler, the leader, the soldier, the robber, the brigand, the warrior, the slayer, the commander, the Ubar?

I thought so.

Was this not ground from which to rule?

What do men seek?

Many traps are baited with silver.

Many seek a cell, if only its bars be of gold?

The wine of riches is a heady wine.

But one knows a stronger wine, one for which many are willing to stake life itself.

What delirium of *kanda*, I wondered, can compare with the rapture of that greater drug? But who, who listens carefully, can fail to hear the dark notes of terror in its bright song, to which the unwary hasten to succumb.

Its wine is the headiest.

I heard guardsmen call the watch, that all was well.

Is the throne not, I wondered, its own prison.

Is it worth the expenditure of blood and gold?

Surely many believe so, certainly if others may be brought to pay the price.

The wine of power is a heady wine.

Men will die to clutch at a scepter.

They will pay anything to rule forever, for a moment.

The cry of the guardsman was echoed, from post to post. So all was well.

But I, I knew, though of the scarlet caste, preferred the sky, the terrain below, mountains, the wind, the surging flight of the tarn, the exhilarating rush of air tearing at the jacket, and, of course, the recreation of the tarnsman, the loot one gathers, so pleasant, the collared, chained slave, at my feet, ready, soft, whimpering, hoping to be touched.

So all was well.

Yet this place could be taken, I knew. Numbers could be overwhelming, pressing incessantly at the trails. To some commanders blood is cheap when there is much of it to be expended. Within the holding itself, mutiny or revolution might occur. Gold might buy an opened gate. Reservoirs can go dry. Larders may be exhausted. Who knows in what corridors may be heard the songs of power?

Drums do not herald the approach of treachery.

It walks on light, soft feet.

I turned away from the parapet.

"Tarl Cabot, tarnsman," said Lord Okimoto, "seems eager to return to his camp."

"I should be with my command," I said.

"You were not when the camp was struck," said Lord Okimoto.

"No," I said.

"Tarl Cabot, tarnsman, was fortunate in that respect," said Lord Nishida.

"It is so," said Lord Okimoto.

"He was summoned to the keep, by command of Lord Temmu," said Lord Nishida.

"Most fortunate," said Lord Okimoto.

"We shall supply, by tarn, what supplies we may secure," I said. "The sky is open."

"It seems," said Lord Okimoto, "that supplies are scarce, and deliveries infrequent."

"The commander," said Lord Nishida, "will do what is possible. We may expect no more."

"Of course," said Lord Okimoto.

"Fields have been lost, burned, acquired by the enemy," said Lord Nishida. "Lines are attenuated. There is occasionally the danger of arrow fire. And there are well over three thousand men in the holding."

"We will do what we can," I said.

"Our people," said Lord Okimoto, "may unsheathe ritual blades."

"Our mercenaries," said Lord Nishida, "do not know our ways nor share them."

"They may be gathered together with some pretext and fallen upon, and the matter is done within Ehn."

"All is not lost," I said.

"I fear," said Lord Nishida, "we lie within the shadow of the iron dragon."

"Let us trust not," said Lord Okimoto.

"While strength remains," I said, "we might rush forth, if only to fall beneath the blades of greater numbers."

"That would be honorable," said Lord Nishida.

"Might it not be a grander gesture to unsheathe the ritual knives, in their thousands?" asked Lord Okimoto. "That is a death for heroes, a noble death, scorning life, preferring honor. Would not rushing about, when all is hopeless, and known to be such, be undignified, even shameful, an act of desperation, contemptible, base, and disgraceful, like the bound tarsk squirming and squealing on the sacrificial altar? If our foes break into the holding and discover, to their dismay, only death and honor, we have cheated them of their victory; they will be awed and the victory will be ours. That would be a grand gesture, an act that would be retold about the fires for a thousand years."

"I trust you will be the first to use the knife," said Lord Nishida.

"Of course," said Lord Okimoto.

"I do not think all men are heroes," I said.

"Some are not," said Lord Okimoto. "They may be attended to."

"Not all agree on what is heroic," I said.

"Those who do not may be attended to," said Lord Okimoto.

"I fear our noble friend, Lord Okimoto," said Lord Nishida, "is unduly pessimistic. Perhaps he has drafted a poem or painted a screen to that effect."

"One takes comfort as one can," said Lord Okimoto.

"All may not be lost," said Lord Nishida. "I do not think the iron dragon has yet spread its wings."

"The enemy is many, and, comparatively, we are few," said Lord Okimoto. "We have lost in the field. The tarn cavalry, on which we were to rely for victory, has been discovered, surprised, and put to rout. It is little more than a third of its original strength, little more than a third of even what survived the voyage onto the homeland."

"And even more would have been lost," said Lord Nishida, "were it not for the precautions of our fellow, Tarl Cabot, tarnsman, who maintained a complement in constant readiness."

"So some might escape," said Lord Okimoto.

"And would there had been more," said Lord Nishida.

"It seems" I said, "the location of the camp was known, and we failed to detect the approach of the enemy."

"I wonder how that could be," said Lord Okimoto.

"Would you care to speak more clearly, noble lord," I said.

"Nothing speaks more clearly than steel," said Lord Okimoto.

"If you wish," I said, "we may continue this conversation so."

"It is often wise, noble friends," said Lord Nishida, "to think carefully before one speaks, particularly if one would speak with steel."

"It is so, of course," said Lord Okimoto.

"If you wish," I said, "I shall resign my command."

"The men," said Pertinax, angrily, "will follow no other!"

"Your friend, the noble Pertinax, is impetuous," said Lord Okimoto.

"I suspect," I said, "that the suspicions of Lord Okimoto, if misplaced, are well founded."

"I fear so," said Lord Nishida, "even from Tarncamp, even from Shipcamp, even from the Alexandra, even from the voyage itself."

"The march of the exploratory probe was apparently well anticipated," said Pertinax.

"The splendid officer, fearful Tyrtaios, so wise in council, so adept with the sword," said Lord Nishida, "has departed the holding, and placed his cunning and skills at the service of great Yamada."

"He could not have known the secret location of the cavalry camp," said Lord Okimoto.

"Others would know," said Pertinax.

"Such as yourself," said Lord Okimoto.

"Of course," said Pertinax.

"And your commander, to whom you seem so loyal," said Lord Okimoto.

"Yes," I said, "and others."

"The fog lessens," said Lord Nishida.

"*Ela*," said Lord Okimoto, "the commander should have sought safety earlier, his departure unnoticed in the fog. Who knows what dangers he might face, did he remain here."

"The commander's place is with the cavalry," said Lord Nishida.

"True," said Lord Okimoto.

"Yet obscurity persists," said Lord Okimoto, "soft ribbons of fog, and drifting cloud, embracing the castle."

"I shall await darkness," I said.

"But an assault might be made before dusk," said Lord Okimoto.

"I shall await darkness," I said.

"There will then be less danger of arrow fire," said Lord Okimoto.

"Following Lord Temmu," I said, "the existence of tarns is to be concealed, insofar as possible, from the enemy, at least from large numbers of its common soldiers."

"Still," said Lord Okimoto. "It is safest to depart from the holding at night."

"Undoubtedly," I said.

"There is little danger of arrow fire when one departs from the holding," said Lord Nishida. "Consider the range."

"Arrow fire," said Lord Okimoto, "need not issue from without the holding."

"True," said Lord Nishida, thoughtfully.

"Too," said Lord Okimoto, "there is the great bow."

He referred to a Pani bow generally anchored in a stout frame, and strung with a thick, oiled cord. It had an unusual range but little else. It required two men to bend it and, out of the frame, it lacked accuracy. Its rate of fire was slow. It was essentially a siege weapon. Its most effective application was to deliver fire arrows. Lord Yamada had not used it, at least as yet, in that capacity, presumably because he was interested in taking the holding, not destroying it. In its frame it resembled a light ballista.

"Lord Temmu," said Lord Nishida, "hopes to cloak the tarn with secrecy, that its appearance in battle may surprise and disconcert the enemy. Given the care with which we strive to conceal this mighty weapon, Tarl Cabot, tarnsman, is well advised to await the cover of darkness."

"If Lord Temmu wishes," I said, "I will remain within the holding. It is not I alone who could command the tarn cavalry. Others may do so, present subcommanders, Torgus and Lysander, and others, as well, any officer who survived the raid on the mountain camp."

"The men will follow only you," said Pertinax.

"Then I have failed as a commander," I said.

"What of Tajima, he of your former world?" asked Lord Nishida.

"My friend, and your spy?" I said.

"If you wish," smiled Lord Nishida.

"To command the cavalry?" I said.

"I am curious as to such a possibility," said Lord Nishida.

"Lord Temmu might appoint him to such a post," I said.

"Of course," said Lord Nishida, "but it is your assessment which is at issue."

"He is young," I said, "but a fine warrior."

"I am sure there are many such," said Lord Nishida.

"I do not think him ready for command," I said. "His judgment is not yet formed."

"I concur," said Lord Nishida.

"Perhaps in time," I said.

"Perhaps," said Lord Nishida.

"He of whom you speak," said Lord Okimoto, "is not of my command, but his skills in the *dojo*, displayed in Tarncamp, were well remarked."

"And in the field, and on tarnback, in the sky," I said.

"He is, as I recall," said Lord Okimoto, "a student of Nodachi, swordsman."

"As are others," I said.

"As our friend, the honorable Pertinax," said Lord Nishida.

"One regrets the waste of such instruction on one not of the Pani," said Lord Okimoto.

"It is true that I am unworthy," said Pertinax.

"Nodachi, swordsman, chooses his students with care," said Lord Nishida. "Who know what he sees, or senses?"

"It is my understanding," said Lord Okimoto, "that this Tajima, liaison between your command and the cavalry, was lost in the attack on the camp."

"We have had no word of him," I said.

"Some of the command, surviving the attack, escaped on tarnback, these reporting later to the castle, and some others, it is conjectured, may have scattered into the mountains," said Lord Nishida.

"It is not known that any so escaped," said Lord Okimoto.

"No," said Lord Nishida.

"The attack was doubtless executed by picked troops, intent on encirclement and extermination," said Lord Okimoto.

"One supposes so," I said.

"It is highly unlikely then that any on foot escaped," he said.

"I do not know," I said. I feared his assessment was well founded.

"How could there have been so little warning?" asked Lord Okimoto. "How could the camp have been so effectively surprised?"

"I do not know," I said.

"Pickets, patrols, guards, outposts, must have been recalled," said Lord Okimoto.

"Who would have such authority?" I asked.

"You, for one," said Lord Okimoto.

"Yes," I said, "I could have done so."

"There are others," said Lord Nishida. "The loyalty of Tarl Cabot, tarnsman, is not in question."

"Is it not?" asked Lord Okimoto.

"Let everything be in question," I said.

"Not everything," said Lord Okimoto.

"Everything," I said.

"It is regrettable," said Lord Okimoto, "that the liaison, Tajima, of whom you speak so highly, is amongst those lost."

"Amongst those as yet unaccounted for," I said.

"His account of the attack might be informative," said Lord Okimoto.

"I am sure it would be," I said.

"I would like to hear it," said Lord Okimoto.

"As would I," I said.

"But I fear none survived, who did not make their escape by tarn," said Lord Okimoto.

"Perhaps," I said. "I do not know."

"It is thought some may have escaped," said Lord Nishida.

"They will die in the mountains or be hunted down and killed," said Lord Okimoto.

"I fear so," I said.

The patrols and kill squads of Lord Yamada were said to be both efficient and zealous, as they wished to retain their heads.

"Lord Nishida," I said.

"Yes, Tarl Cabot, tarnsman?" said Lord Nishida.

"The holding is well invested," I said. "Lord Yamada must have the majority of his land forces, thousands, committed to the siege."

"It is possible," said Lord Nishida.

"Thus," I said, "his holdings, his forts, his capital itself, must be little more than policed, held by token forces, sufficient to do little more than quell dissension or unrest."

"Shogun Yamada has little to fear of such things, as he rules soilsmen, fishermen, craftsmen, buyers and sellers, wary subordinates, even daimyos, with the rod of terror," said Lord Nishida.

"Holdings, forts, may burn," I said.

"The cavalry is not to be committed without orders from Lord Temmu," said Lord Okimoto.

"Let orders be issued," I said.

"To what end?" inquired Lord Okimoto.

"Lord Temmu sought a major engagement whose outcome might turn on the appearance of tarns," I said.

"It is true," said Lord Nishida.

"But he now lacks the men for a major engagement."

"*Ela*," said Lord Nishida, "it is true."

"Surely he understands this," I said.

"Doubtless," said Lord Nishida.

"Then other things must be done," I said.

"True," said Lord Nishida.

"For what is he waiting?"

"Perhaps he meditates," said Lord Nishida. "Perhaps he hesitates, attempting to interpret the wisdoms of bones and shells."

"There is little time to devote to such matters," I said.

"The commander is impatient," said Lord Okimoto.

"I would have an audience with the shogun," I said.

"Given the matter of the camp of tarns," said Lord Okimoto, "the unconscionable losses to the cavalry there, I do not think that would be wise."

"I see," I said.

"Lord Temmu was not pleased," said Lord Nishida.

"Speak then for me, or for the holding, or for the war, or for yourselves," I said.

"Lord Temmu sees no one now," said Lord Nishida.

"Why is that?" I asked.

"One does not question the shogun," said Lord Nishida.

"He is well?" I asked.

"It is thought so," said Lord Nishida.

"He is sequestered?" I said.

"The gates of the castle are closed," said Lord Nishida.

"We must act," I said.

"Do not be impatient," said Lord Okimoto. "The falling leaf descends, completing its journey at its own pace."

"Something must be done," I said.

"Water flows as it wishes, taking what course it wills," said Lord Okimoto.

"It is so," said Lord Nishida.

"Rations diminish," I said. "Time grows short."

"Do not question the way of the wind," said Lord Okimoto.

"Winds change," I said.

"One must obey the wind," said Lord Okimoto. "It cannot be commanded. It must be obeyed."

"One obeys the wind, in such a way as to make use of it," I said.

"Perhaps the commander proposes the first of a series of lesser engagements, compounding ever greater dismay and terror," said Lord Okimoto.

"The emotive impact of the tarn on battle must, of necessity, be brief," I said. "Its appearance, by itself, is unlikely to rout an enemy more than once or twice. It is not a weapon like an armored tharlarion whose charge might shatter walls. It will soon be understood the tarn is a large, and dangerous, but wholly mortal creature. The enemy will soon learn that glaives can cut its body and arrows penetrate its breast, that it can bleed and die."

"Perhaps the commander wishes us to put starving men, unsupported, into the field," said Lord Okimoto.

"If we attack behind the lines of Lord Yamada," I said, "if we threaten treasured assets, palaces and warehouses, and cut the lines of his supply, the siege, if not lifted, might be imperiled. It is common to place the security of what one owns above the prospects of adding to what one owns. Let him hurry back to defend his homeland. Too, even for a shogun of the power of Lord Yamada, it is demanding and expensive to maintain large numbers of men in the field, to supply and support them, and impractical, if not hazardous, to attempt to do so without sufficient resources."

"It is true the weapon of hunger has two edges," said Lord Nishida.

"The commander thinks of raids," said Lord Okimoto.

"Yes," I said.

"It would be premature to reveal the tarn," said Lord Okimoto. "The element of surprise would be precluded."

"Little might be clearly seen, or understood," I said. "Who knows how fire could fall from the sky? Let there be a rush of air, an uncanny cry, and a roof is burning. How are such things to be understood? Might not mysteries be suspected, might not fears flourish, might not superstitions be engaged?"

"I find it difficult to believe that you would suggest so fanciful and unrealistic an action," said Lord Okimoto, "one destitute of the prospects of success and so careless of Lord Temmu's strategic design, to cloak the tarn until its application is opportune."

"Eventually the situation here will become hopeless," I said.

"It already grows hopeless," said Lord Okimoto, "as the cavalry seems unable to supply the holding."

"Fields are few and distant, and many are held by archers and Ashigaru of Lord Yamada," said Lord Nishida. "Tarl Cabot, tarnsman, does what he can."

"He may have made contact with the enemy," said Lord Okimoto.

"And so might have others," said Lord Nishida, "from as long ago as Brundisium and the forests."

"It is at least within our power to die honorably," said Lord Okimoto.

"You think of ritual knives?" said Lord Nishida.

"Of course," said Lord Okimoto.

"Better they repose in the lacquered case," said Lord Nishida.

"One may, of course, postpone the inevitable," said Lord Okimoto.

"Perhaps," said Lord Nishida, "we should permit the commander to retire to his quarters, to rest, for he returns at nightfall to his camp."

"In your camp," said Lord Okimoto, "it is said the men are well fed."

"We have enough," I said.

"Excellent," said Lord Okimoto.

"Perhaps you would care to join us?" I said.

"My place is here," said Lord Okimoto.

"So be it," I said.

"Is your camp pleasant?" he asked.

"It is simple, and sufficient for our purposes," I said.

"You have slaves to serve and content your men?"

"There are no slaves at the camp," I said.

"They were carried away, earlier, by the raiders," said Lord Okimoto.

"Apparently," I said.

"Regrettable," said Lord Okimoto.

No bodies of slaves had been found, following the raid. This, of course, was not unusual. Slaves, having value, as other domestic animals, had little to fear in such altercations. Their fate, as that of other domestic animals, would not be slaughter, but merely a change of masters, a change of owners. It might be quite otherwise with free women. To be sure, they might strip themselves and throw themselves to the feet of conquerors, desperately, piteously licking and kissing the bootlike sandals, begging the collar. If they were found of interest, they might be spared, spared for the collar for which they had begged. Some free women, usually of high caste, if found too plain for a slave, might, to their humiliation, be kept for ransom. Some free women, too, might proclaim themselves slave, following which proclamation they would be slaves. A free woman can freely pronounce herself a slave but, following such a pronouncement, which she, then a slave, is incapable of rescinding, she is a slave, helplessly and fully.

"There were few slaves in the original camp," I said. "Most were housed, as perhaps you know, for safekeeping, in the holding."

"I see," said Lord Okimoto.

My Cecily, for example, had been kept within the walls of the holding, in a slave shed. So, too, had been the Jane of Pertinax. Cecily, the former Virginia Cecily Jean Pym, an aristocratic English brunette, had been mine since her acquisition on a pleasure cylinder associated with a steel world, formerly that of a Kur called "Agamemnon," for the phonetic convenience of humans, claimedly the "Eleventh Face of the Nameless One," now the steel world of Arcesilaus, as we speak of him, claimedly the Twelfth Face of the Nameless One. Pertinax's Jane, whom I had purchased for him in Tarncamp, that he might learn the uncompromising mastery of women, and the rewards and pleasures attendant thereupon, was Gorean, the former Lady Portia Lia Serisia of Sun Towers, of Ar. She had been given an Earth-girl name that she might better realize, and quickly, that she was now nothing, only a man's slave. Pertinax's Earth-name was Gregory White, to which name he was still entitled, if he wished, as he was a free man. He had come to Gor as the timid, docile, pathetically enamored subordinate of an aggressive, ambitious, petty, vain, clever, young blonde woman named Margaret Wentworth. She, arrogant, greedy, and unscrupulous, fond of the perquisites often associated with business and finance, had been a valuable and successful asset to a large investment firm, in the service of which she was expected to use her considerable charms to solicit, acquire, influence, and manipulate male clients. She, dazzled by the prospect of considerable wealth, easily and securely acquired, had agreed to act in the interests of certain unspecified forces. Miss Wentworth, and her subordinate, Gregory White, both English speakers, were brought to Gor and trained in the language and customs of Gor. They were to serve as a link, or liaison, between myself and mysterious parties, deep within the northern forests. They were to make contact with me following my disembarkation on a designated beach north of the Alexandra, and see that I reached a rendezvous deep within the bordering northern forest, where I would be met, for some purpose unknown to them. As it turned out I was to be enlisted in the service of Pani warriors, to equip and train a tarn cavalry, for eventual deployment at the World's End. I knew little of what lay behind these matters. It seemed likely, however, given the mysterious appearance of Pani in the northern forests, and the work on a great ship, so far from civilization, a ship which might be capable of crossing Thassa, that this business would have to do, somehow, with Kurii, or Priest-Kings, or both. In any event, Miss Wentworth, expecting riches, discovered in Tarncamp that she had been perhaps less successful in her attempts to delude, manipulate, and exploit men on Earth than she had supposed. It seems her games, pretenses, deceits, and machinations had been more transparent than she realized. Perhaps she had annoyed, irritated, or merely amused certain powerful men, Gorean slavers or those associated with them. Perhaps some thought she might look less well in a brief, black cocktail dress with pearls, with a drink in hand, than in a rep-cloth slave tunic and collar, bearing drink to a master. What might she look like, being vended naked on a Gorean slave block? However it had come about, she had been, unbeknownst to herself, even whilst on Earth, selected for Gorean slavery. In a sense she was then a slave, though she was herself unaware of her new status and condition. It had been decided for her, by masters. Indeed, it seemed that she, blond-haired and blue-eyed, features rare in the Pani islands, might have been used to fill a special order. In any event, she, originally owned by Lord Nishida, had been given as a gift to the shogun, Lord Temmu. Female slaves, while commonly less expensive than kaiila, and many times less expensive than tarns, are surely amongst the most lovely of gifts. She was now "Saru," named for a small, scampering, largely arboreal bipedalian creature found in the jungles of the Ua basin. I had seen little of her, or of other slaves, of late. I supposed they were kept largely indoors, where they would be in little danger, should a storming take place, or an occasional stone or looping arrow fall into the courtyard space between the walls, and the buildings and the castle itself. When we had arrived at the holding, at the wharves below, we had had some two hundred slaves aboard. Before the defeat of the exploratory force, and the investment of the holding, this number had been reduced, by selling and distribution, to some one hundred and fifty slaves. Several had been given to independent, uncommitted daimyos, in the hope of generating good will, if not a good will of alliance then one of neutrality.

"I trust your journey will be a safe one," said Lord Okimoto.

"I trust so," I said.

"I do not expect to see you again," he said.

"In war there are many unknowns," I said.

"In deceit, betrayal, intrigue, and treachery, as well," said Lord Okimoto.

"It is so," I said, bowing.

Lord Okimoto returned this gesture of respect.

"The commander clearly understands, I trust," said Lord Okimoto, "the cavalry is not to be committed, or engaged, without direct orders from Lord Temmu."

"Of what use is a lance left forever in its rack," I said, "or a sword which fears to leave its sheath?"

"The lance is to remain in its rack until grasped," said Lord Okimoto, "and the sword is to be drawn only by the proper hand."

"Of course," I said.

But who is to grasp the lance, I wondered, and whose would be a proper hand. Obedience is a common path to victory; but it may lead as well to defeat.

"In flight, even in darkness," said Lord Okimoto, "be careful of the course you set."

"There may be someone in the holding," said Lord Nishida, "who would mark such things."

"I understand," I said.

Did they really think, I wondered, that I, or others, tarnsmen, would set a flight line directly to a camp allegedly secret, a line which, well marked, might be followed by seekers, or hunters, on foot? I had ordered my men, in leaving the castle, to choose randomly amongst pieces of silk, each inscribed with subdivisions of four of the eight major divisions of the Gorean compass, and follow that line until it was safe to approach the camp. One of these lines, of course, was the actual line to the camp. It would not do, of course, to systematically avoid the correct line, for what practice might more explicitly call attention to that line? I had every reason to suspect that the intelligence of the enemy was considerable, and acute. As indicated earlier, I had not located the camp at the designated position on Lord Temmu's map, as ordered, but at a different location, known only to myself and the members of my command. Also, as noted, those set to guard the camp, watch passes in its vicinity, and such, were now drawn exclusively from the command itself.

"I wish you well," said Lord Nishida.

"I wish you well," I said.

We exchanged bows, I bowing first, and then I left the parapet.

Chapter Two

I Visit a Field;
The Night Is Dark;
I Must Be Otherwise Engaged

It was cold when I departed the holding.

Pertinax remained behind, that the camp might be contacted in case of need. We kept one or two couriers at the holding.

The dark clouds of early winter obscured the moons.

When I ascended the mounting ladder, I heard a voice cry out, "Traitor!" It had come from the darkness. I buckled the safety strap, and snapped the reins, and my mount leapt from the wall, spread its vast wings, and, after soaring a few Ihn, struck against the air and surged upward.

"Traitor" had been the cry.

I doubted that my absence from the camp at the time of the raid had been an accident. I doubted that I had been withdrawn by design by Lord Temmu. It seemed likely to me that, rather, my presence at the holding had been awaited, that the attack might be made. I did not think, however, that much would have proceeded differently even had I been at the camp. The guard personnel had been instituted as an independent command, that the training and readiness of the cavalry not be compromised. This was essentially a sound military decision as the cavalry's mission would not be well served by, and might be jeopardized by, devoting a large complement of its strength to its own protection. But, as it had turned out, the soundness of this military decision had been predicated on assumptions which did not include

27

treachery, apparently in high places. The pickets, outpost guards, sentries, and such, had been withdrawn, allegedly on the orders of Lord Temmu, which orders, apparently, had been fabricated, but had appeared authentic, given appropriate seals, and a knowledge of passwords, of signals and countersignals. The guard personnel were then relieved, and ordered back to the holding, to assist in its defense, as an attack was allegedly imminent, small, reduced units of Pani then taking their place. The new Pani, as it turned out, were cohorts of Lord Yamada, and served as scouts and guides for the converging raiders. Perhaps if I had been at the camp things might have been different, but it is difficult to tell about such things. As the guard personnel were not housed in the camp itself, and were not under our command, the transition had not been realized until it was too late. At the new camp, as suggested, I had instituted different arrangements. In particular, guard personnel were now drawn from the cavalry itself, despite this depletion of ready personnel. Beyond this, when not at their posts they were housed in the camp itself, where most men now knew one another. There would be no reliefs by strangers. Lastly, they were given to understand that their report lines were now internal to the cavalry itself. In problematical situations, they were not to act, if at all possible, without an explicit authorization administered through recognized officers in the cavalry's chain of command. I remained bitter, of course, for I had not been there. Though I doubted that my presence would have much affected the outcome, if at all, I should have been there! It was my command! But I had not been there! And then I wondered on that. Had it been feared, had I been at the camp, that the attacks might somehow have been anticipated, and foiled? I did not know. It was hard to say. I supposed not. Yet they had awaited my absence. Perhaps, I wondered, that had less to do with military considerations, for I would not have been likely, under the circumstances, to do much to alter an outcome there unless by some happy accident, than political considerations. I ranked high amongst the mercenaries, and certainly, as least as I understood it, in the cavalry, regarded as so crucial to the strategic intentions of the shogun. If doubt could be cast on my loyalty who might trust who? A suspicion of betrayal in high places, particularly amongst one's commanders, can shake and divide units, destroy confidence, undermine morale, threaten discipline, and induce timidity and hesitation. With what will can one obey, and with what heart can one fight, when one fears the enemy is not before you, but behind you?

Abruptly, angrily, I turned the tarn toward the former camp. It was there the columns of raiders had emerged from the passes. I had not been there. I had learned of the raid only from survivors.

The tarn sped on through the night. I felt a bit of snow.

I would scout the old camp.

There would not be much to see now, burned wood, ashes, perhaps rusted weaponry, perhaps bones, scoured by jards and urts.

I would not stay long.

I assumed that the patrols and kill squads of Lord Yamada would be in the vicinity. Lord Okimoto, as I recall, had said they would be about, in the mountains, hunting for survivors, those who might have escaped on foot. And surely some might linger in the vicinity of the camp. Might not some survivors, lost, miserable, desperate, cold, and starving, return, searching for food, perhaps hoping to be rescued?

I should have been there.

Occasionally the clouds parted, and I could see rocks, and mountains, below. Narrow valleys, here and there, were like black wounds.

I would not stay long in the old camp.

I conjectured it was no more than ten or twelve Ehn away.

I looked down, suddenly.

It was tiny and far below, little more than a flicker amongst rocks.

I took it to be the campfire of a Yamada patrol.

It would be visible only from the air.

A light snow continued to fall. In the morning, it would be dangerous for fugitives to move. May a track in the snow not be a long, lingering arrow, one pointing to its unseen target?

I must now be near the first encampment, that decimated weeks ago by the forces of Lord Yamada.

I should have been there at the time of the attack.

I had been at the holding, idle, waiting, doing nothing!

I cried out with rage, startling the bird, which swerved to the left, and lost a beat of the great wings.

"Steady, be steady, friend," I called to him, chagrined, soothingly.

Again the mighty appendages found their beat, and the bird again sped, with no altered signal from the straps, on the course I had set.

Why should I return to the first camp, I asked myself. To reconnoiter, to open wounds I had not borne, or to die?

I had not been at the camp when it had fallen.

Cry out to the hills, fool, I thought, when you are alone. Howl your misery and weep your tears of rage when none are about to hear, when none are about to see. The stone is hard and does not weep; the sword is silent, and speaks only to flesh, and then briefly, swiftly.

How unworthy I was of the scarlet!

The night continued to be muchly dark, but now and again, as occasionally before, the wind tore away patches of cloud, suddenly, and the mountainous terrain below would spring into view.

Only one moon was now in the sky, the largest of Gor's three moons, her yellow moon.

The guide straps were cold in my hands. They are usually supple, like binding fiber, but now they were stiff and pulled like wire. The strap ring with its smaller rings was cold, as well. I lifted my hands, the straps wound about them, to my mouth and blew on them. With the leather of the straps I wiped snow from my eyes. Beneath the jacket I wore a shirt, woven from the wool of the bounding hurt, and beneath the helmet a drawn cap of the same material. I wore tarnboots and leggings of leather. The small buckler was on the saddle to the left. A lance of temwood was in its open boot, to the right. The saddle bow was in its case behind me, and the two quivers, one on each side of the saddle, were closed against precipitation. Saddle knives were in place, and, behind the saddle, one on each side of the small pack, was an Anango dart. Although the saddle knives are balanced for throwing, most of my men preferred the darts. The points of the darts were clear of poison. One leaves poison to the ost, and the striking pins and daggers of free women. That is one reason many warriors require a captured free woman to strip herself, lest they run afoul of concealed devices, a scratch from which might prove fatal. Sometimes the captor inquires politely if the woman's garments contain such devices. If she replies affirmatively she is asked to remove the devices and place them before the captor before stripping herself. If she should fail to surrender any such device she is slain instantly. If she responds negatively, and is found to have lied, such a device being found, she is also slain instantly. Once stripped and weaponless she is assessed, to see if she might be of interest, as such women may be of interest to men, as they should be, as a slave. If she is found of interest, the matter is routinely and summarily accomplished; she is enslaved. If she is not found of interest, she is commonly driven away, naked, and shamed, or, sometimes, held for ransom, naked on a chain. In most cities it is a capital offense for a slave to touch a weapon.

Ho, I thought. What is this? Yes! The beat changes. Now we soar! The bird descends, without instruction. He knows the place. He remembers it, and better than I, in the cold, and darkness. It is so much more familiar to him than his new quarters. He expects to find his cot, warm, dry straw, and raw tabuk on its hook. No, poor fellow, I thought. Such things are gone. Neither of us were here when the Ashigaru of Yamada, with glaives and torches, streamed forth from the mountains. How many, I wondered, might you, in your indignation, have clasped in your talons and torn with your beak, before burned, and struck, you would have foundered, and screamed, and looked one last time at the sky? And I was not here either, dear fellow. I was away, far away, my blade sleeping in its sheath. I was unworthy of my command, for I had survived it.

My heels hit the stirrups as the bird alit.

I looked about, from the saddle.

The ground was covered with a soft snow, which was still, gently, falling.

I had survived my command.

Lord Nishida and Lord Okimoto might have considered ritual knives. On continental Gor routed generals, fugitives about, enemy standards advancing, might cast themselves on their sword.

I descended from the saddle.

I was reasonably confident that I would find, somewhere about the camp, somewhere in the snow and darkness, probably at its periphery, a contingent of the men of great Yamada, Shogun of the Islands. They would be posted here to guard the desolate encampment, to report lest it be reoccupied, to intercept and deal with possible survivors from the attack, perhaps to provide a shelter and retreat, a headquarters, for the patrols and kill squads before they set again about their work. Then, again, I might be alone. I saw no sign; I heard no sound.

The snow continued to fall.

Here, I thought, in a belated moment of honor, I might prolong the battle, and allow the enemy a fit completion of his endeavor. If I had not fought here, at the proper time, I might fall here, at a time of my choosing.

It would be poor atonement, but might it not do?

I lifted my head and stood in the falling snow.

It seemed, for a moment, I heard the cries of rushing men, the clash of blades, the screams of tarns.

"Ho!" I cried. "Tal, Noble Foes! I greet you! I am Tarl Cabot, commander of the cavalry of Lord Temmu. Did you seek me? Have you forgotten me? Behold! I am here! I greet you! I await you!"

There was only silence.

A wind thrust clouds to the west, and the landscape lay a pale yellow about me.

I could sense the tarn behind me, some feet to my right.

The snow no longer fell, but its feel remained in the air.

The sheds and tents had been before me, and there, to the left, the cots, beyond them.

It seemed I could see the fires, the smoke rising.

It was quiet now, and the ashes, the charred planks and blackened poles, would lie beneath the coating of snow.

I did not understand the business of the ritual knife. I did not understand the casting of oneself upon one's sword.

Perhaps that was because I was unworthy.

Once, long ago, in the delta of the Vosk, I had betrayed my codes.

I did understand facing a foe, a weapon drawn. I suppose there are various honors, as there are various men. Yet that each has an honor seemed to me significant. Those without an honor I found it difficult to comprehend. Yet perhaps they were the wisest, or most clever. The urt often survives where the larl perishes. And yet I did not think the urt the better for this. It remains an urt.

Death need not be a defeat; to die well is the final victory.

"Ho!" I cried to the night. "I am here! Greet me!"

It would be doubtless unpleasant to return to one's city, routed and defeated, clad in ashes and rags, to face its councils, to be denied bread, fire, and salt, but better, I thought, that than flight, or falling upon one's sword, for then one might return to war. Life, I thought, sometimes requires a greater courage than death. Different men, different honors. Let each choose his own, or be chosen by his own.

I remembered the parapet.

When things are done, I thought, how might one better sell one's life than splendidly, gallantly, amidst ringing steel?

It is not the worst of deaths to perish in sweat and blood, a sword in one's hand.

But different men, different honors.

"Tal!" I cried. "I am alone. I serve Lord Temmu. Are you not here?"

I was not needed. I had formed and trained the cavalry, and commanded it in the northern forests. Others might command it, Torgus, Lysander, even young Tajima.

"I am here!" I called. "Greet me!"

Where, I asked myself, are they? Surely there would be several here, the Ashigaru and officers, warriors of the two swords, to guard the place, to watch for others, to dispatch the patrols and kill squads.

But there was silence.

The tarn stirred behind me, closer now, still to my right.

No, I thought, they are not here; they are hunting.

"It seems I must come again!" I called to the night.

What would they be hunting? Men, of course. Might any be left, weeks after the attack? Could any have survived, in the mountains, and cold?

Fool, I thought, fool!

I recalled the tiny flicker of light I had seen in my flight. It could have been the camp of a patrol or kill squad, but it seemed a tiny fire, not that serving several men, contented, sure of themselves, with rice boiling in the helmet. It had been positioned such that it could be seen only from the air.

I had failed to think clearly. Sick with grief, and pain, and misery, disturbed and distracted, I had hoped for little more than the self-indulgent gratification of a meaningless sacrifice. I was unworthy of the scarlet, I had betrayed my responsibilities and the remnants of my command. Was this not a treason compared to which my lapse in the marshes was meaningless? I was still the commander of the tarn cavalry, however torn and depleted it might be. There lay my duty, which, for the sake of a childish vanity, I had been on the point of forswearing. One of my men, perhaps more, had need of me. He, or they, had lit their tiny signal, and I, in the madness of my rage and shame, had failed to understand, and respond.

I suddenly became aware of dark shapes about me.

The tarn scratched at the snowy earth with talons.

"Up!" I cried, leaping to the mounting ladder, which swung beside the saddle, and the tarn screamed, and its mighty wings smote the air, and it ascended, I clinging to the mounting ladder. In a few moments I had attained the saddle, and buckled the safety strap. In the moonlight below I could see several figures, peering upward.

I could not concern myself with them.

I was once again Tarl Cabot, an officer, the commander of the tarn cavalry of Lord Temmu.

I could not concern myself with them.

I was otherwise engaged.

Chapter Three

In the Vicinity of a Small Fire

It was merely Ehn later when the tarn, responding to the straps, wings beating, hovering, descending, struck into the snow yards from the tiny fire, concealed amongst the rocks.

I did not descend from the saddle.

The small fire could have been lit by Yamada Ashigaru, to lure in rescuers.

No one was near the fire.

This bespoke wisdom, whether of an enemy or friend. Let others be illuminated in that tiny light, if they were so unwary. Darkness is the friend of assassins, of arrows springing from the night, and it may form the shield and shelter of the fugitive who might, upon the arrival of unwelcome intruders, slip away unseen.

Any, however, of those contingents of Lord Yamada likely to be in the mountains, his patrols and kill squads, would know of tarns, from the raid on the first encampment or reports of the raid, and they, marking the descent of a tarn and its rider, would know that an enemy was in their midst.

"Swords of Temmu," I called, softly, from the saddle. That had been the sign at the time of the raid on the first encampment. It had obviously been available to the raiders.

I awaited the countersign.

But there was but silence, and darkness.

My hand went to the one-strap.

As the fire had been tended, someone was about.

I was not anxious to remain in this place. Some might have

seen the tarn descend, black, brief, swift, against the yellow moon.

My hand tightened on the one-strap.

If there was someone there, in the darkness, I thought, he might be well aware that signs and countersigns had been compromised. How else might the raid on the encampment been as deftly managed? An awareness of the signs would have been initially important, as much so, I supposed, as forged commands, bearing fraudulent seals.

But I had arrived on tarnback, and tarns were alien to the islands, and thus it must be clear I was of the forces of Lord Temmu.

But there were clearly traitors within the command of Lord Temmu. Might there not then be traitors within the tarn cavalry itself?

I dismounted.

It seemed clear to me I had given enemies time to attack, or emerge from hiding, intent upon a kill or capture, of a bird or rider, or both.

"I am of the command of Lord Temmu," I called, softly. "I know you are about. How many are there?"

There was only silence.

I saw the tarn uneasily orient itself. It is much the same with many wild creatures, certainly the sleen and larl. I was then confident of the location of at least one person, and it seemed unlikely there would be more. It was unlikely that groups would have escaped, more likely single persons, if they, in the fighting and confusion.

"You must be hungry, and cold," I said. "I have some food in the saddle packs. Are you alone?"

I walked about the fire. I stayed rather outside its ambiance. Even though it was tiny, one does not peer over a fire, but keeps it behind one. In this way, one is not well illuminated, and, if the fire is large, one is unlikely to be dazzled; let others look into the fire, and strain to see. But it is safest to be in the darkness.

I remained to the side.

I did not remove the blade from the sheath.

It is not wise to draw a weapon when one may be beneath the point of an arrow.

I drew the tarn with its rigid, stalking steps about the fire. It did not resist. Might it know what was in the darkness?

In the cavalry we had often changed mounts. Riders have their favorites, and perhaps, too, the mighty, winged creatures themselves, but it is important that the birds accept different riders. Birds might be slain, and riders separated from their accustomed mounts. Without training a tarn may reject an unfamiliar rider, a rejection often registered by means of a slashing beak and tearing talons.

My foot snapped a branch, and my hand, without my thinking, sped my sword half from its sheath.

I strained to see deeper into the darkness.

Dried branches, dried leaves, and twigs, are sometimes scattered about the periphery of a camp, or sleeping area. Strung cords with their dangling slivers of metal tend to be less favored; they may stir in the wind, like prayer chimes in a temple, which signals a human presence, past or present, and perhaps a camp's periphery. I saw little advantage in them, save to lure in intruders, which might then, after attacking empty bed rolls, be fallen upon. But bandits who know their trade would seldom attack an unscouted camp.

The tarn moved beyond me, and put down its head, and, at the same time, the yellow moon broke through the clouds, and I saw branches about, heaped, from which the fire might have been fed, and a supine figure, crumpled against the rocks.

The branch on which I had stepped was isolated; it was no prepared device of warning, a signal meaningful to one who might be alert, even in sleep, to that particular tiny sound. It had merely been to the side, perhaps stirred, even dropped.

Behind me the fire grew dim.

I did not think it would burn much longer.

The body lay very still.

I feared it was dead.

But the tarn did not turn away.

I took the body in my hands, and shook it, gently.

It opened glazed eyes. I was not sure it saw anything. It must have been half gone, with starvation, and cold. There were dried stains about the cold, stiff, slashed jacket. It must have lost a great deal of blood.

"Swords of Temmu," it whispered.
"Ship of Tersites," I responded, softly.
"Tarl Cabot, tarnsman," it said.
"Tajima," I said.

Chapter Four

What Occurred Subsequently, Again in the Vicinity of a Small Fire

"I was seen yesterday, Tarl Cabot, tarnsman," said Tajima, weakly. "I am sought. I am followed. I heard cries of soldiers. I do not know how long ago."

"There are enemy soldiers at the old encampment," I said.

"There is a new encampment?" he said.

"One better concealed, one less known," I said.

"Good," he said.

"You need not talk now," I said. "Save your strength."

"Some escaped," he said.

"Yes," I said.

"Many?" he asked.

"Less than half," I said.

"There were readied tarns," he said.

"Yes," I said.

"Tarl Cabot, tarnsman," he said, "was wise."

"Tarl Cabot is a poor captain, a poor commander," I said. Well was I aware of this on this night. Lost in self-pity and self-reproach I had risked much for nothing, risked much for no more than a meaningless gesture.

"He is our captain, our commander," said Tajima. "It is his banner behind which we will ride."

"The wisdom was not mine," I said, "but a common wisdom of war. It is done with a tarn cavalry in enemy or disputed territory. A complement is to be kept ready for action."

"I am pleased some escaped," said Tajima. "I was sure there would be some."

"How is it you are afoot?" I asked.

"I gave my tarn to another," he said, "one I thought less likely to survive in the mountains."

"To whom?" I said.

"Ichiro," he said.

"Our bannerman," I said.

"He was unwilling," said Tajima. "I must command him."

"Once, long ago," I said, "when he was prepared to die, I commanded him to live."

"You must escape from here, you must flee, Tarl Cabot, tarnsman," said Tajima.

"I will get you to the tarn," I said. "Can you rise?"

"I do not think so," he said.

"I will carry you," I said.

"Go on, alone," he said.

"There is time," I said. To be sure, I feared the descent of the tarn might have been noted. But then, too, it was unlikely there would be a patrol or kill squad in this particular area at this particular time. In any event, I did not think it wise to linger here overlong. But, too, I was wary of moving Tajima. Sometimes movement can reopen wounds. Yet it must be done, and soon. I must get him to the new camp as soon as it would be practical.

"I do not think so," he said.

"I hear nothing," I said.

"I tried to extinguish the fire," said Tajima, "but I was weak."

"It is well that you did not do so," I said. "Else I would not have found you."

"It would be better had you not found me," he said.

"Why?" I asked.

"There is danger here," he said.

"It is quiet," I said.

"The enemy is near," said Tajima. "I heard their cries. I tried to rise, to extinguish the fire, but I could not do so. I was weak. I lost consciousness. I do not know how long I was unconscious, perhaps a few Ehn, perhaps an Ahn. Then you were here."

"You fear the enemy is about?" I said.

"They were approaching," he said. "I do not know how long

I was unconscious. They are near. I heard their shouts. They will examine each gorge and crevice. In moments they may be upon us."

"We shall leave together," I said.

"No," he said. "Tajima is done."

"No," I said.

"Save yourself," he said.

"I fear to move you," I said, "but we cannot remain here."

"Leave me," he begged.

"No," I said.

"It is snowing," he said.

"It has begun again," I said.

"It is beautiful," he said.

"Your senses wander," I said.

"Surely you see how beautiful it is," he said.

"Beautiful, and fearful," I said. On foot it would be dangerous to move, for the tracks.

I sensed he was in pain. I trusted no wound had opened. But the blood on the jacket remained dry, caked, and cold.

"How goes the war?" he asked.

"Do not concern yourself," I said.

"But I would know, Tarl Cabot, tarnsman," he said.

"Poorly," I said. "The holding is invested, even the wharves are closed. There is little to eat. Lord Yamada is patient. He is like a sleen waiting for a larl to die. In the courtyard an urt brought a silver tarsk."

"What of Lords Nishida and Okimoto?" he asked.

"Both live," I said. "Lord Nishida ponders war, and Lord Okimoto, I fear, the ritual knife."

"He is truly noble," said Tajima.

"Doubtless," I said. "He is fat, as well."

"He is a daimyo," said Tajima, reproachfully.

"A fat daimyo," I said.

"Defeat is dishonor," said Tajima.

"Not if one has fought well," I said.

"Defeat is dishonor," he said.

"Much depends on the defeat," I said. "The leaf torn from the tree suffers no dishonor, nor the grass crushed beneath a passing boot."

"The calligraphy of Lord Okimoto is exquisite," said Tajima.

"Excellent," I said. "He is still fat."

"How fare others?" he asked.

"Well enough," I said, "Torgus, Lysander, Pertinax live."

"What of Nodachi, swordsman?" asked Tajima.

"His whereabouts are unknown," I said. "He disappeared from the holding, days ago."

Tajima leaned back against the rock. I sensed, again, he was in pain. I was alarmed. Then it seemed the pain had passed.

"Go," he said. "Save yourself."

"We leave together," I said. But I did fear to move him. I feared he might die if I should lift him, or die in the pommel straps, if I could manage to get him to them. The fire of life within him did not seem to me that much different from the small, pathetic signal fire, that tiny beacon, now dying, which he had set in the darkness.

He looked up at me.

"You wish to speak," I said, "but hesitate?"

"No," he said.

"Speak," I said.

"—How fares Sumomo?" he asked.

"Why should you care, what does it matter?" I asked.

"I would know, Tarl Cabot, tarnsman," he said.

Sumomo was one of the two contract women whose contracts were held by Lord Nishida. The other was Hana. I knew that Tajima was much interested in buying the contract of Sumomo, but it was not within his means. Sumomo, like Hana, who was somewhat older, was quite beautiful. On the other hand, I personally found her unpleasant and arrogant. She treated Tajima with contempt, even failing to bow to him, despite the differences in their sexes. Amongst the Pani even an older sister will bow first to a younger brother. Tajima was an intelligent, strong, agile, fine young man. For his age he was an excellent swordsman, and was skilled, generally, in the martial arts of the Pani. He was loyal to the cavalry, to his shogun, Lord Temmu, and to his daimyo, Lord Nishida. That he should be taken with the haughty Sumomo, contract woman of a daimyo, who seemingly despised him, and surely treated him with contempt, seemed anomalous. I had never seen Sumomo other than in her decorous robes but I suspected that, properly exhibited, she would fetch a good price in a typical market on the continent, say, in Brundisium, Port Kar, Ko-ro-ba, Ar, or such. The Pani keep slaves, but the cultural status of the contract woman is superior to that of the slave, and considerably inferior, naturally, to that of the free woman. On continental Gor there is no status equivalent to that of the contract woman. All women on continental Gor, and, in the familiar islands, as well, are either slave or free. There is a considerable difference, of course, between being the slave of a peasant, peddler, or herdsman and that of a high merchant or Ubar, but both are identically slaves. In the collar all women are equal, and nothing, mere slaves, though the collars of some may be set with diamonds.

"I know little of her now," I said, "or of the slaves. They are kept indoors. There is the occasional danger of engine-sprung stones, of descending arrows. I would suppose that she is as lovely and disagreeable as ever."

"How beautiful she is," he said.

Yes, I thought, like a silken urt, and perhaps half as trustworthy. I suspected she had ambitions which well exceeded the clauses of her contract. Her treatment of Tajima had never failed to rankle me. Did she not know she was a contract woman, as barterable in her way as a slave, and he a free man, and warrior? "We must to the tarn," I said.

"The blade, the blade," he said.

It was the shorter blade, the companion blade. The warriors of the Pani are seldom far from this tool. The field sword may be kept in its rack, in the hall, but the companion blade is commonly at hand. The Pani warrior often sleeps with it so.

I tied the tasseled hilt of the sword, which was unsheathed, about his right wrist. I did not doubt but what it had tasted blood in the engagement.

I reached behind his back, and placed my other hand behind his knees and lifted him.

I had taken but one step toward the tarn when it lowered its head, the feathers of the neck and crest spreading like a crackling war fan, this considerably enlarging an image which was formidable enough in its natural state, and glared into the dimness beyond the fire.

"Hold!" I heard.

I remained still, Tajima in my arms.

"Control the monster," said the voice, "or a dozen arrows will slay the beast at my mere word."

"Steady," I said to the bird, restless, belligerent, at my side. "Steady, steady."

"I see you are wise," said the voice.

I saw but one foe, helmeted, with a field sword grasped in two hands, across the tiny fire. I supposed there must be others behind him, but I could not see them. He had spoken of a dozen arrows. Then I supposed there might be a dozen bowmen, and perhaps others, as well. But I could not see them.

"Hail Yamada, Shogun of the Islands," said the voice.

I saw no reason to respond.

"Do you speak Gorean?" asked the voice, uncertainly.

"Yes," I said.

"You are not Pani," said the voice.

"No," I said.

"You are a hired sword, a mercenary," it said.

"Yes," I said.

"Hired beasts," he said, "sellers of swords to the highest bidder."

"Steady," I said to the bird, "steady."

"We killed many such monsters," it said, indicating the tarn with the point of the sword.

"It is hard to kill a tarn," I said. "I suspect those killed sold their lives well. Too, it is my understanding that many escaped, and many returned to the wild."

"We have followed the carrion in your arms for days," said the voice. "Now we have caught him."

"Step toward the fire," I said.

He was a large man, with a wide-brimmed, metal-winged helmet. He wore gloves and a heavy jacket.

I thought the jacket might encumber his sport with the blade, but if he had ten men, or so, behind him, I supposed it would not make much difference. I had Tajima in my arms, who, as far as I knew, might have lapsed again into unconsciousness. The body was warm, however, and I could sense its breathing. Too, of course, my own blade, the *gladius*, was sheathed. The sheath was at my left hip, and the sheath strap ran across my body from my right shoulder to the left hip. That is common on tarnback, and when an engagement is not imminent.

"How many men do you have?" I asked.

"Twelve," he said.

"Then you have little to fear," I said.

"And you have much," he said.

I could not see any men behind him. Still, there was much darkness.

"You are brave with twelve men behind you," I said.

"If there were none, I am brave," he said, angrily.

"Let us see," I said. "Let me put my friend, who is ill and weak, and cannot stand, on the ground, and draw my sword. Then let us do contest here, in the falling snow. If I win, I and my friend are free to go. If I lose, you have our lives, and your honor, and have proved to your men your bravery. Do you accept my challenge?"

"I am not a fool," he said.

"I lower my friend to the ground, gently," I said.

"He is dead," said the man, warily.

"I do not think so," I said. "He may be unconscious."

I lowered the limp body of Tajima to the snow. I think he was conscious, but unable to move.

"He is the last of the fugitives," said the man. "His will be the last head we will gather. The others are all dead. It has taken time, but now we have the last of them."

"Do you accept my challenge?" I asked.

"Do not unsheathe your sword," he said, quickly.

"Why not?" I asked.

"You are a mercenary," he said. "Things have become other than they were. Be wise. Change your banner."

My hand went to the hilt of my blade.

"Think," said the man. "Do not draw your sword! You can manage the winged monster! Lord Yamada can use men such as you. Gold, women, a command, will be yours!"

"I have placed the challenge," I said. "Is it accepted?"

"Do not draw your sword!" he said.

Slowly, very slowly, I drew the blade.

"Is it accepted?" I asked.

"I have twelve men behind me," he said.

"I see none," I said.

"You are clever," he said. "You would have me turn my head, and then you would rush upon me with that little sword."

"It is a fast little thing," I said, "rather like the companion sword."

"Kill him!" he cried, suddenly. "Kill him, now, now!"

"I see no one behind you," I said.

"What are you waiting for?" he cried, hysterically, half turning his head. "Kill him! Kill him!"

Then he spun about, cried out once, and then, in his heavy snow boots, plunged into the darkness, and, a moment later, I heard a cry, half of fear, half of misery, which was cut short.

A moment later a short, squat figure emerged from the darkness.

"Nodachi!" I said.

"Master!" said Tajima.

I turned about.

Somehow Tajima had staggered to his feet, that he might meet his teacher while standing, his blade in his hand. He then wavered. I caught him, as he collapsed.

"He is unconscious," I said.

"Build up the fire," said Nodachi. "I have rice. We will boil it in a helmet. When Tajima, tarnsman, has revived, and fed, you must convey him to safety."

"It will be dangerous to build up the fire," I said.

"Not now," said Nodachi, gathering sticks.

"How did you find us?" I asked.

"I found others," said Nodachi. "I then let them find you. I followed."

"There were twelve men, and an officer," I said.

"Paths were narrow, and the night was dark," he said.

"One by one," I said.

"Hunters," he said, "did not know themselves hunted."

"I take it you will gather heads," I said. It is commonly done, that they may be presented to a daimyo, or shogun. Land, position, and authority may be attendant upon the presentation of such trophies.

"No," he said.

"Not even that of the officer?" I asked.

"I found it unworthy," he said.

"You have risked much coming here," I said.

He did not respond.

"How is it that you came alone into the mountains?" I said.

"I sought Tajima, tarnsman," he said.

"Why?" I asked.

The snow continued to fall, softly.

"He is my student," he said.

Chapter Five

Report of a Brief Conversation;
This Took Place in the
New Encampment

I blocked the swift, lashing, whiplike blow of the supple bamboo.

Se'Var had passed, and it was now the second day of the tenth passage hand.

"That was quick," I said to Tajima, "but you are still weak."

Twice more I blocked the blows of the lashing, cord-wound bamboo. "Enough, enough!" I said. "You must rest."

"I am recovered, Tarl Cabot, tarnsman," said Tajima, anxiously.

"You are not," I said.

"I am ready once more for the reins of the tarn," he said.

"The tarn may not think so," I said.

"I do not understand," he said.

"It is nothing," I said. Even the kaiila can sense trepidation, or hesitation, when it is approached, and may shy about, distressing, even resisting, a rider. The tarn, a dangerous beast, half domesticated at best, can be even more skittish or dangerous. It is one thing to train a tarn to accept an unfamiliar rider and another to reduce its predatory instincts, which are often elicited by an appearance of fear, uncertainty, or weakness. What if Tajima might be unsteady, or falter? What if his foot should slip at the stirrup? What if his hands were not sure on the reins?

"I am ready, Tarl Cabot, tarnsman," he said.

"No," I said.

"Now, Commander," he said.

"Be patient," I said. "You may soon return to your post of spy for Lord Nishida, monitoring the whereabouts and behaviors of Tarl Cabot."

"I have my office," he said.

"I do not object," I assured him. "Indeed, I may soon give you interesting things to report."

"But if I may not ascend the tarn?" he said.

"True," I said. "It would then be difficult to report."

"I have learned," he said, "here in the camp, from those in communication with the holding, Pertinax and others, that suspicions have fallen upon you, that you are suspected of treachery."

"Or worse," I acknowledged. "My own suspicions," I said, "fall on Lord Okimoto."

"But he has an exquisite hand," said Tajima. "Have you not seen his calligraphy?"

"Even so," I said.

"He is a daimyo," said Tajima. "One might as well suspect Lord Nishida."

"I do not think so," I said.

"There could be treachery in many places," said Tajima, "in the holding, in the fields, on the roads, here in the camp."

"Next you will be thinking of the cooks and smiths, the readers of bones and shells," I said.

"It is in high places," he said.

"It must be," I said.

"You are in such a place, Tarl Cabot *san*," he said.

"That is true, Tajima *san*," I said.

"Many suspect you," he said.

"And I suspect many," I said.

"What am I to do?" he asked.

"Recover your strength," I said.

Chapter Six

The Dais

"I bring you words of conciliation, of forgiveness, and joy from your lord, Lord Yamada, Shogun of the Islands," said Tyrtaios.

It was now in the holding of Lord Temmu.

"Put aside your doomed rebellion, and attend to the words of your lord," said Tyrtaios.

Several were about, sitting, cross-legged, on the deep, broad dais, of smooth, shining, lacquered wood. Tyrtaios stood on the dais, rather before us, as he addressed us. With him, behind him, and about, not on the dais, were some officers and several Ashigaru of Lord Yamada. In the center of the dais, rather toward the back, like a large, patient stone, sat Lord Temmu. I had not seen him since the meeting at which the site of the new encampment had been specified, a specification which I had ignored. I had little doubt that some on the dais, or about, other than those of my command, realized the camp was not at the assigned site. Perhaps they had sought to arrange an attack there, hoping to duplicate the attack, so fearsomely successful, on the first encampment. On the other hand, if they were to draw this to the attention of Lord Temmu, or Lords Nishida and Okimoto, that the new camp was situated other than in its prescribed location, it would be natural to inquire how they had obtained this information, as the specified location was supposedly secret. How had they come to know that the designated site was not occupied? What would have prompted their curiosity? What would have been their motivation in conducting such an inquiry?

It was my understanding that, better than two years ago, the forces of Lord Yamada had encroached upon, and intruded into, the regions commonly controlled by Lord Temmu. A defensive war had ensued in which the forces of Lord Temmu, considerably outnumbered and, I fear, poorly generaled, had fared badly. Eventually the primary remnants of the land forces of Lord Temmu, those separated from the holding, to which portions had retreated, cut off and undersupplied, had been driven to the very shore of Thassa. They had prepared themselves for what portended to be their last battle. The eve was dark. But when the soldiers of Lord Yamada, with the first light, with fixed banners and brandished glaives, crying out, swarmed to the shore, they found the beach empty. In this I detected the work of Priest-Kings, and a wager, perhaps for the stakes of a world's surface, with Kurii. I knew little of what was occurring, but suspected there were battles behind battles. I suspected the surface of Gor lay at issue. It was a speculation that Priest-Kings and Kurii, weary of skirmishes, of indecision, of stalemates, of continual intrusions and probes, had proposed, if not agreed upon, a game of men, a drawing of cards or a casting of dice, on the outcome of which depended a coveted prize, the surface of a world. I feared the outcome of this dire contest was slated to take place far from known Gor, indeed, at the "World's End," between two Pani contingents. I suspected the armaments involved were to be primitive, neither technologically nor industrially advanced. One supposed both the sophisticated weaponry of Kurii and the engines of Priest-Kings were to be abjured. But then, might they not as well have wagered on a game of kaissa or tharlarion racing at Venna? What were the parameters of this game, if game it was? Could a number of Pani warriors, brought to continental Gor, somehow find their way back to the embattled homeland? Perhaps, if the unprecedented voyage could be accomplished. But for that one would need a ship, a large, unusual ship, perhaps a ship such as that of Tersites. Might they not, too, perhaps by the recruitment of mercenaries, assuming the requisite voyage could be made, manage to achieve a military balance with the numerically larger forces of Lord Yamada? Perhaps, particularly if a new arm were incorporated into their arsenal, an unprecedented arm, unprecedented for the World's End, perhaps that of the trained war tarn. Much of this, of course, was speculative on my part, but there seemed an alarming plausibility in these untoward speculations. But, I thought, if there should be something to this, that a strange, invisible game was afoot, it seemed unlikely to me that it would be a game fairly played, a game innocently played. Too much was at stake. Well was I aware of the subtlety and deviousness of Priest-Kings, well was I aware of the determination and cunning of Kurii. I doubted that either might trust the other. Would the cards not be marked, the dice weighted? Might a hand not surreptitiously move a piece, or insert another? And who is to say on what tiny matters, a sedative pellet scarcely visible, a sliver of iron in the foot, might hang the performance of even the mighty tharlarion? Too, to my dismay, I knew not which pieces were backed by which players. Then I dismissed these arrant conjectures. How absurd to suspect that wars lurked behind wars. The tree, the rock, the sharpened blade are themselves. The motivations of Lord Yamada, greed and ambition, power and wealth, were clear enough, and familiar enough, as were the responses of Lord Temmu, who was, perhaps, not really so different from Lord Yamada himself. Content yourself with the visible. It can be felt; it can bleed. Put aside fruitless, paranoid aberrations.

"I bear, on behalf of my lord, and yours, Lord Yamada, Shogun of the Islands," said Tyrtaios, "welcome, merciful words, words of exoneration, and clemency."

Lord Temmu remained impassive.

"We have spared the holding of Temmu," said Tyrtaios, "from the rain of burning arrows, because of our love for our wayward, misguided servitor, the glorious, honorable Temmu."

It was easy to understand the reluctance of Yamada to destroy, or attempt to destroy, a fortress, castle, and holding as large and beautiful, and as nigh inaccessible and impregnable, as that of Lord Temmu. It had remained secure and undefiled even in the darkest days of the war, even before trapped Pani had mysteriously vanished from a beach several pasangs to the north.

"It is the word of my lord, and yours, Lord Yamada, Shogun

of the Islands," said Tyrtaios, "that peace, amity, harmony, and love, be between us, fully and forever."

Lord Temmu sat in the center of the dais, cross-legged, toward the rear. His reader of bones and shells, a man named Daichi, was behind him, to his left. Ponderous Lord Okimoto was seated to his right, and lean Lord Nishida on his left. I was seated a bit to the side of, and behind, Lord Nishida. Other officers were about, as well. Several minor officers were standing about the dais, before it, on the left and right. Ashigaru guards were present. At the back of the dais, unobtrusive, demure, in their elegant kimonos, and obis, were several contract women. I knew few of them, as they tend to be shy and retiring. I did know Sumomo and Hana, contract women of Lord Nishida, largely from my relationship to Lord Nishida, to whom I usually reported. The only other contract woman I knew by name was Hisui, whose contract was held by Lord Okimoto. I recalled she had once worn about her neck the medallion of the Ubara of Ar. I had decided to accompany Lord Nishida to the World's End. No slaves were present, but that would not be unusual, given the occasion. Certainly I had given it little thought at the time.

"We have been below your walls and before your gates, at the foot of your trails, for months," said Tyrtaios. "The patience of Lord Yamada is known to be prodigious, but it is not inexhaustible. Accordingly, my lord, and yours, Lord Yamada, Shogun of the Islands, is willing, under certain conditions, to grant full amnesty to all rebels."

I expected at least a ripple of interest to course through the assembled Pani, but they seemed impassive. Tyrtaios himself, as I, apparently expected a greater reaction to his words.

Lord Temmu nodded to his right, to Lord Okimoto, appropriately offering his senior daimyo, and cousin, the first opportunity to speak. The lips of Lord Okimoto moved but little sound emerged. He also shook his head, slightly, and moved his hand a little. He generally did not wish to speak publicly, and perhaps particularly not now, as several men of Yamada had accompanied Tyrtaios to the holding. I did not doubt, however, but what his counsel would be forthcoming in private. He was sensitive to, and well aware of, the difficulties attending his speech. Those accustomed to his infirmity scarcely noticed it. If one were within a few feet of him it was not hard to make out his words, once one had become accustomed to the lightness and articulation. The first times I had heard Lord Okimoto, in Shipcamp, Lord Nishida had been of great help, almost acting as an interpreter. Since that time there had been little difficulty in the matter. Tyrtaios, who had served as mercenary liaison to Lord Okimoto, and a guard, on the ship and in the holding, prior to his desertion, similarly, understood him without difficulty. Years ago Lord Okimoto, in serving his shogun, Lord Temmu, his cousin, had sustained a knife wound in his throat. This had impaired, or, perhaps better, changed, his natural speech. He seldom spoke loudly, but I supposed it would be possible for him to do so, if he should wish. In any event, Lord Okimoto, like many of the high Pani, of family and station, seldom raised his voice. This is, I suppose, a matter of seemliness, of decorum. Lower Pani, peasants, fishermen, Ashigaru, and such, seldom share such a reservation, unless speaking to those of a higher station. Amongst the Pani, rank, distance, and hierarchy tend to be strictly observed. One listens with care, of course, to high Pani, as softly spoken as they may be, for an expression, a measured word, a slight difference in an intonation contour, and such, may be quite as meaningful in their case as a shout or scowl might be in the case of another. To be sure, as always, much depends on the individual. I have encountered vulgar aristocrats and aristocratic peasants.

Lord Temmu then, politely, nodded to his left, where, cross-legged, reposed lean Lord Nishida.

If the shogun were to speak at all, in a situation of this sort, he would be likely to speak later, after others had spoken. And, of course, his word, should he wish to utter it, aside from possible formalities, ritual phrases and such, would be, in effect, the last word, the final word. He was shogun.

"We attend the words of noble Tyrtaios," said Lord Nishida, "words spoken on behalf of his lord, noble Yamada, claimant to the islands."

Tyrtaios bowed, slightly, warily.

"It is interesting," said Lord Nishida, "that the great lord would send noble Tyrtaios, who served us well in Brundisium, and in the forests, and who accompanied us on the great ship, and who stood at our side in the holding, as an emissary to our court."

"It is not without thought, Lord," said Tyrtaios. "Lord Yamada knows the affection I bear toward my former fellows, and my desire for their well-being. He thought then that I, most of all, and surely more than others, might convey his lenient appeal and gracious offer. I served you diligently, hardily, and well. I withdrew from your service only under the most powerful of moral incentives, my recognition of the righteousness of the cause of Lord Yamada, Shogun of the Islands. Rather than form a party to conspiracy and rebellion I then chose, as an honorable man, at great personal risk, and with profound sorrow at parting from my friends, to abandon your misguided secession from right and truth."

"The moral integrity and courage of the noble Tyrtaios cannot be but commended," said Lord Nishida.

How a happy a coincidence, I thought, when the dictates of right and the prescriptions of prudence coincide so nicely.

"But it is our humble suspicion," said Lord Nishida, "that the noble Tyrtaios may labor unwittingly, certainly through no fault of his own, under certain misapprehensions. Lord Yamada is not Shogun of the Islands though he may pronounce himself such. He may claim the islands; we may claim the yellow moon; the moon is not concerned. Too, Lord Yamada is not our lord. Lord Temmu is our lord, and, as we do not recognize Lord Yamada as our lord, we do not see ourselves as in rebellion, and thus do not see ourselves as rebels."

"You are rebels," said Tyrtaios, "for you have arrayed yourselves against Lord Yamada. It is a fact of history. He is here. The shadow of his sword is upon your lands. The fields are his. His troops are within your borders. Your holding is invested. The might of steel, victorious and decisive, proclaims him shogun. There is no answer to this. It is done. You have lost. And yet you dare to defy him."

"The holding stands," said Lord Nishida.

"Now!" said Tyrtaios.

I saw Lord Okimoto lean toward Lord Temmu. I could not make out his words.

Lord Temmu nodded.

I did not know what had passed between them.

"The straits in which you find yourselves," said Tyrtaios, "are dire. You cannot hold out. It is known. In the last days, thanks to the compassion and generosity of my gracious lord, Lord Yamada, you have been permitted to trade some goods for food."

At the new encampment I had not known of this. I had only yesterday been summoned to this council.

I did not understand this indulgence on the part of Lord Yamada. It seemed unlikely on the part of a siege master. I was curious as to what goods General Yamada was willing to accept, and why, in exchange, apparently, for supplies, presumably in limited quantities. When the holding fell, as seemed likely, perhaps within days, presumably its goods, gold, silver, jade, jewels, furniture, screens, scrolls, and such, would be his for the gathering. To be sure, some of it might be destroyed, but that was not likely, as Pani tend to be reluctant to damage or destroy objects and materials of value. What Pani, at least of noble birth and refinement, would burn a well-wrought fan, a samisen, a lovely painted screen, or a poem?

"Is it true," asked Lord Nishida, "that you ask Pani warriors, many of whom are men of two swords, to surrender?"

"Surely not, Lord," said Tyrtaios, hastily. "We request only that you desist in your honorable resistance."

"If our resistance is honorable," said Lord Nishida, "why should we desist?"

"It is misguided," said Tyrtaios.

"You spoke of conditions," said Lord Nishida.

"It is requested only that you live in peace and harmony with your lord, Lord Yamada, Shogun of the Islands."

"He is free to leave the lands of Temmu," said Lord Nishida.

"Why should he leave his own lands?" asked Tyrtaios. "These lands are his. The sword has spoken."

"The holding stands," said Lord Nishida.

"Welcome your rightful lord," said Tyrtaios. "He is forgiving and kind, and holds in his heart only affection for his brothers."

"It is said," said Lord Nishida, "that a thousand posts surmounted by a thousand heads line the march of Yamada to the lands of Temmu."

"Those of bandits and recreants," said Tyrtaios.

"What would you have us do?" asked Lord Nishida.

"The conditions are simple," said Tyrtaios. "Lay aside your arms. Abandon this fortress town, this citadel, this castle. Descend unarmed to the plain, rejoicing, in pure garments. Bring gifts to the pavilion of your lord, great Yamada, Shogun of the Islands."

"You would have us descend from the fortress, defenseless, unarmed, amongst hostile forces, as alleged rebels and traitors, humbly bringing supplicatory gifts, and place ourselves at the mercy of Lord Yamada?"

"As friends, and allies," said Tyrtaios.

"We attend to your words with care," said Lord Nishida.

"Lord Yamada is kind, forgiving, and compassionate," said Tyrtaios.

"What man of prudence would say otherwise?" said Lord Nishida.

I thought of the heads aligning a road to the lands of Temmu.

"You may trust Lord Yamada," said Tyrtaios.

"The trustworthiness of Lord Yamada is legendary in the islands," said Lord Nishida.

"Behold," said Tyrtaios, "I bear gifts from my lord, in token of his good will and affection."

As noted earlier Tyrtaios had not come alone. With him had come certain officers of General Yamada, presumably to monitor the proceedings and, later, to report upon them to the shogun, and several Ashigaru. These Ashigaru were unarmed, but each bore a large silk-covered hamper. At a gesture from Tyrtaios they brought the hampers forward, and placed them on the dais, across its front. They removed the silken covers and we noted the hampers were heaped with fruits, vegetables, cakes of rice, smoked fish, layers of dried, salted meat, and stoppered vessels which I supposed might contain sake, and perhaps, considering the continental mercenaries in the camp, none of whom had been permitted, save myself, to attend these proceedings, paga and ka-la-na.

Again I expected more of a response amongst the Pani at these abundances of displayed largesse, but was disappointed. Tyrtaios, too, seemed, surprised at the lack of response amongst the Pani.

Over the past weeks it had become more and more difficult

to supply the holding. This was largely the result of two factors, the number of fields and farms now denied to us by the Ashigaru of Yamada, and the reduction of supplies, the thinning of flocks and the depletion of resources, at those villages still accessible to us. Too, though our supply lines could not be cut, given tarns, they were now considerably attenuated. In brief, supplies were scarce, and growing more scarce, day by day, and it took longer and longer, ever longer, from day to day, to obtain and deliver them to the holding. Too, understandably, peasants, uncertain of the war's outcome, and in danger of starvation themselves, had begun to horde and conceal food. I neglected to convey this intelligence to Lord Temmu, as we were to discipline uncooperative retainers by means of the torch and sword. I personally saw little benefit to be derived from the pursuit of such a policy. Too, I was not a butcher. At the cavalry's encampment matters, though austere, were less harrowing and strained, given the smaller numbers involved, and the availability of local game, tarsk, tabuk, and verr.

"The generosity of Lord Yamada is noted," said Lord Nishida.

"Feast!" said Tyrtaios, gesturing to the heaped hampers of food and drink.

But no one rushed upon the hampers, crying out, crowding, and thrusting, to seize food.

"How soon," asked Tyrtaios, "may we expect to receive your capitulation? How soon may we expect you to abandon the holding?"

"The holding stands," said Lord Nishida.

"You are starving!" cried Tyrtaios, angrily.

"You think matters severe, so truly severe, so severe as that?" inquired Lord Nishida.

"Yes," said Tyrtaios.

"Even if it were true, how would it be known to you?" inquired Lord Nishida.

Tyrtaios did not respond.

I supposed Tyrtaios' claim might have been based on rational conjecture, but I supposed, as well, and more plausibly, that communication, of some sort, existed between the holding and the pavilion of Lord Yamada, far below in the plain.

"It is a matter of time, and not a great deal of time," said Tyrtaios, "until resistance must end, until the holding must fall. In a few days, or less, your men will be too weak to man the walls and hold the gates."

"Meanwhile, the holding stands," said Lord Nishida.

"I warn you," said Tyrtaios, "the patience of Lord Yamada is not inexhaustible."

I feared there was much in what Tyrtaios had said. It seemed likely to me that the garrison, both Pani and mercenary, must soon succumb, if not to the enemy, then to hunger. I myself, several days ago, would have preferred a sallying forth from the holding, to charge, however fruitlessly, upon the enemy, that one might at least, enweaponed, facing the enemy, die as befits the warrior. Even the urt will snarl and attack the sleen rather than die of hunger in its den. But now I feared it was too late, even for the flourish of a last, gallant gesture. Now many men, I knew, could not even rise to their feet.

Lord Nishida turned his head to face Lord Temmu, who sat, cross-legged, near the back of the dais.

"We thank great Yamada for his patience," said Lord Temmu. "Return to your master and tell him that, we, too, are patient."

"Consider your words carefully," said Tyrtaios.

Several hands went to the hilts of weapons.

"He is shogun!" whispered Lord Nishida, quickly, reprovingly.

But not a flicker of annoyance could be marked on the visage of Lord Temmu.

"I meant no discourtesy," said Tyrtaios.

"Cousin," said Lord Okimoto.

"Speak," said Lord Temmu.

I recalled that Lord Okimoto had earlier leaned toward Lord Temmu, and said something, and that Lord Temmu had nodded.

I did not know what had passed between them.

I now supposed that it had had to do with expressing an eventual readiness to participate in the proceedings.

This was unusual.

Lord Okimoto seldom spoke publicly. Presumably this was because of his sensitivity to his impairment. Like most high Pani, he was a proud man. Pani are often embarrassed by what they may conceive as exhibiting a difference, or a weakness, or defect.

The ponderous daimyo did not look about himself.

We prepared to attend closely, for his words were commonly weighty and it was not always easy to decode the light, rasping sounds, like hoarse, sibilant whispers, which escaped his scarred throat.

His gaze was fixed on Tyrtaios.

His words were laden with menace.

It was not a pleasant thing, I was sure, to have Lord Okimoto as an enemy.

"I am offended," said Lord Okimoto to Tyrtaios, "that Lord Yamada would send one such as you to convey his words, a traitor and miscreant. How better could he express his contempt?"

"No insult was intended, great lord," said Tyrtaios. "Recall that I served you faithfully and well, both as guard and as liaison to mercenaries."

"No daimyo would agree to address such words to a shogun," said Lord Okimoto.

"I am a soldier," said Tyrtaios. "I must do the will of my lord, as best I can, as I am commanded."

"You are a foreigner here, a stranger, one not of the islands," said Lord Okimoto. "You do not know our ways."

"The ways of war are common ways," said Tyrtaios. "They possess no insignia, they fly no banners. They stop at no rivers and are held within no walls. They are found on the plains and in the mountains. The quarrel and the arrow are akin, as are the glaive and the spear."

"You will not take this holding," said Lord Okimoto, "while a single man lives."

"Then, great lord," said Tyrtaios, "with all due respect, it must be taken when none live."

"When none live," said Lord Okimoto, "it is then that the greatest victory is won."

"I do not understand," said Tyrtaios.

"There is one victory of which we cannot be deprived," said Lord Okimoto.

"I do not understand," said Tyrtaios, uncertainly.

Lord Okimoto was silent.

"The lifting of the ritual knife," explained Lord Nishida.

"I do not understand," said Tyrtaios.

"The performance of a deed whose tale will be told for a thousand years," said Lord Nishida.

I shuddered, recalling a conversation held long ago, on a parapet damp with fog, early, on a cold morning.

I glanced at some of the officers of Lord Yamada who had accompanied Tyrtaios to the holding. I saw that they understood.

Yes, I thought, ways are different. How hideously strange and unfamiliar are the corridors of culture. How they differ one from another. How strange, I thought, are the wildernesses and labyrinths of propriety. In the vastness and darkness of the forest there are many paths, and it is hard to find one's way, but one seeks one's way, one seeks one's way. I recalled Lord Nishida had asked if Lord Okimoto would be the first to use the knife. "Of course," had said Lord Okimoto.

Tyrtaios turned to the shogun.

"What answer shall I bear to my lord?" he asked.

"Tell your lord," said Lord Temmu, "that the holding stands." He then addressed himself to his men at arms who stood about. "Take that food," he said, "and carry it to the outer parapets, and cast it to the plains below."

Tyrtaios and his party, officers and Ashigaru of General Yamada, then turned about, to take their leave.

Tyrtaios turned back, briefly. "Beware the iron dragon," he said. "It is in its lair. If it is awakened, it will fly."

I did not understand this.

He and his party then withdrew.

Chapter Seven

A Plan Is Conceived

"Why was I not told?" I demanded.

"It was feared you might not approve," said Lord Nishida.

"I do not," I said.

"It is as we feared," he said.

After Tyrtaios and the officers and Ashigaru of Yamada who had accompanied him had withdrawn from the holding, I had made my way to the indoor housing area for slaves, and, to my surprise, found it empty. In the large fire pan were only ashes. The room is large, and there is much freedom of movement within it. It has two narrow windows placed some eight feet above the floor level, and has a single, heavy, timber door. At night, the slaves are chained to the wall, by the neck, an ankle, or, in some cases, by a wrist. Each is given a blanket. The chains were now empty, and there was little indication that the room had been recently occupied. A thought pressed against my mind, but I thrust it away. I supposed that one or more of the slaves might have been less than pleasing and, as a consequence, as a discipline, all might have been moved to the other common holding area, favored in better weather, the kennels under the long shed lining the inner wall of the holding. I had never much approved punishing several for the infraction of, say, one, but I recognized that it was a way of placing considerable stress on the errant individual. Not only is she punished in particular, often whipped, but she is likely to be subjected to the displeasure, ill will, contempt, and abuse of the others, and may even endure additional corporal attentions at their hands. Still, the punishment of several for the mistake of, say, one, seems to me to compromise the very rationale of discipline, which is to link, say, a failure to be fully pleasing, to anticipated, and predictable, consequences. Most slaves are zealous to please their masters. Why then should such a slave suffer for the fault of another? Would this not be likely to dismay, bewilder, and confuse a slave? Similarly, in my view, discipline is not to be arbitrary. Her universe is to be a stable, secure universe, with its well-established borders, expectations, habits, and such. In this respect, her universe is likely to be more secure, livable, and rewarding than that of the free woman, so far above her. Most slaves begin by fearing the master, and strive to be pleasing, fearing not to please him. But then, commonly, as she learns her collar, and realizes it is on her, and locked, she wishes to please him, and fully, with all her heart. Certainly it is pleasant to have a loving slave at one's feet. Is not love the strongest of her chains? To be sure, one must guard against caring for a mere slave. Occasionally she might be whipped, if it seems appropriate, to remind her that she is a slave, and only a slave. This, too, as she loves her bondage, and would not exchange its freedom for the narrowness and imprisonment of the free woman, can be rewarding and reassuring to her, even in its tears. How better can she be informed that she is a slave, than to know herself subject to the whip of her master?

I was not pleased to find the indoor housing area vacant.

There are many forms of discipline, of course. The switch and whip are but two. Short rations and close chains are others. Nudity in the streets is also unpleasant. Being denied an upright posture or speech are others. One of the most effective disciplines has to do with sex. Once her slave fires have been ignited, and, periodically, rage, in all their suffusive, global might, she finds herself, perhaps at first to her terror, dismay, and misery, their helpless, desperate captive and victim. She then has, in her collar, a need for sex which is not even conceivable, save at the terrifying edges of her consciousness, to the free woman. Indeed, the life of a slave female is a life profoundly imbued with sex, a life of profound and radical sexuality. She joyfully abandons herself to what she now is, a female and a slave. In the collar she finds her joy, her freedom, her meaningfulness, and her identity. She has come home to what she is, radically, anciently, biologically, profoundly, a woman, a slave. It is then obvious what might be the nature of a most effective discipline. One spurns her from one's feet. She returns, squirming on her belly, pressing her lips to one's feet and ankles, whimpering, begging to be touched. She is a slave.

I was not pleased to find the indoor housing area vacant.

I fought back against recognizing, or accepting, an intrusive possibility.

More rationally, noting the absence of blankets in the housing area, I conjectured that the slaves, presumably as a discipline, had been moved to the kennels under the roof of the long shed.

My initial reaction to this possibility, aside from my reservations pertaining to mass discipline, as a whole, had been anger, for the weather, for the islands, had been bitter.

I strode toward the long shed.

I fought back an illusive apprehension.

One must be concerned for the welfare of the slave, as for any other form of domestic animal. Though they are likely to bring less than a sleen or kaiila, let alone a tarn, on the market, they do have their value as domestic beasts, much as verr and tarsk. One has an investment in them, as well as in any other form of stock. A tunic and a blanket afforded little enough protection and shelter against the chill of the air, particularly cruel at the height of the holding.

In matters of discipline one must have some sense of proportion, practicality, and fittingness.

The sky was overcast.

The slave is to be treated with the same consideration and solicitude as any other domestic beast; nothing is to be done to her which might reduce or impair her value; you may wish, later, to put her up for sale.

I was angry.

I had now made my way to the long shed, adjacent to the innermost wall of the holding.

"Ho!" I cried.

"Captain?" inquired an Ashigaru, hurrying to me.

I stood beneath the boards of the shed roof, which extended some feet into the courtyard. I was facing the inside of the wall.

"What is this?" I demanded.

"It was deemed appropriate," he said.

Before me, in their lines, now awry, were better than a hundred kennels. The gates, with their close-set, narrow bars, adequate for holding women, were ajar. Each was empty.

My keenest and most unwelcome suspicions were now confirmed, those I had striven to banish, even from the edges of my mind.

Yet somehow, even as I had denied them, I had known them well warranted.

On the dais I had noted that no slaves were present. To be sure, at so august a gathering, one would not really expect them to be in attendance. Yet, I had been somehow uneasy at their absence. But much was ensuing. Might there not have been one or another, lingering by the wall, or passing on some errand? But I had given this little thought at the time. Much had been ensuing.

But afterwards I was intent on visiting the indoor housing area, that I might ascertain the condition of a slave, a particular slave, Cecily, once Miss Virginia Cecily Jean Pym, whom I had collared faraway, on a steel world, concealed amongst asteroids, and, on behalf of my friend and colleague, Pertinax, another, the slender, flaxen-haired, blue-eyed slave, Saru, once Miss Margaret Wentworth.

"Would you like me to look in on her?" I had asked Pertinax.

"It does not matter," he had said. "She is only a slave."

"Do not forget it," I had told him.

She had been put in her first collar at Tarncamp, though she had been, in a sense, a slave unbeknownst to herself even on Earth. Many women on Earth, in this sense, are slaves, unbeknownst to themselves, having been located, marked out, identified, and registered as such by Gorean slavers. They go about their normal lives, completely unaware that they are now slaves. All that is required then is their harvesting. From the point of view of the slavers, their acquisition, chaining, marking, collaring, and marketing are simply matters of ensuant detail. She had been the slave of Lord Nishida who had, after we had arrived at the World's End, bestowed her on the shogun, Lord Temmu. Her coloring was unusual for the islands.

I had anticipated the reunion with Cecily with much pleasure, though I knew it would be brief. The slaves had been sequestered in the indoor housing area, as noted, where they would be safer, but also, by the edict of Lord Temmu, given the rigor of the siege and the scarcity of resources, and the need for the strictest of disciplines, had been denied to the garrison. I deemed this wise. Survival might depend on a keen eye and an undivided attention. Might not a climber, dark in the night, as silent as a snake, attain the parapet, cut a throat, and set meager stores ablaze? Might not a rush to a gate, up one of the high trails, perhaps that from the wharves below, be too belatedly recognized? What if a thousand fire arrows should be launched at midnight, and those who must ascend to the roofs of the castle and other buildings with their dampened mats and cloths not respond with alacrity? The unrestricted presence of the slave, like that of sake, or paga, or ka-la-na, which, too, were currently forbidden, was not to be risked. Not only might their presence be distractive, for who does not fail to note the flanks and figures of slaves, their glances, and the turns of their heads, but, too, it was feared that, if they were about, openly, rather like tabuk amongst starving larls, the mercenaries might seize them and fight amongst themselves for their use. Such squabbles were not only deleterious to discipline, but might result in bloodshed, which might reduce the number of swords at the disposal of the holding. It was felt that each sword was needed; would not each sword, when the major onslaught came, if it would come, be important and precious? Given the honor and discipline of the Pani, and their sense of propriety, even privately owned slaves had been placed in the indoor housing area. For example, Lord Temmu himself had placed his own slaves amongst the others, as had other high officers. The high Pani did not exempt themselves from the hardship and suffering, the long Ahn, the shortness of rations, the denials of pleasures, which they imposed on the men. And I myself, long ago, thinking Cecily safer at the holding than she would be at the new encampment, which I feared might be discovered and attacked, as had been the first encampment, had turned her over to the slave keepers, housing her with the others.

I now well understood the reference to goods which had been

exchanged for food, presumably limited supplies of such, which I had heard on the dais. For some reason, at the time, it had not occurred to me that the goods were slaves. Now that I thought about it, that inference would have been almost inevitable. Pani would seldom destroy valuable objects, and most such objects, then, would be available to the intruders once the holding was taken. On the other hand, under conditions of scarcity, amounting to the brink of starvation, slaves, certainly objects of value, might, as might others, say, the men of the garrison, perish and be lost. If one wished to preserve them, then it would seem plausible to turn them over to the enemy and hope to recapture them later. It would be the same with, say, kaiila. Too, of course, in removing the slaves from the holding, one would conserve resources, not having to feed them, and would also remove a possible object of distraction, even contention, from the holding. They could constitute no distraction then, nor would their use be the prize in any squabble, bloody or not, if they were not in the holding.

"When was this done?" I inquired of the Ashigaru.

"Days ago, Captain *san*," said he.

"I was not informed," I said.

"I am lowly," he said.

"I am interested in two," I said, "Cecily and Saru."

"I do not know the names of animals, Captain *san*," he said. "I count them, like verr."

"They were sold," I said.

"Yes," he said.

"How many?" I said.

"All," he said.

That I supposed would be something in the nature of one hundred and fifty slaves.

"For what were they sold?" I asked.

"Rice," he said.

"Lord Yamada is generous," I said.

"He is a great lord," said the Ashigaru.

"Much rice?" I said.

"Most," he said, "were exchanged for one *fukuro* of rice, some for two."

"That is not much," I said. The most common *fukuro* of rice, or bag or sack of rice, as I had seen it measured out in the holding, and at the encampments, would weigh less than a half stone.

"They are only slaves," he said.

"All were exchanged?" I said. I still wondered about Cecily and Saru.

"All," he said.

I wondered if this were true.

"I should have been informed," I said.

"I am lowly," said the Ashigaru.

I bowed, slightly, turned about, and proceeded to the quarters of Lord Nishida. Men removed themselves quickly from my path.

"Why was I not told?" I demanded.

"It was feared you might not approve," said Lord Nishida.

"I do not," I said.

"It is as we feared," he said. "Would you care for tea?" Lady Sumomo, the younger of his two contract women, was nearby, and ready to pour. Her kimono was of yellow silk. Her glistening black hair was high on her head, and held in place with a long comb.

Tajima wished to buy her contract but, of course, lacked the means to do so. It is easier with slaves, as it is with other beasts. One does not expect to pay much for them. Most are priced reasonably. It is not difficult to pick out a nice one. One examines them, one bids on them, one owns them.

"No," I said. "I am returning to the encampment."

"The onslaught is imminent," he said.

"How do you know?" I asked.

"I do not, of course," he said, "but it seems likely, given the outcome of this morning's conference."

"Were I Lord Yamada," I said, "I would bide my time, letting hunger do my fighting."

"Despite the asseverations of our friend, Tyrtaios," he said, "Lord Yamada is not a patient man."

"You know him?" I asked.

"Yes," he said.

"How is that?" I asked.

"The house of Yamada and that of Temmu have been enemies for years," he said.

"I suspect," I said, "General Yamada has confederates within the holding."

"I fear so," he said. "Tea?"

"I am returning to the encampment," I said.

"Have you leave from Lord Temmu?" he inquired, softly.

"No," I said.

"We expected much from the tarn cavalry," he said.

"I am sorry," I said.

"You are leaving?" he said.

"Yes," I said.

"Things grow dark," he said.

"Yes," I said.

"Lord Okimoto believes you will abandon us."

"He is mistaken," I said.

"You will return?" he asked.

"Yes," I said.

"Lord Yamada," he said, "seems to be well apprised of conditions within the holding."

"It seems so," I said.

"How can this be?" he asked.

"I do not know," I said.

"There are ways in which one might communicate with his pavilion," he said.

"Doubtless," I said.

"For example," he said, "by tarn."

"It is true," I said. "That would be possible."

"Lord Okimoto," he said, "suspects you of treachery."

"I am aware of that," I said. "So, too, do others."

"Such suspicions," he said, "are unfounded."

"I trust so," I said. "What of Lord Okimoto?"

"He is a daimyo," said Lord Nishida. "He is above suspicion."

"Might not a daimyo, consulting likely eventuations, change banners?" I inquired.

"It is unthinkable," said Lord Nishida. "First, one would apply the ritual knife."

"I see," I said.

"You are not sure of that?" asked Lord Nishida.

"No," I said.

"You are not of our people," said Lord Nishida. "Deceit,

treason, treachery, and such are more to be expected amongst others."

"Amongst hirelings, fighters for fee, mercenaries?" I said.

"Lamentably so," said Lord Nishida, quietly.

"Such as Tyrtaios," I said.

"Clearly," he said.

"And others?" I said.

"Possibly," he said.

"Such as Tarl Cabot," I suggested.

"Your loyalty is beyond question," he said.

"The slaves were bartered for rice," I said.

"Even the slaves of the shogun," said Lord Nishida.

"For rice!" I said.

"More valuable than gold at present," he said.

"How long did it last?" I asked.

"Lots were cast into a helmet, and drawn," he said. "Most had nothing. Some were slain."

"Even so," I said, "how long did it last?"

"Three days," he said. "You are angry?"

"Would that the siege might be broken," I said.

"There is no way to do so," he said.

"Tarns," I said.

"Too few," he said.

It was difficult not to share this assessment.

"We should have sallied forth when we had strength, weeks ago, risking all on a desperate charge," I said.

"Numbers cannot be ignored," he said. "The urt gains little by casting himself into the jaws of the larl. In the midst of the Ashigaru of Lord Yamada we would have disappeared like water into sand."

"It would have been honorable," I said.

"Yes," said Lord Nishida, "but, one supposes, less than wise."

"Now the men are weak," I said. "I understand many cannot meet the muster."

"I fear doom is upon us," said Lord Nishida. "I fear, at last, we lie within the shadow of the iron dragon."

"What is this business about an iron dragon?" I asked.

"A figure of speech," he said. "Do not concern yourself."

"But there is a legend involved?" I said.

"Yes," said Lord Nishida. "The dragon is a creature of legend, a mythological beast. When it awakens and spreads its wings, it signifies loss and defeat, the changing of things, the darkening of the sun, the coming of night, the downfall of dynasties, the end of great houses."

I had heard of this sort of thing before. Too, I recalled that Tyrtaios, oddly, had referred to this presumably mythological beast.

"Surely none subscribe to such a superstition," I said.

"Many do," he said.

"Lord Okimoto?" I said.

"Possibly," said Lord Nishida.

"Such thoughts are absurd," I said.

"What lies within the hearts of men," he said, "is seldom absurd."

I rose to leave.

"Do not depart angrily," he said.

"For rice!" I said.

"Better that than that they should languish and perish in the housing area," he said.

"I see Sumomo is about," I said.

The lovely contract woman lifted her head, quickly.

"She is not a slave," said Lord Nishida. "Contract women are refined, trained, and precious."

"Contracts can be bought and sold," I said.

"Do not be angry, Tarl Cabot, tarnsman," he said.

"Perhaps," I said, angrily. "I should remove the cavalry."

"I am sure they would follow you," he said.

"None could stop us," I said.

"None," he said.

"Call the guards," I said. "See that I do not leave the holding alive."

"No," he said. "I trust you. You are Tarl Cabot, tarnsman. You were selected with care."

"Selected?" I said.

"Yes," he said.

"By whom?" I asked.

"Surely you do not think it a mere happenstance that you once found yourself on a remote, unmarked beach some fifty pasangs north of the Alexandra."

"By whom?" I asked.

"That is not known to me," he said.

I shuddered, for I had been landed at such a place long ago, a cold, narrow beach, bleak and stony, deserted, distant from settlements, bordering the northern forests, landed from a slaver's ship, one which had exited the locks of a steel world.

Were there wars behind wars, I wondered.

"You joined us," said Lord Nishida.

"I was curious," I said.

"Of your own free will," he said.

"Yes," I said.

"Had you not joined us," said Lord Nishida, "you would have been slain."

"I see," I said.

"You recall the wands, the perimeter, the guard larls, the fate of deserters," said Lord Nishida.

"Yes," I said.

"Secrecy was of the essence," he said.

"An essence poorly secured," I said. "The camp was discovered, and attacked. Forces were waiting at the mouth of the Alexandra to deny us the sea."

"Enemies are amongst us," said Lord Nishida.

"Clearly," I said.

"How far is the encampment?" asked Lord Nishida.

"Not far, by tarn," I said.

"I did not think the location at the confluence of two rivers was wise," said Lord Nishida. "One need only follow a river north."

"The choice was not mine," I said.

"Tarl Cabot, tarnsman," said Lord Nishida.

"Noble lord?" I said.

"I trust you," he said.

"I am grateful," I said.

"Lord Okimoto does not," he said.

"I am well aware of that," I said.

"Lord Okimoto is senior daimyo," said Lord Nishida.

"I have gathered that," I said.

"He is cousin to the shogun," said Lord Nishida.

"Perhaps he would like to be shogun," I said.

"I do not understand," said Lord Nishida politely.

"It is nothing," I said.

"Not all slaves were bartered," said Lord Nishida.

"I was told all," I said.

"One was not," he said.

"Saru, the slave of Lord Temmu?" I said.

"She went for a *fukuro* of rice," he said.

"What slave then?" I asked.

"It was desired that there would be a hold over you," said Lord Nishida, "a hold in terms of which your service and loyalty might be assured."

"I do not understand," I said.

"Arrangements were made," he said.

"My loyalty is not contingent on such things," I said.

"That pleases me," said Lord Nishida.

"Why did you not tell me that she was held, and not bartered?" I asked.

"There seemed no need," he said, "but now matters are desperate."

"So even you might doubt me?" I said.

"One must be cautious, Tarl Cabot, tarnsman," he said. "It is hard to see into the hearts of men."

"I am sure of it," I said.

"Do not be angry," he said.

"Where is she held?" I asked. "I would see her."

"It is thought inadvisable," he said.

"I do not understand," I said.

"It is not necessary that you do," he said.

"There was no need to hold her apart in the bartering," I said, "as I contemplate no flight, no desertion, no treason, but I am pleased that you did so. In this case your suspicions, if suspicions they be, worked well to my advantage. I accord you my thanks. I regret only that the others were bartered, and for so little."

"Do not concern yourself," he said. "They are mere goods, merchandise, animals, beasts, slaves, and may be worked, tethered, chained, and penned, and enjoyed, as masters wish."

"Still, I am pleased," I said, "that my personal collar-slut, Cecily, was exempted, that she was held apart in the bartering."

"She was not," said Lord Nishida.

"What?" I said.

"She went for a *fukuro* of rice," said Lord Nishida.

"I do not understand," I said.

"It is another beast which was held apart," he said, "not your Cecily."

"I do not understand," I said.

"These arrangements were made long ago," he said.

"By whom?" I asked.

"That is not clear to me," he said.

"Even before the formation and training of the cavalry?" I asked.

"Yes," he said.

"But it is a slave?" I said.

"Yes," he said.

"What slave?" I asked, puzzled.

"That is not known to me," he said.

"Nor known to me," I said.

"Apparently," he said.

"Is there anything special about her?" I asked.

"She is quite beautiful," he said.

"So are thousands upon thousands," I said. "They would not be put on the block if they were not likely to sell, and well."

"True," said Lord Nishida.

"You are sure it is a slave?" I asked.

"Yes," he said.

"Not a free woman?"

"No," he said.

It is difficult to convey to one unfamiliar with the cultural pertinences the social status of the Gorean free woman.

"It does not matter then," I said. "A tarsk is a tarsk. A slave is a slave."

"I am pleased to hear you speak so," said Lord Nishida.

"I leave," I announced.

"Surely there is time for tea," said Lord Nishida.

"The tarn is saddled," I said.

"Tarl Cabot, tarnsman," he said.

"Noble lord," I said.

"Matters are dark," said Lord Nishida. "Lord Okimoto contemplates the ritual knife."

"I have gathered that," I said.

"Lord Okimoto," said Lord Nishida, "has the ear of the shogun."

"So?" I said.

"Should Lord Temmu suggest the ritual knife," he said, "the garrison will unhesitantly comply."

"The mercenaries would not," I said.

"They might be independently slain," said Lord Nishida. "Most are too weak to resist."

"Surely you have contact with the shogun," I said.

"Of course," said Lord Nishida.

"Convince him, at all costs," I said, "to hold out until the passage hand."

"It will be difficult," said Lord Nishida.

"The holding will be supplied," I said.

"How so?" inquired Lord Nishida.

"We have sought supplies in the wrong place," I said.

"I do not understand," he said.

"Perhaps your contract servant might withdraw," I said.

Sumomo was kneeling at the low, oval table, with its surface of inlaid woods, on which reposed the service for tea. She looked up, startled, then glanced to Lord Nishida, and then withdrew.

"You have a plan?" asked Lord Nishida.

I strode to a large framed screen, of painted silk, one bearing the images of mountains and needle trees, at the side of the room, and thrust it back.

Sumomo then, her head down, demurely hurried away, with short steps.

"You have a plan?" asked Lord Nishida.

"Yes," I said.

"Let it be thought," I said, "that I have withdrawn the cavalry, that we have deserted the banner of Temmu."

"I fear few will fail to believe that," said Lord Nishida.

"Good," I said.

"If you will provide to me the details of your plan," he said, "I shall attempt to secure the approval of the shogun."

"Who will then seek the wisdom of advisors, such as Daichi, the caster of bones and shells," I said.

"Doubtless," said Lord Nishida.

"Convince him, merely," I said, "to hold out until the passage hand."

"I will try to do so," he said.

"After the holding is supplied," I said, "keep all but trusted guards off the outer parapets."

"You think you can supply the holding?" asked Lord Nishida.

"Yes," I said. "And it is then that my plan will become practical."

"Surely you may confide the details of your plan to me," he said.

"Forgive me, Lord," I said.

"I am not trusted?" he said.

"It is hard," I said, "to look into the hearts of men."

"That is true," he said, "Tarl Cabot, tarnsman."

Chapter Eight

Lord Yamada Is Supplying the Holding; He Is Unaware of This.

We would wait until nightfall, as we had the last several nights.

"I am not a porter," growled Torgus.

"There are four more panniers to fill," said Lysander.

We were well to the south of the investing forces of Lord Yamada. We were a pasang east of the road lined with posts, each surmounted by a human head. Our proximity to this lengthy, dismal display, I did not doubt, made it easier to enlist informants amongst the local peasantry. In the fields little love was lost where the house of Yamada was concerned. His mercilessly imposed tyranny, wrought by the edge of the sword, was keenly resented. We had soon been apprised of the location of warehouses and the routes and schedules of supply trains. The warehouses in which I was particularly interested were the small, concealed warehouses, scattered about, whose location was apparently unknown even to many of the high officers in the command of General Yamada. Such secret repositories can obviously shorten supply lines and enable a variety of maneuvers and marches, both of advance and withdrawal. In the event of defeat or exile they provide a means of provisioning a flight or supporting an unexpected return and counterattack. A concern for such measures was apparently a characteristic of General Yamada. The other warehouses, large, sturdy structures, on the gates of which were emblazoned the insignia of the house of Yamada, might be left for later, and perhaps for the torch.

"Captain *san*," said Ichiro, issued into my presence, come from the brush to the side. He commonly served as bannerman.

"Report," I said.

"Disguised as a half-blind sutler," he said, "I, together with others, peddlers, camp followers, and such, infiltrated the camp of Yamada. The camp is well-supplied."

"It will not be for long," I said.

"The morale of the men of Yamada is high," he said. "The great onslaught is eagerly anticipated. Great Yamada delays, to make more certain of the incapacity of the garrison to defend itself."

"I thought he might," I said.

I thought him wise in the ways of war, a formidable tactician and leader. One seldom comes easily to the dais of a shogun.

"And in the camp it is said that Tarl Cabot, tarnsman, has deserted the banner of Temmu, and that the tarn cavalry, what remained of it, is fled."

"Good," I said.

"They are muchly amused, and pleased," said Ichiro.

"Excellent," I said.

"I have news from the holding, as well," he said. "Men grow stronger. No longer do they denounce Tarl Cabot, tarnsman. They feed, and rejoice."

"And the parapets are denied to all but trusted guards?" I asked.

"It is so, Captain *san*," said Ichiro. "All others are turned away."

Thus, I thought, even though there be spies in the holding, it would now be difficult, and, hopefully, impossible, for them to communicate with General Yamada. Presumably signals, messages, and such, could no longer be transmitted from the parapets. I had full confidence in the tarn cavalry. And men did not come and go between the holding and the camp of General Yamada. Lord Temmu had seen to this. It was a capital offense to approach a gate without authorization.

"You have done well, brave Ichiro," I said.

He lowered his head shyly.

"It requires great courage to do what you have done," I said.

"It gives me great pleasure to be of service to my commander, and my daimyo, and shogun," he said.

"Few could have done this," I said.

"I am of the command of Tarl Cabot, tarnsman," he said.

"How is Tajima?" I asked.

Ichiro looked up.

"He is muchly recovered, and now resides in the holding," said Ichiro. "He fears the onslaught, and would have it no other way."

I recalled that Tajima, suspecting, and I would suppose correctly, that he might more likely survive as a fugitive in the mountains than Ichiro, had, in the midst of the storming of the first encampment, turned his tarn over to Ichiro and ordered him to flee. I had subsequently feared, had Tajima perished in the mountains, that Ichiro might have had recourse to the ritual knife. To be sure, Tajima survived, and, as nearly as I could tell, was doing well, though I would have still been hesitant to send him forth to meet an enemy. I found it difficult to understand Ichiro, and his sort. He had been ordered away, and thus, in the light of discipline, had had no choice other than to obey his superior, Tajima. If one were to think of the ritual knife, it seemed to me a more plausible occasion for its employment would have been upon the failure to obey the order. From my point of view, of course, living was a more plausible route to honor than death. I was never an enthusiast for leaping on one's sword, and such. Better to die with it in one's hand, facing the enemy. On the other hand, who am I, who once abandoned honor, long ago, in the delta of the Vosk, to speak of it to others? Paths are many; let each seek his own.

"Tajima, I fear," I said, "has an eye for Sumomo."

"Most unwise," said Ichiro.

"He used to watch her in Tarncamp," I said.

"And now in the holding I fear," said Ichiro.

"Most unwise," I said.

"I think so, Captain *san*," he said.

"That is a joke," I said.

"Yes, Captain *san*," said Ichiro.

"We are loading panniers with rice," I said. "Rest now. After dark we will deliver these stores to the holding."

"Yes, Captain *san*," said Ichiro.

Ichiro withdrew, hopefully to secure some Ehn of sleep.

I went to the small shed, to the stores of which we were helping ourselves. "How goes it?" I asked Torgus.

"There will be little left here," said Torgus.

Of the fifty-one tarns which had survived the raid on the first encampment, we were utilizing forty. Each would carry two bulging panniers of rice, one on each side of the saddle. Of the other eleven tarns, six were charged with keeping lines of communication open between the holding, the new encampment, and our storage depot, so to speak, which changed, day by day. The other five were used for reconnaissance and mapping. As yet, I did not think the pavilion of Yamada was aware of our activities. And, even should they be detected, it would take time for word of them to reach his pavilion, as the swiftness of tarns was ours, and he, as kaiila were unknown in the islands, was limited to posts of runners, used to communicate between his camp, his towns, and capital.

"The panniers are ready," said Torgus.

"We leave after dark," I said.

I looked at a brace of panniers.

"The slaves were bartered for one or two *fukuros* of rice each," I said.

"The garrison was starving," said Torgus.

"Each of these panniers," I said, "would hold several *fukuros* of rice."

"Who would know that slaves were so cheap," said Lysander.

"A starving man would give a Brundisium stater, a tarn disk of Ar, for a cup of rice," said Torgus.

"Where are the slaves?" I said. "What was done with them?"

"Such things are not known," said Lysander.

"You have scouts out," said Torgus. "Perhaps they will note cages, a pen, a slave yard, a coffle."

"One or two *fukuros* of rice," I said.

"Most for one, I understand," said Torgus.

"Do you object?" asked Lysander.

"Not to the selling," I said, "it is fitting that they be bought and sold. They are merchandise."

"But so cheaply," said Torgus.

"Yes," I said.

"Lord Temmu had little choice in the matter," said Lysander.

"I understand," I said.

"But you are annoyed," said Lysander.

"Yes," I said.

"Most would be annoyed," said Torgus.

"Yes, I suppose so, most," said Lysander.

Even a pot girl, a kettle-and-mat girl, would most likely bring between twenty and thirty copper tarsks in most markets. And, in better times, one might buy the common *fukuro* of rice, to its usual measure, for as little as one or two tarsk-bits.

"It will be dark soon," said Torgus.

Slave girls are commonly quite vain. Not vain as are free women, arrogant in their freedom and smug in their supposed beauty, whom slave girls commonly look down on, though fear terribly, but vain as slaves. There is a Gorean expression, "slave beautiful," or "beautiful enough to be a slave." Even a free woman so described, feigning her outrage, would, I suspect, be secretly pleased with such an assessment. What woman would not wish to be 'slave beautiful' or 'beautiful enough to be a slave'? The slave, taken and collared, has no doubt as to her attractiveness and desirability. Are such things not proclaimed by the mark on her thigh and the collar on her neck? These are badges of quality, proof that men have found her worthy of bondage, worthy of being put on the block and sold. So it is no wonder that the slave is vain, for she knows that she is a prize, that she is so desirable and exciting that men, in the way of nature, will be content with nothing less than her possession. And so the girls compete, boast of their prices, and the heat of the bidding which took them from the block. And now, I thought, will certain slaves regale their sisters in the pens with accounts of their value, how they were bartered for a measure or two of rice?

"We will gather food again tomorrow?" said Lysander.

"I think not," I said.

"What then?" asked Torgus.

"I shall speak to Lord Okimoto," I said, "who, I trust, will speak to Lord Temmu."

"Why?" asked Torgus.

"It is my part of my plan," I said.

Chapter Nine

What Occurred in the Courtyard of the Holding; What Occurred Later at the New Encampment

The banner of Lord Temmu no longer flew over the castle.

From below there was no sign of life in the holding. The blades of no glaives were visible, borne by patrols.

There was no return fire, or cast stones, to the intrusions of the mighty arrows of the great bow.

Too, somehow, over the last two or three days, rumors had circulated in the camp of Yamada, rumors which, I supposed, only Pani would take seriously, but rumors which, indeed, they might take seriously.

As it was learned later, Lord Yamada, sitting cross-legged in his pavilion, being served tea by his contract women, listening to reports, was incredulous.

He was wary.

He even called forth readers of bones and shells, and, perhaps more judiciously, herbalists, physicians, and chemists.

Then, as the reports went, he rose up and cried out with rage, fearing perhaps in some obscure way that he may have been thwarted, or outdone.

Then, on the third day, word was brought to him that the great gate at the height of the wharf trail, leading upward from the sea to the holding, stood open.

Two or three Ashigaru, impressed from the fields, were sent

to reconnoiter, and they climbed the long path to the gate, in trepidation, fearing much. How tentative they were, and furtive!

Crouching and hesitant, a step at a time, they crept, bit by bit, to the great threshold, and peered within. Moments later, crying out with fear, awed by what they had seen, they hurried back, down the trail, about the wharves, and to the plain, so far below the lofty walls of the holding, on which stood the pavilion of Lord Yamada.

They cast themselves prostrate before the shogun and, eyes on the lacquered boards, not daring to raise their heads, babbled out their report.

Men and officers were gathered about, and, in moments, surgent and uncontrolled, what had once been the scarcely audible stammerings of frightened Ashigaru were being proclaimed, shouted, broadcast throughout the entire camp of the shogun.

Lord Yamada was not pleased. His brow was clouded and his face was dark with fury. He looked from his pavilion to the heights of the holding so far above, almost lost in the clouds, and shook his fists in anger.

"Lord, Lord?" inquired a general.

"Yes, yes!" screamed the irate shogun. "Go, be done with it!"

The shogun then turned away, returning to his private quarters.

Orders scarcely needed be uttered.

The siege was done; gold lay in the clouds; officers sought to muster and organize men, but already hundreds of Ashigaru, and men, even of two swords, were hurrying up the long trail.

Little did it matter to them that a deed massive and potent in its might, a deed which might awe and shame better men, had been accomplished within their own lifetime, a deed the tale of which might be told for a thousand years.

I had returned to the holding and had spoken to Lord Okimoto, and he, in turn, shortly thereafter, had addressed himself to his cousin, the shogun, Lord Temmu.

"I do not well understand the matter of the ritual knife," I had said to Lord Okimoto, "but it is clear you are one who does. So I ask your view on what seems to me a simple matter. My question is this, is it appropriate to lift the ritual knife when success, survival, even victory, is still possible?"

"In such a case," had said Lord Okimoto, "lifting the ritual knife would be not only premature, but would be an error of action; indeed, it would be improper, and thus forbidden."

"The holding," I said, "is strengthened. Supplies are abundant. The men rise up. They look about themselves. Their eyes are clear, their limbs are strong."

"As things are," he said, "one would not take the blade out of its case. There is no point in doing that now. It was different before."

"Our renewed strength," I said, "is not known below."

"I do not think so," he said.

"Excellent," I had said. "Now let me speak more to you. I have a plan."

I supposed that after the months of the siege, the inactivity, the waiting, the watching, the routine patrols, the endless drills, and such, the eagerness, the unruliness, the excitement, the greed of hundreds of the men of General Yamada, rushing as they could up the steep trail from the wharves to the holding, was understandable. At the edges of the encampment below officers sought to control their men, to marshal the platoons and companies as they could, but their success was not notable. At the height of the trail lay the holding with its wealth of gold, silver, silk, sake, vessels, jewels, screens, hangings, perfumes, weapons, robes, instruments, ointments, oils, and such, the treasure and loot of generations amassed by the house of Temmu. Who can discipline an army if it is the army itself which abandons discipline? In warfare, the salvation of the defeated is often contingent on the victors pausing to gather in the stores of the routed force, which delay commonly purchases the time necessary for an expeditious withdrawal. In theory one presses on against a fleeing enemy, denying him rest, precluding a regrouping and stand. In the field manuals the common lesson is to pursue an advantage to the end, to follow up on the victory, never to stop with an incomplete victory, but the field manuals are written with the care and leisure which might accompany kaissa. They are composed in tents by lamplight, after a day's march or skirmishing, even in winter quarters, or even in exile, or retirement, as is thought to have been the case with the *Field Diaries* commonly attributed to Carl Commenius of Argentum. It is not difficult, in the quiet of the night, or the quiet of the study, to analyze with shrewdness, and compose with deliberation. But, unfortunately, those in the ranks are seldom familiar with the manuals, and would not care for them if they were, and many cannot read. And officers, familiar with the manuals, sweating in the midst of fighting, exhausted, hoarse, their arm weary, looking about themselves, discover they are now surrounded by disorganized, swarming men, innocent of, or forgetful of, codes, excited, frightened, violent, celebratory, reckless men who have survived battle, men who are not eager to renew war, to face again the blades of a desperate enemy, men who are now exhilarated to find themselves alive, and are intent on loot, without which the pittance of a common fee is negligible.

Whatever may be the case the trail upward was crowded with hurrying, jostling, panting men eager to make it through the gate at the summit of the wharf trail before it might be shut against them by their own officers. One might, in such a moment, be able to seize and carry away, even concealed in one's garments, enough to purchase a tavern or farm.

Some men apparently died in the climb upward.

Those in the foremost ranks, gasping, legs aching, bracing themselves, pushed from behind, paused as had their predecessors, the timid peasants sent ahead to reconnoiter, at the large threshold.

An awesome sight met their eyes, hundreds of Pani warriors, in white garments, having seemingly performed ablutions and purified themselves, lay crumpled in the remains of what must have been a great number of serried ranks.

Apparently, at a common signal, well over two thousand Pani warriors had had recourse to the ritual knife.

Then there were cries from behind the paused, startled vanguard of looters, cries of wrath and impatience, and men began to force themselves past, at which point, with a great cry, hundreds of men, bent on plunder, burst through the opening.

They swarmed into the courtyard between the inner wall and the fronting of the castle.

There was much shouting, and confusion. Inert bodies were kicked, and white garments trampled upon. Men milled about, their eyes wild, uncertain now where to begin, which buildings to breach, what portals to force. Where would be the deepest vaults and the mightiest chests? Where would lie the greatest treasures? They looked to the castle. "To the castle!" they cried.

Then suddenly, in their hundreds, they stood still, startled, unable to move, struck with surprise, astonished, for, before them, before the portal of the castle, there stood a single figure, this even as others continued to pour over the great threshold.

Lord Temmu was a large man. He was standing; his eyes were wild and fierce, and, over his head, clutched in two hands, he held his field sword.

"Death!" he cried.

In that moment there stood at his side, the short, thick figure of Nodachi, a sword in each hand.

He said nothing, he measured those about, selecting who would die.

Then, behind Lord Temmu on the right stood Lord Okimoto, and on the left, Lord Nishida. "Death!" they cried.

At this signal hundreds of hitherto prostrate Pani, armed, sprang up, and began to fall on the looters, many of whom had cast away weapons, that they not be encumbered in bearing away their booty.

At the same time more than a thousand mercenaries streamed forth from the barracks, sheds, ancillary buildings, and the castle itself, crying out a hundred war cries from a hundred cities.

For some moments looters, unapprised of what ensued on the level; continued to hurry upward, and enter the courtyard, but, momentarily, there was confusion at the threshold as terrified men turned to flee back through the opening. But a line of Pani interposed themselves and a dozen others cut men away from the threshold and swung shut the gate.

In moments hundreds of looters were encircled, crowded together, in the center of the courtyard.

Nodachi then, I am told, cleaned his swords and returned them to his sash, and went to the side, where he sat, cross-legged, and silent.

The tarn cavalry, less than a pasang north of the holding, was mounted, and waiting.

"The banner of Temmu is raised!" called Ichiro.

This, by prearrangement, was coordinated with the initiation of the attack on the looters.

"One-strap!" I cried.

I had requested that Tajima be the one to raise the banner, signaling the cavalry. This did not please him, but I did not wish to risk him against the enemy until I was confident he was fully ready, fully recovered from the harrowing rigors and exposure of his isolation in the mountains. I did not doubt but what, the banner flying, he would race to the courtyard, with two swords, but the delay, I hoped, would be sufficient to reduce the numbers of, and the brunt of the resistance of, the enemy.

In moments the remnants of the tarn cavalry, limited now to fifty-one mounts, was streaking through the clouds over the holding, making its way, in formation, though without tarn drum, to the encampment of Yamada, to fire as many tents as possible.

We began with the tents farthest to the south, selecting tents in the kaissa-board fashion, to conserve our incendiary materials, fire jars lit in flight, as this approach is designed to capitalize on the likelihood that a fire consuming one tent may spread to another. We began with the farthest tents to confuse the enemy as to our mission, that he would merely see us pass overhead, and, more importantly, that the enemy in the fore would see fire behind him, and the mountain and holding before him. This is likely to have its effect on morale. What is behind him, and what does it mean? Too, I assumed General Yamada, from what I had learned of this mighty adversary, would more likely be at the front of his troops than in the rear. Accordingly, he would find himself removed from the immediate locus of the attack, this delaying a personal response to it, and, almost certainly, would assure a delay in his apprehension of the situation, its nature and gravity. Uncertainty and confusion are sometimes as effective as the blade and glaive. Action undertaken in such a situation may easily prove inopportune and unwise. On the other hand, in this situation, small purchase would be obtained.

Any troubling lacuna in the intelligence available to the shogun would be brief.

"Ho!" I called to Ichiro, not yards from me, to whose supple, tem-wood lance was affixed the commander's pennon, and about whose shoulder hung the war horn of command. "About!" I called. "The day is done. Two-strap! Into the clouds, to vanish! Home, Fellows, home!"

Ichiro winded his horn, with the piercing note of assembly, and the riders, as one, wheeled their sky mounts toward the mountains.

Below us, some two hundred feet below, there were screaming, running men. But in moments their cries were behind us, as was the smoke rising from burning tents.

As planned, following our raid, we withdrew to our base, the new encampment. It was just as well, for there would be little purpose in bringing the cavalry to the holding, and, in addition, I was reluctant to see the disposition allotted to the trapped looters, many of whom were not even armed, their greed having encouraged them to disburden themselves of the inconvenience and weight of weapons, in particular, the lengthy, long-bladed glaive. I learned later of the slaughter wrought in the courtyard, and the casting of bodies, some bound and living, from the outer parapets to the valley below. It was not customary in the islands to take prisoners.

At the encampment, the tarns cotted and fed, I called my high officers, Torgus and Lysander, to my tent, that a vessel of paga might be shared.

"Tarns have been seen," said Lysander.

"Some knew of them, from the first encampment," said Torgus.

"But comparatively few," said Lysander.

"True," said Torgus.

"But now matters are quite different," said Lysander. "There is no longer a point in trying to conceal the existence of tarns."

"They are still exotic, strange here, at least unfamiliar," said Torgus. "Better to employ them sparingly."

"But surely employ them!" said Lysander.

"Yes," said Torgus. "Yes!"

It had originally been hoped that a major land battle with the forces of Lord Yamada, a battle decisive for the outcome of the war, might have been brought about, a battle which might turn profitably on the unexpected appearance of the tarn cavalry, a military arm new to the islands. It had been hoped that its entry into the battle, aside from what might be its contribution in terms of fire power, might induce consternation into the masses of a largely ignorant and superstitious enemy. Would not the arrival of such monsters most easily be understood in terms of preternatural agencies? Indeed, Lord Temmu, shortly after the great ship of Tersites had been wharfed below the holding, had sowed the seeds of such alarms by means of spies, spreading rumors of terrifying winged beasts, demon birds, dragon birds, alleged to be favorable to the cause of the house of Temmu. But unfortunately this project had failed of fruition. First, no major land battle had occurred. Indeed, after the probable betrayal of, and surely the discovery and decimation of, the exploratory expedition launched by Lord Temmu, the enemy had advanced in force, later managing to invest the holding. Thus had the siege begun. The exploratory force had failed to rouse the countryside against Lord Yamada and had been unable to set the stage for a major confrontation in which the surprise of the tarn cavalry might be decisive. It had been unsuccessful in its mission, both militarily and politically. Indeed, its remnants, in retreat, routed and worn, harried and driven, had been fortunate to reach the shelter of the holding. Second, the location of, and the security devices of, the first encampment had been betrayed. It had been stormed by picked troops, following which the tarn cavalry itself had been considerably reduced, this impairing its effectiveness as an agency not only of intelligence and attack, but of supply.

Lysander and Torgus turned to me.

"The holding may now be regularly supplied," said Lysander.

"Yes," I said.

"But the siege has not been lifted," said Torgus.

"No," I said.

"Will we not carry the war to the enemy?" said Lysander. "It would be easy to strike behind their lines."

"We will do so," I said.

"I am pleased that Lord Temmu has finally authorized the use of the cavalry," said Lysander.

"He has not done so," I said.

"I do not understand," said Torgus.

"Lord Temmu is under the influence of others," I said.

"What others?" asked Torgus.

"I do not know," I said.

Chapter Ten

What Occurred on the Road North; We Will Later Move South, Having the Business of War in Mind

The fellow below looked up, startled, the shadow of the soaring tarn blotting out the sun.

I wheeled the bird about.

The line of wagons below was long. I think there must have been a hundred or more wagons.

This was the longest train of its sort we had hitherto encountered.

In parts of the line I did not think they were even aware of our presence.

Tarns descended, the forty of the striking arm.

Each wagon was drawn by ten to twelve peasants, rope lines leading to the broad leather belts across their bodies.

As tarns alit several emitted tarn cries, as though to announce their arrival and claim for their own the ground on which, wings snapping, dust in the wind, they stood.

Men fled.

The scream of the tarn is unmistakable, once one has heard it. It is commonly piercing and redolent with challenge and territoriality. The wild tarn will defend its nesting site against larls and sleen. Its hunting strike can break the back of a tarsk, ten hands at the shoulder. Its beak can tear a head from a body and its talons can tear loose the backbone of a larl. I once saw one in Torvaldsland disembowel a Kur, before the ax half severed its head and the Kur began to feed, one paw thrusting its intestines back into its body, holding them in place. Whereas a human being is not the common prey of a wild tarn, the usual objects of its interests being verr and tabuk, the tarn can be dangerous to humans, particularly if a nest is approached. The tarn commonly kills in hunting by breaking the back of its prey, but it can seize a verr and bear it aloft, to drop it to its death, after which it feeds, or carry it to its nest, where fledglings fight for the meat, the swiftest and most aggressive surviving, often at the expense of its siblings. The domestic tarn, on the other hand, like the domestic sleen, is bred for at least the partial tolerance of humans. It does not require live game. There are different varieties of domestic tarns, some bred for war, some for racing, and some for draft purposes, the haulage of tarn baskets, which may contain cargo or passengers, or, in the case of slaves, slave cargo. A tarnster commonly controls the tarn with reins from the basket, unless there is a line of tarns, tied together, which commonly follows a lead tarn, with its own tarnster and basket. The domestic tarn, given the selections involved and their purposes, like the domestic sleen, is usually larger, stronger, faster, and healthier than its wild cousin. It is bred to be such.

I saw men scattering beneath me.

We did not brandish the banners of Temmu but there would be little doubt in whose interest we flew.

For Ihn I scouted the line of wagons, to the end and forward, and then, near the center of the train I brought the bird down.

One commonly commands from the center.

This shortens the lines of communication.

I had seen no guards.

By now I was sure the investing forces of General Yamada were beginning to feel the straits of hunger. It is not only the prisoners of a siege, confined in a holding, who may suffer such an ugly durance, but also their jailers, if no food is brought to them. General Yamada's lines of encirclement, ample to resist and turn back any likely sallying forth from the holding, were numerous, thick, and deep. He had, in effect, his armies in the field, and largely concentrated in the area of the holding. There was no way that limited area could indefinitely sustain large numbers of men. Forces of that size, in such a location, must be supplied from without. There was no dearth of food in the several territories claimed by Lord Yamada as we had determined, in supplying the holding by air. On the other hand, these supplies, if unable to reach his men in sufficient quantities in a timely manner, might as well, from the point of the besiegers, anchored in place, not exist. Several days ago we had begun to disrupt the supply lines of the enemy, striking at supply trains, frightening away draymen, dealing with guards, overturning and burning wagons, seizing stores, and discarding what we could not carry. Our work was often marked by hundreds of birds alighting on the spilled stores, who would soon compete with returning draymen, who would gather what rice they could and carry it away to their villages, where it might be concealed from the tax collectors of Lord Yamada. We would depart, smoke in our wake, leaving behind us the scramblings of hungry men and the cries of clouds of small birds. Soon, if all went well, the siege must be lifted. Even a will of the might of that of Lord Yamada would be unable, indefinitely, to hold thousands of starving men in place. He would have no alternative but to withdraw.

I looked about myself.

Many of the scattered draymen were visible in the fields, several yards off, watching us. This was not unusual. We had no quarrel with such, no more than if the wagons had been drawn by bosk or tharlarion. Too, so positioned, once we departed, they might hurry forth and rush upon the spilled stores. In recent days, and even from the time of the concealed warehouses, it was not unusual for *fukuros* of rice, in many cases, to find their way back to the very villages of their origin.

I had ordered draymen to be driven from the wagons if necessary, but, insofar as possible, to be left unharmed.

Indeed, it was my hope that local peasantries, from which the draymen would be impressed, might eventually be recruited as allies.

There were, of course, given the wagons, a great many of them.

"Where are the Ashigaru archers?" asked Torgus.

"I do not know," I said. In scouting the train I had discerned no archers, no guards.

"Why are these wagons not moving at night?" he asked.

"I do not know," I said. Of late, the supply wagons had begun to enter upon the roads only after the descent of Tor-tu-Gor.

Perhaps, I thought to myself, that there be conditions of maximum visibility.

"Bannerman," said I to Ichiro, "approach our friends in the fields. Greet them. Assure them they are welcome to what we do not take."

Ichiro complied with this request, and, in a few Ehn, returned.

"They do not respond," he said.

They were still standing, not moving, in the fields.

"I do not understand," said Torgus.

"Perhaps they are afraid," I said.

Who could forget the heads further to the south, aligning the road.

"Perhaps," said Torgus.

"I do not like it," I said, looking about.

"Nor I," said Torgus.

I climbed to the top of a wagon. I saw nothing.

Why had the peasants in the fields not responded to Ichiro?

This seemed anomalous.

Commonly we had little difficulty with local peasantries, from which draymen would be drawn. Indeed, we had often received pertinent intelligences from them. Several had proved invaluable in locating rice, in notifying us of supply trains, the times, the routes, the number of guards, and such. Indeed, I did not doubt but what many of the peasants watching from the fields were no more enamored of the policies and practices of Lord Yamada than the fellows who scouted and spied for us.

"Captain *san*," said Ichiro.

"Bannerman?" I said.

"They did not speak," said Ichiro.

"You indicated that," I said.

"Why did they not speak?" he asked.

"Why?" I asked.

"Perhaps they would not speak as peasants," he said.

"Did you see their hands?" I asked.

"Their hands," he said, "were held in their sleeves."

"That is a noble posture," I said.

"Unlike peasants," he said.

"Alert the men," I said.

"Yes, Captain *san*," he said.

Matters were as I had suspected; nonetheless, as rice was at stake, it seemed well to make sure.

I drew my blade and thrust down at the canvas which covered the contents of the wagon.

As I had feared the blade slipped through the canvas, encountered a layer of rice, supported by another canvas, stretched taut beneath the rice, and then met nothing.

I stood up, looking about, and resheathed the blade. I gave no sign of concern or agitation. There was a stirring amongst the men at the side, off from the road. Surely many had marked my action.

"Bannerman," said I. "Sound 'Saddles' and 'One-strap'."

Hardly had the first notes rung out than we heard another sound, the war blast of the *horagai*, and blades in their dozens thrust up through the canvas of dozens of wagons, cutting and ripping, and, emerging from the shreds of rent canvas, were screaming, armed men, many of two swords. At the same time the draymen, whom we had taken as peasantry, uttering the cry "Yamada," rushed toward the wagons, each bearing a dagger. Other covers on wagons were cast aside and archers stood revealed. From other wagons arose Ashigaru, armed with glaives.

The mighty wings of my tarn struck the air, and I saw one fellow stumble, his forearm over his eyes, lost in a sheet of driven dust, and I was aflight. All about me, and down the lines of the wagons, fore and aft, other tarns sprang into the air. I saw wielded glaives below me, and men looking up wildly, scattered amongst the wagons, and daggers were brandished in vain.

I looked back down.

"Cleverly done, great Yamada," I thought. "But better to have had fewer wagons, and some guards in evidence."

The men of two swords were looking up, angrily, their swords already sheathed or sashed.

The sun caught a hundred slivers of light as arrows fell back to earth.

"Bannerman," I called. "Assembly and four-strap."

I brought the cavalry down a pasang and a half from the road. This descent, I hoped, would be marked by the men of Yamada's projected ambush, adding to their frustration. Should they approach we might easily be away before we were within the range of their arrows, let alone their blades, and should they be so unwise as to approach *en masse* the wagons would be behind them, abandoned, and vulnerable.

Following our landing I summoned Torgus and Lysander to me; when the cavalry had been at full force each would have commanded a Century, or Hundred.

"What losses?" I asked.

"None," said Torgus. "None," said Lysander.

"Lord Yamada," I said, "is clever."

"Deception," said Lysander, "is the name of war." Lysander, I was sure, though I had not pursued the matter, had once been of the scarlet. In his background, I suspected, was a woman, perhaps a slave, and perhaps murder.

"The bait," said rough-spoken Torgus, "was too tempting."

"I think so," I said.

"Had we devoted ourselves hastily and uncritically to the wagons," said Lysander, "I suspect there would have been few of us left."

"True," said Torgus.

"Men and mounts are accounted for," said Lysander.

"Perhaps we shall not return immediately to the base," I said.

"How so?" said Torgus.

"I do not think there is enough rice for us to linger about, hoping to secure it," said Lysander, "and what there may be is heavily guarded."

"I have something else in mind," I said, "at least for now."

"Speak," said Torgus.

"It is my understanding," I said, "that the major forces of General Yamada are committed to the siege."

"That is our intelligence," said Lysander.

"Which would mean," I suggested, "the likely vulnerability of certain properties within his domain."

"We are not sure of this," said Torgus. "It seems likely, but it is hard to know. He may have large reserves at his disposal. What if he were to be challenged by a risen population?"

"There is little likelihood at present," I said, "of a native challenge from within his domain."

"No," said Torgus. "Men tremble. Yamada rules by force and terror."

"At the least indication of resistance," said Lysander, "fearful reprisals would ensue."

"Only those loyal to Yamada may carry weapons," said Torgus, "his soldiers, his officers, his police."

I nodded. One always disarms a populace before its enslavement.

"But others might come by arms," said Lysander. "We have the road of the sky at our disposal, the darkness of night, the swiftness of tarns."

"Beware," said Torgus, "of delivering weapons to strangers. The peasantry may prove loyal to Yamada, if only through fear."

"In any event," I said, "as of now, as far as we know, the peasantry is without arms."

"Very well," said Lysander. "We shall discount them, as of now."

"But we need not, do we, discount ourselves?" I said.

"Speak," said Torgus.

"Are you content," I asked, "that the operations of the cavalry should be limited largely to reconnaissance, to the securing of supplies, and such?"

"No," said Torgus.

"What do you have in mind?" asked Lysander, warily.

"Perhaps something more has occurred to you, my friends," I said.

"Raids, of course," said Torgus. "We can strike muchly when and where we please. Yamada's perimeters of defense are lengthy, and his reserves, if he does not fear the peasantry, may well be minimal and scattered."

"It is my understanding," said Lysander, "Lord Temmu has not authorized the use of the cavalry."

"For such a purpose," I said.

"Why not?" asked Lysander.

"Were that known," I said, "much else would be clear."

"We are then helpless," said Lysander.

"Not at all," I said.

"How so?" said Lysander.

"Rogue arms," I said, "are not unprecedented in war."

"I see," he said.

In the chaos of war, beasts might come from afar to hunt amongst the ruins. Often bands of brigands, consortiums of irregulars, even bandits, roamed disputed, ill-defended landscapes.

"Consider this," I said. "There is a war to be fought, and won."

"Discipline," said Lysander.

"Discipline," I said, "is not an end in itself. It is a means. One does not expect well-ordered troops, properly disciplined, in the name of discipline, to march off cliffs or devour poison."

"No," said Lysander.

"A contrived discipline, designed by partisans to produce defeat," I said, "is no discipline. It is to be denied. It is the betrayal of discipline. It is to be eschewed."

"I am uneasy," said Lysander.

"One must choose," I said.

"There are risks," said Lysander.

"There are always risks," I said. "I propose we labor on behalf of the house of Temmu, but independent of the dais. Let us fight in its favor, advancing its interests, independent of its chain of command, as best we can."

"This is disloyal," said Lysander.

"No," I said, "it is a greater loyalty."

"The cavalry," said Torgus, "would be, in effect, a free company."

"Let it seem so," I said, "at least to the enemy."

"If I understand you aright," said Lysander, "it would seem so to Lord Temmu, as well."

"At least," I said, "to those who have his ear, and sway his policy."

"This is dangerous," said Lysander.

"Less so," I said, "than inaction, and a refusal to counter larger numbers."

"You suggest raids," said Torgus, with satisfaction.

"Particularly now," I said.

"Why 'particularly now'?" asked Lysander.

"We have already noted," I said, "two things of interest,

the likely inertia of a peasantry, which would allow limited defensive precautions on the part of Lord Yamada, and the lack of an authorization for raids, which I suspect is as well understood by General Yamada as by those who stand high in the house of Temmu."

"Thus," said Torgus, "raids will not be anticipated."

"Not deep raids, not against his heartland," I said.

"And thus," said Lysander, "the likely paucity of an adequate defense."

"Given a passive peasantry and an inactive, curbed, cavalry, not to be feared, he is likely to be prepared only for pilfering, or, say, isolated acts of brigandage."

"There may be then," said Lysander, "no adequate defense of various holdings of the enemy, let us say, perhaps, warehouses, granaries, castles, palaces, and barracks."

"I would think not," I said.

"Excellent," said Torgus. "When should we strike? A day from now, two days, a week?"

"Yes," said Lysander. "How soon?"

"Now," I said.

"Now?" said Torgus.

"Consider this," I said. "In the train, there were many wagons. Let us suppose one hundred, and let us suppose each was drawn by ten men."

"Many by more," said Torgus.

"But let us say there were a thousand."

"Very well," said Torgus.

"Those men, clearly," I said, "were not of the peasantry."

"No," said Torgus.

"Now," I said, "there were perhaps four or five archers, Ashigaru, warriors, or such in several of the wagons, let us say, in eighty of the wagons. That would give us something like four hundred more men."

"Very well," said Torgus.

"Let us then suppose," I said, "that fourteen or fifteen hundred men were committed to the ambush, and that this would deplete an already restricted home guard, and that these men are far from Yamada's major holdings, and are all afoot."

"Yes," said Torgus.

"I see," said Lysander.

"Captain *san*," said Ichiro. "Enemy contingents approach."

"Are the wagons left unguarded?"

"Yes, Captain *san*," said Ichiro.

"Excellent," I said. "When the enemy is nearly within arrow range, eagerly near, ready to put arrows to the string, you may sound assembly and one-strap. We will then rise up, circle about, burn the wagons, and then fly south."

"They will then hurry south, after us," said Lysander.

"I do not think they will arrive in time to extinguish a thousand fires," said Torgus.

"Perhaps as they hurry south to defend the holdings of Yamada, we will see them below, on the road, on our return," said Lysander.

"We will make it a point to do so," I said.

"What will come of this?" asked Torgus.

"The lifting of a siege," I said.

Ichiro then sounded assembly and one-strap.

Chapter Eleven

I Obtain News from the Holding

"After the closing of the courtyard gates, and the disposition allotted to looters," said Tajima, "the outer parapets were opened again, as was the custom before."

"You seem disturbed," I said.

It had been but a few Ehn since our lookouts had spotted the approaching tarn, which soon alit in a flurry of wind and dust, on the small assembly ground amongst the cots and tents of the new encampment.

As soon as the tarn had been seen the small warning gong had sounded its single note, and I had left the tent I employed as the field headquarters of the cavalry. I shaded my eyes, watching the bird descend.

"It is word from the holding," speculated Lysander.

Tarns and riders were kept in constant readiness to communicate betwixt the holding and the encampment.

"It is Tajima *san*," said Ichiro, beside me.

His lance with the pennon of command was mounted upright outside the headquarters tent, that it might serve to identify the tent and be easily at hand should it be required.

The gong had sounded a single note, that the encampment be alerted to a new arrival. If the gong sounded twice, this suggested the possibility of an unauthorized intrusion. If the gong rang thrice, or repeatedly, this signified the cavalry was to prepare for flight. Beyond that, signals were conveyed by battle horn or drum. Six tarns were kept in constant readiness, usually divided between the holding and the encampment.

I strode out to meet Tajima, who was, I suppose, though he did not care for the role, my eyes and ears at the holding.

"Put Pertinax to such purposes," he had complained to me. Little love was lost between Pertinax and Tajima.

"I am not certain you are yet ready for war," I had said to Tajima.

"I am ready, Tarl Cabot, tarnsman," he had said.

"You are just annoyed," I said, "that you are not here, at my side, to spy on me on behalf of Lord Nishida."

"It is true," he said, "that I am expected to report on you."

"You will soon be well enough to do so," I said.

"I must raise the flag at the castle," he said, "on the closing of the courtyard gates, to signal the beginning of the cavalry attack on the camp of Lord Yamada. By the time I reached the courtyard, there was no blood left for my blade to drink."

"Life is sometimes hard," I said.

"I am not joking, Tarl Cabot, tarnsman," he said.

"Did you fear to be outdone?" I asked.

"By whom?" he inquired.

"Pertinax, for example," I said.

"I trust he was not in the courtyard, or waiting in the ancillary buildings, to rush forth upon the looters," he said.

"This worries you?" I asked.

"Certainly not," he said.

"No," I said. "He was assigned here, with others, to protect the camp."

"Good," he said.

"So he did not outdo you," I said.

"How could that be?" he said. "I am Pani. He is barbarian."

"I, too, am a barbarian," I said. Most Goreans, interestingly, divide barbarians from nonbarbarians on the basis of language. Those who do not speak Gorean, or do not speak it as a first language, are usually regarded as barbarians. Beyond this, I had gleaned that many Pani did this a bit differently, tending to regard anyone who was not Pani as a barbarian, whatever might have been his native language. I suspected that Lord Okimoto had much this view.

"Barbarians," he said, "may be divided into those who are acceptable, and those who are not."

"I see," I said.

"And you are acceptable," he said.

"I am pleased to hear it," I said.

"But Pertinax is not acceptable," he said.

"Why not?" I asked. "Have you detected him casting sidelong glances at Sumomo?"

"Of course not," he said.

"What then?" I asked. "Stealing water, rice?"

"No," he said.

"At one time," I said, "early in Tarncamp, you could have easily killed him."

"Certainly," he said.

"That is not so clear now," I said.

"Nodachi, swordsman," he said, "has accepted Pertinax as a student."

"He does not accept everyone," I said.

"No," said Tajima.

"He believes Pertinax has promise," I said.

"Pertinax is not Pani," he said.

"That does not seem to concern Nodachi," I said.

"How could it not?" asked Tajima.

"He is Nodachi," I said.

"I do not understand," said Tajima.

"Perhaps then," I said, "you have not yet fully profited from his instruction."

I myself did not pretend to understand Nodachi. He was a teacher, and a master. He was wedded to the sword, and it was as alive in his grip as if it were his own hand. There are men who dedicate themselves to an art, to painting, to music, to poetry. They strive for the perfections, the nuances, of shades, of colors, which only they can see, of notes which only they can hear, seeking the perfect drawing on silk, the tree that is living, the never-to-be forgotten cloud, the cascading tumble of sparkling water descending a hill, the perfect line of poetry, the beauty which perhaps only they can fully see, but for which they live. And this strange, short, thickly built man, so unprepossessing, so commonplace in appearance, so ragged in garments with hair so unkempt, this man so solitary, and lonely, so shy, so quiet, so dignified in speech, sought a kindred perfection, but it had to do with a finely honed blade, with skills, with a craft in which a perfection never to be achieved was incessantly sought. I did not understand him. But I knew I had been in the presence of greatness. He was Nodachi.

"Pertinax is not your enemy," I said.

"Nor is he my friend," said Tajima.

"I think he would be such," I said.

"He is not Pani," said Tajima.

"Nor am I," I said.

"But you are acceptable," he said.

"You see Pertinax as different, as not Pani," I said. "You despised him. Now you see him grown in strength, in skills, in learning. You fear he may one day equal, or excel you. This makes you angry, and afraid."

"I am unworthy, Tarl Cabot, tarnsman," he said.

"No," I said. "You are very worthy."

"Why did you not risk me in combat?" he asked.

"I feared you were not yet ready," I said.

"And why did you not risk Pertinax in combat?" he asked.

"I did not think he was ready," I said.

"I will train with him," he said. "I shall try to improve his skills."

"You are truly Pani," I said.

"But you must place us in combat," he said.

"I must do so," I said.

"Why?" he asked.

"Because I am commander," I said.

I had strode forth to greet Tajima.

Auxiliary personnel took the descended tarn in charge, that it might be led to the cots for grooming, for its feeding and watering, its rest.

"After the closing of the courtyard gates, and the disposition allotted to looters," said Tajima, "the outer parapets were opened again, as was the custom before."

"You seem disturbed," I had said.

"I fear I am, Tarl Cabot, tarnsman," he said, "for I bear dark news."

"Lord Temmu has sent you?" I asked. "Lord Nishida, Lord Okimoto?"

"No," he said. "I have come myself, alone, unbidden, that I may report to my captain, my commander."

"Report first," I said, "of the holding."

"Much proceeds well, as you are aware," he said.

"On the surface?" I said.

"Yes," he said. "On the surface. Certainly Lord Yamada is distraught. He cries vengeance on the house of Temmu. He feels betrayed. How is it that the cavalry flew? Was this action not forbidden? He withdraws his troops to protect his towns, holdings, palaces, and fortresses from fire cast down from the sky."

"It will be difficult to do so," I said.

"The siege is lifted," said Tajima. "Our warriors descend the paths to the plain. Only small contingents of Yamada's forces are about. When encountered, they are engaged, commonly successfully. Many withdraw. Our peasants return to their fields. To the north of the holding, Yamada's Ashigaru leave the villages, and make their way south. Their rice sacks are empty. Some die in the mountains. Men sing. Work begins again. Rice which did not exist suddenly appears. *Fukuros* are set aside for the house of Temmu. He is lord and his name is spoken with politeness. Those who control demon birds control the clouds, and those who control the clouds control the sky, and those who control the sky control the earth."

"Scarcely," I said. "The ultimate judge and lord of battle is men afoot, common men, marching, disciplined men, men who breach walls and force their way through gates, who can explore streets and enter rooms where desperate enemies lurk. These are the men who conquer, those who touch the enemy, who sack his treasure, and chain his women, that they be their playthings."

"The cavalry brought an end to the siege," said Tajima.

"The cavalry," I said, "has its values, and purposes."

"In seeking rice, in the time of hunger," said Tajima, "it seems Tarl Cabot, tarnsman, was wise, in not burning and punishing villages, and slaying men and women who withheld rice."

"That was the order of Lord Temmu," I said.

"Which, it seems," said Tajima, "the commander failed to convey to the cavalry."

"It slipped my mind," I said.

"Perhaps the commander is weak," said Tajima.

"Perhaps," I said.

"But perhaps," said Tajima, regarding me narrowly, "there are codes?"

"Perhaps," I said.

"I suspect the codes are not clear on the matter," said Tajima.

"Perhaps," I said.

"Perhaps the peasant is a better ally than enemy," said Tajima.

"That is quite possible," I said.

"In the fields," said Tajima, "we are now welcomed."

"The northern fields," I said, "were long under the suzerainty of Lord Temmu."

"They expect to be honored and protected," said Tajima.

"It would be wise for Lord Temmu to do so," I said. I was not so sure, personally, that there was all that much difference between the tyranny of a Lord Yamada and the benevolence of a Lord Temmu.

"Many Ashigaru of Lord Yamada, after the siege was lifted, were fallen upon by peasants."

"Winds shift," I suggested.

"Doubtless some will find their way south," said Tajima.

"I would expect so," I said.

"Do you think Lord Yamada will welcome them?" asked Tajima.

"Certainly," I said.

"They are in disgrace," said Tajima. "In contempt, he will cast the knife to their feet, that it may be put to use."

"They have obeyed well, and risked much," I said. "Perhaps they should seek a new lord."

"They will not return to him," said Tajima. "They will be *ronin*, men of the waves, men with no lord, mercenaries, free swords."

"Is not Nodachi, swordsman, such?" I asked.

"It is true," said Tajima. "He has never pledged his sword. He owns no lord."

"You spoke of dark news," I said, "yet your report seems benign."

"Indeed," he said, "supplies are ample, and there is talk of marching to the south."

"The offense must begin," I said, "to be abetted with the cavalry."

"Lord Yamada outnumbers us grievously," said Tajima.

Following the disasters of the mutiny at sea, the ambush following the first landing, the fate of the exploratory force, the raid on the first encampment, and casualties of the siege, there were something less than thirty-five hundred men, Pani and barbarians, at the disposal of the house of Temmu. It was estimated that Lord Yamada had at least three times this many in regular troops, and might, if it seemed needed, impress as many again from amongst the peasantry. Indeed, most Ashigaru were of peasant origin. They were not of significant family. Few would become men of two swords.

"Consider the double quiver of the tarn saddle," I said.

"It is true," said Tajima, "that two men with two arrows may be outnumbered by one man with three arrows."

"Surely Nodachi has spoken to you of these things," I said.

"Yes," he said.

The point is to choose one's field and time, and apply force judiciously. Given the reconnaissance of tarns, intelligence, commonly problematical in war, may be increased exponentially. Divided enemies are vulnerable enemies. A larger contingent of an objectively smaller force will often overmatch a smaller contingent of an objectively larger force. One thousand is more than one hundred, but twenty of one hundred is more than ten of one thousand.

"Consider tarns," I said.

"The eyes of the sky," said Tajima.

"Intelligence," I said, "may be as crucial as steel."

"I fear so," said Tajima.

"Recall the fate of the exploratory force," I said.

"Yes," said Tajima.

"It seemed its march, its route, its every move was known to the enemy."

"Yes," said Tajima.

"Had tarns not been withheld at the time," I said, "the exploratory force might have been better apprised of the position and movements of the enemy, and, warned in time, and retracted, spared its decimation, its rout, and the bloody, harrying pursuit to which it was subjected."

"That is likely," said Tajima.

The point at the time, at least in terms of strategy, was to conceal the cavalry until its appearance, presumably at the turning point of a crucial battle, might have a devastating psychological effect on a startled, superstitious enemy, and turn the tide in favor of the house of Temmu. The exploratory force, on the other hand, had failed to scout and assess the enemy, let alone bring about a situation which, properly exploited, would be likely to lead to a major confrontation. The common understanding of its debacle was the superior intelligence of the enemy, an intelligence which, it was suspected, had its origin in the holding of Temmu itself.

"But now," I said, "with tarns at our disposal, our intelligence should be at least equivalent to, if not superior to, that of the enemy."

"I shall hope so," said Tajima.

"The siege is lifted," I said. "Surely it is time now to act, if only to probe."

"Much has changed, Tarl Cabot, tarnsman, since you have visited the holding."

"I am sure of it," I said.

"I have fearful things to communicate," said Tajima.

"But all is going well," I said.

"On the surface," he said.

I recalled that when he had first spoken to me he had seemed uneasy, even disturbed.

"Lord Temmu, Lord Okimoto," he said, "did not approve of your unauthorized use of the cavalry."

"I did not expect them to," I said.

"They are pleased, of course, that the siege is lifted."

"I should hope so," I said.

"The use of the cavalry was not authorized," he said.

"I know," I said.

"It is requested that you report to the holding immediately," he said, "to be interviewed."

"'Interviewed'?" I said.

"The word is carefully chosen," said Tajima.

"I shall be in no hurry to participate in this interview," I said.

"You refuse?" asked Tajima.

"For the present," I said.

"I think that is wise," said Tajima.

"Is that the sum of your news?" I asked.

"No," said Tajima. "I must, with regret, speak three things, one I do not understand, one I am afraid I understand, and one I understand, and would that I did not understand."

"Speak," I said.

"An emissary from the palace of Lord Yamada, Tyrtaios, the mercenary, has come again to the dais," said Tajima. "He begs us to surrender."

"I do not understand," I said. "Is he, or Lord Yamada, mad? The siege is lifted. Major forces have been withdrawn. General Yamada turns his attention to his homeland, circumspect and watchful over his possessions. He is like an angry larl, quiescent in his den. He is not springing forth. He is uncertain. He is waiting. War may soon pound on his gates. His peasantry may be stirring."

"Lord Yamada," said Tajima, "has had read for him the bones and shells, and in these troubled days of strange things and darkness, fears that the iron dragon will awaken, and if awaken, will spread its wings and fly."

"He is afraid?" I asked.

"It seems so," said Tajima.

"And what have the bones and shells to say about iron dragons?" I asked.

"It is said that unless the house of Temmu yields to the house of Yamada the iron dragon will emerge from its den and destroy the house of Temmu."

"That sounds convenient," I said. "Why should this worry Lord Yamada?"

"Who knows what will occur should the iron dragon spread its wings?" asked Tajima. "Its shadow might lie upon the islands. Might not the rice wither and die in that darkness? Who knows the temper and appetite of the iron dragon? How long it has been since it has last flown! What if it is angry? What if it is hungry? What if it is insatiable? Might it not alight upon the palaces of Yamada as well as upon the holding of Temmu? Might its claws not tear the land and cast it into the sea, might not its jaws seize the sun and devour it, plunging the world into darkness?"

"If the bones and shells were read in the holding," I said, "I would expect them to foretell the jeopardy of the house of Yamada, should the iron dragon emerge from its den."

"It is hard sometimes to understand the bones and shells," said Tajima.

"Dear friend," I said, "you are not native to this world, no more than I. The world from which we derive may in many ways be thoughtless, foolish, shallow, decadent, materialistic, and cruel, but it is, at least, a world in which there are no iron dragons."

"Much may depend on what might be an iron dragon," said Tajima.

"On the world from which we derive," I said, "there are no iron dragons."

"This," said he, "is not the world from which we derive."

"There are no iron dragons," I said. "That is a beast of mythology. It is a creature only of stories, a creature of dark, fearful legends."

"You are right, of course, Tarl Cabot, tarnsman," he said. "I spoke foolishly."

"To be sure," I said, "the exploitation of superstition can be a weapon of war, as well as an instrument of prestige, power, and profit."

"The second thing of which I am reluctant to speak," he said, "is one I am afraid I understand only too well."

"I trust," I said, "it is no more important than the first thing, the empty prattle about iron dragons."

"It is reasonably clear, is it not," asked Tajima, "that Lord Yamada has sources of information originating from within the holding?"

"Perfectly clear," I said. "How else explain the massacre at the first encampment, and the ambush and decimation of the exploratory force?"

Many lives, and tarns, had been lost in the massacre at the first encampment, and many more lives had been lost in the defeat of the exploratory force. The great sleen, lame Ramar, first encountered on a steel world, had been housed at the first encampment. I did not know his fate. As the body had not been found, and no reports had been made of his whereabouts, it was supposed he had disappeared during the confusion of the attack. I did not think any Ashigaru would have paused in the tumult of the fighting to attend to the discomfiting of so dangerous a beast. Few would have been so unwise, or so much at leisure, as to attack it, and I doubted that any would have been so foolish as to challenge its departure. Indeed, knowing Ramar I doubted he would have left the encampment without feeding.

"You may recall," said Tajima, "the prohibition of unauthorized personnel on the parapets, prior to the ruse or deceit of the ritual knife."

"Of course," I said. "That was necessary to prevent signals or messages being transmitted to the camp of Yamada, which would have betrayed our plan. Indeed, the success of the plan would have been in no small part due to this precaution."

"Afterwards," said Tajima, "one might ascend again, as before, to the outer parapets."

"This is not merely, perhaps unwisely, to restore a lost privilege," I said, "but to arouse the suspicions of Lord Yamada pertaining to his informants. Why did they not reveal the ruse of the ritual knife? Have they been discovered? Is he again receiving messages? Is it his informants who are sending them, or others? Can he rely on such reports now? And so on."

"I have discovered the spy," said Tajima.

"I trust it is not I," I said.

"No, Tarl Cabot, tarnsman," he said.

"I was suspected by many," I said.

"It is not you," said Tajima.

"I am pleased to hear it," I said. "Surely you have brought your information to Lord Temmu."

"No," said Tajima.

"I do not understand," I said.

"The guilty party stands close to the shogun," said Tajima.

"I was sure this would be the case," I said. "Now you are wary of revealing his identity, fearing disbelief, fearing terrible consequences, possibly lacking adequate proof."

"I did not know what to do," he said.

"Doubtless the situation is sensitive," I said. "It may be best at the moment, to do nothing. An identified spy, unaware of his detection, is not likely to be dangerous. Information may be withheld from him. Watched, he may lead to others. Too, he may be used as a conduit by means of which false information may be conveyed to the enemy."

"I seek the counsel of my commander," said Tajima.

"You are sure you have discovered the spy?" I asked.

"Yes," he said.

"How, where?" I asked.

"In the holding I often maintained a vigil on the outer parapet. From the outer parapet it seemed a message to the enemy might be most easily and safely transmitted, by the subtle and unnoted casting of a note below, to be retrieved by the enemy. A signal of light, from either the second or third parapet, or from a window of the castle, would be far more likely to be noted."

"That is why the outer parapet was substantially closed, prior to the implementation of the ruse of the ritual knife," I said.

"Concealing myself in the shadows," said Tajima, "I saw the note cast down, to the valley below."

"If you had been fully recovered and stationed here," I said, "you would not have made this discovery."

"I am not pleased to have made it," said Tajima.

"Who is the spy?" I asked.

Tajima regarded me, not speaking.

"Lord Okimoto," I said.

"Lord Nishida," said Tajima.

"That is impossible," I said.

"No," said Tajima.

"Impossible," I said.

"He is your friend," said Tajima.

"Even so," I said. "It is impossible. He was master of Tarncamp, he supported the formation of the tarn cavalry and its training. I know him best, saving you, of all the Pani. He is loyal to Lord Temmu. Not the least suspicion could fall upon him. He is a man of exquisite honor. I would trust him with my life."

"I am sorry," said Tajima.

"You are mistaken," I said. "You have misunderstood something. If there is a traitor in high places, it is surely Lord Okimoto, fat, sly, captious, suspicious, censuring, unpleasant, secretive Lord Okimoto, a bloated tarsk, cousin to the shogun, he who would have much to gain from treachery, he who is next in line for the shogunate."

"Lord Okimoto," said Tajima, "acquiesced in the ruse of the ritual knife."

"So did Lord Nishida," I said, heatedly.

"Lord Okimoto," said Tajima, "has a beautiful hand. Have you never seen his calligraphy?"

"Do not be absurd," I said.

"One cannot be evil who uses the brush so well," said Tajima.

"If a rabid sleen could paint," I said, "it might do quite as well."

"I am sorry," said Tajima.

"If there is a spy," I said, "it is Lord Okimoto."

"No," said Tajima. "It is Lord Nishida."

"You saw Lord Nishida on the parapet, and saw him cast a note, or something, to the valley below?" I said, angrily.

"Of course not," said Tajima. "Lord Nishida is a daimyo. He would not go to the parapet, not without others. His absence, or presence, would be instantly noted."

"A confederate then," I said. "Who?"

Clearly Tajima was reluctant to speak.

"Who?" I demanded.

"Sumomo," he said.

"Then," I said, "she is the spy, or in league with the spy, or spies."

"Yes," said Tajima.

"This clears Lord Nishida of suspicion," I said. "She acts independently, or, at least, independently of Lord Nishida."

"No," said Tajima.

"Why not?" I said.

"You do not understand, Tarl Cabot, tarnsman," said Tajima. "You do not know our ways. She is a contract woman. Lord Nishida owns her contract. She serves him. She is not independent. She acts as she must, for him. It is our way. You do not know our ways. Lord Nishida is the spy."

"I do not believe that," I said.

"Why not?" he asked.

"I know him," I said.

"And can you look into the hearts of men?" asked Tajima.

"I think so," I said, "sometimes."

"I see," said Tajima.

"But you have done well," I said. "We now know that Sumomo is at least involved in these matters."

"I am sorry," said Tajima.

"Why?" I asked.

"Because she is beautiful," he said.

"So, too, is the small, venomous ost," I said.

"One last thing I would speak," said Tajima, "though I would not speak it."

"Speak it," I said.

"You have been relieved of your command, Tarl Cabot, tarnsman," he said.

Chapter Twelve

I Hear of Bones, Shells, and Dragons; Some Acquaintances Have Been Renewed

"She is beautiful, is she not," he inquired.

"Yes, even slave beautiful," I said.

"So beautiful?" he said.

"Yes," I said.

"Her hair, and coloring, and the eyes," he said, "are unusual for the islands."

"That is my understanding," I said. "She is a slave, is she not?"

"Of course," he said.

The girl very carefully, holding her right sleeve back with her left hand, poured tea from the blue-and-white ceramic vessel into my tiny cup.

"I had her for a *fukuro* of rice," he said.

"From the holding of Temmu," I said.

"Of course," he said.

"I wonder if she is worth a *fukuro* of rice," I said.

The girl's hand moved, tightened, a flicker of fury flashing across that fair face, but, almost instantly, it resumed its composure. Such indiscretions are not acceptable in a slave. Less may garner a lashing.

I was pleased to note her reaction. The collar does not diminish a woman's vanity; indeed, it may increase it, perhaps to her surprise, for not every woman is found worth collaring. How well must one think of one's femaleness when one finds it collared! The collar itself is a certification of quality, an emblem and testimonial, a warranty, that its occupant has been found of interest, that she is desirable enough to be chained at the foot of a master's couch. She is a beast pleasant to own. Let her understand that. She is, of course, not a free woman and, accordingly, priceless. She does not exist in a reality irrelevant to, or innocent of, assessment. She is well aware that she is an object, a commodity, and that her value is as quantifiable, objectively, given market conditions and buyers, as that of other objects, or commodities, for example, in terms of coins, tarsks, sa-tarna, rice, or such. Two free women may each regard themselves as the superior of the other, each thinking herself more beautiful, more desirable, more exciting, than the other, but, if both were to be collared and placed on the block, well bared to buyers, as is appropriate for such goods, it is unlikely they would go for the same price.

"We had several, many, for so small a price," he said, lifting his tea, regarding me over the rim of the cup.

"I have a friend named Pertinax," I said. "I do not know if he would put out so much for her."

"Pertinax!" she said, startled, softly.

"Beware speaking the name of a free man," I said.

"Be careful, my dear," he said to the slave. "Do not spill tea, even a drop."

"Yes, Master," she whispered, frightened. There are consequences, of course, for clumsiness in a slave. She is not a free woman.

She backed away, with short steps, her hands now in her sleeves, her eyes cast down.

"Is she not overdressed?" I said.

Saru, the former Miss Margaret Wentworth, now far from the mahogany corridors of wealth and power, those which she had once frequented, in her small, manipulative way, in a far city on a distant world, wore a silken kimono, and obi, and figured sandals. Her hair was high on her head, and held in place by pins and an ornate comb. Her garmenture was not unlike that of the contract women I had seen in Tarncamp, in Shipcamp, in the holding, and elsewhere, such as Hana, Sumomo, Hisui, and others.

"Faraway," he said, "across the shimmering breadth of Thassa, it is my understanding that slaves are dressed differently."

"Commonly," I said. "As the slave is an animal, she need not be dressed at all, of course. On the other hand, if her master chooses to permit her clothing, she is to be clothed as what she is, a slave. A rag or brief tunic is more than enough. Such a garment is designed not merely to make clear her beauty, and to make it clear that it is the beauty of a mere slave; it sets off, and even enhances, her beauty. In such a garment she is exhibited; in such a garment she is well displayed as the property she is. Such garments are intended to be provocative, and to leave little doubt as to what is concealed. Indeed, a suitable slave garment can make a woman seem more naked than if she were naked. The garment is little more than a mockery, and invites its removal. In such a garment a woman is in little doubt that she is a slave. She exists for labor and pleasure. Yet, interestingly, such trivial things, a rag or such, can be of desperate importance to the little beasts, and they will often beg for a scrap of cloth, and labor zealously to obtain it, and to retain it, if it is allowed to them."

"It seems we can learn much from barbarians," he said.

"You jest," I said. "I have seen slaves about, and not merely barbarian slaves, collared, tunicked, and less."

He smiled. "It is true," he said, "we know what to do with women."

"At least with slaves," I said.

"With all women," he said.

"But there are free women," I said, "and contract women."

"Women may be sold to contractors," he said, "and contracts, then, may be bought and sold."

"There are free women," I said.

"Yes," he said. "That is true. But I do not think our free women, here in the islands, have quite the pompous, exalted status inflicted on free women across Thassa."

"They do not have Home Stones," I said.

"We have not made that mistake," he said.

"I see," I said.

"Women are not the same as men," he said.

"I have suspected that," I said.

"More tea?" he inquired.

"No," I said.

He, sitting cross-legged, the small table to his left, made a tiny gesture with his left hand, and Saru quickly backed from the room.

"She was the property of Lord Temmu, master of the great holding," he said.

"Yes," I said. "She was given to him, by Lord Nishida."

I watched carefully to see if the mention of Lord Nishida would be registered, and in what way, if at all, on his countenance. But I detected not a flicker of interest, concern, or even recognition on his face.

"Lord Nishida," I said, "is a daimyo, in allegiance to Lord Temmu."

"Lord Temmu, the usurper and unjust tyrant, the scourge of the islands, has two daimyos," he said, "one is Lord Nishida, whom you mentioned. The other is a Lord Okimoto. Do you know him?"

"Yes," I said. "Perhaps you know him, as well."

He smiled.

"You have the simplicity, and crudity, of the barbarian," he said.

"I fear I am insufficiently subtle," I said.

"Lord Temmu," he said, "has two daimyos, I have ten. He has, at most, thirty-five hundred warriors, and soldiers."

"Perhaps," I said.

"Do not pretend ignorance," he said. "I have several times his men."

I did not doubt that.

"There are uncommitted daimyos," I said.

"True," he said.

"And many peasants," I said.

"My peasantry and fields are far more extensive than those of Lord Temmu," he said.

"I understand," I said.

"The peasantry is well in hand," he said.

I did not doubt that. On the other hand, I found it worth noting that he had volunteered this information. Perhaps they were not as well in hand as he seemed to suggest. Certainly we had had the cooperation of certain peasants, putatively his peasants, in our efforts to obtain rice for the holding.

"What of the peasantry laboring in the villages and fields of Temmu?" he asked.

"I am not an authority on such matters," I said.

"You expressed an interest," he said, "in the garmenture of the slave."

"Yes," I said. "I found it excessive, for a slave."

"There was a purpose for that," he said.

"What, noble lord?" I inquired.

"I did not wish her presence to be distractive," he said.

"I see," I said.

"We are alone," said Lord Yamada. "Let us converse."

"By all means," I said.

Whereas I had been willing, under the force of circumstances, recognizing treachery in high places, and the lack of practical alternatives, to conduct the cavalry as a rogue arm, aflight on behalf of Lord Temmu, I was unwilling to transform it into what would be in effect a brigade of bandits under an independent mercenary captain. It had been formed and trained as, and had been intended as, a component in a unified force, engaged in a particular mission.

"It seems," I had said to Tajima, "I might venture to the holding, and participate in the projected interview after all."

"It is a summoning," said Tajima.

"I should then appear," I said.

"I would not do so, Tarl Cabot, tarnsman," said Tajima.

"I think it best," I said.

"You are commander," he said.

"No longer," I said.

"The men will follow you," he said.

"They should not," I said.

"They would die for you," he said.

"I am no longer commander," I said.

"Cry 'One-strap!'" he said, "and the cavalry will be aflight."

"I will not usurp an authority to which I am not entitled," I said. "As appointed commander of the cavalry I was willing, under unusual circumstances, hoping to advance the cause of the house of Temmu, to exercise my own judgment, to act on my own initiative, to act independently of the chain of command, but all that was while I held the post and rank of commander, which post and rank I no longer hold."

"The men," he said, "will follow no other."

"*Ela*," I said. "I have then failed as commander."

"Wait," said Tajima. "Be patient. Wait. Do not go now to the holding."

"I can reach the walls before dark," I said.

Lord Temmu had not seemed angry.

I had bowed, and then sat down, cross-legged, before him.

I looked about myself. We were not on the dais, but within the castle, in a large room near the back portal of the castle, where I had brought the tarn down. An attendant led the tarn to shelter and I had been approached by two Ashigaru, who had apparently been waiting.

"My presence has been requested by Lord Temmu," I had said. They had bowed briefly, and then turned and led the way into the castle.

I looked about myself. Neither Lord Nishida nor Lord Okimoto were present. I found this anomalous, for both commonly attended on the shogun. Daichi, dour and gaunt, the reader of bones and shells, was in the room, sitting to the left of Lord Temmu, and, surprisingly, behind the shogun and a bit to the left, as well, was a contract woman, standing, Sumomo. I recalled that Tajima, in his vigil on the outer parapet, had noted Sumomo's presence there, and had witnessed her casting something over the parapet, presumably to be retrieved by some confederate below. He had surmised, plausibly enough, that Sumomo had acted on behalf of Lord Nishida, whose presence on the parapet, if not indiscreet, would have been likely to attract attention. I knew little of Sumomo other than the fact that she was the younger, and more beautiful, of two beautiful women whose contracts were held by Lord Nishida. I had personally found her unpleasant and arrogant, two features which, I gathered, were unusual in a Pani woman, and certainly in a contract woman. I surmised she was quite intelligent. I thought her inquisitive and cunning, and remembered how she had once lingered, concealed, in the vicinity of Lord Nishida, although she had been dismissed. I did know, of course, that Tajima found it difficult to take his eyes from her. Did not his peregrinations take him often enough into her vicinity? Indeed, I suspected it was less than a fortunate, utter happenstance that he had noted her activity on the parapet. A more casual or less diligent observer might well have missed the quick, subtle gesture which may have sped some missive, probably with its ribbon, to the foot of the cliff on which the parapet was reared. *Ela*, I thought, poor Tajima. I suspected even his dreams were not spared her presence. And I trusted her deportment might be less objectionable in that so-transient dimension. I doubted that her contract was for sale, and, even if it were, it seemed unlikely young Tajima could afford it. He was not a merchant, not a high officer, not a daimyo. Sumomo, as nearly as I could tell, was well aware of the distress and torment which she wrought in the breast of the young warrior and this recognition, rather than bringing about its diminishment or abatement, seemed to have spurred her to its augmentation. Some women enjoy twisting the knife, but this, I understood, was unusual in a Pani woman, whose acculturation tends to discourage such behavior, and certainly for one who was a mere contract woman. However these things may be, despite her acculturation, and her relatively lowly status, she commonly treated Tajima with an unbecoming scorn, contempt, and amusement. Sometimes I wondered if she fully understood that such a behavior might occasion untoward consequences. After all, she was not a Gorean free woman, as across the sea, veiled, hidden in the robes of concealment, a woman exalted and resplendent in status and dignity, a woman safe in her station and secure in her privileges, even one who possessed a Home Stone. She was Pani, and, beyond that, a contract woman. To be sure, she seldom acted like a contract woman, except in relation to, and in the presence of, Lord Nishida. I had wondered sometimes if he had noticed that.

On the floor a bit before, and to the side of Lord Temmu, was a scattering of bones and shells. I did not know how long they might have lain there. I supposed they had been read by Daichi.

Why, I wondered, were Lords Nishida and Okimoto not present? And why would, say, a contract woman be present.

The two Ashigaru whom I had followed into the castle now stood behind me, one on each side.

I would have preferred that they had retired to the side of the room.

Lord Temmu and I sat facing one another. I was not sure, at first, whether I should speak first, or Lord Temmu. Then I recalled that it would be more appropriate for the shogun to be addressed. Does not he who is less in status bow first? Indeed, does not the lesser officer, by word or gesture, first acknowledge the presence of the senior, or higher, officer?

"Greetings, Lord," I said. "It is my understanding that you wish to see me."

"Yes," he said.

"I am summoned," I said.

"Invited," he suggested.

"'Invited'," I said.

"There is rice in the pantries of the House of Temmu," he said. "The gates of the House of Temmu may be opened. The enemy is muchly withdrawn. Men return to the fields."

"I trust the noble lord is pleased," I said.

"Muchly so," he said.

"I then am also pleased," I said.

"How fares the cavalry?" he said.

"Well, my lord," I said.

"It is not at the junction of two rivers," he said.

"No, my lord," I said.

Obviously this had come somehow to his attention, probably from the reconnaissance of scouts now that the forces of Yamada had been substantially withdrawn from the fields to the north.

"The cavalry has been prematurely deployed," he said.

"It can no longer act as an instrument of surprise," I said.

"No longer can it turn a flank in a decisive battle," he said.

"Not in virtue of surprise," I said.

"It has been deployed at your discretion," he said.

"There seemed little choice," I said.

"It has been used as an instrument of attack, far from the holding," he said.

"Yes, my lord," I said.

"This was unauthorized," he said.

"That is true, my lord," I said.

"Who is shogun?" he asked.

"Lord Temmu is shogun," I said.

"Who commands?" he asked.

"Lord Temmu," I said.

"You have heard of bones and shells," he said.

"I have heard of them," I said, glancing at the scattering of debris on the floor, near the shogun.

"They do not lie," said Lord Temmu.

"True, my lord," I said. "They cannot lie, but, as they cannot speak, neither can they tell the truth."

"Barbarian!" cried Daichi.

"They can be read," said Lord Temmu.

"Across Thassa," I said, "there are places where the livers of verr are examined, where formations of clouds are noted, the flights of birds observed, such things."

"That is superstition," said Daichi.

"That seems likely," I said.

"Gross superstition," said Daichi.

"There are many ways in which to obtain one's rice," I said. "Surely one of the most unusual is the reading of bones and shells."

"It requires years to learn to read bones and shells," said Daichi.

"I know a fellow named Boots Tarsk-Bit," I said, "who could manage it in less than an Ehn."

"He must be extraordinarily gifted," said Daichi.

"I think so," I said.

"The messenger, Tajima," said Lord Temmu, "has perhaps relayed to you an account of a reading in the palace of Yamada."

"As I recall," I said, "unless the house of Temmu yields to the house of Yamada, the iron dragon will fly, with possibly disastrous consequences to both houses."

"Yes," said Lord Temmu.

"Lord Yamada," I said, "doubtless fears its flight."

"Of course," said Lord Temmu.

"I trust," I said, glancing at the debris to the side, "you have had your own reader, Daichi *san*, either confirm or disconfirm that reading."

I do not think I had hitherto understood, or taken with sufficient seriousness, the possibility that the shogun might credit the distribution of small objects spilled on a hardwood floor with such portent. To be sure, I knew there was much precedent for such views. Might not the ravings of a lunatic, the occurrence of an eclipse, the conjunction of planets, a monstrous birth, change the courses of states, launch armies, even delay retreats until retreat was no longer possible? I now, suddenly, as I had not before, began to suspect an explanation for dalliance and hesitation, for vacillation, for inexplicable, anomalous tactics, for a sessile strategy of timidity, immobility, restraint, and defense. Such a strategy I had often thought might have been designed by Lord Yamada himself, and now, for the first time, it struck me, like a fist, that it may well have been designed by Lord Yamada himself. Small objects lie about mute, planets go about their business, birds fly where they wish, but such things are interpreted. What are the babblings of an entranced sibyl, moaning and swaying on her tripod, drunk with fumes, without the enlightening interpretations of astute priests? I then understood better why Sumomo was present. Was it not she whom Tajima had discovered on the parapet, casting some object into the night?

"His reading is similar," said Lord Temmu, "but somewhat more extensive, or detailed."

"My reading is, of course, more recent," said Daichi.

"I understand," I said.

"The overlap of the readings, of course," said Daichi, "proves the probity of both readings, which would be inexplicable other than on the grounds of truth and fact."

"How could they agree otherwise," I said.

Perhaps, I thought, if the communication between the holding and the enemy were better they might agree even more closely.

"Speak," said Lord Temmu, to Daichi.

"That the house of Temmu should yield to the house of Yamada," he said, "is clear, but the manner of yielding is less clear. What may be involved is not abject surrender, but accommodation."

"Interesting," I said.

"Rather than surrender," said Daichi, "Lord Temmu would

prefer the termination of his line and the destruction of the holding altogether, even should the iron dragon spread its wings."

"I thought he might," I said.

"Even though the sun be devoured and the land cast into the sea."

"I see," I said. I recalled Tajima had said something of this sort in the encampment. Certainly it had never occurred to me that Lord Temmu would abandon the holding, and such. He would be prepared to accept the consequences for not doing so, however unpleasant, or disastrous.

"The iron dragon does not exist," I said. "It is a beast of legend, a creature of myth. It does not exist. It is not to be feared."

"The bones and shells do not lie," said Daichi, in a terrible voice, pointing to the objects in question.

"Perhaps," I said, "those who read them might—be mistaken."

"It is said," said Lord Temmu, "that they are sometimes hard to understand."

"That is true," said Daichi solemnly.

"How do you read them?" I asked Daichi. It seemed this was important, particularly with two large Ashigaru behind me.

"The readings are similar," said Daichi, "in a sense identical, namely, that the house of Temmu must yield to the house of Yamada, or the iron dragon will fly, and destroy the house of Temmu."

"And Lord Yamada fears the flight of the iron dragon might prove disastrous to both houses?" I said.

"Yes," said Daichi.

"I gather Lord Temmu does not intend to surrender," I said.

"It is only required, to avoid ruin," said Daichi, "that Lord Temmu yield."

"Surrender?" I said.

"Do not read things into the bones and shells," warned Daichi.

"I shall attempt to refrain from doing so," I said.

"I requested Daichi *san* to cast the bones and shells in such a way as to seek the clarification of the message," said Lord Temmu.

"And he has succeeded in doing so?" I said.

"Fortunately," said Lord Temmu. "Would you care for a sip of sake?"

"Not really," I said.

But Sumomo had already drawn to the side, where three small cups resided on a flat lacquered tray. These she filled from a small vessel. I watched her hands carefully. I noted, to my satisfaction, that she poured all three cups from the same vessel.

"You wished to see me?" I said to Lord Temmu.

"Yes," said Lord Temmu.

Sumomo politely, her head shyly down, held the tray first to Lord Temmu and then to Daichi. Each took one of the small cups. That left one cup on the tray.

"Tarl Cabot *san*," she said softly, holding the tray to me.

A slave, of course, would not speak the name of a free man, lest it be soiled on her lips. She might, of course, in discourse, refer to a free man, her master or others, if it were suitable to do so. For example, if she were asked her master's name, she would certainly volunteer this information, with suitable deference. Sumomo, of course, was not a slave, at least *per se*, but a contract woman.

I took the small cup.

Lord Temmu took a sip of sake first. Daichi, the reader of bones and shells, then sipped from the tiny cup.

"I am not thirsty," I said.

"Please," said Lord Temmu.

I recalled that all three cups had been filled from the same small vessel. Too, I had paid careful attention to the small, lovely hands of Sumomo. Also, I was in the castle of the holding. Also, there were two large Ashigaru, armed, behind me.

I sipped the sake.

I recalled from Tarncamp that one was not to throw sake down as one might a paga or kal-da.

"It is excellent, is it not?" inquired Lord Temmu.

"I am sure it is," I said. To be sure, I doubted I could tell one sake from another. To be sure, this one did seem different. It reminded me, somehow, of veminium.

"You wished to see me," I said.

"Yes," said Lord Temmu.

"You are displeased with the raids?" I said.

"Lord Temmu is pleased, of course," said Daichi, "with the provisioning of the holding, the termination of the siege, the freeing of the northern fields."

"He is less pleased with how these things came about?" I said.

"There remains the matter of the bones and shells," said Daichi.

"Enjoy your sake," said Lord Temmu, pleasantly.

I took another sip.

I shook my head a little.

"To whomsoever is appointed to the command of the cavalry," I said, "I would recommend a continuation of the raids on the heartland of Lord Yamada, abetted with judicious skirmishes and attacks of small scale. I think that that is your best route to some sort of truce or accommodation. I doubt that the forces of the house of Temmu could meet those of the house of Yamada on the open field."

"Even with tarns?" inquired Lord Temmu.

"There are too few tarns," I said.

"I fear," said Daichi, "that Lord Yamada has been angered."

"I do not see how that could well be helped," I said. "Perhaps Sumomo could light a lamp," I said.

"Does the room grow dark?" asked Lord Temmu.

I put the tiny cup of sake down, beside my right knee.

"Would you like more sake?" asked Lord Temmu.

"No," I said.

Of course, I thought. The sake was poured from the same vessel. But in one of the cups would be the waiting ingredient, perhaps only a few drops but enough, enough, in the cup which would be given me. But there was little that I could have done in any case. I felt my arms drawn behind me by the two Ashigaru.

"The bones and shells do not lie," said Daichi, "however they are cast, whoever casts them, whether, say, by the reader of Lord Yamada or unworthy, humble Daichi, faithful retainer of Lord Temmu."

I felt my arms corded together.

The room was growing dark.

I could not resist; I felt very weak; I did not think I could rise. I was hardly aware of what was ensuing.

"We must save the house of Temmu," said Daichi. "Allegedly the iron dragon stirs. If the house of Temmu does not yield to the house of Yamada, it will emerge from its lair, will be awing, and will destroy the house of Temmu."

"The yielding will be a small thing," said Lord Temmu. "The

concession is negligible. Lord Yamada wants only peace. He fears the iron dragon as much, perhaps more, than we. He wants little. Our yielding will bring the peace you so foolishly would pursue by tarn and fire, by marches and steel."

"The bones and shells have spoken clearly," said Daichi.

"We now understand the nature of the yielding in question," said Lord Temmu. "It does not solicit a surrender, which we would not give, but only a concession, in effect, a favor, a very little thing from which we will gain a very great deal."

"It will be a small price to pay for peace," said Daichi.

"The extermination of the house of Yamada does not seem feasible," said Lord Temmu.

"You have perhaps guessed the meaning of the bones and shells," said Daichi.

I was put to my side and I felt my ankles crossed, and bound together.

"Lord Yamada," said Daichi, "was not pleased to withdraw, to retreat to protect his holdings, his goods, and fields. His price for peace is to have you delivered to his mercy."

"It is a small price," said Lord Temmu. "Surely you understand this, see its wisdom, and joyfully acquiesce."

I tried, weakly, to pull against the cords, but was helpless. Then I sensed another person in the room, who had entered from the side. I saw the bootlike sandals near me, and then I was kicked, savagely. On the other hand, it did not cause me pain. I could hardly feel it.

I heard Sumomo laugh, merrily.

"We will use two of the messenger tarns," said a voice. "We will leave shortly after dark."

I recognized the voice.

It was that of Tyrtaios.

Then I lost consciousness.

I do not know how long I was unconscious. I suspect I was sedated more than once.

I awakened suddenly, rudely, shocked and shuddering, on a rough, planked floor, in a shedlike edifice, as cold water was cast on my chained, bared body. I tried to rise, but stumbled and fell, for I could move my shackled ankles only a few inches at a time. Several Ashigaru were about. A chain was about my waist, and my hands were manacled behind me, the manacles fastened to the chain. Two ropes were on my neck, of some five or six feet in length, each in the grasp of an Ashigaru, one on either side of me. I was pulled up to my knees by men behind me, and my head was forced down, to the wood.

"What is to be done with him?" asked one of the men about.

"I do not know," said another, "but it will doubtless be done lengthily."

"He is a sorcerer," said another, "whose words conjure demon birds from the sky."

"He has labored on behalf of the rebellious house of Temmu," said another.

"No officers are present," said one. "Strike him!"

There was a moment's pause while I sensed these fellows were looking about, and from one to another.

I grunted in pain, struck twice, by the staffs of glaives.

"Hold," said a voice, "Lord Akio approaches."

Shortly thereafter I became aware of a silken presence before me. I heard a fan snap open and shut, twice, nervously. By the sound, I knew the fan was of metal. Such fans can cut a throat.

"This is the prisoner, the rebel, Tarl Cabot, enemy to the rightful house of Yamada, Shogun of the Islands, delivered to us by the noble Tyrtaios, devoted, trusted mercenary?"

"Yes, Lord," said a voice.

It interested me how one can tell, almost infallibly, from the voice, the diction, the sense of self-acceptance and authority, the rank and station of a Pani speaker. Those of a high house or noble family are seldom confused with those of a lower, or more common, order.

The speaker seemed clearly one of a higher order.

To be sure, such distinctions are not limited to the Pani.

"You, tarsk, are Tarl Cabot?" asked the voice.

"I am not a tarsk," I said. "I am Tarl Cabot."

He must have signaled something to the Ashigaru about, for I was then struck and prodded several times by the butts of glaives.

"Shall we begin the tortures?" asked one of the men about.

As the new arrival had been addressed as "Lord," I supposed him the master of a house, perhaps even a daimyo.

I did not know where I was but it was clear I was somewhere in a territory controlled by the forces of Lord Yamada. My surroundings did not seem auspicious. I did not think Tyrtaios was in the room.

"Has he been fed?" asked the voice.

"No," said an Ashigaru.

"He has only now been revived," said another.

"Are you hungry?" asked the voice.

"Yes," I said.

"'Yes, Lord,'" he suggested.

"Yes, Lord," I said.

"Are you cold?" he asked.

"Yes, Lord," I said, my head down.

"He smells," said the voice. "He is filthy."

"From the straw, from the pens," said an Ashigaru.

Pani are often concerned with cleanliness. Indeed, Goreans, in general, take such matters seriously. Few Gorean cities are without their baths, public and private, which are sometimes extensive and luxurious, with shops, arcades, restaurants, gymnasiums, libraries, and such.

"We have found you troublesome, Tarl Cabot," said the voice. "You have commanded demon birds, dragon birds, brought from across the sea. You have well served the rebellious house of Temmu and have muchly discomfited the rightful, honorable house of Yamada. Yamada, Shogun of the Islands, has not been pleased. Now you are at our mercy. We have waited long to have you as you are."

"Shall we commence the tortures, Lord?" inquired an Ashigaru.

"What of the straw jacket?" asked an Ashigaru.

"Only at the end," said another.

"Be silent," said the voice of the one who had been identified as Lord Akio.

I heard the metal fan snap open and shut.

The Ashigaru were silent.

It was interesting, I thought, how an object, something like a fan, can reveal an emotion which is otherwise concealed.

"Lord Yamada," he said, "intends to see the prisoner."

"Here?" said an Ashigaru, awed.

"You would not expect something this miserable, this stinking and foul, to be brought into his presence," said the voice.

"No, Lord!" said the man.

"Put him to his belly," said the voice. "Smear the excrement of tarsk on his body. Beat and bloody him. See that he is presented appropriately, helpless, foul and prostrate, a captured rebel, a defeated enemy, before the shogun."

I was forced to my belly.

I endured, as I could, the attentions to which I was subjected. I did not cry out.

I do not know how long I sustained the ministrations of my captors. I do not think it was very long as the sand clock, grain by grain, or the water clock, drop by drop, would have it, but, to me, prostrate and chained, my body fouled, and recoiling, shuddering, struck again and again, it was long enough, a time measured in the clock of pain, counted in terms of blows, the number of which soon eluded me.

"What is going on?" had cried a great voice

The men had moved away from me, instantly.

"Is this not Tarl Cabot?" cried the great voice.

"Yes, Lord!" said he called Akio.

"What have you done to him?" cried the great voice.

"Lord?" inquired Akio.

I heard the fan open and shut, as though startled, as though puzzled.

"Unchain him," I heard. "Are you mad? Remove those ropes from his throat. Clean him! Put ointment and salve on his wounds. Rest and nurse him. Then tomorrow dress him regally, in robes of honor, and bring him to the palace."

"We are alone," had said Lord Yamada. "Let us converse."

"By all means," I had said.

Chapter Thirteen

I Have Summoned a Slave;
I Interview a Slave;
What Occurred at the
Termination of the Interview

"Remove your clothing," I said.

She regarded me.

"All of it," I said. "Every bit of it. Completely."

"Please," she protested.

"Now," I said.

I saw she knew how to remove her clothing before a man. She had perhaps been taught that in Tarncamp, after she had been removed from the stables.

"You were overdressed," I said.

She stood beside the garments at her feet, lithe, lovely, slimly erect.

"I think," I said, "these fellows are perhaps too refined, too civilized."

"Perhaps less so than you think," she said.

"Is that how you address a free man?" I asked.

"Perhaps less so than you think, Master," she said.

"I see," I said, "that the collar of Lord Temmu has been removed from your pretty neck."

"As was that of Lord Nishida by the servitors of Lord Temmu, Master," she said.

"Doubtless you will soon be put in another," I said.

"Perhaps," she said, "Lord Yamada does not collar his women."

"I was hitherto, here, in my private quarters," I said, "served by two, both Pani, both collared."

"And you dismissed them?" she said.

"And requested you," I said. "Do you mind?"

"We are slaves," she said. "We may be done with as masters please."

"Do you kick well?" I asked. "Do you whimper, squirm, buck, and moan, and beg well?"

"I cannot help myself!" she wept. "I have become responsive!"

"The grooms in the stable at Tarncamp taught you sex," I said.

"Yes!" she said.

"It was then no longer something with which to tease executives, with which intrigue clients and charm investors," I said.

"I cannot help what has become of me," she said.

"You are now needful," I said.

"Yes," she said, tears in her eyes. "I am now needful!"

"It is interesting," I said, "on Earth you could use the mere suggestion of sex, with its smiles and movements, as a weapon, a tool, as a device of business, use it in the interests of sales, contracts, and accounts, in the interests of opportunity, promotion, and advancement, and all with complete impunity, without risk or compromise, and now, at as little as a word, a gesture, a snapping of fingers, you must hurry to put yourself naked to a man's feet."

"Yes," she said, angrily.

"And," I said, "I suspect that now slave fires, from time to time, burn in your small, lovely belly."

"I cannot help myself," she said. "Men have done it to me!"

"Surely you do not object to being so alive?" I said.

She covered her face with her hands, sobbing.

"You are now in a collar," I said, "whether it is on your neck or not."

She sobbed.

"Remove your hands from your face," I said. "I would see it."

She lowered her hands. Her face was run with tears.

"I suspect," I said, "that the men you teased, tormented, tricked, duped, and manipulated would not mind seeing you as you are now, as a helpless, naked slave."

"Please send me away, to the slave quarters, Master," she begged.

"I did not have you brought here, to send you away," I said. "We shall chat. But first, turn about, and cross your wrists behind your back."

I went to the side of the room, to a wardrobe chest, and withdrew a spool of ribbonlike silk, less than a hort in width, of the sort with which, measured and cut, one might fasten sandals. It was brightly yellow. I cut two lengths of this ribbon. One length I wrapped twice about her neck, and knotted it behind the back of her neck. Is that not where a lock would be? With the other length I tied her hands together, as they were placed, behind her back.

"Every women belongs in a man's collar," I said.

"Here," she said, "men are the masters."

"Perhaps you have not heard of free women," I said.

"Are they so different from me?" she asked.

"Not at all," I said.

"They have just not yet been put in their collars," she said.

"Precisely," I said.

"How different this world is from Earth!" she said.

"Is it so different?" I asked.

"Here," she said, "men are the masters."

"So, too, are they on Earth," I said, "if they but choose to be so."

"I had not known that men such as on this world could exist," she said.

"Of all the beasts a man can own," I said, "surely the female slave is amongst the loveliest."

"Is it pleasant to have power over us," she asked, "to have us at your bidding, to buy and sell us?"

"Of course," I said.

"My belly flames," she wept.

I stepped back from her, and sat down, cross-legged, on a small rug.

"Turn about, and kneel before me," I said.

She did so.

"Must I lower my head?" she asked.

"No," I said.

She regarded me.

"It is pleasant to have a woman so before one," I said.

"Collared," she said, "kneeling naked, bound, helpless."

"Yes," I said. "Do you think I am unlike other men?"

"No," she said. "Why here have men not denied themselves to themselves, why have they not refused to be men?"

"I do not know," I said. "But I do not object. Do you?"

"—No," she said.

"You are far from taxis and elevators, from finance, from polluted canyons of stone, from cacophonous dins, from jostlings and crowdings, from halls of business," I said.

"Yes," she said. "I have been brought to Gor."

"As a slave," I said.

"Yes," she said.

"What do you think of this world?" I asked.

"Earth must once have been like this," she said, "the freshness, the rain, the air, the flight of birds, the blue sky, the water, the food with taste."

"One supposes so," I said.

"What have our people done to our world?" she asked.

"I do not know," I said. "Perhaps they have insufficiently loved it."

"On a world such as this," she said, "one such as I can be only a slave."

"And deservedly so, and correctly so," I said.

"Yes, Master," she said.

"On your former world," I said, "I suspect you never discussed such matters as you are now, while kneeling before a man, while naked and bound."

"No," she said.

"You were not a slave."

"No."

"Perhaps you recall a young woman whose name was once Margaret Wentworth."

"Yes," she said.

"And the free woman pretending to be a slave in the northern forests of continental Gor, with the pompous name 'Constantina'?"

"Yes," she said.

"Miss Margaret Wentworth," I said, "petty, shallow, greedy for money, accepted a commission on Gor, into which, as it was expected to pay well, she did not care to inquire too closely."

"Master?" she said.

"Widen your knees, slave," I said. "Enough. And to abet your endeavors you brought with you a weak, confused, hesitant, foolishly enamored Earth male, one commonly belittled and disparaged, disdained and derided, whose name was Gregory White."

"That is so," she said.

"You enjoyed humiliating and dominating him," I said.

"He is a weakling," she said.

"This Gregory White, in Tarncamp," I said, "did much heavy manual labor, grew lean and powerful, became different, learned weapons, learned the sword and the saddle of the tarn. He has fought. He is an officer in the tarn cavalry in the forces of Lord Temmu, respected, trusted, and relied upon."

"He is an Earth male," she said. "I despise him."

"I see," I said.

"Outside the tharlarion stable, in Tarncamp," she said, "before I was delivered by Ashigaru to the quarters of Lord Nishida, his weakness and pusillanimity, his reluctance to be true to, and satisfy, his masculinity, were sufficiently evident."

"I do not remember the incident in precisely the same fashion," I said.

"He is not Gorean," she said. "I scorn him."

"You were hoping to be his slave," I said.

"No," she said, "no!"

"He found you disgusting, and worthless, and he left you," I said.

"Surely not!" she cried.

"He found you lacking, even as a slave," I said. "You were repudiated, put aside."

"He loved me, he wanted me, he would have done anything for me!" she cried.

"Perhaps Gregory White," I said, "perhaps once. He is now Pertinax, a warrior. Are you worthy to be the slave of a warrior?"

"He is weak," she said. "I can rule him. Even as a slave, I could rule him. I know this. It is true. With a smile, a pout, a glance, a trembling lip, a quavering word, a tear, I could return him to the feeble ineptitude of an Earth male. He is trapped in the toils of convention, a prisoner of the plans of others; he is not his own man but a creation of cultural conditioning, a conditioning founded on alienating a male from manhood. He is too weak to break even the paper fetters of propriety. There is more manhood in a shuddering urt."

"I see," I said.

"May I speak?" she asked.

"Does Saru wish to speak?" I asked.

"Yes," she said, "Saru wishes to speak."

"Saru may speak," I said.

"How is it," she asked, "that Master is in the palace of General Yamada?"

"It seems," I said, "at the request of the general."

"I do not understand," she said.

"That is acceptable," I said. "Curiosity is not becoming in a *kajira*."

"Please," she said.

The less a slave girl knows the less she can betray, deliberately or inadvertently.

I had been very impressed with General Yamada, much as one might be impressed when one has entered a cave and, turning about, finds that one is now under the scrutiny of a charming, watchful larl crouched at the entrance. Lord Yamada was clearly a great leader, a superb tactician, and an astute strategist. It was not surprising to me that victory was no stranger to his warriors and Ashigaru. Had it not been for the intervention of Priest-Kings or Kurii, or both, I think the remnants of Lord Temmu's land forces would have perished on a beach long ago, rather than appearing, seemingly unaccountably, in the vicinity of Brundisium on continental Gor. Had Lord Temmu not had the mighty, nigh-impregnable holding of the house of Temmu at his disposal I suspected that this war would have been concluded long ago, and not to his advantage. Lord Yamada was a pleasant man but he could also nail enemies to the decks of ships and mount heads on posts for pasangs along a road. He was a persistent and efficient fellow, and one of enterprise and calculation. He was also one of singular will, of unswerving resolve, and vaulting ambition. He understood not only the business of marches and sieges, but the politics of logistics and supply. He also maintained, apparently, a network of informers and spies. It had often been suspected that he was as well apprised of the appointments, plans, and secrets of the house of Temmu as those of his own. Personally he was attentive, courteous, and genial. Physically he was large, but bore himself with the poise and grace I had come to expect in Pani of position and family. His features were strong, his eyes keen. It was said he sometimes attended to his own executions.

"Please," she said, again.

"You are *kajira*," I reminded her.

"Forgive me, Master," she said.

The plot of Lord Yamada had now become reasonably clear. Lord Temmu, as many in the islands, particularly in times of doubt and uncertainty, would consult the supposed deliverances of severally scattered bones and shells. This form of inquiry was taken seriously by many. Certainly it was culturally sanctioned and familiar. For the successful pursuit of this matter, of course, one required the services of a skilled reader. Thus, somehow Daichi, presumably a reader of some reputation, and a secret creature of Lord Yamada, had been placed in the house of Temmu. Once ensconced, it would be a simple matter for his readings, thanks to forewarnings, collusions, and arrangements issuing from the house of Yamada, to appear alarmingly accurate. With advanced intelligence it would not be difficult to pave the road to impressive prophecy. Thus, given the legerdemain of ambiguity and obscurity, abetted by occasional, reassuring nuggets of augured gold, it would be possible to convince a gullible patron to pursue courses of action which were less to his advantage than to that of another, in this case, Lord Yamada. I was confident that Daichi, like similar practitioners of kindred arts, might, with the usual amalgam of pretentious pronouncements, awesome gravity, and ponderous theatricality, influence the thinking and action of any client so luckless as to have fallen under his spell. Those who permit strings to be attached to their limbs must expect to be moved by the puppeteer. One would need, of course, some sort of communication between the two houses, which would be easily enough supplied before the siege in virtue of strangers, wanderers, peddlers, merchants, and such, and, during the siege, by envoys, negotiators, messengers, and such, for example, Tyrtaios. And Sumomo's role, I anticipated, was largely that of communicating Daichi's information, available from Lord Temmu, to the enemy, by so simple a contrivance as casting missives over the parapet, to be retrieved below. Similarly, as a contract woman whose contract was held by so high-ranking an official as a daimyo, in this case Lord Nishida, she would have, for most practical purposes, most of the time, a complete liberty of movement within the holding. Certainly she would have no difficulty in receiving information from Daichi, nor, generally, any difficulty in communicating independently with the enemy below.

"Why has Master sent for me?" she asked.

"That seems an unusual question for a female slave," I said.

"Forgive me," she said.

"To be sure," I said, "as I understand it, you went for only a *fukuro* of rice."

"Did any go for more?" she asked.

"I gather, some," I said.

"Oh?" she said.

"But few," I said.

"The men of the holding were starving," she said. "In another week we might have been bartered for a handful of rice."

"Some went for two *fukuros*," I said.

"I regret that I am so displeasing a slave," she said.

"Most went for one *fukuro*," I said.

"Thank you, Master," she said.

"I would suppose that Jane went for but one *fukuro*," I said.

"Who is Jane?" she asked, warily.

"It is not important," I said.

"Please," she said.

"She was the slave of a warrior, Pertinax," I said.

"Surely not!" she said.

"Surely so," I said.

"He has a slave?" she said.

"Had," I said.

"How is that?" she said.

"I bought her for him," I said.

"Master is generous," she said, angrily.

"You are angry?" I asked.

"Of course not," she said, in fury, tears springing to her eyes.

"Good," I said.

"He is a fool of Earth," she said. "He would not know what to do with a slave."

"His Jane," I said, "after some instruction, and not much, was left in little doubt that she was in a collar."

"It is a barbarian name," she said.

"As 'Margaret', or such," I said.

"I hate her," she said, pulling at her bound wrists.

"You are in the presence of a free man," I said. "Remain on your knees."

"Yes, Master," she said.

"I thought you might," I said.

"Of course it is nothing to me," she said, quickly.

"I understand," I said.

"She is of Earth, of course," she said.

"It is not unusual for the women of Earth to be in bondage," I said, "historically, currently, publicly, privately."

"And for those brought to Gor," she said.

"Most, I would suppose," I said, "immediately, or eventually."

"'Eventually'?" she said.

"Certainly," I said, "once her business is done, her specific task completed, it is natural to suppose that she should remain of some value."

"Block value," she said.

"Precisely," I said.

"As in my case," she said.

"As slavers see it," I said, "you were a slave from the moment your name was entered on an acquisition list."

"I see," she said.

"Branding and collaring," I said, "would then be rather in the nature of accompanying details, confirming the matter."

"I see," she said.

"Such things, identifications in their way, are in accord with Merchant Law," I said.

"Tell me more of this 'Jane'," she said.

"There is little to tell of a slave," I said, "other than that she is a slave."

"Of course," she said.

"Are you jealous?" I said.

"Certainly not!" she said.

"Then it does not matter," I said.

"Please, Master," she said, "please!"

"There is little to tell," I said, "other than the fact that she is a lovely slave, an intelligent, shapely brunette, nicely curved, the sort a man likes to sleep at his feet."

"I take it that she is, as am I, a barbarian."

"Not at all," I said. "She is Gorean, once the Lady Portia Lia Serisia, of Sun Gate Towers, a scion of the Serisii, a banking family once of considerable repute and power in Ar."

"'Once'?" she said.

"It no longer exists," I said. "It put gold before the Home Stone."

"I do not understand," she said.

"There was a war, an invasion, an occupation," I said. "Collaboration took place. Assets and skills were turned to profiteering. Then came the restoration of Marlenus, Ubar of Ubars. Law returned, in the form of the red sword. Proscription lists were posted. Impaling poles were weighted. Buildings were burned. Even blackened bricks were carted away and cast into the great swamp. Goreans have long memories."

"Why is she named 'Jane'?" she asked.

"Perhaps," I said, "that she may now know herself as no more than a barbarian, no more than another worthless slave."

"Such as I?" she said.

"Of course," I said.

"And Gregory—."

"Pertinax," I said.

"—owns her?" she said.

"Like a tarsk," I said.

"I suppose that is acceptable," she said.

"I do not understand," I said.

"She is Gorean," she said.

I laughed. "I think it is clear," I said, "that you understand little of these things. You know nothing of Gorean free women. You have never trembled before one. You have never prostrated yourself before one, hoping not to be lashed. You are less valued than the dust beneath the sandals of such a one. She is a thousand times above you, you, a mere slave. Indeed, you are different forms of being, which may not even be compared. You would learn to beg, even to be permitted to kiss the hem of her robe on your belly. The Gorean free woman is exalted, proud, noble, and powerful. She possesses a Home Stone."

"They are not the only free women!" she said.

"Oh?" I said.

"I was a free woman!" she said.

"You had no Home Stone," I said.

"I was free!" she said.

"At best a yet-uncollared slave," I said.

"Is this so different from other women of my former world?" she asked.

"Not really," I said.

"The men of Gor," she said, "think of us as slaves."

"Not just the men of Gor," I said.

"The women, as well," she said.

"Of course," I said.

"As slave stock," she said.

"Yes," I said.

"Suitably enslaved," she said.

"Of course," I said. "Consider your shamelessly bared features, your unconcealed ankles, your small wrists and slender hands, exposed to public view, the nature of your skirts, sometimes high enough to reveal a calf, or even more, the silken undergarments, the clothing fashionably designed to be provocative, clothing in which you might vend yourself for your own profit. You put yourselves on your own block."

"Please do not speak so," she said.

"Such things, of course, are convenient," I said. "They facilitate the inspection and assessment of the slaver."

"Doubtless!" she said.

"But here," I said, "on this world, the profit on you will be taken by another."

"I do not see that we are so different from other women," she said.

"I do not think you are," I said.

Surely much could be done with the robes of concealment, with their layerings and drapings, their bright colors, so ingeniously arranged, with veils slack or disarranged, even diaphanous, the street veil brazenly neglected, with loose, casual hoods from which strands of hair might escape, as though inadvertently, with gloves, with a sleeve too loose, with embroidered slippers, with a hem lifted to ascend a step or curb, such things.

"I hate this 'Jane,'" she said.

"Of course," I said. "It was she who was chained at the feet of Pertinax. It was she who wore the chains you wish were yours."

"No!" she said. "I hold Gregory in contempt! I revile him! He is a weakling!"

"You brought him to Gor with you," I said.

"A servant, a tool," she said. "He amused me. I enjoyed manipulating him, as other men. We have power, you know. I needed a male, and what better excuse for a male than Gregory? He was so simple, so hopeful, so eager to please. He could pretend to be master, as I instructed him, he obedient to my tutelage, while it was I who was mistress. I well ensnared him on Earth, with a word, a gesture, a smile, and then, when he was hopelessly mine, devoted, complaisant, and managed, he would accompany me in my work."

"You hated him?" I said.

"Despised him, rather," she said.

"As I understand it," I said, "you had considerable resources at your disposal. Why then did you not enlist another servitor, one stronger, one more independent, one more formidable, more redoubtable?"

"To accompany me to Gor?" she said. "What if I should find myself at his feet?"

"You wanted a typical Earth male," I said.

"Of course," she said.

"There are deep rivers in human beings," I said. "I do not think you were aware of these waters, and their currents."

"I do not understand," she said.

"Perhaps you were dimly aware of them in yourself," I said, "or your body was, and perhaps you, or your body, were dimly aware of them in Gregory White."

"Absurd," she said.

"When you were serving in the stable at Tarncamp," I said, "you hoped he would visit you, and succor you."

"Perhaps to be kind to me, perhaps to comfort me, perhaps to save me, to free me, to rescue me," she said, angrily.

"Perhaps to steal you and flee with you?" I said.

"Steal me?" she said.

"Of course. You are a property."

"Of course," she said.

"And flee with you," I said.

"Perhaps," she said.

"You would have been destroyed by guard larls within a pasang of the wands," I said.

"Perhaps," she said, angrily.

"I do not think that that was all," I said.

"What else?" she asked.

"It was my surmise that you, in your bondage, now well taught you were a slave, hoped to be his slave."

"Absurd," she said. "Never!"

"Perhaps, on some level," I said, "even on Earth, you wanted to be his slave."

"That is absurd," she said. "Never! Never!"

"Then put that aside," I said. "But perhaps, once you were on Gor, and embonded, you had such hopes."

"Of course!" she said.

"I thought so," I said.

"But for what reason?" she asked.

"Tell me," I said.

"I knew him from before," she said. "We were both from Earth. I could speak to him. We even worked for the same company, though his position was clerical and menial, mine significant and instrumental. We had been brought to Gor together. I knew him well. If he could manage to acquire me, to buy me, or such, then things would be much the same as before. I could rule him, and, though in a collar, be mistress!"

"You would not have been for sale," I said. "Lord Nishida would not have sold you. Aside from your mission to encounter me and see that I was conducted to Tarncamp, you were destined, even from Earth, to be a gift for the shogun, Lord Temmu."

"There are thousands of women on Earth as beautiful as I," she said.

"Or more beautiful," I said.

"Perhaps," she said.

"But your coloring," I said, "the blond hair, the blue eyes, the fair skin, would make you an unusual gift on the islands. Would you not be exotica in the markets? Too, you had come to the attention of slavers. Perhaps other women had not. Too, your character, your mercenary nature, your pettiness, your ambition, your shallowness, your greed, fitted you well for the projected employment. Too, I suspect more than one executive, or client, with suitable connections, relished the prospect of you on Gor, thought you might look quite well, stripped on a slave block."

"Why did Gregory not visit me at the stable?" she asked.

"He may be different from what you remember," I said.

"He did not seek me out, even later," she said.

"Perhaps," I said, "he has seen through you, and has been turned away by what he has seen."

"He loves me!" she said. "A woman can tell! He loves me! He is mine, helplessly and hopelessly mine!"

"Perhaps no longer," I said.

"A smile, a tear," she said, "and he would be again at my feet."

"Is that what you want?" I asked.

"Of course," she said.

"Who is he?" I asked.

"Gregory White," she said.

"He is now Pertinax," I said.

"I have been brought to the quarters of Master," she said. "I am before Master, bound and kneeling. I am a slave. What is the will of Master?"

"What do you think would be my will?" I asked.

"The will of a Master, with a slave," she said.

I rose up, then crouched behind her, and freed her wrists. I returned the one length of ribbon to the wardrobe chest, and then stood before her.

"You have been somewhat trained," I said.

She nodded.

"You are familiar with positions?"

"Yes," she said.

"Assume the position of the she-tarsk," I said.

She went to all fours.

I took a slave whip from the wall and cast it to the other side of the room. "Fetch it," I said, "in your teeth, and return it to me." After a time she lifted her head to me, and I removed the whip from between her teeth.

"You are aware of certain formulas," I said.

"Yes, Master," she said.

"Speak," I said.

"Whip me, Master," she said.

"Have you been displeasing?" I asked.

"I trust not, Master," she said.

"Why, then, should I whip you?" I asked.

"I am a slave," she said. "Master may do with me as he wishes."

"If you are not pleasing," I said, "what will be done with you?"

"I am not a free woman," she said. "I am a slave. If I am not pleasing, I will be punished."

"Why do you think I had you brought to my chambers?" I asked.

"That I might serve the pleasure of my Master's guest," she said.

"And what might that pleasure be?" I asked.

"That I might provide him with the pleasures of a slave," she said.

"But I think I will save you for another," I said.

"I do not understand," she said.

"First obeisance position," I said, unpleasantly.

Instantly, frightened, she went to her knees, her head to the floor, the palms of her hands on the floor, beside her head.

"Do you wish to live?" I said.

"Yes, Master," she said.

"Do you beg to be permitted to live?" I asked.

"Yes, Master," she said.

"Beg," I said.

"I beg to be permitted to live," she said.

"As the worthless, and abject slave you are?" I said.

"Yes, Master!" she said.

"You are the slave of Lord Yamada," I said. "I take it you may frequently be in his presence, may serve him, and such."

"Yes, Master," she said.

"He has withdrawn the majority of his troops from the north," I said. "He is unlikely to remain long on the defensive. What are his plans?"

"I do not know, Master," she said.

I myself, based on my earlier conversation with the shogun, was well aware of plans imparted to me, but, in the case of a Lord Yamada there may be plans unspoken, plans behind other plans, or different plans altogether. I thought some inkling of such matters might have reached the slave. Rumors, for example, abound in the pens. Even the wisp of an allusion, or a seemingly unrelated or meaningless action, the dispatch of a messenger, the nature of the seal on a document, the ordering of a map, may sometimes hint at movements, at routes, at alliances.

"Several slaves, in the number of some one hundred and fifty, were sold for rice," I said. "Where are they?"

"I do not know," she said. "I am *kajira*! I am told nothing. I am *kajira, kajira!*"

"Are they penned, are they sold, distributed, are they in the fields?" I asked.

"I know nothing, Master," she said. "Forgive me! I am only *kajira!*"

"What have you heard," I asked, "of an iron dragon?"

"Little," she said. "It is in stories, it is a fiction, a creature of imagination, a thing of legend, a creature of myth. The Pani slaves speak of it only in whispers."

"Why, if it be such," I asked, "should the Pani slaves so fear it, that they will not even speak aloud of it?"

"I do not know," she said.

"Perhaps they know something you do not," I said.

I did not doubt that the iron dragon was a creature of legend. Lord Nishida viewed it as such. Lord Okimoto seemed less skeptical. He seemed more open on the matter. Perhaps he feared some pebble of truth might lie concealed within the mountain of myth. And Lord Temmu, perhaps under the influence of Daichi, seemed to credit at least the possible existence of such a beast. Lord Yamada, on the other hand, I suspected, despite his alleged fear of its awakening, presumably manufactured for diplomatic reasons, would view such claims as preposterous, spun from no more than the fumes of benighted superstition. What gave me pause in the matter, or at least uneasiness, were the references to such a beast by so unlikely an informant as Tyrtaios, who was not Pani, and would not have been likely to be acquainted with Pani lore. Tyrtaios, as I understood him, a dark realist, as careful and prudential as a knife, was not likely to be the victim of any superstition, let alone that of an alien culture. Yet he had spoken as though this fiction might have had ribs of iron and claws of steel, might be as real as ore and fire.

"Clothe yourself," I said to the girl.

While she rose up, and dressed, I went to a narrow window in the wall, which looked out, onto the night, and the palace courtyard. In the light of the yellow moon, I could see guards below. The window was barred.

"It seems I am a prisoner," I had said to one of the two lovely, briefly tunicked Pani slave girls who had earlier attended on me.

"The bars, Master," had responded one of them, "prevent intruders from entering, from the outside."

"I see," I said.

The window was high above the courtyard, but I supposed an unbarred window might be accessible from ropes, fastened above.

On continental Gor slavers sometimes utilized such a mode of entry. Such a portal might be used as an avenue of egress also, of course, through which a bound and gagged woman might be extracted. Sometimes the woman is not removed from the chamber but sedated. When she awakens she discovers herself bound on her couch, naked and gagged, her limbs rudely, widely spread. She then realizes she has been "marked for slavery." This is sometimes used as a "mode of preparation" for bondage. Sometimes it is spoken of as letting the woman "cook" or "simmer" while awaiting the collar. She realizes how vulnerable she is. She does not know when she will be "collected," only that she is to be collected. It will be done at the slaver's pleasure, of course. She does not know, of course, who might be the slaver, or slavers, or when they will strike. Her fears torment her. Is it he, or another, one who passes her on the street, one who sits near her in the theater, one at her elbow in a market? She may try to flee, her efforts may become frantic. Then, perhaps when she feels safe, another sign or token may be discovered. Perhaps she unrolls a scroll and finds within it a slip of paper, "You are a slave," or perhaps on the very mirror of her vanity, drawn in grease pencil, she discovers an image, the small, lovely, cursive "Kef," much like the one which might be burned into her left thigh, somewhat below the hip. Finally, unable to stand things longer, distraught, frightened, miserable, she may take to courting the collar, traversing high bridges at night, moving on dismal streets after dark, wandering unescorted outside the walls, renting rooms in cheap inns, booking passage on lightly guarded caravans. She may actually cry out with relief and joy when she feels the ropes encircle her robes.

"It seems," I had said, "passage would be difficult from either side."

"Yes, Master," had said one of the slaves.

I regarded her. Pani, like those of continental Gor, obviously chose slaves for their beauty.

"Master?" she said.

"Come here," I said. "Do not kneel."

The slave, summoned, commonly kneels before a free person, waiting to be commanded.

"You are slim, and exquisite," I said. "Try to squeeze through the bars."

"I am not permitted to touch the bars, Master," she said.

I gestured toward the bars, and she hurried to them.

"Try," I said.

She pressed her small body against the bars, trying to insert her body between them, even writhing against them.

"Enough," I said.

She backed away, frightened. It had been clear that not even so small, and lovely, a body could begin to pass though those bars.

I tested them. They were sturdy, and well fixed.

"You may go," I told the slaves.

"All windows in the palace, Master," said the girl whom I

had ordered to the bars, "are similarly barred, even those in the private quarters of Lord Yamada himself."

I nodded, and indicated that they might leave.

They backed away, and then turned, and slipped from the room, gracefully, with the grace of slaves.

I went back to the window. Perhaps, I thought, Lord Yamada has a point in these bars. Might they not make it more difficult for an assassin to gain admittance to the palace, whether through one room or another? Bars do have their purposes, I thought, and not always to confine. Might they not also serve to protect? In any event, I seemed to be no more a prisoner than Lord Yamada himself. I had then gone to the door. I had found it unlocked.

Saru had now finished dressing herself.

She looked at me.

"Master?" she asked.

"Return to the slave quarters," I said.

"Saru is dismissed?" she said.

"Yes," I said.

"Is Saru so poor a slave?" she asked.

"You had best not be," I said, "or you will feel the whip."

"Please!" she said.

"No," I said.

"Do you not understand?" she said. "I am a slave! I did not know what it was to be biologically real, what it was to be wholly female. I now know! It has been done to me! I can no longer be anything but a slave! I no longer want to be anything but a slave! It is my life! I now belong in the collar of a slave! Do you not understand? It has been done to me!"

"I understand," I said.

"Regard me as nothing, if you wish," she said.

"I do," I said. "You are a slave."

It is interesting, I thought, what men can do to women, how one can turn them into slaves. To be sure, one does little more than open a door, little more than draw aside a curtain, and let them see themselves in the secret mirror, into which they had feared to look.

"I am such as is appropriately to be owned!" she said.

"I know," I said.

"I want only to kneel, to kiss the feet of a master, to love and serve him as the slave I am, to please him, and wholly, as the slave I am!"

"I understand," I said.

"In bondage," she said, "at the feet of men, I have discovered who I am and what I am for, and who I want to be and what I want to be for. I have discovered myself, who I am and wish to be! I now inhabit the country of my heart."

"On Earth," I said, "you should have put yourself to the feet of Gregory White, and begged a collar."

"Do not joke," she said. "I need a man, a master. How can I be a woman without a man, without a master!"

"Your slave fires burn, do they not?" I asked.

"Yes, Master!" she said.

"To the slave quarters," I said. "Squirm and writhe there, in your kennel. Sweat on your chain."

"Please," she said. "No!"

"Perhaps, one day," I said, "I will throw you to the feet of another."

"Master!" she wept.

"Get out," I said, "before you are beaten."

"Yes, Master," she wept.

She steadied herself at the portal, with two hands on the jamb. I feared she might fall.

At that moment, throughout the palace, there rang a large gong, the note of which was taken up by, and repeated by, smaller gongs.

"What is that?" I cried out, amidst the din.

"It is the alarm, Master!" she cried.

Chapter Fourteen

The Balcony;
My Conversation with Lord Yamada

"There!" said Lord Yamada, pointing.

"Yes!" I said.

We stood on an extended balcony, near the roof of the palace. Ashigaru were about, several armed with bows.

"It is a tarnsman, against the moon," said Lord Akio, looking upward.

I would have given much for a glass of the Builders.

"It is one rider," I said. "I do not think it is a raid. Hold your fire."

"It is a scout?" said Lord Akio. I heard the metal blades of the war fan ripple briefly.

"An invasion?" said an officer.

"I understand this," said Lord Yamada. "Bring torches! And you, Tarl Cabot, tarnsman, please step forward."

Torches were brought, several held about me, as I stood near the railing of the balcony. The rider was circling, and would shortly be near again.

"Do not loose your arrows," I said.

"They will not," Lord Yamada assured me. "Do you know the rider?"

"It could be one of several," I said. "I have no glass of the Builders."

"Bring a long glass," said Lord Yamada, and a servitor hurried from the balcony.

"The rider," said Lord Yamada, "may be so equipped, with what you call a glass of the Builders?"

"Almost certainly," I said.

"A seeing tube?" he said.

"Yes," I said. "What, I take it, you speak of as a long glass."

"Excellent," said Lord Yamada. "I have been awaiting this moment. As the rider approaches, please stand forward, please, even more so, Tarl Cabot *san*, there, in the light, and please, if you would, lift your hand, pleasantly acknowledging his presence, and inquiry."

"What is going on, Lord?" inquired Lord Akio.

I lifted my hand, waving, to the rider, after which he whirled away.

"It is a representative of our friends," said Lord Yamada, "the cohorts of our guest, Tarl Cabot, tarnsman, come to investigate, come to ascertain his health and well-being."

"We might have brought him down, with arrows," said Lord Akio, nervously, snapping the fan open and shut.

"A difficult shot," said Lord Yamada, "but, if successful, it might have purchased little time, and brought about the end of the house of Yamada."

"How is that?" asked an officer.

"We cannot protect ourselves from the lightning of the sky," said Lord Yamada. "He who has demon birds may come and go as he pleases. He who has demon birds is elusive and may strike unexpectedly, in the day or night, at dawn or dusk. He who has demon birds, in time, could rain fire from the sky, far above futile, angrily brandished glaives, and burn with impunity where archers are not. In a year every fortress, castle, palace, barracks, warehouse, and humble shed of our house could be collapsed and charred wood, the ashes like dry fog, borne on the wind to the sea."

"I did not expect honor and appointment," I said to Lord Yamada, "when I was delivered to you."

"You expected to bear the brunt of a shogun's wrath," said Lord Yamada, "exquisitely expressed over weeks with cords and irons, with needles and clamps, with flaming splinters, perhaps culminating eventually in the horror of the straw jacket?"

"I did not know what to expect," I said.

"Perhaps that was just as well," smiled Lord Yamada.

"Lord Temmu and Daichi, the reader of bones and shells, perhaps were more apprised of various possibilities than I," I said.

"And yet," said Lord Yamada, "they willingly supplied you to me."

"I shall not forget that," I said.

"I did not expect you to forget it," said Lord Yamada.

"You wish the services of the tarn cavalry?" I said.

"Who would not?" he said.

"Surely it remains in the service of Lord Temmu," I said.

"I know more of the house of Temmu than its master," said Lord Yamada. "He expected to deliver you to me, and merely appoint a new commander of the demon birds. Thus, he would gratify me, avoid the flight of the iron dragon, and retain his cavalry."

"That seems, within its limits," I said, "a sensible, well-judged plan."

"But one based on a faulty intelligence," said Lord Yamada, "an intelligence which, if I am not mistaken, you share."

"I do not understand," I said.

"My judgment in these matters," he said, "was sounder than either his or yours."

"How so?" I said.

"I know something of men, of war, and leadership," said Lord Yamada.

"You are shogun," I said.

"The men are yours, the cavalry is yours," he said. "Lord Temmu did not understand this, nor, apparently, do you. It has been so since the place called Tarncamp, far away. You gave men the sky, and the broad-winged tarn. You took soldiers and mercenaries and forged tarnsmen. You formed these men into an arm of war, a cavalry, trained it, and led it, even in a great sky battle across the sea. You brought it across Thassa, nurtured, sheltered, and protected it. You have flown with it, enduring the same hardships and risks, the same hunger, fatigue, cold, and danger as those you led. The men will follow no other."

I did not respond.

"With Tarl Cabot, tarnsman," he said, "goes the cavalry; with the cavalry goes the sky; with the sky goes victory."

"Two approach!" cried Akio, the fan snapping open.

"The long glass," said the servitor, returning to the balcony.

Lord Yamada lifted it, peering through it.

"They are confirming the matter," said Lord Yamada.

He watched the two tarns approaching in the distance, small against the yellow moon.

"Fortunately for Lord Temmu," said General Yamada, "they are confirming that Tarl Cabot, commander of the cavalry, is alive."

"And if they could not make this determination?" I asked.

"Then," said General Yamada, "I think the holding of Lord Temmu would be destroyed."

"That would be unfortunate," I said.

"Yes," said Lord Yamada, "as I wish to possess it."

"It is strange," I said, "that tarnsmen would so scout the palace of General Yamada, here, this night. What would be the likelihood that they might catch sight of me here, in this place, at this time?"

"The likelihood was quite high," said General Yamada. "The rendezvous was arranged."

"I see," I said.

"They feared you would be slain. They were thus contemplating first the destruction of the holding of Lord Temmu, who betrayed you, and, second, the destruction of my holdings, for presumably having slain you."

"I see," I said.

"As you understand," he said, "neither option was appealing. Thus I had only to inform them of your present satisfactory circumstances, and arrange the rendezvous that would confirm the matter."

"How did you communicate with the encampment?" I asked.

"It was only necessary to communicate with the holding," he said, "as there are tarns and riders at the holding, which could communicate with the encampment."

"You know much," I said.

"There are a variety of ways in which one can communicate

with the holding," he said, "flighted vulos, message arrows, signals from the ground, such things."

"What if," I asked, "the cavalry had accepted a new commander?"

"Do not even think of it," said Lord Yamada.

"Then I would have been in your power," I said, "and might expect to bear the brunt of the wrath of a shogun?"

"Of course," he said, handing me the long glass.

"They are closer now," said Lord Akio.

"Do you know them?" asked Lord Yamada.

"Wait," I said.

"Do not fire," Lord Yamada cautioned his bowmen.

The two tarns now wheeled away.

"Yes," I said. "They are two officers, Pertinax and Tajima."

I returned the long glass to Lord Yamada, who handed it to the servitor who had brought it to the balcony.

"Do you find the device equivalent to your 'glass of the Builders'?" he asked.

"Very much so," I said.

"Who are the Builders?" he asked.

"Makers," I said, "artisans, manufacturers, engineers, architects, such things."

"Doubtless there will be joy in the encampment," he said, "when it is learned you live and thrive, and are enjoying our hospitality."

"But I am still in your power," I said.

"And," he said, "now, too, is the cavalry."

"I see," I said.

"We shall be allies, and great friends," said Lord Yamada.

"It seems clear," I said, "that you are well apprised of what ensues in the holding of Temmu."

"One attempts to keep informed," he said.

"Doubtless there were spies even in Tarncamp and Shipcamp," I said.

"Perhaps," he said.

"Doubtless some are highly placed," I said.

"Perhaps," he said.

"I have long suspected Lord Okimoto," I said.

"Interesting," he said.

"My friend, Tajima," I said, "who held the saddle of one of the reconnaissance tarns recently about, suspects the daimyo, Lord Nishida."

"He is certainly highly placed," said Lord Yamada.

"I am sure of two," I said.

"Oh?" said Lord Yamada.

"It was extremely clever of you," I said, "to place the reader, Daichi, in the inner circle of Lord Temmu."

"It took time," said General Yamada. "Years were spent subtly enhancing the reputation of Daichi in the islands, with the result that Lord Temmu must have his services, at whatever cost."

"He preys on the superstition of the shogun, and influences his moves and policies by supposed readings of the bones and shells."

"Most of the readings are stupid ambiguities and obscure nonsense, things which might be interpreted in several ways, one of which is likely, from time to time, to bear some resemblance to something or other which might actually occur, but I take care, naturally, to supply the content now and then, to my advantage."

"The last one was clever," I said, "the business about the iron dragon, the fear of its flight, and such."

"It brought you into my hands," said Lord Yamada.

"It is strange to me," I said, "that Lord Temmu, who is not a stupid man, should take such things seriously."

"Not at all," he said. "If the readings should seem to one uncanny, and fraught with prophetic accuracy, if they should, from time to time, seem to foretell the course of events, even with alarming precision, one might take them seriously."

"But you are arranging and managing the events which are being foretold," I said.

"But Daichi is trusted," he said.

"Of course," I said.

"You said," said Lord Yamada, "you were sure of two."

"But why the references to an iron dragon?" I asked. "That is a matter of legend. There are no such things."

"Are there not?" he asked.

"No," I said.

"Let us then not speak of them," said Lord Yamada.

"Very well," I said.

"You said," said Lord Yamada, "you were sure of two."

"Agents, spies?" I said.

"Yes," he said.

"Daichi," I said.

"Of course," he said.

"Another," I said, "is evident, but unimportant. She is a contract woman, under contract to Lord Nishida. Her name is Sumomo. My friend, and fellow officer, Tajima, discovered her on the outer parapet, apparently casting some missive to the ground below."

"I am sorry to hear she was evident," said Lord Yamada, coldly. "A good spy should not be evident. And I had not, until now, regarded her as unimportant. But I shall now do so."

"Doubtless the missive," I said, "if such it were, was received below."

"She was clumsy," said Lord Yamada, "to permit herself to be discovered in such a compromising act."

"Doubtless her services were useful," I said.

"But now, no longer," said Lord Yamada, quietly. "She is now known. She may be dispensed with. She shall be punished."

"It is not as though your honor is touched," I said.

"But it has been," he said.

"How so?" I asked. "She is a mere contract woman, kept by Lord Nishida."

"She is not a contract woman," said Lord Yamada. "That is a pretense. Do you think I would entrust so sensitive a role to a contract woman?"

"She is not a contract woman?" I said.

"No," he said.

"Some now know her as a spy," I said. "It may be difficult to rescue her, to extract her from the holding."

"Who knows what the bones and shells may say," said Lord Yamada.

"I see," I said.

"She has failed," he said. "I will have her destroyed."

"Surely not," I said.

"I am shogun," he said.

"Your honor is not touched," I said.

"It is," he said.

"How so?" I asked.

"She is my daughter," he said.

I was silent.

"Do not be concerned," he said. "I have many daughters."

Chapter Fifteen

Lord Akio

"You do not mind that you are denied weapons?" asked Lord Akio, a daimyo of Lord Yamada.

It was my understanding that Lord Yamada's daimyos, despite their own lands and holdings, were expected to attend on the shogun several months of each year. In this way they were separated from their own bases of power, and were, in effect, periodic, transitory hostages in the palace. If a daimyo failed to respond at any time to a particular summons, or did not choose to honor his shogun with his presence at expected times, he was regarded, *de facto*, as placing himself in a state of rebellion, the likely consequence of which would be his execution, unpleasantly consummated, the extirpation of his family, the acquisition of his fields, and the appropriation of his holdings.

"Why should I mind," I asked, "when I am accompanied by Lord Akio, a skilled warrior, who will protect me?"

He shook the large, metal fan open.

"This is not a mere decoration, the accessory of an ensemble, a bauble of fashion," he said.

"Still," I said, "it is attractive, with its brightly colored panels, and well matches the tasteful robes of Lord Akio."

"Are you familiar with such fans?" he asked.

"Not really," I said.

"I have others," he said.

"Which match other robes," I said.

"Of course," he said.

"I see," I said.

"Do you think me a fop?" he asked.

"No, Lord," I said. "It is common for nobles to bathe frequently, to dress well, and care for their appearance."

He spread the fan.

"It is a shield," he said.

"I am sure it would turn aside a thrust, an arrow," I said.

It was not much different, in its expanse, from a small buckler, of the sort carried by the cavalry.

"It is, of course," he said, "not simply a shield."

"Oh?" I said.

"It is edged," he said, calling attention to the razorlike brink of the device. "It can cut a throat, or sever a hand."

"I see," I said.

The small cavalry buckler, too, was edged, and, if one were close enough to a foe, might be similarly formidable. I saw no reason to call this to the attention of my companion and guide. On tarnback, of course, it served primarily as a weapon of defense.

We were wandering in the palace garden, a place where a silken print might have sprung into life, where nature and artifice sought to outdo one another. Here were lengths of carefully arranged sand, raked into rhythmic furrows, harmonizing with the contours of the path of colored stones. There there were unusual stones, brought in from the coast, shaped by centuries of tides; and all about were varieties of trees, large and small, some fruit-bearing, some ablaze with blossoms. From the limbs of some of these trees hung lanterns, now unlit, but swaying in the breeze. From the limbs of others hung slender tubes of wood on strings, which tubes, when rustled by the wind, would strike one another, emitting charming notes. We continued on our way, occasionally crossing a rivulet of water on a small, railed wooden bridge, between flowering shrubs and patches of bright flowers, some of which were terraced amongst steps of rocks. Colorfully plumaged birds occasionally fluttered overhead. The Night Singers were now afield, but would return in the evening to proclaim and defend their small territories. I was sure it was no coincidence that Lord Akio had chosen the path he had, for the Pani garden is not merely designed to appeal to the eye, ear, and scent, but to do so in a certain progression, this progression depending on the time of year. Such things, as the notes of a melody, are most pleasing when experienced in a certain order. *Ela*, I felt, there is so much here with which I have so little to do. How much here, I thought, must be wasted on, and lost to, a barbarian sensibility. In my crude way I found myself less rapt with delight than concerned with certain practical assessments, with, say, measuring distances, and calculating times. How long, for example, would it take to traverse, say, the corridor between the gate of the garden, if I could reach it, from the courtyard, or palace steps, and the cover of the garden, and between this cover, and the exterior wall? I considered the height of the walls. Quite high. No trees I noted were near enough to the walls to afford access to the summit of a wall. Too, I supposed that the garden walls would be similar to those of the courtyard itself, and, if this should be so, attaining their summit might constitute a dubious victory. From the sparkle of sunlight by day, and the glint of moonlight by night, I had determined that the courtyard wall, at least that portion which I could see from my quarters, was armed. Anchored in the top of the wall were pieces of broken glass, shards of pottery, and blades, and, strung about the wall, were dangling strips of metal which would be difficult to elude, and which, if not eluded, would produce a jangling of disturbed metal unlikely to pass unnoted. Something of this sort, I supposed, defensive arrangements, would be likely to characterize the garden walls, as well. On the other hand, within the garden walls I saw no sign of the warning apparatus consisting of suspended strips of metal. On the other hand, I would later learn, interestingly, that this lack of an obvious warning arrangement, first, was intended to encourage an approach through the garden to the courtyard, which would then facilitate the entrapment of intruders between the double walls, those of the courtyard and those of the garden, and, second, that there was, in a sense, a warning device in the garden, as well as in the more open, barren courtyard, nearer the palace, a warning device, however, which was armed, so to speak, only after dark. This consisted in the Night Singers themselves, whose song would be silenced if an unfamiliar individual entered the garden, and, when resumed, would be rather different, and would occasionally be interrupted with warning notes, should the individual change his position.

Supposedly these small changes might be registered by guards, whether within or without the walls.

At the moment Lord Akio and I, other than a gardener or so, were alone in the garden.

"Behold," said Lord Akio, with a snap flinging the fan into a circle, and then, with a thumb, locking the blades in place.

"So, now," I said, "it is a circle, a wheel, of sorts?"

"A circle of terror," he said, "a wheel of death."

"I do not understand," I said.

"Do you think I am unarmed?" he asked.

"You might turn a blow," I said, "and, at close quarters, strike an opponent."

"I can hurl this," he said.

"It might be dangerous," I said, "with its weight and sturdiness, functioning as a missile, a flighted, spinning blade, likely to take blood wherever it might strike."

"It is not simply a matter of drawing blood," he said.

"Surely, given its shape it would lack the penetration of a blade," I said, "and, given its shape and weight, it would lack the distance and accuracy of an arrow."

"All weapons have their limitations," he said.

"And their advantages," I said.

"True," he said. "For example, our attractive friend here might not be recognized as a weapon."

"Perhaps not," I said.

"Which is a splendid advantage."

"Doubtless," I said.

"I once decapitated a bandit, who thought me unarmed," he said.

"Oh?" I said.

"You are skeptical?" he inquired.

"Not at all," I said.

"I think you are skeptical," he said.

"It might be done, I suppose," I said, "at extremely close range."

"Behold," he said, "do you see the tender of the garden there?"

"Surely," I said.

The fellow had a long-handled, wooden-toothed rake with which he was dressing the sand near the path we had recently traversed.

"How far would you say he is?"

"Some ten paces, or such," I said.

"Behold," he said, drawing back the circular artifact, its rippled blades locked in place.

"What are you going to do?" I said.

"Demonstrate," he said.

"Do not!" I said.

"It is a peasant," he said, "one not even Ashigaru."

"No matter," I said.

"I do not understand," he said.

"I beg your indulgence," I said. "Do not."

"I am skillful," he said. "There will be little pain, unless I wish it so."

"Please," I said.

"Very well," said Lord Akio. "You are a guest of the shogun." But then he cried to the gardener, "Aside, aside, tarsk, stand aside!"

The gardener turned about, startled, facing us.

"Aside!" said Lord Akio.

Frightened, the man, clutching the rake, moved to his left. He was barefoot. He was clad in little more than a rag. He had his eyes on the device in the hand of the daimyo. I gathered he knew more of it than I. Perhaps he had seen it before.

Not a yard or so from where he stood there was a sturdy sapling of five or six horts in girth.

"Behold," said Lord Akio, and he flighted the device, spinning in its blaze of blurred color, toward the sapling.

There was quick, hard sound, and the device quivered, vibrating, like a startled bird, trapped some two or three horts in the wood. I did not doubt what it might have done if applied to flesh.

"I see," I said.

Lord Akio removed the device from the tree, and, shortly thereafter, it might have been again mistaken for a fashionable accessory.

"Replace this tree," said Lord Akio to the gardener.

"Yes, Lord," said the man.

Lord Akio then turned to me.

"Let us continue our walk," he said. "It is a pleasant day."

Chapter Sixteen

What Occurred on the Fifth Level of the Palace

"This wing of the palace," said the Ashigaru, "is closed to all save Lord Yamada and selected servitors."

"Very well," I said. "I shall turn back."

This was the fifth level of the palace, which contained six levels.

I turned away, but, a pace or so down the corridor, turned about, again. "It seems to be raining," I said.

"I do not know," said the Ashigaru.

"But you do," I said.

"Noble guest?" said he.

"It is nothing," I said.

I turned about, again, and continued on my way down the corridor. I had not gone far when I saw a figure approaching.

It was not easy to mistake those brightly colored, carefully arranged robes, nor the measure of that gracefully sedate tread.

"What are you doing here?" politely inquired Lord Akio.

"Looking about," I said.

The daimyo's arms were within his wide sleeves. I saw no evidence of his fan. I noted the hang of the sleeve on his left arm. The sleeve sheath was held by two straps.

"You are curious?" he said.

"Yes," I said.

"It is possible to be too curious," he said.

"For example," I said, "I would be curious to know if your sleeve dagger has a pearled handle."

"You are observant," he said. "No," he said. "It is tem-wood, with ceramic inlays, yellow."

"Lovely," I said.

"It is a better match for my robes," he said.

"It is a sleeve knife," I said. "Who would know the difference?"

"I would," he said.

Whereas I had been given much liberty of movement within the palace, the garden, and the surrounding grounds, with their shops, pantries, storerooms, and numerous ancillary buildings, including a bakery, smokehouse, and brewery, certain areas were forbidden to me. These, it seemed, were sensitive, perhaps *dojos*, officers' quarters, barracks, arsenals, and such. There were cook houses and eating sheds for the men. One could tell the verr and tarsk pens by smell. There was a small dairy which supplied verr milk, and processed it, as wished, into derivative products, primarily cheeses.

When summoned by Lord Temmu, several days ago, I had arrived at his holding on tarnback. I did not know what had become of that tarn. I had little doubt that Tyrtaios, into whose hands I had been given, to be later delivered to Lord Yamada, was familiar with the reins and saddle of a tarn. If he were of the black caste, as I suspected, that would almost be taken for granted. The Assassin is expected to move with silence, stealth, and swiftness, and depart similarly. His presence at the castle of Lord Temmu suggested that he might have arrived by means of his own tarn. That was not impossible. It did not seem likely he could have arrived publicly, afoot, as a legate or such. After the destruction of the first encampment, we knew that several tarns had been destroyed, and others had been released, by auxiliary personnel, presumably to return to the wild. On the other hand, it was surely possible that a small number might have fallen into the hands of the enemy. We had had, however, no assurances of this. I calculated I had been sedated for some eight days, but did not know how or when I had been brought to the regions controlled by General Yamada. Given the time involved, it seemed plausible I had been transported by wagon or cart from the vicinity of the castle to the palace. On the other hand, I doubted this, given the difficulties which would have been involved. The most rational conjecture was that two tarns had been used, mine, and one brought to the holding by Tyrtaios. In any event, the tarn on which I had reached the castle of Lord Temmu must not remain in the holding. That would have aroused suspicion. Its absence must suggest I had returned to the encampment. I did not think that the messenger tarns held at the castle of Lord Temmu would have been used, as this might have provoked curiosity. I recalled that neither Lord Nishida nor Lord Okimoto had been at the meeting with Lord Temmu, that also attended by Daichi and, to my surprise at the time, Sumomo. I did not now know Sumomo's whereabouts, but had gathered that Lord Yamada, displeased with her, would arrange, by means of the contrived readings of Daichi, that she be brought somewhere into his regions, perhaps to the palace, to be dealt with as a failed spy. All in all then, it seemed to be most likely, despite the time involved, that I had been placed on my own tarn and that that tarn, by a lead, would have been conducted by Tyrtaios to whatever point General Yamada might have designated. I had, however, heard no tarn cries over the past few days and so conjectured that if one or more tarns were at the disposal of Lord Yamada, they were not housed in the immediate vicinity.

"As I am curious," I said, "I would be pleased to inquire if there be tarns about."

"One can be too curious," he said.

"I suppose that is possible," I said.

"Perhaps," he said, "you would like to seize such a mount, and slip away, discourteously declining the hospitality of the shogun."

"That would be rude," I said.

"Barbarians are not noted for their manners," he said.

"True," I said.

"But they may be taught," he said.

"I suppose that is possible," I said. "Are tarns about?"

"You have been well treated, have you not?" he asked.

"Yes," I said. "Are tarns about?"

"*Ela*," he said. "I am a humble servitor of the shogun. I am neither a tarnsman or tarnster. I would not know."

"Apparently there are portions of this level which are closed off," I said, "except for certain individuals."

"Oh?" he said.

"Lord Yamada, and some others," I said.

"Interesting," he said.

"A guard has been placed," I said.

"Interesting," he said.

"It is doubtless that portion of the palace which houses the higher women of Lord Yamada, his wives, concubines and contract women," I said.

"Doubtless," he said.

I had already ascertained, of course, from the Pani slaves who were regularly sent to attend me, that the private quarters of Lord Yamada's higher women was located on the third level of the palace. The private quarters of the shogun himself, as nearly as I could determine from the soon-somewhat-evasive answers of the Pani slaves, were frequently changed, he seldom occupying the same chambers two nights in a row. Apparently ostraka were placed in a small pot and shaken, after which one would be drawn, that dictating the quarters of the evening. Two trusted servitors were then informed of the falling of the lot, that, in the case of an emergency, Lord Yamada might be expeditiously informed. Interestingly, it seemed that his daimyos did not have access to this information.

His palace slaves, of which Saru was doubtless one, and my Pani attendants others, had their quarters in a holding area maintained somewhere beneath the first level. Most of the slaves from the holding of Lord Temmu who had been traded for rice might be anywhere, distributed to daimyos, warriors, and officers, sold, gifted, bartered, put in the fields, put to herding verr and tarsk, perhaps even being held somewhere, in pens or sheds, to be dispersed at a later date.

"I think it may be raining outside," I said.

"It had appeared dismal," he said.

"The wild tarn," I said, "seldom chooses to fly in the rain."

"I know little of tarns," he said.

"But you are not surprised?" I said.

"Not really," he said.

"Many beasts," I said, "prefer to avoid the rain."

"I would suppose so," he said.

"But men," I said, "think little of going about in the rain."

"True," said Lord Akio.

"Particularly if they are clothed appropriately, if they have a raincoat," I said.

"I do not understand the nature of this conversation," said Lord Akio.

"Of straw," I said.

He looked at me, quickly, suspiciously. I sensed his hands had suddenly grasped one another within the concealment of those wide, hanging sleeves. Then his features resumed once more their attentive, benignant cast. "I am surprised that Tarl Cabot, tarnsman, knows of such things, or finds them of interest," he said. "It is true, of course, that many peasants fashion themselves such raincoats."

"What do you know of iron dragons?" I asked.

"They do not exist," he said.

"I am surprised to meet you in the palace, on this level," I said.

"I have an appointment," he said.

"Do not let me detain you," I said.

He bowed slightly, politely, smiled, and continued down the corridor.

I waited for a time, and then turned about. The daimyo was no longer in sight. Apparently he had been admitted into those precincts access to which had recently been denied to me.

I then continued on my way.

In the vicinity of the guard, prior to my withdrawal, I had noted in the corridor, and in the interior passage, that denied to me, alternating residues of moisture, quite possibly, given the spacing, the remnants of tracks, but unusual tracks, perhaps those of a large, unshod, shuffling creature. Doubtless this evidence might have been misinterpreted in many ways, particularly in the Pani islands, except for one detail. When the fur is thick, and matted, and soaked with rain, it has an odor which, once experienced, is not likely to be mistaken.

It was a scent, and a sort of scent, with which I was hitherto well acquainted, from various venues, from the delta of the Vosk outside Port Kar, from the hills of bleak Torvaldsland, the wastes and oases of the Tahari, the expanses of the Barrens, the jungles of the Ua, such places, even from the dens and forests of a steel world.

It was the scent of Kur.

Chapter Seventeen

The Archery Court

"Lord Yamada," I said, "cares to speak with me?"

I had been conducted by an Ashigaru to the shogun's archery court.

"Yes, Tarl Cabot, tarnsman," he said.

The typical Pani bow is quite large, commonly longer, if not heavier, than the peasant bow of the continent. To me it was unfamiliar, given its lack of what I would have supposed to be the natural symmetry of such a weapon. The arrow is released well below the center of the bow. The bow itself is taller than most tall men. The draw is long, contributing to the weapon's striking power, accuracy, and range. Given the length of the draw, a consequence of the bow's construction, the arrow is correspondingly long. Arrows are variously fletched, the fletching curving to the left or right, which determines the rotation of the missile in flight, the left-curving fletching producing what I tend to think of as a clockwise rotation, though, for Goreans, it would be a counterclockwise rotation, and the right producing what I tend to think of as a counterclockwise rotation, but which the Goreans would consider a clockwise rotation. As nearly as I can determine the orientation of the fletching is immaterial with respect to accuracy. Indeed, it is common to use first one and then the other, in pairs. Indeed, an arrow with the left-turned fletching is often spoken of as the first arrow, and an arrow with the right-turned fletching as the second arrow. To be sure, different archers may prefer one fletching to another, one being thought more apt or fortunate than the other. One advantage of the bow's construction is that despite its length it may be fired from a kneeling position, this allowing the archer to avail himself of lower cover and expose less of his body in firing. I had first seen such bows used by the Pani in Tarncamp, in the northern forests of continental Gor. It might be mentioned in passing that I had seen Pani archers with shorter bows, but the longer bow seemed more common, at least amongst the Pani with whom I was most familiar.

Lord Yamada was dressed in a long, white exercise smock, with short, white sleeves. He extracted one of the long arrows from a stand to his right.

"Would you care to join me?" he inquired, pleasantly.

"Perhaps," I said, "if I might avail myself of a more familiar bow."

"Barbarians are delightful," he said.

"Oh?" I said.

"Certainly," he said. "You are inquiring if the tarn which carried you to the castle of Lord Temmu is in the vicinity, masking your interest by a reference to the saddle bow. If that were available, so, too, presumably, would be the tarn."

"It is true," I said, "I am interested to know if tarns are about."

"What would we, mere Pani, know of demon birds?" he asked.

"It seems likely," I said, "your noble ally, the barbarian, Tyrtaios, reached the castle of Lord Temmu astride a tarn, secretly, by night, and likely, as well, that my tarn, for such beasts are of great worth, if it were practical, would have been acquired. Certainly it would not be released, nor would it have been left at the castle. Indeed, I conjecture that it was used in bringing me into your hospitality. If both tarns were used, neither would be overburdened, such a weighting taxing the beast and diminishing its speed, the rider's work thusly being brought more expeditiously to its conclusion."

"Very wise," he said. "I have often regarded barbarians as ignorant and uncouth, but I have never made the mistake, unlike many others, of considering them stupid."

"So I gather that at least two tarns are about," I said.

"Yes," said Lord Yamada. "And I hope to have you soon again on tarnback."

"Good," I said.

"In my service," said he.

"Of course," I said.

"Observe," he said.

Lord Yamada lifted the grip of the bow, with arrow to the string, slowly carefully, above his head, and then slowly, carefully, evenly, considering the target, paralleling it to that objective, lowered it gracefully. A moment later that long bird took flight.

"The preparation for the release," I said, "is interesting. It seems much like a ritual, almost ceremonial. One might almost conceive of such a movement in a ceremony, or stately dance."

"Might you say it is beautiful?" he asked.

"Perhaps," I said. "But the arrow can kill."

"Why can there not be grace and beauty in all things," he said, "the curve of a spoon, the touch of ink on silk, the arrangement of flowers, such things?"

"Perhaps even," I said, "in the flight of an arrow, the stroke of a sword."

"Of course," he said.

I had thought of the frightening, martial grace of a swordsman faraway, a short, unkempt, thickly bodied, ugly man known as Nodachi, Sword, ugly save when his blade was drawn, and his unprepossessing persona seemed somehow enlarged and transformed, transformed into something different, something awesome, something very still, a cloud which might conceal lightning, a night from which a beast might spring, something which, in its way, was, like the crouching, observant larl, both terrifying and beautiful.

"But you must not understand the beauty of this form of archery as a mere cultural oddity," he said, "or a whim of fashion like the color of sandals or the cut of a garment. Things have their purposes as well as their appearances. The lifting of the bow stretches the arms, and postpones the action; this calms the heart and steadies the nerves. The grip is not clutched to waver, but the arrow, as it descends, is gently brought into harmony with the target. Then, after a moment of meditation, it is at peace with the bow, the string, and target. Then, ready, the bird takes wing."

"Things might be done differently," I said.

"Of course," he said.

"Still," I said, "it is beautiful."

"I think so," he said, "but not merely beautiful."

"No," I said, regarding the target, "I do not think it merely beautiful."

"Beauty need not have use," he said. "It is its own justification, of course, the scent of the flower, the marking of the petal."

"True," I said. "But nature has its contrivances. The color of the blossom, the marking of the petal, the scent of the flower attract tiny predators whose labors, unbeknownst to themselves, profit the very hosts whom they despoil."

"But the flower is still beautiful," he said.

"Of course," I said.

"But one must not overlook less contemplative beauties," he said. "There are some beautiful things, even quite beautiful things, of which one might ask of what value would they be without use?"

"The female slave," I said.

"Certainly," he said. "Even barbarians understand that. Consider the women your coins fetch from the auction block. What is the value of that beauty if it is not put to use, if it is not enjoyed, ravished, owned, and mastered?"

"True," I said.

"What value would be that beauty without use?"

"What, indeed?" I said.

"Indeed," he said, "if such beauty were limited to mere contemplation, it would be less beautiful, even annoying, for it would issue in little but torment, and frustration."

"True," I said.

"In such respects it is quite unlike the sunset, and the flower," he said, "on which we are content to gaze with rapturous equanimity."

"Quite unlike," I said.

"Surely you would seldom buy such items for mere decoration or display."

"Certainly not," I said.

"Thus," he said, "we seize them, make them ours, acquire them, and own them."

"Yes," I said.

"It is what they are for," he said.

"True," I said.

"Women are pleasure objects," he said, "and once collared, know themselves as such."

"Of course," I said.

"You spoke," he said, "as I recall, of contrivances of nature."

"Yes," I said.

"The female has her role in nature," he said, "to work, to please, to provide inordinate pleasure to her master."

"True," I said.

We then returned our attention to the target.

"An excellent shot," I said.

The target was a bundle of straw, tied to a post, the bundle shaped into the likeness of a man. The arrow, had the target been a man, would have pierced the forehead. This is a difficult placement of the projectile. The usual target, when practical, is the torso, on the left side.

Five more times I observed General Yamada pierce the target, the arrows then clustered together, within what would have been the size of a fist.

"You are skillful," I said.

"I arranged to have the target formed of straw," he said. "Lord Akio informed me that you might be uneasy if one made use of other targets."

"Quite possibly," I said. "I tender you thanks."

"We will spare no effort to make your stay comfortable and pleasant," he said.

As we spoke, an attending Ashigaru was withdrawing the arrows from the post behind the straw.

"I am to be soon again on tarnback?" I said.

"Did you enjoy the slave, Saru, recently sent to your quarters?" he asked.

"I am saving her for another," I said.

"She is suitably helpless, piteously so," he said, "once suitably caressed."

"I am pleased to hear it," I said.

I recalled the once-arrogant, cool, efficient Miss Margaret Wentworth whom I had met long ago, she in the guise of a slave, on the cold, rocky coast abutting the northern forests, after I had disembarked from a slaver's ship put spaceward days before, from the locks of a steel world, to keep a mysterious rendezvous.

I had taken the key to her collar from her and cast it into the chill waters of Thassa, that she might, whether free or not, know that the device was locked on her neck, and that she had no means wherewith to remove it. She then knew herself, though putatively free, truly collared. She had later been apprised of the bondage of which she had been hitherto unaware. In Tarncamp she had had her head shaved and had been placed in the stables, at the disposition of grooms, that she might learn that she was no longer a free woman pretending to be a slave, but now a true slave, an object and property owned by masters, as much so as a tarsk. It was in Tarncamp that she had been given the name 'Saru', she having been hitherto, unbeknownst to herself, after her name had been entered on an acquisition list on Earth, only a nameless slave. The saru, for which she had been named, was a small, scampering mammal indigenous to the rain forests of the Ua basin. Given her earlier character and behaviors it had amused men that she should now be so named.

"But you are not interested in putting her in your own collar?" he asked.

"I would prefer to save her for another," I said.

"Then you would not object to my putting her in the pens, with other field slaves?"

"No," I said, "but I am surprised, given her coloring and such, that you would do so."

"It is unusual," he said, "but there are others, bought for *fukuros* of rice from Lord Temmu, also from across Thassa, who are similarly characterized, whom I have placed amongst my palace women, given to high officers, and such."

"She is not special to you?" I said.

"No," he said. "She is nothing, only another slave."

This answer surprised me, for Saru was unusually beautiful, as though born for the collar.

But there are men who prefer ka-la-na, and men who prefer paga, even men who prefer mead, or kal-da, even sake.

"Why did you have her serve us, at our first discussion?"

"Did she not come to Tarncamp with you?" he said.

"Yes," I said.

"I thought you might be pleased," he said.

"The general is thoughtful," I said.

"But you were not pleased?" he said.

"I would have been somewhat more pleased," I said, "had she been clothed more suitably."

"As a slave?" he said.

"Yes," I said.

"But then her presence might have been distractive."

"True," I said.

"But you were pleased?"

"Certainly," I said, "to see her in her loveliness, and serving, and as the slave she is."

"Excellent," he said.

"It is my understanding," I said, "that you wish to acquire the services of the tarn cavalry."

The Ashigaru who had withdrawn the arrows from the post to which the target was affixed had now brought them back to Lord Yamada, and placed them in the stand which reposed to the shogun's right.

I gathered the shogun might continue his recreation, or practice.

"We made that clear, earlier," he said.

"Days ago," I said. "But I was brought here today, surely not merely to witness an exhibition of fine archery."

"No," he said. "I wish to inform you that I have arranged the visit of two of your officers. They will see that you are well, and in good spirits. That is important. Too, such contacts are essential as we progress in the matter of the control of the cavalry. I will even permit you to speak to them privately."

"Might I not as easily contact them," I said, "if permitted a tarn?"

"It is important that you remain our guest for the time being," he said.

"I understand," I said. "What two officers?"

"Their names," he said, "are Pertinax and Tajima."

"I know them," I said.

"They are junior officers," he said. "Two others are senior, Lysander and Torgus, each of whom commanded a Century when the cavalry was intact, who will remain with the cavalry."

"It seems you are well informed," I said.

"Thus," he said, "you need not fear that any attempt will be made to disrupt the chain of command."

"You are astute," I said.

"Perhaps you fear I might attempt to avail myself of two additional tarns?" he said.

"The thought might occur to one," I said.

"What would be the value of four tarns," he said, "while the cavalry retains several times that number?"

"True," I said.

"These young officers," he said, "following my instructions, will come with a third. The three will alight at a location undisclosed to me. The young officers will approach on foot, the three tarns left in the keeping of the third man. Thus, if a schedule is not well kept, or if any attempt should be made to obtain the tarns, the tarns, in the keeping of the remaining tarnsman, will take flight, returning safely to your camp, and the cavalry will have lost only two junior officers. Matters, of course, I anticipate, will proceed well, and our two young friends will return on tarnback with their companion to your camp, from which, thereafter, the cavalry will obey my orders."

"And I am to remain here?" I said.

"For the time being," he said.

"A hostage," I said.

"A guest," he said.

"These arrangements," I said, "need not have been imparted to me in an archery court."

"Even a shogun," he said, "has his vanity."

"Ho!" cried the Ashigaru suddenly, pointing upward, to the north, he who had returned the six arrows to the shogun.

In the distance there was a speck, in flight. I watched it make its way toward us. Oddly, for a moment it seemed as though it might be still, fixed in the sky, and the clouds were flowing behind it.

"Good," said the shogun. "It is our friend, Tyrtaios. He is returning with my daughter, Sumomo."

I felt cold.

"She thinks," he said, "that she is being returned to the palace to be rewarded. In a sense I suppose she is, returned to be rewarded as is fit for a failed spy, one whose carelessness might have jeopardized my plans."

"You have many daughters," I said.

"Yes," he said.

"Doubtless you have many sons, as well," I said.

"No," he said, "I have them strangled at birth."

"Why?" I asked.

"They might vie with their father," he said. "They might be ambitious, they might plot, they might desire to sit upon the dais of the shogun."

"I see," I said.

"Sumomo has disappointed me," he said. "Her clumsiness, her indiscretion, need not have been without unwelcome consequences. As with others who have failed me, she is to be executed, slowly, and unpleasantly."

"I see," I said.

"Incidentally," he said, "I must prevail upon you not to inform her of my intentions. That would constitute an abuse of my friendship, trust, and hospitality."

"I understand," I said.

The tarn was now descending.

"It is a single tarn," I said.

"Why risk two tarns?" he said. "Too, Sumomo is light."

"She is carried in honor," I said.

"Would you have her tied to the capture rings?" he asked.

"No," I said. "Not if she is free. Otherwise let her be stripped and fastened down, belly-up, across the saddle apron, where she may be looked upon in flight, and caressed as might please a master."

With a blast of dust, and a snapping of wings, Tyrtaios brought the tarn down some forty or fifty paces away, at the far end, to the right of the archery court.

I considered the distance to that place.

Tyrtaios had his back to me as he was graciously assisting the delicate, richly-clad Sumomo from the saddle ladder to the ground.

"No, please, Tarl Cabot, tarnsman," said the shogun. I noted he had withdrawn one arrow from the stand and put it to the string of the bow.

"Perhaps it would be wise," I said, "if I returned to my quarters."

"Please do so," said the shogun.

Chapter Eighteen

I Encounter Two Friends;
Lord Akio Has Approached

"Tajima, Pertinax!" I cried, elatedly.

I rushed to Pertinax and we clasped hands, and then embraced. Tears burned in his eyes. Tajima stood to one side, very still, but as far as I could read him, he was muchly pleased and reassured. We exchanged bows.

"I am pleased to see Tarl Cabot, tarnsman," he said.

"And I my friends," I said.

"You are a prisoner," said Pertinax.

"A guest," I said, "one not permitted to leave."

Tajima looked about.

"None are near," I said.

I had been permitted to meet them in the open, within the main gate to the grounds.

"The shogun," I said, "looks for allies, not enemies. He wishes to put us at our ease. Thus he refrains from prohibiting our private converse."

"I fear it makes little difference," said Pertinax, looking at the mighty panels of the heavy, now-closed-and-barred gate.

"We are to be entertained," I said. "Expect gifts, and smiles."

"We conjecture," said Tajima, "that you did not desert the holding of Lord Temmu, repudiating your allegiance to that house, but were somehow betrayed into the keeping of the enemy."

"That is what happened," I said.

179

"Lords Nishida and Okimoto," said Tajima, "have been told you turned to the enemy, as did Tyrtaios."

"No," I said.

"The cavalry is still yours," said Pertinax. "It is ready to fly at the first cry of one-strap."

"None but the cavalry anticipated this," said Tajima.

"One did," I said. "General Yamada."

"You were betrayed by the house of Temmu," said Pertinax. "Your sword is now free."

"That you are here, and alive," said Tajima, "indicates that Lord Yamada has designs on the cavalry."

"Precisely," I said.

"Where you should lead, it will follow," said Pertinax.

"Where are your tarns?" I asked.

"The trek of an Ahn," said Tajima.

"We have followed instructions," said Pertinax.

"If we are not back by the Twentieth Ahn, with your orders," said Tajima, "they will depart."

"In whose keeping are they?" I asked.

"In that of Ichiro, bannerman," said Tajima.

"Excellent," I said.

I had hoped it would be so. I had full confidence in the discipline, reliability, and judgment of the bannerman.

"You were betrayed," said Tajima. "Will you now pledge your sword to the house of Yamada?"

"He would pay well," I said.

"You would then serve the house of Yamada?" said Pertinax.

"No," I said.

"I thought not," said Tajima.

"What then is to be done?" asked Pertinax.

"There is little here which can be helped," I said. "You must keep your rendezvous with Ichiro before the Twentieth Ahn."

"What of you?" asked Pertinax.

"You will not be detained in your departure," I said, "for it will be assumed you are returning to camp with my orders, orders which, as we shall manage it, will be supposed favorable to the plans of the shogun."

"But what of you?" asked Pertinax.

"I shall wish you well," I said.

"No, Tarl Cabot, tarnsman," said Tajima.

"We shall not leave you," said Pertinax.

"I have been disarmed," I said.

"So, too, were we, at the gate," said Pertinax.

"We can do nothing," I said.

"We must try," said Tajima.

"Before the Twentieth Ahn," I said, "reach Ichiro, return to the camp, purchase time."

"Only so much time can be purchased," said Tajima.

"We can threaten the destruction of the holdings of Lord Yamada," said Pertinax.

"That would not buy my freedom," I said. "Lord Yamada will not risk me free and in command of the cavalry. I would no longer be in his power. I might lead it against him. Releasing me, he courts destruction. Holding me, it would be no worse. His intent is to keep me hostage, while the cavalry is employed in his interests."

"Surely he has promised you its command," said Pertinax.

"Implicitly, of course," I said. "He is clever. He would dangle that bauble before me, having me on tarnback, in his service, and so on, but he will not do so. He is Yamada, and far from a fool."

"He would not trust you?" said Pertinax.

"He is Yamada," I said. "He is brilliant and charming, cunning and deceitful. He trusts no one."

"He would not even permit you to feign the matter," said Pertinax.

"Perhaps for his amusement, only that," I said.

"What shall we do?" asked Pertinax.

"Prepare to receive gifts, promises, and smiles," I said. "Lord Yamada is a gracious and generous host."

"Someone approaches," said Pertinax.

"A fop," said Tajima, "brightly plumaged."

"He is dangerous," I said to Tajima.

"Surely not," smiled Pertinax.

"Lord Yamada selects his daimyos with care," I said.

"Greetings," said Lord Akio, pleasantly.

"Lord Akio," I said, "these are two friends, officers in the cavalry, Tajima and Pertinax. Tajima and Pertinax, allow me to introduce Lord Akio, a daimyo of Lord Yamada."

Suitable bows were exchanged.

Lord Akio looked up, at the sky. "I think it may rain," he said.

"It is now clear," I said.

"It is the season," he said.

"I see," I said.

"Permit me to escort you to supper," said Lord Akio.

"Gladly," I said.

"But first," he said, "we will stop by the slave pens."

Chapter Nineteen

We Visit the Slave Pens; Selections are Done

"Here," said Lord Akio.

The large shed housing the pens was but a short walk from the courtyard; it was not unlike such sheds elsewhere in the vicinity, rudely planked, and low roofed, used for storage, and the stabling of beasts, verr, tarsk, and slaves. Some such sheds are also used for the housing of rice seedlings, which are later transferred to designated paddies, or wading fields. Harvested grains are commonly dried in the sun in Se'Kara, before the Seventh Passage Hand. Most rice is grown in village fields, several villages often under the rule of a single daimyo. These villages pay the rice tax, supplied primarily in produce, rice itself, to the daimyo, and the shogun receives his tax, usually in kind, as well, from the daimyos. Sometimes, too, the tax is supplied in terms of men, serving as porters, workers, and Ashigaru. Some villages, on the other hand, are under the rule of the shogun himself, so he profits both in virtue of a direct and an indirect tax. To be sure, silver, gold, and copper also function as means of exchange in the islands, either in the form of marked coinages or as plates and bars. Similarly various forms of produce other than rice may be taxed, exchanged by bartering, and so on. Fishing villages, of course, share portions of their catch, fresh, or dried, with their patrons and protectors, these goods gathered by low-level administrative officials. A great deal of the exchange in the islands is effected by barter. It was thus not all that unusual that many of the slaves of the holding of Lord Temmu had been exchanged for rice. What was unusual was the desperation on the part of the besieged to obtain rice, and the ratio of exchange, often as surprising as one *fukuro* for a slave.

"I shall, if you have no objection, wait outside, my friends," said Lord Akio.

"You would not wish to soil the hem of your robes," said Tajima.

"That is true, young warrior," said Lord Akio. "You are perceptive. The Ashigaru in attendance within will see to your selections. They have been informed."

"I gather," I said, "that we will not be served by contract women at supper."

"You may if you wish," said Lord Akio. "Lord Yamada thought that you might find the presence of slaves more pleasing."

I recalled our first tea, which he had had served by Saru, though he had had her decorously garbed, apparently to provide less of a distraction.

"He would not waste the subtleties, the delights and skills, of contract women on such as we?" inquired Tajima.

"No, no, young warrior," said Lord Akio. "Rather the shogun hopes to please you."

"I for one," I said, "am perfectly content with slaves, and would prefer them. I know how to relate to Gorean free women, which is sometimes trying, and often annoying, and I know how to deal with slaves, which is quite simple, but I am uncertain how to behave with your contract women, the modes of address, how to respond appropriately, the ceremonial aspects, and such."

"Lord Yamada is sensitive to your uneasiness," he said.

"I am not a barbarian," said Tajima.

"Forgive me, young warrior," said Lord Akio, "your accent suggested as much."

"Perhaps," said Pertinax, "the shogun might supply a contract woman for my friend."

"Do not speak like a barbarian," said Tajima.

"I am a barbarian," retorted Pertinax, not pleasantly.

I had taken the remark of Pertinax to be well-intentioned. I think he had hoped it would have been genuinely helpful. He was, of course, as I, a barbarian.

A look of distress had crossed the features of Lord Akio. "Does the young warrior desire the services of a contract woman?" he asked.

"No," said Tajima, irritably.

"Why not?" I asked.

"It would be unaesthetic," he said, "to mix the two."

"Quite right," said Lord Akio. "I see the young warrior, despite his accent, is Pani."

"Also, I suppose," said Pertinax, "such a mixture might be offensive to the contract woman, that she would serve with slaves."

"Certainly," I said. "We would not want her to put herself to the ritual knife, or such."

"True," said Lord Akio.

I had thought my remark a joke, but rethought the matter, following the response of Lord Akio.

"Would you not prefer, really," I said to Tajima, "to be served by a slave?"

"Of course," said Tajima, "what man would not? The matter is that of a possible slight."

"I assure you," said Lord Akio, "no slight is intended."

"I am sure that is true," I said.

"Very well," said Tajima.

I did not think he was disappointed.

"I shall wait here," said Lord Akio.

"This place smells," said Tajima.

"Do not be fastidious," I said.

Beneath the roof of the large shed was more than one pen. We were led to one of the larger pens.

"Those selected will be washed, and placed in clean tunics before being bound and led to the palace," said the Ashigaru keeper. Two others were about.

There was no escape for the slaves, even outside the pen, given their condition, garmenture, and such, even were it not for the palings enclosing the general area, but slaves are often bound, perhaps for no better reason than that they are slaves. I suppose that such things, like the collar and the brand, the tunic, and such, help them to keep in mind that they are vendible beasts, objects and properties, slaves.

"You may choose three," said the Ashigaru, "one each, for your personal pleasure."

The light in the shed was feeble. It was furnished from the now-opened door, and various narrow apertures in the ceiling and walls. It took a bit of time to adjust to the light.

We looked through the bars.

The bars of the pen were some three or four horts in thickness, and six horts apart; they reached from the wooden flooring of the shed to the low roof; they were reinforced with crossbeams lashed in place, one a foot Gorean from the ceiling, one a foot Gorean from the floor, and one, about three and a half feet Gorean from the floor, between them.

"I see no Pani here," said Tajima.

"No," said the Ashigaru.

"You would prefer a Pani slave?" I said to Tajima.

"Of course," he said.

The slaves were placed in lines, kneeling, facing away from us, facing the far wall. They had doubtless been placed in this fashion, that they could not see who might be present. Furthermore, as would be expected, they were silent. This is common with slaves who are being inspected, considered, observed, and such. Indeed, it is commonly understood that a slave may not speak without the permission of a free person. "Master, may I speak?" is a common formula for soliciting this permission. Many slaves, of course, have a standing permission to speak. They understand, of course, that this permission is revocable, even instantly, at the discretion of the free person.

The girls were stripped, as is common in slave pens. Would you clothe penned tarsk or verr?

"I take it," I said, "as there are no Pani here, these slaves are from amongst those bought from Lord Temmu, those sold for rice."

"Yes," said the Ashigaru. "They are simple field slaves."

"I see no more than twenty, no more than twenty-five or thirty here," I said. "Lord Yamada received something like one hundred and fifty slaves from the holding of Lord Temmu."

I did recall that, as far as I knew, only one slave had been retained in the holding of Lord Temmu. I did not understand that. Perhaps she was a preferred slave of some sort. I did not think she could have been that much more beautiful than the others, who had gone for rice. I did not know the name of the slave in question.

"There were more," said the Ashigaru, "many more, at first. But they were distributed about, given as gifts, sold, used in trade, bartered, and such."

"Of course," I said. "I trust that some of these are passable."

"The whole lot, the original lot," he said, "was excellent."

"Good," I said.

I had known, of course, that that would be true. I knew most of these girls from Tarncamp, from Shipcamp, from the voyage of the ship of Tersites, from the holding of Lord Temmu. The Pani, on the continent, had made their purchases with exquisite care, sometimes with the assistance of agents, deemed to be authorities on the quality of collar meat. Most purchases had been from the markets and taverns of Brundisium.

"Attend me," barked the Ashigaru to the occupants of that stout pen.

I saw the reaction of the girls, sudden, startled, their alertness, their apprehension, their readiness to obey, instantly. They had been addressed by a free man.

How appropriate it is, I thought, to have women so, in their place, as slaves.

"Attend me, field girls, miserable urts, barbarian beasts," said the Ashigaru. "Three of you, by the beneficence of Lord Yamada, Shogun of the Islands, are to be extraordinarily privileged, are to be permitted, following appropriate ablutions and garmenting, to serve in the palace."

Soft cries, tiny, eager, hopeful cries, inadvertently, escaped several of the kneeling, facing-away slaves.

"Perhaps, who knows," said the Ashigaru, "if you serve well, and beautifully, you might be noticed, you might come to the attention of a free man, if not, perhaps you can steal a mouthful of food, other than the gruel in the troughs which you must feed on, head down, on all fours, as the beasts you are. Perhaps you might even be thrown a scrap of meat. Would you like that? Do you understand?"

"Yes, Master," cried several of the girls.

"But perhaps," he said, "you would prefer the stink and filth, the rudeness, and darkness, of the pen, the long labors, neck-roped, of readying the fields."

"No, no, Master," said several.

"Then attend me, and well," he said. "Stand, facing away. Good. Stand well, stand as slaves! You are not free women. Be beautiful! Remember that you are nothing, only slaves. Be beautiful then, you beasts, you mere lovely objects. Good. Now, clasp your hands behind the back of your neck. Good. You will form a single line and will, in line, at intervals of three paces, come about the interior of the pen. Each will, before the bars, before me, and those who will make their selections, pause, turn slowly, pause again, and then return to your former place, and kneel as you were, facing away. Do you understand?"

"Yes, Master," said several.

"Begin!" he said.

And the inspection of the slaves, slowly, with its pauses, while items were displayed and assessed, began.

"I suspect," I said to Pertinax, "you never saw anything of this sort while working in the offices of Earth."

"Unfortunately, not," he said.

"Here are women, as they should be," I said.

"I know that now," he said. "I have learned it."

"You are fulfilled, in the mastery," I said.

"I have known it," he said. "I will never surrender it."

"What you may not understand," I said, "is the complementarity involved, the female's desire to be owned, to be the property of a master."

The Ashigaru at our side carried a switch, a common accouterment for one in charge of slaves. When he felt each girl had suitably presented herself, pausing, turning slowly before us, and facing us again, he dismissed her with a slight motion of the switch, and the next approached.

I was, of course, looking for a particular slave. What I did not know, of course, given the light, was whether or not she was amongst those confined in the pen.

"What of this one?" inquired the Ashigaru.

"You like red hair," I said.

"It is like fire," he said.

"If her slave fires have been lit," I said, "she would flame in your arms."

"Perhaps I will buy her," he said.

"Next," I suggested.

His switch moved slightly, and the girl, tears on her cheeks, moved away, later to assume her position at the rear of the pen, kneeling, facing away from the gate. We could see her shoulders shaking, the sobbing of her body.

"This one," said the Ashigaru, "is as supple as a reed, as delicate as a talender."

"There are no Pani here," said Tajima.

"No," said the Ashigaru, and the tip of his switch moved slightly, dismissing the slave.

"You will have to take one," I said to Tajima.

"None are Pani," he said.

"Even so," I said.

A brunette, well-formed, her hair slave long, stood before the bars, and turned, and regarded us.

Her lips trembled, but she dared not speak.

Again the switch flicked.

The hands of the women, as directed, were clasped behind the back of their neck. This immobilizes the hands and lifts the breasts nicely. In this way one's view is less obstructed. Too, this stance makes it less likely that the woman, yielding to a foolish lapse, will try to shield her body with her hands. A common examination position in markets is to have the woman stand upright with her legs widely spread, the hands clasped behind the back of the neck or behind the back of the head. The spreading of the legs makes it harder for her to move and easier for her to be caressed, sometimes unexpectedly. Some assessors will put the woman to the floor and she will find herself struggling, startled, perhaps only half comprehendingly, to respond to a rapidly issued series of commands. She is being put through slave paces. This is a device for displaying her body in a diversity of aspects. And the paces might occasionally be halted, that a given pose might be the better assessed.

"Master!" cried a slave, wildly, joyfully.

"That one," I said, indicating the slave.

"She spoke," said the Ashigaru. "She must be whipped."

"No," I said. "Have her sent to the palace."

"Master, Master!" she wept.

"Be silent," I said.

"Yes, Master," she said.

"Do not reach through the bars," said the Ashigaru, lifting his switch. "You stink, you are filthy."

"Yes, Master," she said, quickly, backing away, lowering her head, frightened, before the gaze of a free man.

He motioned her to the side.

"She will be fully cleansed, hair and body, and clad before being taken to the palace," he said.

"Slave clad, I trust," I said.

"Surely," he said.

"That is Cecily," said Pertinax.

"Yes," I said.

She was a dark-eyed brunette, sweetly bodied, and exquisitely featured, highly intelligent and helplessly responsive. Indeed, she had been my personal slave, even on the ship of Tersites. I had obtained her on a steel world. I had first met her on the Prison Moon where I had been confined by Priest-Kings, a confinement which had been ended by a raid of Kurii on that facility, following which I had been taken to one of the steel worlds, on which world, as noted, I had acquired the slave in question. On the Prison Moon, a largely automated prison, it had been intended by the Priest-Kings that I should be defeated and broken as a warrior, by means of an ingenious torture consisting of the counterpoising of desire and honor. In my small, cylindrical, transparent cell, supplied with oxygen, water, and nourishment administered by means of tubes and valves, were two exquisite free women, as unclothed and helpless as I. It was no mistake that I had been confined with precisely these two women. Each, unbeknownst to herself, had her role to play in the machinations of Priest-Kings. It was not a simple matter of placing two stripped beauties within my power, beauties such as one might conveniently take off any slave block on Gor. Surely that would have been cruel enough, but each had been brilliantly selected, with the end in view of my suffering, that I should be torn between desire and honor, suffering indefinitely until, inevitably, I should succumb to the implacable imperatives of nature, and put them to my pleasure. Had they been slaves, there had been no dilemma, but a feast of joy, but both were free women. The first and I, I do not doubt, had been ingeniously matched, physically, psychologically, physiologically, and such, by all the technological and scientific brilliance of Priest-Kings, with the end in view that we should be irresistible to one another. Indeed I had sometimes wondered if she had been, perhaps over generations, given the technology of Priest-Kings, their foresight and their knowledge of the world, bred for me. Certainly we shared a native language, and, to an extent, a common background. She was English, as I, and similarly educated. We had been raised, substantially, in the same culture. Thousands of tiny strands in our biographies, consciously or unconsciously, would be shared. Moreover, we had been matched not simply as man and woman, but, more deeply, clearly, as master and slave. In the container, of course, recently translated to Gor, indeed, awakening to discover her new reality, that of a naked prisoner in a transparent alien containment device, she was dismayed, shocked, frightened, and confused. What had happened to her? Where was she? What was going on? Who had done this? What was the meaning of this radical transformation in her circumstances, the meaning of her startling, unanticipated, terrifying incarceration? The other woman was the human pet of a Kur, for Kurii sometimes keep humans as pets, as well as feed on humans bred for feed, cattle humans. She was, in effect, a primitive, appetitious, uninhibited, untutored, ignorant little animal. She had not been taught any human speech, Gorean or otherwise, and could understand little of Kur, probably no more than a miniature sleen, her name, and some simple commands. She did have, however, besides her raw energy and beauty, enormous ambition, and a quick, fine mind. She had become, thanks largely to the tutelage of a beast, partly human, partly Kur, speeched. The last I knew of her she thought of herself as the Lady Bina. I did not know her present whereabouts. I supposed her somewhere on continental Gor. Much of this had to do with events which had transpired on the steel world mentioned. I was aware that she, and the beast mentioned, who, it seemed, cared for her, and was determined to protect her, were no longer on the steel world. When the Kur raid had taken place on the Prison Moon the English girl, hoping to avoid being eaten, had pronounced herself slave, after which pronouncement, whether she understood it well or not, she was slave. Later, I put my collar on her, making her my slave. Once I had lost my honor in that container, and become a ruination to myself, I am supposing the Priest-Kings would have executed me, or, if satisfied, merely returned me to some wilderness on Gor, where I might eke out a lonely, shabby existence, lost to myself, friendless, excluded, despised, impoverished, and dishonored.

"What of this one?" inquired the Ashigaru.

"Pertinax?" I asked

"I am looking for another," he said.

"Jane?" I said.

"If she is here," he said.

His Jane was Gorean, the former Lady Portia Lia Serisia of Sun Gate Towers, of the Serisii, prior to being reduced to bondage. The House of the Serisii was once a major mercantile house in Ar. During the occupation it had collaborated with the occupational forces and engaged in profiteering. It had been substantially extirpated, and its resources seized, following the restoration of Marlenus, Ubar of Ubars.

Pertinax indicated the slave might return to her place at the rear of the pen.

"There might be another here, in which you might be interested," I said.

"Jane does well at my feet," he said.

"Perhaps another might do as well," I said.

The switch of the Ashigaru flicked once more.

The one before us now had long, light brown hair, almost blond. It fell about her body, loosely.

"You know better," said the Ashigaru.

Frightened, without unclasping her small hands from the back of her neck, she bent down, and then straightened up, tossing the hair behind her shoulders.

I noted no blemish which she might have attempted to conceal. Similarly, as she would not be new to bondage, it seemed unlikely that her indiscretion might be attributed to self-consciousness, or shyness, let alone modesty, which is not permitted to female slaves, no more than to verr and tarsk. More likely it seemed she might have been attempting to provoke attention, curiosity, uncertainty, or puzzlement. Perhaps she hoped to stand a bit longer before us, until she shook her hair back, drawing the curtain away, that we might be dazzled. Sometimes this trick is used by girls in exhibition cages, awaiting their sale in the evening, taking their hair in their hands and lifting it behind their head, which action both reveals her beauty and accentuates it. Still, she, a pen girl, a low slave, a common slave, should have known better.

The Ashigaru pointed her out to one of his fellows. "Five lashes," he said.

The girl cried out with misery and hurried to her place, at the back of the pen.

I myself would have overlooked the matter. I myself am rather fond of such things, of the tiny stratagems, the tricks and devices, of female slaves. I wonder sometimes if they do not understand how transparent such things are. Do they think men do not understand them? In any event, such things, in my view, make them more delightful, ever more helpless, vulnerable, and ownable. They are, after all, only female slaves, and have only their wit and beauty, and their capacity to appeal to males, to improve their lot. They are wholly dependent on masters, as they should be. How helpless they are, how delightfully helpless. Let them strive then to stimulate, intrigue, and please. Let them exert their wiles, but it is on their necks that the collar is locked. Perhaps one might do her best to encourage a male to bid on her, but she cannot make him do so. She is the slave.

"Behold!" I said.

"Yes!" said Pertinax.

Before him, fallen to her knees, her head to the floor, her hands still clasped behind her head, was a dark-haired slave.

She lifted her head, piteously, hopefully, her lips trembling, tears in her eyes.

"That one," said Pertinax.

The Ashigaru motioned her to the side, and she leapt up and hurried to wait, beside Cecily.

I was pleased that Jane had had the intelligence to remain absolutely silent. She had not received permission to speak.

"Shall we go?" asked Pertinax.

"Tajima has not yet made a selection," I said.

"There are no Pani here," he said.

"Even so," I said.

"Two will be enough to serve," he said.

"Wait," I said. "I am sure there will be one more of interest in this flock of vulos."

"Not Pani," he said.

"No," I said.

"I am sorry," said the Ashigaru. "But surely each one here is a suitable sex-tarsk."

"Very much so," I said.

"You have some reason for dalliance, Tarl Cabot, tarnsman," said Tajima.

"Perhaps," I said.

Two more slaves presented themselves, each then dismissed.

Then suddenly a slave rushed to the wooden, polelike bars, and pressed herself against them, as though she might slip through them, or burst them, reaching out, piteously, to Pertinax.

"Gregory," she cried, "Gregory! Gregory White! Do you not recognize me! I am Margaret! Margaret Wentworth! Do you not remember the office, the firm? We were colleagues on Earth! We came to Gor together! Help me, free me!"

But Pertinax had stepped back, that her fingers might not have touched him.

"We were colleagues," she said. "We are both from Earth! See what lamentable fate has befallen me! Why did you not come to see me in the stables at Tarncamp? Why did you not rescue me, and free me! Do you not understand? I have been marked! I am such as may be collared!"

Pertinax was silent.

"Do you not see what has been done to me? Take me out of this terrible place! Take me out of this pen! It is a pen! A pen! Take me out of this pen! It is a pen for slaves, for slaves! Do you not know what is done with us here, what is expected of us, what we must do! Do you not understand the dirt, the filth, the darkness, the long days in the fields, the arduous labors, the digging, the carrying of sacks of dirt on our backs, the being yoked, the carrying buckets of water, the switches of the overseers!"

I put my hand on the wrist of the Ashigaru, for I feared he was ready to switch her extended arms and hands, reaching through the bars.

"You love me, Gregory," she said. "You know you do! You have loved me from the first moment you saw me! I will let you hold me! I will let you kiss me! Choose me, free me!"

"You were worthless on Earth," he said. "And you are worthless now."

"You want me!" she cried. "A woman can tell!"

"Kneel," he said.

In consternation, she slipped to her knees, confused.

"I am Pertinax," he said. "I am a free man."

"You wish to play this game," she said, "as before, when we pretended to be master and slave, to conceal our identities, and that you were my employee?"

"This is no game," he said.

"Yes," she said, "I understand."

"No, you do not," he said. "This is no game."

I saw fear in her eyes.

"You cannot be serious," she said.

"Let us move on to the next girl," said the Ashigaru.

"No, no, no!" she cried. "Choose, choose me!" she said to Pertinax.

But he merely looked down upon her. I could see the marks of the wooden bars on her body where she had pressed herself closely against them.

"Choose me, Gregory," she said. "Please, Gregory, choose me!"

His eyes were stern.

"Please," she said, "please, Master. Please choose me, Master."

"I have a slave," he said.

She looked up at him, her eyes wide in disbelief and fear.

"Next girl," said the Ashigaru.

"Wait," I said. "Tajima, select her."

"She is not Pani," he said.

"No matter," I said.

"Very well," he said. "That one."

The Ashigaru motioned her to the side, where she joined

Cecily and Jane. As Saru, the former Miss Margaret Wentworth, knew my slave was Cecily; she viewed Jane with coldness, a chill which was clearly returned by Jane, who would not have been unaware of the scene at the bars.

"She spoke without permission," said the Ashigaru to Tajima. "How many lashes would you prefer?"

"How many are customary?" asked Tajima.

"Five," said the Ashigaru.

"I shall leave the matter to my fellow," said Tajima, turning to Pertinax.

"Ten lashes," said Pertinax.

"Ten," said Tajima.

"Good," said the Ashigaru, and turned to his fellow. "Ten," he said.

"Ten," said the other.

"Let us leave," said Tajima. "I am not particularly fastidious, Tarl Cabot, tarnsman, but this place does smell."

"True," I said.

We then left the large shed which housed the pens. I trusted we would have an opportunity to wash before supper. Certainly it would take time to prepare the slaves.

Chapter Twenty

Supper in the Palace of Lord Yamada

"My thanks, noble lord," said Pertinax to Lord Yamada.

"It is nothing," said Lord Yamada.

Tajima turned to the side, and bowed politely from where he sat, cross-legged, at the long, low table. We all sat on the same side of the table, side by side, where we might look out the large opened portal before us, the screens removed, onto the moonlit garden.

Both Pertinax and Tajima now had slung about their necks chains of gold.

"Such trinkets, such trifles," said Lord Yamada, "are but tiny tokens of my esteem, and of the wealth of the House of Yamada. They are but a small and unworthy anticipation of treasures to come."

Lord Akio sat to my right. Pertinax was to my left. Tajima sat to the immediate right of Lord Yamada, as seemed fitting, as he was not only a high officer but Pani. Sumomo, in beautiful silks, a daughter of the shogun, knelt between Tajima and Pertinax. I had been startled to see Sumomo at the table. By now I feared she might have been nailed naked to one of the palace gates. I had gathered, earlier, from Lord Yamada that, in his view, she had failed him, even to the point of placing certain plans in jeopardy. I had gathered that her lapse had taken place on the outer parapet of the Holding of Temmu, where she had been detected casting a message, beribboned to facilitate its detection and retrieval, as Tajima had later confirmed my earlier speculation, to a confederate below. Tajima had witnessed this and inferred, naturally enough, that this was done on behalf of Lord Nishida, to whom she was supposedly contracted. One did suppose that her indiscretion would eventually be brought to the attention of Lord Nishida which intelligence, assuming him loyal to Lord Temmu, would terminate her usefulness in his quarters, as a spy. Similarly, one supposed that there was a possibility that this development might bring suspicion on Daichi, given her occasional interactions with, or meetings with, the reader of bones and shells. I suspected that the matter might not be as serious as Lord Yamada feared, and might require little more than some rearrangement of his plans, the ensconcement of a new spy, a fresh, suitable revelation for Daichi to find in his bones and shells, and such, but, as I knew the shogun, his displeasure was not too lightly brooked. He had determined to destroy Sumomo as a failed agent. As he had told me, he had many daughters. Sumomo herself seemed utterly unaware that she might be in danger. This evening Lord Yamada bestowed on her all the attention, interest, friendliness, and kindness of a loving father. One could scarcely conceive a more enviable model of paternal solicitude. I feared she had not the least awareness of the darkness which lay in his heart. I do not even think she even realized why she had been recalled to the palace. I suspected she did not know that her compromising action had been observed. Perhaps she had been recalled in view of new plans, perhaps to be utilized differently, or more importantly. If she had had trepidations at her return to the palace, they seemed to have been assuaged. Lord Yamada, I was sure, had taken great pains to dispel them. But I could not understand her presence at the table. Perhaps it was twofold, first, that her beauty and charm would add luster to the evening; and, second, that the categorical reversal of her fortune, perhaps suddenly manifested, would be found instructive by the guests, as they would then better understand the consequences of having failed the shogun. But, too, it may have been much simpler. Perhaps it simply pleased the shogun, who was reputed to have a fondness for jests. I had heard that more than one individual had been summoned to the palace, thinking to be honored and rewarded, and had perished miserably in the straw jacket.

Three slaves attended on the tables, mostly head down, that

they might not meet the eyes of free persons. Their service, as was appropriate for Gorean slaves, was graceful, deferential, efficient, silent, and unobtrusive. They would kneel to receive their dishes or vessels from the table of the kitchen master, the serving table, toward the back and right of the room, rise, approach the guests' table, kneel, and, their arms extended, their head down between their extended arms, place the dish or vessel, held in two hands, on the table; they would then rise and back away, that they might not turn their back on a free person without permission, and then, sensing they were dismissed, they would return to the vicinity of the serving table, near which they would kneel. They had apparently all been warned, for, though each was a pleasure slave, they knelt in the modest, charming position of what, on the continent, would be referred to as the position of the tower slave, their knees closely together. I did not doubt but what this was because a free woman was to be present, Sumomo. Their backs were straight and the palms of their hands were down, on their thighs. Even kneeling so, so modestly, I found them fetching. Certainly Cecily, Saru, and Jane were three beauties. They were excellent picks from the pen. Putting aside the manner of kneeling, which was suitably decorous, given the occasion, they were, at least, appropriately garmented. Clearly their garmenture had been determined by men. Each was clad identically, and, I was pleased to see, as what she was, a slave.

"Slaves are despicable," said Sumomo.

"They have their pleasantries," said Lord Yamada.

"Their tunics are scarcely covering," said Sumomo.

"Men will have it so," said Lord Yamada.

"You can see so much of their bodies," said Sumomo.

"If you were not present, one might see all of their bodies," said Lord Yamada.

"Disgusting," said Sumomo.

"Do not concern yourself," he said. "They are animals."

"At least they are not Pani," she said.

"There are Pani slaves, of course," he said.

"As these?" she asked.

"Of course," he said.

"I feel faint," she said.

"You are delicate," he said.

"What is that on their necks?" she asked.

"Surely you know," he said, "collars, locked collars, slave collars."

"I have seen slaves without collars," she said.

"So have I," said Tajima, regarding Sumomo.

"It is not necessary, the collars," said Sumomo, uneasily, the fingers of her right hand lightly, thoughtlessly, at her own throat. "One can tell them by their garmenture."

"But garmenture might be changed," said Lord Yamada.

"By their skin color," said Sumomo.

"But slaves come in many colors," said Tajima, adding, "as do flowers."

"They are marked, of course," said Lord Yamada.

"I see no marks," said Sumomo.

"They are there," said Lord Yamada.

"Usually high, on the left hip," I said.

"The left hip?" she asked.

"Most masters are right-handed," I said. "Too, that location is commonly recommended in Merchant law, on the continent."

"The collar is visible, and fastened on the slave's neck," said Lord Yamada.

"Accordingly, there is no mistaking a collar slut," said Tajima, pleasantly, regarding Sumomo.

"Too," I said, "it is quite meaningful. The girl understands its meaning, and so, too, do those who look upon her."

"But why here, this evening," she asked, "are these collared?"

"Because they are slaves, Lady," said Pertinax, glancing at Saru, who shrank back.

"The collar, of course," said Lord Yamada, "does not make the slave."

"Many slaves are not collared," said Tajima, looking at Sumomo.

"On the continent," I said, "slaves are almost universally collared."

"A most excellent practice," said Lord Yamada.

"Still!" protested Sumomo.

"I think I shall institute it in my domains," said Lord Yamada.

Sumomo was silent.

"I thought, beloved daughter," said Lord Yamada, "our guests would be pleased to see them so."

"I see," said Sumomo.

"Tarl Cabot, tarnsman," said Lord Yamada, "are you not pleased to see women in collars?"

"Yes," I said. "Women look well in collars."

"Slave collars," said Lord Yamada.

"Certainly," I said. Indeed, I thought, what beautiful woman's beauty is not enhanced a thousand times, aesthetically and meaningfully, in a collar? Too, does she not then know that she is not a man, but quite different, a lovely work animal, a pleasure object, a toy and plaything, a slave?

"Dear Tajima," I said, in English, quietly.

He reacted, clearly startled, but, almost immediately, regained his composure. I had known from Tarncamp that he was familiar with English, though as a second language. In his way, he was as much a barbarian on this world as I.

"Attend my communication, my friend," I said, in English, "and despite what you may hear, be as you are now, giving no sign of concern."

He nodded, a tiny, almost imperceptible movement of his head.

"Sumomo," I said, "as you now realize, is a daughter of Lord Yamada. Too, she was indeed a spy, as you surmised. As far as I know, Lord Nishida is himself innocent, and unaware of this. You observed her on the outer parapet, apparently communicating with the enemy below. In this act she, unbeknownst to herself, compromised her value as Yamada's agent."

"I brought the matter," said Tajima, in English, "as I am uncertain of the allegiances of Lord Nishida, to the attention of Lords Okimoto and Temmu. It was determined that she would be cast from the parapet to the stones below, at a time corresponding to that at which she had earlier cast the detected message, as it was supposed that at such a time her confederate, or confederates, would be waiting below. In this way, cast from the parapet, she would deliver to the enemy below her last, and final, message."

"How did you feel about this?" I asked.

"I disapproved," said Tajima.

"Why?" I asked.

"There are better things to do with a female spy," said Tajima.

"I agree," I said.

"When the Ashigaru went to fetch her," said Tajima, "she was no longer in the holding."

"She was brought to the palace, here," I said, "on tarnback, by Tyrtaios."

"What are you talking about?" asked Sumomo, testily.

"Nothing," said Tajima, in Gorean.

"Remember," I said to Tajima, in English, "do not betray a reaction. Lord Yamada is now well aware of the disclosure of Sumomo's secret commission, the detection of her action on the parapet, that the nature of her role in the holding of Lord Temmu has been brought to light, as she apparently is not. He is not pleased. He fears plans are in jeopardy, even that the role of Daichi in influencing the shogun might be suspected. He is angry. It is his intention to have Sumomo put to death, I gather most unpleasantly."

"She is his daughter," said Tajima.

"He has many daughters," I said.

"He seems well disposed toward her," said Tajima.

"Lord Yamada is not indulgent where failure is concerned," I said.

"She must be warned," said Tajima.

"You are concerned?" I asked.

"No," he said, "of course not."

"It will not be easy," I said.

"Stop babbling in some barbarous tongue," said Sumomo.

"Forgive us, noble lady," said Tajima, in Gorean.

"What is going on?" inquired Lord Yamada, pleasantly, from his end of the table.

"Nothing, noble lord," said Tajima.

"The small chestnuts are excellent," said Lord Yamada. "Dip them in honey."

"Indeed," I said.

"I thought," said Tajima, turning to Sumomo, on his right, "you were a contract woman."

"Do not insult me," she said.

"Forgive me, lady," he said.

"That was a guise, a role behind which I might abet the projects of my father."

"Are you angry," he asked, "that I failed to recognize that you could not be such, but were instead a noble, and fine, lady?"

"Not really," she said. "Rather, it is a tribute to my talent, and my skill, that you failed to do so."

"You are beautiful enough to be a contract woman," he said.

"More beautiful," she said, "for I am a free woman, and of noble birth."

"You are no more beautiful now than then," he said. "Indeed, you might be even more beautiful, if you were a stripped, collared slave."

"Tarsk!" she said.

"Forgive me, lady," he said.

"And take your eyes from those slaves!" she said.

"No," he said, "they are meant to be seen, to be enjoyed, to be commanded, to be owned, to be mastered, to be relished, to be ravished. It is what they are for."

"Do not think I did not see you hanging about the quarters of Nishida," she said. "I could scarcely stir about without knowing that you watched me, and followed me about. Anywhere in the holding! Nishida, Hana, Hisui, others. Many knew this."

"Perhaps I see you differently now," he said.

"You followed me one night even to the outer parapet," she said.

"True," said Tajima. "What were you doing there?"

"Refreshing myself, in the open air," she said. "What were you doing there?"

"Refreshing myself," he said, "in the open air."

"You were following me," she laughed.

"Perhaps," he said.

"I wager," she said, "you even dreamed of purchasing my contract from Nishida."

"Perhaps," he said.

"Poor fool," she said, "you would have aspired to the daughter of the Shogun of the Islands."

"I did not know you were his daughter," said Tajima.

"I played my part well," she said.

"Excellently," he said.

She then smiled, and seemed well satisfied.

"Why then are you here?" he asked.

"I do not know," she said. "Perhaps I have been removed from the holding of Temmu for my safety. Perhaps, given my value in the north, I am to be permitted an even more important role."

"It is hard to see what that might be," he said.

"True," she said.

Sumomo glanced to the serving slaves, as, head down and deferentially, they attended to the wants of the diners.

"Half-stripped slaves are disgusting," she said.

"Not all find them so," said Tajima.

"They are in collars, like animals," she said.

"They are animals," said Tajima.

"I see men observing them," she said.

"Of course," said Tajima.

"How terrible it must be," she said, "serving men, knowing that you are their beast, and will be punished if not found pleasing."

"They are slaves," said Tajima.

"Who could have the least interest in such creatures?" she asked.

"They sell well," said Tajima.

"Slave!" snapped Sumomo, to Cecily, who, startled, apprehensive, looked to the guests' table, from where she now knelt, near the serving table.

"Approach," said Sumomo.

Uneasily the slave, once Miss Virginia Cecily Jean Pym, approached Sumomo, and knelt before her, her head down.

"First obeisance position," I said.

Instantly the slave assumed first obeisance position, kneeling, head to the floor, the palms of her hands on the floor, beside her lowered head. She was, after all, in the presence of a free woman.

"Kneel up," said Sumomo. "Lift your head. I would look upon your pretty face."

Cecily's lip trembled. She was clearly frightened. She was a slave. She was before a free woman. For those unfamiliar with the Gorean culture, it is difficult to convey the gap between the slave and the free. It is not a gap in degree, but a chasm in kind.

"Mistress?" whispered Cecily.

"How are you here?" inquired Sumomo.

"I was selected from amongst others, in the slave pens," she said.

"Why?" asked Sumomo.

"By men," said Cecily.

"I see," said Sumomo.

"There were many excellent choices," I said.

"Have you stolen any food?" inquired Sumomo.

"No, Mistress!" said Cecily.

"Have you been fed?" asked Sumomo.

"No, Mistress," said Cecily.

"Are you hungry?" she asked.

"Yes, Mistress."

"Perhaps," said Sumomo, "the men will throw you some food later, or feed you."

"We will hope for such kindness, Mistress," said Cecily.

"Doubtless such as you hope to please your masters," said Sumomo.

"Yes, Mistress," said Cecily, "for we are slaves."

"Are you a slut?" asked Sumomo.

"I am less than a slut, Mistress," said Cecily, "for I am a slave."

"Do you know that men sometimes refer to such as you as sex-tarsks?"

"Yes, Mistress," said Cecily.

"Are you a sex-tarsk?" asked Sumomo.

"Yes, Mistress," said Cecily, "for I am a slave."

"You are a pretty little sex-tarsk," said Sumomo.

"Thank you, Mistress," said Cecily.

I did not think that Sumomo was any larger than Cecily.

"You are not your own," said Sumomo.

"No, Mistress, we are the properties of our masters."

"Disgusting."

"We are slaves, Mistress."

"Surely you are horrified to be in collars."

"No, Mistress."

"How is that?"

"We are slaves, Mistress."

"I do not understand."

"Perhaps Mistress might better understand us, and assess our feelings, if she herself were collared."

"What!" cried Sumomo.

"No woman fully understands her sex until she is owned by her master."

"She-tarsk, worthless she-tarsk!" cried Sumomo, leaping to her feet.

"Forgive me, Mistress!" said Cecily.

"You should be whipped, and whipped!" cried Sumomo.

"No, Mistress! Please, no, Mistress!" wept Cecily. Slaves, as other beasts, know the whip, and will do much to avoid its stroke.

"You asked her a question, beloved daughter," said Lord Yamada. "She responded as best she could. Dismiss her. Permit her to continue serving." He then addressed the other diners. "Note the kelp, the bamboo shoots, the fish, the lotus roots, and mushrooms."

"You are dismissed," said Sumomo, angrily, returning to her place, kneeling. "Continue serving."

"Yes, Mistress," said Cecily. "Thank you, Mistress. Forgive me, Mistress!"

"Sake," called Tajima to Saru, who hurried to bring him the second of his three small cups.

I rose to my feet and went to stand to the left of the seated Lord Yamada. I noted that his hand now rested on the tasseled hilt of his companion sword, an accouterment with which men of his station were seldom without. It was at hand, even as they slept.

"Noble lord," I said, "I express my commendation at the excellence of the supper."

"Meat is also available, Tarl Cabot, tarnsman," he said. "I have seen to it. Coast gull, vulo, tarsk, verr, and mountain deer."

"Lord Yamada is thoughtful, and more than generous," I said, "but I speak to him of another matter. Behold, at this table, to your right, is the officer Tajima, Pani, as yourself, and but recently come from the holding of your enemy, Lord Temmu. The noble Tajima will be more informed than I of recent developments which may have occurred in the holding of Lord Temmu. They may be of interest to you."

"You suppose," said Lord Yamada, "he might be reluctant to speak openly of such matters at this point?"

"Yes," I said, "even with your chain of gold now about his neck."

"I understand," said Lord Yamada, softly.

"Men are often disarmed by charm and beauty," I said, "and may willingly, even eagerly, reveal to a woman, hoping to intrigue and impress her, matters which otherwise might be difficult to extract, even by the persuasions of ropes and irons."

"Sumomo," said Lord Yamada.

"Father?" she said, surprised.

"The moons smile upon the garden," he said. "The brook flows brightly between the rocks. The Night Singers rejoice in the branches."

"Father?" she said, puzzled.

"It would please me," he said, "if you would show our insignificant, humble garden to our guest, the noble Tajima, tarnsman."

"Surely not!" she said.

"It would please me," he said, smiling.

"Yes," said Sumomo, suddenly, "of course."

"Is this seemly?" asked Lord Akio.

A woman of the high Pani would not be likely to be unattended in such a situation.

"Ashigaru are about," I said.

"Perhaps," said Lord Akio, "I might accompany them."

"Better to let the young people banter amongst themselves," said Lord Yamada.

I recalled that he had been willing to place Sumomo, in the guise of a contract woman, in the very holding of his mortal enemy, Lord Temmu.

"Perhaps I am not interested in seeing the garden," said Tajima.

"Please, noble warrior," said Sumomo.

"His hands could be bound behind his body," said Lord Akio.

"He is our guest," remonstrated Lord Yamada, dismayed.

"At the first hint of unseemly conduct, great lady," said Lord Akio, "call out, and Ashigaru will be at your side."

"Let us enter the garden, noble warrior," said Sumomo.

"Now I am 'noble warrior'," he observed.

"And wear a golden chain," she said.

"You had little enough time for me before," he said.

Indeed, Sumomo, in Tarncamp, in Shipcamp, on the great ship, and in the holding of Lord Temmu, though supposedly only a contract woman, had treated him with derision and contempt, rather as might have the daughter of a shogun mocked and scorned the attentions of a lowly armsman. I had little understood the adamant nature of her seeming hostility. It had seemed inexplicable to me, particularly as I had taken her to be a contract woman. How could it be that such a woman would not show deference to a Pani male, and a warrior? It would have been simple enough to simply ignore him. But she had not done so.

"Please," said Sumomo, looking over her shoulder at Tajima, and smiling. I doubted that a contract woman could have done it better.

"Very well," he said, as though reluctantly.

He then followed Sumomo down the three steps into the beckoning, moonlit garden.

I did not know if this had been well done, or not, but, at least, Tajima was now in a position to inform the lovely Sumomo of her jeopardy.

I could smell the fragrance of flowers.

"I am not sure of this," said Lord Akio, uneasily.

"There are golden suls," said Lord Yamada, "with butter and cream, from our own dairy."

"If we are to reach our rendezvous with Ichiro," said Pertinax, "we must soon leave."

"There is time," I said. "You seem to have been observing the flanks of Saru," I said.

"She is a worthless slave," he said.

"But she does have nice flanks," I said, "and the collar is pretty on her neck."

"It is pretty on the neck of any woman," he said.

"Of course," I said. "They are, and should be, slaves."

"True," he said.

"Doubtless you recall her from the offices of Earth," I said.

"Of course," he said.

"You find her more pleasing now than before, do you not?" I asked.

"Certainly," he said. "The worthless thing is now as she should be, a helpless, collared slave."

"Perhaps you would like to have your binding cord on her," I said.

"She is not worth the cord that would bind her," he said.

"Still she might look well, helpless, trussed at your feet," I said.

"At anyone's feet," he said.

"True," I said.

I think very little time had passed when Sumomo, holding her kimono about herself, her face dark with anger, ascended the three steps, went behind the table, and resumed her position, kneeling.

Her entire body was trembling, apparently with fury.

"Shall I call Ashigaru?" inquired Lord Akio, anxiously, his right hand within his left sleeve.

"No, great lord," she snapped.

She should not have spoken so, as she, even though a daughter of the shogun, was a female, and he was a male, and a daimyo.

"What occurred, beloved daughter?" inquired Lord Yamada, solicitously. "Did our guest not enjoy the garden?"

"On such a boor, and barbarian," she said, "the bean garden of a peasant would be wasted."

"He was uncommunicative?" inquired the shogun.

"He was communicative enough," she said. "But he is mad, and not to be trusted. He knows nothing. He is ignorant. He speaks absurdities. I could not bring myself to repeat the ludicrous things I heard. He chose not to speak of the holding of Temmu. In the darkness he babbled only nonsense."

"Great lord," I said to Lord Yamada, "I fear the beauty of your daughter, the aroma of the garden, the joy of the evening, the sparkle of sake, the light of the moons, the babble of the water, rendered my officer not himself, but stumbling and incoherent."

"He is young," smiled Lord Yamada. "Sake and beauty have addled the wits of even daimyos, have they not dear Akio?"

"As the shogun has said," he smiled, lifting one of the small cups of sake to the shogun.

Tajima then returned, and took his place, cross-legged, to the right of the shogun.

"Did you enjoy the garden?" asked the shogun.

"Very much," said Tajima. "It is a beautiful garden."

"You did not stay long," said the shogun.

"Too much beauty is overwhelming," said Tajima.

Sumomo smiled.

"I meant the garden," said Tajima.

"Of course," said Sumomo.

"Perhaps he did not trust himself," said Lord Akio.

"My friend would do much to avoid impugning his honor," I said.

"A father is proud," said Lord Yamada, "to be the father of so beautiful and dangerously fascinating a daughter."

"I felt drops of rain," said Tajima.

A small, angry noise escaped Sumomo.

The shogun looked out over the table, to the large, low, opened wall, beyond which lay the garden. "The garden is dark now," he said. "The clouds have gathered."

"True," said Tajima.

"Perhaps another time," said Lord Yamada, pleasantly.

"Perhaps," said Tajima.

"We have eleven varieties of rice here," said the shogun, "variously prepared, in stews, pastes, and cakes, and variously seasoned, with a dozen sauces and herbs. Too, consider the gifts of the sea and shore, from four of my fishing villages, clams, oysters, grunt, bag fish, song fish, shark, eels, octopus, wing fish, parsit, squid."

"You set a magnificent table," I said to the shogun.

"I rejoice if my humble offerings please you," said the shogun.

"She would not believe me," said Tajima to me, in English.

"I had gathered as much," I said, in English.

I heard rain gently falling on the leaves of the trees in the garden.

"The Night Singers are quiet," I said.

"It is the rain," said Lord Akio.

"Perhaps we should have the screens closed," I said.

"Later," said Lord Akio.

"Light lanterns," said Lord Yamada, and attending Ashigaru lit a number of dangling lanterns.

As the lanterns were of diversely colored paper the room was aglow with a medley of illuminations, and yet the colors did not clash but each seemed to enhance the other. I was reminded of the architecture of the plantings, the sequences of flowers, in the garden outside, with their music of aromatic notes.

"Two of our honored guests," said Lord Yamada, "following my arrangements, designed to make clear my trustworthiness and good will, will soon leave, to rendezvous somewhere with one or more compatriots, following which they will return to the encampment of the cavalry. There they will reassure the cavalry of the safety and health of its commander, Tarl Cabot, tarnsman, bear to it my good wishes and assure it of my friendship. It is then my hope that the cavalry, in the light of the despicable treatment of their commander, Tarl Cabot, tarnsman, betrayed into the hands of a putative enemy, but an actual friend, the dreadful perfidy of the house of Temmu, the righteousness of my cause, and the wisdom of an alliance, one both noble and profitable, will pledge itself wisely to the house of Yamada, enlisting under the banner of the Shogun of the Islands."

"This may take some time, great lord," I said. "There would likely be questions, conditions, negotiations, and such."

"Of course," he said. "And in the meantime, we will trust that Tarl Cabot, tarnsman, will consent to continue to enjoy our hospitality."

I nodded, pleasantly.

"Cecily," I said.

"Master?" she said.

I scooped up a handful of rice paste from the shallow bowl to my right, and held it out, across the table.

The slave hurried to me, gratefully, and knelt, and put down her head. I held the rice paste to where she might take it, from the palm of my hand. She fed, ravenously. I gathered it might have been several Ahn since the slaves had been fed in the pen. The first feeding of field slaves is usually at dawn, or earlier, before they are sent into the fields. In the early afternoon water and a handful of millet suffices for them. After returning to the pen, they receive their evening feeding. They are not permitted to linger at the troughs, neither in the morning nor in the evening. Today, given the intended supper in the palace, and the selections to be made, the slaves had been kept in the pens. Thus the millet of the afternoon need not be wasted on them. Accordingly, it seemed probable that the three serving slaves had not fed since the early morning.

"A slave is grateful, Master," said Cecily, looking up.

I motioned that she should return to the vicinity of the kitchen master, which she promptly did.

"Jane," called Pertinax, and she hurried to him, and was fed, as had been Cecily, from the palm of his hand. Then he motioned her away, and she returned to her place by the serving table.

I looked across the floor, to where Saru knelt.

"Your selection, friend Tajima," I said, "has not been fed."

"She was not really my selection," he said.

"That is true," I said.

"She has not been watching me," he said. "She has been watching Pertinax. Have you not noted, as well, her hanging about him, how she positioned herself, that she would be well displayed, so frequently, even in her serving, and such?"

"I was not paying attention," I said. "Perhaps I was distracted by the honeyed chestnuts."

"She was not pleased," he said, "when Pertinax fed the slave, Jane."

"I am not surprised," I said. "Still, you might consider feeding her. Would you not do as much for a kaiila, a verr, a tarsk? It is likely she is hungry."

"She was not my selection," he said.

I looked across the floor to where Saru knelt.

Her face seemed wan. Interestingly, as Tajima had suggested might be the case, her eyes were on Pertinax. She was leaning toward him a little. She seemed a little unsteady. I feared she might faint. Her lips trembled.

"You feed her, if you wish," said Tajima.

"It is not her fault that she is not Pani," I said.

"Sumomo is Pani," said Tajima.

"What are you talking about?" asked Sumomo.

"Nothing," said Tajima.

"I think the slave is hungry," I said to Tajima.

"Let us turn the matter over to Pertinax," said Tajima. "I recall she knew him, even from the forest before Tarncamp, when she, the foolish slave, thought herself free."

"Agreed," I said. "Pertinax, I think a slave would be fed."

"Is she not the selection of Tajima?" he said.

"Of course," I said. "But I fear he is disgruntled that she is not Pani. He is not in a pleasant humor. He leaves the matter to you. I think she is quite hungry, as it seems were Cecily and Jane. Will she be fed or not? It is up to you."

"I see," he said.

Certainly slaves are better in the furs if they have been fed. To be sure, Pertinax and Tajima had a rendezvous to make somewhere with the bannerman, Ichiro.

"Slave," called Pertinax.

She leapt up, and, in a moment, knelt before him, across the table. Before him she seemed more confident, more enlivened.

"I must reproach you, Gregory," she said in English, angrily. "In the pen I was tied, and given ten lashes."

"You spoke without permission," he said, in English.

"But ten!" she said.

"I think I will have you given twenty," he said.

"No!" she said.

Clearly she knew it could be done, at a word. There were several Ashigaru about, and the kitchen master.

"Are you hungry?" he asked.

"Yes!" she said.

"Very hungry?" he asked.

"Yes," she said. "I am very hungry!"

"I see," he said.

There was a hint of a sly smile, or smugness, about her features. I think she still thought of Pertinax in the terms of Gregory White, a Gregory White who, in a sense, no longer existed, at least in the terms in which she thought of him, a Gregory White who had been shy, diffident, insecure, weak, manageable, pathetic, reduced, and confused, the victim of a pathological culture, of a denaturalized conditioning program at odds with the biotruths of a species. That Gregory White, on a new world, and differentially acculturated, had become

Pertinax, a warrior, and tarnsman. Such a man would no longer look upon such as she as some distant and unobtainable object, a goddess, a denizen of remote stars, something far above and beyond him, but now as something quite real, something which she truly was, a live, breathing female, a lovely prey animal at hand, an animal designed by nature for such as he, an animal wanted, an animal to be captured, subdued, owned, and trained, trained to his pleasure, an animal to be mastered.

"Feed me," she said in English.

"Speak Gorean," he said.

"I dare not," she whispered, in English. "I could not dare say such a thing here, not in Gorean, and be understood. I am collared."

"Why are you collared?" he asked.

"Because I am a slave," she said, in English.

"Speak," he said, in Gorean, "and exactly, as you did before."

"I dare not," she said.

"Speak," he said in Gorean.

"Feed me!" she said, in Gorean.

Sumomo gasped. Those at the table looked toward her, surprised.

Pertinax reached into his shallow bowl of rice paste, to his right, and gathered some of this into his palm.

She leaned forward.

But he put the paste into his own mouth, and slowly finished it.

"I do not understand," she said.

"You will go hungry," he said.

"Please, no!" she said.

"Speak properly," he said.

"Please, no," she said, "—Master!"

"Whether a slave is fed or not," he said, "is up to the master."

"Please," she said. "I am starving! Cast food to the floor, if you wish, and I will eat it on all fours, even as a sleen. But I beg to be fed!"

"You are dismissed," he said.

"Master!" she protested.

"Return to your place," he said. "There may be others to be served."

Confused, and frightened, Saru returned to her place, and knelt there.

"She should be whipped," said Sumomo.

"Perhaps later," said Pertinax.

"You believe slaves should be whipped," said Tajima.

"Of course," said Sumomo.

Outside the garden was dark.

It was raining, softly. Beyond the opening, one could see the light of the colored lanterns reflected in the falling drops.

Lord Yamada addressed himself to the kitchen master. "Remove the slaves," he said.

The kitchen master merely looked to the exit from the room, at the back, that leading to the hall, leading to the kitchen, and the three slaves hurried from the room. He followed them.

I gathered that something was to take place which required discretion, something not likely to be permitted to fall upon the ears of slaves.

Secrets are seldom entrusted to slaves. As it is said, the babbling of slaves is like the babbling of brooks. Who knows who will stray by the brook, and at what time?

"Perhaps you, too, should withdraw," said Tajima to Sumomo.

"Why?" she said.

"Our new guests, the noble Tajima and the noble Pertinax, must make ready to return to the encampment of tarns," said Lord Yamada, "to convey my felicitations and suggestions to their fellows, but I think it is only fitting, first, to see if there might be some word to be conveyed to the false shogun of the north, Temmu. Summon Tatsu, reader of bones and shells!"

Ah, I thought to myself, what message will be revealed amongst the scattered bones and shells, to be carried by Tajima and Pertinax to the holding of Lord Temmu where, doubtless, it will be confirmed by the noble Daichi? I thought it would most likely have to do with the possible defection of the tarn cavalry, which might precipitate some unwary act on the part of a suspicious Lord Temmu, which might then incline it more readily toward the house of Yamada. Surely this seemed more likely than a new prattling about a mythical iron dragon, or such.

Shortly thereafter a fellow entered, in simple robes, yellow, carrying an oval box which would contain, I supposed, bones and shells.

This, I assumed was, Tatsu, Lord Yamada's reader.

Lord Yamada, I was sure, placed no more confidence in the ceremonial litter of bones and shells than I, or Tajima, or Pertinax. Lord Temmu, on the other hand, was more than willing to attribute credit to such impostures. It was not simply that readings might be sufficiently ambiguous as to seem to plausibly predict a variety of possible developments, but, upon occasion at least, thanks to the forewarnings, and such, supplied to Daichi, might appear both clear and alarmingly accurate.

"Attend," said Lord Yamada.

Tatsu knelt and opened the box. A moment later a rattle of bones and shells struck the floor, over which Tatsu bent, intently.

"Something is in the garden," said Pertinax.

"Ashigaru," said Tajima, watching Tatsu, whose body rocked slowly over the bones and shells.

I noted the rain, still falling outside, the lantern light illuminating the droplets, and then returned my attention to Tatsu.

Tatsu then turned, hastily, still on his knees, to face Lord Yamada; his face seemed strained, even frightened.

"The bones and shells have not fallen well!" he said.

"I gather," said Lord Yamada, gravely, "they have not fallen well for the house of Temmu."

"I do not understand how they have fallen," said Tatsu.

"You cannot read them?" said Lord Yamada, angrily.

I gathered Tatsu had had his instructions beforehand. How then could he be having any difficulty in the matter?

"I can read them," said Tatsu. "It is only I do not understand how they have fallen."

"They speak of the tarn cavalry," said Lord Yamada, "and of the house of Temmu. They warn the house of Temmu of betrayal, of danger."

"No, great lord," said Tatsu, trembling, "they speak of the house of Yamada, and of danger."

Lord Yamada rose up from behind the table, his hand on the hilt of his companion sword, and strode angrily to Tatsu.

"In whose hire are you?" he inquired. "Who has suborned you?"

"I am loyal to you, great lord," cried Tatsu. "The bones and shells speak of danger to the house of Yamada, of an avenger, a dark figure, one approaching, a lost son, a son of the very blood of the house of Yamada, one who returns, one on whose left shoulder is borne the sign of the lotus."

"There are no sons of the blood of the house of Yamada," said Lord Yamada, drawing from his sash the companion sword. "I will not have sons. Each was strangled at birth."

"There is an empty grave," said Tatsu.

"You lie!" said Lord Yamada. "There is no empty grave!"

"Forgive me, great lord," said Tatsu.

"Cast the bones and shells again," suggested Lord Akio.

"No," said Tatsu. "They have spoken."

"And you shall not again!" said Lord Yamada, and the companion sword, with a movement of Lord Yamada's wide sleeve, entered the reader's heart, and then, as easily, with another motion of that sleeve, withdrew. Tatsu remained kneeling, as he was, for a few moments, as though nothing had happened, and then his body stiffened, and he fell to his side, amongst some of the debris from his reading.

Suddenly Pertinax sprang across the table and seized a dark-clad figure about the waist, lifting it up, and flinging it backward. There was a cry of rage. This figure had apparently emerged from the darkness of the garden, silently. It had been moving swiftly toward Lord Yamada. In its hand, upraised, was a *tanto*, a stabbing dagger. In a moment Ashigaru had closed about the figure and borne it, face downward, to the floor. At its side, crouching, was Lord Akio. His right hand drew from its concealed sheath the sleeve knife, which he thrust into the assailant's neck, at the base of the skull, severing the vertebrae.

"You are safe, Lord!" he cried.

Lord Yamada glared at the assailant's body. It no longer moved.

"Perhaps less safe than before," said Lord Yamada, "as we cannot question this man."

"Such men," said Lord Akio, "are trained assassins. They reveal nothing, even under torture."

"We shall never know," said Lord Yamada.

Pertinax seemed shaken.

"You were brave," I said to him. "You intervened, even though unarmed."

"I did not stop to reflect," said Pertinax.

"Often there is no time to so indulge oneself."

"How is it that you, alone of all," asked Lord Yamada, "noted this peril?"

"When there is nothing to see," said Pertinax, "that is the time to look closely. When all look north, look south; when all look east, look west."

"A teacher?" said Lord Yamada.

"Yes," said Pertinax.

"You will have another chain of gold," said Lord Yamada. "I will owe my life to no man."

"I accept it in lieu of such," said Pertinax.

"We are quit?" asked Lord Yamada.

"Yes," said Pertinax.

"And thus," said Lord Yamada, quietly, "you keep your head."

"Behold, Lord," said Lord Akio, kneeling beside the fallen assailant, who had now been turned to his back. Lord Akio had cut away the dark, close-fitting clothing of the assailant, in such a way as to reveal his left shoulder. "Behold," said he, again. "See, my lord, the sign of the lotus!"

"It is the avenger, of whom Tatsu spoke!" said an Ashigaru, peering downward.

I sopped a cloth with water, and wiped the sign away.

"Dye, or paint, pigment of some sort," said an Ashigaru.

"He is not the avenger," said another, looking at Lord Yamada.

"No," said Lord Yamada. "Examine every man in my domain, whatever his rank, exalted or lowly, warrior or peasant, merchant or Ashigaru, fisherman or porter, whatever he may be, and bring to me any who bear on his left shoulder the sign of the lotus."

"Shall we not kill each so marked?" asked Lord Akio.

"No," said Lord Yamada. "Such a man will not be alone. Where there is one ost there will be others. What nest contains but one?"

"It is an unusual marking," said Lord Akio.

"I bear it on my own left shoulder," said Lord Yamada.

"Command us further," said an Ashigaru.

"Go to the graves of my sons," said Lord Yamada. "See if there is an empty grave."

"Where is Sumomo?" asked Lord Akio.

"She is delicate," said Lord Yamada. "She has returned to her quarters."

"I see," said Lord Akio, pacified.

"Noble guests," said Lord Yamada, addressing Tajima and Pertinax, "please forgive this unexpected intrusion. I trust that it has not diminished in any way the delight of our evening. Surely it has in no way diminished mine. I shall recall the harmony and concord of our gathering with fondness. Take now your chains of gold and assure your compatriots of the cavalry that as much or more awaits them when they take to the saddle in the name of Yamada, Shogun of the Islands."

"Our thanks, great lord," said Tajima, bowing.

"You will be expected at the gates," said Lord Yamada. "You will be passed through. You will be given your weapons. There will be no difficulty. I trust there is ample time, despite the recent diversion, for you to make your rendezvous, wherever you have arranged it to be."

"It is not yet the Eighteenth Ahn," said Lord Akio.

"It has rained," I said. "It may take somewhat longer."

"There will be time," said Tajima, once more bowing.

He and Pertinax then turned to exit the room.

"Wait," said Lord Yamada.

"Lord?" asked Tajima, turning, again.

"The garden is shut," he said. "Exit thence."

"Yes, Lord," said Tajima.

The shogun had indicated the corridor leading back into the palace.

"Also," said the shogun, "I am aware that strong men have interests other than gold."

"Lord?" said Tajima.

"Each," he said, "may take a woman with you, for your own, one of the serving slaves, or another, perhaps from the pens."

"Lord Yamada is most generous," said Tajima.

"I am shogun," said Lord Yamada.

"I fear, however," said Tajima, "that the night sky will be cold, and that the freezing rush of the chill wind, as it is cloven by the speeding tarn, will be harrowing to a tunicked slave."

"Demand two blankets," said the shogun.

"Again our thanks, great lord," said Tajima.

Once more bows were exchanged, and Tajima and Pertinax left the room, traversing the corridor leading back into the palace.

Tajima's solicitude for slaves interested me. Surely he knew that they were slaves. A slave is owed nothing. If she wishes a garment, or a mat, a blanket, or such, let her beg for one, a begging which may then be considered by the master. Indeed, I thought that a chill ride on a tarn, through the blasting wind, bound or chained helplessly against the leather, much exposed, having only her tiny tunic, might be instructive for a slave, something which would help her keep in mind that she is a slave. The slave may be fed or not fed, clothed or not clothed, caressed or not caressed, depending on the will of the master. She is his beast. The slave is almost always distinctively garbed. She is usually garbed in such a way as to enhance her beauty, and make it clear to herself, and others, that she is a slave. Slave garments, incidentally, are almost always extremely comfortable, surely more so than the cumbersome robes of concealment prescribed for the free woman of the continent. In the typical slave garment a woman may move quite freely, doubtless because there is so little of it.

"How did the assailant enter the garden?" asked Lord Yamada.

"One supposes, through the palace," said Lord Akio.

"There must then have been one or more confederates," said Lord Yamada.

"I fear so," said Lord Akio.

Chapter Twenty-One

What Occurred in the Garden of Lord Yamada

The Night Singers were now in the fields.

I sat in the shade, on a bench, near the small bridge which spanned the tiny brook wending its way amongst the rocks, the tiny terraces, the shrubberies, the flowers, and trees of the garden.

It had rained the night of the attack. Accordingly, the Night Singers, as I had gathered from Lord Akio, were silent. Thus, the cessation of their song, commonly resulting from wariness, perhaps an uneasiness occasioned by the entrance of an intruder, or something unfamiliar, in the garden had not occurred. Had it occurred, it might have been noted by guards, or others. Accordingly, I had little doubt that the attack had been coordinated with their silence, to be expected under the circumstances. But rain may reveal as well as conceal. Before retiring I had taken a lantern and, in the dampness, and under the dripping leaves, examined the interior edge of the walls. Surely it seemed unlikely that the assailant would have entered the garden through the palace itself. Too, the height of the wall, I suspected, judging from what I could see of the courtyard wall from my barred room, or cell, to which I was usually confined at night, would have presented its own hazards, of anchored glass, shards, and metal. In the light of the lantern I had carefully scouted the interior edge of the wall until I found what I was looking for. There was little difficulty once I had found the tracks left in the soft soil, and mud. I now knew how I could exit the garden at any time I might wish. Unfortunately I was generally permitted in the garden only during the day.

Near me, the gardener, Haruki, silently, was pruning shrubbery. I had inquired his name in the palace, and had made it a point to greet him, from time to time, in a friendly manner. Initially, I fear this familiarity frightened him; even now he would not converse with me, other than in some brief harmless way, or in response to some simple question about his work or the plantings; he would turn away, and busy himself elsewhere. The Pani were very conscious of rank. Several days ago I think I may have done him some service, when Lord Akio, with a noble's innocence, and no particularly malevolent intent, was ready to show me the deadliness of his flung war fan. Instead I had prevailed upon him to demonstrate his prowess, and the seriousness of the weapon, on a young tree, whose trunk had been half severed, as though with the single blow of an ax, which tree, at the behest of Lord Akio, had been subsequently replaced.

"Tal," I said to Haruki.

"Tal, one who is honorable," he said, softly, his head down.

"I think it will rain today," I said.

"No, noble one," he said.

"How do you know?" I asked.

"The petals of the golden cup are open," he said, "the zar swarm is not aflight, the lavender leaves of the scent tree do not curl."

"You can predict rain," I said.

"Not I, honorable one," he said, "but the garden. The garden knows."

"It is like the weather glass," I said.

"*Ela*," he said, "I know nothing of such a thing."

"It is common on ships," I said, "particularly round ships, merchant ships."

"I am a humble gardener," he said.

"You know this garden well," I said.

"I and others," he said.

"I suspect," I said, "there is nothing you do not know about this garden."

"I must work, honorable one," he said. "I would be excused."

"An empty grave was found," I said.

"I have heard so," he said.

"The body must have been removed from it," I said.

"Perhaps," he said, "it never contained a body."

"That is possible," I said.

"Lord Yamada," I said, "has many wives, and many women."

"He is shogun," said Haruki.

"When sons are born to the house of Yamada they are killed," I said.

"He is shogun," he said.

"From whence does Lord Yamada obtain his women?" I asked.

"From high houses," he said.

"Perhaps from the peasantry, as well?" I said.

"If they are very beautiful," he said.

"I know you have work," I said. "Forgive me for detaining you."

Four days ago, following the slaying of the reader of bones and shells, Tatsu, and the attempted assassination of Lord Yamada, Tajima and Pertinax had left the palace grounds and, as far as I knew, returned safely to the encampment beyond the holding of Lord Temmu.

It seemed clear to me that Lord Yamada had arranged with Tatsu to reveal a reading to his political advantage, which would then be relayed to the holding of Temmu, sooner or later, by Tajima and Pertinax. That reading, once understood, would then, doubtless, be confirmed by Daichi, in a new casting of bones and shells, which would be likely to add to its weight. On the other hand, the reading proclaimed by Tatsu spoke rather of danger to the house of Yamada and of some mysterious figure, supposedly of the very blood of Yamada, referred to as the "avenger." The outraged shogun, believing himself crossed in this dire manner, and doubtless feeling humiliated and betrayed before the company, apparently in a moment's consternation and rage, answered the unwelcome reading with the precipitous retort of the companion sword. I had little doubt that he had almost immediately regretted the hastiness of his action. Surely, shortly thereafter, he had chided Lord Akio, when that noble person, presumably fearing for his shogun's life, had thrust his sleeve dagger into the neck of the assailant, severing the vertebrae at the base of the skull. I did not personally countenance readings of the sort which might issue from a Daichi or Tatsu. On the other hand, I was not at all sure that Tatsu had been the tool of another, had been suborned, or such. He must have known that the delivery of such a reading would be hazardous. Accordingly, I thought it possible he was, as he had claimed, loyal to the shogun, and had chosen this means, that of a reading, to inform the shogun of a sinister intelligence. Perhaps there was, somehow, somewhere, an avenger, one even of the blood of Yamada himself. The morning following the supper the graves, more than fifty of them, had been opened. And, indeed, one had been found empty.

Haruki had now, perhaps gratefully, distanced himself from me, and my doubtless prying, unwelcome questions.

There was much that I did not understand, not merely locally, but about the very strife in which I had somehow become a participant. Long ago, on a dark night on a remote beach, the remaining land forces of Lord Temmu, defeated and routed, confronted with superior force on one side, the victorious warriors and Ashigaru of Lord Yamada, and roiling Thassa on the other, awaited their last battle, in which they would be driven into the sea. But in the morning the advancing forces of Lord Yamada had discovered only the debris and ashes of a deserted camp. Shortly thereafter the Goreans of the continental coast, particularly that in the vicinity of Brundisium, found strangers in their midst, Pani, these survivors of the major land forces of Lord Temmu. These Pani, as I had determined, were as unclear as to the nature of their arrival on a foreign shore, as were those amongst whom they had found themselves. It was obvious, given the technologies involved in such a suspension of consciousness and such a methodology of transition that either the Priest-Kings or the Kurii, or both, had chosen to intervene in what might otherwise have been regarded as little more than a final battle in a minor war in a far place, but why would they have done so? It was my surmise, based largely on intelligences more suspected than delivered in Tarncamp, that the matter had to do with the contest for Gor, or its surface, long waged by Priest-Kings and Kurii, a contest in which an acquisitive and aggressive species sought conquest and victory, and an ensconced species was content to satisfy itself with little more than the defense and protection of its world. The possibility had suggested itself to some, a possibility which seemed plausible to me, that the Kurii, frustrated at the current failure of their designs, and the Priest-Kings, annoyed by probes, and predatory intrusions, might be willing to gamble for a world's surface, which space was seldom traversed by Priest-Kings, and then, commonly, only after the setting of Tor-tu-Gor, Light Upon the Home Stone, whose bright, piercing rays would dazzle and blind their sensory organs, and whose heat at certain seasons and in certain latitudes could scarcely be tolerated by their fragile, delicate bodies. Accordingly, it was surmised, at least by some, that a wager had been made, with humans the cast dice on which the fate of the surface of a world might hang. If the dice fell in favor of the bestial Kurii, the Priest-Kings would surrender to their intrusion and habitation the surface of their world, and should the dice fall in favor of the Priest-Kings, the Kurii would withdraw to their steel worlds, to live in peace, or seek another star. I had no idea whether or not these speculations were grounded in reality, or were no more than the arrant conjectures of an ignorant few who were, perhaps, as little aware of the springs and engines on which the world turned as the grazing tabuk feeding in the meadows, the sheltering wood nearby, or, within that forest, the stolid tarsk turning the soil with its tusks, digging for roots. So let us suppose these mighty species, to whom we were aliens, and of little independent interest, had arrived at an agreement, that we were to be the dice in their dark game, the dice to be cast on the mat of a world. First, how might the dice be balanced; how might they be more equally weighted? The forces of Yamada were large and disciplined, both on the land and sea. They were largely in control of the resources of the crucial islands. Victory sat upon their banners. The devastated forces of Temmu clung to little more than the lofty heights of an ancestral holding. How then could the dice of men and war, those of Yamada and Temmu, be better balanced, be more evenly weighted? The house of Yamada had seized the land and the sea. What if the house of Temmu might be capable of seizing the air? What of tarns, unknown on the islands? Might these monsters not level a game, and adjust its odds with a more gracious equity? Possibly. But how could that defeated remnant of the forces of Temmu, removed to a far coast, return to the war, whose fields lay across the vast, turbulent breadth of Thassa, beyond even the Farther Islands, from whose waters no ship had returned? Let there be then a ship, a great ship, an unusual ship. Could it, unaided, make its way to that board on which the dice were to be cast, the islands beyond the Farther Islands? If not, is the game not done? And if perchance such a ship, a large ship, a transport for men and tarns, as no other before it had done, might brave the perils of Thassa, what then? And the great ship had, worn and tired, after its months at sea, at last drawn up aside the wharf at the base of the great mountain on which, like a nest of tarns itself, half hidden in the clouds, reared the holding of Temmu.

The game, if it were a game, had begun.

The wager, I supposed, if it were a wager, was underway.

Interestingly, I was unclear as to the gambling involved, in particular, who might favor which participant, Yamada or Temmu? For example, it seemed probable that the Priest-Kings had preserved the remnants of the forces of Temmu, but this did not imply that they favored that house. They might have been doing no more than preparing the dice, a preparation in which the Kurii might themselves have collaborated. Similarly, in the very palace, I had recently sensed Kur. Did this mean that the Kurii favored the house of Yamada? Perhaps it was there to monitor matters, and little more. More importantly, I had no reason to trust either Kurii or Priest-Kings with respect to more than a pretence of impartiality. I had no reason to believe that Kurii, long confined to their steel spheres, and desperate to obtain a fresh, unspoiled world after they had ruined their own, would abide a negative result of the wager with equanimity. Too, Priest-Kings, in all their wisdom, must realize that Kurii, suspicious, ambitious, and aggressive, would be unlikely, indefinitely, to peaceably and harmoniously share a world. Matters were further complicated by my realization that factions existed amongst the Kurii, both within worlds and amongst worlds. Indeed, had not such factions rendered their original world little more than a seared wasteland? Too, I knew from my own time in the Nest, long ago, that the Priest-Kings themselves might differ amongst themselves in trust and agenda.

One might speculate as one wished.

I, and others, were before the curtain, so to speak, and it was difficult to know what lay veiled behind that curtain, if anything.

I listened to the brook. I smelled the flowers in the garden. Haruki was elsewhere. The Night Singers were in the fields.

I must return to the palace.

I have not mentioned one thing.

It is perhaps worth mentioning, though it deals with a woman.

It may be recalled that Lord Yamada had been displeased with the foiled espionage of his daughter, Sumomo, who had been placed as a supposed contract woman in the quarters of Lord Nishida, a daimyo of Lord Temmu. Unbeknownst to herself she had been detected on the outer parapet of the holding of Temmu by the warrior, Tajima, seemingly communicating with minions of Lord Yamada, waiting below. This intelligence having been brought to the attention of Lord Temmu and Lord Okimoto, a daimyo of Lord Temmu, it had been determined that she was to be cast from the parapet at a time corresponding to that at which her observed message had been delivered. Tyrtaios, however, presumably at the behest of an angered Lord Yamada, had extracted her from the holding on tarnback before this sentence could be emplaced. She had been ignorant that her work had been discovered, and thought herself recalled to the palace either for her protection or for a new, different assignment. In actuality, Lord Yamada, fearing his plans had been jeopardized by her clumsiness, had had her recalled not for her protection or for a new employment, suitable to her beauty and intelligence, but because he wished to visit his disappointment and displeasure upon her, in a most grievous manner, meting out to her a lengthy and painful death. Tajima, in the garden, had tried to make this clear to her, but he had failed to convince her of her danger. Sent to the garden to pry information from a manipulable male, one likely to be eager to please so beautiful a woman, she had returned, to her chagrin, empty handed to the supper, having succeeded in little more than having found herself regaled with what she viewed as absurdities and ravings. It may also be recalled that Lord Yamada, before Tajima and Pertinax departed for their rendezvous with Ichiro, offered each a woman, who might be kept as their own, and, also, that Tajima, to my surprise, and presumably to that of Lord Yamada, expressed a concern as to the comfort of slaves, on what would be likely to be a cold flight north. Acceding to this concern Lord Yamada authorized a requisition of two blankets. I had little doubt that Pertinax had claimed his Jane; on the other hand, there was much stir in the palace the next morning, for Tajima, I would suppose at great risk, had sought out Sumomo in her quarters, subdued her, and apparently carried her, bound and gagged, and wrapped in the blanket, from the palace, through the outer gate, and onto the road north. It was not difficult to come by this intelligence as the palace was alive with it that morning. Whereas I had little love for the vain, smug, supercilious Sumomo I certainly would have had no wish for her to be put to some prolonged, horrid death, of the sort which might be contrived by Lord Yamada's torturers and executioners. I was thus rather pleased at Tajima's boldness, and hoped that he would get Sumomo into a collar as soon as possible. As I had heard nothing for days I assumed that Tajima and Pertinax and their cargos had made it safely back to the encampment, and, as well, to the holding of Lord Temmu, where their reports would be doubtless eagerly awaited. I had little doubt that Lord Yamada seethed with rage at the abduction of Sumomo. Not only did this preclude the meting out of his justice on his failed agent, but it would be annoying, certainly, to recognize that she had been boldly removed from the palace, literally from amongst his guards. And his annoyance was doubtless not lessened by realizing that his own act, in authorizing blankets, was not only involved in, but was essential to, the success of the matter noted. On the other hand, in his relationship with me, Lord Yamada was his usual charming self, and gave not the least indication of concern. His major goal, as I realized, was obtaining and controlling the tarn cavalry, or at least assuring its neutrality. Too, as I recalled, he had many daughters. By now I supposed a stripped and collared Sumomo was learning to crawl to a man, bringing him his whip, held between her small, fine teeth.

I rose up from the bench and prepared to exit the garden, returning to the palace.

"Greetings, Tarl Cabot, tarnsman," said Sumomo.

"Lady Sumomo!" I said.

"You seem startled," she said.

Certainly I had failed to conceal my astonishment.

Sumomo was in an exquisite kimono, with a lovely obi. In her hair, which was long, and perhaps had never been cut, wound and curled high on her head, was a tall, jade comb. I could see the tips of tiny yellow slippers beneath the hem of her kimono.

"I was told by my father that you were here, and that I might greet you. Do not fear. Nothing is unseemly. Ashigaru are about."

"Yes, Lady," I said.

"You seem surprised to see me," she said.

"Yes, Lady," I said.

"I am but recently returned to the palace," she said, "after recovering from an ordeal, for I am delicate, indeed, only yesterday, drawn by successions of runners, in a two-wheeled hand wagon."

"It was said," I said, "that you were taken from the palace, and that, days ago."

"It is true," she said. "There was an incident. It need not be discussed."

"How could you be taken from the palace?" I asked.

"It need not be discussed," she said.

"It is rumored," I said, "that you were rendered helpless, and silent, and concealed in a blanket."

"It need not be discussed," she said.

"Much as might have been any woman," I said.

"I am returned," she said.

"It is conjectured," I said, "that you were bound and gagged, that you were utterly helpless, even as might have been a trussed slave."

"I am Sumomo," she said, "daughter of Lord Yamada, Shogun of the Islands."

"You were sent to me by your father," I said.

"Yes," she said.

"That you should speak to me?"

"Yes," she said. "I see that you are apprehensive."

"I had two men," I said, "both of value to me, both friends. Are they alive? Are they captives?"

"I shall speak to you of what occurred," she said.

"Are they alive?" I said.

"There were two men," she said, "both known to you, the loathsome Tajima, whom I despise, and a large, barbarian fool, named Pertinax. There was also a slave, with the barbarian name, Jane. I was carried through the darkness, past sentry posts, in the arms of the contemptible Tajima. The slave struggled to match the pace of the men."

Hearing this, I feared, the rendezvous with Ichiro would not be met. Ichiro had his instructions to return to the northern encampment if the rendezvous had not been kept by midnight, the Twentieth Ahn. Too, it did not seem that Tajima, no matter his will or fortitude, his agility and supple strength, could meet the rendezvous on time, bearing Sumomo, despite her lightness and small frame.

"You were carried on the left shoulder of Tajima," I said, "your head to the rear?"

"Certainly not," she said. "I am a free woman."

A slave is often carried in that way, over the shoulder, facing backward, that she may know herself goods, a property, as much so as a crate of larmas, a bundle of tur-pah, a bag of suls. Too, in this way, she does not know to what, or where, she is being carried. Why should she know? She is a slave.

"After a time," she said, "after the guard posts, the blanket was removed, and my ankles were untied; yes, they had been tied; and I was informed that I should accompany my captors on foot. The slave, I think, rejoiced to have this moment to rest. Naturally I refused, by gestures, and shaking my head, to do so. It was clear to me that a meeting must be at issue, and that time might be short. I could thus foil my captors, and trust that we might fall in with one of my father's patrols."

"You are clever," I said.

"Extremely so," she said. "The barbarian oaf, he called Pertinax, upon my refusal, suggested that I might be beaten into submission."

"Were you?" I asked.

"Certainly not," she said. "I am a free woman."

"You were then carried, again?" I said.

"Two ropes were put on my neck," she said, "one before and one behind. The draw of the lead rope was at the back of my neck, and that of the back rope, if it were tightened, would be at my throat."

"Slaves are trained," I said, "to follow docilely on their leashes, as beautiful beasts, the draw, if necessary, always at the back of the neck, to avoid injury."

"I would be drawn forward by the lead tether," she said, "and should I try to hold back, it would draw forward, and the rear draw, then, at my throat, would draw back. This would be quite disagreeable, and so, to relieve any possible unpleasantness, I hurried forward. Too, I realized that I would be well advised to cooperate with my captors, for my life was in their hands."

"Escape was imperative," I said, "and the men impatient, and desperate." All pressure, of course, is to be at the back of the neck, and that applied with discretion.

"Were I a slave," she said, "I suppose I might have simply been whipped into a sobbing, eager obedience."

"But you were a free woman," I said.

"Certainly," she said. "In any event, I am not stupid, and, given the situation, I hurried on, now obedient to my leash."

"As might a slave," I said.

"Perhaps," she said. "But soon," she said, "by pathetic whimpers, and tiny movements of my body, which men cannot withstand, I made known that I now acknowledged myself a helpless woman in their grasp, admitting myself their helpless prisoner, and that I desired to speak."

"What happened?" I asked.

"Men are stupid," she said. "Such wiles were sufficient, though Pertinax was not pleased. My gag was removed, and my hands were unbound from behind my back. I lowered my head, and promised dutiful compliance. The leash, too, was removed."

"You would be silent," I said. "You would do nothing to betray their trust. You would not attempt to escape?"

"I promised all that," she said, "and most earnestly."

"You need not have done so," I said. "But if you promised, it is incumbent upon you to keep your promise."

"Do not be absurd," she said.

"I see," I said.

"Men are stupid," she said.

"What then?" I asked.

It alarmed me that Sumomo was here, in the garden. But it seemed she would not speak, except in her own way, at her own pace. I suspect she was enjoying this unraveling of her account.

"We then continued on our way," she said, "I between the two men, and the slave following, behind and on the left."

"That is the common heeling position for a slave," I said.

"But I walked proudly between my captors," she said.

"Certainly," I said. "You were a free woman."

"The contemptible Tajima," she said, "kept looking at the yellow moon."

"He was judging the night sky," I said, "trying to ascertain the Twentieth Ahn."

"Shortly thereafter he said, 'We are too late!'"

"'Surely not!' said Pertinax."

"'See the moon!' he said."

"'Let us hurry on,' said Pertinax."

"'The bannerman knows his orders,' said the loathsome Tajima. 'He has departed.'"

"'Perhaps not,' said Pertinax."

"'He is bannerman,' said the loathsome Tajima. It seems the barbarian oaf, Pertinax, was unfamiliar with the discipline of our people."

"Discipline," I said, "is to be used with an end in view. It is not its own end."

"'It will be difficult to reach the country of Temmu,' said the witless boor, Tajima. 'It will take days. The patrols of Yamada abound.' I was pleased to hear this intelligence spoken. I was sure I would be soon returned to the safety of the palace. It was only necessary to continue to feign obedience and docility."

I had feared the rendezvous might not be met. The supper had lasted somewhat longer than anticipated. Still there would have been time. Then there had been the incidents of the reader, Tatsu, and the subsequent attack of the presumed assassin, whose charge of death had been disrupted in its progress by Pertinax. Still the projected schedule might have been satisfied, save for Tajima's concern to protect Sumomo from a fate of which she had no inkling, a concern apparently agreeable to, and accepted by, Pertinax. I admired the latter, that he would abet his fellow, at much personal hazard, in that desperate venture. Such delays took time, and, too, more time would have been used in the journey than had been originally anticipated, even beyond the margin of delay allowed for in the original plan, given the unanticipated presence of two women, one of whom, I gathered, had been carried for some time.

"Some twenty Ehn later," said Sumomo, "their fears of the departure of their fellow, to my relief, were confirmed, for the point of rendezvous had apparently been reached, a sheltered glade more than a hundred paces from the road. In the light of the moons, one could see the disturbance of the ground, where the talons of uneasy tarns had torn at the grass."

"'Ho, there!' cried a voice. 'Is there anyone there? Speak the signs, or die!' My heart leapt. This could be only a patrol of my father! The men crouched down, to one side, in the shrubbery, I dragged down with them. 'You will be silent,' said my detestable captor, the abominable Tajima. 'I have your word on this.' 'Of course, Tajima *san*,' I said, as though I might be according him some regard, awaiting my chance to cry out, but then a large hand was on the back of my neck, holding me, and I felt the blade of a knife on my throat. I was in the power of my captor's fellow, the oaf, Pertinax. 'That is not necessary,' said the despicable Tajima. 'You may be wrong,' said the oaf, Pertinax. I decided it would not be an opportune time to cry out. We listened to the patrol, passing within yards of us. Tears sprang to my eyes, but the knife was at my throat. I could feel its edge. It was a guard patrol, as we were within my father's domain. Too, someone had called for the speaking of a sign. Such patrols commonly consist of ten or twelve men, and an officer. The reconnaissance patrols, which may intrude into disputed territory, or enemy territory, commonly consist of two or three men, and an officer."

I nodded. It is easier, obviously, to conceal the movements of a smaller number of men, each trained in stealth.

"My heart sank," said she, "for the patrol had passed. The

fools! I might be lost, or held for ransom. I dared not contemplate that I might be consigned to an even more shameful fate.'"

"You might be quite fetching," I said, "collared."

"Beast!" she said.

"Continue, Lady," I said.

"'It is well past the Twentieth Ahn,' said bold, vile Tajima. 'We will leave the road and move north, while the night lasts. Then we must rest and conceal ourselves, until the darkness returns, and our journey may be resumed.' 'You will never see your base again,' I informed them."

"'Let us gag, strip, and bind her,' said the uncouth barbarian, Pertinax."

"I feared they might do this, for I was in their power. 'No,' said my captor. 'This is a free woman.' I straightened my body, proudly, and cast a look of seething contempt on the barbarian, but quickly turned away, and looked elsewhere, for I was suddenly afraid to meet his eyes. He was not looking upon me as though I was a free woman, but, I feared, as less."

"As a contract woman," I said.

"I feared," she said, "as less, as worlds less."

"As," I suggested, "one in whom one might see the most fascinating and desirable of female beasts, the female slave."

"'Lo!' cried the barbarian, Pertinax, pointing to the sky. We looked upward and, against the yellow moon, were seen three tarns, a lead tarn with mounted tarnsman, and two other tarns, riderless, but each on a long, looping lead. 'It is Ichiro!' said the barbarian."

"'We shall break him in rank, remove from him the honor of the banner,' exclaimed my captor. 'It was his to return to the encampment!'"

"'We are safe!' cried the barbarian. 'Let him have recourse to the ritual knife!' cried my captor. 'I propose a commendation,' said the barbarian. 'The ritual knife!' insisted my captor. 'Let us first return to the camp,' said the barbarian. 'But then the ritual knife would be inappropriate,' said my captor. 'It is hard to have everything, friend Tajima,' said the barbarian. I turned to hasten away, into the darkness, but the hand of the barbarian closed, like iron, on my upper right arm. I was held in place. In moments the tarns had alit not yards from us, and almost on the site of the rendezvous. 'Tal!' called the new arrival. 'Shameful!' cried my captor. 'Your orders!' 'Tal!' said the barbarian, cheerily. The slave, too, I think, was delighted. 'Your orders,' said my captor, 'were to wait until the Twentieth Ahn, and then depart, and return to the encampment!' 'Are you not pleased to see me?' asked the newcomer. 'We are!' asserted the barbarian. 'Noble Tajima, tarnsman *san*,' said the newcomer, 'do not be distressed. I obeyed my orders, and with perfection. I waited until the Twentieth Ahn and departed, but the orders did not specify that I might not return by my own route, which might be circular, nor did they tell me how quickly I was to return to our encampment, only that I was to return.' 'Mere caviling,' said Tajima. 'But surely well caviled, noble leader,' said Ichiro. 'Yes, excellently so,' the barbarian bespoke himself, though his comment was not solicited. 'Perhaps then,' said my captor, 'recourse to the ritual knife is not required.' 'I do not think so,' said the newcomer. 'Certainly not,' said the barbarian. 'Perhaps the orders were insufficiently clear,' said my captor. 'They were obviously obscure, egregiously so,' said the barbarian. 'Welcome then, and well met, friend Ichiro, honored bannerman of the cavalry,' said reprehensible Tajima. I suspected he was well enough pleased, if reluctant to be so."

"I think you are right," I said. I did not claim to find the Pani inscrutable, but it was difficult to deny that they were occasionally puzzling. The matter was doubtless cultural.

"'There is at least one patrol in the vicinity,' said he called Ichiro. 'I noted it on my approach.' 'One passed but recently,' said the barbarian. I shuddered, recalling the edge of the knife on my throat. 'Patrols may have seen you against the moon, as easily as did we,' said the barbarian. 'Let us mount,' said my hated captor. Already the barbarian was in the saddle, the lead on his tarn cut, freeing it for independent flight. To my uneasiness I observed the disposition of the slave. She lay before him, arched over the saddle apron on her back, bound, his. Her crossed ankles had been fastened to a ring to his right, and her crossed wrists to a ring to his left. She lifted her head to him, and he bent down, and, forcing her head back against the saddle apron, crushed her lips beneath his, with the master's kiss, that possessive kiss, wholly at his will, subjected to which the slave well understands his will is all, and she is owned. But, incredibly, she writhed on the leather, responsive, squirming, trying to lift her begging body to his touch. But he then straightened up, ignoring her, addressing himself to the reins. She whimpered, but dared not speak. 'Hurry,' urged he called Ichiro. I looked with dismay on the bound slave, stretched over the saddle apron, before the warrior. 'Do not fear, noble lady,' said my captor, sensing my uneasiness. 'You will be carried before me, in honor, in dignity, well secured with the safety strap, sheltered in the folds of the blanket.' 'Free me,' I said. 'No,' he said. 'I will bring a great ransom,' I said. 'I do not doubt but what your father would pay to have you back,' he said. I did not understand the tone in which he said this. Of course my father would be delighted at my return. I noted that my captor's fellow, asaddle, had already buckled his safety strap about his waist. Thus he could not immediately free himself. I most feared him, for he was a barbarian, untutored and unrefined, rude, uncouth, impatient, violent. I recalled his knife at my throat. 'Remain here,' said the hated Tajima, and he went to sever the lead on the tarn he would mount. All three tarns would now be free to fly separately, obedient to their rider. He then went to the side, to retrieve the second blanket, for my warmth. I backed away. I must run! Then, to my joy, I heard, from the direction of the road, the sounds of men. It was a patrol, perhaps the same which had been so close, that from which we had concealed ourselves. But now it bore two lanterns. I feared it would pass, without realizing our presence! I turned about and ran screaming toward the lanterns. 'Help!' I cried. 'Help! The foe is at hand! Enemies are here! Hurry! Hurry! Seize them! They have tarns! Do not let them escape!' We then heard 'Ho!,' an answering cry, and another, 'Stop! Stand as you are!' We heard, as well, rushing toward us, the shuffle of feet, a movement through brush, the sound of accouterments. Men rushed past me. 'I am Sumomo, daughter of the shogun!' I cried. 'Seize them!' I cried. 'Let not one escape!' I heard the clash of weapons, in the darkness. I heard a cry of pain, the snap of mighty wings, and dust carried even to where I stood, wavering, looking backward. One tarn was aflight, and then a second, and I heard the cry 'One-strap,' and saw a figure dangling from a saddle ring, clinging to it, the third tarn, as that bird, too, now amidst a casting of glaives and a flight of arrows, rose into the sky. I fear I lost consciousness. Later, my identity recognized, a hand cart was arranged for my eventual return to the palace, following my recovery from this dreadful ordeal, with a double escort, two patrols."

"I gather," I said, "that the three, Ichiro, Tajima, and Pertinax, escaped." Certainly I had waited long enough for this intelligence, which I supposed Sumomo had relished withholding from me, until the last moment.

"Unfortunately," said Sumomo. "One may, of course, hope that they were grievously wounded."

"I suspect," I said, "your father is not altogether displeased at this outcome. He has designs upon the tarn cavalry which might be imperiled, should such as Tajima and Pertinax be slain, or wounded. You may recall he honored them, and bestowed upon them golden chains."

"But I was abducted," she said, "his daughter!"

"He has many daughters," I said.

"Beast!" she said.

"It seems," I said, "you were sent here, to the garden, to assure me of the wellbeing of my friends."

"Yes," she said, angrily.

"You might have done so immediately," I said.

"I did not choose to do so," she said.

"You needed not have given your word to your captors," I said, "that word with respect to silence, obedience, and such."

"It was expedient to do so," she said. "It put them off their guard."

"Not Pertinax," I said.

"No," she said, "not Pertinax."

"You forswore your word," I said.

"Of course," she said. "Words are insubstantial, only puffs of air, about for a moment, and then vanished in the breeze."

"Your captors would have been wiser," I said, "to have stripped and gagged you, tied your hands behind your back, and then run you on the double leash to the rendezvous, adding to your speed, from time to time, if it were desired, with a stoke of a supple switch."

"Perhaps," she said.

"And then transporting you as though a slave to the holding of Temmu, to be dealt with there as a spy."

"But I am here," she said, "safe in my father's garden."

"Better you had been tied across the saddle, like the slave," I said.

"I do not understand," she said.

"What did you think of the slave?" I asked.

"Slaves are animals," she said.

"I gather she was responsive," I said.

"She was disgusting," she said, "helpless, and squirming, beside herself with need."

"In the belly of every woman," I said, "are slave fires."

"Not in mine," she said.

"It is only that they have not been lit," I said.

"You are a beast," she said.

"You have not yet been in a collar," I said.

"Apparently you cannot tell the difference between a free woman and a slave," she said.

"The free woman," I said, "is naught but a slave without her collar."

"I see," she said.

"One treats them differently, of course."

"Of course," she said.

"Tajima spoke to you in the garden," I said, "on the night of the supper."

"It was unpleasant," she said. "It was insulting. He was drunk. He babbled absurdities."

"Why do you think he risked much," I asked, "to carry you from the palace?"

"For ransom," she said.

"Scarcely," I said. "Why should he risk golden chains, and handsome prospective emoluments, not to speak of the wrath of the shogun?"

"For what then?" she asked.

"To protect you," I said, "to shield you from a prolonged, unpleasant death."

"You, too, are mad," she laughed.

"I have inquired," I said. "Such deaths may be prolonged over weeks."

"Such deaths," she said, "are inflicted only upon those with whom the shogun is muchly displeased."

"As might be the case," I said, "if one had failed him mightily, so much so as to have seriously imperiled his plans?"

"Such things," she said.

"Beware," I said.

"You think the abduction was not with a ransom in prospect?" she said.

"No," I said. "It was not with a ransom in prospect."

"Excellent," said she, smugly.

"How, excellent?" I asked.

"Permit me, kind guest," said she, "to enlighten you. The contemptible Tajima, a lowly warrior, of no fine family, has dared to aspire to the hand of a shogun's daughter."

"No," I said, "merely to afford the contract of one he believed to be a mere contract woman."

"I played that role well," she said.

"Excellently," I said.

"The interest of the despicable Tajima," she said, "was not unknown to me. Nor could it have been unknown to others! Was it not embarrassing? How often he dallied about, merely to catch a glimpse of me! It was amusing. I often joked with Hana about it."

"You," I said, "though a woman, and Pani, and supposedly a mere contract woman, did not trouble to conceal your contempt. Indeed, you frequently derided and mocked him, publicly. If you did not wish his attentions, why did you not simply avoid him, or ignore him? It was almost as though you wanted to intrude yourself into his thoughts and dreams. Were these things not provocative? What, rationally, might be the motivation of such hostility? I never understood the passion, the feelings, the hatred, which you evinced so freely."

"How desperately he wanted me," she laughed.

"Indeed, desperately," I said.

"I would impose my beauty upon him," she said, "to augment his suffering."

"Why?" I asked.

"It pleased me," she said.

"You regard yourself as beautiful," I said.

"Certainly," she said. "I am among the most beautiful of all women. Hundreds of men have lowered their heads before me, and languished in my presence, even daimyos, so consider the effrontery of a lowly warrior, one of no great family, who would dare to look boldly upon me!"

"He thought you a contract woman," I said.

"He should have realized I was too beautiful to be a contract woman," she said.

"But you played your role so excellently," I said.

"That is true," she said.

"And it is true you are very beautiful," I said.

"That is true," she said.

"I have seen many better," I said, "taken from a slave block."

"You speak boldly for a prisoner," she said.

"I take advantage of the privileges accorded a guest," I said.

"Do not presume too much," she said.

"Are Ashigaru about?" I asked.

"Of course," she said.

"Perhaps there is a way you might slip unnoticed from this garden," I said.

"There is no such way," she said.

"But if there were?" I said.

"I should report it to my father," she said.

"I see," I said.

"I do not understand you," she said.

"Flee," I said.

"Are you mad?" she said. "What is wrong?"

"I hear the gate of the garden," I said. "It is being opened. I suspect Ashigaru are coming for you."

"Certainly they are," she said. "And I will have them find and locate the guards past whom I was smuggled."

"They thought of slaves," I said, "and it would not have been unusual if one, in terror, knowing not to what fate she was being carried, had squirmed in her blanket."

"Their conduct was grievously negligent and wholly inexcusable," she said. "I will have them whipped, and whipped, again, to within a tenth of a hort of their life."

"Lady Sumomo," said the first Ashigaru, politely, "we have come for you." There were two others with him.

"I have been waiting," said Sumomo, unpleasantly.

"Forgive us, lady," said the first Ashigaru. "Has your commission in the garden been discharged?"

"Yes," she said.

This commission, I had gathered, was to inform me of the safety of my fellows, Tajima and Pertinax. Lord Yamada, who was thoughtful and sensitive, must have been aware of my likely concern in that regard, particularly if I might discover the return of Sumomo.

"Please place your wrists behind you, crossed, lady," said the Ashigaru.

"What?" she said.

Her wrists were pulled behind her by another Ashigaru, and, with a short length of binding fiber, fastened together.

"What are you doing?" exclaimed Sumomo.

"Do not interfere," said the first Ashigaru to me. I stepped back.

A leash then, by the third Ashigaru, was snapped about the neck of Sumomo.

"Release me!" cried Sumomo. "This is madness! This is unconscionable! Do you fools not know who I am?"

"You are Lady Sumomo, daughter of Lord Yamada, Shogun of the Islands."

"Release me, immediately!" she demanded. "This is some intolerable mistake, some preposterous misunderstanding, some insane joke!"

She struggled. She could not part her tethered wrists. The leather of the leash danced between its encircling collar and the closed fist of an Ashigaru.

"No, lady," said the first Ashigaru.

"My father will hear of this!" she said.

"It is on his orders that I act," said the man.

"I demand to see him!" she cried.

"He has other concerns," said the Ashigaru.

The leash grew taut.

"What have I done?" she begged.

"Displeased Lord Yamada, Shogun of the Islands," said the man.

"What have I done?" she begged, again.

"You were observed on the outer parapet of the holding of Temmu," I said, "casting a beribboned paper to someone below, apparently communicating with the enemy. Your role was revealed. The use of Daichi to influence Lord Temmu is thought at risk. You were to be cast from the parapet at a time corresponding to your casting of the note below, but you were extracted from the holding of Lord Temmu, by Tyrtaios, that you be spared this fate, though only, I fear, to endure one more to the liking of the shogun."

"He is my father!" she said.

"He has many daughters," I reminded her.

"What fate?" she cried.

"I do not know," I said.

"Please, Lady," said the first Ashigaru.

"Where are you taking me?" she said.

"To the chamber of the long death," he said.

"No!" she wept.

"Its nature has not yet been decided," said the Ashigaru. "I gather it is to be lengthy and exquisite, prolonged in such a manner as to satisfy the shogun. He is consulting with his physicians and advisors, his torturers and executioners."

Chapter Twenty-Two

What Occurred During Tea with the Shogun

"Great lord," I said to Lord Yamada, "I am come to beg the life of your daughter, Sumomo."

"Have tea," said Lord Yamada, gesturing to one of the four contract women in unobtrusive attendance.

"She is loyal to you," I said. "She served you well in the holding of Lord Temmu, at great personal hazard. She admires and respects you, as is appropriate for a dutiful daughter. Her mistake was small, a momentary lapse of caution. Spare her life."

Tea was placed before me on the surface of the table, with its intricate inlays of diverse woods.

"I ask this boldly," I said, "fearing to abuse the consideration with which you have treated me, as your guest."

"As you are my friend, Tarl Cabot, tarnsman," he said, "there is little I would not do for you."

"I ask only," I said, "that you spare the life of your daughter, Sumomo."

"Are you willing to pledge the cavalry to my service?" he asked, regarding me over the brim of the small cup of tea.

"Surely one might consider that," I said. "But one would have to consult with the cavalry, the officers and men."

"Your simple word would not be sufficient?" he asked.

"I would not have it be so," I said.

"But it would be," he said.

"I do not know," I said.

"I do," he said.

"Perhaps," I said.

He took a sip of the tea, and placed it down on the table.

"I am sure," he said, "you do not take me for a fool."

"Certainly not," I said.

"This matter of the cavalry," he said, "has been beset with difficulties and delays. Too much so, for too long. Had you been willing, matters would have been resolved long ago. You have been playing for time while I have knowingly allowed you to do so, exercising considerable patience and forbearance. As I read the situation, the cavalry is estranged from the house of Temmu, given its betrayal of its commander. It would be ready to ride for the house of Yamada; yet you hesitate to have it take to the sky on my behalf. I am not clear on your reluctance in this regard. I think it does not have to do with bargaining, with an effort to extract greater benefits of service."

"No," I said. "The generosity of Lord Yamada is not to be denied. It is not disputed. It is legendary in the islands."

"The other side of the matter," said he, quietly, "is that the disfavor of the House of Yamada is not to be lightly countenanced."

"That is well known, as well," I said.

"I suspect," he said, "that the most I may hope for is the neutrality of the cavalry."

"Given the neutrality of the cavalry, and the forces, and generalship, at your disposal," I said, "the war's outcome may be easily envisioned."

"In the meantime," he said, "I think there is little to fear from the cavalry while you are my guest."

"I am but one man," I said.

"But he is Tarl Cabot, tarnsman," he smiled.

"There is still the coveted holding of Lord Temmu," I said, "it would be difficult to reduce. By now it has doubtless been resupplied."

"It has been," said Lord Yamada.

"Final victory then," I said, "would not be soon at hand."

"Perhaps sooner than you suspect," said Lord Yamada.

"I do not understand," I said.

"Were I assured of the sessility of the cavalry, that it would not act," he said, "I believe things might proceed apace."

"As your guest," I said, "I am in no position to speak for the cavalry."

"It was once decimated," he said.

"It would be difficult to accomplish that end again," I said.

"Its location seems obscure," he said.

"To some," I said.

"I could send a thousand men into the mountains, to search," he said.

"The cavalry," I said, "might fly, and possibly south."

"Hundreds of raids, thousands of fires?" he said.

"Possibly," I said.

"Three tarns," he said, "were captured, during the decimation. Two tarnsmen, who purchased their lives by capitulation, wisely changed their banner."

"Doubtless," I said.

"These were sent recently north, to search for the tarn base."

"Were they successful?" I asked.

"They did not return," said Lord Yamada.

"Then," I said, "they were successful."

I was pleased to get this count on the tarns which had fallen into the hands of the enemy after the decimation. Two of the original three were no longer available to Lord Yamada. This suggested that the tarn of Tyrtaios was the third tarn. Adding in my tarn, secured during my removal from the holding of Temmu, Lord Yamada would have at his disposal only two tarns. I knew the location of neither.

"I do not think the cavalry will act while you are my guest," he said.

"I do not know," I said.

"Yet matters might proceed apace," he said.

"Your armies will march?" I said.

"Abetted," he said.

"How so?" I asked.

"Perhaps by some mighty and unforeseen ally," he said.

"I do not understand," I said.

"It is not necessary that you do so," he said.

"Surely my good will is of some value to you," I said.

"As mine to you," he smiled.

"I beg for the life of your daughter, Sumomo," I said.

"She is beautiful," he said, "but vain, and worthless."

"Spare her," I said.

"Do you want her?" he asked.

"I know one who does," I said.

"The young Pani tarnsman?" he said.

"Yes," I said.

"Surely you understand," he said, "that the justice of the house of Yamada cannot be gainsaid."

"I am your guest," I said.

"I shall mitigate her punishment," said Lord Yamada.

"I am grateful," I said.

"It shall not be the long death," he said, "but something public, something which will make clear to many, daimyos, warriors, Ashigaru, retainers, many, to all, the justice of the House of Yamada. She shall tread the narrow board of the high platform of execution, thence to plunge into the deep pool of death eels far below."

"She is your daughter!" I said.

"I have many daughters," he said. He then sipped his tea, and, a bit later, indicated to the nearest contract woman that his small cup might be refilled.

Chapter Twenty-Three

I Converse with Haruki

The Night Singers were abroad in the fields.

It was late morning.

"Your name is Haruki," I said.

"Yes, noble one," said the gardener, startled. He was standing, pinching off the tips of new branches on the Blue Climber, a vinelike plant with large blue bracts amongst its common leaves, and small yellow flowers, clinging to the railing of the small bridge in the shogun's garden. This minor pruning stimulates new branching.

"I would speak with you," I said.

"I am a gardener," he said. "I am unworthy."

"Recently," I said, "an attempt was made on the life of the shogun."

"I have heard so," he said.

"That is lamentable," I said.

"It is surely so," he said.

"You are skilled in reading weather," I said.

"One cares for the garden," he said.

"You can read rain," I said, "perhaps as much as four or five Ahn, even before the clouds gather."

"I garden," he said.

"It rained on the night of the attack on the shogun," I said.

"I recall it so," he said.

"The Night Singers, returned, were quiet," I said.

"It was the rain," he said.

"The attack took place in the dining pavilion," I said.

"I have heard so," he said.

"But from the garden," I said.

"That cannot be," said Haruki.

"I was there," I said.

"I do not see how it could be," said Haruki.

"On clear nights, in this time of year," I said, "it is my understanding that the garden is alive with the songs of the Night Singers, songs of demarcating territory, of courting, and nesting. It is also my understanding that when these lovely guests are wary, uncertain, apprehensive, or frightened, they do not sing."

"That is true, noble one," he said.

"Thus," I said, "on a clear night, their silence would betoken their concern, and their concern might be occasioned by something unanticipated or unfamiliar in the garden, for example, an animal, or intruder."

"It is true," said the gardener, "that their sudden silence might be so motivated."

"Their silence, then," I said, "could be construed, by those familiar with such things, guards, servitors, even slaves, as a clarion of alarm."

"It is true, noble one," said the gardener. "I have work to do."

"But on a night of rain," I said, "as their songs desist, their silence would be unlikely to motivate an investigation."

"One supposes not, noble one," he said.

"It is interesting," I said, "that the attack on the shogun should coincide with the rain."

"Perhaps it was intended to do so," said Haruki.

"It is conjectured," I said, "that the assailant entered the garden through the palace."

"It would seem so," he said, uneasily.

"But he did not do so," I said.

"How else could he reach the garden?" asked Haruki.

"The assailant," I said, "was armed, and clad darkly. Do you not think it improbable that he could have ventured through a dozen corridors and thresholds and not be noticed?"

"The stealth of such assailants is legendary," he said.

"Doubtless," I said.

"Then," said Haruki, "the garden having been entered earlier, from within the palace, the assailant conceals himself, and, like a sheathed knife, awaits his opportunity."

"Surely you do not believe that," I said.

"There is no other explanation, noble one," said Haruki.

"There is one," I said. "The garden, on a suitable night, was entered from the outside."

"That is not possible, noble one," said Haruki. "There is only one external gate, and it is guarded."

"The assailant did not enter through the gate," I said.

"Through the palace, earlier," said Haruki.

"You know every hort of this garden," I said.

"It is large," said Haruki.

"The garden was entered, from the outside," I said.

"It is not possible, noble one," said Haruki. "The walls are high, and patrolled. Their crests are armed with glass, with blades and shards."

"There is a secret entrance," I said.

"It cannot be," he said.

"I will show it to you, if you like," I said.

"I know of no such entrance," he said.

"Would you care to explain to the shogun that you were unaware of its existence?" I asked. "Perhaps he might believe you."

"No," he said.

"Do not touch the trowel at your belt," I said. "I have no desire to break an arm or neck."

He dropped his hand away from the trowel.

"The night of the attack was one of rain," I said. "Following the attack, I secured a lantern and scouted the garden's perimeter. It was easy, after a time, to mark footprints. Shortly thereafter I located the ring and trap, covered with branches and leaves, and the tunnel entrance."

"Will you now summon Ashigaru?" inquired Haruki.

"No," I said.

"I do not understand," said Haruki.

"Some days ago," I said, "the daimyo, Lord Akio, volunteering to demonstrate the effectiveness of a cast war fan, sought a target."

"Yes, noble one," said Haruki.

"He selected such a target," I said.

"I know," said Haruki.

"I dissuaded Lord Akio, and he, agreeably enough, if somewhat reluctantly, substituted a small tree."

"I know," said Haruki.

"As I understand it," I said, "your life is now mine."

"That is so, noble one," said Haruki.

"I herewith, in all honor," I said, "return it to you."

His eyes widened.

"I seek no debtor or servant," I said, "but a friend, an ally."

"I will reveal no others," said Haruki.

"Nor do I ask you to do so," I said. "But it is my belief that others exist, and we may find them helpful, in pursuing, to an extent, common aims."

"You are a guest of the shogun," said Haruki.

"More his prisoner," I said.

"You wish my help, in abetting an escape?" he said.

"Perhaps eventually," I said, "not now."

"I can be of little help, noble one," he said. "I am a lowly man, a peasant."

"You can come and go," I said. "Few will notice you."

"Your chances of escape are small," said Haruki, looking about. "Ashigaru are about. Men draw in from the fields. The shogun is massing troops, for an attack north."

"That is exactly the sort of help I need," I said. "Information."

"I know little, noble one," he said.

"I do not ask you to reveal others," I said. "But there must be others. In some way it must be possible to move messages about, perhaps even to a great distance."

"Perhaps even to the house of Temmu?" said Haruki.

"Yes," I said, "and if to the house of Temmu, perhaps others might transmit them farther thence."

"To the nest of the demon birds?" he asked.

"Yes," I said.

"The straw jacket is unpleasant," said Haruki.

"I am sure you have already risked that, whatever it is, and more," I said.

"Beneath the trap is a tunnel," he said. "It leads beyond the palace to the vicinity of auxiliary buildings, the dairy, the smoke house, store houses, some workshops, the pens. In the darkness, patrols might be eluded."

"If I wished to hazard that egress," I said, "I would already have done so. I want information and the means to convey it."

"I am lowly," he said, "a humble gardener."

"The most lowly and most humble," I said, "are often the most courageous."

"Surely not," he said.

"I think you are one such," I said.

"The garden needs tending," he said.

"How long have you served Lord Yamada?" I asked.

"Many years," he said.

"I think there is little about the palace you do not know," I said.

"I am an ignorant, simple man," he said.

"Tell me about an empty grave," I said.

"The child was ill-favored," he said, "short-legged, thick bodied, homely."

"But male," I said.

"Yes," he said.

"And thus," I said, "was to have been strangled, as Lord Yamada has it with his sons."

"So that none will rise to challenge him," said Haruki.

"It was you who saved him?" I said.

"Yes," he said.

"You risked much to save such a child," I said.

"There was once a beautiful young woman," he said, "of poor family, of lowly and ignoble birth, of the peasants. She came to the attention of Lord Yamada, who included her, for her beauty, amongst his wives."

"That," I said, "is how you came to the garden?"

"Yes," he said.

"You were her father?"

"Yes," he said.

"I take it," I said, "the male child, however ill-favored, was hers, and your grandson."

"It is so," he said.

"Still you risked much," I said.

"I gave him to others," he said. "He was taken beyond the wading fields. I do not know if he survived."

"It was years ago," I said.

"Many years," he said.

"The child may have died, long ago," I said.

"True," he said. "Life is hard."

"In the dining pavilion," I said, "there was talk of an avenger, one who might wear upon his left shoulder the sign of the lotus."

"There are always such rumors," said Haruki, "for years, meaningless rumors, rumors whispered in the darkness, rumors spoken about small fires while the rice boiled, the rumor of a spared son, a lost son, an escaped son, a returning son, one who would seek his father's blood, who would do vengeance on behalf of his slaughtered brothers."

"But the child bore on his left shoulder," I said, "the birthmark, the sign of the lotus."

"It is borne by many of the strangled sons," said Haruki. "It is borne by Lord Yamada himself."

"Such a sign, fraudulent, was borne by the assailant, he who would have set upon Lord Yamada in the dining pavilion."

"I should have killed the child," said Haruki.

"Why?" I said.

"It bears the blood of Yamada," he said.

"But it was the child of your daughter," I said.

"And so I spared it," he said.

"What of your daughter?" I said.

"She gave Lord Yamada daughters," he said, "but, as she was of lowly birth, these daughters were removed from her, and, when of age, contracted."

"She is now alive?" I said.

"No," he said.

"I am sorry," I said.

"She was very beautiful, more so than many of the other wives, and was a favorite. It is thought she was poisoned by higher-born wives. Lord Yamada chose ten of these by lot, and had them beheaded. Had she been of high birth he might have slain all."

"This was years ago," I said.

"Many years ago," he said.

"Sumomo," I said, "is high born."

"Extremely so," he said.

"Perhaps her mother?" I said.

"No," he said. "Her mother was not brought to the women's quarters until years later."

"You have heard of the projected fate of Sumomo," I said.

"It is merciful under the circumstances," he said. "The plunge to the pool of death eels."

"You would prefer something more grievous?" I said.

"Certainly," he said. "She is the daughter of the shogun."

"I am in need of information," I said, "and the means to convey it."

"I know little," he said.

"And you might find out much," I said.

"I am lowly," he said.

"Do not return to your work," I said.

"As the noble one will have it," he said.

"When do the generals of Lord Yamada march north?" I asked.

"Soon," he said. "The distant daimyos are being summoned."

"That information must reach the north," I said.

"There are many patrols," he said. "Runners might be noted. It is days to the holding of Lord Temmu, if that is the destination you have in mind."

"That first," I said.

"Even the path of the thousand arrows is impractical," he said.

"True," I said. The distances involved would exceed the utility of this device, which is often used to transmit messages between certain outposts or even between separated units, as in coordinating junctions or pincer movements. Obviously the expression, "path of a thousand arrows," is something of a metaphor, as there would seldom be a thousand arrows employed. The procedure, of course, is to relay a message by a number of flighted arrows, the message secured from one arrow, and affixed to the next, and so on. As the chain which is no stronger than its weakest length, this device, too, can be unreliable, as the succession of arrows might be interrupted in any number of ways. The arrows are often brightly colored, and even beribboned. And sometimes whistling arrows are used, much like those which convey signals, initiate attacks, and such. Under certain field conditions, naturally enough, one prefers stealth and silence.

"I see no way to do this," he said.

"Someone must have secured, trained, and positioned the assailant who failed in the attack on the shogun's life," I said.

"Perhaps," he said.

"It is clear," I said, "that Lord Yamada has agents in the camp of Lord Temmu."

"Possibly," said Haruki.

"Similarly," I said, "Lord Temmu, and his daimyos, Lords Nishida and Okimoto, are highly intelligent men. Accordingly, it seems likely they would have agents in the camp of Lord Yamada."

"Possibly," said Haruki.

"I can name one," I said.

"Perhaps," he said.

"And such agents," I said, "must have the means to communicate with their principals."

"Perhaps," he said.

"Expeditiously," I said.

"Once," he said.

"I do not understand," I said.

"The cot of the message vulos," he said, "was a day's trek from the palace. They could not be kept here, or in the vicinity, as suspicion would be aroused."

"That was wise," I said.

"But the cot was discovered, and seized," he said. "It was burned, and the message vulos and their keepers slain. I learned this from a peasant, come to sell a daughter, for her welfare, to a contract merchant."

"Then a messenger, afoot, must set out," I said.

"It will take time, it will be dangerous," he said.

"Nonetheless," I said.

"Who would you put in this jeopardy?" he inquired.

"I will hide in the tunnel, and leave after dark," I said.

"You will be missed before you depart," he said. "Ashigaru will be everywhere. You will be apprehended within the Ahn."

"It must be risked," I said.

"You are serious?" he asked.

"Surely," I said.

"Perhaps," said he, "you are not a spy for Lord Yamada."

"It seems to matter little," I said.

The gardener regarded me, intently.

"You try to look into my heart," I said.

"It is hard to look into a heart," he said.

"The homing bird," I said, "is good for a flight in only one direction, back to its native cot."

"Yes?" said Haruki.

"How are the message vulos of your destroyed cot replenished?"

"By hand-drawn cart," he said.

"This cart," I said, "will attempt a rendezvous with the local cot."

"There are only ashes now," said Haruki.

"That may not be known," I said.

"Unfortunately, noble one," he said, "as wise as your hope might be, that rendezvous was attempted, and failed, which intelligence I have also from the aforementioned peasant, a trap having been laid and sprung. The cartsman and the birds were apprehended."

"Wait!" I said. "I am a fool!"

"How so?" said Haruki, warily.

"Are you assured the message vulos of the secret cot were slain, as well as their keepers?"

"It is thought so," said Haruki.

"Perhaps some bloodied birds were found?" I said.

"That is my understanding," he said.

"Of course," I said.

"I do not understand," he said.

"Lord Yamada is clever," I said. "Would he not keep some birds, who would home to the holding of Temmu, that he might make use of them upon occasion, perhaps to mislead the forces of Temmu, say, putting them at their ease, while he plotted swift and devastating actions?"

"Surely there would be some sign enclosed with the messages, to certify them as genuine, to guarantee their authenticity," said Haruki.

"Doubtless," I said. Otherwise, given the possibilities of spies, birds could be brought from either holding, that of Temmu or that of Yamada, which might then, with false messages, be released to return to either holding. One supposes, of course, that the signs, like signs and countersigns, like passwords and keyed responses, would be regularly changed. "Do you know the sign?" I asked.

"No," he said.

"But the keepers would," I said.

"Of course," he said.

"Perhaps they did not all die quickly," I said.

"I see," he said. "But we do not know the sign."

"But if I am right," I said, "the birds will be at hand."

"In the cot of Lord Yamada," he said, "will be found the birds come from the holding of Lord Temmu, and those birds who are to be transported thence, to return later."

"And," I said, "the apprehended birds, those captured from the secret cot, which will home to the holding of Lord Temmu."

"If there are such," said Haruki.

"There will be," I said. "Is the cot guarded all twenty Ahn, how many keepers are there, how many guards? Might they not be called away, their attention diverted?"

"I shall make inquiries," he said. "But what of the sign?"

"I do not know the Pani script," I said. "I do not know the syllabary in which they transcribe Gorean. If I were to print in continental Gorean script, it would probably be enough. But I will write in another language, which two, I know, in the north, can read, a language which few, if any, in the dominions of Lord Yamada would be likely to know, even recognize. I will now to my room, obtain paper and a marking stick. The message will be ready shortly. You must show me the message cot of Lord Yamada."

"You are too much watched," said Haruki. "I will take the message."

"Can I trust you?" I asked.

"The noble one," he said, "has little choice."

"We are likely to do this successfully only once," I said. Indeed, it was not clear to me that it might be accomplished, even once.

"Inform the house of Temmu," he said, "of the readying of troops, the summoning of daimyos, warn that the word of Yamada is not to be trusted."

"I shall," I said, "and I shall also attempt to devise an arrangement for further communication, one swift but not dependent on caged vulos."

"Tarns?" he said.

"Of course," I said.

"You might also," said Haruki, "inform the house of Temmu of the projected fate of the beauteous Lady Sumomo. They should find that most agreeable."

"You hate all of the house of Yamada," I said.

"Of course," he said.

"But your grandson would be of that house," I said. "In him is the blood of Yamada, and it may be as dark, as narrow, as implacable, as fierce and cold, as his."

"I am troubled," said Haruki.

"But, too," I said, "in him would be your blood, and that of your daughter."

"It is difficult to choose a path," said Haruki.

"I shall convey the projected fate of the Lady Sumomo to the House of Temmu," I said.

"They should find it of interest," said Haruki.

"Perhaps others, too, might do so," I said. "When is she to make the acquaintance of the eels?"

"There are hundreds, half starved," said Haruki. "One can almost walk upon them."

"When?" I said.

"Soon," he said, "when the daimyos are gathered, that they, and others, may take notice, and be apprised of the dangers of displeasing the shogun."

"Lord Yamada has been patient," I said. "But I think he now despairs of enlisting the cavalry, but he needs no more than its neutrality, of which he feels assured."

"As long as you are his guest," said Haruki.

"Yes," I said, "as long as I am his guest."

"Perhaps, one day," he said, "the demon birds will fly."

"Perhaps," I said.

"You wish to summon demon birds?" he said.

"If necessary," I said.

"Do not do so," he said.

"Why?" I asked.

"On that day they will die," he said.

"How so?" I said.

"They will perish in the flames of the iron dragon," he said.

"There is no iron dragon," I said.
"Even Lord Yamada fears the iron dragon," he said.
"There is no iron dragon," I said.
"I have seen it," he said.

Chapter Twenty-Four

The Stadium

"I trust that you will not interfere," said Lord Yamada, pleasantly.

"Your Ashigaru will see to that," I said.

From where I was, in the stands, I could see both the platform of execution, far above and to my left, and the wide surface, some ten paces in width, of the deep, stone-encased pool of death eels. The stones of the pool's circular containing wall were cunningly fitted and bright with color, for the Pani have a finely developed aesthetic sense. The handle of a tool, a wooden hinge, a gatepost, the prow of a fisherman's humble craft, the threshold of a peasant's simple hut, may be models of carving. Even the roofings and walls of their fortresses, structures betokening the dark needs and sober exigencies of fearful times, are graceful, and companions to their background, not intruders. They are such as to be welcomed by the sky, the clouds, and mountains. Even the blades with which the Pani kill are beautiful. The water was still roiling for an attendant, but Ihn ago, had cast a bucket of scraps of raw tarsk into the water, not to feed the massed, swirling, snakelike fish but to excite them, to sharpen their hunger into a frenzy of anticipation.

"A pleasant day for an execution," commented Lord Akio.

"Indeed," said the shogun.

I supposed the day was pleasant enough, at least in itself, as it was neither too warm nor too cold, and the sky was a bright, unblemished, cloudless blue. Too, there was a slight, refreshing breeze.

How could it be then that it seemed I felt the balmy air concealed a veiled chill and the bright sky lied?

"One is surprised," said Lord Akio, "in the light of the prodigious nature of the offense, that the punishment of the criminal should be so mild."

"Lord Yamada is well known for lenience and mercy," said an officer.

"It is his only fault," said Lord Akio.

"It was primarily the petition of our guest, Tarl Cabot, tarnsman," said Lord Yamada, "which swayed me."

"Perhaps a guest presumes too much," said Lord Akio.

"I think I shall withdraw," I said.

"Please remain, dear friend," said Lord Yamada.

"One does not, of course, die in the pool immediately," said the officer.

"It can take a full Ehn," said another officer, "before the bones reach the bottom of the pool."

"It is preferable, is it not, to the straw jacket?" asked another.

"I see little to choose between them," said another.

"It is festival," said Lord Akio. "The straw jacket will be for others, later."

"How so?" I said.

"Peasants delinquent in taxes, thieves, deserters from villages, defamers, the disrespectful, perpetrators of incivility, those forgetful of rank, and such," said Lord Akio.

"I am reminded," said Lord Yamada. "I must seek a new gardener."

I must have started.

"What is wrong?" asked Lord Akio.

"Nothing," I said.

"Why, Lord," I asked the shogun, "do you need a new gardener?"

"As it is your habit, from time to time, to honor my humble garden with your presence, perhaps you know him."

"I know one named Haruki," I said.

"I know you do," said the shogun. "He has been with me for years. I shall miss him."

"I trust he is well," I said.

"Quite well," said the shogun.

"Why, then," I asked, "do you need a new gardener?"

"He is a thief," said the shogun. "He was apprehended in the cot of message carriers."

"What was he doing there?" I asked.

"Such birds, well prepared," said Lord Akio, "are a delicacy."

"He was hungry?" I said.

"More likely he intended to sell the bird to another," said Lord Akio.

"For food," I said.

"It would be of no use to him otherwise," said Lord Akio.

"Perhaps he was curious," I said.

"Curiosity," said Lord Akio, "is unacceptable in one of his rank."

"I have never been in such a cot," I said.

"You need only ask," said Lord Yamada.

"He loved the garden," I said. "It seems a pity to relieve him of his post for so small an indiscretion, particularly in the light of his experience, knowledge, and diligence."

Lord Akio smiled.

"He is a thief," said the nearer officer.

"He will wear the straw jacket," said another.

"When did this crime take place?" I asked.

"Days ago," said Lord Akio. "We are saving him, and others, for this evening, after dark, to line the avenue leading to the courtyard gate."

"There will be a feast in the outer courtyard," said an officer, "to celebrate the justice of the shogun."

"After dark?" I said.

"Illumination," said an officer.

"To light the way to the courtyard," said another.

"Still," said Lord Akio, thoughtfully, "the punishment of the Lady Sumomo seems light, compared to the gravity of the offense."

"I thought," said the shogun, "you aspired to the hand of the Lady Sumomo."

"Before I knew of her grievous iniquity," said Lord Akio. "But Lord Yamada has other daughters."

"Several," said Lord Yamada.

"May I withdraw?" I asked.

"Please remain, dear friend," said the shogun. "I am sure you will enjoy the spectacle, or, at least, find it amusing, or of some interest." He then turned to Lord Akio. "I am sensitive to your concern, beloved Akio," he said. "But one in power must weigh diverse quantities; it is with delicacy that scales are to be balanced; one must proportion right with prudence, truth with utility, appropriate desserts with judicious policy. First, I wished to please Tarl Cabot, tarnsman, as it seemed incumbent on the hospitality of my house to do so, but, too, second, the public execution of a miscreant is likely to have its independent value, as it should be a warning to, and be instructive to, any who might secretly harbor regrettable thoughts."

"Of course," said Lord Akio.

Several hundred were in the stands, mostly men of rank, high followers of Lord Yamada's ten daimyos, who had been summoned to the gathering, several with their warriors, Ashigaru, porters, and servants. In settled times, a given daimyo, in his turn, will commonly spend half of the year in the palace, subject to the scrutiny of the shogun, and the other half in his own dominion, supervising his lands and retainers. When I had come into the power of Lord Yamada, betrayed into his hands by Lord Temmu, however, Lord Akio was the only daimyo then in attendance at the palace. Some others, I gathered, who might have been in attendance, had been released to their lands to marshal resources and men in anticipation of an impending campaign, and then, there, in their lands, to await the summons of the shogun. As I may have mentioned, the failure of a daimyo to respond to the shogun's summons is considered an act of treason, putting at risk his own life and those of others associated with him, his family, his high officers, and his loyal warriors, and would customarily involve, as a matter of course, the confiscation of properties, and the seizure of lands. It might also be noted that while a daimyo is absent from the palace, it is often the case, though not always, that his wife and children will be guests of the shogun.

"A pleasant day, indeed," said Lord Akio, looking about. His raiment was splendid. His colorful fan, with its heavy, edged metal blades, rested across his knees.

"Indeed," agreed the shogun, once again, as pleasantly as before. There were also hundreds of Ashigaru about, though standing before the tiers of the stands. Most, I supposed, would be in the vicinity of their daimyos.

Narrow, rectangular banners, bearing the sign of Yamada, fluttered on the height of the stands. They would be visible from far off. They gave the scene a festive cast. I supposed that they would well mark the likely place of execution.

"The procession to the platform should begin soon," said an officer.

"Behold, it emerges from the courtyard gate," said one higher in the stands.

From where I sat, I could not see the courtyard gate. When I stood, I could do so.

"Can you see?" inquired Lord Yamada.

"Now," I said.

I gathered that it was inappropriate for high Pani, in such a situation, to evince curiosity or impatience, by rising to their feet, as might less couth individuals, anxious to satisfy their curiosity.

Hundreds, however, were doing so.

A group, indeed, had emerged from the gate.

It had turned toward the stands.

Beyond it I could see the broad avenue which led from the east toward the courtyard gate. It was lined, on both sides with what appeared to be cylindrical bundles of some sort.

Another path lay through flowers; it was this path, from the courtyard gate, which was being utilized by the recently emerged group, that now approaching the stands.

"I shall go," I said.

"Please remain," said Lord Yamada.

I could now hear the sound of small gongs, these carried by four solemnly treading, white-robed individuals with black, square headgear of a sort, fastened under their chins with black ribbon. Following these four men with the gongs were two lines of masked, glaive-bearing Ashigaru, each line consisting of five men.

"I cannot see the faces of the approaching Ashigaru," I said. "They are covered."

"Such do the dark work of the shogun," said Lord Akio. "It is best that their faces are not known to others."

"Thus," I said, "when one is about, in the field, the barracks, the *dojo*, or such, one might have at one's elbow, for all one knows, such a one, an executioner."

"The killers, of course," said Lord Akio, "are known to the shogun."

"Only to him?" I said. Indeed, how else could they receive their assignments and be set about their duties.

"And to one another," said Lord Akio.

"Of course," I said.

"They are not known to you?" I said.

"Of course not," he said. "But those who are loyal to the shogun need fear nothing."

"On the continent," I said, "there is the Caste of Assassins."

"Interesting," said the shogun.

"They do not conceal their faces," I said.

"But perhaps they conceal their caste," said the shogun.

"Sometimes," I said.

I could think of at least one individual I was sure was a member of that caste.

The four individuals striking the small gongs were walking abreast. The two lines of masked Ashigaru walked behind them, one line behind the fellow on the left, the other line behind the fellow on the right. Three other individuals were parties to this small procession, two more masked Ashigaru, each of which was behind one of the two center individuals, some steps back, of the four who sounded the small gongs, and a smaller figure, barefoot, and clad in simple white, who preceded them. Her long black hair had been unbound, and fell behind her. Her hands were behind her back, where I supposed them thonged, or braceleted. On her neck were two leashes, each in the keeping of one of the two Ashigaru who followed her.

"The wicked Sumomo!" cried a man.

"To the eels with her!" cried someone in the stands.

The small procession would enter the area of the stands from my right.

"The daimyos and high officers are looking forward to this evening's feast," said Lord Akio.

"It will be scarcely worthy of their attendance," said Lord Yamada.

"A hundred porters labored through the night," said Lord Akio.

"The day after tomorrow," said Lord Yamada, "the drums and horns of war will sound."

"The roads will be filled with Ashigaru," said a man.

"For pasangs," said another.

"Perhaps, great lord," I said to Lord Yamada, "such a march might be premature. What if the cavalry should intervene, on behalf of the house of Temmu?"

"Two golden chains," he said, "may perhaps purchase its quiescence."

"Those were freely bestowed," I said, "and not the fruit of contracting, or bargaining. They impose no obligation on the two distinguished officers to whom they were graciously allotted."

"I think their weight will be felt, dear friend," said the shogun. "Gifts give pause. Who will betray the good will of a benefactor? It will doubtless, at least, slow the responses of junior officers, disengaged from, and uncertain as to, the will of their commander."

"Perhaps not," I said.

"You are not in touch with them," he said. "The chain of command is broken. A link is missing. Vacillation will reign. Decision will dangle in the wind. What junior officer will assume the responsibility for ordering war?"

"I can think of two," I said.

"At present," said Lord Yamada, "I am better aware of what transpires in the camp of the demon birds than many in the camp itself."

"Your spies," I said.

"Dutiful informants," he said. "Much animus burns in the camp of the demon birds. The House of Temmu betrayed their commander. A pebble in the scale could put the cavalry aflight in my interest."

"Surely not," I said.

"I fear so," he said. "And, in the meantime, I trust you will continue to enjoy my hospitality."

"As you hold me, you hold the cavalry?" I said.

"Is it not so?" he asked.

"I trust not," I said.

"If the cavalry does not fly for Yamada," he said, "it will not fly at all."

"But perhaps it will fly for you, great lord," said Lord Akio.

"Surely that is a possibility," I said.

"I judge it remote, dear friend," said Lord Yamada.

"By now," I said, "the holding of Temmu will have been resupplied, its reservoirs replenished, its trails narrowed, its walls strengthened."

"I have the means with which to reduce it," said Lord Yamada.

"A siege might last years," I said.

"There is always a means of last resort," said Lord Yamada.

"I do not understand," I said.

There was one last ringing of the gongs.

"Behold," said an officer. "The Lady Sumomo!"

Chapter Twenty-Five

What Occurred in the Stadium

I looked down, and to my right, at the opening between the two sides of the stands.

"Has she been drugged?" I asked.

"Certainly not," said Lord Akio, snapping his fan open and shut.

"Surely, in the mercy of the shogun," I said, "she has been administered an anodyne, a numbing salve, something to deaden pain?"

"No," said Lord Akio.

"But the eels!" I said.

"It is important," said Lord Akio, "that her punishment be mete, that she will feel excruciating pain however inadequate and incommensurate it may be, compared to what her guilt deserves."

"At least it will be brief," I said.

"Thanks largely, I gather," he said, "to you."

"She has not been drugged, dear friend," said Lord Yamada. "But she is, I take it, stiff, uncertain, numb with fear."

I saw the two leashes removed.

"It is as though she were scarcely conscious," I said.

"One blots out things," he said. "It is like the mind closing its eyes. But she will soon realize what is occurring. They all do, sooner or later."

"She is being taken to the edge of the pool," said a man.

Sumomo, bound, an Ashigaru holding to each arm, ascended the three wide steps encircling the pool.

She looked down, into the pool.

She stood still for a moment, as though not comprehending, and then, suddenly, she uttered a long, weird, terrified scream, and began to struggle in the grip of the two Ashigaru.

"Now she understands," said Lord Yamada.

Sumomo turned toward her father, sobbing, crying out for mercy.

Lord Yamada, with a gesture, indicated that she was to be taken to the height of the platform of execution.

"She is not proud and strong," said a man.

"She is a woman," said another.

"A girl," said another.

"I have seen warriors, on scrutinizing the pool, collapse, sob, and cry out for mercy," said another.

"She has fainted," said a man.

"She is weak," said Lord Yamada. "I had thought she would be strong. It is little wonder she failed me."

"She is a dutiful daughter," I said. "She did her best to serve you."

"She failed," said Lord Yamada.

"Perhaps a sudden blow, while she is unconscious, the stroke of a glaive," I said.

"The crowd has come to see the feeding of the eels," said Lord Yamada.

"You are shogun," I said. "Stop this!"

"The crowd is eager," he said.

"Stop it!" I said.

"It would be dangerous," he said. "There are limits even to the power of the shogun."

"You could stop it," I said.

"And appear a fool?" he said.

"Stop it!" I said.

"I do not wish to do so," he said.

"She is your daughter," I said.

"I have others," he said, "many others."

"I cannot understand you," I said.

"I am shogun," he said.

"Yes," I said, "you are shogun."

"You will be expected at the feast tonight," said Lord Yamada.

The height of the platform was quite high. It was reached by broad and winding steps. Sumomo's bound, unconscious body was held between the two Ashigaru, these abreast, ascending the steps, each with a bound arm in his keeping.

They ascended slowly.

I was sure it would take better than two Ehn, perhaps three, to reach the height of the platform.

The sky, as noted earlier, was a bright blue. The day was neither too warm nor too cold. A slight breeze ruffled the banners set at the height of the stands. They could be seen from a great distance.

Haruki, as I understood it, some days ago, had been apprehended in, or in the vicinity of, the cot where attendants of Lord Yamada housed his small, swift-flighted, messengers. I did not doubt but what some might have come from as far away as the holding of Lord Temmu.

Haruki, I gathered, had attempted to reach the cot, where he would attempt to attach my tiny message, in English, to the leg of one of the vulos captured by Yamada's men from the surprised and seized secret cot, remote from the palace, which vulos would doubtless, for identificatory purposes, be independently caged. He was then to release the bird, and trust that it would home to the message cot of the holding of Temmu. Lord Temmu would then attempt to find an informant capable of understanding the message. And I could conceive of only two, to my knowledge, who would be able to do so, Tajima and Pertinax.

But Haruki had failed.

I should have gone myself, watched or not, and fought to enter the cot and put the bird on its way.

The two Ashigaru, bearing the bound, unconscious Sumomo between them, were nearly to the summit of the platform.

"She will have to be revived," said Lord Akio, concerned, looking up, toward the platform.

"She will be," said Lord Yamada, "abruptly, rudely, the astringent vial held to her nostrils. It is most unpleasant. She will then be held to look down to the pool, far below, while the denizens of the pool, with a stimulatory feeding are aroused and stirred."

"Excellent," said Lord Akio.

"It will then be time to affix the blindfold and place the board," said Lord Yamada.

"It is like the joke at sea, common amongst marauders and corsairs," said one of the officers to another, "where one amusingly disposes of unwanted prisoners."

I had heard of this, on more than one world, and in more than one region of more than one world.

Following the coming onto Port Kar of a Home Stone, the Council of Captains had forbade this practice to its captains. There were, of course, other ports, even outlaw ports harboring the "sleen of the sea," renegade captains, "free corsairs," independent marauders, and such. Much of Thassa lay outside the laws of Brundisium, the range of the mercantile ports, the waters of Port Kar.

The Ashigaru had now reached the summit of the platform, and had placed the inert body of Sumomo on its surface.

"No," said Lord Yamada, "please remain."

I returned to my seat.

I had heard that Haruki, with several others, was to wear the straw jacket. I knew that an unpleasant death of some sort was connected with this practice, but only now, recalling some casual remarks heard earlier, having to do with festivity and illumination, and recalling a glimpse of unusual objects, like cylindrical bundles, lining both sides of the avenue to the main gate of the palace, did the full import of the matter strike me. I was familiar, of course, with the bulky, coarse raincoats of straw commonly worn by the peasants in inclement weather. Surely I had seen dozens of them. I now understood these allusions. From time to time, in one region or another, I supposed hundreds might have shared this fate. Peace and order are often purchased by the torch and glaive.

"Sumomo is revived," said Lord Akio.

I could see that Sumomo, supported by the two Ashigaru, had been brought to the forward edge of the platform, where she might look down to the pool below. At the same time, an attendant, below, as earlier, cast some scraps of tarsk into the water. The crowd reacted, as the water seemed to bubble and explode with a frenzy of activity. Ashigaru near the low, circular retaining wall of the pool drew back, to escape sheets of water, smote about by the violent thrashing of long serpentine bodies.

"The blindfold is being affixed," said a fellow nearby.

"It seems inappropriate to blindfold free women," I said. Slaves, on the other hand, were often blindfolded, hooded, gagged, bound, chained, and such, for they are slaves. Such things make clear to the slave her helplessness, her vulnerability, her unimportance and meaninglessness, her utter dependence on the free. Let her know she is nothing, let her know she is owned.

"It is part of the game, of the amusement," said Lord Yamada. "The criminal is uncertain as to the length of the board, perhaps even its width. Bound, he is urged ahead, even prodded with glaives should he be reluctant. Hort by hort he moves. He tries to feel his way. Will there be a next, uncertain, fearful step, or has the board ended? Perhaps his balance is in jeopardy, and he might not even prolong his life to the end of that narrow, wooden, fateful path, might not even reach the end of the board, and how long is the board, he does not know, and how many steps remain, he does not know, and so on."

"It is torture," I said.

"Exquisitely so," said Lord Akio.

Sumomo stood, unsteadily, at the height of the platform. She was now blindfolded. She wore a gown of simple white, which fell to her ankles. I surmised it was her single garment. At least it guaranteed her modesty. She was not stripped, as might be a slave. She was barefoot, however, as might have been a slave. Doubtless she had never been barefoot in public before. Her hair was unbound. Her wrists were fastened behind her. She was a beautiful female, the sort which, disrobed and displayed, is imminently suitable for the perusal of men, men intent upon acquiring a source of inordinate pleasure.

"Please remain where you are," said Lord Yamada.

There were two of the masked Ashigaru on the platform with Sumomo. The other ten, who had advanced in two lines of five each, from the courtyard gate, were near the bottom of the high, winding stairwell leading to the height of the platform. All attention seemed focused on the platform, even that of the attendant who had served to agitate the restless denizens of the

271

pool. Indeed, the waters of the pool still stirred, and more than once I saw the glistening back of an eel break the surface, and then snap away with a spattering of water.

The banners of Yamada fluttered at the height of the small stadium.

Haruki had failed.

Tonight there was to be festival.

The crowd was very quiet, eyes on the platform.

The two Ashigaru on the platform began to move a long board out, away from the platform, extending it over the pool. The board was long. It was narrow. They moved it out a bit, then drew it back, and then moved it further out, and did this a number of times. So still was the crowd, and so splendid were the acoustics within this cuplike enclosure, that one could, even below, where we waited, mark the scraping of the board on the platform. I then understood why the board had not been directly emplaced. It had been moved in such a way that the criminal, blindfolded, would be unclear as to how much of the board extended over the pool. It might be as little as six or so feet, perhaps eight feet, perhaps as much as ten. As I had expected, however, it was well extended from the platform. In this way, I supposed it would take longer for the criminal to reach its terminus, and this, presumably, would increase the suspense and the entertainment of the crowd. Only the criminal himself, in his uncertainty, would be unaware of the length of the narrow, unstable, precarious, bending, wavering trail allotted for his journey.

At least, I thought, it would not take long. Also, it was not necessary that I watch.

"She begins to traverse the board," said a fellow near us.

It seemed I could not help but watch.

I heard an intake of breath in the crowd.

Sumomo had moved a bit out, onto the board. The two Ashigaru spoke to her, abruptly, derisively. How dared they do this? She was not a slave, who must endure whatever abuse free persons choose to visit upon her. Did they not know that she was a free woman, even the daughter of the shogun? They snarled and urged her forward, and brandished their glaives, impatiently, which movements could not be seen by the criminal, but were doubtless sensed. Then a blade prodded her in the back, sharply, rudely, and she half stumbled ahead, helpless, and blind within the folds of the cloth thrice encircling her eyes.

"She is falling!" said a man.

"No!" said another.

"She will not reach the end of the board," said a fellow.

"She does not even know where the end is," laughed another.

Sumomo wavered on the board. She struggled to retain her balance.

"Walk! Move!" called a man from the crowd.

"Hurry! Do not dally!" called another.

"Get on with it!" cried a man.

"Strike her from the board!" cried a fellow up to the Ashigaru on the platform.

"No, no!" cried a fellow. "She must walk! She must walk!"

"Instruct her!" cried a fellow to the Ashigaru on the platform.

Sumomo cried out, piteously, as a glaive thrust at her back, and she staggered another foot or two out on the board, her head turning, looking wildly, blindly, about. I did not doubt but what her garment, in the back, had been rent. The prodding had not been gentle.

She was not a slave! Let her be accorded the dignity due to a free woman! Might a fellow not be slain for such an impertinence on the continent?

"Proceed," ordered one of the Ashigaru on the platform.

"Move, move!" called the other.

Frightened, uncertainly, Sumomo moved a bit further on the board. She had traversed only some third of the board's length, but, for all she knew, her next step could be her last. Surely she must sense that she was already over the pool, its surface so far below, now rippling, stirred by the agitation of twisting, hungry bodies.

"Walk! Continue!" called a fellow up from the crowd.

I heard bets being taken, as to whether or not the end of the board would be reached.

I suspected the eels well anticipated, by now, perhaps from the past, perhaps from a variety of cues, sounds, movements, and reflections, if not from the two token feedings earlier administered, designed to do little more than sharpen the

ravenous blades of hunger, that food was in the offing. I suspected
they had been starved for days, to ready them for this moment.
Similarly, it is not unusual for trainers and keepers in Ar and
Turia to withhold food from arena animals, that the torments
of hunger might be sorely exacerbated, so cruelly heightened
that the released animal will forgo the caution and probity of its
ways in the wild to indiscriminately rush upon and attack, and
attempt to feed upon, whatever falls within its desperate ken.

Sumomo moved but half a step further on the board, which
now bent slightly under her.

She teetered in place, too terrified to move.

"Mercy!" she cried. "Mercy!"

"It seems she is frightened," said Lord Akio to the shogun.

"I fear so," said the shogun.

"But it is well known she is delicate, and sensitive, as a flower,"
said Lord Akio, possibly attempting to mitigate his former
observation, lest the shogun be displeased.

"She is weak," said the shogun.

"Clearly," agreed Lord Akio.

"She risked her life in your service, in the citadel of your
hereditary enemy," I said.

"She thought herself secure," he said. "She thought it no more
than an amusing adventure."

"She did not anticipate her discovery," I said.

"Sometimes things do not turn out as one expects," said the
shogun.

"Spare her," I said.

"My plans were jeopardized," said the shogun.

"Pity her," I said.

"I am shogun," he said.

"Did you not think she was haughty, and arrogant?" asked
Lord Akio of me.

"That can be taken from a woman," I said.

"How?" asked Lord Akio.

"By the collar, and the whip," I said.

"Do not leave," said the shogun.

"Proceed," said one of the two Ashigaru on the platform to
the distraught criminal on the narrow wooden path, "lest the
shogun become impatient."

Sumomo was then twice jabbed in the back, to urge her forward.

"Will you live one Ihn or several?" inquired one of the Ashigaru on the platform. "Dally, and you will be struck from the board."

"No!" cried more than one man in the crowd. I suspected they had wagered on the matter, that the end of the board would be reached.

The other Ashigaru was looking down, toward us, presumably waiting to see if a small movement by the shogun, a nod, a lifted hand, a dismissive gesture, would signal that the criminal would be dislodged, to plunge to the pool below. To be sure, it was unlikely the shogun would do this, as it might too soon bring the business to its conclusion, prematurely terminating the tension, anticipation, and suspense which, one gathers, add much to the pleasures of the spectacle. In any event, the shogun remained attentive, but quiescent.

The second Ashigaru then, glaive in hand, returned his attention to the plight of the criminal.

"Move," he told her.

Sumomo, half bent over, with great care, bound, blindfolded, barefoot, hort by hort, feeling ahead of her with each step, bit by bit, moved toward the end of the board. I supposed the board was rough to her bare feet. Those feet, I supposed, soft, smooth, and delicate, prior to her journey to the stadium, had encountered no surface harsher or more rugged than the floor of a bath or the polished, lacquered boards of a lady's chamber. As she was moving, so carefully, so tentatively, so slowly, I was sure she would be able to detect the end of the board, when reached, wherever it might be. Then, as the crowd cried out, one foot was half off the width of the board. The board bent. Her body was unsteady. I feared she would tumble to the side, falling to the pool. "Fall!" cried a fellow. It was not difficult to suppose the nature of the wager he had made. Then, as the crowd cried out, she righted herself. "No," said the fellow, dismally, he who had called out. Yet, surely, his wager was not yet lost. I could almost sense Sumomo trembling, and trying to breathe, teetering on the narrow, unstable support which held her from the pool far below, that bending, narrow, unsteady bridge lacking a farther shore. She wavered. She had no clear sense of where she was. She had apparently moved too close to the edge of the board. I supposed, assuming she had been psychologically capable of registering such things, even in a state of presumed terror and stress, she would have had a sense of the board's width before her blindfolding. Similarly, she might be reasonably assured that the Ashigaru on the platform would have made certain that her precarious journey would be well begun. On the other hand, it is extremely unlikely that one, bound, and blindfolded, in traversing such a board, foot by foot, could keep to an undeviating, centered, linear path.

"Move!" ordered the first Ashigaru on the platform.

She moved a hort forward.

"Straighten your body!" he said.

"Move," said the second Ashigaru.

"How long is the board?" asked the first. "Are you near its end? Perhaps, perhaps not. Are there two steps remaining, are there five? Move. Do not fear. You will know when you reach the end of the board. It is easy to tell. You will step into nothing! Then you will fall, and, after a time, bathe with your friends below. Have no fear! They will welcome you! Let us not keep them waiting. Move! Move!"

Sumomo was now at the end of the board.

I decided not to watch.

"Move!" said the first Ashigaru.

"Now!" said the second.

I looked away, up, at the blue sky, the white clouds. On the high walls, encircling the stands, fluttered the narrow, rectangular banners of Lord Yamada, marked with the strange script, vertically aligned, of the Pani syllabary in which, though I could not read the script, were transcribed the phonemes of intelligible Gorean. The same phonemes, obviously, can be transcribed by means of an indefinite number of scripts. I recalled the flowing, lovely script of the Tahari, in which the phonemes of Gorean were also meticulously transcribed. The banners were a brave sight.

I supposed the day was pleasant enough, as Lord Akio had suggested; it was neither too warm nor too cold, and the sky was a bright, an unblemished, cloudless blue. Too, as noted, there was a slight, refreshing breeze.

But wait, the sky, I noted, was not unblemished. There was, high above, a dot, something moving.

"Ho!" I cried. I rose to my feet, looking upward. I pointed. "Beware!" I cried. "Do not move!" I cried to Sumomo. "Do not move!"

"Move!" cried one of the Ashigaru on the platform to Sumomo.

"Do not move!" I cried.

Beside me, Lord Akio, the shogun, and nearby officers, rose up, ignoring what might be the compromise to their dignity, following my gaze.

"It is an assassin!" cried Lord Akio, snapping open his war fan to shield the shogun.

"No!" I said. "It is a tarnsman, out for sport, out for chain luck!"

The shogun, angrily, thrust aside the war fan.

"What is chain luck?" inquired Lord Akio.

"See!" cried an officer. "It is diving!"

The bird was not diving, not from the ambush of the sun, as it might strike the unsuspecting tabuk, commonly breaking its back, but, wings spread was engaged in a soaring descent.

It was approaching rapidly.

The tarn is very beautiful in flight. It is little wonder that men will risk their lives to join such fellows in the sky.

Many in the crowd, now, were aware of the disturbance, the impending arrival of an uninvited guest. I did not doubt but what the brave, displayed, fluttering banners of Lord Yamada had well proclaimed the venue of the afternoon's fearful proceedings.

"Summon Tyrtaios!" called the shogun. "He must be in the saddle within Ehn!"

Haruki, I thought, wildly, had not failed! The tiny message, fastened to the left foot of the vulo, held in its flight against its belly, half hidden in its plumage, days ago, had made its way to the cot in the holding of Temmu!

Suddenly the vast shadow of the mighty bird darkened the stands, and put in flickering, tumultuous shade the disquiet waters of the wide pool, for the tarnsman had pulled the bird up short, and, wings beating, holding its place, the bird shuddered, and hovered but yards below the high board.

"Jump, slave!" screamed Tajima.

Surely he knew she was not a slave!

Crying out in confusion, and misery, Sumomo, obedient, bound and blindfolded, leaped from the board's edge into nothing, and plummeted downward, the skirt of her sheetlike garment torn high about her thighs, and was caught in the arms of Tajima, who threw her on her belly to the saddle apron and wheeled the tarn to the right, and upward, and, as two glaives, hurled from the platform, passed him, one below, and one to the left, spun the bird about and streaked from the stadium.

Consternation reigned below.

"Tyrtaios to the saddle!" cried the shogun.

Tajima, I noted, had addressed the hapless criminal as "slave," had addressed her by this lowest and most degraded of appellations, so utterly and keenly meaningful to a woman, and it was under this demeaning designation that she had unhesitantly responded, obedient to his command.

I smiled to myself.

She had obeyed under the designation, "slave." She had obeyed as immediately and unquestioningly as a new purchase, entered into the domicile of her master.

Did she realize what she had done?

Did she even know, in her helplessness, who had issued the command? Surely it could not be the loathed Tajima, for whom she entertained only contempt.

I watched the tarn climb and depart, and, soon, it was little more than a dot in the sky.

Many were now crowding out of the stadium.

Sumomo, I now realized, though I was not surprised, had lovely legs. This had been clear enough in her leap downward, in which the light garment in which she had been placed, lifted, had billowed about her, trailing her leaping body. Too, when Tajima had put her to her belly, flinging her to the saddle apron before him, holding her in place with his left hand, while grasping the tarn reins in his right hand, he had apparently given little thought to the modesty due to a shogun's daughter. So high on her thighs was the disarranged garment that she might have been a scarcely clad slave, briefly tunicked, taken from a high bridge, awaiting her turning to her back.

Yes, I thought, Sumomo might bring a good price off a slave block.

"What is chain luck?" asked Lord Akio.

"That," I said, pointing to the sky, and the departing tarn, now scarcely visible, with its rider and prisoner.

"I do not understand," said Lord Akio.

"One of the first missions of a young tarnsman," I said, "is to capture a young woman from an enemy city, one with an alien Home Stone. She is taken home and collared. At his victory feast she dances, and serves him, he first, of all present. She then serves others, as his slave. That night, chained to her master's couch, she is taught her collar. She may thereafter be kept as a personal slave, or given away, or sold. It is up to her master."

"It is done thus on the continent?" asked Lord Akio.

"Such things are not unprecedented," I said.

"This is not the continent," said Lord Akio.

"Tajima," I said, "is familiar with the ways of the continent."

"Sumomo," he said, "is a free woman."

"But what if she should be collared?" I said.

"Unthinkable," he said.

"But, if so?" I said.

"Then she is worthless," he said, "only a slave."

"Precisely," I said.

I considered the bared legs of Sumomo. By now, I suspected she was on her back, stretched over the saddle apron, buckled in place, wrists and ankles.

"Most regrettable," said Lord Akio.

"Many do not find it so," I said.

"I do not understand," he said.

"It is nothing," I said.

On the continent, free women, in public, particularly those of the upper castes, are muchly concealed. There are the robes of concealment, the veils, the gloves, the slippers, and such. If a free woman had been as much exposed as Sumomo, she might, in her humiliation, repudiate her compromised, outraged freedom, and seek the collar, regarding herself as now worthy of no more. In the high cities, free women are not permitted in paga taverns. If one is found within the precincts, she is often stripped and put out, into the street. Then, commonly, she begs to be admitted once more, then to know the iron and be fastened in the collar. It is difficult to know about women. Why do some undertake perilous journeys, wander outside guarded walls, frequent lonely streets in poor districts, insult strangers, as though it might be done with impunity, walk the high bridges unescorted in the moonlight, and such? This is sometimes spoken of as "courting the collar." It is almost as though they wished to find themselves at the feet of a master.

There were few left now in the stands.

I was uneasy that Tajima had taken the tarn so high into the sky, and flown north.

Surely those of Lord Yamada, Tyrtaios, and, I thought, one other, for he had two tarns at his disposal, might soon be aflight. Those birds would be rested. Tajima's tarn might have been aflight for an Ahn or more, I did not know, and it was carrying two.

I would have kept the tarn low, for that reduces sightings, and would not have struck out directly north, which suggests a narrow route which might be swiftly determined and followed. It would have been better, I supposed, to go a different direction, and then another, and another, and then, possibly, approach the holding of Temmu, or the tarn encampment, if one wished, from the east, west, or even north. This considerably enlarges the territory which would have to be considered by pursuers, and there would be aflight, at least as far as I knew, at most two.

How soon, I wondered, might Tyrtaios, and perhaps another, be asaddle. Surely Tajima must have considered the possibility of pursuit. I feared he would be an unlikely match for the dangerously skilled Tyrtaios, who, I was confident, was of the black caste, trained in tenacity and guile. The entitlements appertaining to the black dagger are not bestowed lightly. One earns one's position in the black ranks by slaying one's competitors.

I must move swiftly.

The masked Ashigaru, Lord Yamada's secret death squad, the ten who had been waiting at the foot of the platform, and the two who had taken Sumomo to its perilous height, had now departed the stadium.

I must move swiftly, indeed.

Haruki had risked much for me.

As I left the stadium I noted, to my dismay, the departure of two tarns, northward.

There was little I could do.

Chapter Twenty-Six

What Occurred Outside the Stadium

"Do not gainsay me," I said, angrily, to the guard on the road, that leading to the palace. "Have you not heard? The daughter of the shogun was carried away. Tonight there is no festival."

"I have no authority to release the prisoners," said the guard.

"I am the authority," I said, severely. "I bring the command of the shogun. Release them from the posts and straw jackets, rope them together and I shall conduct them to the designated pen."

"Who are you?" inquired the guard.

"Is that not clear from my habiliments?" I said, impatiently.

"Those of the secret executioners of the shogun," said the guard, uncertainly.

"Do you wish me to remove my mask?" I asked.

"You are not to be known," he said.

I reached to the mask, as though to tear it from my head.

"No! No, noble warrior!" he said.

My hand was tight on the mask, angrily so.

"It would be my head, were I to see your face," he said.

"Precisely," I said.

"The prisoners will be released and bound," he said.

"And deliver them into my keeping," I said.

"What pen is designated?" he asked.

"Are you curious?" I asked.

"No!" he said. "No, noble one!"

He summoned other guardsmen to assist him. There were twenty prisoners, bound to posts, each heavily enwrapped in a bulky straw jacket, the sort worn by peasants in foul weather. Now, of course, each jacket was dry, tinder dry.

"It is disappointing," said the guard.

"Doubtless," I said.

"We had hoped for a splendid feast," he said.

"It was planned," I said.

"Fortunately," said the guard, "we had not yet added colored resins and chromatic oils."

"Yes," I said, "most fortunate."

I gathered that these additions to the jacket, surely superfluous in a prosaic, routine execution, were connected with the celebratory nature of the intended feast, presumably resulting in more colorful, fiercer, longer lasting flames.

Soon the twenty were well bound, and roped together, relieved of the thick straw jackets, which remained by the posts.

The guard surveyed the coffle of prisoners.

"We can burn them later," he said, "when the occasion is happier, and more auspicious."

"Perhaps," I said.

"Perhaps then, too," he said, "we might add the tarnsman and Sumomo to the festivities."

"Perhaps," I said.

"How many men do you wish to accompany you?" he asked.

"None," I said.

"Surely some," he said.

"The location of the designated pen," I said, "is not to be revealed."

"I understand," he said.

This is not unusual, that prisoners will be held in undisclosed locations. There are two major reasons for this. First, it is intended to complicate, if not frustrate, attempts to communicate with prisoners, attempts to rescue them, and such. Second, it is thought to instill fear in the general populace. Who knows where the prisoners have been taken, how long they will be held, and what is being done with them in these unknown locations? By such means an authority may see to a population's alarm, lack of ease, and intimidation.

"And," I said, annoyed, lifting the glaive, "do you fear that I, a wearer of the mask, and he chosen to convey the command of the shogun, am incapable of managing a small herd of twenty tarsks, helpless and tied together?"

"No, noble one," he said.

"Thus," I said, "you keep your head."

"The noble one is gracious," he said.

I did not wish to talk further with the guard, and I waved him, and his fellows, away. The Ashigaru from whom I had borrowed the robes and mask was in a nearby shed, bound and gagged. I had not broken his neck. I assumed he would, after a bit, regain consciousness. Sooner or later, of course, he would be missed, and a search would be mounted.

I addressed myself to the bound prisoners.

"Follow me!" I said. I then turned about and made my way toward several of the ancillary buildings in the vicinity of the palace. I did not even look behind me. I knew they would follow me, in line. Pani of the peasant classes tend to be polite, stolid, resigned, and reconciled, at least until a breaking point is reached, at which time they may become as secretive and clever as the urt, as subtle as the ost, as dangerous as the cornered sleen, as fierce as the enraged larl, discovering the claiming stains of a competitor in his territory.

Once we were out of sight, I would introduce myself to Haruki. He would know where it was, it was somewhere here about, here, outside the palace grounds, the concealed entry to the secret tunnel which led to the garden. With some fortune we might conceal ourselves in the tunnel until dark, after which it would be every man for himself. Surely I thought that I had long enough prevailed on the hospitality of the shogun, and might now, with good grace, take my leave.

Chapter Twenty-Seven

We Have Departed from the Tunnel

"Wade," said Haruki. "There will be no tracks."

Hundreds of paddies, like ridged, geometrical lakes, now reflecting the orbs of the moons, dotted the landscape for pasangs about the lands of Lord Yamada. This is also the case about the holdings of many daimyos, and, of course, about local villages, most of which were subject to one daimyo or another.

The only weapon I bore was a dagger, a *tanto*, relieved from the fellow I had dealt with following my exit from the stadium. As he had not been a warrior, he had not carried the two swords. I had discarded the glaive for it was large, and impossible to carry in a concealed manner. I supposed it would have been speculated that it might have been retained. If so, its presence might have been noted, provoking an investigation. The glaive combines the features of the stabbing spear and ax. It can take a man's head off, but, in the thick of battle, shoulder to shoulder with one's fellows, one would seldom have the opportunity to employ it with such an end in view. It is used more to stab and slash. It may be thrown but in battle this is seldom done. Certainly it lacks the lightness and fleetness of the javelin and the weighty penetration of the typical Gorean war spear, familiar on the continent. It can function, rather as the heavy staff, though bladed, both defensively and offensively. Rather, too, as the pike and halberd, it may be used both to break an enemy's ranks and, when necessary, to keep him at bay. If the Pani had access to the lofty kaiila I would not doubt that the glaive would be designed additionally, like the halberd, with its hook, to dismount a rider, putting him at the mercy of the dagger. On the continent, street contingents, raised in times of need to supplement a city's standing troops, commonly make do with knives, clubs, sharpened poles, and stones. Some cities maintain semi-military units, skirmishers, light bowmen, and slingers. Slingers may use stones or metal pellets. These are more dangerous than many understand, particularly at a short distance, and in great numbers, when a sheet of missiles in their thousands can strike foes as might a deadly hail. Certainly one of these hornet-like projectiles, almost invisible in flight, can blind a man, break a head, and cut him open. Tuchuks, incidentally, commonly do not close with the enemy, certainly not in masses, but depend on the bow and the cast quiva, or saddle knife. Whereas shield and lance may be used for fencing with an isolated foe, commonly another Tuchuk, they are most often used for riding down isolated enemies who are afoot. In battle, if troops are massed, the kaiila can be penned in, and immobilized, this rendering it susceptible to a common form of attack, being stabbed from beneath in the belly, by a crouching, lunging foe, following which the animal becomes unmanageable, is likely to throw the rider, and may eventually bleed to death. As mentioned, Tuchuks seldom close with their foe. It is not necessary. In this sense, in their way, they resemble the caste of peasants, masters of the great bow.

It had been dark in the tunnel.

There was no candle, no lamp. In such as place even the sleen would be blind.

I had conjectured it was in the vicinity of the Twentieth Ahn. The nineteen prisoners who had been sentenced to the straw jacket with Haruki had slipped, one by one, from the tunnel.

"Are you still there?" I asked Haruki.

"Yes, noble one," he said, from, I judged, a few feet away.

"The others have gone, have they not?" I said.

"One by one," he said.

"I heard no cries, no warnings, no clash of arms," I said.

"They are of the countryside," he said. "They are indistinguishable from many others. Few concern themselves with such men. They move silently. They will avoid the searching torches."

"They will return to their villages?" I said.

"They will be accepted in others," he said.

"Though strangers?" I said.

"There is fear and dissatisfaction in the fields," he said. "He of one village in such times may not be a stranger to those in another village."

In Gorean, as in several languages, the same word is used for "enemy" and "stranger."

"It seems there might be retaliation on a fugitive's village," I said.

"It is possible," said Haruki, "were the village known, and the fugitive considered dangerous. But it is not customary to punish the innocent for the crimes of the guilty. Such a practice is not likely to elevate respect for the law."

"I see," I said. To me that seemed a wise view. I was pleased to learn that this degree of enlightenment, or what I took to be a degree of enlightenment, prevailed in the islands.

"Too," said Haruki, "villages are sources of wealth. One cannot tax bleached bones and ashes. Few will cast gold into the sea."

"True," I said.

"And it is possible that murdering many for the crimes of one, or a few," said Haruki, "might occasion resentment."

"That is conceivable," I said.

"One might even, over years, dig a tunnel," he said, "which might open into a garden."

"Quite possibly," I granted him.

"We are no match for gentlemen of two swords," he said.

"I would suppose not," I said.

"But even they," he said, "must sometimes sleep."

"But with a sword at their side," I said. That would be the companion sword.

"That must be taken into consideration," he said.

"You are locally known," I said. "Why have you not left the tunnel?"

"Those who have departed," he said, "did so individually. It is easier to conceal one man than two, or three. If one man is apprehended, that is preferable to the apprehension of two or three."

"Why have you not left?" I asked.

"Soon," he said, "those who departed will be little noted. They will be Pani amongst Pani, shadows amongst shadows."

"Why have you not left?" I asked.

"You are not Pani," he said. "If nothing else, your garb, and accent, would betray you."

"I accept that risk," I said. "Leave, while there are still Ahn to daylight."

"We will leave together," he said.

"No," I said.

"You will need a guide, someone to introduce you into villages, someone to speak for you," he said.

"I will be a handicap," I said.

"Are you prepared to leave?" he inquired.

"Two are more likely to be apprehended than one," I said.

"We will go now," he said. "I think the interval has been sufficient."

"Go," I said to him.

"Follow me," he said.

In the total darkness, touching the sides of the small tunnel, in which one could not stand upright, I followed Haruki.

Then we were at its far terminus, that which emerged in brush, not far from several of the smaller, ancillary buildings.

"I have one regret," said Haruki.

"What is that?" I asked.

"I shall miss the garden," he said.

We must, by now, be two or three Ahn from the palace grounds.

I would have preferred, in our projected escape, to have forced my way into one of the slave pens, one with which I was familiar. There would be, I had conjectured, two slaves there of interest, one to me, and the other, I suspected, in spite of what he might claim, to a friend of mine. Haruki, however, with an earnestness which seemed incongruous with his normal composure, had forbade this venture and I, however reluctantly, had acknowledged the wisdom of his counsel. First, the pens were guarded and locked shut. Second, there were several in the pens and the likelihood of removing an occupant or two without some sort of outcry or contretemps was unlikely. Thirdly, the slaves in which I was interested might not be in the same pen as before. The contents of that pen might have been rather special, being white-skinned slaves obtained for rice in the north, during the siege of the holding of Lord Temmu. Tajima, I recalled, had been annoyed at the lack of Pani slaves held behind those stout wooden bars. Presumably they had been gathered together and displayed for us with the supper of Lord Yamada in mind, white slaves who might be of interest to white masters. By now they might have been scattered about, transferred to any number of pens throughout the domain of Lord Yamada, where their labors might now be applied to the arrangement and care of the liquid meadows from which the shogun hoped to obtain his rice. Indeed, several might have been distributed amongst the shogun's daimyos, for diverse purposes, field slaves, slaves to a daimyo's wives, personal pleasure slaves to warriors, to officers, and even to the daimyo himself. And I recalled that Saru might even, for all I knew, be shackled at night in the palace itself. And, additionally, of course, adding a pair of slaves, and white-skinned slaves at that, would be unlikely to augur well for the success of our flight.

"Besides," had said Haruki, "the march begins at dawn, and coffles might accompany the march."

"Is that possible?" I said.

"Certainly," he said.

I supposed that was possible. After all, there would be camp grounds to be cleared, fuel to be gathered, water to be carried, food to be cooked, clothes to be laundered, and troops to be entertained, and in the way of the slave, kissing, caressing, dancing, mat service, and such. And woe to the slave who does not do well on the mat. A free woman may disdain such things, or fail in them, even miserably, but a slave is to be pleasing, fully pleasing, and in the way of the slave. She is owned. She is a slave.

I considered the position of the moons, reflected in the water of the paddy, about my ankles.

"We are moving west," I said.

"If all goes well," he said, "in a day or two, we may circle about, and make our way north. We will travel largely at night. We will sometimes rest in selected villages, known to me, where we will be sheltered. When I deem the way is safe, some days from now, you may continue on, to the holding of Temmu or, if you prefer, to the nest of the demon birds."

"You will not accompany me?" I said.

"There is no place for me in the holding of the hated Temmu," he said, "nor in the aerie of demon birds."

"I had thought," I said, "that by now, for pasangs about, the countryside would have been scoured by hunters, intent on man quarry."

"Much was done last night," he said, "with torches."

We had evaded search parties four times earlier, though each time in the vicinity of the palace.

"Do not forget the campaign begins at dawn," he said. "Men must be marshaled. Daimyos have gathered. The drums and horns must sound. At such a time one does not commit hundreds of men, perhaps a thousand or more, to a search for a handful of peasants."

"I see," I said.

"We are not of great interest to Lord Yamada," he said.

"I might be," I said.

"True," said Haruki.

"He might prefer to have me returned to the hospitality of his holding," I said.

"He is unlikely to postpone the march of thousands of men for such a purpose," said Haruki.

I supposed this was the case, given the exigencies of logistics.

"He is not certain of the cavalry," I said.

"The noble one forgets," said Haruki, "that the cavalry is likely to suppose you are still in the palace."

"True," I said.

"Accordingly," he said, "Lord Yamada, has little to fear, at least at present, from the intervention of the cavalry."

"But later?" I said.

"Perhaps not then, either," he said.

"I do not understand," I said.

"It is a thought I have," he said.

"I must return, as soon as possible," I said.

"It will take you days to reach the north," said Haruki.

"Yes," I said, angrily. To move directly north, of course, would considerably increase the risks of discovery. I feared that Tajima, in his flight, had made that mistake.

"I trust that the noble one, who is now to the west, and far from the road north, does not intend to shorten his journey by hastening east and joining Lord Yamada's march."

"Lord Yamada," I said, angrily, "will have a start of days."

"The noble one is correct," observed Haruki.

"I would that I had a tarn," I said.

"That would be helpful," said Haruki.

How the pasangs slipped away, beneath those mighty, beating wings!

"I looked about, I inquired," I said. "I knew there must be two tarns, somewhere. Now I know they must have been housed close to the palace."

"Why do you say that?" asked Haruki, wading ahead of me.

"When in the stadium the tarnsman made away with Sumomo, Lord Yamada issued orders that Tyrtaios, his servitor, was to be asaddle within Ehn, in pursuit. Indeed, on the palace road, Ehn later, I saw two tarns aflight, northward. Thus, the tarns must have been on the palace grounds, perhaps housed in the palace itself."

"It is my understanding that such birds occasionally utter a loud, shrill cry," said Haruki.

"Yes," I said.

"You were in the palace, and on the palace grounds, for days," said Haruki. "Did you hear such a cry?"

"No," I said.

"Then," said Haruki, "it is likely some means of communication linked the palace with a more distant point."

"There are the laws of Priest-Kings," I said. "Such devices are prohibited."

"You have in mind secret, forbidden devices?" asked Haruki.

"Yes," I said.

"I know little of Priest-Kings, or their laws, or thoughts," said Haruki, "or that there are Priest-Kings, or that they think, but there are many ways to communicate quickly, to transmit even complex messages, explaining situations, issuing instructions, indicating directions, and such. In daylight, flags may be used, and mirrors, and at night, the movements of double torches, or the light of a single lantern, revealed, and shielded, alternately."

"Yes," I said, dismally, resigned, "yes." How quick I had been to suppose illegal deceit and even perilous, surreptitious dishonesty, a betrayal of principles and understandings, a departure from implicit rules without which a game, even a mighty game on which might depend worlds, would be forsworn and treacherously subverted! But I recalled, too, that I had seen tracks on a rainy afternoon in the palace, and had sensed in a corridor the odor of wet fur, a particular scent, one I had never forgotten, one I had hitherto encountered, at various times and places, the scent of Kur.

"I am puzzled," said Haruki.

"In what way?" I asked.

"Why do you think Lord Yamada has initiated this campaign?" asked Haruki. "Why has he acted now?"

"He believes the cavalry immobilized," I said.

"I think there is a darker reason," he said.

"I do not understand," I said.

"Lord Yamada is an extremely intelligent man, but also one of infinite caution."

"It is my understanding," I said, "that he arranges matters with care, and leaves little to chance."

"I am a humble one, of limited understanding," he said.

"Speak," I said.

"I think," he said, "something may have changed."

"It is 'your thought'?" I said.

"Yes," he said. "Why does he march now? Why does he risk the intervention of the cavalry?"

"So, why?" I asked.

"I think," he said, "Lord Yamada may have received assurances. How else can we explain what he is doing, given the ruination the cavalry might visit upon his troops and holdings."

"'Assurances'?" I said.

"He is doubtless wary of the cavalry," he said, "but I do not think he now holds it to be the same dreaded, decisive unknown, on which the fate of islands might depend."

"How so?" I said.

"It is growing light," said Haruki. "We must seek shelter."

Chapter Twenty-Eight

In a Yamada Village We Await Nightfall

I sat cross-legged in the small hut, across from Haruki, fingering millet into my mouth. The village was one of several, most avoided, west of the road north.

It was the third day following our departure from the tunnel.

"Perhaps we will be betrayed," I said to Haruki, looking about.

"I do not think so," said Haruki.

"But this village is clearly subject to Lord Yamada, is it not?" I asked. I had seen the sign of Yamada, recognized from his banners, carved into the two gate posts.

"Yes," said Haruki. "Indeed, it is one of his prime villages, one of his largest, and most prosperous villages."

"But you have sought shelter here," I said.

"Here, I suspect," he said, "our presence might be the least suspected."

"I fear betrayal," I said.

"It is here, in such a village," said Haruki, "where the burdens of the shogun are most sorely felt, that we are least likely to be betrayed."

"I see," I said.

"We occupy, and but briefly," he said, "a small shed on the outskirts, as some others, not even within the palings. Officially the elders have no understanding that we are here."

"It will soon be dark, and we must move, again," I said.

"Does the noble one like his new clothing?"

"I have seldom been as grateful for the gift of a few rags," I said.

"It is such things that peasants wear," he said.

"I am pleased," I said.

"When about," he said, "have recourse to the hood, keep your head down, walk bent over, perhaps you have been injured, be humble, be timid, do not meet the eyes of others, be Pani, be peasant, let me speak for us."

"I fear I am poorly disguised," I said.

"Be of good heart," he said. "We trek alone, and, amongst others, keep much to ourselves. Farther north, where we are unlikely to be sought, such precautions will not be necessary. Here, I think no more than a few marked your difference, your strangeness. Most do not even know we are here."

"I am still uneasy," I said.

"I know you have been troubled," he said.

"I fear for a friend," I said, "who is young and inexperienced."

"The tarnsman?" he said.

"Yes," I said. "He is Tajima, an officer in the cavalry. With daring, and sustaining great risk, he fled with Sumomo, the shogun's daughter, rescuing her but a moment before she would have plunged into the pool of death eels."

"What is your concern?" asked Haruki.

"He fled directly north," I said, "and so high that he might have been noted over a wide area. His line would be an easy one to mark and follow. His tarn would have been aflight before reaching the stadium, perhaps for Ahn. It may have been weary, perhaps nearly spent. It would be burdened. It would carry two. Pursuit, on fresh tarns, was soon mounted."

"I see your concern," said Haruki. "Please come with me."

"Where are we going?" I asked.

"To a nearby hut," he said.

Chapter Twenty-Nine

We Will Depart from a Yamada Village

I swung open the small, rickety, slatted gate of the hut, awry on its wooden hinges, and peered within.

"It is hard to see," I said.

"There," said Haruki, "at the back of the hut, in the corner."

"Yes!" I said.

A small figure sat there, her back against the wall, in a simple white garment, her legs drawn up. She was barefoot. Her ankles were close together, for they had been crossed, and bound. Her hands were behind her, where I surmised they, too, had been crossed, and bound. Her hair was undone, and behind her. About the upper part of her head, thrice wrapped, was a blindfold.

"Who is there?" she pleaded, softly, stirring, moving her head as though she would peer through the thick layers of cloth which swathed the upper portions of her face.

"Be silent," said Haruki, "lest you be gagged."

I gathered the female was to be permitted to speak only when it pleased her captors.

"It is Sumomo!" I whispered.

"Perhaps, as of now," said Haruki.

"'As of now'?" I said.

"Yes," he said.

"How is she here?" I asked.

"By capture acquisition," said Tajima, from the threshold. He carried, in one hand, a small lamp, a bit of tallow, with a wick, in a shallow bowl. In the other hand, he carried a small sack.

I felt flooded with relief and joy and were he another, and the time and place different, might have rushed upon him, to seize him in my arms, but I remained where I was, acknowledging his polite bow.

But I think he may have been as pleased as I.

"I recognized him, outside," said Haruki.

This made sense to me, as Haruki might well remember him from the palace of Yamada, on the fateful afternoon and evening of the supper.

"How are you here?" I asked. "I feared you overtaken, slain or captured, two tarns, rested and fresh, in pursuit."

"It seemed obvious that a pursuit would be mounted," said Tajima. "Accordingly, I would, for a time, set a simple course, high and level, north, one easy to anticipate and follow, and then take the tarn down to reduce sightings and veer westward. Unfortunately, given the surprising promptness of the pursuit, which I had not anticipated, a matter of little more than a few Ehn, this stratagem failed of its intended effect. I could soon detect two far behind me but growing closer. So it continued for better than an Ahn. I could not lose them. The outcome of this matter, I feared, was clear. Shortly thereafter I took my mount into the cover of clouds, within which I would be briefly concealed, shifted my course, descended, landed, and freed the bird, which then, rising, would presumably seek its cot in the north."

"You were then dismounted," I observed.

"No more than you," said Tajima.

"Perhaps the tarn would be again spotted and followed," I said.

"That was my hope," said Tajima, "that it would be again noted by the pursuers who might follow it, being led further and further from our position."

It would be hard, from a distance, for a time, to ascertain that the bird was unmounted.

"The tarn, unburdened," I said, "might have eventually reached the cot."

"We shall hope so," said Tajima, "its seeking fellows each

bearing, presumably, a male of full weight, saddles, various accouterments, and such."

"I think you were fortunate," I said.

"I think so," he said.

"How is it you are here?" I asked

"One supposes for the same reason that you are here," said Tajima, "the need for shelter and food, for concealment, the desire for a refuge unlikely to be suspected, one not fond of the exactions of the shogun."

"I had thought," I said, "you had planned to fly directly north and at a height more suitable for reconnaissance than stealth."

"That would have been quite unwise," said Tajima.

"Clearly," I said. "I am sorry."

"Be not so," said Tajima. "You train your tarnsmen well. If there is a fault here, it is mine, for I too much gambled on surprise and seriously underestimated the alacrity with which a pursuit could be brought aflight."

"I would not have anticipated it, either," I said.

I recalled how dismayed I had been when, en route to the palace road, to free Haruki and his fellows, if possible, I had seen the two tarns streaking northward, and one mounted doubtless by dangerous and pertinacious Tyrtaios, who, I feared, possessed the subtlety, training, and weaponry of the darkest of castes. I knew the black dagger was not easily attained; it is won in but one way, the ascent, as it is said, of the nine steps of blood. In many cities the caste is outlawed, but there are those, in such cities or elsewhere, who will pay for its services.

Tajima lifted the tiny lamp and surveyed the prisoner.

She lifted her head. Probably she sensed the light through the blindfold.

"I trust," I said, "you have freed her limbs occasionally." It was not as though she was braceleted, or chained.

"Yes," said Tajima. "But I have left the blindfold in place."

"You are thinking of removing it now?" I said.

"Soon," he said.

The prisoner started. She was frightened.

"There is a lamp," said Tajima, addressing himself to the prisoner. "Do not look directly upon it until your eyes have accustomed themselves to the light."

The lamp, of course, was quite dim, and barely illuminated the single room of this hut, or shed. On the other hand, it would doubtless be painful if directly looked upon by one who had long been the prisoner of a blindfold.

Tajima placed the small source of illumination on a shelf to the side. He then put down the sack he had brought into the hut on the floor, near the sitting prisoner. I heard it touch the floor. It contained, whatever its other contents might be, some metal.

"Do you know, captive," he asked, "whose captive you are?"

"No," she whispered, frightened.

"I think you do," he said.

"No!" she sobbed.

"Surely you know my voice," he said.

"Let it not be he!" she pleaded. "Let it not be he!"

"You looked well," he said, "turned, bound belly up, well extended, nicely stretched over the saddle apron of a tarn."

"Tarsk!" she said.

"A pleasant thing to see a female bound so," he said.

"Tarsk!" she said.

"As a slave," he said.

"Tarsk, tarsk!" she hissed.

"I am going to kneel you," he said.

"I am a free woman!" she said. "I do not kneel before men!"

Tajima reached down and lifted her beneath the arms, and placed her on her knees before us.

"Remain as you are," he cautioned her.

Obviously she was furious at this humiliation, but she remained on her knees. How different she was from the impassioned, eager, tender, vulnerable loving slave who wants so much to be on her knees, and knows she belongs there, before her beloved master.

"Are you a free woman?" inquired Tajima.

"Certainly!" she said.

"She is barefoot, and has but a single garment," said Haruki. "And the garment is rent, and soiled."

"Twice," said Tajima, "tarnsmen returned, circling about, at a great height, and we must conceal ourselves, once in the reeds and mud near a small stream, once in leaves and brush."

"She needs a bath," said Haruki. Pani, even of the peasants, are likely to be particular about such things.

"Tarsk!" she hissed.

"You are sure you are a free woman?" asked Tajima.

"Yes!" she said.

"When I commanded you from the board, over the pool," said Tajima, "I addressed you as 'slave', and under that designation you obeyed."

"That is sufficient," I said. "In that act she pronounced herself slave."

A free woman can freely pronounce herself a slave, of course, but this is her last act as a free woman. Her freedom is then gone. She is then only another slave, another vendible beast and property.

"I responded so to save my life!" she said.

"That matters not in the least," I said.

"I do not know why I did that!" she cried.

"But it was done," I said.

"I do not know why I did it!" she said.

"We do," said Tajima.

"Why?" she said.

"Because," he said, "you are a slave."

"No!" she said.

"Do you wish to be returned to the board, to swim with the eels?" he asked.

"No, no!" she wept.

"Now, of course," he said, "as you are a slave, you would be not only bound and blindfolded on the board, but stripped, as well."

"I hate you all!" she cried.

"Beware," said Haruki, "a slave is to be obedient, respectful, deferent, and pleasing."

"Wholly pleasing," I said.

"I am not a slave!" she said. "Free me! Remove the blindfold!"

"Are you hungry?" asked Tajima.

"Yes," she said. "I am hungry. I am terribly hungry!"

"Are you prepared to beg for food?" he asked.

"Tarsk!" she cried.

"I suspect," said Tajima, "she is now as hungry as a slave."

"As other slaves," I said.

I recalled the pathetic hunger of Cecily, Jane, and Saru at the supper of Lord Yamada. Indeed, as I recalled, Saru had not been fed at the supper. Hopefully, she had been given something later, either in the pen, or before her shackling in the palace. Perhaps, on the other hand, she must wait until the following day.

"I am not a slave!" she said. "Feed me!"

"She seems insufficiently deferent," I said.

"As I recall, from the supper," said Tajima to the prisoner, "you believe slaves should be whipped."

"I am not a slave," she said.

"But, if you were," said Tajima, "what then?"

"If I were a slave," said Sumomo, "I would, of course, be subject to the whip, as any other slave."

"I think you are a slave," said Tajima.

"No," she said.

"Do you have a name?" asked Tajima.

"Yes," she said, "Sumomo, free woman, daughter of Lord Yamada, Shogun of the Islands!"

"Slaves," I said, "do not have names, unless it pleases masters to give them one."

"I am not a slave," she said.

"But you are hungry?" said Tajima.

"Yes!" she said.

"Are you prepared to beg for food?" he asked.

"If necessary," she said.

"You may do so," he said.

"I beg food," she said.

"Properly," he said.

"Please!" she said.

"Properly," he said.

"I beg food," she said, pathetically.

"'I beg food,' what?" he asked.

"No!" she said.

"'I beg food,' what?" he said.

"I beg food," she whispered, "—*Master*."

"You heard?" inquired Tajima.

"Of course," I said, "the slave has begged food. It is not

unusual for a slave to beg food, particular if she has not been fed recently."

"And in so begging," said Tajima, "the woman proclaims herself a slave, and makes herself a slave, does she not?"

"Yes, if she is not already a slave," I said.

"And in so begging," said Tajima, "the slave acknowledges herself a slave, does she not?"

"Yes," I said. A slave's food, of course, as her clothing, and such, is at the discretion of her master. Indeed, some masters require small rituals at feeding times. "I beg food, Master," "Please feed me, Master," "Your slave would be fed, Master," "Please, Master, feed your slave," and such. Certainly, in such ways the girl is reminded that she is a slave.

He then cupped some millet, not rice, in his hand, and fed the slave.

"She eats like a ravenous slave," said Haruki.

"She is a ravenous slave," said Tajima.

"Please, more," she said. "Please more—Master."

"That is enough," said Tajima. "We must be careful of your figure."

An angry noise escaped the captive.

"She is slight, but seems exquisite," I said. "I speculate she would look well on the block."

"It is now dark," said Haruki. "We must soon leave. I trust you will accompany us, noble Tajima."

"Of course," said Tajima.

"We cannot take this woman with us, as she is," I said.

"Certainly not," said Tajima. "I am prepared." He then reached to the prisoner's blindfold. I gathered she had worn it since it had been affixed by an Ashigaru, high on the platform by the eel pool. "Do not look directly at the lamp," said Tajima, again warning the prisoner.

"Who are you?" she said, suddenly.

"Surely you suspect," he said. "Surely you know. Surely you can recognize my voice."

"You tarsk," she cried. "You tarsk!"

She struggled in the cords.

"I hate you," she said. "I hate you!"

The blindfold, slowly, carefully, unwrapped, was drawn from her head.

She regarded her captor, indeed, her master.

"Yes," he said, "it is my bonds you wear."

"I hate you," she wept.

"You are the property of Tajima, officer in the tarn cavalry, liaison to the forces of Lord Nishida, daimyo to the shogun, Lord Temmu," I said.

She squirmed angrily, helplessly, in her bonds.

Then, after a time, her struggles subsided.

She was well secured.

"We cannot take you with us, as you are," said Tajima.

He then, slowly, and carefully, removed her bonds.

She regarded him, wonderingly, frightened.

No longer did she regard Tajima with derision or contempt, if she had ever truly done so. It was clear to her that she was in his power, and he could do with her what he might wish.

"Stand," said Tajima.

She rose, unsteadily, to her feet, for her ankles had been bound. She caught her balance, and stood before us, frightened, bent over.

"Straighten your body," said Tajima.

"Slovenly posture is not acceptable in a slave," I said.

"I am not a slave," she said.

"Straighter," said Tajima.

She straightened her body.

"No," he said, "not stiff, not rigid, but slim, supple, slender, so gentle and lovely that you might bend in the wind. Be as soft and delicate as the petal of a talender, as graceful as the fresh, young willow by the side of the stream."

"Tarsk!" she said.

"Better," said Tajima, considering her posture.

"Let me go," she said.

"Will you flee to the eels?" inquired Tajima.

"No!" she said.

"It is nearly dark," said Haruki. "Cut her throat and leave her behind. It will be more merciful than the eels."

"Do not!" she begged.

"I do not think that she is fully pleasing," I said.

"We can fetch a whip," said Tajima.

"How am I to be?" she asked, plaintively.

"Be such that men will want you," I said, "such that they will bid on you, that they will want you in their collar."

"I do not understand," she said.

"Be such that free women will hate you," I said.

"Tarsk," she said, "urt, sleen!"

"Stand as what you are," I said, "stand as the most exciting, beautiful, helpless, vulnerable, and desirable of women, as a slave."

"I am not a slave!" she cried.

"Head down," said Haruki. "Do you dare look into the eyes of a free male without permission?"

"That is it," I said.

"Good," said Tajima.

I regarded her, as I had learned to regard women on Gor, to see them unclouded by hypocrisy, pretense, convention, and lies, to see them as they are, so fascinating, so special, so different, so wonderful, so designed by nature to be owned, collared, and mastered. Her face was lovely, her figure exquisite. Her wrists were slender, and would take bracelets nicely. Her feet were small, and her ankles were trim. Such ankles take shackles well. Light chain would hold her with perfection, as any such small lovely beast. Yes, I thought, she might do well on the block. How pleasant it is to buy women.

"Excellent," I said.

"Beast," she said.

"Her hair," I said, "is slave long." Indeed, it fell behind her almost to her ankles. Perhaps it had never been cut.

"Inappropriate, however," said Tajima, "for a field slave."

She looked up, startled.

"Do not move," said Tajima.

"What are you going to do?" she cried, alarmed.

He had approached her with an unsheathed knife. He now stood behind her, one fist knotted in her hair.

"Do not resist," he warned her.

"Do not!" she begged.

"You cannot be taken with us, as you are," I said. "You might be mistaken for Sumomo, the daughter of the shogun."

"I am Sumomo," she said, "daughter of Yamada, Shogun of the Islands!"

"You are no longer Sumomo," I informed her.

"Hold still," said Tajima.

"She will have to have a new name," said Haruki.

"If she is to have one," I said.

"True," said Haruki.

Not all animals, of course, are named. Consider a flock of verr, a herd of tarsks. Still it is common for slaves to be named, as this makes it easier to refer to them, to command them, and so on.

Tears welled in the eyes of the slave as Tajima, cut by cut, cropped her hair. Indeed, in my view he had cropped it rather short, even for a field slave.

"Good," said Tajima, stepping back, well satisfied with his work.

I feared that Tajima had relished the slave's shearing. To be sure, she had not treated him well, in Tarncamp, and elsewhere.

Disbelievingly, awed, with dismay, she put her hands to her head.

"What have you done to me?" she said.

"Very little," he said, "as of now."

He then sheathed the knife, and came around the girl, and stood, with us, appraisingly, before her.

"The white garment would surely be recognized," I said.

"Certainly," said Tajima.

"It is all I have!" she said.

"Remove it," he said. "Do not fear, I have arranged another."

"A slave is not permitted modesty," I said, "no more than any other animal, but unclothed you would obviously be conspicuous. Certainly nudity is easily noticed."

In public, female slaves are almost always clothed. The most obvious exceptions to this are of an instructive or punitive nature. When a girl is new to the collar she is sometimes denied clothing in public. This well impresses on her that she is no longer a free woman. She is soon likely to plead for a rag or tunic. Similarly, a slave who has been displeasing may be denied clothing in public, as a punishment. Obviously a nude slave has little status amongst clothed slaves, even given the usual nature of the clothing likely to be permitted to a slave. Also, as an aesthetic note, one might remark the fact that most slave garments are extremely attractive on a woman. Indeed, they are designed with this in mind, the striking enhancement of her beauty. Many women have no sense as to how beautiful they really are until they find themselves in the garments of a slave. What garmenture could be more stimulating, more attractive, more provocative, or feminine? How could a woman be more female than in such a garment, other than, say, being chained nude to a master's slave ring, or such? Too, I fear that such garmenture, and the collar, as both much enhance a woman's beauty, have their appeal to her vanity. What woman, slave or free, objects to being beautiful? Indeed, what free woman has not conjectured how she might appear, so excitingly and beautifully clad? Nudity, incidentally, is not so rare amongst Gorean men, particularly those engaged in heavy labors. One thinks little of it in such situations.

"I am to be disguised?" she said.

"Rather," said Tajima, "clothed appropriately."

"I do not understand," she said.

"It is dark," said Haruki, looking outside.

"Would you prefer to retain your white gown?" I asked.

"No," she said. "It is light and thin. It conceals me but inadequately. I fear it even hints at my lineaments. It is humiliating and disgraceful." She then turned to Tajima. "Where are my robes?" she said.

Tajima bent down and drew from the bag he had brought to the hut, a small wad of cloth. This he threw against the slave, who caught it, and then held it from her.

"What is this?" she said.

"It is the tunic of a field slave," said Tajima.

"I cannot wear this," she said.

"Cut her throat," said Haruki.

She backed away into a corner of the shed where the light of the tiny lamp scarcely reached.

"We must reach the next village before dawn," said Haruki.

A few moments later the slave emerged from the gloom, the white gown clutched in her hands.

She now stood before us, in the sleeveless, brief rag of a field slave.

"Ah," said Haruki.

"Excellent," said Tajima.

"Remember your posture," I cautioned her.

"Beasts!" she said.

Haruki no longer suggested doing away with the captive. Tajima was clearly pleased, which reaction, I suspected, did not displease the captive. Yes, I thought to myself, a good price, certainly.

"Put the gown there," said Tajima, indicating the coils of hair he had shorn from her.

She complied, and then stepped back, more into the gloom, again.

"I will take these things out and burn them," said Haruki.

"My thanks, gardener *san*," said Tajima.

I thought it a shame to waste the hair, as woman's hair, given its tensility and weather-resistance, makes excellent catapult cordage, much better than hemp and common cordage. It is prized by artillery men on the continent. On the other hand, it was clearly important that such evidence be destroyed, as it might link us, or the village, with a shogun's daughter.

"Step forward, slave," said Tajima.

"I am not a slave," she said.

"Stand here," he said, "before me, in the full light of the lamp. I would look more fully on my property."

"I am not your property," she said. "I am a free woman."

"You are not a bad looking slave," he said.

"Tarsk!" she said.

"I am pleased to own you," he said.

"Tarsk, tarsk!" she said.

"Beware," I said.

Haruki soon returned to the hut. I gathered he had disposed of the hair and gown in one of the night fires. He also, interestingly, held in one hand some loops of knotted rope.

"Here," said Tajima to the slave, pointing to the floor of the hut, at his feet, "here, before me, go to all fours, and keep your head down."

"What are you going to do?" she asked.

"What am I going to do, what?" he asked.

"What are you going to do—Master," she whispered.

How careless she had been on the outer parapet, in casting an object to the valley below. How was it that she had failed to exercise a greater caution? How anomalous an action that had been for a woman of her obvious intelligence. Did she not recognize the jeopardy, the risks, involved? She had doubtless, of course, felt herself secure, alone and unobserved. That was understood. That must be the case. Had she not communicated with a confederate or confederates below, similarly, on several occasions? But how had it been that on that occasion she had, apparently, shut out the very possibility of detection? What was different on that night?

Might she not be observed?

Could she have been unaware that Tajima might have drifted near her, as he, to her contempt and amusement, had so often done in the past?

How was it that it had not even occurred to her that he, or another, might have been about? How could such a possibility be forgotten? Why should it be forgotten? What could explain such a lapse? Had she closed a gate, which she refused to open?

I had never understood the passion of that contempt, the intense cruelty of that amusement, lavished on the hapless Tajima.

She had not even accorded him the respect prescribed for a female with respect to a male in the Pani culture, let alone that of a supposed contract woman with respect to a free male.

Why should she have treated him so, so derided and hated him?

Should she not, at least, have been flattered by his interest?

Would it not have been enough to ignore him or avoid him?

Is civility so costly?

"Remain as you are," he said.

Tajima then left the hut. The loops of knotted rope dangled from Haruki's hand. I saw them. I do not think the slave did.

In a few moments Tajima had returned to the hut. In his hands, cupped, I saw, in the light of the lamp, he held what seemed to be a quantity of dirt, of ash, of soot.

"No," begged the slave.

"Keep your head down," he said.

He then, judiciously, applied these materials, some dirt, some ash and soot, to the slave and her small garment.

"Now," I said, "one could not tell her from a field slave."

"She is less than a field slave," said Tajima. "She is a pleasure slave."

"No!" wept the girl.

"Head down," said Tajima.

"Disguised as a field slave," I suggested.

"Precisely, Tarl Cabot, tarnsman," said Tajima.

"You would use the daughter of the shogun for pleasure?" asked Haruki.

"Certainly," said Tajima.

"I am a virgin!" said the slave.

"Not for long, dirty little slave," said Tajima.

"You will soon learn to jump, squirm, and beg," I informed her.

"Keep your head down," said Tajima.

"Is a detail not missing?" I asked.

"Yes," he said, and reached, again, into the sack he had brought into the hut.

I heard, again, a slight sound of metal, possibly something impinging on slave bracelets or shackles.

We noted the object withdrawn from the sack.

"What is that?" she said, frightened.

"Would it not encircle your neck, nicely?" asked Haruki.

"What is it?" she said.

"Perhaps the daughter of the shogun is stupid," said Tajima.

"I am not stupid!" she said.

"Surely you know what it is," I said.

"It cannot be!" she said.

"It is," said Haruki, "it is a collar, a slave collar, a collar for a slave."

"No!" said the girl.

"Yes," said Tajima.

"A lock collar," I said.

"Of course," said Tajima.

"Do not put it on me!" she said.

"Keep your head down," said Tajima.

"Do not collar me!" she begged.

"Head down," said Tajima.

"I trust that it is not engraved," I said.

"Not yet," said Tajima.

"All slaves need not be collared," she said, intensely.

"On the continent," I said, "it is prescribed by Merchant Law."

"Do not collar me!" she begged. "If I am collared, everyone will see me as a slave, know me as a slave, and treat me as a slave!"

"You are a slave," said Tajima. "Let it be proclaimed to the world."

"That is proper," I said.

"Have mercy," she said. "No!"

There was a snap and the device, encircling her throat, was closed.

She sobbed, tears falling to the floor of the hut.

She who had been the unpleasant, difficult, lofty, haughty Sumomo was now on all fours, collared.

"On the continent," I said, "slaves are slaves, and are clearly to be identified as such." How beautiful a woman is in a collar, and how meaningful is the collar on her neck!

"You will have to hold her tightly," said Haruki.

"How so?" said Tajima.

"It must not be blurred or spoiled," said Haruki.

"I do not understand," said the girl.

"I thought we must wait," said Tajima, "to the holding of Temmu, or to the encampment of tarns."

"What are you speaking of?" asked the slave.

"As soon as I learned of your presence here," said Haruki, "given the possible eventuations involved, I instructed the village metal worker to have an iron ready."

"An iron?" said the girl.

"You are a man of excellent forethought," said Tajima.

"I shall fetch the brazier," said Haruki. "We will attend to the matter privately. The less that the village knows the better. You had best bind her and hold her mouth."

"What are you going to do?" said the girl.

"Mark you, of course," said Tajima.

"Mark?" she said.

"Yes," he said.

"No!" she cried.

My hand stifled what might have been a scream on the part of the slave. Her eyes were wide, and wild, over my hand.

Tajima attended to her binding.

In a bit, Haruki returned, bearing, on its carrying ring, insulated with folds of cloth, a brazier, from which two handles protruded.

The girl's thigh was washed and dried, and the matter was expeditiously attended to.

After an Ehn or so, I removed my hand from her mouth.

I did not know the brand, but, I gathered, in Pani script, it unambiguously identified her as a slave.

"I am marked, marked!" she said.

"Yes," I said, "marked as what you are, a slave."

"No," she wept. "No!"

"Rejoice," I said. "It is possible, now, that your father would not even regard you as worthy to be fed to his eels."

"More likely," said Haruki, "as a branded little beast, he would merely throw you to them naked."

"It has been done to me," she said. "I wear the slave mark."

"It is a lovely brand," I said. "Like the tunic, the collar, and such, it is designed not merely to identify you as a slave but to enhance your beauty, as well."

"Is it pretty?" she said.

"Yes," I said, "it might be the envy of many free women."

"But its meaning!" she said.

"True," I said. "Its meaning is clear, and indisputable."

Her bonds, applied to assist in controlling her movements during the application of the iron, were removed, and she was again placed on all fours before her master, Tajima, he of the tarn cavalry.

"Let us beat her," said Haruki, the cluster of knotted ropes once more dangling from his hand.

"Please do not beat me, Master," said the slave.

"But you recognize you are subject to the whip?" said Tajima.

"Yes, Master," she said.

Tajima took the ropes and said to the slave, "I shall toss these ropes to the side of the hut. You will fetch them on all fours, lift them in your teeth, and then return before me, on all fours.

You will then lift them in your mouth to me, and, when I accept them, you will kneel, and await my pleasure."

She looked up at him, wonderingly, frightened.

He flung the ropes to the side of the hut.

In the dim light of the small lamp we watched her make her way to the ropes, pick them up in her teeth, and then return to her place before Tajima. She lifted her head to her master, timidly, the ropes dangling from her mouth. Tajima took them from her, gently.

"Kneel," he said.

He then looked into her awed, uplifted eyes.

I knew that expression on a woman's face. It is not unusual when the woman is kneeling before her master.

"Kiss my feet," he said.

"Yes, Master," she whispered, bending forward, and putting down her head.

Had I detected a thrill of submission in those simple words?

Had the radical sexual dimorphism of the human species suddenly become real to her?

Did she understand it at last?

Did she sense the possible fulfillments, and liberation, of the collar, the joy of a sensed, unalloyed, apprehended truth, a truth which it would now seem to her pointless, even absurd, to deny or dispute, a truth in the light of which she, now a slave, would, to her joy, have no choice but to live?

We watched, for several Ihn, while she addressed herself to the performance of her simple task, so replete with its symbolism of acknowledged social chasms, the difference between slave and master.

"Look up," said Tajima.

The slave complied.

"You lick and kiss the feet of a master well," said Tajima. "You are clearly a slave, and belong on your knees before a man."

"Yes, Master," she said.

It is a common Gorean view that all women are slaves, only that some are collared and some are not yet collared.

I have often been puzzled as to why free women commonly hate and despise slaves. Do they see the slave as a rival? Do they resent the preference of men for the slave? Do they envy

the slave? Do they fear the slave in themselves? Do they object
to the slave's openness and freedom, to the liberation of her
femininity, to her desire to selflessly love and serve, to her
happiness, to her passion, to her sexual fulfillments, to her
categorical ownership by a master whom she must serve, who
will have, and without qualification, whatever he wishes from
her? In any event, the relationship between the free woman
and the slave is scarcely symmetrical. The free woman is free,
and the slave is a slave. Whereas the free woman may hate and
despise the slave, and treat her with all the cruelty, harshness,
and contempt she pleases, the slave may not reciprocate in
the least. It could be her death to do so. The slaves, in their
vulnerability and weakness, so unguarded and defenseless,
subject to sale, to the chain and whip, live in terror of free
women.

"As I recall, from the supper," said Tajima to the prisoner, the
knotted ropes dangling from his hand, "you believed slaves
should be whipped."

"I was not then marked, not then in a collar, Master," she said.

"You have changed your view?" he said.

"It is my hope that Master will not whip me," she said.

"But you are now subject to the whip, are you not?" he asked.

"Yes, Master," she said. "I am now subject to the whip."

He then held the loops of knotted rope to her face.

"Kiss the whip," he said.

"Yes, Master," she said.

We watched while the slave tenderly pressed her lips to the
ropes, and then looked up, into the eyes of her master.

It was a beautiful, and touching, ceremony, enacted in
the dim light of the lamp, in a small hut on the outskirts of a
Yamada village.

"You have now returned the rope, and deferred to it," said
Tajima. "You may now beg to be beaten if you are not fully
pleasing."

"I beg to be beaten," she said, "if I am not fully pleasing."

"You realize it will be done to you," he said.

"Yes, Master," she said.

"You may now retire to the corner," he said, indicating a
dark corner of the hut, to which the dim lamplight scarcely

penetrated, "and kneel there, grasping your ankles with your hands, until summoned forth."

"Yes, Master," she said.

"And you will keep your head down," he said.

"Yes, Master," she said.

I saw that Tajima, despite his Earth origin, knew how to treat a slave. She is to be kept with perfect discipline. Perhaps he had learned this in Tarncamp, or Shipcamp. Surely there had been enough slaves there, for work, and the pleasure of men.

"Master," she said.

"Yes?" he said.

"Am I Sumomo?" she asked, timidly.

"Not unless I have it so," said Tajima. "And if I should have it so, it will be a slave name, put on you by my pleasure."

"Yes, Master," she said.

The slave drew back.

"What will you name her?" I asked.

"What do you think of 'Sumomo'?" he said.

"I scarcely think that the most judicious of choices," I said.

"Nor I," he said.

"Forgive me," I said.

"What do you think?" he asked.

"She is a beautiful slave," I said.

"Her hair is wretched," he said, "and her body filthy."

"Doubtless there is a comb, and slave tub somewhere," I said.

"Doubtless," he said.

"There are many beautiful names," I said.

"Has she earned a beautiful name?" he asked.

"Perhaps not yet," he said. "Slave," he called.

"Master?" she said, from the half darkness.

"Are you kneeling, your ankles grasped in your hands, your head down?" he inquired.

"Yes, Master," she said.

"You are 'Nezumi'," he said.

I heard sobs, from the darkness.

"What is your name?" he inquired.

"'Nezumi', Master," she said.

"I do not know the name," I said.

"It is an old word for an urt," he said.

"I see," I said.

"I shall return the brazier and irons," said Haruki. "In the meantime, prepare to depart. Few know we are here, and it is dangerous."

Chapter Thirty

We Have Paused at an Inn to Gather Intelligence

"Sake, more sake!" said the Ashigaru, striking the low table with the metal cup.

"Nezumi!" called Tajima.

Nezumi hurried to the table bearing the earthen vessel.

"That is a sorry slave," said the Ashigaru. His two fellows laughed.

"How so?" asked Tajima.

"The hair," said one of the Ashigaru.

"True," said Tajima.

Nezumi was actually far more presentable than earlier. Her body and hair were now washed, and her garment. She was still barefoot, of course, and the garment was still the tiny rag of a field slave. Tajima had tried, with his knife, to shape her hair a bit. It would, of course, in time, grow out.

"She is cheap, and all I could afford," said Tajima. "How fares the march north?"

"The pace is leisurely," said the Ashigaru. "The shogun moves with deliberation."

"It spares the men," said one of the Ashigaru.

"You are rice thieves," said the innkeeper.

"Requisitions must be made," said their leader.

I did not think the innkeeper would have spoken as he had if a warrior had been present. It might have meant his head. The Ashigaru, like most, were of the peasants, and took no umbrage at the annoyance of the innkeeper.

Near the door of the inn, inside, were several sacks of rice, while, outside, a handcart waited.

I was to one side, behind a silken screen, sitting cross-legged with Haruki, before another table. Such screens may afford privacy, for example, dividing a larger space into semi-secluded, individual dining areas. The screen, on the house side, so to speak, was decorated with a fanciful image, that of a large, winged, fearsome beast. "It is a dragon," had said Haruki. Such images were not infrequently encountered in the islands, but, more commonly, one encountered images of a gentler, more tranquil nature, snow-capped mountains, forests, winding streams, placid villages, and such. There seemed to me many contrasts, if not paradoxes, in the Pani culture. Perhaps where life may be short, and jeopardy is often afoot, when the morning may not guarantee the evening, one is more likely to see and appreciate beauty, and fix it, as one can, for a moment of contemplation. It was a culture with a place for both the blossom and the glaive, a culture where one might, a sword within reach, unroll a painting and, bit by bit, meditate upon its elements, where a warrior might attend sensitively to the delicacy of his calligraphy and a general might compose poetry on the eve of battle.

"The shogun marches against the lands of Temmu," said Tajima.

"Of course," said one of the Ashigaru.

"No attempt has been made at swiftness of approach or stealth," said Tajima.

"A lame man may move more rapidly than an army," said another of the Ashigaru.

"One cannot conceal the movements of thousands of men," said the leader.

"The shogun moves with the implacability of the seasons," said another. "In this way the onslaught, in its inevitability, will be the more feared."

"Let the tarsks of the traitorous rebel, Temmu, the Wicked, cringe in anticipation," said the leader.

"But are there not demon birds to fear?" inquired Tajima.

"I have seen them in the sky," said one of the Ashigaru. "They do nothing; they watch, and go away."

It was easy to hear this conversation from behind the screen. We were some fifteen days now from the palace of Lord Yamada. After the fourth day we had begun to move east, and had thought to then parallel the northern road. In this way we hoped to reach the countryside controlled by Lord Temmu apart from the march of Yamada, but not that far behind it. Our practice, until recently, had been to house ourselves in selected villages, some known to Haruki, and some scouted by him, in the daylight Ahn, and then move, again, at night. To be sure, we had been unable to obtain much intelligence from the villages. We had finally, after avoiding villages for three days, approached this inn. It lay in the territory of one of Lord Yamada's daimyos, on a road leading to the northern road. Travelers, coming and going, from various points, merchants, and others, shelter and refresh themselves at inns, and, accordingly, inns are likely to be repositories of information and what might purport to be information, repositories of rumors, news, reports, and conjectures. What we had not counted on at the inn was that we might encounter foragers of Yamada in its precincts. We had not, of course, encountered them further west. Fortunately this encounter, to this point, had proved not only innocuous, but propitious with respect to our needs. From whom more informed might we garner the intelligence we sought than from Ashigaru of the shogun himself? When three of them had spilled into the inn, Tajima had hailed them, greeted them like long lost brothers, and, to their pleasure, stood for several rounds of sake.

"That is a field slave, is it not?" had growled a stout peasant, seemingly a high man in one of the villages at which we had taken shelter.

"Of course," had said Tajima.

"There are fields to be seeded," he said.

Nezumi had looked up at him, from her knees, wildly. She had knelt at his first appearance in the doorway of the hut. A slave commonly kneels upon the appearance of a free person. It is a common slave deportment.

The fellow carried a switch. I gathered he might be in charge of the village's field slaves.

He had apparently become aware of our presence shortly after we had entered the gate, shortly after dawn.

"Are you strangers?" he asked.

"Wayfarers, sojourners, and guests," had said Tajima. I remained in the back of the hut.

"You are aware," he said, "that this village lies under the suzerainty of Lord Yamada, Shogun of the Islands."

"Fortunately for us," had said Tajima, "for times and roads are dangerous, and the protection of the great lord's law is welcome."

There had been no mistaking the insignia of Yamada carved deeply into the two gateposts of the village.

"We have a coin for rice," had said Haruki.

"A coin?" said the fellow, surprised.

"Yes," said Haruki.

The common means of exchange were in terms of commodities, millet, rice, silk, coarser cloth, and such.

"Let me see your coin," said the peasant.

"Have you seen one before?" asked Haruki.

"Of course," said the fellow, belligerently.

Haruki removed a string from about his neck, and drew it forth, from beneath his long, gray shirt. On this string were seven or eight copper disks, each penetrated by a small, square opening, through which the string was threaded.

"They are shaved," said the fellow.

"No," said Haruki.

"Let me see," said the fellow.

"Do not approach more closely," said Haruki.

"He has two swords," said the fellow, looking uneasily at Tajima.

"That is true," said Haruki. "Thus, it would not be wise to approach more closely, unless permitted."

A shaved coin is one from which a clip or filings of metal have been removed, which clips or filings, melted down in sufficient numbers, may be reformed into new coins, plates, or ingots. Copper, of course, and bronze, is seldom shaved. On the continent silver and gold coins are not unoften shaved. Accordingly, much transaction in various markets and "Streets of Coins," takes place with scales. Valuable coins, of course, might also be debased, but if the coins are minted, struck by hammers from the molds, that is commonly done by a municipal authority, publicized or not. Much depends on trust, of course. For example is it not surprising, if one stops to consider it, that something of value, say, a *fukuro* of rice, or a slave, might be exchanged for a tiny piece of metal, of whatever sort? I had heard of one city in which the state had issued small black leather packets sewn shut, which packets were alleged to contain a golden tarsk. It was a capital offense in that state not to accept, and value, such a packet as containing a golden tarsk, and it was a capital offense, as well, to open such a packet, to see if it actually contained such a tarsk. The problematicity involved here is obvious. The packet contains a gold tarsk or not. If it does, the packet is unnecessary. Just use the gold tarsk. And if the packet does not contain a gold tarsk, then one is defrauded. So the packet is either pointless or a lie. The ultimate success or failure of this inventive economic adventure was never determined, as the city was attacked by several neighboring municipalities, was burned to the ground, and had salt cast upon its ashes. Sometimes, of course, such schemes might be more successful, as when a paper currency might be used, which can then be multiplied and produced in any amount deemed useful by an appropriate, armed authority.

"He is *ronin*," said the peasant, regarding Tajima, "one of the waves, two swords with no daimyo."

"But two swords," said Haruki.

"I will bring you a *fukuro* of rice, from the storehouse," said the peasant, "for your coins."

"One coin for four *fukuros* of rice," said Haruki.

As far as I could gather, this offer was quite generous on the part of Haruki, perhaps exceedingly so. It was hard to tell, however, for, as I have suggested, most exchange was done in terms of commodities. For example, a daimyo's taxation levied on his subject villages, as noted earlier, was usually done in terms of rice, or, if the village was a fishing village, in terms of dried fish, or such.

"I am not a high, noble person," said Haruki, "who may be fooled, deluded, and tricked by the first grasping, greedy peasant met on the road. I am of the peasantry myself. Do you not think I know our tricks?"

"Let me see the slave," he said.

"Why?" said Haruki.

"A man," he said, "astride a demon bird, with the banner of Yamada, visited our village."

"Interesting," said Tajima.

I assumed this must have been either Tyrtaios or his colleague, probably the colleague, as Tyrtaios would more likely be in closer contact with Lord Yamada.

"We are warned to watch for two fugitives, presumably afoot, a man, possibly a warrior, and a woman, a high lady."

"But we are rather three, and a mere pretty-legged beast," said Tajima. "Do you detect a high lady in our company?"

The peasant, glaring, moved back, away from the threshold.

"Girl," he said.

"Master?" she said, frightened.

"Crawl to me on your knees," he said, "your right wrist grasped behind you in your left hand, and kneel here, outside the hut, in the sunlight, your head back, that I may look upon you."

Nezumi struggled forth, awkwardly, into the sunlight. Slaves obey free persons.

In the slave houses, girls being trained for the pleasures of men, namely, being taught the subtleties, skills, behaviors, and dispositions of the pleasure slave, are taught how to move, and now not to move. There is to be grace, submission, loveliness, and vulnerability in all things. She is, after all, a slave. She is not to conceal, deny, deride, resent, hate, or suppress her femininity, but to accept it, and liberate it, to rejoice in it, to revel in it, that she will be the fullest and most perfect of women, her master's slave. Nezumi had not crawled well. She had not even known enough to draw back her shoulders, that the loveliness of her breasts would be accentuated beneath the thin, scarcely concealing rag of the field slave.

"She is collared," said the peasant.

"Of course," said Tajima.

I remained much back, in the darkness of the hut.

"Oh!" said the slave.

"This brand is fresh!" said the peasant, suspiciously.

"Yes," said Tajima. "I bought her recently, and thought it judicious to mark her."

The peasant dropped the hem of the garment.

"What butcher dressed her hair?" he asked.

"I bought her so," said Tajima.

"Keep your head up and back, girl," said the peasant.

He gazed for some time on her features. Free Pani women seldom veiled themselves. Accordingly, if he had ever seen the daughter of the shogun in the past, he might well have identified her. Had he done so I supposed that we would have had to kill him. On the other hand, perhaps it would have taken a familiar, keen eye, one well acquainted with the girl, to behold the features of the sophisticated, delicate, elegant Sumomo in the uplifted, sullied, frightened visage of Tajima's Nezumi.

"She is unkempt, and filthy," he said, "a sorry slave."

"But she has pretty legs," said Tajima.

The peasant snapped the switch he carried smartly into the palm of his hand. Nezumi flinched.

"If you are to stay in the village," said the peasant, "if you are to enjoy our hospitality, you will earn your rice. There are stones to be carried, wood to be cut, and water to be drawn."

"That is eminently fair," said Tajima.

"How does this slave take the switch?" he asked.

"With reluctance, I wager," said Tajima. "I have not much switched her."

"Put your head down," said the peasant to Nezumi.

"Oh!" she cried, startled, in pain. The switch had lashed down, viciously, catching the slave on the left shoulder, near the neck.

Perhaps it was the first time she had ever been struck.

I had no doubt but what the blow had stung.

Nezumi sobbed, shaken, her head down.

"See?" said Tajima, affably.

I could note the welt rising, even now.

"You men will follow me," he said. "As for you, lazy girl, on your feet! That way, to the wading fields. Run! You have already escaped two Ahn of work! Run, run!"

Nezumi leaped to her feet, sobbing, and hurried in the direction indicated. The peasant pursued her briefly, laying his switch against the back of her thighs.

The peasant then strode off, toward the center of the village.

"I fear Nezumi knows nothing of the work in the wading fields," I said.

"She will imitate the other girls," said Tajima.

"I trust the other girls will treat her well," I said.

"Your trust is misplaced," said Tajima. "She is new, and has already missed two Ahn of labor."

"Will there be an overseer?" I wondered.

"Of course," said Tajima, "but it will probably be a First Girl."

"I see," I said.

"Do not fear," he said. "She will have a switch."

"I shall try to remain composed," I said. "Do you not object to the fellow switching Nezumi?" I asked.

"No," said Tajima. "It will be good for her, and we must remember that we are guests here."

"We would not wish to be discourteous," I said.

"No," said Tajima.

"What of me?" I asked. "I am not Pani. I fear I will be conspicuous."

"The fellow had little interest in you," said Tajima. "It is well known there are several barbarians, mercenaries, amplifying the forces of Lord Temmu. He will presumably take you for a deserter, one wise enough to recognize that the cause of Lord Temmu is a lost cause."

"Ho!" cried the peasant, turning, several yards ahead, and waving us on.

"Let us forward," said Tajima, starting off.

"With a good heart," I said.

"If you wish," said Tajima. "I myself have never been fond of manual labor."

A few Ahn later we returned to the hut, with two *fukuros* of rice. Nothing more had been said of coins. Shortly thereafter Nezumi, limping and muddy, with various welts on her thighs and arms, joined us. "My back is sore," she said, "my muscles ache. I hobble. I have been switched. I can barely move."

"How many field slaves were there?" asked Tajima.

"Ten," she said.

"Where are they now?" he asked.

"Penned," she said.

"At least," said Tajima, "we were not suspected."

"Do not be so sure, noble one," said Haruki.

"How so, gardener *san*?" said Tajima.

"I do not think he knows us, noble one," said Haruki, "but I think he is suspicious. If we are not those whom the rider of the demon bird sought, we may be others of interest. While we were detained with labors, busied so, two fellows left the village. I do not know their errand, but it may portend difficulties for us. Similarly, there was no difficulty about two *fukuros* of rice."

"Our wages," I proposed, "and some consideration for the application of Nezumi in the wading field."

"It is all too easy," said Haruki.

"You are overly suspicious," said Tajima.

"I know these people," said Haruki. "I am one of them."

"What do you suggest?" I said.

"We will rest now and wait until dark. We will then break through the back of the hut, and leave thusly. The hut entrance may be watched. In my work today I examined the palings of the village. They are high, well-fastened, and deeply planted, but scalable from within in secrecy."

"We have no rope," I said.

"In my hewing of wood," he said, "I left one trunk, tall and slender, fit for a paling, concealed amongst several others not yet turned into kindling, or dressed, not yet readied for the adz or plane. That trunk I notched in such a way that it might, leaned against the palings, afford the semblance of a ladder."

"Wise Haruki," I said.

"Excellent," said Tajima.

"What of Nezumi?" I asked.

"If necessary," said Tajima, "she can be bound and gagged, and a sling arranged for her."

"Do you think she knows," I asked, "that she is truly on a chain?" Sometimes it takes a woman a little time to understand this, that she is on a chain. To be sure, the more intelligent the woman the sooner she understands this, that she is helpless and without resource, that she is utterly incapable of altering her condition, that she exists in, and only exists in, a state of categorical and unqualified bondage. Then, restored to herself, and fulfilled in a thousand ways, she would not have it otherwise. In her collar, at the feet of strong men, to her joy, she has found herself.

At last she is a woman owned, wholly owned, without compromise or condition, as she wishes to be.

"I think she suspects," said Tajima. "She may have to be beaten a bit."

"I suspect," I said, "that you should soon subject her to the attentions of the master. It is easy to caress even a free woman into the throes of begging submission."

"Prior, perhaps," said Tajima, "to their collaring."

"She is a virgin," I said. "She has no sense, as of now, of the raging of slave fires."

"She might prove interesting," said Tajima, "when they begin to burn in her belly."

We glanced to lovely Nezumi, who was asleep.

"I do not think she can trek the night," I said.

"We will take turns carrying her," said Tajima.

After leaving the village in which we feared we had provoked suspicion, and having ample rice, we avoided villages for a time. We did not know if we were pursued or not. We had certainly detected no evidence which suggested that we might be the object of a pursuit. Haruki may have been overly suspicious. One might hope so. It did seem best to proceed cautiously. We were little aware of what might be going on, in the great events of the islands. This lack of intelligence was keenly frustrating. "We must seek a road," said Tajima. "If we encounter an inn we are unlikely to be suspected, as men come and go, and where all are strangers none is a stranger. We are more likely to be welcomed by an innkeeper than feared, or shunned. What innkeeper does not want patrons, what merchant does not want customers?"

It was late afternoon.

After the fall of darkness we would trek again.

I glanced to Nezumi, who was asleep. She was beautiful. A sleeping slave is often very beautiful. The light chain, some two or three feet in length, ran from her neck to the trunk of the small tree about which it was fastened. She was clean now, and her tunic had been washed. In her sleep she was unaware it had come high upon her thighs.

Tajima was proceeding carefully, sensitively, with his slave. There are of course a thousand thousand variations in the mastery. Sometimes more is accomplished by what is not done than by what is done. Women are different and slaves are different. Much, for example, may be done with postponement, neglect, and anticipation. Sometimes a slave becomes so distraught, even beside herself, with anticipating the inevitable that she can stand it no longer, and throws herself to her belly before her master, sobbing, and begs her usage. "I am your slave! Please have me, Master! Ravish your slave! She is yours. Have mercy, Master! Ravish me, ravish your slave!" Too, when a woman is not frequently and well used, such being the common practice of masters, she begins to fear that she may no longer be desired, that he is considering another slave, that she may be taken to the market. All the fears and harrows which may afflict a free woman in an ambiguous relationship are multiplied in the case of the slave, who is without recourse, other than her collar and beauty. The free woman, for example, cannot be simply stripped and sold. Sometimes a slave will even beg the whip, that she be reassured that her master still cares for her, if only enough to beat her. Slave beatings, incidentally, are quite rare, and almost always of a punitive nature. The slave is pleased to be subject to the whip, which situation is quite meaningful and excites her, but she seldom cares to feel it. So she is likely to behave in such a way that there will be little cause, or temptation, to use it on her. Why should she be beaten? She is doing her best to be a good slave, to be wholly pleasing to her master. To be sure, sometimes the slave may be beaten to remind her that she is a slave. Few things so impress her bondage on her as the lash. Under the lash she is in no doubt that she is a slave. Interestingly, the slave, in her tears, often welcomes, and is grateful for, this confirmation of her helplessness, vulnerability, and servitude. It reassures her of that of which she wishes to be reassured, that she is a slave, the property of her master.

Two days ago, at our camp, Tajima had had her disrobe before us, and turn slowly, and then stand still, before us.

"A slave may be looked upon," he informed her.

"Yes, Master," she had said, tears in her eyes.

He had then put her to her chores in the camp. After our

small repast, which she cooked and served, naked, utilizing some simple vessels and bowls extracted from the packs of Haruki and Tajima, she was allowed to feed, and don again the rag of the field slave.

Yesterday, at our camp, he had had Nezumi precede him to a small pool he had discovered, amongst the trees. There he had permitted her, kneeling at the pool's edge, to wash her garment.

She rose to her feet.

She eyed the water longingly.

She turned to face him, clutching the small, damp garment in both hands. "Please, Master," she said.

"Do you intend to make a request?" he asked.

"Yes, Master," she said.

"Kneel," he said, sharply.

Swiftly she knelt. She still had much to learn. The slave is not a free woman. The slave commonly addresses requests, petitions, supplications, and such, to the free person from a kneeling position, which is appropriate to her condition. Indeed, this position, suitable to the negligibility, shamefulness, and degradation of her status, is often assumed in the presence of the free.

She put the small, washed garment down beside her.

"You may speak," he said.

"May I bathe, Master?" she asked.

I could understand her desire to bathe, for her body bore not only some residue of Tajima's early ministrations in the camp where we had first made contact, his application of dirt, ashes, soot, and such, designed to confirm her status as a field slave, but now, as well, the stains and flakage of dried mud from the wading field, and the dust, mixed with sweat, of our journey north.

"You merely wish to escape," he said, "to splash across the pool and hurry into the brush."

"No, Master!" she said.

He viewed her, his arms folded.

"We are in the wilderness," she said. "There is nowhere to go!"

"Slaves are sometimes hysterical and desperate," he said. "Slaves are not always wise. It would be inconvenient, if you attempted to escape."

"I am naked," she said. "I am collared. I am branded!"

"Still," he said, thoughtfully.

"There is nowhere to escape to," she said.

"True," he said.

"At most," she said, "even with a start of days, if successful in eluding one master, I could only hope for a different collar, to be subject to a different whip."

"I see," he said.

"I am not stupid, Master," she said. "I know there is no escape for slaves. I need not be taught it by the lash, or the cutting of the tendons in my legs. I do not want an 'I have been displeasing' brand burned into my forehead, for other girls to see, to greet with laughter and mock."

"Remain as you are," he said, "and grasp your ankles and close your eyes."

Shortly thereafter he returned to her side. She heard a snap, and sensed something on her neck, about the collar.

"May I release my ankles and open my eyes, Master?" she asked.

"Yes," he said.

"I am leashed," she said.

"You may now bathe," he said.

She thrust her head down, quickly, to his feet, kissed them gratefully, and, turning about, waded into the water.

"She is a lovely slave," I said.

The leash was a tether leash, of some feet in length. Such leashes are often used with a back-braceleted slave, allowing her several feet of movement, access to food and water, and such. The common leading leash is much shorter, but, it, too, is longer than is necessary for mere leading. Its looped coils, held in the leash-master's hand, are convenient not only for disciplinary purposes, for example, if the girl does not walk well, but are long enough to bind her, hand and foot, if such should be desired. Similarly it might be noted that the snug double belting of the common camisk, usually of cordage, thongs, or binding fiber, is not designed merely to emphasize the woman's figure, and in such a way as to make it clear it is the figure of a slave, but to serve a similar purpose.

"Wash well, dirty little slave!" he called.

"Yes, Master!" she called.

"There is something attractive in a leashed slave," I said. "In the high cities, on the continent, particularly on holidays, masters often promenade their slaves, on the boulevards, in the plazas, on the high bridges. If the master pauses to converse, the slave instantly kneels."

"I would hope so," said Tajima.

"She struggles with her hair," I said.

"There is not much to struggle with," he said.

"You saw to that," I said.

We saw the head of Nezumi, with the leash collar, and part of the leash, plunge several times under the water, while her small fingers tore at the scraggly stubble left to her.

"It will be clean, at least," he said.

"What there is of it," I said.

"Lord Nishida had the hair of the blue-eyed, blond-haired slave, Saru, cropped when she was assigned to the tharlarion stables."

"That is common with stable girls and mill girls," I said. "Sometimes the head is shaved."

"She is wading more deeply into the water," said Tajima.

"Give her more slack," I said.

"I can see only her head now," said Tajima.

"She is modest," I said.

"Slaves are not permitted modesty," he said.

"Nonetheless," I said, "most are modest. That makes it easier to control them, in virtue of their clothing or such."

"I would suppose so," said Tajima.

"In the privacy of a domicile, however," I said, "many, alone with their masters, are shamelessly naked. Too, some masters, indoors, will permit their slaves only their collars."

"It is pleasant to be served by a naked slave," said Tajima.

"It is," I said. "Such things are not only for the stripped high women of a conquered city serving the victory banquets of conquerors."

"Before they are branded, and collared," said Tajima.

"Usually before," I said, "that they be made more keenly aware of their humiliation. Later they will think nothing of serving masters naked, and will be grateful for being permitted to do so, as it is a great privilege for a slave to be allowed to serve free men."

Tajima began to draw on the leash, and the head and shoulders of Nezumi could be seen. Her small hands were on the leash strap, almost protestingly, as though she might be tempted to hold back.

Tajima began to reel in the leash, and she, hands holding to it, could not help but move toward us, step by unwilling step.

Tajima did not cease to draw in the leash until she stood before us, a few feet away, the water to her knees. Her hands were still on the leash.

"Have you finished bathing?" inquired Tajima.

"Yes!" she said, curtly.

"Take your hands away from your body," snapped Tajima. "Do not attempt to conceal yourself."

"Forgive me, Master," she said, frightened.

"You will soon know what it is to be exposed, and as a slave," he said.

"She has already served naked," I said, "about the camp, gathering boughs, making couches, fetching water, cooking, serving."

"But she has not been bound, for slave exhibition and torment."

"What have you mind?" I asked. "I trust you do not subscribe to the practices of the savages of the Barrens, the staking out, the insects, the smearing with honey, such things."

"Certainly not," he said.

"The denial of food, close chains, the switch, the whip?" I asked.

"You will see," he said.

He then bent down, picked up the washed slave tunic, and, shortening the leash, drew Nezumi, apprehensive, frightened, stumbling behind him, to the center of the camp.

He threw her tunic to the grass.

She reached for it.

"No!" he said, and she drew back her hand, frightened.

"Sit there," he said.

He then removed the leash from her neck, and, with its length, wrapped it closely about her legs, binding them together. She then sat there, frightened, her legs bound closely together. As her hands were free, she could have undone the straps, but she was wise enough to stay as she was, sitting quietly on the grass, watching, waiting, unable to rise.

When Tajima had spoken of slave exhibition and torment I was not clear on what he might mean. In a sense all slaves are exhibited as slaves. Does the tunic, the ta-teera, the camisk, the collar, the bracelets, the shackles, the chain, and such, not manifest the slave? Everything exhibits the slave, for she is a slave. Some modalities may be as simple as the exposition cage in which girls may be displayed prior to being brought to the block, or as subtle as the skills of the auctioneer presenting merchandise for the interest of possible buyers. What of slave shelves, public cages, sales racks, sales wagons, exhibition poles, and such? Is not any slave in a coffle or on a rope exhibited? What of leashed slaves on promenade? What of those chained to the throne of a Ubar? Is not any girl fastened to a public slave ring exhibited? What of the girl ordered to assume "examination position," standing, legs widely spread, hands held behind the back of her head or neck? What of a girl being put through slave paces, or being danced in a tavern, or war camp? What of the slaves kneeling about the steps of a public building, or below a public platform, on which an ambassador is being ceremonially welcomed, some of whom may have been taken from his own city? What of the slaves ordered into the streets in their briefest and most colorful tunics when visitors of note are in the city? Is this not a display of a city's taste and wealth, and a suggestion of the prowess of her men at arms?

What had Tajima meant? It seemed he might have meant anything.

It seemed there must be an infinite number of modalities of slave exhibition. What is the last natural number?

Certainly any slave must expect to be exhibited, for she is a slave.

Tajima cut, and sharpened, four stakes, each of which he notched at the blunt end.

He then, with a heavy rock, drove two of these stakes well into the ground, and then drew Nezumi between them, extended her arms, and fastened her wrists, with thongs, to the two stakes. Then she lay between them, arms stretched out, her legs still fastened together. He then put the last two stakes in the ground, undid her legs, and fastened each ankle to its appropriate stake. The thongs resided in the notches in the high ends of the stakes, so they could not slip.

"Behold," proclaimed Tajima, looking down, pleased, upon his handiwork, "the daughter of Lord Yamada, supposed Shogun of the Islands, a slave, and the slave of Tajima, servitor to the daimyo, Lord Nishida of Nara, Tajima, officer in the tarn cavalry of Lord Temmu, commanded by the warrior Tarl Cabot."

The slave struggled a little, but could do nothing to free herself.

"What think you?" asked Tajima.

"It is hard to conceive of a woman better exhibited," I said, "unless perhaps she was bound naked on a spinning exhibition rack, her hands tied over her head."

"And you, Haruki, gardener *san*?" he asked.

"She is quite different from she whom I once knew as Sumomo," said Haruki. "She whom I once knew as Sumomo was a free woman, delicate and refined, as fragile, soft, and exquisite as the petal of a veminium, but, too, petty and unpleasant, cruel and deceitful, arrogant and haughty, impatient and short-tempered, clad in rich garmenture, with silken slippers, with long hair, glistening like dark stars, curled high about her head, fixed in place with a high, black, jade comb."

"And what do you see now?" asked Tajima.

"A naked, well-bound slave," he said.

Tajima stood over the slave, looking down upon her. She was well spread for the inspection of men.

"Why are you bound so?" inquired Tajima.

"I do not know, Master," she said.

"You tried to hide yourself in the water," he said, "and, emerging, you tried to conceal your body."

"Forgive me, Master," she said.

"A slave may be looked upon," he said.

"Yes, Master," she said.

"Say," said Tajima, "'I am a slave and may be looked upon'."

"I am a slave, and may be looked upon," she said.

She pulled at the thongs, and tears welled in her eyes.

"'Whenever and however men may wish'," he added.

"Whenever and however men may wish," she said.

"Keep it well in mind, girl," he said.

"Yes, Master," she said.

"You may thank me for this lesson," he said.

"Thank you, Master," she said.

She twisted helplessly in the thongs. She looked well, so secured, but would not any slave?

"At least," I said, "she is now presentable. Even her tunic has been washed."

"Perhaps now," said Haruki, "she is more appealing to her master."

"No!" said Nezumi, pulling suddenly, helplessly, at the thongs.

I saw she was frightened.

"She is well tied for exhibition," I said to Tajima, "but how for torment?"

"Please do not hurt me, Master," she said. "I will try to be a good slave. I will try to be pleasing. I will try not to disturb the Masters. I will carry burdens. I will tidy camps, I will prepare couches, I will gather nuts and berries, I will gather wood, I will carry water, I will cook!"

"The torment I have in mind for her," he said, "is not one of insects, or burnings, not one of irons, not one of tongs and pincers, not one of the lash of leather, such things."

"What then?" I asked.

"I will make her the victim of her own body," he said. "Her own body will be her torturer."

"And, in time," I said, "when she begs for relief?"

"Then," he said, "I shall grant her relief or not, as it might please me."

"Excellent," I said.

"I do not understand, Masters!" she wept.

"Do you wish to watch?" asked Tajima.

"No," I said.

"No," said Haruki.

"It will not be dark for some Ahn," he said. "That will be enough time."

"More than enough," I said.

To be sure, on Gor, it is not unusual for a master to allot several Ahn, even a full day, to such a business.

"What are you going to do?" cried Nezumi.

As she struggled, I noted that Tajima had tied her legs in such a way that her knees might be drawn up, and back, a bit, lifted some inches from the grass.

Haruki and I withdrew.

It seemed most judicious to let Tajima attend to his slave, in his own way.

If torture were to be involved, I recalled, it was to be an internal matter, one inflicted on her by the means of her own body. That was to be the instrument in terms of which she would be afflicted, apparently to whatever degree Tajima might wish. I recalled he had said that he would make her the victim of her own body, that it would be her torturer.

"What are you going to do, Master?" she begged. "Do not hurt me. I will be a good slave! I will be humble, and obedient. I will be solicitous to please! I will crawl to you! I will bring you the whip in my teeth! I will kneel before you! I will beg to kiss your feet! I will tie sandals, and wash clothing! I will polish leather, I will try to sew, I will cook! Do not beat me! Be merciful! I am only a slave!"

I will make her the victim of her own body, he had said. Her own body will be her torturer.

"What are you doing, Master?" she cried. "I am helpless, I am naked, I cannot resist! No! No! How dare you! I am the daughter of Lord Yamada, Shogun of the Islands. Oh! I hate you! I hate you!"

How careless she had been, I recalled, to have cast that beribboned missive from the outer parapet.

"Please, Master, stop!" she cried. "Desist, stop, stop! Yes! Thank you, Master! You are kind! Master is kind! No, no, not again! I beg you to stop! Stop! Please, Master!"

"Interesting," said Tajima. "Do you know how you just moved, how you yanked against the thongs?"

"Tarsk!" she screamed. "Let me go!"

"I do not think you wish to be unbound," he said.

"I hate you," she cried. "I hate you! Oh!"

"Interesting," he said. "Let us see."

"No!" she cried. "Oh!"

"I thought I saw your little belly leap, and jerk," he said.

"No," she said. "No!"

"I must have been mistaken," he said.

"Yes," she said. "Oh! Oh!"

"No," he said. "I was correct. I was not mistaken."

"Let me go!" she said.

"I think you are going to writhe," he said.

"No!" she said.

"Do you think you are a free woman?" he asked.

"Let me go!" she said.

"Dullness, inertness, a lack of feeling, insensibility, passivity, dormancy, the suppression of nature, self-fear, self-denial, frigidity, torpidity, and such, is acceptable in a free woman," he said.

"Let me go!" she begged. "Oh!"

"Indeed," he said, "I know of places where such biological denials and maimings are the object of indoctrinations, and are to be praised, where nature is to be subordinated to superstition and ideology, in the interests of pathological minorities, whose interests and livelihoods are involved, where women are encouraged to take pride in their inertness, and deride their more natural, more vital, helpless sisters."

"What are you doing to me?" she wept.

"We shall rest," he said. "Did your belly lift?"

"No, no!" she said.

"You draw back in the thongs," he said.

"Let me go!" she begged.

"But you look pretty, tied so," he said.

"Please," she wept.

"When you were in the elegant, sedate robes of a contract woman," he said, "I wondered what you might look like, so fastened."

"And perhaps when I was in the robes of a shogun's daughter?" she said.

"Possibly," he said.

"Beast!" she said.

"It is on your throat that I detect a collar. It seems it is you who are the beast."

"Beast!" she cried.

"Perhaps," he said, "but a free beast, as opposed to an owned beast, a domestic animal which may be penned, given away, or sold."

"I hate you!" she said.

"Such things I spoke of," he said, "dormancy, and such, are acceptable in a free woman."

"Please, untie me," she said.

"Do you think you are a free woman?" he asked.

"No," she said. "I am a slave!"

"But perhaps you do not know much of bondage yet," he said.

"I am naked," she said. "I am collared! I am branded!"

"But perhaps you know little of bondage at this point," he said.

"I do not understand," she said.

"Do you think it is merely a lack of clothing, a ring or band on your neck, a mark on your thigh?"

"Let me go," she begged.

"It is a condition," he said, "a form of being, an entirety, an existence, a suffused reality, a wholeness."

"Please be kind to me, Master," she said. "Oh!"

"Do not protest," he said. "What has the slave to say of such things? In all things she is subject to the master's pleasure. It is done to her, and will be done to her, as the master wills."

"Please untie me, Master!"

"The slave," he said, "is wholly different from the free woman. The free woman is free, the slave is a belonging, a property. The free woman does as she pleases; the slave hopes to be found pleasing. The free woman stands proudly; the slave kneels at the feet of her master, submissively, her head down. The free woman is a person; the slave is a purchasable, vendible animal, a domestic beast."

"Please do not hurt me," she said. "I know I am now a beast. I will try to be a pleasing beast."

"What of this?" he asked.

"Master?" she said. "Ai!"

"Interesting," he said. "Would you prefer to be blindfolded?"

"No!" she said.

"The correct response," he said, "is 'As Master pleases'."

"As Master pleases!" she cried.

"No," he said, "I think we will dispense with the blindfold.

Perhaps some other time, for that involves a different modality of sensations. I enjoy studying your features, which, Nezumi, slave girl, I admit are exquisite, surely marvelous, the thousand subtleties of expression, the soundless words and cries of the eyes, the turning of the head, the trembling of the lips."

"Mercy," she said.

"But such things as I mentioned with respect to free women," he said, "dormancy, and such, are not acceptable in a slave."

"I cannot help how I am!" she said. "Oh!"

"I do not think you know how you are," he said, "but I think you suspect."

"No!" she said.

"Have you heard of slave fires?" he asked.

"Yes!" she said.

"I gather," he said, "they can be quite tormenting to a woman."

This was true. I suppose it might be wondered if men should put such fires into the belly of a woman. Perhaps it is cruel. Doubtless this should not be done to a free woman, unless as a prelude to her collaring. The slave, of course, is a different matter. One need not concern oneself with slaves. One does with them as one pleases. They are only slaves, and exist only for the service and pleasure of masters. Indeed, such fires are almost always lit in the belly of slaves, as it improves the stock. Hot slaves bring higher prices. It is pleasant, incidentally, to see a woman in the throes of slave fires. How piteous she can be, before one, helpless, suffering with need. To be sure, such fires are seldom instilled in the women of my former world, unless, of course, they are embonded. Then they are as helpless as any other slave. Earth males, I conjecture, though I have not polled the matter, seldom encounter women, helpless, beautiful, and naked, crawling to their feet, pleading for relief. It is common in slave houses, prior to sales, to deprive the merchandise of relief for two or three, even for four or five days, prior to the sale. Such a girl, brought to the block, so poignantly alive, so needful, is likely to leap to the slightest touch of the auctioneer's whip.

"I know nothing of such things," she said.

"Perhaps you might speculate," he said.

"No!" she said. "Oh!"

"Did not your hips jerk?" he inquired.

"No," she said, "no, no!"

"Let us see," he said.

"Aii!" she exclaimed.

"That is clearly such a response," he said.

"Tarsk!" she said.

"One would think you had been six months in the collar," he said, "not a few days."

"I hate you," she said.

"Are you aware," he asked, "that you have lifted your belly to me?"

"Never!" she said.

"I shall press it back down, to the grass," he said. "There. Keep it down, worthless slut!"

"Do not speak so to me!" she said. "I cannot help myself! You are doing this to me! I am naked, I am bound! I have no choice! Oh, oh!"

"Do you want a choice?" he asked.

"—No," she said.

"What are you?" he said.

"A slut," she said. "A worthless slut, your worthless slut!"

"You are less," he said, "a slave."

"Yes, Master," she said, "I am less than a worthless slut. I am a slave."

"Whose slave?" he asked.

"Yours, Master!" she cried.

"Remain still," he said.

"I cannot!" she wept.

"Do so," he said.

"Permit me to move, Master," she said.

"Perhaps," he said.

"Please, please," she said.

"Very well," he said.

"Ahhh, yes!" she wept. "Oh, yes!"

"Are you grateful?" he asked.

"Yes, yes!" she said. "Thank you, Master!"

"Shall I untie you?" he asked.

"No, Master," she said.

"Interesting," he said.

There was silence, for a time.

Doubtless he was continuing to address attentions to the slave.

"Aii!" she said.

"Steady," he said.

"I do not understand this," she said. "Oh!"

"Steady," he said.

"What is going on in my body?" she said.

"Little, as yet," he said.

"No!" she cried. "What are you doing to my body?"

"Nothing," he said.

"What have you done to my body?" she asked.

"Nothing," he said.

"I am different!" she exclaimed.

"Possibly," he said.

"I am sweating," she said. "I am enflamed!"

"You should see your body," he said, "and its condition."

"Oh!" she cried.

"Steady," he said.

"I am afraid," she said. "I do not think I can endure this!"

"You are in no position to resist," he said.

"What are you doing to my body!" she said.

"Awakening it," he said.

"Master!" she said, frightened, awed.

"I think you will soon whimper and moan," he said. "Later you may plead, and beg."

"I do not know what is going on in my body," she said. "I have never had such feelings, such sensations."

"It is nothing to fear," said Tajima. "It is all quite natural, quite normal."

"I am afraid," she said.

"Be not so," he said. "I think we are now ready for subtler caresses."

"Ohh," she said, softly.

I heard nothing more for a time, but then heard a small cry, and a rhapsodic series of soft whimpers.

"Shall I stop?" inquired Tajima.

"No, no, Master," she moaned. "Do not stop, please do not stop!"

"You realize your helplessness?"

"Yes, Master," she said.

The slave was wholly at the mercy of her master.

"You plead, you beg?" he asked.

"Yes," she whispered, "yes, Master!"

"I shall carry you to the summit of the mountain," he said, "to the edge of the cliff, to the brink of the bridge."

"Yes," she said, "yes!"

"And then," he said, "I shall abandon you."

"I do not understand," she said. "Ohhh, Master, Master!"

A bit later, she cried, softly, questioningly, wonderingly, poignantly, "Master?"

I hoped Tajima would be merciful to the slave.

I suspected, by now, the lightning, set to the bowstring of the heavy, dark, surging, turbulent clouds, was prepared to flash, the thunder to roll forth, to the beat of its drums, roaring like an avalanche in the Voltai, precipitating its tons of falling rocks to the valley below.

"Please, Master!" she cried suddenly, frightened, miserably. "Continue! Do not stop! I am there, there! I am ready! I am poised! I shall burst! I cannot help myself! I am bound! I am helpless! I ache! I cannot stand it! Be merciful, Master! Be merciful! Please, Master, be merciful to your slave!"

I waited for a time, uneasily, and then, to my satisfaction I heard the slave cry out, suddenly, explosively, wildly, joyously, disbelievingly, her cry almost instantly stifled by Tajima, presumably his hand clapped over her mouth. Who knew what might lurk about, in this pleasant grove, with its small pool?

There was silence for a time.

I could not even sense the twisting of the body in the grass, nor hear the pulling of the leather against the stakes.

"Oh, Master!" said Nezumi. "Master!"

"Rest now," he said. "Descend slowly. I shall unbind you, and neck chain you, as usual. Later we must trek."

"Yes, Master," she had said.

"More sake," said the leader of the three Ashigaru, foragers for Lord Yamada's march.

Inside the inn, near its door, as noted earlier, were several sacks of rice, while, outside, a handcart waited.

"Have you not had enough?" asked Tajima, pleasantly.

"Perhaps we should think of reporting," said one of the Ashigaru to his leader.

"Rice is gathered," said the leader. "There is plenty of time."

"True," said the fellow, sleepily.

"I am sure," said the innkeeper, "the noble one, he of two swords, is generous, as are all of his quality, and would not mind an additional round of sake, to warm friends on the road."

"Certainly not," said Tajima.

Behind the dragon screen, with Haruki, I was annoyed, as the innkeeper seemed clearly interested in selling another vessel of sake. I was not surprised, however, as, in these perilous times, this inn, off the northern road, might well be less frequently patronized. In unsettled times, dangerous times of unrest and war, the routes of merchants are often altered. There would be less to sell, particularly items of value, in the fortresses, villages, and towns of local daimyos if the daimyos, and most of their officers and Ashigaru, might be absent, not to mention that the approaches to such places would become more hazardous. In such times roads are lonely and bandits grow bold.

"So then, perhaps another round," said the leader of the Ashigaru, with affable incoherence.

"By all means," said Tajima.

But I sensed he was anxious to be on his way.

We might be pursued, and, in any event, there might be others about, other foragers, perhaps less congenial than those with Tajima, even scouts or patrols, assigned to flank the march of Lord Yamada.

"Must we not load the rice and report to the storage master?" said the third Ashigaru to the leader, stumbling somewhat in his diction.

"It is true," said the second, gloomily. "It would not be well to be missed." His articulation was not much superior to that of his fellow.

"There is time," said the leader, "time, time, time."

I feared that one or another might fall asleep.

"Perhaps not," said Tajima. "We are well met, but I must not detain you from your duty."

"Duty," said the leader, "is for warriors, for officers, for those of quality."

"Perhaps we should be on our way," said one of his fellows. But I did not think he was eager to, or cared to, or was able to, spring up, rush to the rice, place it on the cart, seize up the handles, and haul it away.

"Another round?" proposed the innkeeper.

"Yes, yes!" said the leader.

"Of course," said Tajima, pleasantly enough.

Nezumi then must have filled another vessel, and replenished the cups. I suspected Tajima himself had drunk little. It would be important for him to keep his wits about him. I supposed the innkeeper was secluding his own girls, probably locked in a shed somewhere. There was no need for their presence or services, as Nezumi was at hand. Too, it is difficult to assess the nature of armed men, and their interests, particularly in troubled times. They are not local folks come for an evening or the common patronage of an isolated inn. Some may even be bandits, not Ashigaru, and one cannot always be sure of Ashigaru either, particularly out of the sight of officers. Some are likely to be unwilling recruits, in effect, impressed from their villages for various terms of service. Indeed, bandits are largely derived from the peasantry. Many a throat has been cut for a *fukuro* of rice. Occasionally common folk are beaten or killed, houses plundered and burned, women and stock stolen. Even isolated warriors, particularly if *ronin*, or fugitives from lost battles, may be set upon, robbed and killed, with relative impunity. What daimyo is there to protect them, or proceed with the dark retaliations of the Pani? The three fellows with Tajima, on the other hand, seemed good fellows. To be sure, if the guests were to spend the night, the innkeeper's girls would doubtless be demanded, for he would surely have some, and they would be turned out. In many inns on the continent there is an extra charge for the girl; here I suspected, but did not know, certainly for this inn, what might be the case. The innkeeper, of course, was well aware that Haruki and I were about, but, as we were behind the screen, I doubted that the Ashigaru were aware of our presence, or, if aware of it, were in the least concerned. Our separation from Tajima and Nezumi had been thought to be judicious, given that my presence might have occasioned curiosity amongst other patrons of the inn, should such materialize. As it turned out, this separation would prove fortunate.

I heard Nezumi suddenly cry out in alarm.

I leaped to my feet, but Haruki's hand, seizing my sleeve, gave me pause.

"Do not squirm, girl!" said the leader of the Ashigaru.

"Here now," called Tajima, as though drunk himself.

"Give her to us," said the leader. "We will sell her in the camp, and divide the price."

"An excellent suggestion," said Tajima. "But I fear she would bring so little that the profit would not justify the bother."

"True," said the leader. "Look at her hair."

I gathered then that he must have released Nezumi.

I did not think her hair was all that miserable now, as Tajima had tried to remedy the vengeful butchery of his earlier barbering, or, at any rate, not all that miserable, at least for a field slave.

"I am tired," said the leader. "I think I shall rest."

"Fumitaka is already asleep," said one of the Ashigaru.

"I fear we must be on our way," said Tajima.

"So soon?" said the leader.

"I fear so," said Tajima.

Haruki indicated the kitchen entrance to the eating hall, through which we might exit, to rendezvous outside with Tajima and the slave.

Certainly we had dallied overlong in this place.

I had scarcely risen to my feet, when I heard a new, and a very angry, voice. "Besotted dolts!" it cried. "Drunken tarsks! Two Ahn you are late at the checkpoint! Who will vouch for you? Who will bring you to the camp, and conduct you safely to the rice wagons? Your spoil is at the door, the cart is empty! Dally at an inn, will you! Do you not know there are bandits about?"

I noticed the innkeeper move quickly past us, exiting through the door to the kitchen.

"We were inveigled into drink, noble one!" cried the leader of the Ashigaru. "It is the fault of that noble one. Ai!"

I gathered he had been struck.

"Yes, Officer," said Tajima. "It is all my fault. I did not wish to hold these fine fellows from some appointment, but merely to pass the time of day with jolly companions."

"I shall jolly them!" said the voice, and I heard some more blows, and protests, now, perhaps, from the other two Ashigaru. "On the floor, on your bellies!" cried the angry voice. "I shall consider taking your heads!"

"Mercy, noble one!" said the leader. "Who will pull the rice cart?"

"Ho," said the voice, seemingly suddenly pacified, and interested. "You have two swords." He would be addressing Tajima.

"As do you, warrior *san*," said Tajima.

I gathered that polite bows might have been exchanged.

"These oafs are unreliable, and insufferable," said the voice.

"Thoughtless, perhaps," said Tajima.

"They are without honor," said the voice. "They are lazy, greedy beasts. One could line them up behind any banner at hand. They would eat by day and desert by night. They are as skittery as a jard and as sly as a barn snake. More allegiance would be proffered by a turtle."

"They are foragers, probably recently impressed," said Tajima. "They are not with the march. One must not judge all Ashigaru by these happy fellows, many of whom are disciplined, loyal, well-trained, reliable, valuable, dangerous men."

"They are all peasants," said the voice. "They think only of their stomachs, only of eating and drinking, of sitting about and escaping work. Unfortunate that one must fill the ranks with such."

"Surely they have their place, and well support the work of we nobler sorts," said Tajima.

"Who are you?" asked the voice.

"*Ronin*," said Tajima.

"This is an unusual place to be washed ashore," said the voice.

"It is my hope the current will carry me to the house of Yamada," said Tajima.

"The shogun always has a place for those who manage sharp swords well," said the voice.

"One would hope to be found suitable," said Tajima, humbly.

"Where is the innkeeper?" asked the voice.

"I do not know, he was here," said Tajima.

"I do not like it," said the voice.

"How so?" said Tajima.

"He is doubtless a peasant," said the voice.

"Perhaps," said Tajima.

"Is that an inn slave?" asked the voice.

"No," said Tajima. "She is my slave. I bought her for work and girl sport."

"She is obviously of the peasants," said the voice.

"Obviously," said Tajima.

I could not see the reaction of Nezumi, for the dragon screen.

"That is the one good thing about the peasants," said the voice, "aside from raising our rice, that they also, upon occasion, produce lovely daughters, suitable for the collar and the contract, useful for serving and pleasing men of quality."

"Precisely," said Tajima. "It would be inappropriate to expect such delights from women of quality."

"True," said the voice. "I think I shall now take the heads from these louts. Stay where you are, tarsks. Do not move."

"Perhaps I could offer you a drink?" said Tajima.

"Just one," said the voice.

"Perhaps you might spare them," suggested Tajima.

"Why not?" said the voice.

"But only one drink?" asked Tajima.

"Perhaps, two," said the voice.

Behind the dragon screen, Haruki whispered to me, "I am afraid."

"Why," I asked, "gardener *san*?"

"The innkeeper is missing," he said.

Chapter Thirty-One

The Inn Has Visitors

Haruki had scarcely confessed his apprehension when, suddenly, with boisterous shouts and a rushing of bodies, several men crowded into the inn, hurrying through both the main entrance and, I gathered, the rear entrance, as they emerged into the eating hall through the door leading to the kitchen.

I heard Nezumi scream.

"Do not touch your weapons," I heard, "or you die!"

The *tanto* was ripped from my belt, and Haruki, too, was relieved of his knife. Our hands were then tied behind our backs.

"Excellent swords," I heard, from the other side of the screen.

With a miscellany of blades and clubs Haruki and I, after a bit, bound, were ushered about the screen. The three Ashigaru still lay on their bellies on the floor. Tajima and another fellow, a stout fellow, but clearly a warrior, were sitting cross-legged on the floor, their arms tightly bound. Nezumi, trembling, knelt in one corner.

In the center of the eating hall, as though bestride the room, in a short jacket and fur boots, was a short, thick-bodied man. I took him to be the leader of the intruders. He had a wide face, large arms for his body, a scraggly mustache which drooped to his throat, and eyes which, in a human, seemed almost feral. Interesting, I thought, that a man so short should be in charge of at least fifteen ill-clad brigands. But decision and aggression, intelligence and vanity, authority and command, do not all have similar habitats. Leaders are where one finds them, and leadership is not measured by height and weight, nor by age or station. It is one of those rarities which, expressed, is both intangible and unmistakable.

The innkeeper, or he whom I had taken to be the innkeeper, now reappeared. "It took you long enough to respond to my signal," he said.

"It took you long enough to signal," said the leader of the intruders.

"Others had arrived," he said, "among them one with two swords. Such are dangerous. I thought it well to drunken him, with the rice guards. He might then be less to fear. How many men would you wish to lose?"

"He does not appear drunk to me," said the short, thick-bodied leader of the intruders.

"Perhaps, at the edge of death, one sobers quickly," said the innkeeper or he whom I had taken to be the innkeeper.

"Shall we carry out the rice and burn the inn?" asked one of the men.

"No," said the leader. "It serves as a splendid trap."

"The foragers have done well," said another, "as have we. There is much rice, hard to obtain with the exactions of the shogun for pasangs about."

"An entire handcart," said another.

"The villages will be pleased," said another.

"Is there not loot in the inn?" asked a man.

"What there was, we carried off, long ago," said he whom I had taken to be the innkeeper. "We kept the inn girls, that we might, if it seemed appropriate, display them, and have them serve, utilizing them for purposes of disguising our tidy trap."

"They know you are not their master," said a fellow.

"He was bribed away," said a fellow.

"That or be slain," said another. "He chose wisely."

"The girls," said he whom I had taken to be the innkeeper, "would abide our sham, giving not the least signal of our deception, or have their throats cut."

I saw that Tajima and the warrior with him, apparently he who had so liberally castigated the heedless, if not derelict, foragers, had been disarmed, as well as bound. Their weapons seemed now to be in the hands of, or sashes of, various of the intruders. It is frequently the case that brigands arm themselves from the spoil of their victims. Indeed, a superb Pani sword, composed of matched steels, with its successive temperings, layerings, and edgings, usually the product of several smiths, which takes weeks to bring to its perfection, is booty of no small price. Warriors will commonly kill a peasant who is found in possession of one. One supposes that a peasant is not entitled to such a weapon, that such a weapon should not be entrusted to a peasant, indeed, that it is forbidden to them, that it dishonors so fine a weapon if it should be so unworthily, so shamefully, possessed, and that a peasant, in any case, could not afford such a weapon, and so has stolen it, and, as warriors are reluctant to part with such things, on which their lives may hinge, that a warrior must have been killed to obtain it. The warrior might have been an enemy, to be killed on sight, but considerations of class, and propriety, become involved. It is not unknown for an enemy to avenge the death of an enemy, if the enemy was thought to have been inappropriately slain. Warriors who seek one another's head may have more in common with one another than either of them will have with an individual of a different quality, even a supposed ally. Too, perhaps it is unwise to allow, say, a peasant, or merchant, to possess an object of such lethal beauty; who knows what may occur in the night, or if one should be careless in crossing an unfamiliar threshold?

"You are Arashi, the bandit, are you not?" said the fellow, the warrior, tightly bound, sitting cross-legged on the floor, next to Tajima.

"I am Arashi, the patriot," said the leader of the intruders.

"It is known you are about," said the warrior.

"But not seen," said Arashi.

"It is thought you were crucified," said the warrior.

"Five times," said Arashi, "but they were others, not even of my band. Perhaps such reports, promulgated by such as you, mollify the shogun."

"They gave you different names," said the warrior.

"And the leaders of five bands were thought apprehended and executed?" asked Arashi.

"Yes," said the warrior.

"But innocent men died."

"Yes."

"And I remained unseen," said Arashi.

"I see you now," said the warrior.

"Who are you, noble one?" asked Arashi.

"I am Yasushi, twenty-third constable of the march of Lord Yamada, Shogun of the Islands," said the bound fellow next to Tajima.

"He came alone to the inn," said he whom I had taken to be the innkeeper, "to inquire after three foragers, the rice guards prone before you."

"He is a fool, to risk his life and swords, to inquire after foragers."

"A brave fool," said Tajima.

"You fellows," said Arashi, kicking one of the prone foragers, "why are you on the floor, so?"

"We were commanded to the floor," said the leader, "that our heads might be the more easily taken."

"You are bigger fools than he," said Arashi.

"No," said Tajima. "It is a splendid tribute to the discipline maintained within the ranks of the cohorts of Yamada."

"It is second only," said Arashi, "to the discipline maintained within my own band."

"An unreliable concourse of self-seeking dolts and bumpkins," said Yasushi.

"There is no man here who will not, at my command, cut his own throat," said Arashi.

"Order several to do so," said Yasushi.

"One must be prepared to kill swiftly and savagely to maintain such discipline," said Tajima.

"True," said Arashi.

"And soon risk a knife in the back," said Tajima.

"Not as long as I can provide rice," said Arashi.

"Rice is scarce in the villages?" said Tajima.

"Yes," said Arashi.

"There is an alternative to force, and fear," said Tajima.

"Loyalty, honor?" said Arashi.

"Yes," said Tajima.

"I have heard of such things," said Arashi. "In the villages they are not real. In the villages hunger is real, death is real."

"Rise against Yamada," said Tajima.

"Challenge, rather, the rising of Tor-tu-Gor, the tides of Thassa."

"I do not think it wise for you to remain too long in this place," said he whom I had taken to be the innkeeper.

"Gather up the rice by the door," said Arashi, gesturing to some of his fellows. "Load the cart. We are soon away."

Three of his band left the hall.

Arashi then returned his attention to the three prone Ashigaru.

"Ai!" said one of them, kicked.

"There is much rice," said Arashi. "It is little wonder you paused to celebrate."

"One grows thirsty, high one," said the leader of the three foragers.

"How is it you were so successful?" inquired Arashi.

"Men are generous when they are kneeling, head down, and a glaive is at the back of their necks," said the leader.

"You were unwise to stop here," said Arashi. "You would have done better to hurry back to the North Road."

"It is true, high one," said the leader. "But wisdom may not appear until the moons have risen."

"You were fools to lie here, docile, like trussed verr, waiting to be butchered," said Arashi.

"Not really, high one," said the leader. "The rice might be lost, if we were not to transport it back to the camp."

"Clever rogues," said Arashi. "Now we shall see how clever you really are. I offer you a choice. Join my band or die."

"We are your men," said the leader of the three foragers.

"Despicable peasants!" cried Yasushi, he who had identified himself as the twenty-third of Lord Yamada's march constables.

I had no idea how many such constables serviced the march. As there were several thousand men involved, hundreds of warriors and a great many Ashigaru, I supposed it must be several. Aside from the business of scouts, patrols, skirmishers, spies, and such, ancillary to the major movements of men, a march must be ordered, supervised, policed, and supplied. Banners are not likely to fly on the rice carts but without the rice carts the banners may not fly at all.

"Who are these?" inquired Arashi, now giving us his attention.

Haruki and I, bound, had been standing to one side.

"Two wayfarers," said he whom I had taken to be the innkeeper. "One is clearly foreign, as may be seen from the eyes and skin, and the firelike hair. I take him to be a deserter, a mercenary fled from the holding of Temmu, one forsaking a doomed cause."

"Then at least one man here is wise," said Arashi. "Mercenaries have no loyalty, save only to gold or rice."

"The other is clearly Pani, and of our sort."

"I imposed upon him," I said, "that he serve me as intermediary and guide."

Arashi turned to his men, and gestured to the bound warriors, and to Haruki and myself. "Search them," he said, "and rifle their packs, if such there be."

"You should be soon gone," said he whom I had taken to be the innkeeper.

"Here!" called one of the intruders, tearing the string of coins, not many coins, to be sure, from the neck of Haruki. My wallet contained a better trove, but it contained no more than what it bore when I had been drugged long ago in the holding of Temmu. Similarly disappointing, I am sure, were the meager gleanings extracted from the two warriors. Yasushi, in his search for missing foragers, had carried but two coins, and of bronze, folded in his sash, and Tajima, in his venture to obtain a slave, had carried but one, of copper. Their swords and knives, however, given their exquisite smithing, were of considerable value. On that score Arashi and his men had no cause for disappointment. Tajima's Nezumi, too, of course, had some value, but, given the condition of her hair, and as she had not been bid upon, it was not clear what it might be.

"These two," asked Arashi, indicating Haruki and myself, "are not with the young warrior, and the slave?"

"No," said he whom I had taken to be the innkeeper. "They dined secretly, and separately, concealed behind the dragon screen. I think they fear detection. One is a fugitive, and the other, it seems, is an abettor of his flight."

"But unwillingly so," I said.

"He is of the peasantry," said Arashi. "We may put the choice to him."

I realized then, to my unease, that the choice, or such, was not to be put to everyone. I tested the ropes. I was well tied.

"Do not turn to me, high one," said Haruki. "I am a humble gardener. You have no flowers to tend and I would consume rice. Too, I have no skill in cutting throats."

"Please, be off," urged he whom I had taken to be the innkeeper.

"The rice is loaded," said one of the intruders, entering.

"So hurry," said he whom I had taken to be the innkeeper.

"I would have more here than rice," said Arashi.

"There is no more," said he whom I had taken to be the innkeeper.

"There are girls in the shed," said a fellow. "Six."

"I need them," said he whom I had taken to be the innkeeper, "to serve, to maintain the facade of authenticity."

"Put them on a rope and tie them to the back of the rice cart," said Arashi.

"No!" said he whom I had taken to be the innkeeper.

"We will find someone to sell them, in a Yamada camp," said Arashi.

"What am I to do for inn girls?"

"Hungry peasants will bring in other daughters," said Arashi. "But buy only the most beautiful, for we may wish to sell them later."

It might be mentioned that it is not only hungry, desperate peasants, driven to extremities, who sell their daughters. Others may do so, as well. The matter is cultural. It is not unusual, for example, for proud, wayward daughters to be marketed. The life of such a girl changes. It is difficult to be proud and wayward when one is owned. And, of course, there is always money, or goods, to be made from the sale of a daughter. That is a temptation. Also, it might be mentioned, some daughters request their sale, if only to escape the drudgery and limitations of the villages.

"Yes, chieftain *san*," said he whom I had taken to be the innkeeper.

"Attend to it," said Arashi to some of his men, and they exited.

As I have suggested, most exchange in the islands is done not in terms of coins, or notes, from one establishment or another on some Street of Coins, but in kind, in terms of rice, millet, fish, cloth, and such. And, although I may not have made this hitherto explicitly clear, amongst such commodities, as I suppose may be obvious, may be numbered women.

And in war, of course, women, on the islands, and certainly on continental Gor, are accounted loot, and what loot could be lovelier, or more desirable? One of the delights and remunerations of victory is appropriating the most beautiful of the enemy's women for your slaves, to have them collared at your feet, obedient and helpless, yours to do with as you wish.

What man does not desire a slave?

What man can be happy without a slave?

And what slave can be happy without her master?

"Master!" wept Nezumi, plaintively, and hurried to Tajima, who did not even appear to notice her.

"Master, Master!" wept Nezumi.

"Put her on the girl-rope, with the others," said Arashi.

"Master!" cried Nezumi, as she was seized by the arm and yanked to her feet, and conducted, stumbling, weeping, outside, through the main entrance, where the rice cart, now heavily laden, I supposed, was waiting.

No sign of any expression was on the face of Tajima.

He seemed utterly impassive.

Arashi had one of the swords, a field sword, and, grasping the tasseled handle in two hands, divided the air with it, twice. "Whose blade is this?" he inquired.

"Mine," said Yasushi. "Do not befoul it."

"It is ill-balanced," said Arashi.

"Not for the hand for which it was made," said Yasushi.

"You and your fellow are officers," said Arashi. "What ransom might you bring?"

"He will bring none," said he whom I had taken for the innkeeper, indicating Tajima. "He is *ronin*, a transient stranger, one with no rice giver, one with no master, one with no lord."

"Nor will I," snarled Yasushi. "I wear the ropes of a bandit. I am dishonored. The shogun would have me bound, and caged with starving urts. All I ask from you is a blade, with which I might end my disgrace."

"Surely both might bring some ransom," I suggested, "one as a potential recruit to the cohorts of Yamada, the other as a brave and valued constable."

"They are witnesses to our deeds, and faces, chieftain *san*," said he whom I had taken to be an innkeeper.

"And what of these two?" asked Arashi, indicating Haruki and myself.

"Similarly," said he whom I had taken to be the innkeeper.

"I request the blade," said Yasushi. "It is my right."

"We do not share codes," said Arashi.

"You deny it to me?" asked Yasushi.

"Yes," said Arashi.

"Then I must act," said Yasushi. "You leave me no choice. You are under arrest. You are to free me, and then you, and your band, are to return with me to the camp of Lord Yamada, Shogun of the Islands, to stand judgment."

"Are you mad?" asked Arashi.

"No," said Yasushi. "I have done my duty. You have been placed under arrest. The words have been spoken. The order has been issued."

"Brave fellow!" cried Tajima.

"I think you are mad," said Arashi.

"No," said Yasushi.

"You think words are things," said Arashi, "but things are things, not words. The name of water does not assuage thirst, nor the name of food fill a belly. So, too, the name of arrest does not arrest. A decree without the sword is no more than a sword without a blade. There is no law without the bow and glaive."

I was reminded of a saying I had heard long ago. "The laws of Cos march with the spears of Cos."

"What are we to do, chieftain *san*?" asked one of the intruders.

"Free him," said Arashi.

"Chieftain *san*?" said a man.

"Free him," said Arashi. "Then strip him, and nail him to the floor."

"Yes, chieftain *san*," said two men, hurrying to Yasushi.

"Despicable tarsk!" cried Tajima.

"He, too," added Arashi.

"I trust all is prepared outside," said he whom I had taken for an innkeeper, "the cart ready, the girl-rope filled with its occupants."

353

"We will pause long enough to see this carpentry done," said Arashi.

"What of these?" asked one of the intruders, indicating Haruki and myself.

"We shall let them observe," said Arashi, "and then, after a time, we shall be done with them, all of them."

"One is of the peasantry," said a man.

"He made his choice," said Arashi. "The other is a deserter, and he who deserts one cause will as promptly desert another."

"Yes, chieftain *san*," said the man.

He whom I had taken to be the innkeeper, nervous, clutching his hands, went to the main entrance.

"Is all in readiness?" inquired Arashi.

"The cart is laden," said he whom I had taken to be the innkeeper, "and the girl-rope is in order, the sex-tarsks appropriately strung in its keeping."

"Good," said Arashi.

Yasushi was struggling in the keeping of two of the intruders. Tajima was struggling in his ropes.

"But chieftain *san*," said he whom I had taken to be an innkeeper, "I do not see your men."

"What?" said Arashi, looking up, quickly.

At that moment he whom I had taken to be an innkeeper, staggered back, and fell, a long Pani arrow, thrice-fletched, buried in his heart.

Chapter Thirty-Two

What Occurred Later in the Inn

In the eating hall of the inn consternation reigned.

Within, men looked wildly about, uncertain, weapons in hand. Some of the intruders plunged through the door leading to the kitchen, to seek the rear entrance of the inn. Shortly thereafter I heard cries of dismay, and some of death. I heard buffeting, falling, and cries of anger, and a slamming and barring of the rear entrance. No arrows flew through the front entrance. The Pani archer seldom releases his missile without a clear target. Yasushi, half unroped, but still muchly bound, his shirt torn, had an arm free, and was tearing at his ropes. His captors stood back, looking to Arashi, who looked outside, obliquely, quickly, muchly concealing his body. Another arrow struck the door jamb, quivering in place. I could see the shadow of its movement, on the other side of the jamb. "Kill them!" ordered Arashi, but the glaives of two of the three foragers warned his men away from Yasushi and Tajima, the latter helpless, but spilled to his side. Some inn girl, or, perhaps Nezumi, screamed outside. I hoped they had the common sense to fall to the dirt or conceal themselves behind the substantial shielding provided by the layers of sacks of rice. Haruki and I backed against the dragon screen which fell, and, stumbling, ruining it, fell behind it, and then struggled up, past the low table, our backs to the side of the inn. We seemed well neglected, given the tumult within, from which we were largely separated. From our position we could see the eating hall, and partly into the kitchen. One of the three foragers, their leader, was cutting the ropes from Yasushi.

"We are your men, noble one!" he assured Yasushi. "Hurry!" cried Yasushi. "Hurry! And I will have you all, careless, foolish, dallying dolts, flogged in camp!"

"Yes, noble one," said the leader, happily, his knife parting the ropes on Yasushi's ankles.

One of the intruders made as though to leap on Yasushi, but the thrust of a glaive forced him back, bloodied.

Another girl, outside, screamed.

The leader of the foragers then addressed himself to the bonds of Tajima. I looked wildly about. Clubs and swords, knives, and one glaive, were in the grip of the intruders. Two glaives, alone, were interposed between a number of distraught, confused intruders and Yasushi and Tajima. I did not think two such weapons, however well wielded, could resist any organized charge or attack. Unlike the companion sword or the shorter *tanto*, and unlike the typical Gorean *gladius*, they are not intended for close work. Arashi flung shut the doors of the inn, and, as four arrows splintered half through the wood, he succeeded in barring the portal.

"There cannot be many of them!" he cried.

"There may be a thousand!" said a man. "They may be as leaves, as the sands of the shore!"

"Probably there are no more than ten," said Arashi. "Doubtless we outnumber them, even with losses!"

I had, of course, no knowledge of what might be the case outside the inn, but it was brought home to me, forcibly, the common military strategy of confusing one's enemies as to the nature and quantity of one's strength. An enemy's suspicions, and fears, often work to one's advantage. Let him conjecture the worst.

Were there a hundred men outside, or ten, who, concealed, shifted about and distributed their fire? Were there a hundred men outside, or ten, who applied themselves efficiently, under conditions of limited vision, on a covered bridge, in a pass, or at the rear door of an inn not far from the North Road?

Ten men can defeat a hundred if ten attack five, and attack five again, and again.

Even in the earliest, preserved records of war, on both Earth and Gor, it is clear that a sophisticated variety of tactics was already in place, and familiar. There are men who study war with same avidity and attention as others study the materials of the earth and the movements of the stars.

"No more than ten!" said Arashi.

I suspected the conjecture of Arashi was correct, but what if it were not?

"A hundred!" speculated a fellow.

"Ten!" shouted Arashi, angrily.

"Ten may be warriors!" said a man.

Obviously those outside, or some of them, had bows at their disposal. This lovely weapon was not possessed by the bandits, who, simple, ignorant men, made do, for the most part, with knives and clubs.

Indeed, might not ten men, each with ten arrows, match even a hundred, if that hundred could not reach them, and bore but knives and clubs?

To be sure, shooting penned verr is poor sport.

"If there are many," said Arashi, "let them try to enter!"

A few men might hold a bridge, a pass, a threshold.

"In darkness," he said, "we will rush forth, and break, and scatter!"

"There will be watch fires," said a man.

"We will bear tables," said Arashi, "and, so shielded, sustain the first volley, and then disappear in the darkness."

"There may be many," said a man.

"If there were many," said Arashi, "they would force the doors."

Arashi, I thought, was shrewd. I thought he knew more of war than would be expected of a peasant, and bandit.

I also supposed that he would be aware of another possibility. To be sure, it was one he would be likely to keep to himself. It would not hearten his men.

"I smell smoke!" cried a man.

I could hear a fierce crackling from above.

"The roof is on fire!" screamed a bandit.

I could not see the fire, for the sleeping loft, reachable at one end of the eating hall by a ladder, but I could hear it, and, shortly thereafter, began to feel the heat, and the burning of the air.

Some of the bandits were in the kitchen, by the rear entrance, which they had blocked. Most, seven, not counting their leader, Arashi, were in the eating hall. They stood about, confused, frightened. At the side of the eating hall, backed against the wall, now unthreatened, perhaps forgotten in the distress and tumult, were Tajima and the constable, Yasushi. Both were unarmed. The foragers, two with glaives, the other with a drawn knife, were still between them and the bandits. Tajima was looking about, wildly. Well did the young warrior recognize the imminent danger, which was not at all limited to the blades and clubs of bandits. Yasushi had his eyes fixed on Arashi. He opened and closed his fists, as though he would that a weapon might somehow appear in them.

Arashi swept his hand toward Tajima, Yasushi, and the foragers. "Kill them!" he cried.

The bandits milled, wavering.

Who would be the first to fling himself upon the brandished glaives of determined Ashigaru?

Yet, I was sure the bandits, despite the danger, and despite their fear, and their dread of the unknown quantity of the forces outside, would respond to Arashi's command.

Indeed, given their misery and confusion I thought they might have been willing to respond to any order addressed to them with sufficient authority, perhaps by anyone.

The two glaives and the knife, I was sure, could not withstand a concerted attack of several desperate men.

"Kill them!" cried Arashi, again.

"Come back!" cried Haruki. But by the time he called out, from back where we had been standing, ill at ease, apprehensive, observant, unobtrusive, even discounted, against the wall, I was across the room. The nearest bandit, poised to attack, facing the foragers, had no time to react. He had barely lifted his head, startled, trying to register the sound, the possible movement, behind him, when the weight of my shoulders struck against the back of his knees, and he pitched backward, suddenly, awkwardly, forcibly, miserably, half paralyzed. I was on my feet. I jammed my heel down on his throat. His blade, a field sword, that purloined from Tajima, was loose in his hand. I stomped on his wrist and the hilt was free, and then, with a sweeping kick, I slid the loose blade across the floor, between the Ashigaru, to Yasushi, who seized it up with a cry of elation.

I crouched down, my hands tied behind me.

I was not attacked.

Two of the bandits, like sheaves of wheat, reeled back, cut from the path of the exultant Yasushi. The others drew back. One threw his blade to the floor.

I could hear the fire roar through the roof, above the sleeping loft. I heard a plank fall. Near the ladder I could see sparks. The sleeping loft, once the fire reached the straw matting, would erupt with flame.

Arashi turned, wildly, seeing Yasushi, armed. He brought up his own field sword and blocked the fierce blow which might have taken his head. His own attempt to strike was turned aside, smartly, twice, by Yasushi, almost indifferently.

"Do not fear," said Yasushi. "I want you alive."

"Die!" cried Arashi, rushing upon him, flailing.

"I fear," said Yasushi, "you cannot touch me."

"Ai!" cried Arashi, in pain.

"But I can touch you," said Yasushi.

Arashi winced, drawing back, his shirt bright with blood.

The four bandits in the eating hall, left of the seven, fled from the hall into the kitchen.

"Flee," they cried to their fellows blockading the door.

"Arrows!" cried one, protestingly.

"A warrior, a warrior inside, is armed," cried one of the fugitives from the eating hall.

"It is a larl, a larl with fangs of steel," wept a man. "It is loose!"

"Unbar the door. Escape!" cried another.

Tajima, securing a companion sword from one of the fallen bandits, severed the bonds on my wrists. They parted easily, almost falling away from the blade. Such a blade, lifted, can divide silk.

I heard the heavy wooden bars removed from their mounts at the back door to the inn. Crates, too, which had been piled against the door, were cast aside. I heard an arrow splinter into the door.

I did not know what lay without, in the back, but I did not envy the miserable, fear-stricken bandits who, crying out, burst outward, buffeting one another, into the sunlight.

The three foragers, now each with a glaive, stood back.

Arashi and Yasushi had the main room, the eating hall, muchly to themselves.

The inn grew hot.

Smoke was about, like cruel, dark, dry air.

I retrieved the *tanto* which had been taken from me, from one of the two bandits whom Yasushi had scarcely noticed, acknowledging them merely with two dismissive gestures of steel. I then relieved Haruki of his bonds.

"Behold Yasushi!" exclaimed Tajima. "See the swordwork. The man is a master!"

Yasushi, now, was doing no more than playing with the desperate, half-frenzied Arashi.

"We must depart the inn," I said. "When the roof falls it may take the loft with it, and the ceiling will cave in."

Haruki was coughing.

He was far from the pleasantries, the colors and perfumes, of his garden.

"That man is a master!" said Tajima, awed.

"Let us leave," I said.

"But who is without?" said Tajima.

"It does not much matter," I said.

A crash came from above.

"The roof falls!" I said.

Hopefully the loft floor would hold, if only long enough for us to make our escape.

There was a great, crackling roar of flames above, and a new wave of heat, and I could see the brightness above through the cracks in the ceiling, cracks I had not even noticed until now, until they were bright with light.

"Kill me!" pleaded Arashi.

"I want you alive," said Yasushi.

I did not know the fate of the bandits who had exited the inn through the rear entrance, nor, indeed, those whom the fellow I had taken for the innkeeper had failed to discern, when he had thought to inquire into the preparations for departure.

Yasushi then struck the blade from the hand of Arashi, who then stood before him, weary, bleeding, unarmed.

"You are under arrest," said Yasushi.

Arashi glared angrily at the floor.

"Bind him," said Yasushi, to the three Ashigaru, the foragers, "two leashes, and the other will herd him with a glaive."

"Yes, noble one," said the leader of the foragers.

"I suggest it is time to leave the inn," I said.

Yasushi handed his field sword to Tajima, and regained his own weapon.

"It is ill-balanced," said Arashi.

"Not for the hand for which it was formed," said Yasushi.

Both warriors then, Yasushi and young Tajima, were soon armed with their own weaponry.

I threw down the bars with which Arashi had secured the door. I feared the ceiling, the floor of the loft, would soon crash down, with a blanket of showering, burning planks.

Smoke permeated the room.

The wall of the eating hall, to the left as one would enter, was aflame.

The main entrance to the inn had then been flung open.

Arashi, his upper body swathed with rope, two rope leashes on his neck, each in the keeping of an Ashigaru, stood framed in the doorway.

He was thrust forward, into the courtyard.

Then behind him, his shirt torn, a sword in each hand, stood Yasushi. "I am Yasushi," he announced, "a march constable of Lord Yamada. This man is Arashi, the bandit. He is my prisoner."

I saw no one outside, but I knew they were there.

No sooner had Yasushi, Tajima, Haruki, and myself exited the inn than the ceiling collapsed.

We looked about.

"Where are they?" I asked.

"About," said Yasushi.

"Master!" cried Nezumi, who was the last on a rope coffle, a neck coffle, its free end tied to the back of the laden rice cart. The girls' hands were tied behind their back. The inn girls wore inn tunics, sleeveless and revealing, and Nezumi less, the tunic of a field slave. On continental Gor, girls are often coffled naked, which protects tunics against the dust of the trail, and such, and are usually chain-coffled, rather than rope-coffled. The chain affords superior security. It is harder to make off with a chained slave than a roped slave. Too, it is thought that a chain has an excellent effect on a woman. A woman on a chain is in little doubt that she is a slave. "Oh, Master!" cried Nezumi, joyously. "You are alive, Master!"

Tajima strode to her, angrily. "On your knees," he said. "Head down!" "Yes, Master!" she said. The other girls, alarmed, swiftly assumed this position, as well, one quite meaningful to a woman, a position suitable for a woman, a position of slave submission. "Were you given permission to speak?" asked Tajima. "Forgive me, Master," she said.

"I see no one," I said.

"They do not wish to be seen," said Yasushi.

"Perhaps arrows are trained upon us now," I said.

"I would suppose so," said Yasushi.

Tajima then approached Yasushi.

"You are a master swordsman," said Tajima, humbly, bowing to Yasushi, who returned this courtesy. Tajima, of course, had bowed first, and more deeply. "It is rare to see such skill," said Tajima. "You are a master."

"Long ago," said Yasushi, "on the palace grounds of Lord Yamada, Shogun of the Islands, I profited from the instruction of an itinerant master."

"May I ask, noble one," inquired Tajima, "his name?"

"You may," said Yasushi. "His name was Nodachi."

Chapter Thirty-Three

We Will Depart from the Vicinity of the Inn

"There," said Haruki.

Several yards away, rising from the grass, was a tall figure, clearly a man of two swords.

Almost at the same time several other figures emerged, as well, some with bows. And four others appeared, too, two from behind each side of the collapsed, burning inn, and one of each of these two held a bow.

"Warriors, all," said Haruki, marveling.

"Strange," I said. Usually Ashigaru would be more in evidence.

"How many?" I asked Haruki.

"I see twenty, with a high officer," said Haruki.

"I, too," I said.

"Tal," said Yasushi, bowing.

"I am Kazumitsu," said he who seemed most prominent amongst the now visible participants in this recently concluded, small siege, "special officer to Lord Yamada, Shogun of the Islands." He who had identified himself as Kazumitsu was a tall, angular man, with a lean face. His hair, as with many of the warriors, was bound in a knot at the back of his head.

"You have done well," said Yasushi. "You have engaged the band of my prisoner, Arashi, the bandit. I suspect few escaped."

"None escaped," said the angular man.

"Excellent," said Yasushi.

"I do not understand," I said to Haruki. "I do not see why

twenty warriors would pursue Arashi, and his band, with not even one Ashigaru."

"It does not bode well, noble one," said Haruki.

"Many have sought Arashi, and failed to find him," said Yasushi. "Rather it is he who finds others. He moves unseen, like the wind, he strikes like lightning, and vanishes as swiftly. How did you mark his path, how did you locate him? Many, for months, have failed? How is it that you, of all, found him?"

"We did not find him," said Kazumitsu.

"I feared as much," said Haruki.

"I do not understand, Kazumitsu *san*," said Yasushi.

"Arashi was a mere impediment," said Kazumitsu, "an obstacle, to be cleared away."

"I am uneasy," I said.

"Consider warriors," said Haruki, "twenty, consider the absence of Ashigaru, consider one who leads, a special officer to the shogun."

"A formidable force," I said, "to pursue a small outlaw band, a band easy to conceal, and accustomed to move with stealth."

"Yes, noble one," said Haruki.

I recalled the village where we had worked, and where Nezumi had been sent to the wading fields. We had feared that, in that village, we might have provoked suspicion. Haruki had informed us of two men who had slipped from the village. It was the village from which we had stolen away, using Haruki's makeshift ladder, high enough to clear the palisade.

"This party then," I said, "was not searching for bandits."

"I fear not," said Haruki.

"I fear its nature," I said.

"It is clearly an unusual party, a special party," said Haruki.

"A pursuit party?" I said.

"I fear so," said Haruki.

"And we," I said, "are the object of its pursuit?"

"I fear so," said Haruki.

"There was no sign we were pursued," I said.

"Sometimes," said Haruki, "there is no sign."

I noted now that several of the warriors had gathered about us.

"We must to the North Road," said Yasushi. "There is rice to deliver to the rice wagons."

Kazumitsu went to within a few feet of the burning inn, and, for several Ihn, sometimes moving about, looked into the raging debris.

"The rice should be delivered," said Yasushi.

Kazumitsu turned back to our party.

"The rice," said Yasushi.

"There is no hurry," said Kazumitsu. "We will wait until the fire subsides. We will then seek amongst the ashes."

"Why?" asked Yasushi.

"There are bodies there," he said. "We will gather heads."

Chapter Thirty-Four

Yasushi and Kazumitsu Hold Converse; This Occurs in the Vicinity of a Prison Pen

"I fear these are not those whom you seek," said Yasushi, addressing himself to a taciturn, attentive Kazumitsu, outside the vertical wooden bars, the palings, of the prisoner pen in which we were incarcerated, a temporary pen in the road camp of Lord Yamada's march. "As I understand it you were instructed to apprehend for inquiry a party of four who visited, some days ago, Lord Yamada's village of the Two Veminiums."

"There were four apprehended," said Kazumitsu.

"But these two," said Yasushi, indicating Haruki and myself, "are not with the other two. They dined separately."

"It is easy to dine separately," said Kazumitsu.

"Trails may be confused," said Yasushi.

"Two matters are involved," said Kazumitsu. "The rider of a demon bird has visited a hundred villages, alerting them to watch for a tarnsman and Sumomo, the stolen daughter of the shogun."

"It is thought," said Yasushi, "that the bold tarnsman and his fair captive, Sumomo, outdistanced their pursuit and that she is now a prisoner in the holding of Temmu, the Wicked, or somewhere in a nest of demon birds."

"No," said Kazumitsu. "The pursuit was being successfully effected. The pursuers were closing. Then the gap enlarged, and the pursuit proved fruitless. From this it is conjectured that the pursued tarn was no longer burdened, while those of the pursuers were."

"I see," said Yasushi, satisfied.

"Thus," said Kazumitsu, "the alerting of the villages."

"It is speculated the mysterious tarnsman and his prize are afoot?"

"Yes," said Kazumitsu, "and doubtless attempting to reach the holding of Temmu, or the camp of the demon birds."

"Doubtless," said Yasushi.

"And amongst the four," said Kazumitsu, "are a warrior and a woman."

"The warrior," said Yasushi, "who is named Tajima, is *ronin*, and seeks to serve the shogun. He does not flee the shogun but has come far to serve him. You intercepted him on his way to the dais. The woman, whom I gather you have inspected, is scarcely a shogun's daughter. Such a thought is absurd. Look well upon her. She is a lowly, cropped-hair, collared field slave."

"Any woman may be collared, and have her hair cropped," said Kazumitsu.

"Who would dare inflict on a shogun's daughter the degrading yoke of bondage?" asked Yasushi.

"What of the other two?" said Kazumitsu. "All were in the inn."

"A coincidence," said Yasushi.

"It may not have been a coincidence," said Kazumitsu.

"Perhaps not," said Yasushi. "They may have met on the trail."

"They may well be the four reported in the village of the Two Veminiums," said Kazumitsu.

"It is possible, if not likely," said Yasushi. "Consider the separation in the inn. But even if it is so, that these are the four you sought, of what interest or importance would they be, for anyone, a free warrior, zealous for a shogun's rice; a field slave; a foreigner, probably a deserter from the camp of Temmu; and a peasant?"

"Why does Yasushi, a march constable, concern himself in these matters?" asked Kazumitsu.

"In an inn," said Yasushi, "we shared danger, and war."

"Ah," said Kazumitsu.

"Too," said Yasushi. "I fear for you."

"I do not understand," said Kazumitsu.

"You are, as I have it," said Yasushi, "a special officer, and, it seems, your special office, presumably shared with others, is to locate and apprehend an unknown tarnsman and a high lady, Sumomo, the daughter of Lord Yamada."

"That is true, noble constable," said Kazumitsu.

"Thus I am concerned for you," said Yasushi. "The shogun is not a patient man. If you present this motley four before him, hazarding the claim that this *ronin* warrior, who wishes only to see him, is a tarnsman, indeed, the one who abducted his daughter, and that a field slave is his daughter, I fear for your head."

"I see," said Kazumitsu.

"Surely these words will be difficult to dislodge from your mind," said Yasushi.

"What am I to do?" asked Kazumitsu.

"At the moment, nothing," said Yasushi. "Your prisoners are all in custody. There is nothing to fear on that score. In the morning, as a march constable, I shall petition an audience with the camp lord, second under the shogun himself. He will be familiar with Sumomo. He need only look at the field slave, and see that she is not Sumomo. You may then see to the release of the prisoners, and let the warrior enlist his weaponry in the service of the shogun, and later marshal your men and resume your search."

"And what if the field slave is Sumomo?" asked Kazumitsu.

"You cannot be serious," said Yasushi.

"What if it is Sumomo?"

"Then," said Yasushi, "you will report to the shogun, your office well discharged, and accept his gratitude."

"Then," said Kazumitsu, "until morning."

He then left the vicinity of the thick, heavy bars, the palings.

"Have no fear, my friends," said Yasushi. "You will be free by noon tomorrow."

I pressed myself against the opening between two of those stout, vertical bars.

"Noble one," I said.

"Yes?" said Yasushi.

"Perhaps the camp lord has never seen the gracious daughter of the great shogun."

"Have no fear," said Yasushi. "He is an intimate of the shogun himself, and a daimyo who has been in frequent attendance in the palace. He will be quite familiar with Sumomo. Do not be concerned. He will see immediately that the field slave is not Sumomo."

"Good," I said.

"Then you will all be free," said Yasushi.

"Excellent," I said. "Who is the camp lord?"

"You would not know him," said Yasushi. "He is an exalted personage, a most high and favored daimyo, Lord Akio."

Chapter Thirty-Five

In the Prison Pen

"We are lost!" said Tajima, sitting, cross-legged, with us, on the dirt, inside the prison pen. "Lord Akio knows me, from the day of the supper with Lord Yamada, and will certainly recognize Sumomo. He will thus know me for the abducting tarnsman and will publicly announce her identity, and then I shall be put to death, doubtless without great haste, and Nezumi will be returned to Lord Yamada, to endure some fearful fate, perhaps the eels once more, though now, presumably, fed to them as a stripped, blindfolded slave."

Nezumi was not with us in the prison pen.

One would not put an attractive slave, even a cropped-hair field slave in a pen with more than fifty virile males, unless as a punishment. Sometimes a free woman, from a conquered, hated city, is cast naked into a cage or pen of male slaves. Later, when the slaves are whipped back, and she is drawn forth, shaken and shuddering, she is fit for the collar.

We did not know Nezumi's location.

"For me," said Haruki, "I, as I, too, will be known, and the matter of the message vulos will be recalled, will perish unpleasantly. I would not expect to be twice rescued from the straw jacket."

"You, Tarl Cabot, Tarnsman, may be spared," said Tajima.

"I would not think so," I said. "My value to Lord Yamada seems considerably decreased. He is marching on the holding of Temmu. Thus, for some reason, which I do not understand, it seems he is prepared to discount the danger of the tarn cavalry. That I should be in his power is apparently no longer important to him. Too, the freeing of the fellows by the road, in the business of the straw jackets, I suspect, will be laid to my account, and regarded as confirmed by my flight. Clearly I have not conducted myself as his ally, or possible ally."

"There is, too, I fear," said Tajima, "another consideration."

"What is that?" I asked.

"Our friend Yasushi," he said, "in his attempt to protect us, all of us, made much of the possibility that we were not connected, that we might not be the four sought, or such, or, if the four, that there was nothing of importance in our association, which might have been merely casual."

"Yes?" I said.

"Accordingly," said Tajima, "Lord Akio, who will doubtless surmise your likely identities, and may easily inquire into the matter, if in doubt, need not report your presence to Lord Yamada. In guileful innocence, as though accepting the speculation of the noble Yasushi, he may give no account of you. This will free him to deal with you independently, with impunity, as he may wish."

"I do not think," said Haruki, "the noble lord is overfond of a gardener, one who frequents a cot of message vulos."

"Nor," I said, "of a barbarian tarnsman, who has taken to the saddle on behalf of Lord Temmu."

"I think he fears you," said Haruki.

"That does not improve the situation," I said.

"Not at all," said Tajima.

When we had come to the march camp of Yamada, it had been something of a procession. I think both our captor, the officer Kazumitsu, and the march constable, the honorable Yasushi, with his captive, Arashi, the bandit chieftain, did not deign to seek some modest or secret entry into the camp, but, rather, entered in such a way as to proclaim their satisfaction with their day's work. The camp must have been some two or three pasangs in diameter. The circle is the geometrical form containing the most area for its perimeter. On continental Gor temporary camps are usually laid out in squares, moated and palisaded if possible, with blockhouses at the corners and two gates, and a reticulation of straight streets, in terms of which the

units are ordered. As nearly as I could determine the Yamada
camp was divided into several flaring areas, rather as a series
of spokes in a wheel might divide intervening surfaces. There
were ten or more, I was told more, as apparently some previously
unallied daimyos seem to have declared for Yamada, with their
officers and men, and supplementary personnel. The tent of
each daimyo lay near what would be the center of the wheel, the
hub of which was occupied by the command tent of the shogun
himself. His own forces, which were considerable, occupied two
or three of what we have spoken of as "intervening surfaces."
Interestingly enough, although I supposed scouts, outrunners,
guards, and such must have been about, the camp itself was
not fortified, even by a deep ditch, the dirt from which would
have been piled high behind the ditch, to form a wall. I did not
know if this apparent lack of care was a function of the distance
from the lands of Temmu, a sense of the weakness of the forces
of Temmu, or was merely to be attributed to the arrogance of
a mighty shogun. After all, the fearsome larl does not build
ramparts behind which to tremble, fearing the depredations
of urts. This arrangement did present, of course, a relatively
porous perimeter which, by individuals, or small groups, might
be penetrated with relative ease. Indeed, at certain points, there
seemed to be a traffic of sorts from outside the camp into the
camp, and from within the camp to the outside, this seeming
to consist mostly of local peasants vending millet or vulos,
herdsmen with a verr or a tarsk or two, some sellers of salted
fish, for the sea was not far away, peddlers with their carts,
various sorts of craftsmen, and such. Occasionally the master
of a merchant wagon would trundle in, with a trove of silk, and
clothing, sometimes a fine sword. Occasionally a peasant would
appear with a daughter to rent or sell.

The procession of which I have spoken was ordered as
follows. First came Arashi, the bandit, swathed with ropes, two
rope leashes on his neck, each in the grasp of a glaive-bearing
Ashigaru, two of the foragers first met in the inn. Behind Arashi
came the third Ashigaru, the third of the foragers, and he,
particularly in the vicinity of the camp, would poke Arashi in
the back with the point of his glaive. Each time this occurred
Arashi must announce, in a loud, clear voice, under the threat of

being stripped and publicly flogged, "I am Arashi, the bandit. I am the prisoner of Yasushi, Twenty-Third Constable of the march of Lord Yamada, Shogun of the Islands." Following Arashi and his guards came Yasushi and Kazumitsu, walking abreast, that there would be no precedence amongst them. Following Yasushi and Kazumitsu, came Tajima, his arms bound to his sides. Following Tajima came the heavy rice cart, drawn by Haruki and myself. The cart, in its front and sides, was decorated with several heads. Most of these dangled from the top railings of the cart, tied in place by the hair. There were also three heads, scarcely recognized as human heads, or even as heads, for they were burned beyond practical recognition, mounted on three of the cart's vertical posts, rather as on stakes. There were eighteen heads in all. Tied to the top, back railing of the cart was the coffle rope, with its seven occupants, their hands tied behind their backs, six in the tunics of inn slaves, and one, the last, in the tunic of a field slave. I feared the trek had been difficult for them; the distance had been several pasangs, Tor-tu-Gor merciless, the road rough, and, as one moved north, frequently steep. Flanking this procession, and following it, were the twenty warriors who had constituted the command of the special officer, Kazumitsu.

"All is lost," said Tajima.

"Perhaps not," I said.

"How not?" asked Tajima.

"Your tarn, loosed, unburdened, may have reached the encampment of tarns," I said.

"It is possible," said Tajima.

"Then," I said, "all may not be lost."

"How so?" said Tajima.

"Its saddle would have been empty," I said.

"So?" said Tajima.

"So," I said, "all may not be lost."

Chapter Thirty-Six
Two Men Call for Tajima

It was now the next morning.

By now, perhaps the eighth Ahn, we supposed that Yasushi would have visited Lord Akio, and Lord Akio would have had an opportunity to make his determination with respect to Nezumi, who was not with us, discovering her to be the former Sumomo. It would then be an immediate inference that the Pani warrior with us was he who had made away with Sumomo. A further identification, presumably inevitable, would be that it was the young tarnsman, Tajima. Then, the descriptions of Haruki and myself, as the other two of the "four," would presumably suffice for our identification, even before we might be brought before him.

"Enjoy your millet," I encouraged Tajima, wiping the last bit of grain out of the wooden bowl with my finger.

There were some fifty or sixty prisoners in the pen, all male. Most were peasants.

"How can you eat?" inquired Tajima.

"I am hungry," I said.

"I will not eat," said Tajima.

"Haruki feeds," I said.

"He is a peasant," said Tajima.

"I am eating," I said.

"You are a barbarian," he said.

"So are you," I said, "a barbarian, though Pani."

"I do not wish to die with a full stomach," said Tajima.

374

"There is little danger of that," I said, "given what is in your bowl."

"True," said Tajima.

"Eat," I said. "Keep up your strength."

"Do you think it fitting?" he asked.

"Certainly," I said.

"Very well," he said.

"Behold," said Haruki. "Kazumitsu approaches."

To be sure, approaching the pen was the special officer. His twenty men, with full accouterments, were with him.

"I will sell my life dearly," said Tajima.

"Do not bother doing so, as yet," I said.

"How so?" said Tajima.

"His men," I said, "have their field packs."

Kazumitsu, with his men, arrested their march outside the bars of the pen. We went to the bars. The special officer bowed. "It is well I did not approach the shogun," he said. "The noble Yasushi has saved me embarrassment, and perhaps my head. You are not those for whom I sought, the four. I regret my error and any inconvenience I may have caused you. Lord Akio has examined the slave, Nezumi. She is a common field slave, and certainly not the gracious, exalted daughter of the shogun."

Tajima, Haruki, and I received this communication with silence.

"I am humbled by my error," said Kazumitsu, "but I do not think the matter of sufficient import to warrant recourse to the ritual knife."

"Certainly not," I said.

"You are a barbarian," said the officer. "What do you know of such things?"

"Forgive me," I said.

"I think you are right," said Tajima.

"I deem it so," said the officer, "and accept your view as welcome, though unnecessary, confirmation."

"What of the rest of us," asked Tajima.

"You, perceptive young warrior, will be soon fetched before an officer of the camp, to pledge your service to the shogun. That is, as I understand it, your desire."

"What of myself, and my friend?" I asked, indicating Haruki.

"Friend?" said Kazumitsu.

"Yes," I said.

"Interesting," he said. "You two, who were, as it seems, merely coincidentally in the inn with the others, are to be held for questioning until tomorrow morning. You, the foreigner, are presumably a deserter from the holding of Temmu, the Wicked, and might have information of interest pertaining to the forces, dispositions, and appointments of the holding, and the other, even as a guide, or follower, might prove similarly useful."

"We are pleased to be vindicated," I said.

"The warrior will be soon released," he said. "The officer of the guard has been so instructed. You and he of whom you have interestingly used the word 'friend', are to be interrogated tomorrow, after which you may go as, and where, you please."

"Lord Akio is generous," I said.

"Such great lords are wise and just," he said. "I must now resume my search for the mysterious tarnsman and the shogun's fair daughter." He then bowed graciously, turned about, and departed with his men.

"I do not understand," said Tajima.

"Lord Akio wants Nezumi for himself," I said.

"I will kill him!" said Tajima.

"Surely not over anything as negligible as a slave," I said.

"I shall find another reason," said Tajima.

"You need not search long," I said. "Reasons are as easily found as Ka-la-na grapes in autumn, as easily as grains of sand on the beaches of Thassa."

"Surely you do not suppose Lord Akio failed to identify Nezumi?" said Tajima.

"Not at all," I said, "nor the rest of us."

At this point the officer of the guard approached the pen gate. Outside the gate he waved Tajima to the gate. "I salute you, future ally," he said. "I have with me two of the shogun's officers, of the palace itself, who will conduct you in honor to a suitable officer, before whom you may pledge your service to the shogun."

Tajima bowed, while the gate was opened.

"Those two men," whispered Haruki, "are not men of the

shogun. I know them. They are of the personal guard of Lord Akio."

"I wish you well, my friends," said Tajima. "I do not expect to see you again."

"You may," I said.

"How so?" inquired Tajima.

"The saddle of the returning tarn was empty," I said.

Chapter Thirty-Seven

We Must Arrange to Leave the Pen

It was now the Eighteenth Ahn of the same day, that on the morning of which we had been briefly visited by Kazumitsu, and had learned of our supposed exonerations by Lord Akio.

"I fear for the noble Tajima," said Haruki.

"Fear for yourself, as well," I said.

"I am a mere peasant," he said.

"On continental Gor," I said, "the Peasants is a proud caste. It is the ox on which the Home Stone rests."

"That is a saying?" said Haruki.

"A very old saying," I said.

"What is an ox?" asked Haruki.

"A large, strong animal, a mighty animal," I said.

"What is a Home Stone?" inquired Haruki.

"It is the meaning, the difference," I said, "that for which men will kill, that for which men will die."

"It is very important?" said Haruki.

"Very much so," I said.

"It is hard to understand," said Haruki.

"It is less to be defined than cherished," I said.

"It is as the garden?" said Haruki.

"Yes," I said, "and as Thassa, as fields of Sa-Tarna, as the crags of the Voltai, the skerries of bleak Torvaldsland, the steaming flower-strewn basin of the Ua, beyond Schendi, the gleaming stars of the sky."

"It is perhaps then not so lowly to be of the peasants," said Haruki.

"Not at all," I said.

"It is the ox on which the Home Stone rests," said Haruki.

"That is the saying," I said.

"And it is an old saying," said Haruki.

"A very old saying," I said.

"I am pleased," said Haruki.

"Do not despair of Tajima," I said. "I suspect he is still alive, though in the power of Lord Akio. Lord Akio is a resourceful man. He may arrange things in such a manner as to appear to have personally apprehended the thieving tarnsman who so shamefully spoiled the sport of the plank and eels. Surely the shogun would find that impressive."

"What of Nezumi?" asked Haruki.

"I think Lord Akio wishes her for his own," I said. "Indeed, few men would be unwilling to have a slave such as Nezumi at their feet. He may be particular with respect to his appearance and attire, but I am sure he is man enough to have better things to do with a beautiful slave than feed her to eels."

"I see," said Haruki.

"I am also sure, of course," I said, "he would be willing, as would the shogun, to sacrifice her instantly for political reasons, but why do so, if there is no advantage in doing so?"

"Where is she now?" asked Haruki.

"I am sure," I said, "she is somewhere in the camp, probably chained to a stake in some obscure tent, perhaps near the camp's border, being held incommunicado. It is easy enough for a slave to be moved about, to disappear and reappear where one wishes, in one house or another."

"You conjecture that both Tajima and Nezumi are alive," said Haruki.

"As of now," I said. "I think we, at present, are in much greater danger."

"We are supposed to be interrogated in the morning," said Haruki.

"And then released," I said.

"Yes," he said.

"Do you believe that?" I asked.

"No, noble one," said Haruki.

"It is dark now," I said. "I am sure Lord Akio wishes to do

away with me, surreptitiously, for a variety of reasons, and you, as a witness of various things, are in no better way."

"No, noble one," he said.

"We are not expected to see the morning," I said. "His guards will visit the pen tonight. We are to be either slain here, or, taken out, done away with elsewhere."

"*Ela*," said Haruki, sadly.

"But we shall not wait for them," I said. "We shall escape."

"The bars are closely set and deeply planted," said Haruki.

"Perhaps not so deeply planted," I said. "This is clearly a temporary pen, to be taken down and reassembled in successive camps."

"What of the prisoners?" asked Haruki.

"Those who are retained, neither released nor killed," I said, "would be taken ahead to the next camp, under guard, perhaps coffled."

"The bars, I suspect," said Haruki, "would be planted deeply enough."

"True," I said, "but there are some fifty or sixty stout fellows here."

"The camp is armed," said Haruki.

"Yamada is complacent, security is lax," I said. "Too, I am sure we have allies within the camp."

"How so?" asked Haruki.

"I anticipate that Tajima's tarn, unburdened, managed to reach its cot in the encampment of tarns," I said. "The empty saddle, undamaged, uncut, not bloodied, and such, will suggest that Tajima abandoned the tarn, and would try to reach the holding of Temmu or the encampment of tarns on foot. If he managed to do so, well and good. On the other hand, given the intensity and extensiveness of searchings, the broadcast alertings of villages, and such, which would presumably be anticipated, it would be quite possible that he would be captured, and, if captured, would be brought to Lord Yamada, not back at the palace, but here, where Lord Yamada would be, in one of his march's road camps. Too, of course, in any event, one would hope that Lord Temmu would have the common wisdom of attempting to penetrate such camps with spies. Indeed, these spies, if recognized, might not even be apprehended, but, rather, ignored, that they might return to the holding of Temmu with disconcerting, dire tidings of the might of Lord Yamada's advance."

"Much of this is conjectural," said Haruki.

"True," I said. "It is now up to you to enlist allies, and arrange an escape."

"I?" said Haruki.

"Of course," I said. "You are a peasant."

"And it is on such as I," said Haruki, "that the Home Stone rests?"

"Precisely," I said.

Chapter Thirty-Eight

We Note Lanterns on a Stormy Night; We Deem It Wise to Depart

A guard fire was maintained only near the gate of the pen. The officer of the guard had his tent in its vicinity. The guard, those not on watch, were tented within hailing distance. A pair of Pani guardsmen remained with the guard fire, by the gate. Another pair of Pani guardsmen, one with a torch, at intervals, patrolled the pen's perimeter. In this fashion, the far side of the pen, away from the gate, received only intermittent attention.

I strained at the paling, lifting, then trying to loosen it, moving it backward and forward, and from side to side. In this work, I was assisted by two sizable peasants. Almost at our feet, two others, with empty rice bowls, tore at the dirt, scraping it away from the foot of the paling.

"Torch!" whispered Haruki, our lookout.

Immediately we melted away from the bars, and assumed postures of sleep.

We worked in relays, and at more than one point in the pen. Some might have better fortune in this work than others. Perhaps one paling was less deeply anchored than another. Ideally, men might slip in small numbers through more than one opening in the bars. If one potential egress was discovered, others might not be suspected.

Haruki had done his work well, and recruits were about, aplenty. Those who were not immediately involved in our work pretended sleep, many near the gate.

If some feared escape and would not join us, they refrained, at least, from giving an alarm. To be sure, I would not wish to give such an alarm, while separated from the guards who were on the other side of the bars.

It was our hope that several exits might be simultaneously readied. Both a clandestine vanishing, or, unfortunately, if necessary, an explosive scattering, of fugitives from diverse points is likely to be more confusing to guards, and less easily tracked, than the traces of a single line of men, not yet scattered, availing themselves of a single aperture.

I stepped back from the paling, sweating.

"How does it proceed, noble one?" inquired Haruki.

"My body aches, and my hands are bloody," I said.

"Good," said Haruki. "Then the work is going well."

"It is hard to see how these fellows can keep at this," I said.

"I am sure some palings are loosening," said Haruki.

"We do not have long to do this," I said. I was sure that men of Lord Akio, with suitable credentials and orders, might arrive at almost any moment.

"I fear that is true," said Haruki, looking back toward the gate.

"With more time," I said, "one might tunnel under the palings."

"In places, that might be possible," said Haruki. "Whereas the palings appear to be the same height, not all need be of the same length."

"You have done well to recruit these fellows," I said.

"I feared failure," he said. "There is much selfishness, and much suspicion, amongst villages. Each is out for his own."

"How then did you succeed?" I asked.

"Torch," he whispered, suddenly.

It then, in a moment, became again as though all slept. I watched the torch, now at the gate, through half-closed eyes, begin its circle of the perimeter of the pen. To my unease, I sensed that it had stopped not far from where we worked. Then, to my relief, after a time, it continued on its way.

"It is going to rain," said Haruki.

"No," I said, "the night is clear."

"The night will be overcast, and the darkness will deepen," said Haruki. "That is good for our work. Too, the guards will seek shelter, and it will be difficult to kindle their torches."

"The night is clear," I said.

"What is not good," said Haruki, "is that tracks may linger in rain-softened soil."

I was silent.

He had his head lifted, and seemed keenly alert. "Good," he said, "the rain will be heavy and, in time, tracks will be obliterated."

"The night is clear," I said, and then felt a drop of rain.

"We must dislodge palings swiftly," said Haruki. "It must be near the Twentieth Ahn."

I joined several others, stout fellows, working about the palings. These were strong men. Smaller fellows addressed themselves to the earth about the palings, about this high, smooth fence, the points of which were fastened together with lashings several feet above our heads, some with rice bowls and others with stones, and their bare hands.

A gentle rain began to fall. The yellow moon was partly obscured. The white moon was not in the sky, nor that smaller orb, called in Continental Gor, the Prison Moon.

"It is moving," I whispered to the fellows with me. I licked the blood from my hand. It was raw from the wood, and slick now with rain, as was the wood.

I heard thunder, far off, and saw a flash of lightning beyond the camp.

"Here, too," said one of the fellows nearby.

The rain had purchased time, as the rounds of the guards, which were desultory at best in this lax camp, had now ceased.

Men worked at various points.

I suspected the pen guards had not considered the possibility of concerted action, not amongst peasants. They would not anticipate any general challenge to the integrity of the facility they supervised, not amongst peasants. They would rely upon, and take much for granted, the docility and obedience commonly to be found in the peasantry. Peasants are expected to abide unquestioningly the will and words of the gentry.

I wondered how Haruki had managed to recruit his small legions.

I wished, of course, to free as many men as possible, both for my own sake, to confuse matters, and make pursuit more difficult, and for theirs, as well, that at least some might make their way back to their villages.

"A little more," said the man beside me.

The palings were lifted up a foot, carrying with them the lashings near their points, and then bent outward. Almost at my feet the sharpened foot of a paling, bent forward, thrust up dirt. I bent down, and could feel the point.

"More, a bit more!" said the fellow beside me.

It was now raining heavily.

There was a flash of lightning and the camp, through the palings, suddenly appeared, in a cold blast of light, and then, as suddenly, vanished in an alarming crash of thunder.

We thrust forward against the palings.

"Not enough," said a man.

"Noble one," said Haruki. "Look back. Look to the gate. It is too late. A party approaches."

I wiped rain from my eyes, and looked back, to the gate.

There was a party there, of some ten or twelve men. They wore hoods and shawls, to protect them from the rain. None wore the straw jacket of the peasantry. None carried glaives, the common weapon of the Ashigaru. I gathered they were officers and warriors, all. Some did carry sheltered lanterns which threw forth a dim light. They were being met by the officer of the guard.

"We are to be removed from the pen in darkness," said Haruki. "Few will note our departure. None will know what has become of us. None will care what has become of us. We will have vanished. The rain and darkness will cover their work."

"The gate opens," said a man.

"We cannot break through the palings," said a fellow.

"We will," I said, "we, and the others. Together, now!"

At various points, to my left and right, for others, too, had made progress such as we, I heard the soft cries and utterances, sudden and forceful, of desperate and straining men.

"They approach," said Haruki.

"Lift," I said, "extend the palings, force them apart!" I got my back against one paling and, with my feet, both feet, bracing myself against it, thrust against the other. "There is your door," I said. "Crawl, slip through, take your leave, go!"

Yards to the side I heard the movements of other men. Others may have been more successful than we.

I heard a creak of timber. From somewhere I heard the splash of a paling into the mud. The high lashings must have torn loose.

"What is going on there?" I heard, from somewhere within the pen.

I heard another sound, from the other side, and saw a paling thrust aside, swinging on its overhead lashing.

"On your hands and knees," I said. "Through the opening, quick. *Harta! Harta!*"

One man after another squeezed through that narrow aperture.

"Unsheathe your blades!" cried a voice. "What you come upon, kill! Lanterns forward! Lanterns forward!"

Only Haruki remained behind.

"I shall block the opening, noble one," he said.

"No, you will not," I said, unpleasantly.

"What is life without its garden?" said Haruki.

"I do not know," I said. "Hurry!"

"Must I?" he asked.

"Yes," I said.

"As you will, noble one," he said.

"Find Tarl Cabot!" cried a voice, from somewhere in the midst of the approaching lanterns.

I thought my back might break, but Haruki crawled through the opening, and I threw myself free of the heavy paling which then fell back, as it could, into place. That particular opening had doubtless not been one of the best, but it had sufficed. Palings, in their strength, in the depth of their planting, in their securings and lashings, and such, would differ amongst themselves. I hoped the pursuers would attempt to make use of the same opening, as it would presumably present them with the same difficulty it had us. In the darkness and rain easier openings might not be scouted, or noticed. As soon as I was beyond the palings, I cried out, "Bowmen of Temmu, fire on the first tarsk who emerges from the pen!"

I moved back in the darkness with Haruki. The lanterns had stopped, and I sensed some indecision and milling about. Less pleasantly, I sensed cries, and movements, in the darkness about me. The camp, this portion of the camp, was apparently becoming aroused.

"Fools, there are no bowmen of Temmu in the camp. Break through, here, where the tarsks fled!"

I heard men grunting.

That massive vertical bar would not be easy to move.

"Where is Tarl Cabot?" cried an angry voice from within, a voice redolent with authority.

"Here!" I called out, from the darkness.

That, I thought, would keep them at this point in the fence. Perhaps, I thought, they could use a few stout fellows, such as I had had at my disposal, to move the palings. But then I doubted they had any peasants in their party.

"You did well, friend Haruki," I said, "in your recruiting. How did you manage it, peasants, and peasants from different villages, suspicious, grasping fellows, wary of men of quality, working together, joining in such a common effort?"

"I told them, noble one," said Haruki, "that they were the ox on which the Home Stone rests."

"Did they understand?" I asked.

"I do not think so, noble one," said Haruki, "but they were pleased."

We then, in the pourings of rain, in the flashings of lightning and the crashings of thunder, with startled, confused men rushing about, slipping a bit in the mud, scrambled away, to lose ourselves, as we might, amongst the corridors of tents.

Chapter Thirty-Nine

Pertinax;
There Is Work to be Done

I stepped back behind a tent and a squad of Ashigaru hurried past, bearing glaives.

I did not think the laxity characterizing the perimeter of the camp was to be long in place.

In the distance, I could hear the ringing of an alarm bar.

Rain still fell, but the brunt of the storm had passed.

The yellow moon was now visible, only partly obscured.

I surmised that the fugitives, including Haruki and myself, would be expected to depart the camp as quickly as possible. I hoped that many, under the cover of the storm and darkness, might do so, reaching the open country. Haruki and I, however, would not be amongst them, at least not now. There was a different business to which we wished to attend.

I sought Tajima. I had dispatched Haruki to locate Nezumi. To be sure, I was less than sanguine about the success of either mission. We were to rendezvous where I supposed we would be the least suspected, within sight of the high banner surmounting the command tent of the shogun himself, at the hub of the great wheel which constituted the camp.

I turned the corner of the tent, and found the point of a sword at my throat.

Then the sword was lowered.

"Tarl!" said the fellow.

"Pertinax!" I said.

"What are you doing here?" whispered Pertinax. "Surely you

are behind, not here, but much away, faraway, held in the palace of Yamada."

"I escaped," I said. "Lord Temmu must be warned."

"He is well aware of the march of Yamada," said Pertinax.

"There is more," I said.

"With you in command," said Pertinax, "if you care to invest the cavalry, Yamada, as before, can be forced to withdraw."

"Yamada is no fool," I said. "The beast who puts his nose in fire is not likely to do so again. He would not advance north unless he felt justified in dismissing the threat of the cavalry."

"How can it be dismissed?" asked Pertinax.

"I do not know," I said, "but he is marching north. I am much pleased to encounter you."

"I and Ichiro," he said, "have been in this camp for several days."

"You seek Tajima," I said.

"He could not be dissuaded from madness," said Pertinax. "He set forth on some desperate adventure, one involving the worthless Sumomo. His tarn returned to its cot, the saddle empty. Neither it nor the bird bore signs of war. It was then, we conjectured, freed deliberately; there would seem no reason for doing this unless it was in imminent danger of being overtaken; Tajima, then, must be afoot, and at risk of capture. If he were captured, it is likely he would be brought to the shogun, and the shogun, as you know, is here."

"And you and Ichiro came to scout the camp," I said.

"Yes," he said.

"Sumomo," I said, "was to be fed to death eels."

"We heard so," said Pertinax. "It was to intervene that Tajima left the encampment of tarns."

"His intervention was successful," I said. "He carried away the shogun's daughter."

"But surely she is not in chains now, at the encampment of tarns."

"No," I said.

"What became of her?"

"Tajima put her in his collar."

"The shogun's daughter?"

"Yes," I said.

"Excellent," said Pertinax.

"And she is now here, in this camp."

"I did not know that," said Pertinax.

"And so, too, is Tajima," I said.

"I know that," said Pertinax.

"You know that?" I said.

"Ichiro and I slipped into this camp to find him. We searched long and unavailingly. We were unsuccessful for days. We were planning to withdraw, in despair, until yesterday."

"You know where he is?"

"In the compound of Lord Akio," said Pertinax. "I observed him, under guard, conducted to that place."

"We must free him," I said.

"That is our hope," he said.

"You and Ichiro risked much to enter this camp, to seek him," I said. "You will risk a great deal more, should you attempt to free him."

Pertinax shrugged, and sheathed his sword.

"I thought," I said, "there was much uneasiness between you and Tajima, that there was much rivalry between you, much envy, and jealousy, and competition for priority of station."

"On the part of Tajima perhaps," said Pertinax. "Not on mine."

"Tajima resented that Nodachi, the teacher and swordsman, would accept you as a pupil."

"I am unworthy to be his pupil," said Pertinax.

"That is not for you to say, but Nodachi," I said.

"I am not Pani," said Pertinax.

"That is apparently not the criterion in terms of which Nodachi selects his students," I said.

"I am not Pani," said Pertinax.

"Neither are the moons or tides," I said, "nor the sword."

"Ichiro," he said, "watches near the compound of Lord Akio, camp lord here, lest Tajima be moved."

"But you are here," I said.

"I return from scouting the perimeter," he said, "and have planned an escape route."

"You will have to revise your plans," I said. "Several have escaped from the prison pen."

"I hear the alarm bar," he said.

"Security is certain to be increased at the perimeter," I said.

"We cannot remain here," he said. "The camp will be searched, every tent, every hort."

"Doubtless," I said.

"We will sell our lives fearlessly," he said.

"That is all right for heroes," I said, "but it is not the way of men who win wars."

"I do not understand," he said.

"Wars are won not only by the sword," I said. "Dying for a cause seldom does a cause much good."

"I do not understand," he said.

"Dying nobly is all well and good," I said, "but it is, at best, a last resort. It does not stand high amongst the priorities for success."

"Oh?" he said.

"Those who are eager to die," I said, "are likely to be obliged by the foe."

"What of honor?" he said.

"Death and honor seldom have much to do with one another," I said. "It is easy to die honorably. To live honorably is much more difficult."

"What of Tajima?" he said.

"We must renew our acquaintance with the young tarnsman," I said.

"Good," he said.

"But there is a problem," I said.

"What is that?" asked Pertinax.

"Tajima," I said, "is not likely to leave the camp without Nezumi."

"Who is Nezumi?" he said.

"She who was once Sumomo," I said, "now no more than a rather pretty, marked, collared slave."

"I do not know where she is," said Pertinax.

"I have a friend about," I said, "a Pani gardener, named Haruki, you do not know him, but were it not for him, a colleague and guide, it is unlikely I would be here. I have put him about searching for Nezumi. We think she is being held by Lord Akio, incommunicado, probably in some far, nondescript tent near the perimeter, far from the shogun's command tent and the compound of the camp lord, Lord Akio, most likely concealed amongst other slaves."

"What are we to do now?" asked Pertinax.

"The rain has stopped," I said. "It will soon be light. We must move quickly. I hope to meet Haruki near the center of the camp. I trust he will have come upon some useful intelligence."

"Tajima is being held near the center of the camp," said Pertinax, "in the compound of Lord Akio."

"Let us hope things work out nicely," I said.

"They seldom do," said Pertinax.

"One may always hope," I said.

Chapter Forty

A Diversion Is Planned;
I Visit the Camp Lord;
Tajima Is Missing;
Tajima Is Found

"You are certain Tajima was taken into that tent?" I said.

"Yes," said Pertinax.

"And, Commander *san*," said Ichiro, "he has not been taken elsewhere."

"There are but two guards, at the entrance," said Pertinax.

"I am sure there are several, elsewhere," I said.

"We see none, Commander *san*," said Ichiro, bannerman of the cavalry.

"They are there," I said.

"It is a trap?" said Pertinax.

"Tajima is the bait," I said. "It was doubtless laid as soon as word from the prison pen reached Lord Akio."

"I had thought we might cut the canvas, at the rear of the tent," said Pertinax.

"It might still be done," I said.

"But if there is surveillance, and guards at hand?" said Pertinax.

"Think," I said, "as might Lord Yamada."

"I am not sure I care to do so," said Pertinax.

"What," I asked, "is more valuable than the bait?"

"I do not know," said Pertinax.

"He who laid the trap," I said. "Yamada would willingly sacrifice a lesser value for a greater."

"So?" said Pertinax.

"In our position," I said, "he would think nothing of sacrificing Tajima in order to strike at Lord Akio."

"We are not Yamada," said Pertinax.

"Surely we would not sacrifice Tajima *san*," said Ichiro.

"Lord Akio might think so," I said.

"You plan a diversion?" said Pertinax.

"Yes," I said. "I will need a blade."

"Take my sword," said Pertinax. "In your hands it is an efficient tool of death."

"And in yours," I said. "Give me, rather, your knife."

Pertinax handed me the knife, hilt first.

"Is the knife not a more likely weapon for an assassin?" I said. "Consider how easily it is concealed and how, well flung, it greets its target."

I put the knife in my belt. I would have preferred a Tuchuk quiva, for its weight and balance, but one must make do with what may be at hand.

"This," I said, "is my plan."

"Demon rider!" said Lord Akio, rising to his feet, spilling tea.

Two contract women cowered in the background.

"Make no sound," I said. "In two steps I could be at your throat."

He glanced to the contract women.

"They will remain where they are," I said, "or your throat is mine."

"Remain," he said to the two women.

"You should be better guarded," I said. "Where are your men, out searching for Tarl Cabot, or lying in wait, within or outside a nearby tent?"

"There are guards," he said, "outside. Did you not see the banner of the camp lord?"

"Perhaps by morning," I said, "there will be a new camp lord."

"How did you get in?" he said.

"In the same fashion you expected one to enter the tent of Tajima, the tarnsman prisoner, by cutting the back of the tent.

How easy and inviting you made such an entrance appear. You did not anticipate this. If you had, you might have invested fewer guards in your other plans."

The tent of the camp lord, incidentally, was not a simple tent, but a large tent, lavish and well-appointed, one containing several rooms, or joined apartments. Although it had rained heavily outside, earlier in the night, it was nicely dry within. It was lit by a number of hanging lamps.

He looked down, quickly, a darting glance to the other side.

"You would not have time to reach the war fan," I said.

"You would give up your friend, the tarnsman?" he said.

"Who would not, in kaissa," I said, "sacrifice a Spearman for a Ubar?"

"I do not understand," he said.

"Who would not, in a dark game, sacrifice a lesser piece for one of greater value?"

"You are more astute in the ways of statecraft than I had realized," he said.

"One learns from masters," I said.

"What have you come to do?" he said.

"Leave the companion sword as it is, lying by the table," I said. "Do not place your right hand in your left sleeve."

"What do you want?"

"Your head," I said. "Lord Temmu would prize it. His women would carefully wash and clean it, comb and perfume its hair, blacken its teeth, and mount it in a place of honor."

"Perhaps we can talk," he said. "There are diamonds, gold, silver, jade, women."

"I have not come here for such things," I said.

"Do not approach!" he said, backing away.

"I congratulate you on your present attire," I said. "It does credit to your wardrobe. Doubtless you would be distressed, if it were to be stained, to run with blood."

"Come no closer!" he said.

I could have reached out and touched him.

"I am prepared to bargain," he said. "I will give the prisoner to you and you may leave the camp with impunity."

"Lord Yamada," I said, "would not allow you to surrender the prisoner."

"The great lord," said Lord Akio, "does not know he is my prisoner."

"Why not?" I asked.

"I wish to surprise him," said Lord Akio.

"Lord Yamada," I said, "does not like surprises. He would expect you to have surrendered the prisoner instantly."

"Lord Yamada," he said, "may not always be shogun."

"At a supper," I said, "an assassin was foiled in the attempt to kill the great lord. His shoulder bore the false sign of a lotus. Before he could be interrogated, presumably under torture, which few men can withstand, you slew him, a knife to the back of the neck."

"It was regrettable," he said, "a sudden, thoughtless act, which, in the moment, I could not help, an act expressing my horror, my indignation, my outrage, at the attempt on the life of my beloved shogun."

"That you did not immediately present Tajima, the tarnsman, to the shogun suggests you were holding him for a purpose, perhaps that he might later figure in a staged capture, redounding to your benefit. That you did not immediately return the shogun's daughter to him, and his justice, might serve a similar purpose, or perhaps, more likely, while it might be assumed or alleged that she had perished, she might be retained, her curves suggesting that she might prove of slave interest."

"Do not kill me," he said.

"You offered to free the tarnsman and guarantee us safe passage from the camp?" I said.

"Yes," he said. "Yes, surely yes!"

"How do I know you will do so?" I asked, as though considering the matter.

"You have my word," he said.

"Should I trust you?" I asked.

"Of course," he said. "You have my word, the word of a warrior, of a daimyo."

"Very well," I said. "I will trust you."

"Permit me to withdraw, to arrange the matter," he said, backing cautiously away.

"It will not take long?" I said.

"Not at all," he said. "Only a few moments. You will wait here, will you not?"

"Certainly," I said.

"Perhaps you will have some tea while you wait," he said.

"I have your word?"

"Of course," he said.

As soon as Lord Akio had left this compartment, or portion, of the long, large tent, I turned to the contract women. "Leave, ladies," I said. "I have no time for tea. I must be about burning a tent."

I had hardly said this when, from a few yards away, some canvases separating us, I heard Lord Akio crying out, screaming wildly, "Guards, guard, guards!"

I then withdrew, swiftly, stopping only long enough to scatter oil from four or five of the lamps I passed, igniting the spillage. The interior of the tent was protected by layers of canvas from the outside, and weather, and, with its furnishings, its mats, chests, screens, and such, would burn splendidly. As soon as I emerged in the early morning light from the slit I had made in the canvas, I cut several of the tent ropes. The guards, as I had surmised, large numbers of them, would be arrested in their pursuit by the flames, and further discomfited when the roof's layered canvases, those in this portion of the tent, the ropes cut, would collapse. Once finished I no longer hurried, but walked slowly about, and even stopped, for a time, with several others, to watch the steam rise from the damp, collapsed canvas, this generated by the heat from within.

"So where is Tajima?" I said. "We must be on our way."

"I do not know," said Pertinax.

"I do not understand," I said.

"The guards were drawn away," said Pertinax. "There must have been forty or fifty of them. They seemed to spring from everywhere."

"It seems there was an emergency," said Ichiro. "They hurried to the tent of the camp lord."

"This presented us with our awaited opportunity," said Pertinax. "The prison tent abandoned, left unguarded, we cut the canvas in the back, reached Tajima, severed his bonds, and drew him forth."

"So where is he?" I asked.

"I do not know!" said Pertinax.

"There was a fire, too," said Ichiro.

"I know," I said.

"Tajima said he had an errand to attend to," said Pertinax.

"He does not even know where Nezumi is," I said. "I do not know. Haruki is trying to determine the matter. We are to rendezvous with him, in the vicinity of the tent of the shogun."

"Is that not conspicuous, Commander *san*?" said Ichiro.

"Where better to conceal an object," I asked, "than to place it where seekers will not look?"

"We have not long to wait," said Pertinax. "Tajima approaches."

"Where have you been?" I asked.

"Attending to a matter," said Tajima.

"I see no little beast, closely collared, heeling you," I said.

"Do you refer to the small, collared beast, Nezumi?" he asked.

"It is possible," I said.

"How could it be?" he asked. "I do not even know where she is."

"What then was the matter to which you wished to attend?" I asked.

"It is not important," he said.

"The alarm bar is still ringing," said Pertinax.

"It has to do with an escape from the prison pen," I said to Tajima.

"It is strange that it should still be ringing," said Pertinax.

"Perhaps, not," said Tajima.

"How so?" asked Pertinax.

"Another escaped," said Tajima, "more recently."

"I did not know that," I said.

"Arashi," said Tajima.

"How do you know that?" I asked.

"I freed him," said Tajima.

"He is a blood-thirsty rogue, and cutthroat," I said.

"But likable," said Tajima.

"At the inn," I said, "he would have killed you."

"But not in a mean-spirited way," said Tajima, "only as a matter of expedience."

"Still," I said.

"One must not be petty," said Tajima.

"Why not release a mad sleen instead," I said. "Because there was no mad sleen at hand?"

"Arashi," said Tajima, "is a bandit, a brigand, a villain, and such, but he is also a leader, a firebrand, a hero amongst many in the villages."

"I see," I said.

"He would be a dangerous enemy," said Tajima. "I would rather have him as an ally."

"He is a brigand," I said. "Arashi is the ally only of Arashi."

"What if the peasants should rise?" asked Tajima.

"Peasants do not rise," I said.

"True," said Tajima. "It would be regarded as inappropriate."

"If they should rise," I said, "they would soon subside."

"The river returns to its banks," said Pertinax.

"After washing many things downstream," said Tajima.

"You would have done better," I said, "to have freed a mad sleen."

"But Tarl Cabot, tarnsman," said Tajima, "there were none at hand."

"Haruki should be in the vicinity of the shogun's tent," I said.

"Let us join him," said Tajima.

"Are you willing, dear Tajima," I said, "to leave the camp without Nezumi?"

"No," he said.

"Haruki may have word of her," I said.

Chapter Forty-One

We Rendezvous;
Notes Are Exchanged;
Haruki Misses His Garden

"I am pleased to see you alive, noble ones," said Haruki.

"Probably no more than we to be so seen," I said.

"Have you found Nezumi?" asked Tajima.

"How is that you are anxious about a slave?" asked Pertinax.

"I am not anxious," said Tajima.

"It is just a matter of idle curiosity," I said.

"In a way, of course," said Tajima.

"Nonetheless, friend Haruki," I said, "have you located the unimportant, even despicable, slave, in whom Tajima has little, or no, interest?"

We moved back a bit amongst the tents, as a squad of glaive-bearing Ashigaru, in double file, sped past.

"That is the sixth search squad dispatched into the camp while I have been here," said Haruki.

"There were doubtless others before," I said, "probably from shortly after we left the pen."

"I suspect more are being organized," said Pertinax.

"They will scour the camp, every hort," said Tajima, grimly.

"They cannot scour every hort at the same time," I said. "The point, then, is to be where they are not scouring."

Tajima looked at me, narrowly.

"The safest way to assure that end," I said, "is to follow the search party, wary, of course, of its turning back."

"A single seeker, astute and suspicious, might do so," said Haruki, "turn back, but a directed party is almost certain to have its route delineated in advance, a route from which it is unlikely to deviate, indeed, one from which it might be dangerous to deviate, given the discipline of Lord Yamada."

"And such routes," I said, "in the name of a misguided efficiency, would not be likely to intersect with, or duplicate, one another."

"I think so," said Haruki.

"Too," I said, "considering the size of the camp, the number of fugitives, and the large number of peasants, tradesmen, craftsmen, deserters from the holding of Temmu, and such, in the camp, one might pity the search squads. Their work is likely to be arduous, confusing, and frustrating."

"Nonetheless," said Pertinax, "I will struggle to withhold my pity."

"Barbarians are strange," said Haruki.

It must not be thought odd, or unprecedented, that a large number of strangers, so to speak, would be present in a camp of this size. This was not a camp of flying columns or forced marches. Large camps, transient cities of tents, attract their multitudes, rather as a flowering meadow its cloudlike swarms of tiny, four-winged zars. Indeed, I had gathered from Pertinax and Ichiro this camp had not been moved in several days. I supposed this had something to do with logistics, given the need to acquire and store supplies for so large a force. On the other hand, it is possible that Lord Yamada's seeming dalliance was otherwise motivated; perhaps negotiations of some sort were underway; perhaps certain pieces in his game of war were being rearranged with scrupulous care; perhaps it was merely that the advance of his might, approaching now and again with its glacial implacability, might dismay a foe, eroding morale and precipitating desertions.

"What of Nezumi?" I asked. "I am interested in that matter, even if Tajima is not."

"First," said Haruki, "many officers have slaves in their retinue."

"It is unlikely," I said, "that Nezumi would be in a particular retinue."

"True," said Haruki.

It was not surprising, incidentally, that a number of slaves might be in the camp. Strong men want their slaves, and, on Gor, will have them. In a war camp, free women, and even contract women, would be rare. On my former world, large camps were often accompanied by numbers of putatively free women known as "camp followers." In Gorean camps such women would be seldom found. If such a woman were to enter a Gorean camp, given the pervasiveness of female bondage on Gor and its cultural approval, she would soon find herself in a collar and on a chain. The free woman can be a nuisance; the slave is a convenience. Who would want a free woman, when one can have a woman at one's feet, realizing she must obey?

"I expect," I said, "Nezumi would be concealed amongst other slaves. To have her isolated, as though she might have the status of a prisoner, perhaps a special prisoner, might excite comment, even arouse suspicion."

"Have you found her?" demanded Tajima.

"Patience, young noble one," said Haruki.

"Poor Tajima," said Pertinax, I thought unnecessarily.

"Would you care to meet me in a *dojo*," said Tajima, "with bamboo whips?"

"Not really," said Pertinax. "As you are a dear friend, I would not wish to hurt you."

"Remember, Tajima," I said, "Pertinax and Ichiro have entered this camp and risked their lives to find you and free you."

"What difference does that make?" asked Tajima.

"I thought it might make one," I said, "perhaps a little one."

"Not at all," said Tajima.

"Very well," I said.

"It seemed likely to me, as well," said Haruki, "that Nezumi would be concealed amongst other slaves. There are twelve major slave enclaves in the camp."

"Have you found her?" asked Tajima.

"Haruki will not have had time to examine twelve enclaves," I said.

"Eight of the enclaves are slave pens," said Haruki, "and four are slave tents."

"Nezumi is to be concealed," I said. "The slave pens are too open, so dismiss them."

"I agree, noble one," said Haruki.

Given the recent storm, the pounding rain, the drenching miseries, the cold, and such, I thought it might have done Nezumi some good, helping her to learn her collar, to have been in a slave pen, but I did not think that that, for political reasons, would have been her housing.

"Have you found her?" asked Tajima.

"Yes, and no," said Haruki.

"Perhaps you could be more clear," I said.

"Have you found her?" pressed Tajima.

"I think so, young noble one," said Haruki, "but I am not sure."

"How can you not be sure?" asked Tajima.

"I made inquiries," said Haruki, "pretending that I was inquiring for an officer, what might be the arrangements for the inspection and purchase of slaves."

"What did you find?" I asked.

"In only three of the four tents are slaves available for public purchase," he said.

"Then she is in the fourth tent," I said, "that not open to the public."

"At present," said Haruki.

"And where is that tent?" I asked.

"It is isolated, remote, near the perimeter of the camp," said Haruki.

"She is there," I said.

"I did not see her, of course," said Haruki.

"No matter," I said. "She is there."

"I have been told the way," said Haruki, pointing.

"Excellent," I said. "That is the route taken by the recent search party. We shall follow it."

"What if it turns back?" said Pertinax.

"That is unlikely," I said, "for it would be examining the same path twice, once going, once coming."

"But what if it should turn back?" asked Pertinax.

"We will follow it in a tandem fashion," I said, "with an ample interval amongst ourselves. Thus we will not appear together, or not obviously. He at point, he first in our group, should be able, easily, and at a distance, to detect the approach of a squad of searchers, and will be able to signal us, enabling all of us, if all goes well, to disappear amongst the tents. If the evasion is successful, we will rejoin, near the point of scattering."

"I will go first," said Haruki. "I have been told the way."

"I fear Pertinax and I will be conspicuous," I said, "as we are clearly barbarians."

"Do not fear too much," said Pertinax. "We are not all that conspicuous. There are several deserters in the camp, barbarian mercenaries, fled from the holding of Temmu. I have been in the camp for five days, unquestioned."

"Things have changed," said Tajima. "Many who have been unquestioned, Pani and others, may now find themselves questioned."

"Well, then," said Pertinax, "it is only a slave. Let us give up the whole matter."

"No," said Tajima.

"Ah," said Pertinax, triumphantly. "Then she is important to you."

"Not at all," said Tajima, annoyed. "Not in the least."

"Why, then?" asked Pertinax.

"For the same reason I would buy her," said Tajima.

"And what is that?" asked Pertinax.

"She has pretty legs," said Tajima.

"We may still be questioned," said Haruki.

"Sometimes," I said, "the best answer to a question is a dagger thrust between the ribs."

"I miss my garden," said Haruki.

Chapter Forty-Two

What Occurred in the Slave Tent

"I am sure that is the tent," said Haruki.

"I hear no whimperings, no plaintive cries of distress," said Pertinax.

"They are slaves," said Tajima, "not free women."

"They have been warned to silence," I said. "Ichiro, can you speak with authority?"

"I fear not, Commander *san*," said Ichiro. "I can speak loudly."

"That often suffices," I said.

"I shall enter first," said Tajima.

"No," I said. "You, Haruki, and myself, might be recognized."

"Surely none here, at this far point, would know us," he said.

"We can not be sure of that," I said. "Recall the procession of Kazumitsu and Yasushi, in which they paraded their prisoners. Similarly, we three were publicly penned."

"What am I to do, Commander *san*?" asked Ichiro.

"First," I said, "it would be well to reconnoiter, to find out what forces are to be dealt with."

"Two Ashigaru are at the entrance," said Ichiro.

"There will be at least a whip master inside," I said.

"There may be others inside, as well," said Pertinax.

"Ichiro," I said. "Approach the entrance, demand to see the whip master, proclaim that you have come on behalf of the camp lord, Lord Akio, who plans a pleasure feast and will require the services of, say, four slaves, which you are authorized to select."

"I fear, Commander *san*," he said, "even if I speak loudly, he will require some certification of the genuineness of this request."

"Of course," I said, "but, in the meantime, you will note the interior of the tent, and, in particular, the presence of any additional guards."

"What, then?" asked Ichiro.

"You will profess anger, threaten the whip master, insult him, deplore his incompetence, and vainly strive to convince him to allow you to proceed with your mission, the selection of a handful of feast slaves. He will be uneasy, but will remain adamant, as he must, at which point you will turn about, assuring him you will return shortly with the required authorization, in writing."

"He will be able to read?" said Ichiro.

"Presumably he, or another," I said. "It seems there would have to be at least one person on the premises capable of reading written orders."

"It could be done with pass signs," said Pertinax.

"Let us hope not," I said. "But if that is the case, then Ichiro will invent a pass sign, discover it is no longer current, that a mistake has been made, or such, and, again, will assure the fellow of his quick return, with everything in order."

"If all goes well," said Ichiro, "I shall then rejoin you."

"Yes," I said, "and if all does not go well, we will sell our lives dearly, as Pertinax would be likely to suggest, as there would not seem much else to do."

"Master!" cried Nezumi.

"I have the key," said Tajima.

Ichiro had done his work well. There were five to deal with, two Ashigaru at the entrance, two more within the tent, and the whip master, who was an officer and warrior. It was a large tent. Within it were housed some forty slaves. The tent, as most such large, long tents depended on several poles to support its roof, and was further secured by a number of tent pegs, or, as the Americans will have it, stakes, and ropes outside. While Haruki kept watch, Tajima and I kicked, loosened, and drew up several of the tent pegs or stakes, at the back of the tent, which would produce a sagging at that point. These tent pegs, or stakes, were large, pointed, rounded pieces of wood, most of which were something like a foot and a half in length, and two to three horts in diameter. I mention these measurements as it may make more clear the application to which they were shortly to be put. When two Ashigaru came about the tent to investigate the local collapse of canvas they encountered Haruki, apparently bewildered, who called their attention to the loose ropes and sagging canvas, not that this situation really required his exposition. I fear they might have been unkind to Haruki, but they had little opportunity to do so, as Tajima and I, armed with the tent pegs, or stakes, if you will, approaching from different sides, struck them, from behind, heavily. It was shortly thereafter that the other two Ashigaru came to look into the matter, perhaps curious to know what was delaying their fellows. Behind the tent, they encountered Haruki, seemingly bewildered, indicating the two mysteriously prone Ashigaru, whom our new arrivals, the other two Ashigaru, quickly joined. Meanwhile Ichiro had entered the slave tent and had his companion sword, easily handled at close quarters, at the throat of the officer. We joined Ichiro and the officer, both now well within the tent, as soon as we had dragged the four Ashigaru to the back of the tent, outside, and tucked them under the sagging canvas. We then slipped into the tent under the canvas, as well, as that was most convenient. The whip master was reluctant to supply the master key to which the ankle locks of the slaves would answer but it was easily rifled from his person. He was then conducted to the rear of the tent, which was half collapsed, where he beheld four unconscious Ashigaru. He did not have long to behold them, however, as, thanks to another blow of a peg, or stake, such things having been brought within the tent, wielded now by Tajima, he joined them, to share for a more or less indefinite time their untroubled condition. We left Haruki to bind and gag the four Ashigaru and the officer, as it was not clear how long they would remain in their state of inert serenity. Interestingly, there was, within the tent, a canvas partition which separated the main portion of the tent, in a linear fashion, from the area where the slaves were housed. This was unusual in a slave tent, for in such a tent, given the inspection, the buying and selling, and such, of the slaves, the slaves are usually publicly exhibited, as on a slave shelf, on platforms, in cages, in cells open to the street, and such. In such venues one does not have the privacy available in a professional slave house, or in the purple booths, admittance into which is restricted. I suspect the reason for this division in the tent, by means of the canvas partition, was less to protect the slaves from roving, appraising eyes, for slaves are accustomed, as other animals, to being openly regarded, than to minimize the possibility of a particular slave being identified, even casually or accidentally. A consequence of this arrangement, of course, was that the slaves had no clear understanding of what had occurred on the other side of the partition.

As mentioned earlier, there were some forty slaves in the tent. They were in a single line, held on a common chain, anchored at each end to a large ring fixed in a heavy, trunklike piling, of which a foot or so was visible above the ground. Each was fastened to the chain in the following fashion. A portion of the chain was looped twice, closely, about the left ankle, following which the shackle, or tongue, of a padlock was threaded through two links of the chain, and snapped shut, this closing the loops. In virtue of this arrangement girls could be conveniently added to, or removed from, the chain. A further convenience was afforded by the fact that the padlocks answered to a single key, the master key.

"Oh, Master!" wept Cecily.

How I had missed her in my arms!

"Master!" cried Jane, the former Lady Portia Lia Serisia of Sun Towers, of Ar, to Pertinax. I had purchased her for Pertinax in Tarncamp, long ago, not merely for his pleasure, but that he might learn how to handle a woman, as a woman should be handled, as a slave.

"Gregory!" cried Saru, the former Miss Margaret Wentworth, of Earth, who had come to Gor, thinking to be enriched, with Gregory White, now Pertinax. Unbeknownst to her, she had been brought to Gor, requisitioned, for Lord Nishida, who wished to give such a woman, young, shapely, fairly complexioned, blond-haired, blue-eyed, and beautiful, as a gift to Lord Temmu, his shogun. Whereas there was no dearth of beautiful women, both free and slave, in the islands, her complexion, and her hair and eye coloring, would be unusual at the World's End.

"On your bellies, all of you, facing away, hands at your sides, palms up," I said.

The slaves, well trained to obey free persons, instantly, and unquestioningly, complied, with the exception of Saru, who struggled to her feet and held out her hands to Pertinax. "Gregory!" she sobbed. "Gregory!"

"Must a command be repeated?" said Pertinax. The repetition of a command is commonly a cause for discipline, unless there is a serious reason to suppose that the command has not been heard, or has not been understood. In this case, it seemed clear the command would have been both heard and understood. Failure on the part of a female slave not to respond instantly and unquestioningly to a command can mean the whip for her.

"Oh, of course, Gregory," she said, smiling, and quickly assumed the prescribed position.

She extended her left ankle behind her, lifting it a little, to facilitate access to the padlock which held her in place.

"I know why Nezumi is here," said Tajima. "But how is it that these other three, your Cecily, and Pertinax's Jane, and the fair-haired slave, Saru, are here, as well?"

"It is unlikely it is a coincidence," said Haruki. "The three slaves, and the other, were associated. Recall the supper of Lord Yamada."

"Yes," said Tajima, uncertainly.

"Ichiro," I said, "when you first approached the whip master on the ruse of acquiring slaves to serve a pleasure feast, did he express surprise or skepticism?"

"No, Commander *san*," said Ichiro. "His concern pertained only to the assurance of an authorization."

"When recently in the tent of the camp lord," I said, "Lord Akio remarked that Lord Yamada may not always be shogun."

"Interesting," said Haruki.

"At the time of Lord Yamada's supper," said Pertinax, "Lord Akio slew the would-be assassin, despite the fact that the fellow had already been subdued by Ashigaru."

"That preventing an interrogation which might have proved illuminating," I said.

"You think Lord Akio plots against Lord Yamada?" said Tajima.

"I think it is obvious," I said.

"But Lord Yamada is his shogun," said Tajima.

"The code of the warrior," I said, "is sometimes easily put on and off, as easily as one of the splendid garments of Lord Akio."

"The slaves, and the shogun's daughter, were all witness to this," said Pertinax.

"Perhaps, then, that is why they have been kept together," said Haruki, "that they might be supervised and controlled, or, if one wished, disposed of without difficulty."

"I do not think so," I said. "I think Lord Akio has little to fear from slaves. I think the matter would have more to do with emulation, satisfaction, and vanity. As I see it, Lord Akio is the most prominent daimyo of Lord Yamada. Certainly he was much at the palace, and, now, is the camp lord of Lord Yamada's march. In the event of Lord Yamada's demise I suspect that Lord Akio would be the presumptive shogun. I think that most of the lesser daimyos would accept him as, and even acclaim him to be, the successor to Lord Yamada. To be sure there might be a civil war about the matter. It is hard to know. Add in now, in addition to Lord Akio's presumed uncontested ascent to the shogunate, his likely jealousy, envy, and hatred of Lord Yamada, and his long-thwarted ambition to ascend to the dais of the shogun, his possible interest in the shogun's daughter, now a vulnerable, available slave. Would it not be a triumph for him, a delightful vengeance on Lord Yamada, and a lovely sop to his vanity, to organize similar suppers, even feasts, for his daimyos, officers, and retainers, feasts served by lovely but lowly barbarian slaves, indeed the very same who served the supper of Lord Yamada, that at which the critical and haughty Sumomo was present, only now feasts in which she herself, the former Sumomo, serves as only another slave, to the gratification and amusement of her master, amidst the very slaves she so regaled and despised?"

"Only now," said Pertinax, "a supper, or suppers, or feasts, that need not be so decorous, as no free women would be present."

"Certainly," I said, "if no free women are present, why should the slaves be clothed?"

"I will not leave without Nezumi," said Tajima.

"You have the key," I said. "Take her off the chain."

In a moment Tajima had freed Nezumi of the chain, and she knelt beside him, her cheek pressed tenderly against his thigh.

"Did you hear our conversation?" he asked her.

"Yes, Master," she whispered.

"You shall not serve Lord Akio in the manner suggested by Tarl Cabot, tarnsman, if I can help it," he said.

"Yes, Master," she said.

"Unless," he said, "I choose that you shall do so."

"Yes, Master," she said.

"But, I suspect," he said, "you will frequently so serve me."

"I am a slave," she said. "I am to be as Master wishes me to be, and to be done with as Master pleases."

"Give me the key," said Pertinax. "I will fetch myself a slave."

"Hurry, Gregory, hurry!" said Saru.

"Keep on your belly," I said, "and keep your hands at your sides, the palms up."

She shook the chain a bit on her ankle, as though vexed, but obeyed.

The palms of a woman's hands are excruciatingly sensitive, particularly if touched lightly, as with the tracing of a fingernail. Exposing her palms to a male, even over a distance, can be arousing to a woman. It is almost like unsheathing, or offering, herself. I had little doubt that if I were to touch the exposed palms of almost any of the slaves, they would have shaken with need. I did not doubt but what in almost any of these slaves the slave fires had been lit. How helpless they are then. How much that makes them ours! How wonderful it is to have a slave!

"Oh, Master," sobbed Jane, softly. "Yes, yes!"

"Gregory?" said Saru.

Freed of the chain, Jane instantly knelt before Pertinax.

In the position of the pleasure slave the woman kneels as an obvious pleasure slave. There is no doubt as to what she is for. Masters may, of course, instruct their slave as to how to kneel before them. Most commonly she kneels back on her heels, her head up, her back straight, and the palms of her hands down on her thighs. In the position of the common slave, or the tower slave, on the continent, the knees are held closely together; in the position of the pleasure slave, they are separated, spread vulnerably. This accentuates the softness of her thighs. As mentioned, there is to be no doubt as to what she is for. Whereas most commonly the head is raised, that the master may observe the beauty of her features and read her tiniest expression, and note how beautifully her throat is encircled with his collar, some masters prefer the slave's head to be lowered, submissively. Indeed, some masters do not permit a slave to look into their eyes, unless commanded to do so. Some masters, too, prefer for the hands to be held behind the back, as though bound, the head either up, or lowered, submissively. I considered Jane, before Pertinax. The palms of her hands, I noted, were not down on her thighs, as is usually prescribed, but the backs of her hands were on her thighs, and the palms were exposed to Pertinax, almost pleadingly. Another way a slave may supplicate the master's attention is to place the bondage knot in her hair. Sometimes, of course, the master has other things to do, perhaps finishing a kaissa game, and the slave must wait to be caressed. This is acceptable, as she is only a slave. Sometimes the master allows her to simmer, or heat, perhaps helplessly bound. Let her cope as she can with her slave fires; she is a slave; let her be tormented almost to madness in her need; she is a slave. How ready she is then! How then she leaps to the touch of a hand, of lips, or tongue!

I took the key from Pertinax.

"Thank you, Master," said Cecily, freed from the chain. She went gratefully, unbidden, to first obeisance position, kneeling, head to the ground, palms of her hands beside her head.

The former English beauty, Virginia Cecily Jean Pym, had well learned on Gor, to her joy, that she was a slave.

"Gregory!" said Saru. "Gregory?"

"Tajima has his Nezumi," said Pertinax. "I have my Jane and you your Cecily. Let us leave."

"We cannot remain here," I said. "And it will be hazardous to be about in the camp, and hazardous to leave the camp."

"Gregory!" called Saru, insistently.

I was pleased she had the sense to remain on her belly, with her arms at her sides, the palms of her hands facing upward.

"We will need three tunics," I said. "I expect they may be found on the other side of the partition."

The tent was a sales tent, though obviously it had been closed for sales, presumably to better conceal the shogun's daughter. Being a sales tent it seemed likely it would be equipped with certain devices and goods. In some markets, the seller will provide a tunic for the purchased slave, and a whip for the buyer. More often, such items may be purchased. In either case, they are likely to be available. I had seen some chests, and bundles, in the main area of the tent, to the side, which observation I regarded as promising in this regard. Certainly I would not look forward to conducting three naked slaves through the camp, an action unlikely to pass unnoticed.

"You will attempt to evade the perimeter guards," said Pertinax.

"I think not," I said. "Given the escape, the number of fugitives, and such, I would expect the perimeter to be infested with Ashigaru."

"I do not think we can long remain in the camp," said Pertinax.

"You and Ichiro," I said, "must have arranged some means of returning to the holding of Temmu or the encampment of tarns, surely not on foot."

"Certainly," said Pertinax, "a point of tarn rendezvous to be scouted from tarnback each day at the tenth Ahn, but that point is pasangs from the camp, and we had not anticipated any great difficulty in leaving the camp."

"Which anticipation must now seem miserably naive," I said.

"Unfortunately," said Pertinax.

As I had suggested earlier, the camp had been, possibly by intent, or carelessness, or arrogance, relatively open, but that situation, I was sure, no longer obtained.

"What do you suggest, Tarl Cabot, tarnsman?" said Tajima.

"We must leave," I said, "from the point from which our departure would be least expected."

"The Merchant Portal?" said Ichiro.

"Yes," I said.

This was the authorized entrance and departure point in the camp, utilized by a variegated traffic of peasant venders, itinerant craftsmen, peddlers, merchants, recruits, deserters from the forces of Lord Temmu, and others.

"It will now be heavily scrutinized," said Haruki.

"We will need a wagon or cart," I said.

413

"There are many near the point," said Pertinax. "Near the market, where vegetables and fruits are sold."

"Good," I said.

"Let us be on our way," said Pertinax.

"No!" cried Saru. "No, no, Gregory! Do not leave me!"

"Do not break position," I warned her.

"Gregory, Gregory White!" she exclaimed, over her shoulder. "You cannot leave me behind! I am Margaret, Margaret Wentworth! We are both of Earth! Remember New York! Remember the office! We came to Gor together! You want me! You love me! You will do whatever I want! Free me! I am chained! Free me! Take me with you!"

"Fetch three tunics," I said to Pertinax.

"And a whip," said Tajima.

"Oh, yes, Master, yes!" said Nezumi, pressing her lips to Tajima's thigh. Slaves fear the whip, but it thrills them to know that they are subject to it, are truly subject to it. Few things bring a woman's slavery home to her better than the sight of the whip which may be used upon them, if they should fail to be pleasing, fully pleasing.

"Do not break position," I warned Saru.

"Please, please, oh, Master!" she wept. "Permit me to break position!"

"Very well," I said.

"Thank you, Master!" she wept, and scrambled about, rising to her feet and dragging against the chain fastened to her left ankle.

"The rest of you remain as you are, precisely," I said.

A shudder of linkage coursed down the chain. Then the slaves were as before. Most, I am sure, given their positioning, were not clear on what was transpiring.

"Gregory!" cried Saru, looking about.

"He is gone," I told her.

"No," she cried, "no!"

"He will be back, shortly," I said. "I think you had best welcome him on your knees."

"But I know him, from Earth!" she said.

"You knew Gregory White," I said. "I am not sure you know Pertinax."

"I do not understand," she said.

"Gregory White was a timid, retiring, easily abashed, enamored, manipulable weakling, an employee, a subordinate, whom you enjoyed ordering about, humiliating, tormenting, and demeaning," I said. "Pertinax is strong, supple, agile, skilled and trained, a warrior and tarnsman, the possessor of a code."

"But Earth!" she protested.

"This is not Earth," I said. "And you are not on Earth. This is Gor. Here your Gregory White is Pertinax, a warrior and tarnsman, and you are a stripped, chained, collared slave."

"I need only have a moment alone with him," she said. "I need only smile, shed a tear, let my lips quiver, my body tremble, my voice shake, and all will be as it was before. I shall recall him to his better nature, his true nature."

"He has now found his better nature," I said, "and here, on Gor, his true nature. Do you think he will betray the blood which is his, the heart which he has at last found, severe and hardy, in his own breast?"

"I can make him weak!" she said.

"Perhaps once," I said. "And that may be why he avoided you for months in Tarncamp. But I do not think you can do so now."

"I am strong," she said. "I am powerful. I can trample and destroy him!"

"How so?" I asked.

"He loves me!" she said.

"You are not a free woman," I said. "You are a slave, a beast. Perhaps you might hope at best, if you are fortunate, that he might find your flanks of interest."

"No!" she cried.

"Why is this slave standing?" asked Pertinax, returned from the other side of the partition.

"Get on your knees," I snapped, and, instantly, the former Miss Margaret Wentworth, the slave, Saru, went to her knees.

Pertinax cast a tunic to the ground before Jane, before Cecily, and Nezumi. Each gratefully clutched the tiny garment.

Pertinax handed a slave whip to Tajima, who briefly held it to the lips of Nezumi, who kissed it, joyfully.

The slaves looked to me.

"You may clothe yourselves," I said.

The three slaves stood, and slipped into the bits of cloth allotted to them.

How pleasant it is to be the masters of women.

"Where is my tunic, Gregory?" said Saru.

Pertinax turned his back on her. "I have some bracelets, as well," he said, "and, here, a coil of rope."

"Good," I said. "Back-bracelet them and put them in neck coffle."

"Gregory, I am here, Margaret!" said Saru.

The three slaves then stood before us, gracefully, as slaves, their hands braceleted behind their backs, in a rope coffle, neck-fastened.

"Gregory!" said Saru.

Pertinax turned to face her, and she shrank back.

"Who are you?" he asked.

"Margaret," she said, "Margaret Wentworth."

Pertinax turned to me. "Do you see a Margaret Wentworth here?" he asked.

"No," I said. "I see a slave, who might be given what name masters might please."

He then turned back to the slave. "Margaret Wentworth," he said, "was a free woman, petty, vain, venal, ambitious, conniving, sly, hypocritical, dishonest, pretentious, lying, and arrogant, but free, one despicable in many ways, but free. A free woman is permitted whatever nasty indulgences, whatever flaws and faults, she pleases, but the least suggestion of such a thing in a slave can be a cause for discipline."

This was true. The free woman need please only herself. The slave is to please the master. The free woman is responsible only to herself. The slave is responsible to her master. She is owned.

"Gregory," she said, putting out her hand.

He seized her by the hair, and struck her twice, first with the flat of his hand, on the left cheek, and then with the back of his hand on the right cheek.

She looked up at him, aghast, in awe.

"You struck me," she said, reproachfully. "No! Do not turn away!"

He turned back. I feared he might be angry. The slave is not to be struck in anger. She is to be struck, if she is to be struck, to discipline her, to improve her. She is to be trained as the animal she is, and in her training, the whip is occasionally useful.

"Why did you strike me?" she asked.

"I found you displeasing," he said.

"What do you think you are?" she asked.

"A free man," he said, "and you are a slave."

"A slave," I said, "does not address a free man by his name."

"We have dallied enough," said Pertinax. "Let us be on our way."

Scarcely had we turned away, when the slave cried out, "Masters, do not leave me! Do not leave Saru! Please, Masters, take Saru with you. Do not leave her behind on her chain!"

We turned about, and saw that the slave had prostrated herself on her belly before us, her ankle pulled as far forward as the chain would allow. Her left leg was stretched taut, behind her. Her hands were extended, lifted. Her head was up, from the dirt, tears streaming down her face. "I am contrite, Master!" she wept. "I beg forgiveness! I am only a slave who begs a master's forgiveness!"

Pertinax regarded her, angrily.

"I know," I said, "you had many reservations about the moral character of Miss Margaret Wentworth, but now it is the helpless, chained slave, Saru, who is on her belly before you, begging your forgiveness."

He glared, down, at the prostrate slave.

"What do you see there?" I asked.

"A slave," he said.

"That is what is there," I said.

"Obviously," he said.

"It is incontestable," I said, "that many faults and blemishes, of diverse sorts, personal and moral, characterized the former Miss Wentworth, but it is not to be overlooked that she was also a beautiful woman. Indeed, she was designated for Gorean slavery, and the slavers of Gor, I assure you, are not easy to please. They are not just chaining the women who flee from burning cities. They choose with taste and discrimination. Miss Wentworth was beautiful, even on a world contaminated with lies, hypocrisy, and pollution. And here, we have the slave, Saru, on a fresh, clean, natural world, marked and collared. So marked and collared, surely her beauty is much enhanced, as is ever the case when a woman is marked and collared, proclaimed female, and slave."

"Let us be on our way," said Pertinax.

"You can see she is beautiful," I said.

"There are many beautiful women," said Pertinax.

"Stand closer to her," I said.

He did as I suggested, looking down.

Saru put down her head, and her tears fell on his feet, as she kissed them, again and again. Then, tenderly, she lifted his foot and placed it on her head. He then stepped back, and she looked up at him, her eyes bright with tears.

"I love you," she said, "—Master."

"Lying slave," he sneered.

"I dare not lie, Master," she said. "I am a slave!"

"Speak," he said, coldly.

"I always loved you, even on Earth," she said, "even when I despised you for your weakness. Do you not understand? I wanted to be taken in hand, and put to your feet. I longed for, and needed, a master, not an associate, a pet."

"Do not blame Pertinax," I said. "Few can stand against the weight of centuries of denial, superstition, and madness. Culture was determined to banish nature, to rob men and women of their selves. He was endeavoring, as so many others, trusting innocents unaware of what was being done to them, to fulfill alien prescriptions, to fulfill pathological stereotypes, engineered stereotypes in terms of which the 'true male' was to be defined, a male without maleness. Is the political agenda here so difficult to determine? Can one not sense what lies concealed behind the veils of rhetoric? Is it so difficult to detect what the advertisements are out to sell, under a hundred false labels? But faraway, and never wholly forgotten, for it lies in the blood, and genes, is the burning fire, the hunt, the club, and thong."

"Forgive me, Master," she said, "for all the wrongs I have done you, all the cruelty I showed to you. I hoped to find in you the master I had sought so unsuccessfully to drive from my dreams."

"We must be going," said Pertinax.

"Surely you wanted me," said Saru, "if only in your collar, or on your leash!"

Pertinax extended his hand to Tajima, without looking at him. "Whip," he said.

He was handed the whip, and he gestured, peremptorily, to Saru that she should rise up, to her knees.

He then held the whip to her, and, weeping, she held it in both hands, and, head down, licking and kissing, lavished upon it the ecstasy of the submitted slave.

"I love you, I love you, Master!" she said.

Pertinax pulled the whip away and returned it to Tajima. I handed Pertinax the key and he thrust it into the ankle lock of the slave.

"Take your place," said Pertinax to the slave, and she hurried to stand behind the other slaves.

"We will fetch her a tunic, bracelet her, and add her to the coffle on the way out," I said.

"This is all well and good," said Haruki, "but we may all be dead within the Ahn."

"It is still light out," I said. "The Merchant Portal will be most closely scrutinized after dark. It is my hope that few would expect us to depart through the Merchant Portal, and in the full light of day."

As the bracelets were being placed on a tunicked Saru, and she was being added to the coffle, Tajima turned to me. "Do you think she will make a good slave?" he asked.

"Why do you ask?" I asked.

"She is not even Pani," said Tajima.

"No matter," I said.

"Do you?" he asked.

"Yes," I said. "The woman actually enslaves herself, when she yields to the slave in her heart and belly."

"When she acknowledges to herself what she is, and wants to be?" said Tajima.

"Yes," I said.

"Do you think Pertinax is strong enough to be a master?" asked Tajima.

"Yes," I said. "He is no longer of Earth. He is now of Gor. If at any time Saru should be so foolish as to dare to doubt her bondage, she will be soon reminded that she is owned, and wholly. Indeed, given their antecedents, their experiences on Earth, and such, Pertinax may not be excessively patient with her. Let us hope then that she is a dutiful and pleasing slave, and fully so. The whip is not pleasant."

"If Pertinax is not satisfied with her," said Tajima, "do you think he would sell her?"

"Certainly," I said. "She is a slave."

"Do you think she will be pleasant on the mat?" asked Tajima.

"Slave fires," I said, "are already in her belly. Pertinax may not be aware of that."

"He has a pleasant surprise in store," said Tajima.

"I think so," I said.

"You think she will writhe well on the mat?" asked Tajima.

"I think so," I said, "and if Pertinax should be otherwise occupied, I think she will beg to do so."

"Four," said Haruki, looking at me closely, "seems a nice number."

"Yes," I said. "It balances out better than three."

"I do not understand," said Tajima.

"We are thinking about appropriating a wagon," I said. "And the most likely harnessing will come in pairs."

"And we will need some harnessed draft beasts to draw the wagon," said Tajima.

"Yes," I said.

"Yes," said Tajima, "four is better than three."

We then, with our tunicked coffle, left the slave tent.

Chapter Forty-Three

We Reach the Merchant Portal

I cinched the harness straps on Cecily.

"We are only women, Master," she said.

"We selected a small wagon," I said.

"It does not seem to me so small," she said.

"It was convenient," I said.

"I see," she said.

"It is empty," I said.

"It will be heavy, nonetheless," she said. "I do not know if we can draw it. We are but women."

"That it is empty will not arouse suspicion," I said, "as we are planning to leave the camp."

"Still," she said.

"The men will walk," I said.

"We will do the best we can," she said.

"Haruki and I," I said, "drew a loaded rice wagon pasangs to the camp."

"We are women, Master," she said.

"And much of the way was uphill," I said. "And much of your way, as we are leaving the vicinity of the camp, should be downhill."

"But not all of it," she said.

"No," I said.

"Surely we are not to be used as draft beasts," she said.

"It is one of the things slaves are good for," I said. "On continental Gor it is not unknown for women to draw wagons, and carts, even plows."

"But large women," she said, "work slaves, the slaves of peasants. I fear we are not such."

"You look well in harness," I said.

"I fear we will be unable to draw the wagon," she said.

"You will do very well," I said.

"What are you doing?" I asked Haruki.

"Cutting a switch," he said, "in case the beasts need encouraging, or hastening."

Pertinax now had Jane and Saru harnessed.

Nezumi had been hitched up first by Tajima.

"Cecily is right," I said to Haruki. "The wagon is heavy for four slaves."

"Do not fear, noble one," said Haruki. "I have a switch." He then cut the air with the switch, with a swift hiss, and the slaves stirred uneasily in their harnessing.

I turned to Tajima. "We could use some bosk," I said, "kaiila, or a small draft tharlarion."

"There are no bosk or kaiila in the islands," said Tajima. "But since the ship of Tersites has proven that Thassa can be crossed, if with great hazard, such stock may be brought to the islands, perhaps in the next few years. And the only tharlarion I have discovered about I could lift in one hand."

"I have my switch," said Haruki.

"We will walk beside the wagon," I said. "That will make matters manageable. And once we are beyond the camp, we can abandon the wagon and proceed on foot to Pertinax's and Ichiro's rendezvous point. It should be scouted at the tenth Ahn tomorrow."

"Will there be enough tarns?" asked Haruki.

"I do not know," I said. "As Pertinax and Ichiro sought Tajima and, possibly, Nezumi, there should be enough for at least three men and a slave."

"The slaves are light," said Tajima.

"A raiding tarnsman," I said, "can fasten two women to the saddle rings and one if he wishes, across the saddle apron."

"There is likely to be at least two in the scouting party," said Tajima, "each with his own tarn, and perhaps each with an accompanying tarn."

"I do not anticipate difficulty," I said.

The slaves were now hitched where we had drawn the wagon, rather at the end of the wagon yard.

They were arranged in two pairs. The first pair consisted of Cecily and Nezumi, Cecily on the left, as one would face forward; the second pair consisted of Jane and Saru, Jane on the left, as one would face forward. I put Nezumi in the first pair as I did not wish it to seem that I might be trying to conceal her. Too, I supposed few would expect the shogun's daughter to be in this position of prominence, or, indeed, harnessed to a wagon at all, as a common slave, to be sure, the common slave she now was. Also, as she was Pani, it made sense she would be given precedence over the other three, who were not Pani.

"See that you pull your weight," said Jane to Saru, "or I will call your laxity to the attention of Master Haruki and he will lay his switch on you, and well."

"Yes, Mistress," said Saru.

"Barbarian," said Jane, scornfully.

"Yes, Mistress," said Saru. "Forgive me, Mistress."

Pertinax had made it clear to Saru that Jane was "first girl," and so, naturally, Saru addressed her as "Mistress." "I am second, Master," Saru had said to Pertinax. "So, as I am the lesser slave, the inferior slave, I must try harder, so much harder, to please my master!" "And your mistress," said Pertinax. "Yes, Master," said Saru. "And keep your head down," said Pertinax. "Yes, Master," she said. "Forgive me, Master."

Pertinax put his hand to the side of her face, and she twisted her head, pressing her lips, quickly, almost furtively, on his wrist. "I am yours," she whispered. "I love you, my Master!"

"Avert your eyes," said Pertinax.

"Yes, Master," she said.

"Beware, slave," said Jane, "for I have whip rights over you."

"Yes, Mistress," said Saru. "Forgive me, Mistress."

I reviewed the slaves.

Each was collared. A woman in a collar is beautiful. Not only is the collar an aesthetic enhancement of a woman's beauty, but, in the psychological dimension, it makes her a thousand times more exciting and attractive. She is a slave. She can be owned. She can be bought and sold.

Each, too, was marked, high on the left thigh, under the hip.

Jane, Cecily, and Saru wore the common kef, familiar on the distant continent. Nezumi wore a Pani brand, selected for her by her master, Tajima.

These marks were now, if one cared to look, in plain sight, as the slaves were naked.

Near the wagon yard we had removed the slaves from the coffle and relieved them of the bracelets which had secured their hands behind their backs. Before their harnessing we had also removed their tunics. Women used in draftage, for wagons, carts, plows, and such, are usually stripped, for the work is likely to be both dirty and sweaty. This arrangement is likely to be the most comfortable for the beasts and, too, it protects the tunics from undue soiling. It also guarantees, of course, that there will be nothing between the body of the slave and, if it is desired, the stroke of a switch or whip.

"I think we are ready to essay the exit," I said.

"I am uneasy," said Pertinax.

"We are all uneasy," I said. "Why are you uneasy?"

"I think your plan is wise," he said, "bold, even brilliant."

"It would be nice if it would also work," I said.

"However," said Pertinax, "it is exactly what Nodachi would expect. 'Look for the enemy where he cannot be'."

"Nodachi?" I said.

"Yes," he said.

"If Nodachi were about," I said, "I might do what is expected, as that would not be expected."

"But," said Pertinax, "in your case he might expect that."

"What then would you suggest?" I said.

"'Let the decision be made by the bird springing unexpectedly from the brush'," he said.

"Nodachi?" I said.

"Yes," he said.

"He is a wise man," I said. "The darting upward of such a bird cannot be predicted. It is irrelevant to the calculations of hunters and hunted. One cannot penetrate thought where thought is not involved."

"I take it to be a random-selection device," said Pertinax.

"It is," I said, "one of the shrewdest devices in the quiver of games, including the game of war."

"Forward," said Haruki, slapping his switch on the side the wagon.

The four slaves, slipping in the dirt, put their slight weight, straining, against the traces. The harnessing was taut. The wagon did not move. Again Haruki struck the side of the wagon, smartly, with the switch.

Nature had not selected women such as these, so lovely, so beautiful, so vulnerable, so deliciously and helplessly female and feminine, for the lifting of stones and the hauling of wagons. They had been selected to be at the feet of men, to serve men, and to give pleasure to men, their masters.

One of the girls, I think Saru, began to cry.

"Again, forward!" said Haruki.

I went behind the wagon and, bracing myself, thrust it forward. The wheels began to turn.

"Forward!" said Haruki. Again the switch slapped the side of the wagon.

Once the vehicle is in motion it is easier, naturally, to keep it in motion. Still, from time to time, particularly on upgrades, I, Pertinax, Ichiro, and, I think, even Tajima, would assist the struggling slaves.

"Saru is well harnessed," I said.

"I saw to it," said Pertinax.

"Perhaps more tightly than was necessary," I said.

"She is a slave," said Pertinax.

"The harnessing," I said, "well accentuates her figure."

"All their figures," said Pertinax.

"On Earth," I said, "in her chic, well-chosen, fashionable ensembles, in the offices, in meetings, in boardrooms, in restaurants and cocktail lounges, in her meretricious flatterings of, and hypocritical solicitations of, clients, in her application of shallow, lubricious charms to cloud and sway judgment, in her sly hintings at gratifications which would never be bestowed, I would suppose she never expected to find herself a naked slave, hitched to a wagon on Gor."

Such experiences are useful, of course, as many other such experiences, for example, scrubbing a floor naked, in chains, in helping a woman to learn her collar.

"I imagined her in a thousand such ways," he said, "even

chained naked beneath my desk at the office, everyone else clothed and going about their business, scarcely noticing her, to be cast scraps when it pleased me."

"Good," I said.

"Many a night," he said, "I imagined her lying on the floor at the foot of my bed, naked, bound hand and foot, there if I should choose to make use of her."

"Splendid," I said.

"And how often, in my mind, I marched her naked on her leash, before me, on familiar, busy streets, pausing from time to time to exchange pleasantries with others, who were also walking their slaves, the slaves then kneeling, head down, beside us, while we conversed, until, with a snap of the leash, we put them to their feet again and continued on our way."

"Excellent," I said.

"And now," he said, "she is a Gorean slave."

"Excellent," I said.

"I think now," he said, "she was always a slave."

"But now in her collar," I said.

"Yes," he said, "now in her collar."

"Where she belongs," I said.

"Yes," he said.

"What if she should be displeasing," I asked, "in the least?"

"Then she will be disciplined," he said, "promptly, and effectively."

"Good," I said.

The camp was large, and the wagon yard lay near its center, by the market.

"That way," said Pertinax.

Pertinax and Ichiro, perhaps as much as three or four days ago, had apprised themselves of the location of the Merchant Portal.

It was better than a pasang away.

The wagon creaked. The wheels came to my shoulders. The slaves strained against the harness. Occasionally Haruki's switch cracked against the side of the wagon. Now and again, we thrust against the wagon, until it would again roll freely, if slowly.

"There are the white stones," said Pertinax, at last.

"We are nearing the exit?" I said.

"Yes," said Pertinax. "Keep within the two lines of white stones. Once we have reached the stones, we are not to depart from them."

"The stones are widely spaced," I said.

"Yes," said Pertinax, "to allow wagons, coming and going, to pass one another, and keep within the stones."

More Ashigaru were about now, and I made it a point to avoid their eyes.

"Ashigaru," I said.

"Do not concern yourself with these," said Pertinax. "Their only concern here, near the perimeter, is to make sure that those entering or leaving the camp do so at the same point."

"The Merchant Portal," I said.

"Yes," said Pertinax, "but it is not an actual portal, a gate, or such, only a point on the perimeter which is to be monitored for traffic."

"There it is," I said. Before us we could see some fellows on foot, some arriving, and some departing. Two wagons were approaching. A man passed us carrying a cage of vulos. Toward the perimeter a man and a boy were herding a small flock of verr into the camp.

"There seems little difficulty in entering the camp," I said.

"I expect," said Pertinax, "it may not be as easy to leave it."

"True," said Haruki. "It is easier to step into a trap than remove its teeth from your ankle."

"I see the inspection point," I said. "There seem four there, three Ashigaru and an officer."

"But many Ashigaru are about," said Ichiro, "who might be easily summoned."

"We must turn back!" I said.

"We cannot," said Pertinax. "The stones! And there are fellows, and a wagon, behind us. We must proceed."

"Look," I said. "Ahead! My plan has failed!"

"How so?" said Pertinax.

"The officer!" I said.

"What is wrong, Commander *san*?" said Ichiro.

"We are discovered," I said.

"Move forward," called a voice from behind us.

"You know the officer?" asked Ichiro.

"Yes," I said, "unfortunately we have met."

"I do not know him," said Pertinax.

"Nor I," said Ichiro.

"Tajima, Haruki, and I know him," I said.

"We must proceed," said Pertinax. "Perhaps he will not recognize us."

"He will recognize us," I said.

"How do you know?" said Pertinax.

"He has been waiting for us," I said, "waiting here, at the least likely place for us to be found."

"I do not understand," said Pertinax.

"I know him from elsewhere, first from an inn," I said. "He is Yasushi, a constable of the march."

"He is waiting for us?" said Pertinax.

"Yes," I said.

"I do not understand," said Pertinax.

"He is a student of Nodachi," I said.

"Move forward," again called a voice from behind us. "Move forward!"

"We cannot turn back," said Pertinax, his hand on the hilt of his sword.

"We are lost," I said.

Chapter Forty-Four

Yamada Advances

We stood on the outer parapet of the holding of Temmu, high above the valley below. I think it must have been about the eighth Ahn.

"We have the assurance of the tarn cavalry, that it will fly on behalf of our house?" said Lord Temmu, gazing over the parapet.

"Yes," I said, "and Lord Yamada has been so informed."

"Yet he advances," said Lord Temmu. "He must be a fool."

"Lord Yamada is no fool," I said.

"I would that we could understand this," said Lord Nishida.

"It is difficult," said Lord Okimoto.

"Would that I had a skilled and honest reader of bones and shells," said Lord Temmu.

"If men with minds and memories are confused and baffled," said Lord Nishida, "how can bones and shells do better, which have neither?"

"Do not doubt the bones and shells," said Lord Temmu.

"But sometimes," said Lord Okimoto, "they are hard to read."

"True," said Lord Temmu.

The reader, Daichi, had disappeared from the holding of Temmu, I had learned, shortly after the discovery of Sumomo's espionage. This seemed judicious considering the likely linkage between them. Fortunately for Sumomo she had been removed from the holding by Tyrtaios before she was to have been cast from the outer parapet to the ground below, at the very time it was supposed that her next secret message would be anticipated below. The former Sumomo, now Tajima's slave, Nezumi, and the slaves Saru, Jane, and Cecily were all at the encampment of tarns. We thought them safer there, from war, and, in the case of Nezumi, from the dark justice of Lord Temmu. If she were housed in the holding of Temmu, it seemed likely that she, even with cropped hair and in the garment of a field slave, would be recognized as the former Sumomo, and dealt with accordingly.

"Daichi," said Lord Temmu, "was a fine reader. Else I should not have employed him. Many thought so. Only he was suborned, and lied. He did not report truly what the bones and shells proclaimed."

"He labored in the service of Lord Yamada," I said.

"He betrayed the bones and shells," said Lord Temmu.

"I am pleased," said Lord Nishida, "that you have been reinstated as commander of the tarn cavalry."

I bowed, politely.

"The cavalry," said Pertinax, "never owned another."

It is interesting, I thought, the relationships between politics and reality, between words and deeds, between laws and enforcements, between formalities and facts. Lord Temmu had relieved me of my command, as he thought, but the cavalry, as I understood it, had remained mine, and now, with no change in things, Lord Temmu had supposedly returned my command. But the reality was that the cavalry had repudiated in fact, if not in name, its allegiance to Lord Temmu, following his betrayal of me into the power of Lord Yamada. The cavalry was now, in fact, if not in name, an independent unit. I was not now to be commanded as a subordinate but courted as an ally.

"I do not understand the advance of Yamada," said Lord Okimoto. "Why should he not fear the cavalry? It lifted the siege, it ruined camps, it shocked troops into disarray, it disrupted supply lines, it burned storehouses, it spread havoc throughout villages, towns, and fortresses of Lord Yamada, it forced the withdrawal of his army, to protect the core of his homelands."

"Perhaps he is a fool," said Lord Temmu.

"Perhaps," said Lord Okimoto, "he has assurances that the cavalry will not fly."

"How could that be?" asked Lord Nishida.

"Tarl Cabot, tarnsman," said Lord Okimoto, "was a guest in

the palace of Lord Yamada, for several days. Who knows what negotiations took place between them, what agreements were made, what arrangements instituted."

"The cavalry," I said, "is stationed now in the hills nearby, not at the encampment of tarns. Banners on the summit of the holding could signal it instantly. In an Ehn it could be aflight."

"But will it be aflight?" asked Lord Okimoto.

"If Lord Okimoto wishes," I said, angrily, "I can withdraw the cavalry."

"Please do not do so," said Lord Temmu.

"Then it would obviously not be aflight," said Lord Okimoto.

"Dismissing the interesting question of the cavalry, its intentions, its allegiance, its reliability, and such, the holding has been resupplied," said Lord Nishida. "It could withstand a siege for thousands of years."

"But the towns and countryside could be devastated," said Lord Okimoto. "Our villages could be burned or accept the exactions of Lord Yamada. We would hold a mountain and he would possess a world."

"Lord Yamada has been informed," I said, "that if his advance does not cease, and he does not retire to his ancestral lands, the cavalry will fly."

"How do we know it will do so?" asked Lord Okimoto.

"You have my word," I said.

"The word of a barbarian," said Lord Okimoto.

"The advance continues," said Lord Nishida.

"Lord Yamada is a fool," said Lord Temmu.

"What does Lord Yamada know that we do not?" said Lord Nishida.

"Perhaps," said Lord Okimoto, "that the cavalry will not fly."

In the distance we could hear drums and battle horns.

"Tajima," I said.

He had been silent. Now he put down the glass of the Builders. "Yes, Tarl Cabot, tarnsman," he said.

"Signal Ichiro on the summit," I said. "Signal 'Saddles' and 'One-strap'."

"Yes, Tarl Cabot, tarnsman," he said.

We had approached the Merchant Portal with considerable

trepidation. Had we departed from the road, or wide path, that lined with white stones, Ashigaru would have investigated. It was not practical to turn back, and, had we done so, that, too, would surely have provoked attention, and, presumably, would have resulted in some sort of inquiry, the outcome of which would have been likely to have been our discovery and undoing.

"Hold!" said Yasushi, holding up his hand, palm forward. With him were three Ashigaru, which, now, to my surprise, I recognized as the three fellows whom Tajima had entertained in the inn a few pasangs to the west, the fellows who had been disappointingly casual about fetching their gathered rice to the supply wagons, but had been more than helpful in apprising us of local military and political matters with which we, due to our prior journey, had been woefully out of touch.

"You escaped from the prison pen," said Yasushi.

I glanced about. There were more than a hundred Ashigaru within hailing distance.

"Two of us," I said.

"How did you manage that?" he asked.

"We organized peasants," I said.

"But few would be from the same village," he said.

"Nonetheless," I said, uneasily.

"Interesting," he said. "Why did you bother? It was dangerous. You were to be released the next morning."

"We did not wish to wait," I said.

"The entire camp," he said, "is being searched for fugitives, you two, some slaves, a young warrior, several peasants, and Arashi, the bandit."

"How have you been?" I asked.

"Well," he said, "and you?"

"Fine," I said.

"Where are you off to?" he asked.

"That probably depends on you," I said.

"That wagon," he said, "and probably the slaves, are stolen."

"If you like," I said, "we can leave the wagon, say, within a pasang."

"I like your draft animals," he said.

The slaves were obviously frightened. To be sure, as slaves, they were in no particular danger. In many situations where free persons would be instantly put to the sword, no one would think of injuring a slave, no more than one would think of injuring any other property of value, say, a glazed, red-figured vase from Turia, or a domestic animal, say, a blond-maned, silken kaiila. Free women in jeopardy, say, a blade at their throat, rather than accept an honorable death as a free person, as is prescribed, may declare themselves slave, after which they are stripped and bound, and, despised as the slaves they now are, are held for the iron and collar. Sometimes, wild and distraught, frantic, in a sacked, burning city, free women will even disguise themselves as slaves, that they may be spared. Their ruse discovered, usually by genuine slaves, they are beaten and cast naked to the feet of masters, to be assessed, and, if found suitable, marked and sold. The exception here, of course, was Nezumi, who, if recognized, might have been remanded to Yamada's executioners for the eel death, or worse. Indeed, it was not clear that Nezumi was in a much better way should she come to the attention of Lord Temmu, as she might then be decollared and cast to the rocks at the foot of the outer parapet of his holding.

"You are in the presence of free men," I said.

Swiftly the slaves, in a rustle and jangle of harness, knelt.

"Heads down," I said.

"Yes," said Yasushi, "a pretty lot."

"We did not have the resources, or opportunity," I said, "to hire a number of good fellows to draw the wagon."

"It is not even your wagon," said Yasushi.

"True," I said.

"I think you are a clever fellow," said Yasushi. "That is why I thought you would elect this egress from the camp. It is public and dangerous, but shrewd and bold. There are fewer Ashigaru about, watchful, ready to kill on sight. An urt would be fortunate to slip from the camp otherwise."

"I was not clever enough," I said.

"I was afraid," he said, "that you might encounter others here, and it would go badly for you."

"That is why you arranged to be here?"

"Of course," he said. "I, and the three required Ashigaru."

"I recognize them," I said.

"Shoji, Akiyoshi, and Fumitaka," he said.

"By sight," I said. "Tal," I said.

"Tal," they said, "noble one."

"Better get your beasts up," said Yasushi.

"Up, *kajirae*," I said.

With a sound of harness, the girls, I think uncertain, bewildered, stood.

"You are holding up the line," said Yasushi. "Pass."

"Are we not to be arrested?" I said.

"No," he said.

"Why not?" I said.

"Did we not share danger and war?" he said.

"I wish you well," I said.

"I wish you well," he said. "Do not leave the wagon faraway."

"Over that hill," I said.

"That will do," he said.

We then moved from the camp. A quarter of an Ahn later we unhitched the girls and abandoned the wagon. Shortly thereafter, the slaves tunicked, rope-coffled, and back-braceleted, following the lead of Pertinax and Ichiro, wary of patrols, we turned north. The next afternoon, we were picked up at the rendezvous point and were on our way to the encampment of tarns.

Overhead was the snap of wings, like whips, and, below, on the parapets, flighted shadows darted on the walkways, and then, smaller, on the valley below.

"The cavalry is aflight," said Lord Temmu, with satisfaction. "Lord Yamada is a fool. He has made the greatest mistake of his life."

I was afraid. Lord Yamada was not a man from whom mistakes might be expected.

"Lord Yamada was informed of this," said Lord Nishida. "Yet he advances! How can it be?"

"He did not think the cavalry would fly," said Lord Okimoto. "Otherwise it would be madness to advance. I, too, thought it would not fly. I thought arrangements were in place."

"That Tarl Cabot, tarnsman, was traitorous?" asked Lord Nishida.

"On what other grounds might Yamada advance?" said Lord Okimoto.

"On those of madness," said Lord Temmu.

"I should be with the cavalry," I said, "and so, too, others, Tajima and Pertinax."

"No," said Lord Temmu. "I want you here."

"That I might be slain for treachery, if all did not proceed as planned?"

"You may command from here, by the summit, by flags and signal horns," said Lord Temmu.

"You are not needed to supervise a routine slaughter," said Lord Nishida.

"Lord Yamada was warned," I said. "I did not think he would advance. I expected him to withdraw, rather than risk the decimation of his forces, the loss of towns and fortresses."

"Yet he has advanced," said Lord Okimoto. "It is clear he did not believe you."

"The attack has begun," said Tajima, peering through the glass of the Builders.

"He was warned," I said. "He had my word."

"The word of a barbarian," said Lord Okimoto.

"Know you so little of the continent?" asked Lord Nishida. "It was the word of one who is of the scarlet caste, the word of a warrior."

"His troops will be showered with unanswered arrows," said Lord Okimoto. "Men will seek cover and dare not move. His supply train will be burned. Foragers and scouts will venture forth only with hazard. His march will be arrested. Then the cavalry may return to his ancestral lands to burn and pillage."

In the distance, even without the glass, one could see formations in disarray.

"This is not war," said Tajima, grimly. "It is like shooting tethered verr."

"Victory is upon our banners," said Lord Temmu.

"Hail to Lord Temmu, Shogun of the Islands!" cried an officer. This cry was taken up on the outer parapet, by officers and Ashigaru. It resounded as well on the inner parapets, and I heard it faint, below, in the courtyard of the holding.

"Let the drums pound," said Lord Temmu. "Sound the horns of victory!"

"Hold!" cried Tajima, the glass of the Builders trained on the horizon. "Hold!"

"What is it?" I cried.

"There!" said Tajima, pointing. "There!"

In the distance, hard to determine initially, from the morning sun, there was a speck in the distance.

Lord Temmu seized the glass of the Builders, and peered through it. "It is a bird," he said.

"It is far off," said Lord Okimoto. "It is a tarn."

Lord Temmu handed the glass to his daimyo.

I knew that Lord Yamada had at his disposal at least two tarns.

"Yes," said Lord Okimoto, uncertainly, "a tarn."

"I fear not," I said.

"Give the glass to Tarl Cabot, tarnsman," begged Lord Nishida.

Lord Okimoto passed me the glass, and I trained it on the approaching speck, still far off.

"What is it?" asked Lord Nishida.

"I do not know," I said.

"It is a tarn," said Lord Okimoto.

"No," I said. "It is not a tarn. It does not have the wing beat of a tarn."

"It approaches, does it not?" said Lord Temmu.

"Yes," I said. "And now more swiftly."

"It is a tarn," said Lord Okimoto.

"No," I said. "It is not a tarn. It is not the wing beat of a tarn. Too, it is hard to judge from the distance, but, too, I think it is too large for a tarn, much too large."

"Speak," said Lord Temmu.

"Surely you can make it out now, with the glass!" said Lord Nishida.

"Yes!" I said.

"What is it?" demanded Lord Okimoto.

"I have never seen anything like it," I said. Then I cried out, "Clear the parapet!"

At that very moment the wall of the parapet a few feet to my right burst apart, stones rising in the sky, a hundred paces, and then falling, gracefully. The walkway to the right was half torn away, and smoked with blackened stone. I could feel the heat from where I stood. The air was acrid, and stinging. Men coughed, many seeking the ladders and stairs to the ground below. The object had passed over us, and a moment later there was an explosion in the courtyard below and behind the parapets, and a geyser of dust sprang up behind us, and, almost at the same time, a twisting skewer of fire tore forth from what seemed a maw of the thing, and a segment of the castle roof, the keep of the holding, was afire.

The large object then ascended into the sky, swiftly, smoothly, much as a floatable object submerged will ascend to the surface when released. I had not seen such a movement in many years.

The sight of this thing, the noise, the smoke, and flames, the spillage of rocks and the spumes of dust, brought the tarn cavalry wheeling about, to do battle, to protect the holding.

"No!" I cried, from the damaged parapet. "No!"

The large object faced south, not really moving, seemingly suspended, just rocking a little in the air, much as a ship might rock in the water.

It had been years, too, since I had witnessed solid objects which could remain in place, as did that object, with little or no visible motion, silent, seemingly effortlessly suspended, almost as though alive, waiting.

"Go back!" I cried, from the parapet.

The first tarn flew at the object, the tarnsman's lance couched.

"No!" I wept.

A burst of flame rushed forth from what seemed the maw of the thing and the bird and rider, in a flash of fire, were incinerated before our eyes, and, blackened and smoking, enridged for a moment with lingering fire, a scattering of remains tumbled to the valley below.

A dozen tarns, from the sides, swept toward the seemingly patient, still thing, in the sky, quiet as though waiting, and arrows and Anango darts struck sparks and rang against it.

"No," I cried, looking up, helplessly, from the outer parapet. "Get out! Escape! Go! Flee!"

Lances shivered, and cast knives, quivas, caromed away.

"Tajima!" I cried. "Signal Ichiro, on the summit, signal, 'Retreat' and 'Scatter'! 'Retreat' and 'Scatter'!"

The large object now turned about, gracefully, the large, slow-moving wings orienting it. I do not think it was even aware that it was under attack. Rather, it was as though it wished to learn if that might be the case, as such things might be expected. The maw of the thing was then aligned with another bird and rider, and another burst of fire was emitted from what seemed the maw of the thing, and another rider and bird seemed to discolor the sky as though burning debris might have been cast suddenly on blue tiles. One could then see the residue descend against the hills beyond.

The object then, almost as though mounted on a spindle, turned about, examining the sky about.

I saw some sparks of light, and noted more broken arrows falling from its sides, to the ground below.

Ichiro on the summit winded his battle horn, and the ranks of the tarnsmen seemed to erupt about, as though cast by an invisible hand into the wind.

Another bird and rider perished in a blast of fire, and remains descended, smoking, to the ground.

Ichiro blew, again and again, the horn of battle.

Tarns, and riders, withdrew, in all directions. At most one such pair might be sought at a time.

But the object showed no interest in pursuing any of the riders or mounts.

Nor did it renew its attacks on the holding.

It then turned about, again, and slowly circled over the holding, as though it wished that its presence, and nature, might be unmistakably noted, and, perhaps, recalled.

It then, soft as a winged cloud, turned south, and, wings slowly moving, disappeared over the forces of Lord Yamada, which were now reassembling. Indeed, they were beginning to prepare the trenches and redoubts which would serve for a siege.

There were men on the roof of the castle, extinguishing the flames.

The air about still hung with smoke.

A breeze came from the north, and it would clear the air.

"It could have destroyed the holding," said Tajima, looking after the object.

"Lord Yamada does not wish to destroy the holding," I said. "He wants the holding."

"What now?" asked Pertinax, wiping grit and stains from his face.

"The next move in this sport," I said, "is Lord Yamada's."

"A truce," said Lord Nishida. "Negotiations."

"I would conjecture so," I said.

"I will never surrender the ancestral holding," said Lord Temmu.

"We will fight to the last man," said Lord Okimoto.

"You may have to," I said, "in the ashes."

"We will need every sword," said Lord Okimoto. "We must marshal them. Where is Nodachi? His sword is worth a dozen swords."

"Even a sword worth a dozen swords," said Lord Temmu, "is useless against a thousand swords."

"What if the thousand swords are wielded by but one hand?" I said.

"I see," said Lord Nishida.

"One sword," I said, "applied in a certain way, at a certain time, might do the work of ten thousand swords."

"True," said Lord Nishida.

"Where is Nodachi?" said Lord Temmu.

"He left the holding days ago," said Lord Nishida, quietly.

"Why?" asked Lord Okimoto.

"He said he seeks Lord Yamada," said Lord Nishida.

"Lord Yamada is with the march," I said.

"How do you know?" asked Lord Nishida.

"His headquarters tent and banner were with the camp," I said. "They were stationed at the hub of the camp, at its very center."

"Did you see him?" asked Lord Nishida.

"No," I said.

"Nodachi seeks him," said Lord Nishida.

"Did you dare to look upon the thing in the sky?" asked Lord Temmu.

"Yes," I said.

"You saw its nature?"

"Of course, great lord," I said.

"The brutality, the size, the fangs of steel, the scales, the vast, skinlike wings, the ridged, spikelike tail, the claws of steel, the shining eyes about the head, the breath of fire?"

"Yes, great lord," I said.

"We must attempt to die well," said Lord Temmu.

"All may not be lost," I said.

"Surely you know what we face?" said Lord Temmu.

"I did not believe it existed," said Lord Nishida.

"I never doubted it," said Lord Okimoto, "but I did not hope to see it."

"Daichi referred to such a thing," said Lord Temmu.

"As was advised by Lord Yamada," I said.

"You are skeptical?" said Lord Temmu.

"I fear so," I said.

"But you have seen it," said Lord Temmu.

"Of course," I said. "I have seen what I have seen. I know what I have seen."

"It has come from its cave," said Lord Temmu.

"Perhaps it was released, unchained," said a man.

"But who would dare to release such a thing, to unchain it?" asked Lord Okimoto.

"Yamada," said Lord Temmu.

"What do you think it is?" I asked Lord Temmu.

"You saw its size, its shape, the wings, its terribleness, the tail, the scales, the claws, its ferocity, its fangs, its breath of fire."

"Of course," I said.

"It is the iron dragon," said Lord Temmu.

"No," I said. "It is not. It is a device. You may call it an iron dragon, if you wish, but it is not your feared iron dragon of legend, which is a myth. It is a contrivance, somehow controlled, either from within or from some distant point. On a distant world, a far world beyond the moons, a steel world, inhabited by fierce denizens, I saw such things, animated by an ensconced brain, its body the device itself."

"The iron dragon is such a thing?" said Lord Nishida.

"Something similar," I said.

"But not the same?"

"I do not think so," I said. "When it was attacked, it seemed unaware of the assault. If it were governed by an ensconced brain, I think the brain, housed in the object itself, would, in its own interest, have had things arranged in such a way that it could sense an attack, perhaps being aware of impinging sounds, or responding to vibrations following strikes on the surface, or fuselage, such things. I do not know, but I suspect it was controlled from afar, perhaps from a great distance."

"Perhaps from as far as the palace of Lord Yamada?" asked Lord Nishida.

"Precisely," I said.

"How could anything so far away guide or control it?" asked Lord Okimoto.

"The means exist," I said.

"From far away, how could one see?" asked Lord Okimoto.

"The means exist, Lord," I said.

"I do not understand what is going on," said Lord Nishida.

"As long ago as Tarncamp," I said, "you suspected."

"We are pieces on a board we do not understand," said Lord Nishida, "in a game of giants we do not see."

"And a game, I suspect," I said, "not fairly played."

"What are you going to do?" asked Lord Nishida.

"Seek Nodachi," I said. "I think he will lead me to Yamada."

"Beware the iron dragon," said Lord Temmu.

"I think I know its lair," I said, "and the intelligence, or intelligences, which animate it."

"You will go by tarn, of course," said Lord Nishida.

"I and some others," I said, "if they wish it."

"I am with you, Tarl Cabot, tarnsman," said Tajima.

"I, too," said Pertinax.

"What of us here?" asked Lord Temmu.

"There will be negotiations," I said. "Lord Yamada desires the holding. You may threaten to destroy the holding rather than surrender it. If you do this well, dallying and caviling, the business will take days."

"I see," said Lord Temmu.

"Pretend to believe in the iron dragon," I said.

"That will not be difficult to do," said Lord Nishida.

Chapter Forty-Five

Friends Converse on a Hilltop, A Distant Palace in View

"You once said you had seen the iron dragon," I said to Haruki.

"In the sky, to the west of the palace," said Haruki.

"Only once?" I said.

"Yes," he said.

"It was doubtless a practice flight, a test flight, or such," I said, "one to assess its handling or performance, perhaps to familiarize an operator with the pertinent controls."

"I do not understand such things, noble one," he said.

"Do you know its nest, its lair?" I asked.

"No," he said.

"I think I do," I said, "and I think I know the intelligence, or intelligences, which govern it."

"There is much to fear," said Haruki.

"That is the palace of Yamada in the distance," said Pertinax.

"Consider the fifth level of the palace," I said, "from this side, toward the north."

"I see nothing unusual," he said.

"Nor should you," I said.

"You think that is the housing of the device?" asked Pertinax.

"I am sure of it," I said.

"As far as I know," said Tajima, "it has not flown since the attack on the holding of Lord Temmu."

"What is not seen is often more frightening than what is seen," I said.

"And once briefly glimpsed, and then concealed," said Tajima, "imagination may be permitted to enlarge its menaces and terrors."

"I think so," I said. "If it were frequently seen it would be obvious that, however awesome it is, it is not a living, breathing dragon, no egg-sprung beast of flesh and blood, but a contrivance of sorts, terrible though it may be. It would be obvious that it is not the iron dragon of myth and legend, the source of which is lost in history, but a surrogate of that, a counterfeit."

"It is terrible enough," said Haruki.

"But it would have lost its mantle of mystery, its most fearsome feature, the aura of the unnatural and incomprehensible; it would no longer be something unfamiliar and inexplicable which transcends reason and the world as we know it; it would no longer be something astonishing and unwelcome, emerged from another dimension or world, from a suspected, feared, foreign order of reality. It would no longer be the iron dragon. It would be a machine, complicated and powerful, but a machine, something of this world, and a machine can be built, can be countered, can be dismantled, can be destroyed."

"I have never seen such a machine," said Pertinax. "It is no ordinary machine. Consider the fluidity of its movement, how it can turn in the air, no visible sign of its propulsion, its capacity to remain in place unsuspended."

"I have seen such things," I said.

Long ago, in the Nest of Priest-Kings, in the Nest War, I was familiar with such things, the flat, circular transportation disks which could be used to speedily negotiate the vast intricate corridors and halls of the nest. I had even managed such a device.

"It utilizes gravity," I said, "countering its drag, minimizing and maximizing its effects, shaping its geodesics."

"That is impossible," said Pertinax. "There is no way to control gravity."

"Once," I said, "there may have been no way to control water, fire, or wind, or other forces."

"It is impossible," said Pertinax.

"The technology exists," I said. "Even worlds may be moved."

"It is beyond science," said Pertinax.

"Much depends on the science," I said.

"Gravity is unlike other forces," he said. "It cannot be manipulated."

"The iron dragon exists," I said.

He was silent.

"Much of the dragon was doubtless designed, fabricated, and assembled in the islands," I said, "the framework, the metal plating, and such, but the crucial elements, having to do with propulsion, surveillance, and controls, are almost certainly derived from the continent."

"How then are they here?" asked Pertinax.

"I do not know," I said, "but I suspect we brought them here ourselves, in the ship of Tersites."

"Contraband?" said Pertinax.

"Of a sort," I said. "We brought them to the islands and then, perhaps part by part, they were smuggled south, to be delivered to a waiting party or parties, leagued with the forces of Yamada."

"Lord Nishida," said Pertinax, "spoke strangely of a board, and pieces, and a game of giants."

"I suspect," I said, "we are unwitting participants in such a game. Permit me to speculate, and do not try to understand all of what I say. I may be wrong, and it may not be wise to know too much of such things. Gor is a natural world, a fresh, green, unspoiled world, one much as once was Earth, a jewel world, a green, living diamond in space. It is lovely, and precious. It is also a world housing a species which, from your point of view, would be alien. I will not attempt to describe them, as you might not care to hear what I might say. They are spoken of as 'Priest-Kings'."

"Handsome, godlike creatures, like men," said Pertinax.

"They are often so conceived," I granted him. "But there is another species involved, too, in these things, which, too, for similar reasons, I shall refrain from describing. They are commonly spoken of as Kurii. The Kurii, long ago, it seems, destroyed their native world, and the remnants of their warring races migrated into a number of steel worlds, artificial habitats, which lurk within the cover of thousands of the great stones of space, which, on Earth, we speak of as the asteroid belt. Both Priest-Kings and Kurii possess technologies which are well beyond those available now on our home planet. To shorten matters, the Kurii seek a new world, and covet Gor. Skirmishes and altercations have taken place for generations between these two species, the Kurii wishing to obtain this world and the Priest-Kings, naturally, to retain it. In temperament the Kurii tend to be imperialistic, tenacious, ambitious, and fierce, and the Priest-Kings, on the whole, tend to be pacific and nonaggressive, content, on the whole, to defend their world, rather than seek out Kurii in their strongholds and methodologically destroy them. The speculation then is that rather than continue this intermittent war of generations, with its probes and pursuits, that Kurii and Priest-Kings, or portions of such, have agreed on a wager, with the surface of Gor the prize."

"The surface?" said Pertinax.

"The Priest-Kings," I said, "are a largely subterranean species."

"I see," said Pertinax.

"This wager was to be played out far from the continent," I said, "rather, at the World's End, here, in the islands. The forces of Yamada were to be ranged against those of Temmu."

"Yamada's forces are mighty," said Pertinax, "those of Temmu weak."

"To balance the matter," I said, "foreign mercenaries, and, more importantly, tarns, hitherto unknown in the islands, were to be supplied to Temmu."

"So the die is honest and the coin fair," said Pertinax.

"Supposedly," I said.

"A game played with living pieces," said Pertinax.

"As many games," I said.

"Do we know on which side which giant is wagering?" asked Pertinax.

"I do not know," I said. "The matter is obscure."

"I suppose it does not matter to the pieces," said Pertinax. "They fight, and win or lose, live or die."

"The evidence is mixed," I said. "Sometimes, from various things, I am sure that Kurii favor Temmu, even from Tarncamp, and, at other times, from various things, particularly here, in the islands, it seems clear they favor Yamada."

"If the iron dragon utilizes gravitational technology, as you suggest, and that is within the provenance of Priest-Kings," said Pertinax, "then it is clear the Priest-Kings favor Yamada."

"But," I said, "that technology may have been supplied to Kurii, and I have evidence which suggests that that is the case."

"I do not understand," said Pertinax.

"I think one thing is quite clear," I said, "and that is, if we are indeed enmeshed in some game of giants, it is not a game which is being honestly played. For example, though the iron dragon clearly incorporates the technology of Priest-Kings, it just as clearly violates the laws of Priest-Kings, and would thus, in countering the effect of the cavalry, seem to tip a balance in favor of Yamada."

"Interesting," said Pertinax.

"With so much at stake," I said, "in effect, a planet, for Kurii would not long be likely to peaceably share a world with Priest-Kings or any others, and surely Priest-Kings would realize the danger of admitting a technologically advanced, aggressive species like the Kurii to their world, it seems probable that neither player is willing to abide defeat, and will therefore take whatever measures are deemed useful to ensure victory, or its semblance."

"So much for fair play and sportsmanship," said Pertinax.

"But all this," I said, "is speculation."

"But the iron dragon is real," said Pertinax. "And steel, and blood, and danger."

"Yes," I said.

"What is wrong?" asked Tajima. He and Haruki had been sitting with us, quiet, listening, on a hill, overlooking the palace of Yamada in the distance.

"I am troubled," I said.

"How so?" said Tajima.

"Long ago," I said, "I was placed by a ship on a beach bordering a portion of the northern forests, north of the Alexandra."

"You were placed there for a purpose," said Tajima.

"But for what purpose?" I said.

"Whence issued the ship?" asked Tajima.

"The ship departed from its berth on a steel world," I said.

"Then Kurii favor Temmu," said Pertinax.

"Not necessarily," I said. "It might have been entailed by

the wager, that a tarn cavalry be formed, to even the strengths of war."

"How then does this advance our inquiry?" asked Tajima.

"This is not what troubles me," I said. "It is something different. I learned that I was to be conducted to a rendezvous in the forest, to encounter some who might enlist my services. I was, of course, not eager to enlist my services in obscure causes. I was then informed that an influence might be exerted over me. I was told that they would have a hold over me, in the nature of a woman. This made little sense to me, and, apparently, not to my informant, either, she who then still regarded herself as Miss Margaret Wentworth. In any event, I was conducted to Tarncamp, where nothing was said of a woman. And, too, it was not clear to me, in any case, how one might have a hold over me, and, of all things, because of a woman. I knew no such woman. It made no sense. I dismissed the matter. I did agree to form and train a tarn cavalry. I think the lure here was most the challenge. Could it be done, and well? And there is commonly little to choose from, when one considers warring factions, in both of which are likely to be found the plausible and the implausible, the worthy and the unworthy, the noble and the base, the honorable and the dishonorable. And are not battle and contest, too, their own lures? For a warrior, surely. With what zest then one comes alive! And there was mystery here, too, and, more important, I suppose, adventure. Do distant horizons not call to the hearts of men?"

"I do not think you bestowed your sword casually," said Tajima.

"No," I said. "I think it had to do, as well, with Lord Nishida. Sometimes, when matters are dark, the skies of meaning confused, and the hundred inconsistent reports vie for one's attention, one chooses men, not rhetorics. One chooses a man, rather than a cause, or, perhaps, it is the man who is the cause. One tries to assess probity, integrity, and honor, and they may be more visible, more evident, in a man than in words, than in the janglings of warring assertions, than in a thousand competitive claims and calls."

"Even with the emergence of the iron dragon," said Tajima, "the tarn cavalry is of great value to Lord Temmu."

"And I do not think," said Pertinax, "he is that sure of it."

"Nor is Lord Okimoto," I said.

"When the garrison of the holding of Temmu was on the brink of starvation," said Tajima, "slaves were sold cheaply, for rice."

"That is true," said Pertinax. "Jane, Cabot's Cecily, Saru, others, perhaps some one hundred and fifty others, all collar beauties."

"As I have heard it," said Tajima, "all but one."

"What one would be spared?" asked Pertinax.

"Perhaps one whose possible value was thought to exceed the pleasures derivable from her body," said Tajima.

"Do you know her name?" I asked.

"No," said Tajima.

"There is an obvious explanation why one would be withheld from the vending," I said.

"Yes, Tarl Cabot, tarnsman?" said Tajima.

"She would be a favorite of Lord Temmu," I said.

"That is it," said Pertinax.

"Yes," said Tajima, thoughtfully, "no other explanation is possible."

"You are convinced?" I said.

"I think so," he said.

"But you are not sure?"

"It is hard to be sure," said Tajima, "of many things."

Pertinax looked into the distance, toward the east.

"You think the iron dragon is housed on the fifth level of the palace?" he said.

"Yes," I said.

"We wish to obtain access then, I take it, to the palace of Yamada."

"Certainly," I said.

"How may this be effected?" he asked.

"Not easily," I said, "if at all. One cannot well cut one's way in through the main portal. Roof doors are doubtless bolted. Windows are barred."

"There is the tunnel," said Haruki.

"If it has not been discovered and filled in," I said, "one supposes, following the assassination attempt, precautions would be in place, denying an approach to the supper chamber from the garden, a sealed entrance, bars, guards, or such."

"Access is unlikely?" said Pertinax.

"As I see it," I said, "the main difficulty is being able to do something within the palace, if one should attain access to it, and, if one is interested in such things, coming out alive. Let us suppose we could approach the iron dragon, eluded guards and such, perhaps even alarms. What could we do to damage such a monstrous thing, let alone destroy it? It would be like trying to pull a Tur tree up by the roots, like pounding on a mountain with one's fists."

"If there is nothing to do here," said Pertinax, "we must return northward."

"Haruki," I said, "has scouted the local towns and markets."

"With what end in view?" asked Pertinax.

"For word of a master swordsman," I said.

"Nodachi?" said Pertinax.

"In the holding," I said, "Lord Nishida informed Lord Temmu that Nodachi had departed the holding, to seek Lord Yamada."

"For what reason?" asked Pertinax.

"That one sword, I gather," I said, "may do the work of a thousand swords, perhaps that of ten thousand swords."

"Surely no more than we," said Pertinax, "will he be able to approach Yamada."

"I think he will manage to do so," I said.

"How?" asked Pertinax.

"I do not know," I said. "But he is a gifted, strange, and unusual man."

"And you came south," said Tajima, "to seek Nodachi."

"Yes," I said, "that he might lead me to Yamada."

"Yamada is in the great siege camp, at the foot of the holding," said Tajima.

"Perhaps," I said. "But, in the earlier camp, we did not see him, as Lord Nishida reminded us, nor did we have any evidence of his presence there, other than circumstantial, a banner, a command tent, and such."

"He must be there," said Tajima.

"Nodachi had been missing for days," I said, "even before our return to the holding."

"So?" said Tajima.

"If he thought Yamada with the march," I said, "would he not merely have waited?"

"This man of whom you speak, this Nodachi," said Haruki, "may have been mistaken."

"True," I said.

"Yamada must be with the march," said Tajima.

"If that were so," I said, "would not Yamada be dead, or the head of Nodachi flung to the ramparts of the holding?"

"Still," said Tajima.

"One does not always lead from the front," I said. "The wisest of generals often commands from the rear."

"You think Yamada is there," said Tajima, looking away, to the east, "in the palace?"

"I suspect so," I said. "I suspect he will be at the center of command, while his generals can manage things at the periphery. Perhaps trouble brews amongst the peasantries, which might erupt in his absence, while on campaign. Too, if I am correct, that the iron dragon is housed in the palace, it is likely that he would wish to be in its vicinity, that he might the most conveniently put it to his purposes."

"Still," said Pertinax, "we have made little progress here. It seems access to the palace may not be practical. Lord Yamada might be with the march. We do not really know. We cannot even be really certain the iron dragon is housed in the palace, and, if it were, we could do little about it. And we know nothing of the whereabouts of Nodachi. Certainly Haruki, who has been about, inquiring unobtrusively, diligently, after strangers, after unfamiliar warriors, after any new, unknown master swordsman in local towns and villages, has little word on the matter."

"I am not ready to return," I said.

"We are with you, of course," said Pertinax.

"But Haruki has been inquiring after a master swordsman," said Tajima.

"True," I said.

"If swords are sheathed," said Tajima, "how does one know a master swordsman?"

"We furnished Haruki with a description," I said.

"It might fit a thousand persons, or none," said Tajima.

"But few who would fit that description," I said, "would be likely to be a two-sword person."

"True," said Tajima. "But what if two swords are not carried, or are not obviously carried?"

Nodachi's cast of feature and form of body suggested a peasant origin. His face was unreadable, like stone. I did not understand the nature of the mind that might lie behind that face. I was sure it was deep, and I knew it could be dangerous. I suspected he cared for little but lonely places, meditation, and steel. He killed swiftly, efficiently. No motion was wasted. I had never seen him smile or heard him laugh. His body, not well shaped, was short, thick, gross, broad in frame. His arms were long. His typical garb was frayed and ragged, mean and uncared for, his hair, as I knew it, was shaggy, long and badly cut, unusual for the Pani, even for the peasantry. He was apparently not concerned with his appearance. How he was in himself, I suspected, was important to him, not how he might seem to others. Outwardly he was plain, even ugly and shabby. It was hard to know what lay within. Certainly there was little in the appearance of Nodachi which suggested the refinement, carriage, and authority of the typical Pani warrior. The Pani tend to be class conscious, and I think few would have taken Nodachi seriously, until they had met his eyes. He was not as other men. It was said he was the blade's brother.

"I am sorry I have failed, noble ones," said Haruki.

"You have not failed," I said. "For all we know, Nodachi may have returned to the holding."

"Is there anything of note, gardener *san*," asked Tajima, "in the towns and villages?"

"I do not think so, noble one," he said.

"Anything?" pressed Tajima.

"Nothing of interest to the noble ones," said Haruki.

"What?" I asked.

"A beggar," he said, "a mountebank, a gambler, a madman, who will wager his head against a bowl of rice."

"And thus he earns his rice?" asked Pertinax.

"It is said, one bowl a day," said Haruki.

"What is the nature of this wager?" I asked.

"It is said word of it has carried even to the palace," said Haruki.

"What is its nature?" I asked.

"I know this only by hearsay," said Haruki.

"Speak," I said.

"A grain of rice is placed on the forehead of a slave," said Haruki. "The madman then strikes fiercely at the grain of rice, and divides it, without even creasing the forehead of the slave."

"And if he fails to divide the grain or should injure the slave?" asked Pertinax.

"Then," said Haruki, "his head is forfeit."

"And he has been successful?" I said.

"I have heard so," said Haruki.

"I would see this madman," I said.

Chapter Forty-Six

What Occurred in the Market Square

"Please, no, Master!" wept the slave.

"Make use of this one," said the peasant. "She is scrawny."

"You do not mind losing her?" said a man.

"No," said the peasant.

"I have not seen this before," said a warrior, in the livery of Yamada.

"There is a trick here," said another, in the same livery, though, I gathered, of lesser rank. "I shall discover it, and expose this fraud."

"The mountebank approaches," said a man.

Tajima, Pertinax, Haruki, and I were in the crowd, hopefully inconspicuously so. Tajima and Haruki were clearly Pani, and would be likely to evoke little attention or comment. Pertinax and I were hooded, but not in such a way as to suggest an intended concealment. While barbarians, so to speak, were not common this far south, they were not wholly unknown. It was estimated, given the hardships of the early spring, the rigors of the first siege, the threat of the second siege, the overwhelming superiority in numbers enjoyed by Lord Yamada, and the fearful advent of the iron dragon in the skies over the holding of Temmu, that better than two hundred mercenaries had defected to the banners of Yamada. These were employed variously, as traitors have their uses, particularly in missions Yamada did not care to entrust to Pani, whose primary loyalty might be to their daimyo and not to the shogun.

"Let me go, Master!" begged the slave, struggling, her wrist in the peasant's grip.

She was pretty, but not collared. Most Pani slaves were not collared. Many, however, were marked. I did think she was pretty enough to collar. On the continent, almost every slave is collared. It is prescribed by Merchant Law. I did not personally, incidentally, regard the slave as scrawny. I would have said excitingly slender, rather like Nezumi, back, I trusted, at the encampment of tarns. I did gather the master was not wholly pleased with her.

"Please, no, Master!" she begged.

"Be silent," he said.

We were in the Yamada market town closest to the palace itself. It was called Chrysanthemum of the Shogun. The performances of the magician, the gambler, or such, supposedly, day by day, had approached this point. As mentioned, two warriors, from the palace itself, were in the crowd.

The crowd was of a goodly size, and, day by day, village by village, town by town, it seemed the fame of the magician, or fraud, had spread.

"It is a trick," said the warrior who had insisted he would expose the magician.

"We are here to determine that," said the other, who, I took it, was his superior.

The slave cried out with terror, broke away from the peasant, and tried to force her way through the crowd, even to falling to her hands and knees, and crawling, but she was in short order seized, held, and returned to her master, indeed thrown to the ground before him.

"Switch," he said, and was soon handed a flexible, peeled, supple branch.

The slave was then beaten.

She had been displeasing.

She was sobbing, and her body, her arms and legs, bore the numerous snakelike marks of her master's wrath. Even the brief rag she wore was creased in places, and parted in others.

"Put her on her feet, tie her to the post," said a man.

The slave was yanked to her feet, and, sobbing, thrust back against a post, and, with several loops of rope, bound in place.

"Tie her head back, by the hair, against the post," said a fellow.

She cried out with misery.

"Good," said a fellow.

The magician, as we shall refer to him, for that seemed to be the description most often used of him, had viewed the scene with the slave impassively.

"No, no, no!" cried the slave, struggling against the ropes, shaking her head, as she could, wildly, back and forth.

"If she moves," said a man, "and her head is split, the wager is done, and the magician wins."

"Of course," said a man.

"There is a trick here," said the skeptical warrior. "She is a confederate of the mountebank."

"No," said the peasant. "Not so. I have owned her from the age of eleven. She is a work slave, in the fields by day, in the kennel by night. This is the first time she has been to the market."

I thought she was rather slight for a work slave. Perhaps that was what the peasant had in mind when he had spoken of her as scrawny. Most work slaves are strong sturdy women. I would have guessed her to be something in the order of seventeen or eighteen years old. To be sure, women mature deliciously, and early. Throughout most of human history on Earth, women were commonly mated at the age of fourteen or fifteen. Few would have reached the age of twenty without being mated. On continental Gor, it might be mentioned, women are often companioned similarly, but less so in the high cities, presumably for cultural reasons. Males, on the other hand, mature much more slowly. Whereas much is obscure here, the selections involved seem to favor early maturity in the female which increases the length of her beauty, the length of her attractiveness, the length of her child-bearing years, and such, and to postpone maturity in the male until he is capable, in strength, agility, determination, coordination, cunning, ambition, tenacity, and such, to compete with other males for, say, position, territory, and women.

"Do not be afraid, slave," said the skeptical warrior. "You are in no danger. It is a trick."

He then scowled at the magician, whose face betrayed no emotion.

"Fraud," he said.

The magician remained impassive.

"This is interesting," Tajima whispered to me. "There are two warriors here, from the palace."

"So they are curious," I said. "We are all curious."

"No common soldiers are here," said Tajima, "no Ashigaru, no common warriors. They are both officers. See the accouterments. The sashes of rank. High officers."

"So?" I said.

"They have a purpose here," said Tajima.

"They are just curious," I said.

"I think another is curious, as well," said Tajima.

"Who?" I asked.

"The shogun," he said.

"Get on with it," said the skeptical officer.

"I have seen this," said a man to the slave. "Put your head back, so your forehead leans back. Close your eyes. Do not move, not in the slightest, do not even breathe until it is done."

"Are you volunteering the use of your slave for another, or are you yourself wagering?" a fellow asked the peasant.

"I have heard of this," said the peasant. "I wish to see it. I am wagering, a bowl of rice against a head."

The peasant drew a thread of copper coins from his wallet, removed from it a single, tiny coin, and held it up.

"For rice," he said, "my stake."

"He is rich," said a man.

This was quite possible. There are rich peasants, and poor warriors.

"Remember to hold still," said a man to the slave, whose eyes were clenched shut.

I think she needed no encouragement in this particular.

The magician then placed a grain of rice on the girl's forehead.

"He has a sword!" said a man.

This had appeared from the robe of the magician. Surely it had been there, but not obviously.

"It is a companion sword," said the skeptical warrior, scornfully. "It can be handled with the delicacy of a knife."

"Begin," said the peasant, stepping back, interested.

"Do not move," again a man advised the slave. I myself doubted that she could have moved, even had she desired to do so. She seemed frozen with fear.

I scarcely saw the blade move toward the slave when it was drawn back.

"The stroke was short!" laughed the skeptical officer.

The magician then touched the grain of rice, lightly, and it fell into two pieces.

A cry of astonishment and pleasure coursed through the crowd.

"Brilliant stroke!" said a man, awed.

"Skilled fellow!" cried a man.

"He could peel a tospit in flight!" said another.

"Bring the bowl of rice!" cried the peasant.

A fellow rushed away, to seek a vendor.

"Fools!" cried the skeptical officer. "Can you not see how it is done? Are you all such dolts! The blow was short, the grain of rice was already split!"

"Ah!" said a man.

A murmur of disappointment coursed through the crowd.

"So that is how it is done?" said a man.

"Yes!" laughed the skeptical officer. "What ignorant fellows, you are, what dupes!"

"Take the magician's head!" said a man.

"Rice thief!" said another.

The skeptical officer, and his companion, I think of higher rank, turned away.

"Is that how it is done?" a man asked the magician, disappointed.

"No," said the magician.

The two officers, hearing this, or sensing the crowd's reaction, turned back.

"No," said the magician, again.

"I am Izo," said the skeptical officer, angrily, "of the guard of the shogun. I am a warrior. Do you, mountebank and peasant, lowly one, despicable fraud, speak my words false?"

"I suggest," said the magician, who looked up, I was reminded of the way a larl might raise its head, "the honorable one is mistaken."

"Do you call Izo, of the guard of the shogun, a liar?" asked the warrior, his hand on the tasseled hilt of his companion sword.

The crowd drew back from about the magician.

"Come away," said his companion, gently. "We have seen

what we wished to see. We have learned what we wished to learn."

"No!" said the skeptical officer.

"He is a simple mountebank, an innocent fellow seeking rice," said his companion. "Spare him. Do not soil your sword."

"My honor is not satisfied," said Izo, the skeptical officer.

By now the fellow who had rushed away for the bowl of rice had returned, apparently with a vendor's man, who held, cushioned by layers of cloth, a large bowl of steaming rice in two hands.

"Take that away!" said Izo.

"Do not," said the magician. "It is mine. It has been fairly earned."

"Admit here, publicly, you are a fraud," demanded Izo.

"No," said the magician.

"You are a fake, a fraud!" said Izo.

"No," said the magician.

"Come away," said the other officer, to he whom I took to be his irate subordinate.

"I will fetch a grain of rice," said Izo, "raw, uncooked, whole, not split, and place it on the forehead of the slave."

"You may do as you wish," said the magician. "I have earned the bowl of rice. I do not need another today."

"See!" cried the officer. "He acknowledges deceit, and fraud!"

"No," said the magician.

The officer turned away, disgusted.

"Fetch your grain of rice," said the magician, quietly.

"No, Masters! Please, no, Masters!" cried the slave.

The officer had then turned back.

"Examine it, and place it yourself on the forehead of the slave," said the magician.

It did not take long for a grain of rice to be brought to the officer, who examined it closely, and then, satisfied, holding it between two fingers, placed it carefully on the forehead of the miserable slave.

"Where is the magician?" asked a man.

"Gone," said another.

Izo laughed.

"No, he approaches," said another.

Izo turned about, annoyed.

The magician was indeed approaching. But now, gripped in two hands, he carried a different sword, the heavier, longer of the two swords often carried by a warrior, the field sword.

"Is the grain of rice acceptable, and placed to your satisfaction?" asked the magician.

"It is," said Izo.

The magician now stood before the bound slave, on whose forehead had been placed the grain of rice. She had her head back, pressed against the post, and her eyes closed tightly. She was, I think, holding her breath. He regarded her intently, measuring the distance. He moved his left foot, in its sandal, a little forward. I saw the tiny ridge of dirt moved before it. The sword, held in its double grip, held in both hands, was raised, until both hands were literally behind his head. The blade was as still as an ost before its strike. Then, like the ost, so swift one could not mark its movement, but was only aware of it a moment after, it had struck.

Two tiny halves of a grain of rice lay parted on the girl's forehead, and she cried out, suddenly, expelling breath, and had fainted in the ropes.

Men cried out, awed.

"So it is easily done!" cried out Izo. "I did not understand that! If a nondescript peasant, a lowly one, can do it, so can anyone! Bring another grain of rice!"

The magician, with one movement of the field sword, severed the knot of hair which held the slave's head back, against the post. Her head, she unconscious, fell forward, some cut hair falling about the post. His blade then entered itself amongst the ropes which bound her, and they leaped away from her body, and she slumped to the foot of the post.

"How dare you free her?" exclaimed Izo, angrily.

"You would kill her," said the magician.

"Tarsk!" cried Izo.

"Run!" said the rich peasant to the girl, and she sped away.

"Behold," said the magician, taking a grain of rice from a fellow who had, in response to the officer's demand, fetched it. The magician then placed it half in a tiny crack in the post, about where the girl's forehead would have been. He then stepped back.

"It is easy," said the magician.

With a cry of rage the officer drew his field sword, poised it, and struck at the post. The blade had entered the post half a hort from the grain of rice, and sunk a full hort into the wood.

It was with some difficulty that he managed to extricate the blade.

There was much laughter from the crowd.

And then stillness, for the lowly are not to mock their betters.

"It is easy," said the magician, "if one trains for Ahn a day, for years."

I do not think I had ever seen such rage on the countenance of a Pani warrior as I then beheld on the visage of the officer.

"Ragged, gross creature," he cried, "shaggy, ugly beast, ungainly tarsk!"

"All that you say is true," said the magician. "I am ill-dressed and ungroomed. I am homely. I am ill-favored, and ill-formed. In such a way I was born, and in such a way I live. I am an offense in the eyes of many."

"Loathsome peasant," said the officer.

"I am a peasant," said the rich peasant, not pleased.

"Peasants," cried the officer, glaring at the magician, "are not permitted two swords, or one. Cast down your illegitimate weapons, seize up your proper tools, the digging stick and rake!"

"I trust he will not disarm himself," I said to Tajima. I myself would have been unwilling even to turn my back on the warrior.

"He will not," said Tajima.

The magician turned away.

"No," I whispered.

"Is my sword sharp?" cried the officer. "Perhaps I shall test it, on the neck of a peasant!"

Several in the crowd moved away. It was not unknown for Pani warriors to try their weaponry on living targets.

"Come away," said he whom I took to be the senior of the two officers. "We have seen what we were sent to see. We have learned what we were sent to learn."

"No!" said Izo, the hitherto skeptical officer, furiously, "no!" His field sword was still in hand, indeed, gripped in two hands.

The magician stood to one side, his back to the officer. His head was down.

"He is in grave danger," I said.

"No," said Pertinax.

"His back is turned," I said. "He cannot see."

"He sees," said Tajima. "Consider the sun."

"Yes," I said. The magician had placed himself in such a way that the sun was behind him. Accordingly, whatever might approach, even if not heard, would cast a warning shadow. A critical distance would be involved. Then, should the shadow move—!

"Watch," whispered Tajima.

"I do not think I care to watch," said Pertinax.

It was over very quickly, the two blades did not even meet. The officer's head rolled a dozen yards before it was arrested in the dirt, the eyes staring up at the sky, as though startled.

The magician was then facing the other officer, waiting, his weapon ready.

But the other officer's weapons were still thrust in his sash. He bowed to the magician, slightly.

"You have slain Izo," he said, "the finest sword in the shogun's guard."

The magician bowed slightly.

"I am Katsutoshi," he said, "captain of the shogun's guard."

Again the magician bowed slightly, acknowledging the honor paid to him, that he would be addressed by such a personage.

"Izo was a rash fool," said Katsutoshi.

"It is unfortunate," said the magician.

"Word of you has reached the shogun himself," said Katsutoshi. "We were sent to report upon you."

"I am unworthy to be brought to the attention of so great a lord," said the magician.

"What is your name?" asked Katsutoshi.

"I do not know," said the magician. "I may have no name."

"What is your class, your craft, or trade?" asked Katsutoshi.

"My class is my own," said the magician. "My craft is the sword, and my trade the same."

"Where is your land, your home?" asked Katsutoshi.

"I am found in remote places," he said. "My home is in the darkness of the forest, on deserted beaches, in mountain caves."

"Who is your daimyo?" asked Katsutoshi.

"I am of the waves," said the magician. "I have no daimyo."

"That may soon be remedied," said Katsutoshi. "I think you will soon have a lord."

"I serve the sword," said the magician.

"We shall meet again," said Katsutoshi, bowing.

The magician returned the bow.

The captain of the guard then left the market.

The crowd began to dissipate.

The vendor's man approached with the bowl of rice. "This is yours, noble one," he said. "It is paid for by Eito, the great peasant."

"And where is Eito *san*?" asked the magician.

"He has hurried away, to fetch his girl," said the vendor's man.

"Place it on the earth, there," said the magician.

"Why is that?" I asked Tajima. "There are strangers about," said Tajima. "At such a time both one's hands are to be free."

"Has he seen us?" I asked Tajima.

"Of course," said Tajima.

"Tal," said the magician.

"Master," said Tajima, bowing.

"Master," said Pertinax, bowing.

"Tal, noble one," I said.

Bows were exchanged.

"This," I said, "is our friend, Haruki."

"Forgive me, noble one," said Haruki. "I am unworthy to greet you. I am but a humble gardener."

"It is I who am honored, gardener *san*," said the magician. "Flowers are beautiful and those who love and tend them are themselves of most noble mien."

"Tal," said Haruki.

"Tal," said the magician.

"We sought you," I said.

"Your presence was not entirely unexpected," said the magician.

"You have heard of the iron dragon?" I said.

"Yes," said the magician. "And word like fire has swept the roads and fields, the towns and villages, that it has flown."

"It has flown, Master," said Tajima. "We have seen it."

"And the holding of Temmu still stands?" asked the magician.

"I fear," said Tajima, "only on the sufferance of Yamada."

"Lord Yamada," suggested the magician.

"Lord Yamada," said Tajima.

"It is my hope to be received by him," said the magician, "that I may kill him."

"I have sought you," I said, "that I may be led to Lord Yamada."

"Do you dispute his head?" asked the magician.

"No," I said. "My concern is not his life, or his death. There is more here than is obvious on the surface."

"One sees the hurrying of the leaf, the crash of the tree, but not the wind," said the magician.

"It is thought," I said, "that behind one war there is another war."

"One of unseen houses?" said the magician.

"Yes," I said.

"How may I be of assistance?"

"Take four with you, into the palace," I said.

"You do not seek Lord Yamada?" asked the magician.

"Only to seek another," I said, "a greater beast."

"The iron dragon," said the magician.

"Yes," I said.

"I will need four to accompany me," he said.

"Good," I said.

"Ho!" cried a voice, and we spun about.

"It is the peasant, Eito!" said Tajima.

"And the slave!" said Pertinax.

It was indeed the fellow who had supplied the slave for the magician's demonstration, and had purchased the rice which the vendor's man had given to the magician. At his side, held by the hair, bent over, her head at his hip, stumbling beside him, was the young, lovely, scantily tunicked slave. The garmenting of slaves, if garmenting is permitted, is up to their masters. That was one of the first lessons Nezumi had learned.

"Noble one," said the peasant, holding up, addressing the magician.

The magician bowed, slightly.

"Twice," said the peasant. "The noble one divided a grain of rice on the forehead of this miserable creature, but was paid but once."

"There was but one wager, and so but one prize," said the magician.

"Izo, sword of the shogun's guard," said Eito, the peasant, "slew four men of my village."

"I am sure that was not necessary," said the magician.

"And you slew Izo," said the peasant.

"That, I fear, was necessary," said the magician.

"I am pleased, my village will be pleased," said Eito.

"Then I, too, am pleased," said the magician.

"Behold," said Eito, "I have fetched forth this ill-begotten, worthless, scrawny creature, but even warriors, I have noted, have looked upon her with interest."

I found that easy to believe. Her slave curves were slight, but surely of interest. In two or three years even the Pani might think of collaring her, to keep her more securely theirs.

"Rice is expensive," said Eito. "And coins are rare."

"Nothing is owed," said the magician. "Keep her."

"For what you have done," said Eito, "slaying Izo, the scourge of a dozen villages, the village itself would not suffice."

"Keep her," said the magician.

The slave herself dared not speak.

Eito released his grip on the girl's hair. "Stand up, stand straight, worthless creature," he said. "Put your hands behind your head. Bend backwards!"

Yes, I thought, slave curves. How beautiful are women!

"She is not pay, noble one," said Eito. "She is not even a gift. But I will unclaim her in your presence."

"Do not do so," said the magician.

"Then," said Eito, "we will take her back to the village, cut her throat, and leave her for the feeding of jards."

"Unclaim her," said the magician.

"You are unclaimed, slave," said Eito. He then smiled, bowed, and took his leave.

Eito, I thought, was a clever fellow. It was no wonder that he, though of the peasants, had a string of coins.

The girl looked at us, frightened.

"Get on your knees," I told her.

Swiftly she went to her knees, before us.

I did not want her to bolt away, either in foolishness, or terror.

Kneeling is not merely a posture of submission; it is also a posture in which the slave realizes she is relatively helpless.

It is interesting, how the same position, say, kneeling, can be experienced. It might be experienced as unspeakably humiliating and degrading to a free woman, even debasing, but, to a slave, it is experienced as welcome, warm, fulfilling, desirable, and appropriate. It is a lovely expression of the servitude for which she has longed and in which she revels. It is a lovely expression of her submission to her master, her surrender, wholly, as a female, to him. She is no longer hers, but is now his. On her knees, submitted, is where she is and wants to be. She wants to love and serve, wholly and selflessly. She does not want to be her master's equal. She wants to be her master's slave. Even free women understand this, for they, too, are women.

"You are now an unclaimed slave," I told her.

"Yes, Master," she whispered, frightened.

"As a rightless slave," I said, "you may be claimed by any free person."

"Yes, Master," she said.

"And you will then belong, wholly, to that person," I said.

"I understand, Master," she said.

"And there is nothing you can do about it," I said.

"I know, Master," she said.

Sometimes women are enslaved, but not claimed. They must then wait, in trepidation, perhaps being inspected and appraised, to see who will claim them. They are free, of course, as they are unclaimed, to beg to be claimed by a given male. Similarly even an owned slave who is up for sale may utter the "Buy me, Master" solicitation. Indeed, the "Buy me, Master" solicitation is not unoften required of girls exhibited in selling lines, on slave shelves, in exposition cells and cages, and such.

"No one will want me, Master," said the girl. "I am only a work slave, and not even a good work slave. That is why my master used me in the wager. I am the smallest and weakest in my kennel."

"There are many sorts of slave," I said. "There are field slaves, draft slaves, female fighting slaves, racing slaves, many sorts."

"And pleasure slaves, Master?" she whispered, looking up.

"Yes," I said.

"I am scrawny," she said.

"Not at all," I said.

"I know nothing of pleasure," she said.

"You have never moaned and squirmed," I said, "caressed as a man's plaything?"

"No, Master," she said.

"You may have the experience," said Pertinax.

"Certainly we must search for someone to put slave fires in her belly," said Tajima.

"Yes," said Pertinax. "It might be interesting. Do you have anyone in mind?"

"Anyone in the cavalry," said Tajima.

"What of Ichiro?" asked Pertinax.

"Why not?" said Tajima.

"What is your name?" I asked the slave, who was visibly disconcerted.

"Whatever Master wishes," she said.

"What were you called in the village?" I asked.

"Aiko," she said.

"That is a lovely name," I said.

"Thank you, Master," she said.

"We will keep it for a time, until you have a master," I said, "and he can then think about it."

"Yes, Master," she said.

"In the meantime," I said, "stay with us, and do not tell anyone you are unclaimed. I do not want to lose you to the first fellow who glances at your ankles."

"Yes, Master," she said.

"Do you think she is pretty enough to collar?" I asked.

"Yes," said Tajima.

"Yes," said Pertinax.

"I am unworthy of a collar," she said.

"Do not underestimate yourself," I said. "Besides, masters collar their slaves or not, as they please."

"Yes, Master," she said.

On the continent, of course, almost all slaves are collared, even pot girls, and kettle-and-mat girls. It is prescribed, as indicated earlier, by Merchant Law. When young women of Earth are brought to the Gorean markets, they are sometimes unclear as to their status. For example, might not even a free woman be herded about, with switches, naked and chained? On the other hand, once their thigh has encountered the searing iron, leaving behind for all to see a lovely *kajira* mark, once they find their neck fastened in an attractive, locked metal collar, clearly a slave collar, once they find themselves in a single, simple, brief garment which could be naught but the garment of a slave, they are in little doubt as to their status. If any doubt should linger, it is dispelled when they are sold.

"It would be better that she not be here," said the magician.

"One did not wish to have her throat cut," I said. "One would not wish her to be given over to the feeding of jards."

"No," said the magician. "But there is killing to be done."

"One need only claim her," I said, "and then one may sell her, or give her away."

"True," said the magician.

"The peasant Eito," I said, "though seemingly well to do, and presumably peaceful and law-abiding, respectful of authority, and such, was clearly pleased at the slaying of the warrior, Izo. He even unclaimed a slave in our presence."

"The rule of Lord Yamada," said the magician, "is one of edged steel and terror. He is a tyrant. There is much unrest amongst the peasantry."

"That is why, I suppose," I said, "the peasantry is to be disarmed, and kept in its place."

"The peasantry is dangerous," said the magician.

"There are a great many of them," I said.

"The peasants may be discounted," said Pertinax. "They are simple people, quiet, peaceful people, who stay much in one place, people with limited ambition and vision, who are happy with small comforts, and look for little more, people concerned with fields, and crops, plantings and harvestings."

"Arashi, the bandit, is of the peasantry," I said.

"But," said the magician, "they can go mad. They can be like a raging beast with no head."

"And then, in the end," said Haruki, who had long been silent, "men die, and villages are burned."

"Will you join me for supper?" inquired the magician.

"We will be pleased to do so," I said.

The magician then indicated that the girl should rise from her knees, for she had not been given permission to break position, pick up the large bowl of rice, and accompany us.

We then followed Nodachi, the swordsman, from the market square.

Chapter Forty-Seven

What Occurred on the Archery Range

"It is the test of twelve arrows," said Lord Yamada. "You have perhaps heard of it."

"Yes," said Nodachi, "and that none have survived it."

"I am not a fool," said Lord Yamada.

"It was not thought so," said Nodachi.

"Nor is my patience inexhaustible," he said.

"It was not thought so," said Nodachi, not moving within the ropes which held his body bound to the post, his hands free, in the exercise yard.

"I am in touch with the negotiations being pretended in the holding of Temmu," he said. "Message vulos keep me informed, and I have intelligence by tarn, as well. The pretended negotiations, obviously not in good faith, were a transparent ruse to buy time, but for what? Temmu has no army rushing to his rescue. My forces lie before the holding. He is trapped. The tarn cavalry cannot withstand the fire of the iron dragon, which is even now poised to spread its wings. So time was bought for what, obviously an attempt on my life. And I have awaited your tiny league of assassins with interest. Was it not amazing that an allegedly remarkable swordsman should approach through the villages and towns at just such a time? Is that not an astonishing coincidence? And accompanied, as well! Yes, three or four must be available to assure matters. One might not be enough. I viewed you at the gate, with the Builder's glass, on the walks, approaching through the garden, even to the great portal itself.

And so there was our swordsman, and his cohorts! And what cohorts, their features concealed with wind scarves! Who could they be? Would they not be, if possible, individuals familiar with the palace and its grounds, those who would have been within its rooms and corridors, who would know their way about? And the grounds! Did I not, through the Builder's glass, see one of your number adjust the vines of the blue climber on the railings of the garden bridge? Who but a gardener, and the finest of gardeners, would note, or be disturbed by, so small a fault in such a place?"

"We are fools, indeed, great lord," said Nodachi, "but there was little else to be done. We did what we could. We failed."

"I have discontinued the mockery of negotiations," said Lord Yamada. "The siege is laid. Time is on the side of those who control the rice."

"If the rice can be obtained," said Nodachi.

"It can be harvested with the sword," said Lord Yamada.

"It is often so," said Nodachi.

"Do you think, swordsman," asked Lord Yamada, "that the fool Temmu, the wicked, will surrender his holding?"

"No," said Nodachi.

"Nor I," said Lord Yamada.

"Do you think he understands that it can be destroyed by the iron dragon?"

"Yes," said Nodachi.

"Does he wish it destroyed?" asked Lord Yamada.

"No," said Nodachi.

"Nor I," said Lord Yamada.

Nodachi did not respond.

"I am prepared to offer a truce," said Lord Yamada. "And gold, and amnesty to him and his men, should they withdraw from the holding."

"Lord Yamada is generous," said Nodachi.

"They need only withdraw unarmed," said Lord Yamada.

"It is the generosity of the ost," said Nodachi.

"Do you think that Temmu will destroy the holding, rather than surrender it?" asked Lord Yamada.

"Yes," said Nodachi.

"I do, as well," said Lord Yamada. "The matter is thus perplexing."

"The great lord desires the holding," said Nodachi.

"As it seems the holding is to be destroyed, in either case," said Lord Yamada, "either by the breath of the iron dragon or the torches of Temmu, one may as well be done with it, and free the iron dragon."

"But the great lord desires the holding," said Nodachi.

"We shall offer the truce, and the bounty for surrender," said Lord Yamada. "If it is declined, we shall issue an ultimatum. On the third day following, the iron dragon will fly. The holding will be destroyed. It will be mine or cease to exist."

"It is a lofty, mighty, and beautiful holding," said Nodachi.

"Walls will crumble, the mountaintop will be black, ashes will blow out to sea," said Lord Yamada.

"Does the great lord not fear the tarn cavalry?" asked Nodachi.

"No longer," said Lord Yamada. "The iron dragon can burn it out of the sky."

I feared this was true.

No sooner than Nodachi, Pertinax, Tajima, Haruki, and I had been admitted through the great portal we had been set upon by dozens of waiting Ashigaru, purportedly placed to lead us into the presence of Lord Yamada.

We were swiftly subdued and bound.

"This, I take it," had said Lord Yamada, when we were brought, helpless, before him, "is the remarkable swordsman of whom you spoke?"

"It is, Lord," said Katsutoshi, captain of the shogun's guard.

"An unprepossessing fellow," had commented the shogun.

"But dangerous, Lord," said Katsutoshi. "The sword is as his hand, the blade like the stroke of lightning, a flash, and the matter is done."

"You slew Izo," said Lord Yamada, "the first sword in my guard."

"He was angry," said Nodachi. "One's anger is often the friend of one's foe."

"In all my lands," said Lord Yamada, "I myself am the finest sword."

Nodachi, in his bonds, bowed.

"It might be sport to try your skills," said Lord Yamada.

"This humble one, great lord," said Nodachi, "is ever at your service."

"What sport that might be," said Lord Yamada, "but, *ela*, it is regrettable, a penalty of the shogunate. The shogun does not cross swords with upstarts, vagabonds, mountebanks, magicians, common warriors."

"Propriety is understood," said Nodachi, again bowing.

"Perhaps the shogun is afraid," I said.

Lord Yamada looked at me, hurt.

"Forgive me, Lord," I said. "I spoke foolishly."

"It is pleasant to see you in the palace once more," said Lord Yamada, "but one might have hoped for happier circumstances."

"True," I said.

"I had high hopes for you," he said.

"I fear I have disappointed you," I said.

"I liked you," he said.

"And I you," I said.

"And yet you would kill me?" he said.

"If it should prove practical," I said, "quite possibly."

"Such is war," he said.

"True," I said.

"I no longer need the tarn cavalry," he said.

"I understand," I said.

"I now have the iron dragon," he said.

"I saw it," I said, "at the holding of Temmu."

He then turned aside from me. "And here we have two fine young officers," he said, "one barbarian, one Pani, this one Pertinax, that one Tajima."

Both Pertinax and Tajima bowed, politely, in their ropes.

"Perhaps one of you interfered with an execution," he said.

"Perhaps," said Pertinax.

"Where is Sumomo?" asked the shogun.

"Sumomo no longer exists," said Tajima.

"She is dead," said Lord Yamada.

"No," said Tajima, "she has been renamed; she is now in the collar of a slave."

"Excellent," said Lord Yamada. "Was it you who fastened the collar on her neck?"

"And pressed the burning iron into her thigh," said Tajima.

"Excellent," said Lord Yamada. "And do you derive great pleasure from the use of her body?"

"Yes," said Tajima.

"You make her leap and squirm, and moan and cry out, as a slave in your arms?"

"Yes," said Tajima, "as the slave she is."

"Splendid," said Lord Yamada. "I always thought she had the belly of a slave, but then, do not all women, properly handled?"

"You are not angry?" said Tajima.

"No," he said, "the execution was to serve a political purpose, which no longer exists. All that is now wiped away. Other things being equal, it is a waste to feed a beautiful young thing to ignorant, unappreciative, voracious fish. It is much better to have it in a collar, trembling at your feet."

"It is unfortunate," said Pertinax, "that we had no opportunity to return golden chains, Tajima one, I, two."

"Do not concern yourselves," said Lord Yamada. "They are yours, all yours, and delightedly bestowed."

"Thank you, Lord," said Tajima.

"Thank you, Lord," said Pertinax.

"Besides, with the fall of the house of Temmu, I might well recover them, and surely much more."

"Yes, Lord," said Tajima.

"Yes, Lord," said Pertinax.

Lord Yamada then turned to Haruki.

"The garden misses you," he said. "The garden is one of my pleasures, and since your departure a hundred tiny flaws have asserted themselves, unnoted by your inept successors."

"I fear so, Lord," he said. There were tears in his eyes.

Lord Yamada then turned back to Nodachi. "It is my understanding," he said, "that you are keen of eye and quick of body."

Nodachi was silent.

"Tomorrow," said Lord Yamada, "we will test your skills on the archery range."

"I do not know the bow," said Nodachi.

"Nor, I suspect," said the shogun, "the arrow."

"I see," said Nodachi.

At the time I did not understand this brief exchange. But, tomorrow, apparently, it was to become clear.

The shogun then turned, again, to me. "I am sure you did

not trek south," he said. "Therefore, there will be tarns about. I do not think they could be concealed in the vicinity, but, rather, are some pasangs away. It does not matter. We will find and acquire them."

I did not respond to this.

Lord Yamada was, of course, substantially correct. Some pasangs from the palace, in a deep draw, Ichiro had concealed four tarns, his, and three others, those with which Pertinax, Tajima, and I, Haruki behind the saddle of Tajima, had flown south. I had no doubt, as we had been captured, the countryside would soon be examined, that such mounts might be discovered. Hopefully, Ichiro could make away before he, and the mounts, might fall into the hands of the enemy. What particularly concerned me was that Ichiro would be unaware of our plight. We had contacted him and informed him of our plan before approaching the palace. We did not know, of course, at that time, if we would be called to the palace or not, and, if so, if we were to be allowed to approach the shogun, when that would be. We had not been in touch with him for some five days now. We had given the slave, Aiko, into his keeping, as there seemed no part for her in our plan, even if we had been willing to risk her in so dubious and hazardous a venture.

"It is the test of twelve arrows," had said Lord Yamada. "You have perhaps heard of it."

"Yes," had said Nodachi, "and that none have survived it."

There were several in the exercise yard, a length of which served as an archery range. I recalled I had once been called to attend on Lord Yamada here, and had been apprised of his skill with the great Pani bow. It was here, too, that Tyrtaios had brought his tarn down, delivering the unsuspecting Sumomo to the mercies of her father.

Amongst those present were some five or six officers, some warriors, and several Ashigaru, some with glaives, others with bows, mostly small bows, some with quivers behind their left shoulder, some with quivers at their left hip. The daimyos of Lord Yamada were apparently north, with his generals, supervising the siege. Tajima, Pertinax, Haruki, and I were bound, our arms tied behind us. Each of us wore a leather collar, with a metal ring in the back. Through this ring a rope was threaded, and knotted about each ring. Each end of this rope was in the keeping of an Ashigaru.

Lord Yamada wore a white exercise smock, as before. Several paces behind us, some forty paces, for it had been paced out, was an arrow stand. In this stand were twelve long arrows. Beside it, in a bow rack, resting horizontally, on projections, were four great bows, unstrung. This stand and the rack were flanked by two Ashigaru.

"It will be interesting," said Lord Yamada, "to see the outcome of our test. As you are doubtless well aware, it is not unknown in the islands. It has been used both in courts of law as a procedure for deciding guilt or innocence, and, more commonly, as an amusing manner of execution, in which the naive subject tortures himself into hoping that he may survive. As you are obviously of low birth, a simple, honorable beheading would not be appropriate. But, too, in virtue of your alleged skills, and my own curiosity pertaining to the accounts I have of you, we are putting aside the straw jacket, crucifixion, and such."

"This humble one is honored, great lord," said Nodachi.

"To the best of my knowledge," said Lord Yamada, "no subject, at any time in the islands, has survived this test."

"That, too, great lord," said Nodachi, "is my understanding."

"What are we to make of that?" asked Lord Yamada.

"Perhaps," said Nodachi, "that many were guilty."

"Or insufficiently skilled," said Lord Yamada.

I supposed the matter was much the same, in either case.

"I have performed this test eleven times," said Lord Yamada. "No one survived more than the second arrow."

Nodachi bowed, politely, slightly, acknowledging this intelligence.

"Katsutoshi, captain of my guard," said Lord Yamada, "will remain at hand, to supply the companion sword."

Nodachi bowed again.

"Come, friends," said Lord Yamada, "let us withdraw."

The crowd, including we four prisoners, then withdrew from the post to which Nodachi was bound, his hands free.

We then arranged ourselves in the vicinity of the arrow stand and the bow rack.

"Do not fear," said Tajima.

"There is much to fear," I said.

"He is Nodachi," said Tajima.

"Do not be naive, my dear friend," I said.

"He has meditated," said Tajima. "The arrow is known to him. The bow, as well. Do not fear. All are friends."

"I do not understand," I said.

"He is as the arrow," said Tajima. "He shares its flight, its swiftness, its intended destination."

I did not respond to this.

Pertinax was obviously concerned.

Lord Yamada selected the first bow, the highest bow, and strung it. As the bow was large, I had not expected it to be strung so easily. Lord Yamada had performed this action fluidly. I then realized he was much stronger than I had understood. The Ashigaru nearest the arrow stand then handed him one of the long arrows.

"Are you ready?" called Lord Yamada to Nodachi.

"Yes, Lord," called Nodachi.

Lord Yamada then put the arrow to the string. "Arm him," he called to Katsutoshi, who then handed the companion sword to Nodachi, and stepped to the side.

"The distance is forty paces," said Lord Yamada. "It is my hope that he will survive the first arrow."

"He will do so," said Tajima.

I saw the large bow lifted, and then lowered, being trained on the target. Again, I was impressed, in spite of myself, with the combination of grace and elegance, with menace.

I had had ample evidence before of the skill of Lord Yamada with the implement in hand, though before he had placed himself considerably farther from the target.

I lifted my head a little.

I did not think there was any wind.

The arrow flashed from the bow.

There was a cry of surprise, and pleasure from the crowd.

"Splendid!" called Lord Yamada.

Nodachi inclined his head, bowing.

He had struck the arrow away with a tiny flick of the companion sword.

Lord Yamada extended his hand, in which the Ashigaru placed another arrow.

"Let us hope well for him," said Lord Yamada. "One once managed two arrows, but none three."

"Superb!" called Lord Yamada, clearly impressed, as the parts of the second arrow skittered to the side.

"High fortune to you!" called Lord Yamada. "May you do well!"

I heard bets being taken, some amongst officers, others amongst Ashigaru.

The crowd then cried out with amazement, and pleasure.

A new record had been set, apparently, at least with respect to previous outcomes of this sport on the grounds of Lord Yamada.

"It is enough!" I cried, astonished, laughing. "Free him!"

"One other did nearly as well," said Lord Yamada.

"No!" I cried, in misery.

An Ashigaru strung the second bow, the draw of which, I feared, was stronger than the first. This bow was strung with some difficulty. I gathered Lord Yamada did not wish to weary or strain himself with preparing the bow, but preferred to accept it, set for use.

He then advanced to a marker farther down the court, which would be not forty, but thirty, paces from the target.

"Do not!" I called to the shogun.

But I was paid no mind.

The two unused bows and the nine unfired arrows were now beside the shogun, a little behind him, these brought by Ashigaru. The first Ashigaru carried the nine arrows. He who had strung the second bow now carried the two unused bows. A third Ashigaru, who seemed short, and brawny, was slightly in the background. I assessed him a very strong individual. He reminded me of the professional wrestlers who, with their troops, handlers, and drummers, sometimes visited the local villages and towns.

Again, at the closer range, an arrow flashed from the bow.

The crowd, and we prisoners, who had now followed Lord Yamada to the new marker, that set at thirty paces, were absolutely silent.

The only sound had been that of the snap of the flat of a blade against a slender, narrow, swirling cylinder of wood.

We regarded one another.

"Four!" whispered an Ashigaru.

No longer did Lord Yamada extend cordial greetings to the subject of his test, nor did he accord him any longer a pleasant commendation, but merely extended his hand, that a new arrow be placed within it.

The third bow, the shogun having advanced to the twenty-pace mark, was strung by the stout, brawny fellow.

Nine arrows had been expended when we, following Lord Yamada, moved to the ten-pace marker, where the fourth bow was strung, this also strung, though now with difficulty, by the stout, brawny fellow.

"Surely it is enough, Lord," I said.

But the shogun's attention was on Nodachi, bound, hands free, the companion sword in hand, awaiting the tenth arrow.

Deflected arrows, and the parts of deflected arrows, were about. Some of the deflected arrows, given the force with which they were sped, lingering even after the deviation suddenly introduced into their trajectory, had seemed to spring to the clouds, and others had bounded over the walls of the enclosure, or struck against the far wall. About, too, were parts of arrows, strewn yards about.

"Do not, Lord!" I cried.

"Ten!" cried an Ashigaru.

"Desist!" I begged.

But I do not think that either Lord Yamada or Nodachi heard me.

I think that these two inhabited a world alien to that of better than a hundred observers, a world shut away from other worlds, a world in which each stood at an opposite end, a narrow world, the two poles of which were linked by a wirelike, invisible path no broader than the breadth of an arrow.

"Eleven!" breathed an officer.

"Arrow!" cried Lord Yamada.

The final arrow, the twelfth arrow, was handed to him, and the shogun set it to the string.

The great bow was lifted, and lowered, and the missile, leveled, trained on its target.

The shogun's hand trembled on the bow. Sweat was on his

brow. It was difficult even for the shogun, with his considerable strength, to draw back that string. It was difficult to conjecture the force with which that long, narrow, poised, iron-tipped missile would be impelled.

"Fire," I thought to myself. "Fire!"

But the shogun was in no hurry to release the string.

"Now," I thought, "it is no longer a simple test of skill, of eye and hand, but one of nerves, as well. How can one adjust that delicate balance of muscle and time, how sustain so long, unwavering, that patience, that alertness, that intentness, that intensity of focus, how long manage to survive that indefinite season of uncertain readiness? Lightning was kindled, unhurried, waiting, in the dark sky. When would it strike?"

The face of Nodachi seemed expressionless. One might have thought him of stone, save for the eyes. Those eyes, dark, fierce, and glittering, were very much alive.

"Twelve!" cried more than a dozen throats in the crowd.

"Twelve! Twelve!" I cried.

The blade had caught the arrow behind the head, and, as the arrow slid on the blade, pressed to the side, the blade had caught in the wood and shaved the long, graceful missile lengthwise leaving behind it two almost equal parts, even to the fletching.

These two segments fell at the feet of Nodachi.

Even as we cried out with astonishment and pleasure, and Lord Yamada, shaken, tried to grasp what had occurred, Nodachi thrust the companion sword amongst the ropes which fastened him to the post, and the ropes parted, darting to the sides, as though fleeing from the blade.

Katsutoshi, captain of the shogun's guard, drew his sword and leaped between Nodachi and the shogun.

At the same time at least a dozen arrows were trained on Nodachi.

"You have done well," said the shogun to Nodachi. "Put down your sword."

"Stand back!" cried Katsutoshi.

"Stand aside," said Nodachi to the captain of the guard.

Katsutoshi almost quivered with tension, in an on-guard position, facing Nodachi, two hands on his field sword. This choice of weapons gave him the advantage of length of blade, as well as heaviness of stroke.

"Put ten men against me, or one hundred," called Nodachi to the shogun, "but be yourself, mighty lord, the last man in that line."

"Stand aside, Captain," called the shogun to Katsutoshi.

"But, great lord!" protested the captain.

But he stepped aside. No command of a shogun is to be disregarded.

"Think carefully before you approach, clever swordsman," said the shogun. "Five paces before you could bring me within the compass of your blade, you would be greeted by fifteen well-fletched birds of death. Glaives would grow about you as a forest. Nor could you block the storm of steel that would contest your passage."

"Ten men, or a hundred," said Nodachi.

"Do not tempt me to betray my station," said Lord Yamada. "It is not seemly that the shogun should stain his sword with a blood less elevated than his own."

"My blade would meet your blade," said Nodachi. "Twelve arrows assert its right, twelve arrows plead its cause."

"Would that I were not shogun," said Lord Yamada.

"But you are shogun, Lord," said Katsutoshi.

"*Ela*," said the shogun. "It is true."

"The shogun," said Katsutoshi, "has slain daimyos."

"Surrender your sword," said the shogun.

"You see that I cannot," said Nodachi. "It has been lifted, in war."

"Unwisely," said the shogun.

Nodachi inclined his head, briefly.

"I am sure, great lord," said Katsutoshi, "from what I have seen in the town, Chrysanthemum of the Shogun, and here, that his skills would be remarkable."

"Join my guard then, bold, outspoken swordsman," said the shogun. "I would have such a sword at my side."

"It has been lifted, in war," said Nodachi.

"To attack me," said the shogun, "is suicide, even if I do not draw my blade."

"The sun is bright. The sky is blue. The day is calm," said Nodachi. "It is not a bad day to die."

"Then attend me well, fellow," said the shogun, "you who value your life so lightly, for on this day others, too, will die."

"That is not honorable," said Nodachi.

"Do not concern yourself with us," I called to Nodachi.

"No, Master," said Tajima

"No, Master," said Pertinax.

"No, noble one," called Haruki.

"It is not honorable," said Nodachi.

"I am shogun," said Lord Yamada.

"My sword," said Nodachi, bowing, and handing his sword, hilt first, to Katsutoshi, the captain of the shogun's guard.

Chapter Forty-Eight
We Have Tea with Lord Yamada

"We have as yet," said Lord Yamada, "not discovered the whereabouts of the tarns which brought you south."

"Perhaps, great lord," said Tajima, "we came on foot."

"Scarcely," said Lord Yamada, lifting his tiny cup of tea.

"Had we come on tarn," I said, "it seems, after a suitable interval, with no contact, such a party, if it existed, might have departed, returning north."

"That is possible," said Lord Yamada.

I sipped my tea, and then put it down on its saucer. Four sat, cross-legged, about the inlaid, lacquered table, Tajima, Pertinax, the shogun, and I. Behind three of us, Tajima, Pertinax, and myself, stood an Ashigaru, armed with a large, weighty beheading sword.

"I wished to speak with you three," said the shogun, putting down his cup. "Ah!" he said. "Of course! You are concerned with your fellows. Do not fear. Both are well. The swordsman is encelled, of course. Too, as he is neither an officer nor a tarnsman, and outside the command structure of the cavalry, I saw no point in including him in our group."

"There was another," I said.

"He is in the garden, working," said Lord Yamada. "It has suffered much during his absence."

"He will be concerned to put things right," I said.

"I trust so," said the shogun. "I have been much distressed with its condition. But, too, as the swordsman, he is neither an officer nor a tarnsman, and thus, in my view, not a suitable participant in our discussion. Too, of course, both are lowly, which fault bars them from the discussion of matters of moment, such matters being the province of the higher orders."

"What are we to discuss?" I asked.

"What do you think?" he asked.

"The cavalry," I said.

"Of course," he said.

I had been incarcerated separately, but comfortably, for the last few days. Shortly after meeting Tajima and Pertinax in the hall, before we joined Lord Yamada for tea, I had discovered that each had also been kept in isolation. We had, accordingly, had no opportunity for interaction, no opportunity to share views, plan an escape, or such. I had now gathered that Nodachi was most likely encelled similarly. It had come as a surprise that Haruki was allowed the freedom of the garden. The garden, I gathered, was of interest to Lord Yamada. These aesthetic interests, surprisingly to a barbarian, were not that uncommon amongst the Pani nobility. Lord Okimoto, as I recalled, attended to the elegance of his calligraphy. Indeed, the fineness of his hand, I had gathered from Tajima, ruled out the possibility that he might be in league with an opposing house. I found the logic implicit in this assurance difficult to fathom. Lord Yamada, for example, who was apparently sensitive to the delicacy and hue of flowers, and the melodies of their arrangement, could strangle sons, behead enemies, burn and crucify dissidents, and tranquilly administer the test of twelve arrows. I did not know, of course, if the secret entrance to and from the garden still existed or not. I did gather that Haruki was still about. I would not have been surprised, of course, that the secret entrance might still exist and Haruki might still be about. He might have been unwilling to abandon his friends. In the humble gardener I sensed a nobility that would have graced a warrior, a daimyo, even a shogun. But too, of course, there would be work to do in the garden, particularly if it had not been well tended of late.

"And in what way, and to what end, great lord," I said, "are we to discuss the cavalry?"

"You understand, of course," he said, "from the demonstration in the vicinity of the holding of Temmu, that the cavalry cannot meet the iron dragon. It would be burned from the sky."

"But," I said, "what if it does not choose to meet the iron dragon?"

"Precisely," said Lord Yamada.

"It may not choose to be incinerated in the sky," I said.

"That, too, is my speculation," said Lord Yamada.

"In which case," I said, "avoiding open combat, eschewing a direct confrontation, which might be suicidal, it might still constitute a force to be reckoned with."

"Perhaps," said Lord Yamada.

"Let us suppose," I said, "that the cavalry maintains several tarns."

"It does," said Lord Yamada.

"In which case," I said, "the cavalry might be in several places at once, whereas the iron dragon can be in but one. Where the iron dragon is not, the cavalry might be."

"The dragon can destroy the holding," said Lord Yamada.

"But is that not to be destroyed in any case?" I asked.

"Sooner or later we can find the encampment of the tarns," said Lord Yamada.

"Found," I said, "it may disband to reform. And what might be found is where it was, and not where it is. A camp might move, frequently, unpredictably. And there might be many camps, suitably remote, suitably concealed."

"I am cognizant of such possibilities," said the shogun.

"So, too," I said, "will be the senior officers of the cavalry."

"The mercenaries, Torgus and Lysander," he said.

"Perhaps," I said.

"You see, great lord," said Tajima, "your villages and towns, your fortresses, your storehouses, even your palace, all these remain in jeopardy."

"Not while I hold Tarl Cabot, tarnsman, prisoner," said Lord Yamada.

"I am unimportant," I said.

"Not to the cavalry," he said.

"Matters pause then," I said. "The cavalry is not defeated. It is a threat. Yet it is quiescent. What then is the purpose of our discussion?"

"I would like a guarantee of the inactivity, the neutrality, of the cavalry," he said.

"Do you not have that, in your view, while I am your prisoner?" I said.

"I want more than that, of course," he said.

"What more?" I asked.

"The cavalry itself," he said. "I want its eyes, and its wings."

"Perhaps that would be a suitable subject for a further discussion," I said.

"No!" said Tajima, shocked.

"Tarl!" protested Pertinax, who had been silent until now.

"Your young friends," said Lord Yamada, "have much to learn of the ways of the world."

"True," I said.

Tajima and Pertinax were silent, darkly so.

"Nothing need be decided on at present, of course," said Lord Yamada. "But it is my hope that you will all, at your leisure, think upon what I have suggested."

"We shall do so," I assured the shogun.

"Meanwhile," said the shogun, "I trust you have all been well cared for."

"It would be nice to leave a room, at will," said Pertinax, "even a pleasant, well-appointed room."

"Yes," I said, "I am sure we have all been well cared for."

"Perhaps you would like a slave sent to your quarters, for your comfort and convenience, and pleasure," said Lord Yamada.

"No," we said.

"Lord," I said.

"Tarl Cabot, tarnsman?" he said.

"We have been your guests for days," I said. "I do not understand why only now we have been summoned to share tea with you. Our small discussion might have taken place days ago."

"But it did not," he said.

"No," I said.

"Why not, do you think?" he asked.

"There is something special about today," I said.

"Yes," he said.

"Perhaps," I said, "you have by now offered the truce, and the bounty for surrender, and your overtures have been rejected, as expected."

"Excellent," he said.

"Accordingly," I said, "the projected ultimatum was issued."

"Yes," said Lord Yamada.

"Two days ago?" I said.

"Yes," he said.

"Then," I said, "tomorrow is the third day following the issuance of the ultimatum, the day on which the iron dragon will fly."

"At dawn," said Lord Yamada, "the iron dragon will spread its wings. The forces of Temmu are trapped in the holding, and the holding will be destroyed."

"Unfortunate," I said.

"Most unfortunate," said Lord Yamada. "More tea?"

"I have rethought the matter of the slave," I said. "Please have one sent to me this evening. Too, please have her sent naked as that will save time. Too, I like them in collars."

"It will be so," said Lord Yamada. "Would you like points inside the collar, or, perhaps, a high metal collar with points on the upper rim, so that she keeps her head up?"

"A simple, plain, comfortable collar will do," I said, "as long as it is locked on her neck."

"It will be so," said Lord Yamada.

"Will you excuse me!" asked Tajima.

"And me!" said Pertinax.

"Of course," said Lord Yamada. He then glanced to the Ashigaru who were behind Tajima and Pertinax. "Please conduct our young friends to the guards outside, that they may be returned safely, and without incident, to their quarters."

Lord Yamada then looked at me.

"More tea?" he said.

"Yes," I said.

Chapter Forty-Nine

I Find a Use for the Pani Pillow;
I Depart the Incarceration Chamber;
I Enlist Allies

I had dined well on roast vulo, rice, and chestnuts.

To one side lay several strips of cloth, which I had torn from a coverlet. The room in which I was incarcerated, with its heavy door and its barred window, was not, on the whole, untypical of Pani taste. It was pleasant, simple, and uncluttered. It contained one screen, by means of which the room might be divided, two chests, against one wall, that to the left as one would enter, for storage, a low, rectangular table, and some woven floor mats. Near the sleeping mat had been one of the heavy, rounded, wooden Pani pillows. I had never become accustomed to sharing my rest with one of these hard, sturdy, but, viewed from a distance, rather attractive, objects. It did not constitute my idea of a pillow. I preferred to leave such matters to the Pani themselves. I thought, however, that I might put it to use this evening.

I had scarcely finished the final chestnut, which I had been saving for dessert, when I heard steps outside the door. When I was visited in my room, usually to be served food, it was brought by a slave, attended by an Ashigaru. It was my hope that a similar arrangement would be in place this evening. When I was conducted outside the room, as was the case for sharing tea with the shogun this afternoon, there were usually six Ashigaru in attendance. That would not do at all, for this evening.

The steps seemed to be those of a single male, which was all to the good. I assumed the promised slave would be at hand, either preceding the fellow or heeling him, depending on his decision. I would not hear the slave, of course, as she would be barefoot. I had not specified the nature of the slave but I hoped she would be a barbarian, namely, a typical Gorean *kajira*, such as was brought to the islands on the ship of Tersites, primarily as gift objects, sales objects, and trade objects. Such would be well aware of her collar, and its meaning. Such would most likely be terrified to disobey a free male, particularly one of her own race, who would see her uncompromisingly as the slave she was. Gorean masters are seldom lenient with their slaves. They may love their slaves, but they treat them as slaves. They never permit them to forget that they are slaves, only slaves. I was not certain how a Pani slave might react. I trusted that not all barbarian slaves had been sent north with the troops. Also, given the shogun's likely sensitivity to such matters, I supposed he would have had the thoughtfulness to supply me with a barbarian, as my taste ran to such, and, presumably, in his thoughtfulness, one of unusual loveliness. It is pleasant, of course, to have slaves at one's disposal. What male does not want one or more? On Gor, many males have a clear understanding of what women are for, and how they may be uncompromisingly put to the purposes of their sex.

There was a polite knock on the door.

It opened, of course, only from the outside.

"Yes?" I said, pleasantly.

"I bring you a girl for your pleasure, noble one," said the voice.

"She is, I trust," I said, "a barbarian."

"Yes, noble one," said the voice.

This pleased me.

"Is she beautiful?" I asked. It seemed well to inquire into this.

"Yes, noble one," said the voice, "as barbarians go."

"Is she as I specified?" I asked.

"Yes, noble one," he said.

"Naked?" I said.

"Yes, noble one."

"But collared?"

"Yes, noble one, she is collared."

I bent down and picked up the heavy Pani pillow, of hard wood.

I heard the door unbolted, and then heard the two security bars drawn back.

"Lift her in your arms, and carry her within," I said, "and place her on the sleeping mat."

I saw the door swung back.

I stepped to one side.

I was sure now the Ashigaru had the slave in his arms. He paused at the threshold, presumably to locate the sleeping mat. There would be no difficulty in this, as I had placed it prominently before the dividing screen.

The Ashigaru, the slave lifted in his arms, stepped boldly into the room and boldly into the heavy block of curved wood that Pani were accustomed, however incredibly, to utilize as a pillow. The slave tumbled onto the floor, startled, crying out, and I administered a second blow to the stunned Ashigaru, this one to the back of the head.

I put aside the pillow and closed the door.

"No noise," I said to the slave. "Absolute silence, if you would continue to live."

She nodded, frightened, her lip trembling.

I cast her a swift glance, enough to determine that the shogun had exquisite taste, and was generous. Momentarily, she seemed about to cover her body with her hands, perhaps a reflex dating back to the time of her freedom, but withdrew her hands instantly, and swiftly, unbidden, frightened, knelt in first obeisance position, head to the floor, the palms of her hands on the floor, on each side of her head. As her hair had fallen forward, it was easy to see the collar on her neck, fastened not with a lock but a plug rivet.

"On all fours," I said to her. "Crawl to the sleeping mat."

She was then on the mat on all fours.

"*Bara!*" I snapped.

Instantly she assumed the *bara* position, prone, her ankles crossed, her wrists crossed behind her body, her head turned to the left, her cheek on the mat.

So simply a slave may be positioned, to be bound hand and foot.

"May I speak, Master?" whispered the slave.

"No," I said.

I dragged the Ashigaru away, well into the room, and placed him behind the dividing screen. I did not expect individuals to be about at this Ahn, but it is hard to know about such things. Too, even after I left the room, and resecured the door, with the bolt, and the bars, someone might investigate. If so, the presence if the Ashigaru would not be immediately evident. I was satisfied, given the blows he had sustained, particularly the second, that he would be unconscious for some time. It was the first time, incidentally, that I had discovered a use for the Pani pillow. It served nicely as a club. I now removed the outer garments of the Ashigaru. I was under no delusion that I might be mistaken for an Ashigaru at close range, by either barbarians or Pani, but the case might be otherwise at a distance, and in ill-lit corridors. More importantly, considering my plan, I hoped that, in a certain situation, I might be identified as an Ashigaru simply on the basis of my garmenture. When one is unfamiliar with a life form, or disinterested in a life form, one is unlikely to be particularly discriminating where individuals of that life form are concerned. Who distinguishes one gray urt from another gray urt, and few would pay much attention to the difference between a gray urt and a red urt. They are all urts. I recalled that on the steel world of Agamemnon, I had often, at first, confused one Kur with another. Indeed, it had been difficult for me, at first, to distinguish a male Kur from a female Kur, a difficulty which would be incomprehensible amongst Kurii themselves. It might be mentioned, in passing, that no similar difficulty occurs amongst Kurii where humans are concerned. Any Kur can instantly tell a male human from a female human, in virtue of the radical sexual dimorphism characterizing the human species. After putting the outer garments of the Ashigaru to one side, together with the knife, a *tanto*, which I had removed from his sash, his only weapon, I used some of the strips of cloth torn from the coverlet, and fastened his ankles together, and then his wrists, behind him. I then, with more of the same materials, gagged him. Coming about the screen, the knife, and outer garments, of the Ashigaru in hand, I encountered the slave, still in *bara*, as she had not been given permission to break position. It took only a moment, as she was conveniently placed, to tie her ankles and wrists, and she then lay in *bara*, trussed. I then rolled her to her back, to get a better look at her. She had long, light brown hair, nearly blond. It was now, as I had turned her, about her head and face. I brushed it aside, to better examine her features. I thought, in many markets, she might fetch as much as two silver tarsks.

I then pulled her up by the hair to a sitting position.

"Oh!" she said.

"I remember you," I said, "from the slave pen. You were rejected as several others, as a serving slave, to serve at the supper of Lord Yamada. You performed the slave girl's trick, of having your hair about your body, and then bending over to loosen it, and then straightening up, head back, to fling it behind you, thus to startle us with the sudden revelation of your beauty."

"Yes, Master," she whispered, looking at me.

"You sought to achieve an advantage over your sister slaves," I said, "who must display themselves as commanded, uniformly."

"No!" she said.

"Oh!" she sobbed, cuffed.

"Do not lie to a free man, slave," I said.

"Forgive me, Master," she said.

She tried to back away, but could not do so, as my left hand was still in her hair.

"It earned you five lashes, as I remember," I said.

"Yes, Master," she said, paling, presumably remembering the incident of her disciplining.

"I might have given you ten," I said.

"I am a slave," she said, closing her eyes. "I am at the mercy of my masters."

"You are pretty," I said.

"A slave is grateful, if she is found pleasing," she said.

"Open your eyes," I said.

"Yes, Master," she said.

I then, ripping some of the torn cloth, formed a wadding which I thrust into her mouth. A moment later it was tied in place, with two broad loops, knotted behind the back of her neck.

I then went to the door, opened it a bit, and, carefully, looked out.

The corridor was empty, and muchly dark.

I was on the third level of the palace.

I did not know where Nodachi might be encelled, or where Haruki might be housed, but I knew, from the afternoon, when we were to be fetched together to the tea of Lord Yamada, the incarceration chambers of both Tajima and Pertinax. They were on the same level as this, the third level.

I returned to the interior of the room, to assume the outer garb and knife of the unconscious Ashigaru.

I looked down on the seated, bound slave.

"You look well," I said, "naked, bound, in a collar."

She made not the tiniest sound, not even the tiny, almost inaudible whimpers permitted to her in the gag.

"On your back," I said.

She immediately lay back.

The slave is not a free woman. The slave is to obey instantly, unquestioningly.

Failure petitions discipline. The slightest hesitation is likely to be rewarded with punishment.

They are to be in no doubt that they are slaves.

"In Pani custody," I said, "you are doubtless familiar with the lashings of the mat."

She whimpered once, briefly, pathetically.

In gag signals, one sound betokens "Yes," and two sounds, "No." She would know that from the continent.

I reached down to pick up the garb I had removed from the unconscious Ashigaru.

She turned to face me, on her side, tears in her eyes. She began to whimper, piteously.

"Stay on your back," I said.

She went to her back.

She continued to whimper, and began to squirm on the mat. I looked down upon her, and she lifted her belly to me, pathetically.

"You are pretty," I said.

Again she whimpered.

Her belly was again lifted from the mat.

"Do you petition the lash of the mat?" I inquired.

I wondered how long it had been since she had been caressed. As she was a Gorean *kajira*, I had no doubt she was the victim of the slave fires which free men, perhaps cruelly, had seen fit to light in her belly.

How much that makes them ours!

Are not her needs the mightiest of her chains?

Once the slave fires burn in a woman's belly, she is undone; she can no longer be free; freedom is no longer an option; it is forever behind her. She is then the property of masters.

Again she lifted her belly, and whimpered, piteously, once, and then again more desperately, more pathetically, once, again.

Her eyes were bright with tears.

I recalled that she had been sent to me for my pleasure.

The slave is nothing, of course, a beast, a plaything, a domestic animal, an object, a property, a vendible possession. She may be neglected, overlooked, scorned, and spurned. No notice need be taken of her. Her emotions, feelings, and needs are unimportant. They may be ignored. They are of no consequence. One must guard against caring for her. She is a slave.

I looked down on the pathetic, needful, bound thing, at my mercy, on the mat.

She was to be ignored.

There is, of course, in the slave, a humanity, a vulnerability, a helplessness, a need, a radical femaleness which is foreign to the free woman. Perhaps the free woman can dimly sense this if she could dare to imagine herself stripped and rightless, owned, and collared.

How then could she be more basically, more fundamentally, more radically, a female?

She whimpered, again.

It is no wonder that men make them slaves.

I looked to the closed door.

I thought it quite possible that I might be dead within the Ahn, perhaps less.

I bent down, to unbind the ankles of the slave.

I unbolted the portal of the incarceration chamber and moved back the two bars.

That should alert Pertinax.

I then knocked on the door lightly. "Pertinax," I whispered. "Pertinax."

"Tarl?" I heard.

"Yes," I said.

As soon as he opened the door, Tajima, whom I had already released from his chamber, and I, slipped inside.

Naturally I had resecured my chamber, with the bolt and bars, as soon as I had left, and we had done the same for that of Tajima. One passing these chambers would suppose their occupants to be safely confined within. Surely, eventually, an inquiry would take place when the Ashigaru who had conducted the slave to my chamber failed to report back to his station, but I did not expect this to take place immediately. Perhaps the Ashigaru had been requested to wait. Presumably not every delivered slave is retained until morning. One might be dismissed, after a longer or shorter time. Perhaps one would be tried out, and another requested. To be sure, usually the delivered slave is the property of her temporary master until morning. If the room were looked into, I hoped the bound slave, on the mat, clearly ready for slave use, would dispel suspicion. As the door had been secured from the outside, I hoped it would be supposed that the prisoner was still within, and, presumably, behind the screen. One might then exit, relock the door, and, if interested, attend to the matter of relocating the missing Ashigaru. Perhaps he had reported in, in the meantime. In any event, I was sure we would have at least a few Ehn at our disposal.

"I thought," said Pertinax, "your acceptance of a pleasure slave, one to grace your sleeping mat for the night, betokened a possible interest in colluding with the shogun."

"Not as yet, at any rate," I said.

"So, too, did I," said Tajima. "Forgive me, Tarl Cabot, tarnsman."

"Leave such speculations to Lord Okimoto," I said.

"How did you obtain the garments of an Ashigaru?" inquired Pertinax.

"I have them on loan," I said.

"No one is going to think you Pani," said Pertinax.

"Something might," I said.

"What is your plan?" asked Pertinax.

"It has two parts, and then stops short," I said.

"'It then stops short'?" said Tajima.

"One can plan only so far ahead," I said. "First, Tajima will don these garments. An Ashigaru might well think him an Ashigaru, which would be unlikely with us. We will be as his prisoners. Second, we shall attempt to obtain a similar garmenture for ourselves."

"But no one would take us for Pani," said Pertinax.

"Something might," I said.

"I do not understand," said Pertinax.

"Perhaps, if we are fortunate," I said, "you may see."

It took only a moment to remove the garments of the Ashigaru, and another moment for Tajima to assume them.

"Here, Pertinax," I said, "put your wrists behind you, crossed, and I will wrap this bit of cloth about them, from my room. Your hands will be easily freed, and quickly, but they will seem as though bound. I do not expect anyone to check into the matter. Tajima will serve me similarly. We must appear his bound prisoners. That should allow us to approach another Ashigaru, or so, easily."

"Very well," said Pertinax.

In a moment I had looped the cloth two or three times about his wrists and tucked it in. He could free himself almost instantly, when he wished. From a distance, however, and if not closely examined, he would appear bound. With some additional strips of cloth, Tajima then supplied me with a similar pretense of helplessness.

We then left Pertinax's chamber and Tajima, the *tanto* in his sash, closed the door, putting the bolt and the bars in place.

"Our objective," I said, "is the fifth level."

Pertinax and I, then, our hands seemingly bound behind us, preceded Tajima down the corridor.

"We turn here," I said. "Then the stairs, then the fifth level."

"What then?" asked Tajima.

"At a certain point on the fifth level, a point known to me," I said, "we will encounter one or more Ashigaru, one during the day, but now, at night, perhaps two. I hope two. I do not think more."

"And what then?" asked Tajima.

"We acquire, I hope, two more uniforms," I said.

"And what then?" asked Tajima.

"Then," I said, "we will see."

Chapter Fifty

Certification

Tajima, Pertinax, and I were now in the narrow side corridor on the fifth level of the palace, the same access to which had been denied to me several weeks ago, by its guard.

Each of us was now clad in the garments of an Ashigaru. Two of us were armed with a glaive, Tajima and Pertinax, and each of us had in his sash, that of a common Ashigaru, a *tanto*.

"I fear this disguise," said Pertinax to me, "is unlikely to be convincing."

"Much depends on what one wishes to convince," I said.

We had then come to the end of the darkened side corridor. The main corridors were lit with lamps. So, too, were most of the side corridors. This one was not.

We could do little other than feel our way.

Some creatures, of course, have excellent night vision. I mentioned nothing of this to my friends, Pertinax and Tajima. I did tell them that if they should be confronted by a darkness within a darkness, and sense that deeper darkness surging forward, like a hurricane of night, to meet it with the poised, braced glaive.

"I feel the portal," said Tajima, "it is heavy, and of iron. My fingers trace riveted bands of reinforcing iron."

"Good," I said. Such a portal could withstand for a time anything likely to be brought against it, axes, rock hammers, beams of wood.

"There is light within," whispered Pertinax.

"Good," I said. There was a slight streak of yellow, like a bright line, beneath the door.

"Do we call out?" asked Tajima.

"It is likely we have already been heard," I said.

"Consider the door, its weight and presumed thickness, that we have spoken softly," said Tajima.

"Nonetheless," I said.

"What lies behind this door?" said Pertinax.

"Be ready," I said.

"What are you guarding?" had asked Tajima.

"You do not have an officer's sash," had said the Ashigaru.

"I am still curious," said Tajima.

Tajima had paused before the entrance to a side corridor, to the left, one off the second of the two main corridors on the fifth level of the palace.

"It is none of your concern," said the Ashigaru.

"I would see," said Tajima.

"Be on your way, with your prisoners," said the Ashigaru.

"Still," protested Tajima, looking toward the entrance to the side corridor.

"You cannot enter," said the Ashigaru, lowering his glaive to block the corridor. At the same time, another Ashigaru, who had been leaning on his glaive in the background, half asleep, lifted his head, shook it, and advanced toward us.

"Begone," said the second Ashigaru, unpleasantly.

"Barbarian tarsks," said Tajima, addressing us, Pertinax and I, "back against the wall, there, and lower your heads, submissively."

Pertinax and I then went to the wall of the main corridor, that on the west side of the palace, beside the entrance to the side corridor. This would place us behind the two Ashigaru, should they advance into the main corridor.

"You do not need to admit me," said Tajima. "Just tell me. I have a bowl of rice on this. It is a treasure room, is it not?"

"There is no place for prisoners on the fifth level," said the second Ashigaru.

"I know," said Tajima. "I brought them, that I might have a pretext for moving about in the palace, discharging a seeming errand."

"There is no place for prisoners on the fifth level," said the second Ashigaru, again, angrily.

"I needed them to reach this level," said Tajima.

Common Ashigaru, of course, were not permitted to move about the palace, at will. They would need some office, or errand, to justify their presence.

"There is much discussion in the meal hall about the fifth level," said Tajima.

"This corridor is closed to all but high ones," said the first Ashigaru.

"Why?" asked Tajima. "Remember the bowl of rice."

"It is not our bowl of rice," said the first Ashigaru.

"Begone," said the second.

"Very well," said Tajima. "But if you will not speak, then neither will I."

"About what?" asked the first Ashigaru.

"About what was overheard by a slave serving in the officers' meal room," said Tajima.

"What?" said the first Ashigaru.

"Nothing," said Tajima, backing away.

"Speak," said the second Ashigaru, lifting the butt end of his glaive.

"I must return these prisoners," said Tajima.

"Wait," said the second Ashigaru.

"I wish you well," said Tajima.

"We have seen things," said the first Ashigaru, "that would raise the hair on your head, that would shake and terrify you."

"There is a bowl of rice at stake," said Tajima. "A treasure room?"

"There are beasts," whispered the second Ashigaru, "large, shaggy animals, who come and go."

There are at least two then, I thought. That was not good. On the other hand, one should have anticipated more than one. What if one should suffer a mishap, or become disabled? Surely Kurii would not rely on but a single operative in the palace.

"They enter and leave the portal at the end of the corridor," said the first Ashigaru.

"We do not know what is within," said the second. "It is a den, an arsenal, a treasure room, we do not know."

"If even you do not know," said Tajima, "then I have neither won nor lost my bowl of rice, nor the other his."

"No," said the first Ashigaru. "Now, what is your news? What, of import, was overheard by the slave in the officers' meal room?"

"Approach," said Tajima, looking about. "This is not for the ears of prisoners."

The two Ashigaru then approached Tajima and, looking about, leaned toward him, presumably that we might not overhear what might be communicated.

"What was overheard?" asked the first Ashigaru, half whispering.

Tajima looked about, as though to reassure himself that the corridor was empty, and that there was no danger of being overheard.

"As I said," whispered Tajima, "nothing."

At that point Pertinax and I had seized the two Ashigaru.

"You think they have heard us?" asked Pertinax.

"Probably," I said, "but they may not have understood us."

"How so?" asked Tajima.

"Presumably they are alone," I said. "If that is the case, their mechanical devices are not likely to have been activated."

"Mechanical devices?" said Pertinax.

"You will see," I said.

"What is behind this door?" said Tajima.

"A Kur," I said. "I fear more than one."

"What is a Kur?" said Pertinax.

"I shall not attempt to describe it," I said. "Unarmed, it can dismember an adult sleen."

"It is a fearsome thing," said Tajima.

"It is not likely to survive the attack of a larl," I said.

"It is mortal," said Tajima.

"Of course," I said.

"Then we can kill it," he said.

"It has been done," I said.

"Frequently?" he asked.

"By others of its kind," I said. "They are much like men."

"Is it easy to kill?" he asked.

"No," I said.

"Is it frequently killed by men?" he asked.

"No," I said, "not frequently. Be ready."

I then stepped forward and, lightly, struck three times on the heavy iron door.

We heard something move within. We heard a shuffling sound, and a scratching, as of claws on a metal surface.

"I think it is large," said Pertinax.

"It is," I said.

Then, from the other side of the door, there came an issuance of sounds, of a sort with which I was quite familiar, but it was doubtless new, and perhaps disturbing, to my friends. Initially, it would strike one as the sort of sound one might expect from a large, predatory animal, a tiger, a leopard, a lion, a larl, a sleen. Indeed, if one listened only briefly, or did not listen carefully, one might have supposed that something of that sort was on the other side of the door, perhaps caged, perhaps chained, but, if one attended more carefully, one began shortly to suspect, and it was a most unsettling suspicion, particularly at first, that this stream of sound was being subtly articulated, subtly modulated, in such a way as to suggest something more than a mere stream of sound, that these sounds might not be simple reflexive cries or questioning or warning signals, but sounds bearing meaning, that these sounds were phonemes, and would be linked with the mysteries of meaning, with morphemes, the remarkable, conventional, intangible inventions which make possible intelligible discourse, except that these organisms, emitting these sounds, with their power, energy, ferocity, and terribleness, with their tendency to violence, were not human. Kur, with its dialects, is as much a complex native language as any familiar to humans. What is the lever or the wheel, compared to the meaningful sound? What a rare moment when a simple organism, shambling and brutelike, in lost millennia, first lifted its head to the sky, and realized, in a stunning, magical moment, that a sound might mean.

The door swung open, heavily.

There was a dim, yellowish light within, though I supposed it bright enough for the chamber's occupants. It eerily illuminated the chamber. I was reminded of the denlike apartments I had encountered on a far world, a steel world, save that there was here, in the recesses, a shallow cistern and, on a wall to the left, as one would enter, a number of slabs of meat, fastened on hooks. I had somehow expected a variety of pipings, a number of vessels, glassware in the form of beakers, cylinders, and retorts, racks of complex equipment, conduits, valves, and tanks of sorts, things more to be expected in a laboratory or workshop. My first reaction was one of disappointment, and consternation. This seemed no fitting support facility, no adequate housing, for a device as large and sophisticated as that I sought. Had I been so wrong? There seemed no hanger here, or cage, large enough for the enormous, mechanical beast of prey I wished to find, and feared to find. Then I recalled from the Nest of Priest-Kings the bleak, tiered housings of transportation disks. Where a device utilizes gravity, its fuel is always at hand. No mighty tanks of propellant need fill storage yards. Too, Priest-Kings would not be likely to entrust Kurii with a sophisticated technological apparatus unfamiliar to them which might be dangerous or difficult for them to control and manipulate. Too, I suspected that vital parts of the machinery would be sealed away from the curious, and armed in such a way that any attempt to examine them would result in the destruction of the equipment and, doubtless, the release of a quantity of lethal energy, either in radiation or explosiveness, which would destroy the prying beings who might presume to acquaint themselves with a forbidden technology. Indeed, a version of the blasting flame death itself might be linked to such an unauthorized inquiry. I was pleased to see the food and water, enough to sustain even life forms as large and voracious as Kurii. This portion of the palace, with its door and supplies, might form a defensible redoubt capable of resisting intrusion for days. But where was the great mechanical beast I had hoped to discover, and then disable?

There were two Kurii in the room, one facing us, half bent over, as Kurii often stand, on the other side of the threshold, and one back, near the cistern, little more than a large mound of fur, a haunch of meat in one paw.

I supposed this was the first glimpse of Kurii entertained by Pertinax and Tajima.

I did not envy them the experience, particularly under these circumstances, in the ill-lit corridor. The Kur before us had the light behind him and thus we could not well see its features. It was like a large blackness before us, a living blackness.

A noise issued from the thing before us. It was, largely to me, and perhaps entirely to Pertinax and Tajima, a growl.

Both were behind me, with glaives.

"Tal," I said, cheerily. "I bring word from Lord Yamada. He wishes your presence, immediately."

The flat of a paw was held up before us. We were to remain where we were. The beast then turned away from us.

"Be ready to kill, or die," I said to Pertinax and Tajima.

The beast did not yet have its translator activated.

Had it been activated, my greeting would have been transformed into Kur.

I looked about.

Where was the large device I sought? What if it were not here? It would soon be light.

At dawn the iron dragon was to spread its wings.

In a moment the beast had returned to the threshold, the translator slung about its neck on a chain. One of its long, thick, tentaclelike digits pressed the switch on the face of the machine.

"Tal," I said, again. "I bring word from Lord Yamada. He wishes your presence, immediately."

This was translated into audible Kur. It was often fascinating to me, to hear Gorean, or any other suitable language, depending on the device, transformed into an alien form of speech.

"As you can see," I said, "we are Ashigaru, soldiers of Lord Yamada. We come to summon you, rather, to invite you, into his presence. A matter of considerable moment has arisen."

This message was apparently accepted without demur by the beast. I expect this surprised Pertinax, but I had counted on this being the case, and, luckily, it had turned out to be the case.

Similarly it had not seemed to concern the beast, nor did it seem to notice it, that none of us wore an officer's sash. Yamada, I was sure, would address these things through an officer, and perhaps one as highly placed as Lord Akio, one of his daimyos.

"Haste is of the essence," I said.

It was my hope, of course, that we could get these two things out of the way, on one pretext or another, and somehow obtain access to the interior chamber. I had hoped, of course, for a more normal door, one which we might be able to force in the beasts' absence.

"I am afraid there is going to be blood," I said to Pertinax and Tajima, in English. "I shall do my best with the first. You two, with glaives, prepare to meet the second."

This utterance apparently came out, as I had hoped it would, as something unintelligible in Kur. This translator, as I had hoped, was either not capable of handling English or, if it could, then, at least, it was not currently set to English. Most Kur translators, as I understood it, at least on Gor, were set, as one would expect, for Gorean alone. Too, few Kurii understand spoken Gorean without a translator, and few can do little more than produce a grotesque mockery of human phonemes. To be fair, of course, few humans can do much with the phonemes of Kur either. As an analogy one would not expect a tiger, even an intelligent, rational tiger, if such could exist, to recite Shakespeare well, and a Shakespearean scholar would not be likely to soothe or satisfy a Kur audience with a rendition of even the simplest of their revered poets. Indeed, he would be well advised to refrain from the attempt. Kurii are both short-tempered and fanged.

"I did not understand you," came from the beast's translator. The words were emitted noncommittally, routinely, but the attitude of the beast suggested suspicion.

"I am sorry," I said, in Gorean.

"I understand that," said the beast.

"Good," I said. "Perhaps your translator briefly malfunctioned. Perhaps it should be attended to. Please report as soon as possible to the shogun."

The beast turned off the translator, and said something in Kur. The second beast half rose up, so that he was half standing, and he threw the meat he had been feeding on to the side of the room. It struck against the wall. He also came forward a pace or two.

In the background, leaning against the wall, was a Kur ax, its haft some seven feet in length, its socketed, double-edged blade some two feet in width.

It is light in the hands, or paws, of a Kur, but it is not a practical weapon for a human.

"Be ready," I said to Pertinax and Tajima.

The first beast then reactivated the translator.

"You bring a message from Lord Yamada," it said.

"Yes," I said. "You and your fellow are commanded, are invited, rather, forgive me, into the presence of the shogun, to attend upon him as soon as possible."

"You are the corridor guards?" asked the beast.

"No," I said. "We come from the dais of the shogun."

It did not seem wise to me to attempt to pass ourselves off as the corridor guards. They might be known. Presumably they would have names.

"What does the shogun have in mind?" he asked.

"We are humble soldiers," I said. "We are not privy to the secrets of the shogun."

"But you are authorized to convey the shogun's invitation?" he said.

"Of course," I said.

"How do I know that?" he asked.

"How else would we have the courage to approach your august presence?" I asked.

"Certify," he said.

"'Certify'?" I said.

"Yes," he said, "certify."

"I do not understand," I said.

"I do not think you will leave the corridor alive," came from the translator. The words were evenly spaced and equable, but the mien of the beast was now clearly menacing, extremely menacing.

"Report to the shogun," I said, severely.

The second beast, that now a pace or two behind the first, snarled. Whereas this noise seemed to me no different from the noises the translator had been dealing with, rendering them into intelligible Gorean, no Gorean emerged from the machine. It was then, I gathered, a simple snarl.

"The confirmation device, the authentication signal, the sign, the password, is simple," said the first beast. "Certify."

"It has been changed," I said.

"To what?" he asked.

"To this," I said, drawing the *tanto* from my sash.

The beast lunged forward, and I drove the blade, two hands on the handle, bracing it against my body, deep into its chest.

My head was buried in its fur, and I felt the heat of its breath on my neck. I sensed Pertinax and Tajima hurrying about me.

The other Kur had spun about, rushed to the side, and now had the great Kur ax lifted, ready to strike, when two glaives were thrust into his body, again and again.

The first beast had fallen before me.

It was still alive, and the translator was still on.

"Forgive me," I said to the beast, kneeling beside it.

"Well done," said the beast. "Now I will not die the tarsk death."

"I would have had it otherwise," I said.

"It will do you no good," said the beast.

I was not heartened by this remark.

Tajima and Pertinax seemed shaken, numb, almost dazed; in the cry of the moment they had reacted almost reflexively, and were only now better aware of what had occurred; they stood near the fallen Kur, looking down, the blades of their glaives drenched with blood, oddly paled in the yellowish light.

"It is thus, with steel," I said, "that we certify ourselves."

"It is the way of warriors," said Tajima.

"It is well," I said, "you responded as quickly as you did. Had the strike of the ax been launched you might both have been cut in two. Few things can stand against a Kur ax."

Pertinax and Tajima came then to stand next to me.

"Now," I said, "my friends, you have met Kurii."

"What a gross beast," said Pertinax, looking down on the first Kur.

"Do not speak ill of it," I said. "It was a warrior."

Chapter Fifty-One

We Must Undertake an Inquiry

"It is not here," I said, miserably.

"This is the fifth level of the palace," said Pertinax.

"And it is here we encountered the beasts," said Tajima.

"It must be here," said Pertinax, angrily.

"It is not," I said.

That was clear enough. Its bulk would have been impossible to conceal, certainly in the space to which we now had access.

"The roof?" said Pertinax.

"The roof was visible from afar," I said. "The dragon or, more likely, its housing would have been evident, when we scouted the palace from a distance."

"One of its wings would not fit in this place," said Tajima.

"It must be here," said Pertinax. "There must be a secret panel, leading to an adjoining chamber, one cavernous in nature, one where the walls might draw back, that it might fly."

"Search then for such a vast chamber," I said. "But I do not think you will find it."

"It must be here, somehow adjoined with this chamber," said Pertinax.

"I do not think so," I said. "While I was Lord Yamada's guest, I examined the palace with care, not simply to familiarize myself with the premises, but to seek avenues of escape, and note points of possible attack. I recall no such space. I had hoped the corridor which was sealed away and guarded, that to which I had no access, might lead to such a space, the dragon's cave, but it does not."

"There must be a secret panel," said Pertinax.

"Search for it then," I said.

Pertinax began to examine the walls, even the floor, with care.

"It is nearly dawn," said Pertinax.

"The iron dragon is to fly at dawn," said Tajima. "We will be unable to stop it."

"The trussed Ashigaru will shortly be discovered," said Pertinax.

"Doubtless, by now," said Tajima.

"The door," I said, "will hold indefinitely."

"And we are trapped within," said Tajima.

"I had thought the housing for the device would be accessed from the corridor," I said.

"But it is not here," said Pertinax.

"So it is obviously elsewhere," said Tajima.

"Of course, it need not be here!" I said.

"What do you mean?" asked Pertinax.

"Continue to search for your panel," I said. "It exists."

"I do not understand," said Pertinax.

"It is here, in this secret, guarded place, we encountered the beasts," I said.

"Yes?" said Tajima.

"They must be its technicians, its controllers, its operators," I said.

"That is likely, Tarl Cabot, tarnsman," said Tajima.

"Dawn," I said, "is at hand, perhaps moments away."

"And the beasts were here," said Tajima.

"Precisely," I said.

"The dragon need not be here," said Pertinax.

"But it must be controlled from here!" said Tajima.

"Search!" I said. "Let us all search for the panel!"

Chapter Fifty-Two

The Secret Room;
What Was Found Within
the Secret Room

"It must be dawn," said Tajima.

"Almost," I said. "Go, see!"

On the side of the chamber, on the wall, facing west, there was a steel-shuttered aperture which Tajima slid back. The opening was small, a matter of horts. It was, however, apparently, the only direct access the chamber had to view the outside.

"It is dark," said Tajima.

"You are facing west," said Pertinax.

"It may be dawn," I said.

Gor, as Earth, rotates toward the east.

Toward the rear of the chamber, fixed in the wall to the right, as one would enter, Pertinax had located a small metal object, circular, less than a hort in diameter, covered with a mesh of fine wire.

"I see nothing inexplicable, or anomalous, other than this," had said Pertinax.

"That has to be it," I had said. "The lever, the switch, the key!"

"It would meaningless to most Goreans," said Tajima.

"By intention," I said.

"I have tried to turn it, I have pressed it," said Pertinax.

"But," I said, "my dear friend, you have not talked to it."

"What?" he said.

"It looks, does it not," I said, "like a receiver, or small microphone?"

"Yes," he said.

"I wager," I said, "that is, in effect, what it is. The panel is voice-sensitive. Some message in Kur would spring the lock and open the panel."

"*Ela!*" moaned Pertinax. "We are lost."

"Not at all," I said, "you have succeeded splendidly. This victory is yours!"

"We do not know Kur," said Tajima.

"But the panel has been found," I had said. "Fetch the Kur ax, and help me, both of you, one after the other, to wield it."

Four or five feet of the wall had soon splintered apart, and collapsed, before us, succumbing to the attentions of the great ax. I yanked boards aside and revealed a small room, containing what appeared to be a console of sorts, and, behind it, a large frame, in which were mounted six viewing panels.

"Now," said Pertinax, "we use the ax, and destroy these things."

"Not yet," I said. "That would not harm the dragon."

"It would be inoperative," said Pertinax.

"Temporarily," I said.

"Better that than nothing," said Pertinax.

"Compared to the dragon," I said, "I am sure the control devices are relatively simple, and possibly easily replaced."

"You do not know that," said Pertinax.

"No," I said. "And I may be wrong. But I think the dragon itself is the target of interest."

"We do not know where the dragon is," said Tajima.

"No," I said, "but I am certain it is controlled from here."

"Destroy the control apparatus," said Pertinax. "We have the ax. We can do at least that."

"Later," I said.

"At least the dragon will not fly at dawn," said Pertinax.

"I hope it will," I said, sliding onto the bench before the console.

"What are you going to do?" asked Tajima.

"I hope," I said, "—release the dragon."

"Do not trifle with these things," said Pertinax. "They may be armed."

"Withdraw," I suggested.

"No," said Pertinax.

"No, Tarl Cabot, tarnsman," said Tajima.

"You were ready," I said to Pertinax, "to strike it with an ax." Pertinax was silent.

"This equipment," I said, "has been designed to be operated by Kurii, a visually oriented organism presumably unfamiliar with the technology internal to the dragon. I have no doubt that an attempt to examine that technology would be dangerous to the highest degree. Priest-Kings do not care to share secrets on which the fate of worlds may hang. This control apparatus, however, I suspect, is not armed. That precaution would not be necessary, and it might, if accidentally triggered, bring the entire mission of the iron dragon to naught. Further, I suspect we have nothing here which exceeds the technology of the Kurii themselves, and nothing here, by intent, which an average Kur, or human, cannot manage."

"Can you manage it?" asked Pertinax.

"Possibly," I said. "The board is very simple. There are only a few switches. There must be a way of opening the dragon's gate, so to speak, of activating the dragon itself, of opening its eyes, so to speak, and so on."

"How is it to be guided, controlled?" asked Tajima.

"That is the easiest," I said. "By its reins."

"It has no reins, Tarl Cabot, tarnsman," said Tajima.

"They are here," I said, "embedded in the board, this mounted sphere. Long ago, in a distant place," I said, "I utilized something much like this."

I needed not speak to them of the great nest in the Sardar, nor of the Nest War, nor of the fierce aerial battles within those mighty chambers, nor of transportation disks and flame tubes.

"And this lever, given its curved, linear housing," I said, "I suspect will activate the dragon, and regulate its speed."

"But it seemed to breathe fire and it could blast walls," said Tajima.

"Like a gun," I said, "pointed to its target."

"And where is the trigger?" asked Pertinax.

"I do not know," I said, "but consider these two switches on the right, in their recesses. There is no danger of accidentally tripping them. That is interesting, is it not?"

"One for a torrent of fire, one for missiles, or rays, of a sort?" said Pertinax.

"In any event," I said, "we will not try them unless we are successful in getting our dragon out of its cave and into the open air. There is no point in turning its hanger or housing into a furnace or a shambles of debris."

"There are six small spheres in what appear to be cups," said Pertinax, pointing to the board, "and each sphere has what seems to be a dial next to it. What is all that for?"

"I do not know," I said, "but as there are six spheres and six dials, I would suppose it has to do with the six viewing screens."

We then heard a pounding on the heavy iron portal, probably from the butts of glaives.

"The guards have been found, and released," said Tajima.

"It sounds so," I said.

We could also hear shouting from behind the door.

"It must be dawn, by now," said Pertinax.

"Lord Yamada must be furious," said Pertinax.

"I doubt that he is informed, as yet," I said. "I expect, rather, he is ensconced in some coign of vantage, where he is eagerly awaiting the flight of the iron dragon. Indeed, I think I know the place."

"Surely, Tarl Cabot, tarnsman," said Tajima, "we must not keep the shogun waiting."

I threw one switch.

"At least the chamber did not explode," said Pertinax.

"Nothing happened," said Tajima.

"I am sure something happened," I said. "The first switch in order presumably either activates the screens or opens the dragon gate, so to speak. Since the screens are not activated, namely, the dragon has not yet opened its eyes, I am hoping the dragon is free to fly, that the gate has been opened, or the roof rolled back, or such."

"Try the second switch," said Pertinax.

I threw the second switch.

"Nothing happened, again," said Tajima.

"Something happened," I said. "I am sure. I can feel the tremor in the board. Too, listen, carefully."

"It is a soft hum," said Tajima.

"I am sure the dragon is activated," I said.

"But motionless?" said Pertinax.

"I hope so," I said.

"Try the third switch," said Pertinax.

"Ah!" cried Tajima, pleased.

"There!" said Pertinax.

"The sky, Tarl Cabot, tarnsman!" said Tajima.

We could see clouds.

"And rock walls all about, and even what must be the floor, as of a cave!" said Pertinax.

"Our dragon has opened its eyes," I said.

"Its six eyes," said Tajima.

"But it will seem, and act, as if it has but two," I said. "That would contribute to the illusion."

"Can you control it?" asked Pertinax.

"I think so," I said. "In any event we shall soon know."

I did not think there would be much difficulty beyond this point, at least with controlling the movements of the dragon. One used the sphere for orientation, as one had with a transportation disk, and the other switch, that associated with the sphere, analogous to a throttle, to regulate power.

"What is the role of the six spheres and the six dials?" asked Pertinax.

"Our mystery controls," I said.

"Those," he said.

"Let us see," I said.

"Ah!" said Tajima.

I had lightly rotated the sphere which I, for my convenience, would think of as Sphere One, in its recess, or cup. It was obviously associated with the side camera to the left. Manipulating the sphere then, as I determined, oriented the camera, changing the screen from the default position to a selected position, say more to the left or right, higher or lower, and such.

"What are the dials for?" asked Pertinax.

"We shall soon know," I said.

"Wonderful," said Pertinax.

The dials regulated the magnification of the image on the pertinent screen. Depending on the use made of the dial, altering the default setting on the camera, either the field was reduced and the image magnified, or the field was enlarged and individual images were reduced.

"One could read a banner at a pasang," said Tajima.

"But little else at the time," I said.

"What are we going to do now, Tarl Cabot, tarnsman?" said Tajima.

"Now," I said, "we are going to release a dragon."

Chapter Fifty-Three

The Dragon has Spread Its Wings

"It is in flight!" cried Pertinax. "I see it!" He stood before the small, steel-shuttered aperture, the metal panel slid back, which provided the only direct visual access to the outside.

"Let me see," said Tajima, and Pertinax stepped aside.

"I can see the palace," I said, "on the screen. It is less than a pasang to my east."

"'Your east'?" said Pertinax. "You are in the palace."

"To the east of the dragon," I said.

One thinks of oneself from a certain perspective, that natural to an organism. Is one not always behind the phenomena, so to speak? Is the world not always conveniently at hand, about one as usual? Is one not always, for example, the center of the visual field? Suppose, then, your sensory experiences were somehow dissociated from their common site. Would it not then be natural, almost immediately, to psychologically situate yourself in accord with the coercions of custom and familiarity? Though I knew myself in a small room, in the palace of an island shogun, I had much the sense of oneness with the enormous beast through whose eyes, so to speak, I was experiencing the world. It was not so much that I seemed within it, as a pilot might be within an airborne vehicle, or even as though it might be a body, which I might temporarily inhabit, but rather it seemed as though it was I, myself. I seemed not so much within it, as it, it itself.

"I shall bring it about," I said. "I am going to circle the palace, three times, slowly, in a stately fashion, at a low altitude. I want the dragon to be visible, unforgettably visible to as many as possible."

"There is the fifth level, the compartments on the western side of the palace," said Pertinax.

"That is where you are," I said.

"There is the courtyard, the exercise yard, the archery range, the barracks, the work sheds, the stadium," said Pertinax.

"I know the stadium," said Tajima.

"That is the location of the eel pool," I said to Pertinax.

"Guards, Ashigaru, officers, are about," said Tajima.

"This is the first time most of them will have looked upon the dragon," I said.

"Many are awed," said Pertinax. "Many cover their eyes."

"Others wave, and cry out, eagerly, and smile, and run beneath it, even in its shadow," said Tajima.

"Would you not rejoice," I asked, "in the presence of so mighty an ally?"

"The iron dragon flies for Yamada," said Tajima.

"That is their supposition," I said. "At a given point, I shall hover. There! Examine the screen to the left, as I adjust the camera and increase the magnification."

"Lord Yamada!" said Pertinax.

"On the balcony of observation," I said. "I thought he would observe, and presumably from such a place. Indeed, it was there that I was displayed long ago, that any concern the cavalry might have entertained with respect to my welfare might be dispelled."

"He is in full ceremonial regalia," said Tajima.

"I suspect," I said, "that this brief encounter, or something like it, that of dragon and shogun, would have been prearranged."

"Those with him," said Tajima, "seem to be crying out. Banners are lifted. Swords are raised in salute."

"They are probably cheering," I said, "but we cannot hear them."

"The dragon," said Tajima, "has spread its wings."

"Yes," I said.

The wings, of course, given the technology involved, were not necessary for flight, though I supposed they might provide some lift. They did move in flight, giving the illusion of propelling the great, mysterious, aerial beast. Do not all dragons have vast, fearful batlike wings? In a sense then, the wings were quite essential, to convey the illusion. Indeed, lacking wings, or seeming wings, this remarkable machine might not have been instantly identified, in the minds of thousands, with the fabled iron dragon of legend. In the psychology of war such a thing might rout armies.

"Lord Yamada raises his hand," said Pertinax.

"Rather grandly," I said.

"What is a state without theater?" said Pertinax.

"Do not object," I said. "Men often live in terms of symbols and gestures."

"And die similarly," said Pertinax.

"Yes," I said. "And worthily. What else so ennobles life? Without his symbols and gestures man has only the dumb succession of pointless seasons, the repetitive, meaningless cycles of insects, the vacuous rootings and ruttings of tarsks."

"He sweeps his hand toward the north," said Tajima.

"He is sending us on our way," said Pertinax.

"Then," I said, "we had best be gone."

"I suppose," said Pertinax, "with a bit of experimenting, we might blast the observation balcony off the wall of the palace."

"Probably," I said, "but our business lies in the north."

"What is in the north?" asked Pertinax.

"Yamada's armies," I said, "his camps and siege works."

"He thinks the dragon will destroy the holding of Temmu," said Pertinax.

"Let us suppose he is mistaken," I said.

I then slowly oriented the dragon toward the north. I would fly relatively low, and relatively slowly for a time, even, now and then, deviating from a direct route, that the nearby towns and villages might note our flight. Then, after a time, I found the northern road, and opened the throttle, so to speak, and, marked on the appropriate screen, the ground below rapidly slipped away.

Chapter Fifty-Four

The Dragon Has Flown

"I have not heard guards outside, for several days," said Tajima.

Substantially, we had not left our small redoubt since what we took to be the last passage hand. We had occasionally, glaives ready, opened the door briefly, to reconnoiter the corridor, which led to the main corridor on the western side of the palace. We had opened the door the first time on the second day of our isolation, near the twentieth Ahn, both to reconnoiter and to rid ourselves of the bodies of the two dead Kurii. We trusted that, at that time, little would be known of what, if anything, had transpired within the chamber of the Kurii. Whereas it would be known that we were no longer in our respective incarceration chambers and had neutralized two Ashigaru near the corridor entrance, little else would be known. For example, little was known at that time other than the fact that the door to the chamber of the Kurii was secured and that the iron dragon had flown north, presumably on its mission to deal out destruction to the holding of Temmu. Thus, from the point of view of Lord Yamada, it seemed his plans were being implemented although the Kurii were surely unresponsive. As the iron dragon was in flight, it seemed all was well from his point of view, that of the self-proclaimed Shogun of the Islands. And who but Kurii might manage the enormous mechanical beast? Who else might risk bringing such a dreadful thing forth from its lair? Who else might dare to pilot such a thing? And who else would have the skills to do so? Most likely it would be supposed that we had failed to obtain an entrance to the chamber of the Kurii, and had fled elsewhere. Perhaps we had obtained an entrance to the chamber of the Kurii and had perished within, and perhaps had been eaten. Some Kurii do feed on human. It is not that they are cannibals, no more than a human could be considered a cannibal if he fed on verr or tarsk. And if the Kurii were unresponsive, who would be so rash, at least upon reflection, to reprimand so large, unpredictable, and dangerous a form of life?

So, the first time we had opened the door, near the twentieth Ahn on the second night of our stay in the chamber, we had propped up the bodies of the two Kurii, with boards, behind the door, so it would appear, at first, they were standing in the portal. We then opened the door. As the corridor was still dark, as before, the apparent will of the Kurii was still being respected, that of the darkened corridor.

As we had met with no opposition, and encountered no sign of our enemy, we eased the two carcasses, supported as they were, outside the door. No dozens of arrows thudded into the bodies. We then returned to the chamber and closed and barred the door.

"This ruse will not be long effective," had said Pertinax.

"Perhaps until morning," I had said.

"The corridor was dark," said Tajima. "There was no arrow fire."

"Lamps will be brought," I said. "An inquiry will be made."

Although the two bodies had been arranged so as to suggest the semblance of life, an appearance which might be maintained almost indefinitely in the dark, even a casual perusal under better conditions, even from a distance, would quickly dispel that illusion.

We thought it unwise, as well as noisome, to keep the bodies longer in the chamber.

"There is no sign of the men of Yamada," had said Tajima.

"They are there, about, somewhere," I had said.

"Can they get at us in here?" had asked Tajima.

"Eventually," I said. "Not immediately."

"There is food and water," said Pertinax.

"Too," I said, "this chamber has been designed to resist forcible entry."

"How long will it be until they realize what has happened?" asked Tajima.

"On foot," I said, "days, but there will be message vulos, and Yamada has two tarns, one flown by Tyrtaios. If one or both are at the front, it will be much as with the message vulos."

"Do you think he knows now?" said Tajima.

"Probably not," I said.

"By morning?" said Pertinax.

"He should at least suspect by morning," I said.

"And when he knows?" said Pertinax.

"Then," I had said, "there will be lamps in the corridor."

This conversation had taken place, as suggested, days ago. There were now lamps in the corridor. The two dead Kurii had been dragged away by noon of the day following their placement. They were doubtless buried by now. The Pani tend to be fastidious about such things.

"It is amazing," had said Pertinax, turning back from the observation port, "you can fly the monstrosity."

"A dragon, in its way," I said, "can be beautiful, like a storm or fire."

"Jane is beautiful," he said.

"And Saru?" I asked.

"Perhaps," he said.

"I think," I said, "that at one time you would have thought her the most beautiful woman in the world."

"I was not then familiar with Gorean slaves," he said.

"She is now a Gorean slave," I said.

"A common slave," he said.

"Of course," I said.

"One amongst countless others," he said.

"But perhaps you would like to own her, the former Miss Margaret Wentworth, now a Gorean slave, and have her subject to your whip," I said.

"How is it that you can manage the device?" he said.

"In bondage," I said, "even a formerly plain woman can be beautiful."

I supposed this had to do with their then being in their place in nature, being owned and subject to a master.

"Margaret Wentworth," he said, "was mercenary, shallow, cheap, arrogant, dishonest, and untrustworthy."

"And beautiful," I said.

"Not bad looking," he said.

"And she is now in a collar, on Gor," I said.

"At least now," he said, "she has some value, what men will pay for her."

"And what would you pay for her?" I asked.

"A tarsk-bit," he said, "would be too much."

"Scarcely," I said.

"I do not see how you can control the dragon," he said.

"The central sphere is the major control device," I said. "I am familiar with sphere-guidance from a different venue, a different place, a different time. We shall experiment with the recessed switches when we are in the open, and less likely to be observed."

"Still," he said, "I am impressed."

"Remember," I said, "these controls have been designed for a visually oriented organism, and one presumably unfamiliar with the technology involved. Accordingly, they are designed to be easily understood and conveniently manipulated."

"What is this business about a visually oriented organism?" he said.

"Nothing," I said.

"I see," he said.

I pointed to one of the six screens. "That is the northern road," I said.

"Yes," he said.

"What is your plan, Tarl Cabot, tarnsman?" asked Tajima.

"We shall fly north," I said, "and greet the garrison of the holding of Temmu, and then we shall be about our business."

"And what is our business?" asked Tajima.

"The imperilment of the house of Yamada," I said.

"How long will it take to reach the holding of Temmu?" asked Pertinax.

"On foot, days, on tarnback, several Ahn," I said. "I expect that the dragon, if urgency were involved, could manage the matter in less than two Ahn, perhaps in a single Ahn."

"If urgency were involved?" said Pertinax.

"It is not," I said. "It is enough if we simply move with some swiftness, bringing to those on the ground some sense of the speed and power of the dragon."

"You are bargaining for maximum visibility," said Pertinax.

"The more the better," I said. "But, of course, of brief extent."

"As a cloud," said Tajima, "swiftly on its way, portending a storm."

"You freed Arashi," I said, "in the great road camp."

"I do not know if he managed to escape the camp," said Tajima.

"You spoke to him of the peasantry?" I said.

"Of course," said Tajima, "but only in allusions. I did not negotiate. I would not insult him, nor incite him."

"You bestowed his freedom as a gift," I said.

"Yes," said Tajima.

"What did he say?" I asked.

"He accepted it, and said nothing, and slipped away," said Tajima.

"He is an ungrateful, worthless cutthroat," said Pertinax.

"The peasant is conniving and greedy," said Tajima. "He is to be kept in his place with edged steel."

"But you freed Arashi," I said.

"One does something, and then one must wait to learn what one has done," said Tajima. "Is it not always the case?"

"The peasantry is a great beast," said Pertinax. "It is slow to wake, but dangerous when hungry and afoot."

"Under what conditions does the beast wake?" I asked.

"One supposes," said Tajima, "in times of destruction, of chaos and disorder."

"I think so," I said.

"And then," said Pertinax, "after the fire and the wind, the prowling and rending, the beast returns to its den, and once more there are only peasants, the beast forgotten, and the cycle begins again, the begetting and feeding, the living and dying, the planting, the tending, and harvesting."

We then continued on, in our flight, though we did not leave the small room, the vicinity of the simple console.

I think perhaps two Ahn elapsed.

"You will try the recessed switches?" said Tajima.

"Why not, now?" I said.

"Now?" said Pertinax.

"I will orient the dragon," I said, "toward the sea to the east."

"Ai!" cried Tajima.

"And now the other," I said.

"This thing is hideous," said Tajima. "It must be destroyed!"

Although we were placidly ensconced in a small room in the palace of Lord Yamada, we could sense from the screens, the shuddering of the dragon, as, first, a torrent of fire appeared on the forward screen, and, a moment later, it seemed a stream of light sped away, diminishing in the distance.

"What is that?" asked Pertinax.

"I do not know," I said. "I think it may be the trail of a projectile."

"When the dragon attacked the holding of Temmu, a wall was shattered," said Tajima.

"That suggests a projectile of some sort," I said.

"This is a terrible thing," said Tajima. "We must destroy it."

"First," I said, "the cause of Yamada must find itself beneath the shadow of its wings."

"Then!" said Tajima.

"Then," I said, "one must be very careful. One cannot simply crash it, or the secret of the dragon will be publicly revealed, that it is a mere contrivance."

"Take it to sea," said Pertinax, "and let the waves conceal it."

"The device conceals a forbidden technology," I said. "It must be armed in such a way, some way, to protect this technology from discovery and imitation."

"I would not be the one to try that door," said Pertinax.

"No," I said. "The device would doubtless self-destruct and simultaneously destroy its unwise interrogator."

"So, simply crash it into the sea," said Pertinax.

"That may be too obvious, and too simple, my dear friend," I said.

"How so?" said Pertinax.

"Kurii," I said, "have designed gigantic habitats in space, which house the remnants of warring communities, races or nations. They are familiar with weapons of enormous power. They are the masters of space flight. Surely they might use sophisticated devices to locate and retrieve a large object fallen into the sea. The arming devices, assuming they exist, as seems likely, might perhaps, with sufficient ingenuity, be neutralized.

Indeed, perhaps the very waters of Thassa herself might, after an Ehn, or after months or years, disarm the defensive devices presumably implanted in the machine. I, for one, do not know."

"What then is to be done?" asked Pertinax.

"If you were the masters of this technology," I said, "what would you do?"

"What?" said Pertinax.

"I would keep within my means the capacity of destroying it, remotely."

"Why would they do this?" asked Pertinax.

"Do you think they would trust Kurii?" I asked.

"No," said Pertinax.

"Doubtless the surveillance of those responsible for this technology is neither universal nor perfect," I said, "but I would think they, or, more likely, some small group involved in this matter, would have the means, electronic or otherwise, of tracking the dragon."

"Perhaps," said Pertinax.

"Would you give a loaded gun to a blood enemy?" I asked.

"No," said Pertinax.

"Why not?" I asked.

"I would be afraid he would turn it on me," said Pertinax.

"And therein," I said, "I think, lies the solution of our problem."

"I am not sure I understand," said Pertinax.

"Behold the front screen," said Tajima.

"There, in the distance," said Pertinax, "it is the holding of Temmu!"

"Below," I said, "is the south siege camp, that to the south of the holding."

"It is large," said Tajima.

"So, too, was the road camp to which we were taken by Kazumitsu," I said. "Other camps will be strategically located, to enable the encirclement of the mountain of the holding. The wharves, too, will be guarded, to prevent an escape by sea, even in small boats."

"Eventually," said Pertinax, "the holding is doomed."

"The dragon has not yet spoken," I said.

"See the trenches, the earthen walls, the redoubts, the guard posts," said Tajima.

"Yamada's generals," I said, "prior to the arrival of the dragon, might well fear a sortie from the holding."

"The dragon has now arrived," said Pertinax.

Such sorties from a besieged holding, city, or such, providing a sufficient number of troops is available, are not that uncommon. There have been numerous instances not only of the clash of armies before walled, besieged cities, sometimes almost daily, often involving challenges and conflicts of champions, but there is always the danger of destructive, nocturnal raids, designed to burn tents and spread panic, or, often, to disable or destroy siege engines, siege towers, and such. To be sure, in the present instance, siege towers were impractical, given the height and steepness of the escarpment surmounted by the holding of Temmu. Too, the garrison of the holding, given its slightness, would be unlikely to mount a sortie in force. Still the threat of raids, almost certainly under the cover of darkness, would not be discounted by the generals of Lord Yamada. Too, walls, trenches, frequent watch fires, and guards would be likely to minimize the escape from the holding of even small numbers of individuals. In short, under familiar circumstances, the almost impregnable security of the holding and the relative slightness of its garrison, one would expect a prolonged siege, perhaps for years, until hunger and thirst would force either the garrison to capitulate or the enveloping forces to withdraw. In such a situation, of course, the enveloping forces are likely to have the advantage, given the extent of their logistical base and the openness and stability of their supply lines. But, as before, one cannot always count on familiar circumstances. As earlier, the cavalry had forced the lifting of the siege, so now, it seemed, the iron dragon might render it unnecessary, demolishing the holding.

"What are you doing?" asked Tajima.

"At low altitude," I said, "I am going to circle the south camp, and the nearby siege works, three times."

"Maximum visibility?" said Pertinax.

"Maximum effect," I said. "People see with their hearts, with their fears and hopes, their beliefs and expectations, as well as their eyes. Seeing is a mysterious, complex business; it is not a matter of just opening one's eyes. An identical image may strike terror into one fellow and hearten and inspire another. One fellow may see what is not there, wanting to see it, and another not see what is there, even before him, as he does not want to see it."

"Some are fleeing," said Pertinax.

"Others are being rallied by officers," said Tajima.

"Many, now," said Pertinax, "seem to acclaim us, waving to us, lifting banners, brandishing glaives, as though to urge us on."

"It is much as it was at the palace of Yamada," said Tajima.

"They must remember the dragon's attack on the holding," said Pertinax.

"Even so," I said, "many will fear the dragon. Who can look into the heart of a dragon?"

"As you do not attack, and continue to circle," said Tajima, "surely many will lose their fear, and see the dragon as their ally, a monstrous beast who spreads its wings on behalf of the house of Yamada."

"That is my hope," I said.

"What if this hope, this optimism, this confidence, were to be dashed?" asked Tajima.

"Yes," I said, "what then?"

"You do war with the mind," said Pertinax.

"The mind is a dangerous weapon," I said. "It is never to be discounted."

Following the benign display of the dragon over the vast, southern camp, which we took, from its location, its proximity to the northern road, facilitating communications with, and the movement of supplies from, Yamada's heartland, to be the headquarters of the besieging forces, we moved, in a similarly serene and stately manner toward the holding of Temmu. It was easy for us to suppose the trepidation with which the garrison of the holding might view the dragon's approach, particularly given its earlier attack on the holding. That earlier attack, of course, had been more in the nature of a demonstration than an assault in earnest. Its purpose had been little more than to convince the house of Temmu that the dragon was dangerous, powerful, irresistible, and flew for Yamada. Now, however, the negotiations, the terms for surrender, the supposed guarantees of safety for the garrison, and such, had been concluded. The shogun, Temmu, and his daimyos, Lords Nishida and Okimoto, predictably, had refused to evacuate the holding. Lord Yamada's ultimatum had been issued, and rejected, and this now was the third day, toward noon, following the rejection of the ultimatum, the day on which the iron dragon was to take to the sky. The holding would be his, or it would cease to exist, had said Lord Yamada. Walls will crumble, the mountaintop will be black, ashes will blow out to sea, he had said. I could see the rationale of this decision. Lord Temmu would destroy the holding before allowing it to fall into the hands of Lord Yamada. That being the case, why might not the iron dragon strike? Surely Lord Yamada would not care for the inconvenience, the delay, and the economic hardships of maintaining a second siege, perhaps lasting years, to obtain a prize which would be destroyed before it could be grasped.

Dalliance was unacceptable.

"Terror courses the walls of the holding," said Tajima.

"We will circle, three times," I said, "as we did at the southern camp."

"Some flee," said Pertinax, "seeking shelter. In the courtyard some fists are raised, and shaken. Others threaten us with futile weapons."

"I see arrows looping upward," said Tajima.

"Some may strike the dragon," I said, "but we will be unaware of the sound of such contacts."

"Had they Yamada's great bow, that in the valley, its missiles might reach us," said Pertinax.

"But without effectiveness," I said. "The hide of the dragon is plated with scales of steel. It would be as unavailing as an angry, absurd straw flung against a cliff of stone."

"Perhaps they will raise the banners of truce, and beg for mercy," said Pertinax.

"No," said Tajima. "They are warriors."

"Still," said Pertinax.

"They are pledged to their daimyos," I said, "and their daimyos to the shogun."

"Still," said Pertinax.

"What mercy," I said, "the mercy of Yamada?"

"True," said Pertinax, grimly.

"And who," asked Tajima, "would sue a dragon for mercy?"

"Perhaps Lord Temmu will engage the cavalry," said Pertinax.

"The cavalry is no longer a minion of the house of Temmu," I said. "It is an independent arm, a sovereign force."

"It may be committed," said Tajima, "even if the engagement be suicidal."

"At best," said Pertinax, "the cavalry could do little more than attack the cameras, little more than blind the dragon."

"The success of such an attack would be unlikely," I said, "if the dragon chose to defend itself. Too, I would suspect that the cameras are either shielded or inconspicuous."

"Still," said Tajima, "the cavalry might fling itself upon the dragon, however madly, however futilely."

"It will not do so," I said. "Before leaving the holding, on our venture south, I transmitted orders to Torgus and Lysander."

"You explicitly forbade such an engagement?" asked Pertinax.

"Certainly," I said.

"We have now completed the second circle," I said. "By now the forces of Temmu should be alarmed or resigned, and those of Yamada reassured and inspirited."

"You are counting on the awe and superstition of the common soldier?" said Tajima.

"And many who are less common," I said, "for example, high officers, even generals, even the shogun, Lord Temmu, and his daimyo, Lord Okimoto."

"Many believe in the iron dragon," said Pertinax.

"Or do not disbelieve," I said. "Remember, few have inspected the dragon closely. In the minds of almost all it is not a device, not a machine, however complex and formidable; it is a gigantic, living beast, a startling, monstrous, fabulous, terrifying creature, hinted at in a thousand legends, employed even to frighten children. And those who did not believe now need only lift their eyes to the sky and behold the spread of these mighty wings, the thing come alive, as from nowhere."

"It is a machine," said Pertinax.

"Few will understand that," I said. "Priest-Kings and Kurii guard their secrets well."

"So most," said Tajima, "will see it as a living being."

"And no ordinary living being," I said, "simply large and

dangerous, but rather a mysterious being, come from unknown worlds, come with obscure intent, a being both purposeful and portentous. The beat of its wings drives the currents of destiny; its approbation dignifies and ennobles houses; its frown foretells stricken futures. It is a thousand times more potent than the patterns of bones and shells."

"And now?" said Tajima.

"Now," I said, "the third circle is complete, and it is the house of Temmu which the dragon has examined and not harmed. It is that house which it has saluted, that house which it has taken beneath its wing."

"The holding stands," said Tajima.

"And now the dragon turns south," said Pertinax.

My hand hesitated for a moment, and then reached toward the recessed switches.

"I have not heard guards outside, for several days," said Tajima.

"Nor I," I said.

"They must be there," said Pertinax.

"I do not know," I said.

"What is going on, beyond the door?" said Pertinax.

"We cannot stay here forever," I said.

"It is seventeen days," said Tajima, "since the iron dragon visited the forces of Yamada in the north."

"That is enough time," I said, "for whatever was to happen to have happened."

"What happened is one thing," I said, "whatever it may be. Why it happened is another thing."

"Would Lord Yamada know?" asked Pertinax.

"What he knows," I said, "is likely to be little different from what is known by thousands of others, namely, that the iron dragon favored the house of Temmu, and then disappeared, perhaps to return to its mysterious realm of origin."

After the attack on the south camp and the siege works associated with it, I had circled about the mountain of the holding, burning hundreds of tents, blasting earthen ramparts, and pouring fire into better than a hundred trenches. Following this, I had turned the dragon east, and, over Thassa, set a course as directly as I could for the Sardar Mountains, the supposed domicile of the gods of Gor, the Priest-Kings. It had been my supposition, first, that the path of the dragon would be monitored by whatever group was responsible for its existence, and, second, that there would be a provision implicit in the thing itself for its destruction. As I had indicated earlier, no one would be likely to put a lethal weapon into the hands of a blood enemy, for it might be turned on one. Presumably then a provision would be in place to protect the donor or supplier against this most unpleasant possibility. What I did not know were the parties or arrangements involved in the construction of, and management of, the dragon. Given the disunity of the steel worlds I doubted that it would be more than one administration of one such world, if that, which would be involved on the part of the Kurii. I was much less certain about the involvement of the hierarchy of the Nest, largely determined by order of birth, in the matter. I suspected, but did not know, that the possible wager, or game, having to do with the surface of Gor, assuming it existed, was not a congenial, approved stratagem of the hierarchy as a whole, but that it would more likely be the stratagem of an aggressive faction within the hierarchy, acting on its own, and possibly secretly. If the latter conjecture was warranted, it would be important to that faction not to be discovered, at least prior to the success of its efforts. If that was the case, I suspected the dragon would be destroyed almost as soon as it was determined it was no longer behaving as expected. Indeed, the matter would seem far more urgent and dire once it was clearly turned toward the Sardar. In such a case there could be no triumphant result of a successful experiment with which to regale a world or a hierarchy, or portions thereof, supposedly having resolved a controversy of generations, but a clear threat to the Sardar itself, perhaps mounted by Kurii. If the hierarchy as a whole was a party to the wager, or game, so to speak, I would expect a delayed reaction to the dragon's inexplicable behavior and change of course, one perhaps involving inquiries, consultation, and such; on the other hand, I expected the reaction would be precipitate if a clandestine faction were involved, which, first, would be tracking the dragon closely, and thus would be almost instantly alerted to these surprising changes in its behavior, and, two, might fear a premature exposure as plotters, and failed plotters, rather than receiving an eventual acclamation as visionary public servants.

"What are you doing?" had asked Pertinax.

"The iron dragon," I had said, "has done its work. It is also a dangerous device. I think it best if it now disappears."

"That is Thassa beneath it," said Tajima.

"I see fishing boats," said Pertinax.

"Where are you taking it?" asked Pertinax.

"Have you heard of the Sardar?" I asked.

"I know little about it," he said. "I have heard of it. It is the home of the mythical Priest-Kings, is it not?"

"Perhaps they are not mythical," I said.

"You are laying in a course for the Sardar?" asked Pertinax.

"What happened?" cried Tajima.

The six screens had suddenly gone black.

"I was," I said.

"How can you guide the dragon now?" had asked Pertinax.

"It is no longer there to guide," I had said.

"I do not understand," had said Pertinax.

"The dragon," I had said, "is dead."

"Lord Yamada doubtless feels betrayed by the dragon," said Tajima.

"Perhaps by Kurii," I said.

"The two Kurii are dead," said Pertinax. "We killed them."

"Were there more than two?" I asked. "Did one or more others kill the two? Did others appear? Did others kill the two, and then interfere?"

"He would not know," said Tajima.

"I do not think he supposes we are involved," I said. "Presumably we could not overcome Kurii, and, even if so, presumably we would be unable to manage the device. No, Kurii, other Kurii, would by far be the more likely conjecture."

"It has been seventeen days," said Tajima.

"I do not wish to remain here indefinitely," said Pertinax.

"Nor I," I said. "Open the door."

Chapter Fifty-Five

A Woman Flees Before Us;
We Encounter a Prisoner

"When we reconnoitered before," said Pertinax, "there were lamps in the corridor. Now it is dark again."

"I do not understand," I said.

"It is quiet," said Tajima.

"Nodachi," said Pertinax, "said, 'Beware of silence'."

"Arrows make little noise," said Tajima.

"We will be careful," I said.

We edged slowly down the corridor, until we reached the main corridor on the west side of the palace.

"There is some light here," I said.

"It is dim," said Tajima.

The main corridor stretched out on both sides, and, as far as we could tell, was empty.

"Someone must have tended the lamp," said Pertinax.

"But when?" said Tajima

"I suspect that there is little oil left in the lamp," I said.

"Should there not be guards here?" asked Pertinax, grasping the glaive he carried, looking about.

"There were before," I said.

"Where are they?" asked Tajima.

"I do not know," I said.

"Seventeen days," said Tajima.

"We need an informant," I said.

"What are we to do?" asked Tajima.

"We will attempt to locate Nodachi and Haruki," I said, "and then attempt to make contact with Ichiro, and the tarns, and then take flight north."

"Nodachi will not go with us," said Tajima.

"He must," I said.

"He will not," said Tajima.

"Why not?" I asked.

"He wishes to kill Lord Yamada," said Tajima.

"That plan failed," I said.

"One does not need a plan," said Tajima. "One needs only a sword and Lord Yamada."

"Lord Yamada may not even be in the palace," I said.

"Nor Nodachi, now," said Pertinax.

"I think the corridor is empty," said Pertinax, peering into the gloom.

"Let us search for Nodachi, and Haruki," I said. "They are not likely to be on the fifth level."

We spoke softly.

But I had the sense that if we were to shout, our voices would have rung in the corridor.

We moved softly, but, still, it seemed we could hear our footsteps.

It seemed a hollow sound.

The small lamp, behind us, as we passed it, went out.

Pertinax spun about, glaive lowered.

"Steady, friend," I said. "Its fuel was exhausted."

"Why was its fuel low?" asked Tajima.

"I do not know," I said.

"It should have been tended," said Tajima.

"Yes," I said. "But it seems it was not."

"Why?" asked Tajima.

"I do not know," I said. "It would be gratifying to encounter an informant. The stairs are at the end of the corridor."

"Hold!" I cried.

We had descended to the second level of the palace, and had encountered no one, until this moment.

She had turned about, several yards before us, and faced us, momentarily, seemed for a moment glad, even overjoyed, and then her expression turned to fear, and she turned and ran.

"Would that I had a bola," I said.

"It is a female, she would be simple enough to pursue," said Pertinax.

I thrust out my arm, abruptly, and halted him, in midstride.

"No!" I said. "Do not pursue her."

"As you wish," said Pertinax, puzzled. "Might she not constitute our needed informant?"

"Perhaps, perhaps not," I said. "In pursuing her you would pass opened chambers, which might not, as the others, be empty. You might rush about a blind corner, to encounter glaives or bows. She may be a decoy girl, a lure girl."

"I do not think so," said Pertinax.

"Nor I," I said, "but I do not choose to risk your life on the matter."

"She seems no slave," said Tajima.

"She is briefly and ill-clad," said Pertinax.

"But not slave-clad," said Tajima. "She wears no tunic."

"Barefoot, and little but a rag clutched about her," said Pertinax.

"But no tunic, or no remnant of a tunic," said Tajima.

There are various garments which slaves, when permitted clothing, must wear. Usually they are brief and revealing, little more than mockeries of a garmenture, garments appropriate for their debased condition, that of property girls, that of owned objects. But in all their variations, which may be manifold, such garmentures clearly identify their occupant as a slave. It would not do, at all, to confuse one with a free woman. Indeed, on the continent, it can be a capital offense for a slave to don the garments of a free woman. The free woman would not stand for it, and free men would not permit it. They enjoy seeing slaves clad as slaves. As the slaves are owned, why should men not have them clad as they wish, clad for the pleasure and delectation of men? And the slave, once she understands that she is truly a slave, even to the mark and collar, delights in such things, delights in her display, delights in her frank, honest, shameless exhibition and brazen exposure, that in which she has no choice and to which she dare not object, even should she wish to do so. How else could a woman be more herself, more radically female, than as slave? The hatred borne by free women to helpless slaves is legendary. What was of interest was that the woman, of whom we had caught a brief glimpse in the corridor, though barefoot and half naked, was not tunicked, or comparably clad, as a slave. She clutched about her, in her flight, no more than a simple cloth, which might have been derived from any number of possible origins, even from the shreds of more refined habiliments.

"I think that is a free woman," said Tajima.

"Too ill-clothed," said Pertinax.

"Even so," said Tajima.

"Free or slave," I said, "she may be a lure girl."

"I do not think so," said Tajima.

"Let us not wager our lives on the matter," I said.

"In any event," said Pertinax, "she is gone now."

"Slaves were shackled in the basement," I said. "If there is slave housing there, shackle rings or pens, there may be cells, as well."

"The palace is deserted," said Pertinax.

"It seems so," I said. There was debris here and there in the halls, unthinkable in a Pani dwelling, even discarded scrolls, some torn, and some blackened with soot, as though partly burned.

Tajima lifted up a charred painting, on a wooden panel, of a delicate forest scene, with a pond, and cranes. "This is barbarism," he said.

"Hatred," I said, "is often blind."

"I do not understand the desertion of the palace," said Pertinax.

"It may not be deserted," I said. "Here are stairs. Have your weapons ready."

"Yes," said Tajima. "These are holding areas."

"But they are empty," I said.

We had passed walls, with inserted slave rings, and by each ring a mat, and blanket.

In some cases there was a half-eaten bowl of rice near a mat.

"The slaves are gone," had said Tajima.

"They have been freed," said Pertinax.

"Do not be foolish, friend," I said. "Either they have been moved, as one might herd a flock of verr to a new location, or they have been stolen."

"'Stolen'?" said Pertinax.

"Of course," I said, "they are properties, slaves."

"I see," said Pertinax.

"It would be only a change of collars, and masters, for them," I said.

"Excellent," said Pertinax.

On the continent there is a familiar saying, that only a fool frees a slave girl. Indeed, in the frequent wars amongst cities, in the waxings and wanings of victories, in the advancing and receding tides of conflict, it is not unusual that a woman captured from one city and routinely enslaved may on another day, in the fortunes of raiding and war, fall into the hands of men of her original city. She is not then liberated. That would be unthinkable. One can see the mark on her thigh, and note the collar on her neck. She has been spoiled for freedom. She will be kept as a slave, for that is what she now is. Normally, she will be sold out of her original city, unless perhaps someone, say, a formerly spurned suitor, wishes to buy her.

"The pens, and cages, and slave boxes, were empty, too," said Tajima.

"And the cells, as well," said Pertinax. "Their doors are all ajar."

"I see one," I said, "which is not."

Tajima and Pertinax hurried to the closed door.

"Slide back the panel first," I warned them.

I did not wish them to fling open a door behind which might wait a drawn bow, a raised knife.

"Ah!" cried Tajima.

Tajima and Pertinax slipped back the four bolts. The door was then swung back.

Tajima and Pertinax then bowed. "Master," they said, heads lowered.

Nodachi rose to his feet, stiffly, and returned their bow.

"Does Lord Yamada yet live?" he asked.

"I do not know, Master," said Tajima.

"We must learn," said Nodachi.

I looked into the cell. There was some water left in the shallow cistern to the right, little more than a puddle on the floor. I saw no food.

"Most cells are empty," I said.

"Prisoners were freed," said Nodachi.

"But you were not," I said.

"I declined," said Nodachi. "I did not regard it meet to be freed by such as they."

I found it difficult to understand the sensibility involved, but proprieties are often subtle and elusive. Perhaps one was to be fastidious with respect to favors received. Some debts are perhaps best not incurred.

"Who are 'they', noble one?" I inquired.

"Peasants," he said.

"In the palace?" said Tajima.

"Storming, and rampaging about," said Nodachi. "I fear there was much discourtesy, perhaps even theft and vandalism."

"I fear there was, Master," said Tajima.

"Where were the soldiers, the officers, and Ashigaru?" asked Pertinax.

"I do not know," said Nodachi.

"I am sure they will return," I said.

"Wild may be the peasants," said Tajima, "but they did not burn the palace."

"The palace is the seat of the shogun," said Nodachi. "They feared to do so."

"Perhaps you are hungry," I said.

"One meditates," said Nodachi, "but the stomach is an unwilling partner."

"I saw rice outside, some rice, Master," said Tajima, "by the slave rings."

This was true, and it suggested that the slaves had been moved precipitously, or, as the case might have been, seized and carried away precipitately.

"Perhaps you will bring me a little," said Nodachi.

"But it is the rice of slaves, Master," said Tajima.

"We will not tell the stomach," said Nodachi.

"Yes, Master," said Tajima.

"Even amongst the higher orders," said Nodachi, "it is said that some eat the rice of slaves."

Tajima hurried from the cell, to fetch rice.

"Tajima, Pertinax, and I have been detained, so to speak, for several days," I said. "We know little of what has occurred."

"*Ela*, my friend," said Nodachi, smiling, looking about, "I, too, have been detained."

Tajima returned shortly with two heaping bowls of rice, presumably the result of pooling the meager contents left behind in several of the small slave bowls we had noted earlier.

Nodachi first offered us the rice, but we politely refused.

I thought, he must be starving.

Nodachi then sat down, cross-legged, and, using his fingers, fed.

He did this calmly, and without haste, in a seemly manner.

"We shall leave the door open," I said, "and you may exit, or not, as you wish."

Nodachi, not rising, inclined his head, politely.

"We hope to venture north," I said. "It is our hope that you will accompany us."

"That is wise," said Nodachi. "Do not delay on my account."

"Come with us," I said.

"I have an audience with Lord Yamada," said Nodachi.

"Is he aware of this audience?" I asked.

"It is my hope that he suspects," said Nodachi. "I would prefer that."

"The palace is deserted," I said.

"That is unlikely," he said.

"The peasants have gone," I said.

"They fear the return of troops," said Nodachi.

"Troops may not be returning," I said.

"What does not exist may still be feared," he said.

"Lord Yamada," I said, "may not be in the palace."

"It is the seat of the shogun," said Nodachi.

"I think we will delay our departure," I said.

"Do not do so on my account," he said.

"We will do so on our account," I said.

"Is that wise?" he said.

"One is not always wise," I said.

Nodachi set aside the last of the two bowls from which he had fed, and rose to his feet, smiled, and bowed graciously.

"We shall require weapons," he said, "something more suitable than glaives and *tantos*."

"Perhaps there is an arsenal," said Tajima.

"Peasants will have taken everything of value," said Pertinax.

"Only what they can find," said Nodachi. "Only what they did not fear to touch."

"I do not understand," I said.

"There will be a trophy room," said Nodachi.

Chapter Fifty-Six

We Obtain an Informant

"Oh!" she cried, seized.

I turned her about, and saw that she was comely.

I thought this a natural place to find her, or another. Surely our seemingly frightened wraith in the corridor, she who had fled from us, seemingly so distraught, earlier on the second level of the palace, might still be in the palace. If she was a free woman, as we speculated, she might in such times fear to leave the building. In a time of peril even its hazards might seem preferable to those of the outer grounds or the open country, which might be roamed by raiding peasants, by bandits, by renegades, by hungry, desperate soldiers, like animals, freed of the rod of discipline. It was the kitchen of an Ashigaru guard station within the palace itself. Might there not be scraps of food in such a place, even scrapings from the sides of garbage bins? Might not such locations then be frequented by such an individual, or individuals, trying to survive like urts in the collapse of a society or civilization? I had located it and other such facilities in my peregrinations about the palace before my escape with Haruki, after the incident of the eel pool and the straw jackets. I had set Pertinax and Tajima separately on their way about the palace, searching for weapons. I did not know where Nodachi might be, but I suspected he was searching for a trophy room, wherever it might be, whatever it might be. I had seized her from behind, and then turned her about.

"Yes," I said, looking down into her terrified, uplifted eyes, "you are beautiful. You are worthy of a collar."

"A collar?" she said.

"Of course," I said.

"No, no!" she wept. "I am a free woman!"

We had speculated that this might be the case.

"Perhaps you are a slave," I said. "Perhaps I shall have you strip yourself before me, that your body may be examined for a slave mark."

"No!" she said. "I am a free woman. I am Lady Kameko, of the household of the shogun!"

"You are a lure girl," I said, "with confederates."

"No," she said. "I am alone!"

Now, that seemed quite likely to me, after Pertinax, Tajima, and I had explored so much of the palace, which now seemed barren and empty, unkempt, and deserted.

"If you are not a lure girl," I said, "why did you flee from us, on the second level?"

"First I thought you were Ashigaru, returned to restore order, and rejoiced, but then I saw that you, and another, two of the three, were barbarians, and I was afraid, and fled."

"You claim to be a free woman," I said.

"I am a free woman!" she said. "Lady Kameko, of the household of the shogun!"

"Perhaps you are a mere contract woman," I said, "whose contract may change hands, and be bought and sold, much as though you might be a slave."

"No," she said, "I am a free woman, and a free woman of the higher orders."

"Considering your garmenture," I said, "I find that hard to believe."

"Upon the departure of soldiers," she said, "peasants, laughing, curious, angry, riotous, streamed into the palace. They fell upon me, tore away my clothing, threw me to the tiles, and used me, several, like rutting tarsks, as a vessel for their pleasure."

She squirmed in my hands.

"But you are clothed now," I said.

"The beasts ransacked the palace," she said. "Perhaps their simple women are now clothed in the kimonos, the sashes, the obis, and silks, of fine ladies. I found the shred of a garment, and put it about me."

"You are well-featured and trimly formed," I said. "I think you might sell as a slave."

"What are you going to do with me?" she said.

"You inquire as to your fate?" I said.

"Yes!" she said.

"You are a helpless prisoner, and beautiful," I said. "Speculate."

She turned her head to the side.

"I fear the men of Temmu march south," she said.

"It is possible," I said.

She looked up at me. "I must not fall into their hands!" she wept.

"Perhaps," I said, "you have already done so."

"No!" she cried. "Have mercy! I am a free woman!"

"As of now," I said.

I then pulled her by the upper right arm out into the hall.

"Tajima, Pertinax!" I called. "To me! To me! We have found our informant!" I also added, for good measure, several other names, choosing them at random. I thought this a good thing to do, as it would suggest that our party was a strong one, consisting of several men. That, I thought, might discourage inquiry, or attack.

Chapter Fifty-Seven

We Gather Intelligence;
We Look Forward to a Decent Meal;
We Wish to Find Nodachi;
We Will Search for a Particular Room

"You will kneel here," I said. I helped her kneel, easing her into place, as I had thonged her wrists together behind her back. "As you are a free woman," I said, "you may kneel with your knees closely together."

It is common on the continent to interrogate slaves in a kneeling position. Indeed, slaves are often in a kneeling position before free persons, unless busied about their duties. Indeed, some masters prefer for the girl to be prone, or supine, or lying on their side, facing them. It depends on the master. Binding the slave's hands behind her back, of course, emphasizes her helplessness, and helps her to keep clearly in mind that she is a slave, wholly subject to free persons. One would not be likely, of course, on the continent, to subject a free woman to such an indignity, unless one had a collar in mind for her.

"This, my friends," I said, "is a free woman, an exalted high lady, one of the sort to whom you would, in the normal course of things, not dare to lift your eyes, the Lady Kameko, of the household of Lord Yamada."

"Of the hated household of Lord Yamada," snarled Tajima.

"Would you care to be stripped, my dear?" I asked her.

"No!" she said.

"You are to be interrogated," I said. "You are a woman, before men, so straighten your body."

"Perhaps I do not choose to do so," she said.

"Would you prefer to do so," I said, "before, or after, you have been stripped and lashed?"

She straightened her body.

Men wish women to be beautiful. Is the beauty of women not one of the pleasures of men?

The slave, for example, is required to be as beautiful as possible before men, even before a hated master, as well as, naturally, graceful, obedient, deferent, and submissive.

And as a woman is graceful, obedient, deferent, and submissive, soon she finds herself graceful, obedient, deferent, and submissive.

"To me," I said, to Tajima and Pertinax, "she seems quite attractive, indeed, particularly lovely, but I am no fit judge of Pani beauty." I turned to Tajima. "What do you think?" I asked.

"Fit for a secondary, or tertiary, slave block," he said, "in a village market."

Her eyes flashed with fury.

"I have fashioned a rope leash here," I said. "Would you care to put it on her?"

"With pleasure," said Tajima.

It was doubtless the first time the Lady Kameko had been leashed.

"Now, dear lady," I said, "I and my confreres have been for several days out of the palace, so to speak, though, interestingly, in the palace. As a consequence, much must have ensued in our absence, so to speak. You will speak clearly, openly, fully, truthfully, and, as you are a woman and a captive, modestly and deferentially. We wish to know, in detail, what has recently transpired. You will answer any question put to you to the best of your ability. If we suspect you are holding anything back, or lying, you will be punished for any such indiscretion precisely as would be a slave. Is that understood?"

"Yes," she said.

After the attack of the iron dragon on the camps and the siegeworks of Lord Yamada in the north there was, as we would have supposed, a great deal of consternation and confusion. A thousand rumors must have sped about the islands. It seems that Tyrtaios and his colleague, the two tarnsmen at the disposal of Lord Yamada, had been held at the palace, and the first information pertaining to the new, startling developments in the north were a result of the communications borne by several message vulos. These reports, certainly at first, given the confusion at the front, the haste with which they were drafted, and the limitations on content imposed by the nature of the small, swift carriers, as well as the contradictory nature of some of these accounts, seemed to have created little more than alarm and perplexity in the south. Despite Lord Yamada's announcements of a great victory in the north, it soon became clear that his armies had been thrown into disarray. This was less because of any damage, however severe, wrought by the dragon, than the fact that the attack had taken place. The iron dragon, it seemed, had withdrawn from the cause of Yamada and espoused that of the house of Temmu. This matter, of course, went far beyond the physical details of a brief military engagement. It was as though there had been a cosmic shift in allegiances, as though the world itself had turned its back on Lord Yamada. The dice of the future had rolled awry; the very cards of destiny had proved unpropitious. It was as though a thousand castings of the bones and shells had uniformly rattled, in a thousand holdings, a knell of doom against the house of Yamada. Terror had been cast into the hearts of thousands of brave men, men who would face a common, charging, comprehensible foe with readiness and resolve, with bow and lowered glaives, but who had no heart to withstand the singular and incomprehensible, the mysterious, unnatural, and weird. Into such realms arrows do not fly; no steel blade can halt the coming of darkness, the fall of night.

Daimyos deserted the shogun, withdrawing their men, hurrying to their own holdings. Units melted away; supplies were abandoned. The road to the south was filled with disorganized, routed troops, with stragglers and refugees. Many had now passed even beyond the grounds of the Yamada heartland, continuing to move further south. Who would dare to attempt to hold, or stop, such desperate, frightened men? In the confusion, the chaos, and disorder, in the sudden disarrangements of power, in the lapse of authority, peasants rose, many following a charismatic leader named Arashi, himself of the peasants. The beast in the hearts of men had broken its tether, and was now afoot, free, prowling, and ravening.

Lord Yamada had sent Tyrtaios north to apprise him of the situation, but he had returned only days later, with dire reports and small comfort. Later he, and his colleague, took flight, it was rumored to pledge their swords to the house of Temmu, to which house they had seemingly been long devoted, and in whose interest they had labored secretly.

Five days ago Yamada's household troops, most of his staff, his wives, his chattels, verr, tarsks, and slaves, had been moved south.

Three days ago the deserted palace had been overrun by looting, riotous peasants.

The location of Lord Yamada, and perhaps that of some of his closest associates, who might have remained with him, was not known.

Lady Kameko feared, but did not know, that contingents of Lord Temmu were advancing south. Certainly the common wisdoms of war would recommend such an action. One expects the wise commander to press an advantage, allowing his foe no respite. Whereas the forces at the disposal of Lord Temmu were small compared to those which had maintained the siege in the north, the variables involved in the equations of war had changed dramatically. The thousands of Lord Yamada were disorganized and routed, in chaotic retreat, unnerved by panic and superstition, having no stomach for standing against an enemy on whose behalf had flown the iron dragon. Who would choose to hold ground or counterattack under a sky in which might suddenly appear the stern, beating wings of fate's implement, a gigantic dragon sprung alive from legend and myth, capable of palpable arson and destruction, appearing in a world where the canvas over one's head might burst into flame, where trenches could be flooded with fire as with water, and where the very stones of one's path might glow and melt before one's eyes?

I was not clear, of course, whether Lord Temmu would pursue his advantage or not. He tended to be a cautious and defensively minded commander. In Daichi's absence, who now would read the bones and shells for him? Lord Nishida, I was sure, would urge pursuit; Lord Okimoto, I suspected, would advise restraint, until intelligence, and more intelligence, and more intelligence, might be gathered. Lords Nishida and Okimoto had at their disposal, from the continent, something like three hundred and fifty Pani warriors, and some eleven hundred barbarian mercenaries and mariners. Lord Temmu had some two thousand warriors. As nearly as I could estimate the matter, from the outside, so to speak, the house of Temmu, altogether, could muster something in the neighborhood of thirty-five hundred men. This might, of course, be supplemented by deserters from the house of Yamada, new recruitings of Ashigaru from the northern villages, and, possibly, the pledges of hitherto uncommitted daimyos, and, even, possibly, those of daimyos who, in the light of recent developments, might withdraw their support from the house of Yamada. The role of the cavalry in all this was not clear, and it had remained a substantially independent force since the betrayal of its commander to the house of Temmu's foe, Lord Yamada. I conjectured it might fly somewhere in the neighborhood of fifty tarns. It was difficult to know if one or more tarns might have been lost, or recaptured. Fifty tarns, of course, might provide invaluable intelligence, telling attacks at carefully selected points, and, equipped with flame vases, threaten any number of structures, even the palace of Lord Yamada itself, with relative impunity.

It remained unclear at this point, of course, whether or not Lord Temmu would seize the tempo of war and invest troops in consolidating his advantage, and, if so, in what numbers.

"Why did you remain in the palace?" I asked the Lady Kameko.

"Contingents, different parties," she said, "left at different times. We were to be in separate groups."

"That some groups might elude pursuit," I said.

"Perhaps," she said

"Your group was then to leave," I said.

"I was frightened," she said. "I went as far as the gate. The others were hurrying. Soldiers escorted them. We were to travel lightly. My ornaments were left behind. I hurried back to fetch them. I bundled them. When I came again to the gate, the others were gone, and I saw soldiers, not in formation, on the road. I was alone. I dared not present myself to them. They did not seem men under appropriate discipline. I was a woman. I was afraid. I hurried back, into the palace, to hide, and I have been afraid to leave it."

"I think, perhaps," I said, "you did not wish to leave the palace, that you were afraid to do so, and, accordingly, neglected to bring your belongings, this providing an excuse to return for them, and, incidentally, to lose contact with your supposed escape group."

"Surely not!" she exclaimed.

"What of your ornaments?" I said.

"Peasants took them," she said, bitterly.

"And, it seems, your clothing, as well."

"Yes!" she said.

"Most slaves are better clothed than you," I said.

"I was at the mercy of ravaging, greedy beasts," she said.

"Perhaps you would prefer a garment which might be somewhat more concealing," I said.

"Yes," she said, "please, please!"

"The tunic of a slave," said Tajima.

"No!" she said. "Never, never that!"

Pertinax laughed, and Lady Kameko, shrinking back, looked at him, uneasily.

"Body!" I snapped.

Instantly she straightened her body.

The responses of a female captive, as those of a female slave, are to be unquestioning and immediate. Men have little patience with a female captive, and, less, indeed, little or none, with a female slave. I conjectured that the Lady Kameko may have owned slaves, and would have promptly attended to their condign punishment, given the least infringement of her will or pleasure.

Tears had sprung to her eyes.

"What do you conjecture to be the fate of your ornaments, and, say, your silks?" I asked.

I thought it well for Pertinax and Tajima to be apprised of certain matters, extracted from the recent biography of Lady

Kameko, and how better could they be so apprised than by means of Lady Kameko herself. Too, I thought it well for Lady Kameko, on her knees, and clad as she was, to supply this information. Let her, so situated and so clad, despite what trepidation she might feel, speak openly and clearly of these matters, of her fate at the hands of peasants, of what had been done to her, of her reduction, humiliation, and debasement, of her treatment as no more than a slave, knowing full well how free men might then view her, particularly free men of the enemy, how they might, say, glance at her now-bared throat, seeing it inevitably as an attractive mounting point for a suitable, circular metal enhancement.

"I do not know," she said. "They may have been sold in the far towns. Some of the ornaments may have been buried, to be sold later. Perhaps both the ornaments and silks now adorn uncouth tarsks, the homely, gross women of doltish peasants."

I recalled Aiko.

She had not seemed to me homely, gross, or such. To be sure, I did not know her antecedents. In her village she had been one of Eito's work slaves. He had unclaimed her, before Nodachi. As a slave, then, she was subject to the claim, and possession, of any free person who might care to make such a claim. To be sure, few knew her to be unclaimed. We had left her with Ichiro, that she might not compromise certain efforts upon which we might venture.

"The interests and appetites of the peasants, as I understand it," I said, "were not to be fully satisfied by the mere appropriation of jewelry, clothing, and such."

"No!" she said.

"Speak," I said.

"Please, no!" she said.

"Now," I said.

"My back and belly, and knees, are sore from the tiles on which I was used," she said. "I was stripped, put to the floor, handed about!"

"Excellent," said Tajima, "high lady, of the hated house of Yamada."

"Tarsk!" she said.

He jerked her from her knees to her belly, and drew her to

him, turning and twisting, thrashing about, across the floor, by the rope leash. He then seized her hair, and forced her head up, to regard him. She was terrified. "Beware," he said, "I may not be pleased."

"I am a free woman!" she said. "Ai!" she sobbed, his hand twisting in her hair. "Forgive me," she said.

I lifted her away from Tajima, and replaced her before us. She was shaken.

She pulled a little at her wrists, thonged together behind her back. The rope leash was still on her neck.

"You are fortunate, that you are not a slave," I said, "not yet a slave."

Pertinax laughed, and she cast him a frightened glance. I wondered if he might want a Pani slave. She was quite beautiful. If he did not want her, he could always sell her. I thought that Tajima's disparaging conjecture as to a secondary, or tertiary, block in a village market was less than realistic.

"Are there others, like you, hiding in the palace?" I asked.

It seemed likely to me that this might be the case. Some, I supposed, might have feared to join the escape parties, risking the open country, and, surely, might not have anticipated the entry of peasantry into the august corridors of the shogun's palace.

"I think so," she said. "The palace is vast and the rooms many."

"Free women?" I asked.

"Yes," she said, "the slaves were taken away."

"There will be collars enough for all of them," said Tajima.

"Please, let me go," she said.

"You are too beautiful to free," I said.

"Surely you know what you are," said Tajima.

"What?" she said.

"Booty," he said.

"No!" she said.

"Suppose," I said, "the holding of Temmu had been overrun. What do you think the fate of its free women would be?"

"They are lesser women," she said.

"Surely as high, or higher, than you," said Tajima, annoyed.

"No!" she said.

"Collars are not fit for such as you?" he asked.

"Certainly not," she said.

"You have heard of the Lady Sumomo?" he inquired.

"Surely," she said.

"Perhaps she is as high as you?" he asked.

"A thousand times higher," she said. "She is the daughter of the shogun."

"She who was the Lady Sumomo," said Tajima, "is now a slave."

"I do not believe it!" she said.

"She is now in a collar," said Tajima, "my collar."

"No!" said the Lady Kameko.

"Perhaps I will put you at her disposal," said Tajima, "that you may be as a slave's serving slave."

The Lady Kameko regarded Tajima, and shuddered.

"It pleases men," said Tajima, "to take high women and make them slaves."

This was true. Even the daughters of Ubars had been put in collars by raiders and conquerors.

"Do not put her at the disposal of a woman, even a slave," said Pertinax. "Let her petition her life, on her belly, at the feet of a male."

"Free me!" she wept.

"You are too beautiful to free," I reminded her.

"A kettle-and-mat girl, a pot girl," said Tajima.

"Be serious," I said.

"Who would want her?" said Tajima. "She has been in the hands of peasants."

"Do not be overly fastidious," I said.

"You could always have her scoured, and brushed, and combed," said Pertinax.

"We could give her to an Ashigaru, when the men of Temmu arrive at the palace," said Tajima.

I was not sure, personally, that men from the holding would be committed this far south.

"We thank you, noble lady," I said, "for the information you have furnished. As noted, we have been out of touch for several days."

"May I speak?" she asked.

Pertinax laughed.

She cast him an angry glance.

It is common for slaves, not free women, to ask for permission to speak, before daring to speak.

Free women, at least on the continent, commonly speak boldly, as, when, and how they wish. To be sure, it was common amongst Pani women to be deferent in the presence of males, those, of course, of their own level, station, or class.

"You may," I said.

"I have spoken, as I have heard," she said. "I have seen little of this with my own eyes. Is it true that the iron dragon flew?"

"Yes," I said.

"Where is it now?" she asked, trembling.

"It disappeared," I said.

"Vanished?" she said.

"Yes," I said.

"Will it return?" she asked, frightened.

"That is a subject for speculation," I said.

"Let the men of Yamada, in terror, fear the sky," said Tajima.

"If it came once," said Lady Kameko, "surely it may come again."

"Let the shogun sit uneasy upon his dais," said Pertinax.

"It might come again, with fire and destruction," said the Lady Kameko.

"It seems so," I said.

"Why would it fly for the house of Temmu?" asked Lady Kameko.

"Or why for the house of Yamada?" I asked.

"Who," said Tajima, "can look into the heart of a dragon?"

"I have served you well," she said. "I have spoken fully, and freely, and to the best of my ability. Surely you are satisfied. So untie me, take from my neck this coarse, horrid leash, and let me go."

"Remove the leash," I said to Tajima.

"If you wish," he said.

Lady Kameko cast him a look of disdainful triumph.

"And unbind her wrists," I said.

"Very well," said Tajima.

"Hurry," she snapped.

"Now," I said, "with the leather which bound her wrists

fasten her ankles together, shackling her, allowing her steps of only three or four horts in length."

"What are you doing?" she demanded.

"Keeping you in the vicinity," I said. "If you take a step, even a small step, beyond the length permitted by the leather, you will plunge awkwardly to the tiles. Do not fear. You will soon learn to measure your movements in such a way as to respect the limits imposed by your restraints. As Tajima is a warrior, you would find it difficult to undo the knots. On the other hand, if you should either try to do so, or seem to try to do so, you will be beaten. If you attempt to hobble away, to escape, or struggle unseen with the leather, you will be leashed again. When not under direct observation, your wrists will be tied behind your back and your ankles will be crossed and bound. At night this arrangement will be in place, and you will be tied by the neck to some post, or convenient object, as well."

"I see," she said, angrily.

"You might also understand," I said, "that if any unwelcome or displeasing sounds should escape your lovely lips, we may, at our discretion, prevent the future escape of such by a suitable, effective, and unpleasant application of leather and cloth."

"I understand," she said, frightened. "May I speak?"

"Surely," I said. She was, after all, a free woman.

"What is the purpose of all this?" she asked.

"We are men," I said. "We wish a woman to serve us, to look after us, to clean, dust, launder, prepare bedding, cook, and such."

"I am not a slave!" she said.

"But we have no slave," I said.

"I am the Lady Kameko!" she said.

"But a woman," I said.

"But not a slave!" she said.

"Make her a slave," said Tajima.

"No!" she said.

"How do you think women become slaves?" I asked. "Some by birth, but, commonly, by appropriation, by seizure, by capture."

"I do not understand," she said.

"Surely the men of Yamada," I said, "as well as those of

Temmu, not to mention a common practice across the sea, do this all the time."

"But I am the Lady Kameko," she said.

"It makes no difference," I said. "You are a woman. You are captured, and can be pronounced a slave."

"Do not so pronounce me!" she begged.

"I can fashion a collar from leather, or rope," said Tajima. "We can always, later, brand her, search out a lock collar, and such."

"No!" she said.

"Captives are subject to discipline, are they not?" asked Tajima.

"Certainly," I said.

"Approach me, Lady Kameko," said Tajima. "Closer."

With tiny movements she came and stood before Tajima. "Keep your hands at your sides," he said. He then fastened his hand in her hair. "A bit ago," he said, "when I was to untie your hands, you told me to hurry. Perhaps you remember. I was displeased. Be sure to keep your hands at your sides."

He then cuffed her, twice, the palm of his right hand, and then the back of the same hand.

He then released her hair.

"Please lie on your stomach, Lady Kameko," I said, "with your hands at your sides, the backs of your hands on the floor."

"Obey quickly," snapped Tajima.

"Forgive me!" she said.

We regarded her, prone, before us.

"She is pretty is she not?" I asked.

"Yes," said Pertinax.

"Poor stuff," said Tajima.

"I, for one," said Pertinax, "am tired of the raw meat from the chamber of the Kurii."

"It would be nice to have it roasted, or boiled," I said.

"There is probably some rice left in the basement holding areas," said Tajima.

"It will be pleasant," I said, "to have, after such a long time, a good meal."

"Very much so," said Pertinax.

"A kitchen is not far away," I said. Indeed, it was in a kitchen that I had apprehended the fugitive, the hiding Lady Kameko.

"Now," said Pertinax, "we need only a cook."

"Oh!" wept the Lady Kameko, recoiling from the blow of a sandal.

"There is our cook," said Tajima, stepping back.

"I know nothing of cooking," she whispered, frightened.

"You will do well," said Tajima, "or you will be beaten."

"If you do well," I said, "and you beg prettily enough, earnestly enough, we may allow you to eat, too, after us, say, a handful of rice, a shred of meat."

She moaned.

"After supper," I said, "and after you have cleaned up the pans, the pots, and utensils, and have prepared some sort of bedding for us, if possible, we shall retire, and rise early, in the morning."

"We must find Nodachi," said Tajima.

"He was searching for a trophy room," said Pertinax.

"I expect he has found it by now, although we have not done so," I said.

"Perhaps not," said Tajima. "The palace is large, rooms are numerous, and some may be secret."

"We will have an advantage," I said. "We will have a guide."

"I do not know the location of a trophy room!" said Lady Kameko.

"In the morning," I said, "freed of your shackles, but leashed and bound, you will guide us to it."

"I know of no such room!" she said.

"Surely you have heard of it," I said.

"Of course," she said, "but I have never been there. I do not know where it is."

"Then you are not one of the women," said Tajima, "who attend to such trophies, who care for them."

"No," she said.

"Why should trophies need tending, or caring for?" asked Pertinax. "What sort of tending and caring?"

"The women will have fled the palace by now," said Tajima. "The room will be deserted."

"Perhaps the peasants have found it, and despoiled it," said Pertinax.

"They could take," I said, recalling the words of Nodachi, "only what they could find."

"That suggests a secret room," said Pertinax.

"And only," I said, again recalling the words of Nodachi, in this case a cryptic allusion, "what they did not fear to touch."

"Why should they fear to touch trophies?" asked Pertinax.

"Much, my friend," said Tajima, "depends on the nature of the trophies."

"Nodachi," I said, "seeks weapons."

"It is not unlikely," said Tajima, "that among certain trophies might be found weapons."

"What is the nature of these trophies?" said Pertinax.

"If we are successful in finding the room," said Tajima, "you will see."

"They are hunting trophies?" said Pertinax.

"How does one attain, and maintain, the shogunate?" asked Tajima. "How is order established, and kept?"

"By force, by war, by terror?" said Pertinax.

"And what sort of trophies might a daimyo or shogun, if he were so inclined, garner in such pursuits?" asked Tajima.

"I see," said Pertinax.

Chapter Fifty-Eight

We Will Arm Ourselves

"I think," said Nodachi, a field sword across his legs, as he sat cross-legged in the trophy room, "Lord Yamada is in the palace."

"Surely not," I said. "His troops have moved south."

"Fled south," said Nodachi.

"You have scouted the grounds?" I said.

"Yes," he said. "The signs are clear. No stand was made. There are no entrenchments. The road is not blocked. Even now, stragglers pass the grounds."

"Master," said Tajima, "surely the legendary discipline of picked troops is sustained."

"Doubtless," said Nodachi, "here and there, under prize officers, but not enough to hold back Lord Temmu, should he choose to march."

I did not know if he would commit troops to the south, and, if so, in what numbers.

"Surely, Master," said Pertinax, "Yamada—."

"Lord Yamada," suggested Nodachi.

"Yes, Master," said Pertinax. "Forgive me. Surely Lord Yamada will have withdrawn south, perhaps to rally his men."

"I do not think so," said Nodachi. "The iron dragon has flown."

"Why," I asked, "do you think Lord Yamada is in the palace?"

"He is shogun," said Nodachi.

"All is lost for him," said Tajima. "He has by now donned pure garments, and had recourse to the ritual knife."

"I do not think so," said Nodachi. "It is his way to put others to the knife."

"We followed your signs," I said.

"I did not think it an accident that you are here," said Nodachi.

It was now two days later, following our apprehension of the Lady Kameko. We had searched in vain for the trophy room, until Tajima, this morning, on the fourth level, had seen the tiny image of a sword scratched on a tile. "Nodachi!" he had said, pleased. "Yes!" had said Pertinax, similarly pleased.

It was scarcely noticeable, such a tiny mark.

I had been concerned to investigate room after room, in a methodical fashion. We had encountered no one in the corridors or the rooms, but, now and then, we had come upon the suggestion that others might be in the palace, presumably other fugitives, as the Lady Kameko.

"'By means of small things one sometimes sees large things'," had said Tajima, with satisfaction.

"You were looking for small things?" I said.

"One is to look for many things, both small things and large things," said Tajima.

"Nodachi?" I had asked.

"Of course," had said Pertinax.

We had then searched diligently for these tiny scratches, which, if Tajima and Pertinax were right, had been left for us.

The evening of our apprehension of Lady Kameko she was kind enough to cook for us, and attend to a number of other small conveniences and pleasantries on our behalf. It had been necessary only to strike her twice across the back of the thighs with a switch, found in the kitchen, useful for encouraging scullery slaves, serving slaves, and such. Tajima attended to the matter. She was, after all, a high lady, of the hated house of Yamada. We allowed her to feed after our supper, for which privilege we deemed she had begged prettily enough, and earnestly enough. She would feed on all fours, head down, from a pan, not permitted to use her hands. We felt this was appropriate, given the sort of captive she was, a free woman of the house of Yamada. As a free woman she may have felt this intensely humiliating. As a slave she would be grateful to be fed. Most slaves, of course, eat with the master, though he will take the first bite, and they are permitted to use their hands to feed themselves. In such a situation the master commonly sits, either cross-legged, or on a bench or chair, while the slave kneels. She may, too, be fed occasionally by hand, in which case, naturally, she takes the food in her mouth, and may not otherwise touch it. There are hundreds of small details by means of which a slave is trained, and levels to which she may aspire, earned by diligence and pleasingness, for example, as suggested, eating with the master and using her own hands to feed herself. None of us put the Lady Kameko to use, this despite her rude handling by peasants. She was, after all, a free woman. I suppose it is easy to be mistaken about such things, but I think the Lady Kameko had mixed feeling in this matter. Was she not attractive? Too, it seemed possible that the attentions to which she had been subjected by aroused admirers, ravaging peasants, might have shaken her in her sexual sleep, and hinted at what it might be to be sexually awake. Certainly when we were tethering her for the night, and such, certain small movements, and attitudes, her wide, expectant, frightened eyes, and tiny noises, seemed to say, "Here I am. I am helpless. I am yours to do with as you please. I cannot stop you. I am yours. What are you going to do with me?" "Slut!" had said Tajima, and kicked her contemptuously, and she shrank back in her bonds. "They are all slaves," said Pertinax. "Happily," I said. So, I thought, that high lady, so superior, distant, and frosty, must now begin to cope with a possibly dismaying realization, that she has the belly of a slave. In the morning, following some residue of the previous evening's meal, sumptuous compared to the miserable fare of the chamber of the Kurii, we had begun our search, the object of which was to rejoin Nodachi and locate the trophy room in which, we hoped, might be found weapons. The first day, we put the Lady Kameko, on her leash, her hands bound behind her, to the fore, as we supposed that she, despite her denials, must know the location of the trophy room. "To the trophy room," ordered Tajima, with a flourish of his switch. She threw herself to her knees before him, her head down to his feet, trembling. "I do not know where it is, noble one!" she wept. As she, after enduring some threats, some shovings, some pushings, some kicks, and more than one blow of the kitchen switch, collapsed weeping on the tiles, Tajima, switch in hand, turned about, and regarded us, annoyed. "She may not know where it is," said Pertinax. "I think Pertinax may be right," I said. "There is no serious reason, in a muchly deserted palace, in a dangerous, lawless time, why she might not lead us to the trophy room, if she knew its location. What would she have to lose? Dalliance on her part would be inadvisable, perhaps painful. Presumably she would lead us to it quickly enough, if she could." "Consider, too," said Pertinax, "the location of the room may not be generally known. Indeed, it might be a concealed, secret room, as that in the chamber of the Kurii." "True," said Tajima, thrusting the switch in his sash. "Get up," he ordered the Lady Kameko. "Keep your head down." "Yes, noble one," she said. "Loop the leash about her neck," I said. That was done. "Lady Kameko," I said, "we now have had about as much good out of you as we are likely to have. You are not a slave, and free women are not worth that much. You may go." "'Go'?" she said. "Yes," I said. "Where?" she asked. "Wherever you wish," I said. "You are a free woman." "I do not understand," she said. "Flee," I said. "Where," she said, "to what? I am half naked and helplessly bound. I would be at the mercy of anyone, a peasant, a soldier, a beast. I might starve." "True," I said, "but your fate would be that of a noble free woman."

"Of the hated house of Yamada," said Tajima.

"Let us be on our way," I said to Pertinax and Tajima, and we turned away from the distraught Lady Kameko.

We had proceeded but a few steps, and we heard her plaintive cry from behind, and the pattering of her bare feet on the tiles.

"Take me with you!" she begged.

"There is no place here for free women," said Tajima.

"Do not hate me so!" she wept.

"You are of the house of Yamada," he said.

"Mercy!" she wept.

"We must continue our search," I said.

"I am a helpless woman!" she cried.

"Of the house of Yamada," Tajima reminded her.

"I am a female!" she wept. "I am smaller than you! I am weaker than you! I am different from you, so different! And I need food! And I need shelter, and protection! I am at your mercy! Please, please!"

"We must be on our way," I said.

She hurried to stand before Pertinax.

I found that of interest.

"Please!" she begged.

"No," he said.

"I am a female," she said. "I am young! I am beautiful!"

"A kettle-and-mat girl," said Tajima.

"Many have sought my hand," she said, "and I have refused them all!"

"A pot girl," scoffed Tajima.

I supposed then that she must have been rich, and of independent means, prior to the ruination of the house of Yamada, for the matings of high Pani females are generally arranged and supervised as closely as those of slaves.

"Regard me," said Lady Kameko to Pertinax. "Am I not of interest?"

"Perhaps to tarsks, to peasants," said Tajima.

"Please, noble barbarian?" she said, to Pertinax.

There was no mistaking the zealousness of her appeal.

Why, I wondered, would she apply so fervently to Pertinax?

I supposed him a handsome enough fellow. Certainly he was cleanly cut, tall, sinewy, and such. Perhaps she thought him weak. If so, she would find that she was mistaken. He was no longer the pathetic, diffident Gregory White who had crept about in the officious shadow of Miss Margaret Wentworth, now the slave, Saru, tentative and pliant, hoping to please. He was now Gorean. He had learned war, and the uses to which women may be put.

"Please!" she said.

Clearly her situation was desperate.

"Abandon her," said Tajima. "Let her be left behind. She is a slut of the house of Yamada. Did you not see the disgraceful, mute pleadings of her small, curved body last night? She shames her station, and freedom. Even in tight thongs of leather she well displayed the mere goods which are she!"

"No, no!" wept the Lady Kameko.

"This is a slave," said Tajima, "not a free woman."

"She is free," I said.

"A cavil," said Tajima. "Did you not see her move in her bonds?"

"Still," I said, "free."

"Could a slut chained on a shelf, a wretched *kajira* reaching through bars, soliciting buyers, have done more?" asked Tajima.

"Mercy!" she wept.

"Be respectful, friend," I said to Tajima. "Remember that she is free."

"She," said Tajima, "is not one of your distant, exalted free women on the continent, one of mighty towers and high cities, resplendent in the rich, colorful robes and veils of concealment, one possessing a Home Stone. This is a face-stripped slut of the house of Yamada, a brief cloth tied about her worthless body."

"I beg indulgence in my plight," said the Lady Kameko to Pertinax.

"None for her," said Tajima.

"She is free," I insisted.

"A slave masquerading as a free woman," said Tajima.

"Regard me, noble one, handsome, blond warrior," said the Lady Kameko to Pertinax, "behold me, helpless and destitute, a high lady of a great house!"

"A fallen house," said Tajima.

"I stand before you," said the Lady Kameko to Pertinax, "utterly helpless, barefoot, ill clad, my hands tied behind me, a rope leash wound about my neck!"

Tajima drew the switch from his sash. "I shall whip this worthless slut from our presence," he said.

A small gesture of my hand deterred him.

"Noble one," said the Lady Kameko to Pertinax, "am I not of interest?"

"Perhaps to tarsks, to peasants," said Tajima.

"Consider me!" she begged.

"Away with you!" said Tajima.

"Regard me," said Lady Kameko to Pertinax.

And Pertinax, once the diffident, timid Gregory White of Earth, now a tarnsman of Gor, did indeed regard the Lady Kameko.

"Am I not of interest?" she asked.

She trembled in place, scrutinized.

"Please, noble one," she said.

"Please!" she whispered.

It was very quiet in the hallway.

"Kneel before me, kiss my feet, and declare yourself a slave," said Pertinax.

Swiftly the Lady Kameko knelt before Pertinax, her hands tied behind her, the coarse, rope leash about her neck, put down her head, and kissed his feet.

She then looked up. "I am a slave," she said.

It was done, I thought. A free woman can utter such words, but she, then a slave, cannot retract them. No longer had the Lady Kameko a name. She was now a property, a vendible beast.

"I claim you," said Pertinax.

"I am owned," she said.

"Here," said Tajima to Pertinax, handing him the switch. "Strike her, twice, that she will know she is subject to your whip."

Pertinax gave her two smart blows, one high on the left arm, the other, a back stroke, high on the right arm. Tears were in her eyes. He then held the switch before her and she lifted her head, and bent forward a little, and humbly licked and kissed it. He then returned the implement to Tajima.

She kept her head down. She was no longer useless, or a burden. She was now a slave.

"We will now be on our way," I said.

"Heel me," said Pertinax to his new slave.

"Yes, Master," she said.

Following the tiny swordlike scratches on the tiles, landings, and stairs, scratches which were spaced at different intervals, we had descended from the fourth level to the second level, and, eventually, had arrived at what seemed a stout wooden wall.

"The scratches end here," I said.

"Thus," said Tajima, "the end of our search is here."

"The wall seems solid," I said.

"The palace is large, and many passages are narrow and intricate," said Pertinax. "Perhaps the scratches do not lead to a trophy room, but merely blaze a trail, that Nodachi might not inadvertently retrace his steps."

"If that is the case," I said, "he may not have found the trophy room."

"The palace is intricate," said Tajima, "but it is not a maze."

"We do not know," I said, "that the scratches were made by Nodachi."

"The sword is his sign," said Tajima. "He did not know our whereabouts. He left them for us, that we might follow."

"The scratches end here," said Pertinax.

"If he were set upon, or gave up the search," I said, "the last scratch would be parallel to the corridor, not perpendicular to it."

"Precisely," said Tajima. "We are thus at the trophy room."

"It is well concealed," I said.

"But it must be easily accessible," said Tajima. "Free women must be able to come and go, to tend the trophies. The shogun might wish to view them from time to time, to display them to guests, and such."

"Search the wall," I said. "There must be a panel, or pivot."

"And where?" asked Tajima, smiling.

"At the last scratch," I said.

"Yes," he said.

A moment later the wall turned.

"Tal," said Nodachi, sitting, waiting for us.

"Tal," I said. "Perhaps you heard us, on the other side of the wall."

"Yes," he said, "Tarl Cabot, tarnsman."

"Perhaps," I said, "you might have opened the wall, or informed us how it might have been opened."

"No, Tarl Cabot, tarnsman," said Tajima. "Nodachi is Nodachi. It is up to us to discover the secret ourselves."

"I see," I said. We then bowed to Nodachi and said, "Tal," which bows he politely returned, with an inclination of his head.

"I think," had said Nodachi, a field sword across his legs, as he sat cross-legged in the trophy room, "Lord Yamada is in the palace."

I had doubted that that was true.

Tajima had speculated that Lord Yamada, in defeat, would have had recourse to the ritual knife.

This, too, had been doubted, by Nodachi.

If Lord Yamada was dead, it seemed the contest, if it existed, betwixt wagering Priest-Kings and Kurii had been decided. I knew not what this might bode for the future of Gor. Indeed, I was not clear on which side either force had placed its wager. Did Priest-Kings favor Lord Temmu or Lord Yamada? Which, if either, was favored by Kurii? Surely both Kurii, or some Kurii, and Priest-Kings, or some Priest-Kings, had collaborated in the readying of, and the flight of, the iron dragon. It seemed Kurii, or some Kurii, might have favored Lord Temmu, as I had been brought within his compass on a northern beach long ago, in a ship departed from a steel world. But was this in virtue of an agreement between Priest-Kings and Kurii? Tiny bits of evidence suggested one interpretation, and tiny bits of evidence suggested another. Perhaps, for all I knew, there was no wager, only the suspicion of, or the rumor of, a wager. And if there was a wager, I had no assurance that its outcome would be respected by either Priest-Kings or Kurii. Were these not independent, powerful, sovereign species, under no shared law, subject to no common sovereign, capable of imposing its will, but rather stood opposite one another in a state of nature, rather as two larls might face one another, snarling, contesting territory. And who would presume to give law to the savage larl?

She who had been the Lady Kameko was outside, in the corridor, kneeling, bent over, bound. The name 'Kameko' had been put on her, as a slave name. The tie in which she had been placed was an efficient and familiar slave tie. In it the slave leash is utilized. The slave is knelt. Her head is to the floor and the leash is taken back, before and under her body, and then used, tautly, to tie her ankles together. By the taut leash her head is held in place, tightly, down to the floor. Her wrists were left as they had been, tied behind her back. One has then, before one, a helpless, aesthetically attractive, compact slave package or bundle, so to speak. It is a tie in which a woman is in little doubt that she is a slave.

"We have not found Haruki," I said.

"He is in the garden, at work," said Nodachi.

"Even in a time of madness, dissolution, the failure of discipline, of social and military chaos?" I said.

"It is well that the garden be tended," said Nodachi.

"Does he know that you are free?" I asked.

"No," said Nodachi.

"You think that Lord Yamada remains in the palace?" I asked.

"Yes," said Nodachi. "He is shogun."

"Perhaps you think he will come here, to revel in his trophies?" I asked.

"To console himself with past glories?" asked Tajima.

"Lord Yamada is shogun," said Nodachi. "He looks to the future."

"He has no future, Master," said Tajima.

"He will then die, attempting to bring it about," said Nodachi.

I was uneasy in the trophy room, and Pertinax sat near the door, so to speak, where we had pivoted the wall.

I thought the air was better there, near the corridor.

The former Lady Kameko, now Kameko, was, as noted, outside, in the corridor, where she would await the pleasure of masters. Pertinax had removed her clothing before binding her.

Slaves are animals, and animals need not be clothed.

There were, I conjectured, more than two hundred heads in the trophy room, on shelves, on tables, suspended from the ceiling. The air in the trophy room was oppressive with the perfumes used to preserve, and anoint, the heads. The long black hair of each was oiled and combed carefully. The teeth of several had been dyed black, which, in the eyes of some, particularly high ladies, I had learned, is accounted a beautification, a fashionable and aristocratic embellishment, an enhancement of charms, rather, I suppose, like the drug-dilated pupils of Renaissance ladies, or, depending on the culture, whitening powders, rouges, lipsticks of motley colors, eye shadows, and other variations of cosmetic ingenuity. The eyes of several of the heads had been replaced with jewels or precious stones, mostly, it seemed, jade.

"The palace is large," I said.

"Lord Yamada will be in the room of the great dais," said Nodachi, "in the prime audience chamber, where taxes and tributes are presented, where vassal daimyos are received."

"He is not hiding?" I said.

"Lord Yamada does not hide," said Nodachi.

"But you are here," I said.

"I have been waiting for you," he said. "Arm yourselves."

Chapter Fifty-Nine

What Occurred in the Audience Chamber

"Greetings, great and noble lord," said Nodachi, bowing. "I have come to kill you."

The audience chamber, though I had not seen it before, probably because it was reserved for formal occasions, state functions, and such, was surely a centerpiece in the palace of Lord Yamada. It was a large room, spacious, and deep. The dais was a foot or so above the level of the general flooring. The boards of the flooring, and those of the dais, were of dark, polished wood, and the walls, also of dark wood, were ornamented by numerous characters, designs, and images of light wood, inlaid in the darker wood. The characters were in Pani script, in which they transcribe Gorean, rather as those in the Tahari transcribe Gorean in their own flowing script. These characters were unintelligible to me. The designs seemed on the whole, to me, swirling and abstract, though they may have been meant to suggest the surging of waves and the curling, startling movements of wind. The images were of natural objects, such as trees, flowers, and animals, predominantly birds, and, amongst them, predominantly, of water fowl. The dais itself was sternly severe. There were various portals in the room through which it might be entered or left. Nodachi had entered through the main portal, facing the dais, walked to the dais, bowed, and politely announced himself. The light in the chamber seemed poor to me. It was supplied by small lamps, some of which were mounted in the walls, and some of which hung from the ceiling, descending, in some cases, to within a yard or so of the floor. One would, in such a case, move carefully amongst them. Perhaps they were intended to illuminate small tables about which one might sit, cross-legged. But there were no such tables in the room now. Given the lighting, I would not, personally, have preferred such a venue for the work of steel. Better an open court, on an overcast day, where one need not be concerned with the glare of the sun. Occasionally there was a screen in the room, near the walls, which screens were decorated rather in the fashion of the walls, save that the screens were paneled with silk, and the images, and such, were painted on the silken panels.

"How dare you, magician, and charlatan," said Lord Yamada, "enter my presence unannounced?"

"Forgive me, great lord," said Nodachi, "but I announced myself."

Lord Yamada sat cross-legged on the dais, richly and formally robed, as though holding court, as though he might be expecting a loyal daimyo or some petitioning ambassador, and not vengeful, deadly enemies, perhaps hundreds, to appear before him.

"The house of Yamada has fallen on hard times," said Nodachi.

"It stands," said Lord Yamada.

"Only as long as you," said Nodachi.

There were two with Lord Yamada, standing, behind him, one on either side. In a sense I knew both. One was Yasushi, whom I knew from the battle of the inn, before we were taken into custody by Kazumitsu, the special officer of Lord Yamada, who had been searching for Sumomo and her abductor. The other was Katsutoshi, whom I recalled from the village, where Nodachi had twice divided a grain of rice, once with the companion sword, and once with the field sword. Katsutoshi, as I recalled, had identified himself as the captain of the shogun's guard.

"Where are your armies, great lord?" inquired Nodachi.

"Regrouping in the south," said Lord Yamada.

"I fear not," said Nodachi. "The iron dragon has flown. Many, officers and warriors, have fled to lesser, farther islands. Roads are filled with roving bands. Daimyos have withdrawn to their holdings. Dismayed warriors seek new daimyos. Ashigaru have returned to villages."

"I now dismiss them, all," said Lord Yamada. "They have failed. I order them away."

"You are not heavily defended," observed Nodachi.

"Did my guards not object to your passage?" asked Lord Yamada.

"They object no more," said Nodachi.

"I gave no command that you be released," said Lord Yamada.

"The door of my cell was left open," said Nodachi.

"By your friends?" said Lord Yamada.

"It is so," said Nodachi.

"Greetings, Tarl Cabot, tarnsman," said Lord Yamada. "And to your fellows, Tajima *san*, and the noble barbarian, Pertinax *san*."

We three bowed to Lord Yamada, acknowledging his greeting.

"The palace was overrun, by peasants," said Nodachi.

"None dared to enter this chamber," said Lord Yamada.

"Why have you not fled, great lord?" I asked.

"I am shogun," he said.

"I fear the men of Temmu may march south," I said.

"They do," said Lord Yamada. "They have defiled the road for days."

"There is still time to flee," I said.

"I am shogun," he said.

It was my surmise that the wager betwixt Kurii and Priest-Kings, if it existed, would not be considered resolved until either the house of Yamada or that of Temmu would be crushed into a nullity.

"How magician," asked Lord Yamada of Nodachi, "did you survive the test of twelve arrows?"

"Does that concern you, great lord?" asked Nodachi.

"Yes," said the shogun.

"One must care for the arrow, understand the arrow, think as the arrow, and be as the arrow," said Nodachi.

"That is absurd," said Lord Yamada.

"The test was passed," said Nodachi.

"If the men of Lord Temmu have been on the road for days," I said. "They must be near."

"It is expected," said Lord Yamada, "that they will arrive within the Ahn."

"And you choose to receive them here?" I said.

"Certainly," he said. "It is my audience chamber."

"You are ill defended," said Nodachi.

"One cannot be better defended than by those who are loyal," said Lord Yamada.

"I have no quarrel with two brave men," said Nodachi.

"Nor they with you," said Lord Yamada. "I am expecting visitors. I permit you to withdraw."

"You understand," said Nodachi, "that I have come to kill you."

"I recall you have said so," said Lord Yamada.

"Your garden is lovely," said Nodachi.

Lord Yamada inclined his head, politely.

"Let us repair to the garden," suggested Nodachi.

"Why?" asked Lord Yamada.

"I think it would be a good place to die, amidst the flowers and trees," said Nodachi.

"There is no good place to die," said Lord Yamada.

"We must loosen steel," said Nodachi. "I insist."

"It is improper," said Lord Yamada. "You are a peasant, a charlatan, a magician, a mountebank. I would dishonor my steel."

"Perhaps, great lord," said Tajima. "You might find it within the perimeter of your honor to lift your sword in certain circumstances, say, to avenge a grievous insult to your house?"

"Perhaps," said Lord Yamada.

"Excellent," said Tajima. He then turned curtly about, and exited the chamber, only to return a moment later, dragging the leashed, naked, bound Kameko behind him. He then threw her to her knees before the dais. "Perhaps you recognize this naked, bound slut!" he said.

"Certainly," said Lord Yamada, "though I am accustomed to seeing her more fully dressed."

"She was an exalted, high lady in your house!" said Tajima.

"Once," said Lord Yamada.

"Be outraged! Be enflamed! Fight!" cried Tajima. Then, as Lord Yamada did not move, but seemed impassive, Tajima, in disgust, threw the leash to the floor.

"Have I taught you nothing, dear friend?" said Nodachi. "It is you who are enflamed, not the great lord. Steel does not well obey the furious hand. As you are, you might not survive three touches of engaging steel."

At this point, the leash loose, Kameko leaped to her feet, ran to the dais, ascended it, and put herself to the feet of Lord Yamada.

"Save me, save me, great lord!" she cried.

She put her head to his leg, sobbing.

We tensed, but made no move.

Lord Yamada said something to Katsutoshi, who left the shogun's side, and shortly returned, carrying an object, wrapped in cloth.

She who had been the Lady Kameko raised her head to the shogun. "Please, great lord," she said, "remove this hated rope from my neck, this degrading leash, cut my hands free, clothe me, and then kill them! Kill them all!"

"Turn about, as you are, on your knees," he said, "that your back is to me, and your face to our visitors."

She was then facing us.

Lord Yamada rose to his feet, behind her.

"Are you a slave?" asked the shogun.

"No!" she cried. "No!"

"Slaves," he said to her, "may be punished for attempting to escape, and for lying."

"Great lord?" she said.

"Is she a slave?" asked Lord Yamada.

"Yes," said Pertinax.

"Whose slave?" asked Lord Yamada.

"Mine," said Pertinax. "This very day she declared herself slave, following which irrevocable act, I, perhaps foolishly, put claim on her."

"There are witnesses, of course," said the shogun.

"I," I said.

"And I," said Tajima.

The shogun then seized Kameko's long hair and, with a stroke or two of his blade, cut much of it away. He then put out his hand for the object which Katsutoshi had brought to the dais. Katsutoshi slipped the cloth away, and handed the object to the shogun.

He then lifted the object over her head, and then down, and about her neck, and snapped it shut.

Kameko cried out with misery, collared.

The shogun threw the tiny key to the floor before Pertinax, who retrieved it, and slipped it in his pouch.

He then threw the slave from the dais, and she rolled to the feet of Pertinax.

"There is your slave," he said.

"My thanks, great lord," said Pertinax.

"I trust," said the shogun, "you will see that she is suitably punished for attempting to escape, and for lying."

"Yes," said Pertinax.

"As she is now collared," said Lord Yamada, "I trust that there will be no further confusion or doubt as to the fact that she is a slave. I would also advise you to have her marked as soon as possible."

"Yes, great lord," said Pertinax.

"And, my dear," said the shogun to the distraught slave, "I suspect it will be a long time before you are permitted clothing."

Pertinax then bent to the slave and, with the leash, tied her ankles together. She had, thus, been placed in a variation of the most common slave tie, which is simply, usually with two short thongs, ropes, straps, laces, or such, to bind the slave hand and foot. This is a comfortable tie, but, in it, the slave is bound helplessly, and efficiently. A less pleasant version of this tie is to pull back the ankles and tie them, rather closely, to the hands, behind her.

"You understand, magician," said Lord Yamada to Nodachi, "that I cannot cross swords with you, as you are not of my level."

"I must beg your permission to permit me to do so," said Nodachi.

"Yasushi," said the shogun, resuming his sitting position, cross-legged, "kill the peasant."

"*Ela*, lord," said Yasushi. "I cannot, for he is my teacher, the master, Nodachi. The bond between student and master is inviolate."

"True," said the shogun. "I did not understand. Forgive me."

He then turned to Katsutoshi. "Loyal Katsutoshi," he said, "you are the finest sword in my guard."

I had no doubt as to the skills of Katsutoshi, were he the finest sword in the shogun's guard. This distinction, I gathered, had become his following the demise of the warrior, Izo, in the market town, Chrysanthemum of the Shogun. Izo, as it may be recalled, had been dispatched with ease by Nodachi. Blades had not even touched.

The shogun then indicated Nodachi. "Go," he said, "kill him."

Katsutoshi bowed to the shogun. "You send me to my death," he said. "I go."

"I have no quarrel with this brave man," said Nodachi. "Please be so good as to interfere."

Both Tajima and Pertinax whipped out companion swords, taken from the trophy room, and stepped between Nodachi and Katsutoshi, who descended, lightly, from the dais.

"Be behind me," I said to them.

"No," said Nodachi. "They must learn."

Tajima first engaged Katsutoshi. Blades, under the lamps, flashed. I was much impressed with both combatants. I soon realized how it might have been that Katsutoshi had won his captaincy, at least in part.

Suddenly Tajima had lost the blade, and it struck the floor.

Katsutoshi put his foot upon the blade, and Tajima backed away.

"The blade is to be held neither too lightly nor too tightly," said Nodachi. "Held too tightly the wrist locks, the blade is less nimble; held too lightly, the blade may fly away, like a startled vulo."

"I have failed, Master," said Tajima.

"Not at all," said Nodachi. "I am proud of you. Few could stand against you. Your opponent is a master swordsman."

Pertinax stepped forward.

"You must be as in the *dojo*, alert, and calm, cool, quick, steady, but not as in the *dojo*," said Nodachi, "for here you must be more, even more, for here it is different, for here you are facing steel which intends to cut you, swift steel intent upon entering your flesh, quick steel which is intent upon shedding your blood, clever, cunning steel which wants to kill you."

I wished that Pertinax had in his hand the Gorean *gladius*, in which he had been trained. He was no master of the companion sword, nor would he have been of the field sword. Nor was I.

"Step in," I said to Nodachi.

"I would not dishonor my pupil," said Nodachi. "He must learn."

"And he may die," I said.

"Then he will die well," said Nodachi.

Blades struck smartly together.

"The blade, the blade," said Nodachi. "Remember the *dojo*, gifted barbarian, the exercises. Do not watch his eyes, they will lie, watch his blade, his wrist, for the blade must follow the wrist."

"He is holding his own," I marveled.

I recalled that Nodachi had accepted him as a student, something which had once disturbed Tajima, and, I think, Lord Okimoto.

"*Ela*," said Nodachi. "The last exchange!"

"What is it?" I asked.

"Young Pertinax is being drawn into a trap. Consider the exchanges! What he will think is an opening will not be an opening. The wise enemy does not present his foe with gifts. He has forgotten!"

One fences with the mind, of course, as well as the body. In the Kaissa of steel, as in the Kaissa of the hundred-square board, beware the seeming mistake, for it may not be a mistake. Beware the too-vulnerable piece, for it may be unwisely seized. Beware the tethered verr, for the hunter lurks in his blind. Is deception not the name of war?

"*Ela*," said Nodachi, "he is not yet ready for such a foe."

"I am," I said, companion sword in hand, taken from the trophy room. In whose hand had it once leapt and soared?

"Hold," said Nodachi. "Do not interfere. See, Tajima lives."

"Pertinax may not," I said.

"He will live," said Nodachi. "It is not he, but I who am the quarry of the noble Katsutoshi."

"Ai!" cried Pertinax, and his right sleeve was drenched with blood, and he moved his sword to his left hand, and lifted it, awkwardly.

"Lower your sword!" cried Tajima.

"Do so!" I ordered him, and Pertinax, blood running down his right arm, lowered his sword.

"Do not kill him," I said to Katsutoshi.

"I am not a butcher," said Katsutoshi.

"I shall regret killing so noble a foe," said Nodachi.

"It will not be necessary," I said.

"Do not interfere," said Nodachi. "I am his quarry."

"He will not reach you," I said.

I stepped between Katsutoshi and Nodachi.

"Please step aside," said Katsutoshi, politely.

"On guard," I said.

"I have an appointment with the master," said Katsutoshi.

"It would be your last," I said. "You will not keep it."

"I must," he said.

"You will not," I said.

"Forgive me," he said, and I parried the thrust.

He was very quick.

He backed away, a pace.

"That is not your weapon of choice," he said.

"No," I said.

"You grasp it in an unusual fashion," he said.

"Perhaps," I said.

"Are you accustomed to it?" he asked.

"It is a blade," I said, "a sword."

To be sure, I would have preferred a different blade, the shorter, broader *gladius*, designed for closer work, for stabbing, for moving within the guard of heavier, longer weapons.

He thrust, and I parried, again.

There are styles of fencing, as well as variations in blades. Tajima was familiar with the two swords of the Pani warrior, and we had often sported in the *dojo*, he with one or both of the Pani swords, and I with the familiar *gladius*. The *gladius* is often used with shield, or buckler. The Pani swords, like the rapier, the foil, and saber, are designed for both defense and offense. The *gladius* too, of course, may function in both modalities, without shield and buckler, though Gorean infantry commonly combines it with the shield, and the arena fighter with the buckler. From the sporting contests with Tajima I was familiar with the feel of the blade, then against the *gladius*, and its movements, and its reach. I was less familiar, of course, with handling such a weapon. A fine companion sword, with its balance and edge, is a masterpiece of the smith's craft.

He thrust twice more, and I parried twice more.

I had observed him, of course, in his exchanges with Tajima and Pertinax. This was an advantage, of course, which one seldom has in dealing with a foe. I had seen him at work, and he had not seen me. Commonly, in encounters of steel, strangers meet and one dies.

It is difficult to touch, or cut, a skilled swordsman who is content with defense. But he who defends only will eventually die, for no defense is forever impenetrable. When one extends to the attack, one exposes more of the body, and risks more, but without risk there is no victory, only eventual defeat.

We indulged ourselves in a brief exchange.

I am sure that Katsutoshi was testing me, reading my blade. So I presented him with certain results to his test, and let him misread my blade.

"Ai!" he cried, suddenly, startled, and the weapon dropped from his hand, to the dark, polished floor.

He looked at me, wildly.

"Kill me!" he commanded.

It had followed his low feint, for which I had been waiting, used against both Tajima and Pertinax, intended to bring the opponent's blade down, thus opening the way to a straight thrust over the momentarily descended blade. But no straight thrust would follow that feint, for in the instant his blade was occupied in this subterfuge, lowered, threatening, the arm extended, I did not move to defend but struck over the lowered blade, striking to the right wrist.

In that hand he would never hold another sword.

He had spared Tajima and Pertinax, neither a match for his skills. I would spare him.

"Kill me!" he cried.

"Neither of us is a butcher," I said.

He backed away, bleeding.

Now, I thought, he will not rush to his death. Nodachi would have killed him. Why? Because he stood between him and Yamada, the shogun.

"Young friends," said Nodachi to Tajima and Pertinax, "you have done well. I am pleased with you. You have had a most valuable lesson, at the hands of a master swordsman, the noble Katsutoshi, captain of a great lord's guard."

Katsutoshi inclined his head, honored.

"My young friends," said Nodachi. "You have advanced in the tutelage of war. You are worthy of the codes of steel. I am proud of you."

"Master," said Tajima, bowing.

"Master," said Pertinax, bowing, his hand pressed to his arm, to staunch the bleeding.

"Master," said Kameko, lying at the feet of Pertinax, "I am pleased that you live."

Pertinax reached down with his left hand and drew her up, to her knees.

Women look well on their knees.

"What is on your neck?" he asked.

"A collar, Master," she said.

"What sort of collar?"

"A slave collar, Master."

"And why is that?" he asked.

"Because I am a slave, Master," she said.

"Whose slave?" he asked.

"Your slave," she said.

"You are a pretty slave," he said.

"It is my hope to please my Master," she said.

"I think I will be pleased to own you," he said.

"And I, to be owned by you," she said.

"You will learn your collar," he said.

"It is my hope that you will teach it to me," she said.

"I will teach it to you," he said, "—with perfection."

"I would have it no other way, Master," she said.

Nodachi then stepped between us, between Tajima, Pertinax, the slave, and I, and Katsutoshi, and advanced to a place before the dais.

He bowed politely to the shogun. "Now, please," he said.

"I," said the shogun, "did not come to the dais easily. There were many steps, and many were covered with blood."

"It is often so," said Nodachi.

"I am the finest sword in the islands," he said.

"Then it will be I who will die," said Nodachi.

"You are not of my station, my level, my class," said the shogun.

"Forgive me," said Nodachi.

"You are determined in this matter?" asked the shogun.

"Yes," said Nodachi.

"Then," said the shogun, "let us repair to the garden."

Chapter Sixty

Swords Meet Amongst Flowers;
The Insects Are Not Disturbed;
A Gate is Sundered

"Let us consider matters, here, on the raked sand," said Lord Yamada, "that we may not risk trampling flowers."

Nodachi nodded his acquiescence.

Tajima, his weapon recovered, Pertinax, wadding his shirt against his wound, and I, had accompanied Nodachi and the shogun to the garden, having taken our way through the open chamber leading to the garden, that chamber in which, some time ago, we had been entertained at the shogun's supper. Yasushi and Katsutoshi had followed, Katsutoshi's right hand hidden in his wide sleeve. Pertinax had untied Kameko's ankles in the audience chamber and wrapped the leash about her neck. Unbidden, she then, head down, heeled him to the garden, her wrists still thonged behind her back. He had then knelt her down on the small bridge, that whose railings were entwined with the vines of the blue climber. He had then, with the leash, fastened her neck, closely, to one of the stanchions supporting the rail, just under the rail. Before he removed his hands she had pressed her lips timidly against the back of his hand. Clearly she now understood there was a collar on her neck. When a woman is collared she often experiences a great sense of relief. A thousand frustrations are behind her. She is now, helplessly, gladly, in her place in nature, owned by a male. Her identity is now on her. She knows how to be, how to act, how to speak, how to love. As other slaves, reveling in the liberation bestowed by their collars, she would wish to be a good slave, and a pleasing slave, a fully pleasing slave. From her point of vantage, she could see what ensued, a few yards away. Haruki, who had been working in the garden, stood in the background.

"Weapon?" inquired Lord Yamada.

"You are shogun," said Nodachi, "great and noble one."

"Very well," said Lord Yamada. "Companion sword."

I had expected that to be the choice, rather than the larger, longer, heavier field sword, usually wielded with two hands.

The graceful companion sword is shorter, and lighter. Its speed is such that many find it difficult to follow its flights. As unnoticed as the wind, it can appear as suddenly as the pouncing sleen, cut like a razor, and strike like the tiny, venomous ost.

Lord Yamada thrust his field sword into the sand, and so, too, did Nodachi. Nodachi wore a short-sleeved gray jacket of simple, rough cloth, as many peasants. Lord Yamada divested himself of his stiff, ornate, outer robe.

I did not expect Lord Yamada to stand long against Nodachi, but I did not know his skills. He had claimed to be the finest sword in the islands. I had known Lord Yamada to lie, for strategic and state reasons, but I had never known him to boast. I recalled his remark about steps leading to the dais, many of which were covered with blood. In any event, Lord Yamada's demeanor and attitude suggested no apprehension concerning the outcome of the imminent contest. Indeed, I suspected, with a sudden coldness in my body, he might welcome this occasion, for a distractive interlude, pending returning to the audience chamber, to await the arrival of enemy troops, hundreds of violent men thirsting for his blood, competing for his head. What loyalty he had inspired, I thought, that Yasushi and Katsutoshi had stood with him on the dais, waiting, in that large, lonely, untenanted audience chamber.

"You are not now dividing grains of rice, magician," said Lord Yamada.

"No, great lord," said Nodachi.

"There is no trickery here," said the shogun.

"And none was there," said Nodachi.

Suddenly Lord Yamada, startling me, rushed at Nodachi, and there was a brief, fierce, exchange, and both men stepped back.

Lord Yamada smiled.

"It seems then we are to do war," he said.

"Yes," said Nodachi.

"Are you prepared?" asked Lord Yamada.

"I was," said Nodachi, bowing.

"Grains of rice do not strike back," said Lord Yamada.

"Should they do so, one must be prepared," said Nodachi.

There then commenced a lengthy, remarkable duel.

Sunlight flashed on swift blades.

We remained silent. There was no sound in the garden but the sudden ringing of steel, followed by silence, and then beginning again. In the silence we could hear Lord Yamada breathing, and the hum of insects. The garden was very beautiful. I supposed it had profited from Haruki's return. Sometimes a breeze stirred the leaves. Zar flies were about. I brushed one away.

There was a streak of blood on the right cheek of Nodachi.

"It seems magicians can bleed," said Lord Yamada.

"Shoguns, as well," said Nodachi.

"A scratch, only," said the shogun, annoyed, a stain of blood discoloring his left sleeve, high on the arm.

"The touch of the point was too low for the eye," said Nodachi.

"Too high for the throat," said Lord Yamada.

"One intervenes, as one can," said Nodachi.

"But you were cut," said Lord Yamada.

"Your garment is stained," said Nodachi.

"I hear men at the gate!" I said.

"Soldiers," said Pertinax.

"Peasants!" said Tajima.

"I fear they have come for you, Lord," said Yasushi.

"You fight well, peasant," said Lord Yamada to Nodachi, "better than any I have crossed steel with. Seven times I planned to kill you, and did not do so."

"One intervenes, as one can," said Nodachi. "Five times, I thought I had you on my point, and five times I failed."

"One intervenes, as one can," said the shogun.

"I must improve my skills," said Nodachi. "I must perfect them."

"He who is on the path to perfection is doomed," said the shogun. "It is a path with no end."

"Yet," said Nodachi, "some must follow it."

I heard the clamoring of men, and the breaking of timber. "The gate is being forced," I said.

"Mountebank," said Lord Yamada, "I have an appointment. We must end this. You must pardon me."

He then addressed a medley of blows to Nodachi so swift and fierce, so varied, and so deftly met that Tajima cried out in awe. Clearly the shogun had launched that onslaught that it might constitute the bloody terminus of this strange, lengthy engagement. Nodachi, in the rhythms of combat, in its tides, in its alternation of offense and defense, had now elected to withstand this storm of steel rather than penetrate it, and seek in it some advantage. One may not slay a hurricane but, rather, strive to survive it. I feared then that Lord Yamada might indeed be the finest sword in the islands. But Nodachi met this attack, and lived! Then Nodachi, commonly so skilled in stance, and ready in response, slipped in the soft sand. Tajima cried out, in misery. I saw the shogun's blade slash down. "No!" cried Tajima. "I live," said Nodachi, straightening up, and tearing away the shreds of his jacket from his left side. But Lord Yamada had not pressed the advantage. Rather, startled, shaken, panting, gasping for breath, he regarded his antagonist. "The avenger!" he said. "I am no avenger," said Nodachi. "The mark, the sign of the lotus, on the left shoulder!" cried Haruki, wildly, tears in his eyes. Lord Yamada backed away. "I have had it since birth," said Nodachi. "It is only another blemish, one of many." "The empty grave!" cried Lord Yamada. "Yes," said Haruki. "I did not strangle him. He lives. This is he! He is the son of my daughter, who died in your palace, of woman's poisons!"

"She?" said Lord Yamada.

"Yes!" cried Haruki.

"Of what are you speaking?" said Nodachi.

"He," said Lord Yamada, "this short, gross, squat, malformed beast?"

"He is your son," said Haruki.

"Such cannot be of my blood," said the shogun. "I will not have it."

"He is the avenger!" cried Haruki. "See the sign, the sign of the lotus!"

"I am no avenger," said Nodachi. "I am Nodachi."

"He has come back, noble lord!" said Haruki. "He has come back, to avenge a cemetery of brothers, a thousand wrongs, a generation of tyranny!"

"This is not true!" said Nodachi. "I am alone, I am of no family!"

"Lord Yamada is stunned," said Tajima.

"He cannot defend himself!" said Pertinax.

"Strike!" said Tajima.

"Seize your opportunity," said Pertinax. "Thrust, now, to the heart!"

"Kill him!" said Haruki.

"But he cares for the garden," I said to Haruki.

Lord Yamada's sword was lowered. I sensed he could not raise it, nor employ it now in the work of war. But he regarded Nodachi, unflinchingly, as shogun.

"You?" he asked.

"I know nothing of this," said Nodachi.

Haruki wildly rushed upon the shaken, inert shogun, and tore down his robe to the waist.

How dared he touch the person of the shogun?

On the shogun's left shoulder was the odd mark, which so resembled a lotus.

Then Haruki turned about, to face Nodachi. "He is Yamada, tyrant and murderer!" he cried. "Strike! Kill him! Kill him!"

"Do so," said Lord Yamada.

Nodachi bowed. "Father," he said.

"Kill him!" said Haruki.

"It is not honorable to kill one's father," said Nodachi.

I heard Kameko scream.

"The gate is broken through," I said. "Men pour in!"

Chapter Sixty-One

Visitors;
A Plan Is Formed

It was not the men of Temmu who first burst through the gate, overcoming guards, but some thirty or forty soldiers, mostly officers, many of whom still wore the livery of the shogun.

"Greetings," said Lord Akio.

"You would be welcome," said Lord Yamada. "How is it that you have broken the gate?"

"Guards were adamant," said Lord Akio.

"Word might have been brought to me," said the shogun.

"A thousand men of the holding of Temmu are less than an Ahn away," said Lord Akio.

It was as I thought. Lord Temmu would be thrifty in his commitment of troops. Still, a thousand men would be a sufficient force when opposed to empty roads and abandoned fields.

Lord Akio, I conjectured, had no more than forty men with him.

"You have come to die with me?" asked the shogun.

"We have come to live," said Lord Akio.

"Excellent," said Lord Yamada. "You bring news of the rallying of troops, of resistance to invaders!"

"Disarm yourself, surrender the shogunate," said Lord Akio.

"It was you who slew the would-be assassin!" said Lord Yamada.

"Certainly," said Lord Akio. "Few men can resist torture."

"It was I," said Haruki, "who admitted the assailant into the garden, by a secret way."

"I had supposed so," said Lord Yamada.

"And you permitted me to remain with the garden?" said Haruki.

"Of course," he said.

"The straw jacket?" said Haruki.

"You were apprehended," said the shogun. "One must respond to expectations, one must maintain order."

"Many are content with oppression," said Haruki.

"It seems not all," said Lord Yamada.

"No," said Haruki.

"Tyrants could not exist," said Lord Yamada, "were they not welcome."

"Can it be?" asked Haruki.

"A tyrant may be replaced," said Lord Yamada. "But the mask of the savior, removed, reveals merely the face of the new tyrant."

"Men do not wish to rule themselves," said Pertinax, "but only to be well ruled."

"The choice, dear Haruki, gardener *san*," said Lord Yamada, "is always, and only, one amongst masks and tyrants, he who wears the mask and he who disdains doing so."

"And the great and noble lord disdains doing so," said Haruki.

"I am as I am seen," said the shogun.

Lord Yamada then turned to Lord Akio.

"You have not come to succor the shogunate," said Lord Yamada to Lord Akio.

"No," said Lord Akio, "but to seize it."

"If troops of Temmu are at hand, as you say," said Lord Yamada, "it would be a prize but briefly held."

"Perhaps longer than you surmise," said Lord Akio.

"You have an arrangement with the house of Temmu," said Lord Yamada.

"Of course," said Lord Akio, lifting his war fan, spreading its wings, and locking them in place.

Such a device is difficult to evade.

"You have come for my head," said Lord Yamada.

"A gift for Lord Temmu," said Lord Akio.

"Come and take it," said Lord Yamada.

"Do not resist," said Lord Akio. "The iron dragon has flown."

"It flies no more," I said.

Lord Akio gestured toward us, impatiently. "Kill them!" he said.

The first two men who reached us, fell before the whipping, almost invisible, sword of Nodachi.

The forty some who were still with Lord Akio paused, startled, disconcerted. They had seen little but two of their fellows fall. It was though the wind itself, unseen, had drawn blood.

"Those with glaives, forward," said Lord Akio.

The glaive, of course, outreaches even the field sword.

"Swordsmen, surround them!" called Lord Akio.

"Back," I called. "To the bridge!"

The bridge, entwined with the blue climbers, arched in a lovely manner, for a length of some thirty-five or forty feet over a narrow, decorative pond, on the surface of which bloomed white and yellow water flowers, rising from flat, green pads; below, in the pond, which was shallow, one could see the slow movements of colorful fish. No more than two men could stride that bridge, abreast. Either ascent could thus be well defended. The highest point of the bridge was some five to seven feet above the water.

In the pause which followed Nodachi's swift, almost casual, felling of Lord Akio's two men, that small, eager, ill-fated vanguard unwisely addressing themselves, woefully unsupported, to their foray, both he and Lord Yamada had replaced their companion swords in their sashes and drawn up their field swords from the sand where they had deposited them, following the election of the companion sword as the instrument for resolving the matter which lay between them. The blow of the field sword can fell a small tree, or cut away the head of a glaive.

We fenced away sporadic, tentative attacks about us, drawing back to the bridge.

Few seemed willing to cast themselves recklessly upon us.

The lesson of Nodachi, it seems, had been well noted.

"Kill them! Kill them!" shouted Lord Akio.

I had no doubt that the Ashigaru, some ten or so, with Lord Akio would enter the pond, but the obstacle of the floor of the bridge, and its height, would, I hoped, neutralize to some extent the effect of the glaives wielded from below, by wading men with uncertain footing.

Kameko, kneeling, her neck tied closely to a stanchion near the height of the bridge, her hands tied behind her, squirmed.

"Be still," snapped Pertinax, his jacket soaked with blood at the right shoulder. He grasped his companion sword in his left hand.

"Yes, Master," she whispered, frightened.

"Do not be afraid," said Pertinax. "You are a domestic animal. Unless you are cut by a diverted blade, you will simply belong to another."

"I do not wish to belong to another, Master," she said.

"You are a slave," he said. "Your wishes are unimportant. They are of no more interest than those of a verr or tarsk."

"Yes, Master," she sobbed.

The portion of the bridge nearest the gate, and the raked sand, where contest had been done, was held by Nodachi, and, at his side, Lord Yamada. I sent Tajima and Yasushi to hold the farther portion of the bridge, that nearest the far wall, and the supper pavilion. I surmounted the center of the bridge. I could see both sides, and judge the pond below. In this way I might apprise my fellows of new dangers, direct a defense, and, in the case of need, on either portion of the bridge, supply it, immediately. A commander has obligations which take precedence over his personal preferences. He must not succumb to the dark hunger, covet the zest of battle as he may. His priorities are elsewhere. Mostly I feared bows, but none were carried that I had seen amongst the followers of Lord Akio. With me were wounded Pertinax, sword in his left hand, and Katsutoshi, his right hand in a reddened sleeve. "I may throw myself on glaives," said Katsutoshi, "and thus discomfit or disarm two or three, clearing the road for our steel." "Do not," I told him. "I am useless," he said. "There is no line to be opened." "Watch!" I said. "Lord Akio has spread his war fan and locked its blades in place," he said. "He is dangerous," I said. "He looks for his opportunity. His own men obscure his targets of choice." I assumed these would be Lord Yamada, and Nodachi, in that order. The spinning war fan is a terrible weapon, but once discharged, it is not easily recovered. "Watch," I encouraged him. "I shall," he said. "Momentarily," said Pertinax, "Ashigaru will enter the water." "It would be well," I said, "were you not wounded, had you retained your glaive." "*Ela*," said Pertinax. "It is true." "Even so," I said, "even as you are, it might be well to have one in hand." "I think so," said Pertinax. I thought him strong enough to handle one in his left hand, at least for the purposes of fending and jabbing. He would have the advantage of height, striking down, with the uplifted faces of the enemy almost within reach. Normally the glaive is held in both hands, the left hand before the right. The left hand guides the blade, the right hand, and body, supplying the driving force behind the thrust. "It is awkward to use the glaive from below, from the pond, thrusting upward," I said. "Perhaps one of those good fellows will loan you his." "I shall see to it," said Pertinax, placing his companion sword in his sash, "seizing it, tearing it away, with one hand, even if I have to lift him over the bridge." I feared that Pertinax, in his zeal, might worsen his wound. I looked about. "Where is Haruki?" I asked. "I do not know," said Pertinax, looking about.

The leadership, it seemed by default, had fallen to me. I would have chosen Lord Yamada as the commander of our small force, but he had ranked himself at the side of Nodachi.

They would await the foe, side by side.

Who was I to dispute his decision?

He was shogun.

"Storm them!" cried Lord Akio. "Like wind and rain, like lightning! Carry all before you!"

Lord Akio's men, from two sides, rushed onto the bridge.

Thickets of clashing steel sparkled.

Ten or more Ashigaru, bearing glaives, splashed into the water, five at least to each side of the bridge. I saw the fish dart away, and then the pond was muddied.

Swordsmen, some yards on the bridge, crowded, before and behind, were trying to force their way higher on the bridge, both to the left and right.

One swordsman reeled over the railing, into the pond.

Blades of glaives thrust up at us, striking wood, splintering railings, tangling in the vinous blue climbers. Men slipped and fell in the pond, in the muddy water, amidst the disturbed white and yellow flowers. Pertinax seized a thrusting glaive behind the blade and yanked it up, with two hands, blood running down his right arm, shaking loose a startled Ashigaru from the shaft, he plunging back into the water. I feared he had opened his wound, as there was fresh blood at his shoulder, and staining his sleeve, and running down his wrist. Pertinax then thrust at another, who slipped back, screaming, bleeding, his face half cut away, and then Pertinax swung the tool of war to the other side of the bridge, threatening another below, which fellow stumbled back in the muddy water, removing himself from the ambit of the weapon.

I saw an officer fall before the stroke of Yasushi, once a pupil of Nodachi.

Tajima fenced back a second attacker.

I looked wildly about. I held back a moan of misery. New figures were at the gate, unopposed.

"Draw back, draw back!" called Lord Akio. "All is well! Reinforcements arrive!"

"We cannot hold," called Lord Yamada. "There are too many. Die well!"

"Who can read the fortunes of war?" said Nodachi.

"What is written largely and boldly is easily read," said Lord Yamada.

"And may be as easily mistaken," said Nodachi.

"I saw how you handled your sword, stunted monster," said Lord Yamada to Nodachi. "I fear my blood is indeed within you."

"Blood is but the beginning," said Nodachi.

"You are a fool, skillful, misshapen brute," said Lord Yamada.

"Each must choose his own path," said Nodachi. "You chose to wed power. I chose to wed the sword."

"You are a fool," said Lord Yamada.

"Victories differ," said Nodachi. "One's victory is another's defeat. Each must strive for his own victory."

"You tread the path of fools," said Lord Yamada.

"It is my path," said Nodachi, "I have chosen it for myself. I fear few have done as much."

"Then tread it well," said Lord Yamada.

"I shall endeavor to do so," said Nodachi.

There must have been forty or fifty men now filing through the gate, many, as several of those with Lord Akio, still in the livery of Yamada.

Ela, I thought to myself. The matter is done! We had held

the bridge well, our narrow, wooden field of battle giving our smaller number the equalizing advantages of height and narrowness of access. Indeed, on some of the narrow, graceful, soaring bridges of the high cities of the continent, arching amongst lofty keeplike cylinders, there were many accounts of such high and dangerous passages being defended by one or two men against dozens. Odds of ten to one are considerably qualified when nine of the ten must remain inactive, when the ten must meet the one singly, one at a time, only one at a time.

My despair was occasioned by noting that several of the newcomers carried bows, and full quivers of the long Pani arrows.

Lord Akio's men had moved back, to allow the approach of the newcomers. Even his Ashigaru, those in the pond, water to their thighs, waded back, glaives held at the ready, away from the bridge.

Two floated in the water, face down.

"We cannot resist the flighted arrow," said Pertinax.

The bridge, our salvation against the odds arrayed against us, would be our doom with archers, as it would hold us in place.

We would be as vulnerable as penned verr.

I prepared to cry us from the bridge, to regain the land, to fight amidst our foes, that archers must have patience, confronted with moving, confusing targets, that they must be cautious and often hold their fire, lest they strike allies.

I was suddenly apprehensive.

With the drawing back of the men of Lord Akio, both ends of the bridge were now open.

Fighting bodies were no longer interposed between Yasushi and Tajima and the foe at their portion of the bridge, nor, at the other portion of the bridge, that closer to the gate and the raked sand, between Lord Yamada and Nodachi and the foe.

Lord Yamada and Nodachi had turned to look up to me, at the height of the bridge.

Were they awaiting my cry, to abandon the bridge?

"Beware!" cried Katsutoshi.

I had seen the motion, the preparation before, the grace and power of that movement, long ago in the garden, when Lord Akio, forgoing a living target at my behest, as I was a guest of the shogun, had demonstrated the effectiveness of the war fan on a young tree, close by the side of the gardener, Haruki.

I assumed his target was Lord Yamada, but never learned, for Lord Akio suddenly stiffened, and the fan fell behind him.

Warned, Lord Yamada and Nodachi had swiftly turned, but only to see Lord Akio, in his exquisite robes, crumple to the ground.

One of Lord Akio's men raised his sword to strike Haruki, who stood there, a long, four-pronged garden fork, used for turning soil, bloody to the socket, in his hands, but the blow failed to fall, and the bearer of the lifted sword spun away, his blade lost, he grasping at a long Pani arrow in his throat, blood running through his fingers.

Two more of Lord Akio's men were struck by arrows, and the rest fled from the garden, through the gate.

The officer apparently in charge of the newcomers approached.

I knew him, for I had met him before, and, indeed, had had unpleasant dealings at his hands.

"Greetings noble lord," said the officer, bowing to Lord Yamada.

"Who is your shogun?" said Lord Yamada.

"Yamada, of the house of Yamada, great lord," said the officer.

"You have not come to seize the shogunate?" said Lord Yamada.

"No, great lord," he said. "I would defend it as long as I could, but I fear it is doomed."

"It stands," said Lord Yamada.

"The perfidy of Lord Akio is broadcast," he said. "He is in league with the house of Temmu. The forces of Temmu, a thousand or more, are nigh."

"How then are you here?" asked Lord Yamada.

"I have come to die with my shogun," he said.

"Though the iron dragon has flown?" asked Lord Yamada.

"Yes," he said.

"You, noble Kazumitsu, special officer, trusted servant, are now daimyo," said Lord Yamada. "All lands and goods, treasures, houses, fortresses, men and chattels of the traitor, Lord Akio, are now yours."

"The men of Temmu are nigh, great lord," said Kazumitsu.

"Gardiner!" called Lord Yamada. "Approach!"

Haruki, the long fork still in hand, in two hands, approached Lord Yamada.

I feared he might raise the fork against the shogun.

"How dared you strike one so far above you, one of the nobility?" asked Lord Yamada.

"To save your life, noble lord," I suggested.

"No," said Haruki.

"Why then?" asked Lord Yamada.

"Lord Akio," said Haruki, "did injury in this place."

"He failed," said Lord Yamada.

"He succeeded only too well," said Haruki.

"I live," said Lord Yamada.

"His victim does not," said Haruki.

"What victim?" said Lord Yamada.

"The victim of his cruel and needless crime," said Haruki.

"I do not understand," said Lord Yamada.

"In this very garden, Lord Akio gratuitously slew a lovely tree, in the shimmering glory of its youth."

"I see," said Lord Yamada.

"I have avenged it," said Haruki.

"It seems you have saved my life, as well," said Lord Yamada.

"The occasion, if not welcome, was opportune," said Haruki.

"I will not owe my life to another," said Lord Yamada. "What will you accept, in lieu of my life, that your head be spared?"

"I return your life," said Haruki. "I ask nothing in return."

"You shall take something, or I shall have your head," said Lord Yamada. "What will you have, a golden chain, ten flocks of verr, ten herds of tarsk, a house, a dozen slaves?"

"I would that I might be permitted to tend your garden," said Haruki.

"The post is yours," said Lord Yamada.

"I fear it will be but briefly held, great shogun," said Kazumitsu. "The troops of Lord Temmu are nigh."

"Men swarm now at the gate!" cried Pertinax, from the height of the bridge.

"Hold!" I cried. "Those are not orderly troops. An avalanche, a flood, sweeping all away in its path, could not be less disciplined."

Kameko screamed, struggling helplessly, in her tether.

"I will not die at the hands of such!" announced Lord Yamada.

"One often has little choice in such matters, father," said Nodachi.

"Peasants!" cried Yasushi.

"Hundreds," said Pertinax, pointing.

"Swords ready!" cried Lord Yamada.

The storm of men, like lava pouring through the gate, bearing arsenals of stolen weapons, glaives, and swords, and dozens of implements of farming, rushed forth upon us, and was as though it would engross us, when it stopped, but yards way.

A burly figure, large and thick, emerged before us.

"Where is the noble warrior, Tajima, of the house of Temmu, of the service of Lord Nishida, of the cavalry of Tarl Cabot, tarnsman?" cried Arashi.

"Here!" cried Tajima, rushing forward, then stopping, abruptly, bowing, which bow Arashi, leader of the horde, returned.

"We have risen!" cried Arashi.

"And much destruction have you wrought!" said Tajima.

"The iron dragon flew!" said Arashi.

"Have you not done with looting?" asked Tajima.

"Much may be done in the shadow of the iron dragon's wings," said Arashi.

"The sky is clear," said Tajima.

"The men of Temmu march," said Arashi. "They are on the road now, but their foragers range widely. They will overrun the land. Villages will burn, fields will be harvested and drained, our flocks and herds will be taken, our women will be carried away."

"How can you, a bandit, object to banditry," asked Tajima, "whether that of a dozen greedy rovers or that of an army?"

"When an army passes," said Arashi, "there is little left to steal."

"Why are you here?" asked Tajima.

"The world crumbles," said Arashi. "Our blood has raced. We have had our time. Now we do not know what to do. We need law, time to tend our fields, leaders, the protection of the mighty."

"The mighty are fallen," said Tajima.

"You are Arashi, the bandit?" asked Lord Yamada, striding forward, field sword gripped in two hands.

"Yes," said Arashi.

"You are in the presence of the shogun," I informed Arashi.

"Yes, great lord," said Arashi, bowing.

"I shall have you crucified," said Lord Yamada.

"Not today, Lord," said Arashi, gesturing behind him, at the restless, massed peasants.

"Noble leader," I said to Arashi. "You have not come to loot an empty palace, nor steal from the destitute."

"No, noble one," said Arashi.

"Great lord," I said to Lord Yamada. "It is no accident that these troubled men have entered the palace grounds."

"Unbidden," said Lord Yamada.

"Yes," I said, "even unbidden."

"Some men cannot live without a tyrant," said Haruki, "either to obey, or defy."

"And service to the shogunate," I said, "surely sponges away many stains."

"We crave no pardon, great lord," said Arashi.

"Why have you come, bandit?" asked Lord Yamada.

"To pledge to my shogun a thousand Ashigaru," said Arashi.

The peasants behind him stirred, shouted, and lifted, and shook, their weapons of diverse sorts.

"Your crimes are no more," said the shogun, "but now return to your villages."

"How so, great lord?" said Arashi, startled.

"You are not Ashigaru," said Lord Yamada, "but the metal from which Ashigaru may be formed."

"We are your metal, great lord," said Arashi, "shape us into your tool of war!"

There was acclamatory shouting from behind him, and it rang in the grounds of the shogun.

"There is no time, brave fellows," called Lord Yamada. "The men of Temmu march. They are on the road, they are near."

"We shall meet them!" cried Arashi.

"You would be cut to pieces, destroyed," said Lord Yamada, "perhaps to a man. Return to your villages, and hope that you may be spared."

"And what will you do, great lord?" asked Arashi.

"Wait here, to die," said Lord Yamada.

"No, great lord," I said. "You are shogun. You will march. You will advance to meet the enemy, though there be but ten behind you."

"And would you, Tarl Cabot, tarnsman," he asked, "be one of those ten?"

"I am," I said.

"That is a good way to die," said Kazumitsu.

"I am with you, great lord," said Katsutoshi.

"And I," said Yasushi, coming forward.

"Where Tarl Cabot, tarnsman, goes, I go," said Tajima. "He is my friend."

"No more than mine," said Pertinax. "I am with him."

"There will be more than ten," I said. "I have a plan. We will need the men of Arashi, but they will not be engaged. They are not trained. But their quality will be unknown to the forces of Temmu. We shall spread them about, and scatter them. Let them be glimpsed amongst trees and brush. They will move. They will not be closely seen. It will be difficult to assess their numbers. Caution will suggest there are many even where there are few. Lord Temmu has committed only a portion of his forces south. Meeting the appearance of stout resistance they will slow their pace, hold, and reconnoiter. This is the only pause I require, the opportunity to parley. Indeed, with them, I trust, will be members of the cavalry. This will allow me to communicate with the cavalry itself, which is important. The forces of Lord Temmu in the south, I speculate, will be commanded by either Lord Nishida or Lord Okimoto, or both. I know both. Both are rational men. I can speak with both. What I have to say will, I think, convince either Lord Nishida or Lord Okimoto, or both, to withdraw, or camp, and seek orders from the holding of Temmu, conveyed by tarnsmen. Personally, I need only communicate somehow with the cavalry itself."

"We will march," announced Lord Yamada. "Tarl Cabot, tarnsman, arrange matters with Arashi. See to the details of things. That is not the role of a shogun."

"Yes, great lord," I said.

"Great lord," said Tajima, "I do not know the details of the plan of Tarl Cabot, tarnsman, but perhaps the mighty have not fallen."

"They have not," I said.

"Will you march with me, son?" asked Lord Yamada of Nodachi, the swordsman.

"I am at your side," said he, "father."

Chapter Sixty-Two

How Matters Turned Out;
I Look Eastward

It was a bright morning, with a pleasant wind, and I stood on the heavy planks of the great wharf, that at the foot of the long trail which led upward, within its walls, to the holding of Temmu, far above, almost obscured by clouds.

At the wharf, restless at its moorings, was the *River Dragon*, with its large, battened sails and high poop, brought across Thassa from Brundisium, on the continent, by Captain Nakamura. The ship of Tersites had demonstrated the possibility of reaching the World's End, and, then, the *River Dragon*, in turn, inspirited by the success of the ship of Tersites, had dared Thassa, as well, but then eastward, and had managed to make the great harbor at Brundisium. It had then returned to its native port in the lands of Temmu. Here it had been refitted, and was now prepared to essay the bold and dangerous, but now-proven-practical, trip again. I would be aboard her.

"There is peace now, in the local waters," said Captain Nakamura, "save for occasional pirates."

"I am pleased," I said.

"Many arrangements were made in Brundisium, for my return," he said. "We shall bring kaiila, and bosk, back to the islands, and the eggs of large tharlarion."

"But no dragons," I said.

"I do not understand," said the captain.

"It is a joke," I said.

"The humor of barbarians is fascinating," he said. Then he

597

looked down at the large, shaggy, sinuous beast by my side, Ramar, the lame sleen, brought from the camp of tarns, some one hundred and twenty pasangs north of the holding of Temmu. I learned he had often patrolled the perimeter of that camp, in the sleen's territorial manner, as we had hoped, this much increasing its security, and he had on more than one occasion dealt with interlopers, or spies, who had attempted to infiltrate its precincts. This was determined by guards who detected the remains. He rubbed that large, triangular head against my leg, and I fondled his head, roughly. Had it been another's hand, it might have been snapped away. "And sleen, too," said Captain Nakamura. "They have many uses."

"Tarns' eggs were brought west from the continent on the ship of Tersites," I said. "They have now been removed to the camp of tarns, and several have hatched."

"Interesting," said Captain Nakamura.

The cavalry had reserved to itself tarns, and their training. It was one of the provisions stipulated in the "Agreement."

"Forgive me," said Captain Nakamura, "but I must be about my duties."

We exchanged bows.

"With the tide," he said.

"With the tide," I said.

The first gong had already sounded.

In the past months the skies had been clear. The shadow of the iron dragon had fallen on neither the lands of Yamada nor those of Temmu. Rumors abounded, normally spoken in whispers or hushed tones, for who knew the hearing of dragons. A thousand stories were about, in village markets, in the *dojos* and barracks, in courtyards and fields, in fortresses and sheds, about campfires, even in the corridors of palaces.

It had returned to its secret lair to guard its treasures, perhaps to sleep for another thousand years; it had returned to the country of mystery from which it had emerged, some fearful land, a far land of rock and flame; a vast, noxious crevice in the bowels of the earth, a dark, freezing country beyond the moons.

In any event, it seemed that the iron dragon had departed from the islands, and might never return.

The skies were clear.

Accordingly, given the nature of men, life began to form itself again in the ancient patterns of coming and going, farming and hunting, fishing and gathering, gaining and losing, accumulating and squandering, building and destroying, planning and plotting, loving and hating. Peasants returned to their villages; goods and wives returned to their houses and holdings; ornaments and coins were unearthed; fields were tended; palisades were rebuilt; gates were repaired; traders sought customers; and warriors, hungry and barefoot, weary, weapons in their sashes, drifted back toward rice and daimyos.

"You see your danger," I had said to Lords Nishida and Okimoto, "thousands of warriors and Ashigaru."

"The road was clear, there was no resistance," said Lord Okimoto.

"Does that not seem to you odd," I asked, "that you would not see the enemy until you were deep within his country, a hostile country, and far from reinforcements and supply lines?"

"It is a trap?" said Lord Okimoto.

"Obviously," I said.

"I warned of this," said Lord Okimoto to Lord Nishida.

"If," I said, "you have several thousand troops, you may make a good show of it."

Lord Okimoto looked displeased, visibly.

"You might be able to break through, and withdraw north."

"Break through?" said Lord Okimoto.

"Yes," I said, "clearly you must understand that you are surrounded."

I had arranged that portions of Arashi's men would hover about variously, behind and to the sides, as well as to the fore, allowing themselves to be detected, but not clearly. Surely scouts would have notified Lords Nishida and Okimoto of such sightings.

"I urged Lord Temmu to commit more troops to the south," said Lord Okimoto.

"Perhaps five thousand?" I said.

To the best of my knowledge, Lord Temmu could not have brought four thousand men south, even with deserters and recruits, let alone five thousand. Indeed, had he emptied his holding and left it vacant, to urts and jards, he could not have brought five thousand men south.

Lord Nishida remained taciturn, not speaking.

"Lord Yamada," I said, "has marched forth to meet you. He awaits you on the road."

"Surely he is dead," said Lord Okimoto.

"He is not," I said.

"He has been defeated, and deserted," said Lord Okimoto.

"That is your intelligence," I said. "I inform you that it is inaccurate."

"But Lord Akio—" said Lord Okimoto.

"Lord Akio is dead," I said.

"Yamada lives?" said Lord Okimoto.

"Yes," I said, "and commands his army, of thousands."

"But," said Lord Okimoto, "the iron dragon has flown."

"The skies are clear," I said.

"Why have you come here?" asked Lord Okimoto.

"I object to pointless slaughter," I said.

"Yamada waits?" said Lord Okimoto.

"For now," I said. "He trusts you will advance further, deeper into his trap."

"And if we do not?" said Lord Okimoto.

"Beware the fall of darkness," I said.

"What is your recommendation, Tarl Cabot, tarnsman?" asked Lord Nishida, politely. "That we turn about, and hasten north?"

"No, Lord," I said. "I fear there is no time. I would recommend you hold here, and fortify your camp."

"We have been betrayed," said Lord Okimoto. "We have been informed the troops of Yamada are scattered, and most fled south, that he is vulnerable, and without support."

"He has marched to meet you, and waits upon the road," I said.

"We are assured he has no men," said Lord Okimoto, uncertainly.

"This by whose assurance?" I asked.

"By that of Lord Akio," said Lord Okimoto.

"Lord Akio," I said, "is dead."

"—no men," said Lord Okimoto.

"And what are the reports of your scouts?" I said.

"That his minions are as the sands of the shore, and the leaves of trees," said Lord Okimoto.

"Fortify the camp," I said. "You may then survive the night. In the morning you may reconnoiter. If you deem it wise, you may then advance, or, if not, communicate with the house of Temmu, by message vulo, and await a response from the house of Temmu, brought by tarnsmen."

"We shall await the word of Lord Temmu," said Lord Okimoto. He turned then to a subordinate. "Fortify the camp," he said.

I thought it fortunate that Lord Okimoto, cousin to Lord Temmu, was the ranking officer, the high daimyo, of this small invasion force, probably no more than a thousand men. Lord Okimoto was no coward, but he was amongst the most careful of commanders, his caution predictably exceeding his audacity. Lord Nishida, I thought, was a better commander, one capable of more judiciously balancing risks. Sometimes the arrow must rest on the string; at other times, the bow is to be drawn, and the arrow loosed.

The tarnsmen would almost certainly be of the cavalry. Communications would not be trusted to Tyrtaios, and his fellow, allegedly deserted to the banner of Temmu.

I would thus be able to transmit certain orders to the cavalry. Indeed, should time permit, I might, after these days of imprisonment and escape, be able to rendezvous with Ichiro, if he were still in the vicinity. He had had four tarns in his keeping, those on which he, Tajima, Pertinax, Haruki, and myself had ventured south, Haruki behind the saddle of Tajima. Also in the keeping of Ichiro we had left Aiko, the unclaimed slave from the market village. Few knew of course, she was an unclaimed slave. Such are exceedingly rare, and are seldom long unclaimed. Indeed, any slave whose master's identity cannot be readily established, is unknown, or is in doubt is likely to be promptly claimed. It is much the same with any other domestic animal, say, a kaiila or verr. Slaves, after all, have value. The slave collar commonly has two purposes. It, like the brand, proclaims its occupant a slave, and will normally, as most collars on animals, identify the beast's master. The brand is commonly concealed by even a brief tunic. The collar, on the other hand, prominent on the beast's neck, is to be clearly visible. This arrangement is demanded by free women in order that the worthlessness and degradation of the slave be dramatically contrasted with their own freedom, dignity, and station, and required by men, as it is appropriate that slaves be collared. Also, men like to see women in collars.

In fortifying the camp, as palisading was absent, a deep ditch was dug at the perimeter of the camp, and the removed earth was then piled at the edge of the ditch closest to the camp, this heightening the climb toward the camp. Various camp wagons were also brought toward the perimeter, that ensconced defenders, when not resisting intrusion, might be sheltered from arrow fire.

"I trust you will remain our guest," said Lord Okimoto.

"I suspect I will have little choice in the matter," I said.

"You are perceptive, for a barbarian," said Lord Okimoto.

Lord Nishida smiled.

It turned out, however, that I soon, unexpectedly, departed from the camp. Haruki, not required in our perilous ruse, that of peasants and feigned readiness for war, had made his way to Ichiro's hiding place, which, happily, had not been discovered in the long interval between our early visit to the market village to investigate stories of a mountebank, a master of sword tricks, and the present. Ichiro then brought the four tarns, three on leading straps, to the grounds of the palace of Yamada. With him, of course, came Haruki, and Aiko, bound, belly up, wrists back and down, ankles over and down, over the saddle apron of Ichiro. That night, about the Twentieth Ahn, the silhouette of a tarn was cast briefly on the white moon, and, a bit later, the snap of mighty wings disturbed the canvas of several tents.

"Tarn!" I heard cry. "Tarn!"

I was near the center of the camp. I was, after all, a guest. Similarly, I doubted I would be welcomed near the perimeter, as an intent of unauthorized departure on my part might be suspected. Too, of course, most of the Ashigaru and warriors were at the perimeter.

I hoped that the tarnsman would have a similar assessment of the situation, particularly as the camp had been hastily fortified, and an imminent attack might be anticipated.

"It is too soon for a response to the message vulos!" cried a man.

"No," cried another. "It is a tarn."

"So soon?" said another.

"It cannot be otherwise!" said a fellow.

"Retreat!" cried a fellow.

"Leave fires, withdraw in darkness!" said another.

"To what?" said a man. "Who knows what lies in wait, in the night."

"Some have already fled," said a man.

"No," said another. "They would be stopped at the ditch!"

"What if the guards have fled?" said another.

"Let us see!" said another.

"Remain in place!" said a voice, presumably that of an officer.

I feared some of these men were not thinking clearly. It was indeed far too soon for any tarnsman-brought response to messages sent forth this very afternoon. But, of course, the thousand men or so with Lords Nishida and Okimoto were only too aware of the camp's fortification, and the seeming appearance of hostile troops in the vicinity, hostile troops in undetermined numbers. What had begun as an unopposed march to claim an uncontested and inexpensive victory had suddenly, within an Ahn or so, turned into an apparently desperate situation, sustaining a possible siege without the benefit of suitable defenseworks against a foe which might be present in overwhelming numbers. It was not surprising, then, that nerves were taut and thoughts might seize on hopes, not facts.

"Fire on the flighted monster!" cried a man.

"Arrows to the string!" called a fellow.

"No!" said another. "It must be a response from the holding of Lord Temmu!"

"It is too soon," said a man.

"It must be from our lord," said a man. "The beast, Yamada, has no tarns!"

The two tarns which had been at the disposal of Lord Yamada were no longer available to the shogun. Tyrtaios and his fellow, masters of these two tarns, had disappeared. It was conjectured by some they had forsworn the service of Yamada and fled to the banner of Lord Temmu, apprising him of their secret, unswerving fidelity to his cause.

How would the rider, whom I surmised would be either Tajima, Pertinax, or Ichiro, locate me?

Whereas the camp was not nearly as large as the vast road camps of the earlier advance of Lord Yamada on the holding of Temmu, it was large enough.

One could scarcely descend, and inquire, tent to tent.

Were I a prisoner, a hostage, or a detained guest, it seemed rational to suppose that I would be somewhere near the center of the camp.

But where?

The center of the camp, of course, would be thinly defended. As the tarn cavalry was either neutral to, or allied with, the house of Temmu, and as there was too little time for mining, an assault must take place at the perimeter. Certainly that was where it was anticipated.

Had I been in the wilderness, a small fire, visible only from above, would signal my position.

But there were dozens of watch fires in the camp.

I seized up a large, thick, burning brand from the nearest fire, and held it to a tent, and then, to another tent, and another, until there were four tents afire.

"What are you doing?" cried a fellow, but he was then struck, heavily, with the fiery club, and desisted in his inquiry.

I was then standing, well illuminated, in a clear area, looking upward, I suspect anxiously, a blazing tent several yards away, on each side. I heard men shouting, and converging toward my artificial, geometrically arranged conflagrations. From the air the spectacular oddity of this arrangement should be obvious. Who would not investigate such an anomaly?

The great wings snapped over my head, dust pelting me, flames roaring to the sides, as though driven by the wind, the tarn hovering, and I grasped the flung, uncoiling, knotted rope, and, in a moment, was swinging wildly beneath the climbing tarn, the camp growing small behind me.

"Well done, Ichiro, bannerman!" I called.

"It is nothing, Commander," he shouted.

But it was something, in my view. I thought that I might

604

claim Aiko, who was open to claim, and give her to him. Surely, in his long concealment with the tarns, waiting for Tajima, Pertinax, Haruki, and myself to return, he would have had an opportunity to form some interest in Aiko's lovely and delicate lineaments.

Whereas I have spoken of an "Agreement," that expression was, to some extent, a euphemism. It was more in the nature of a decree, or ukase, imposed by those in a position to impose and enforce it, in this case, the cavalry, now commanded by young Tajima, tarnsman.

I am sure the terms were neither congenial to Lord Yamada nor to Lord Temmu.

Whereas war was forbidden to neither of them, it was forbidden between them. If the altercation between these two houses was indeed wagered on by mysterious gamblers, perhaps treading the depths of a vast nest in the Sardar, or in orbiting worlds of steel, it would lack a resolution. In this game there would be no winner, nor loser. The dice would disappear, the coin would vanish. The pieces, the game unresolved, would be dashed from the board. I did not even know if the wager had existed, or, if it existed, on which side which gambler might have wagered. But there would be truce between the two warring houses, and enemies might live in peace, however unwillingly, glaring at one another balefully. The holdings, the palaces and fortresses, the houses and villages, were vulnerable from the air. There would be no shield against fire from the sky. Not even the high holding of Lord Temmu, citadel which had withstood a hundred sieges, over a thousand years, would be immune from foes who might companion themselves with clouds. I think few understood this ruling, other than myself, and perhaps Lord Nishida.

I had little optimism, of course, even if the contest had been allowed to come to its conclusion, that a losing party would abide its outcome. It was hard to imagine Kurii ceasing to hunger for the green fields of Gor, and it was hard to imagine Priest-Kings voluntarily sharing their world, even its surface, with so aggressive, dangerous, and territorial a life form as the destroyer of a planet and the maker of steel worlds.

"How long do you think this arrangement will last?" had asked Lord Nishida, over tea.

"At least," I said, "until the interest of unseen others has turned aside."

"The gamble, if it existed," said Lord Nishida, "is over, as this war is over. Stasis has been achieved. That is our resolution. A new wager would require a new war."

"I trust so," I said.

"In time," he said, "blades will be sharpened, and the two houses will be again at one another's throats."

"Let it not be so," I said.

"They are opposed houses," he said.

"For a time," I said, "the cavalry will keep the peace."

"A peace," he said.

"One is better than none," I said.

"Unless one cares for war," he said.

"Of course," I said.

"You are a warrior," he said.

I was silent.

"The cavalry was once decimated, nearly destroyed," he said. "It might be so again."

"I think not," I said. "Security is enhanced. Spies are stationed. Signals are emplaced. Retreat camps, hidden in the mountains, might permit rearming, and regrouping."

"There is always the danger of dissension and corruption within the cavalry itself," he said.

"There is no guarantee," I said, "that the sea sleen will not swim, that the larl will not hunt, that the ost will not strike."

"Tajima is a good officer," he said.

"He served you well," I said.

"And you," he said.

"Pertinax will accompany me to Brundisium," I said.

"And others?" said Lord Nishida.

"Those who wish to do so," I said.

"Brave, loyal men may replenish the cavalry," said Lord Nishida.

"Many decisions will be made by the tarns themselves," I said. The tarn, an aggressive, terrible bird, senses diffidence, hesitation, and fear. And some, for no clearly understood reason, will not accept certain riders. Many men have been maimed, even torn to pieces, by these dangerous "brothers of the wind." But men will seek their saddles. They will risk death to share the flight of the tarn.

"Rutilius of Ar, one perhaps of interest to you," said Lord Nishida, "now serves in the kitchen of the castle."

"I see," I said.

Rutilius of Ar was once Seremides of Ar, master of the Taurentian guard. He had lost a leg in the Vine Sea, on the voyage to the World's End. He had supported Talena, the "false Ubara" of Ar. There was a price on his head, on the continent. The bounty on Talena herself, who had been mysteriously removed from Ar, during the restoration of Marlenus, Ubar of Ubars, was a fortune, such that it might purchase a city, ten thousand tarn disks of gold, each of double weight.

"The location of Tyrtaios, and Straton, his fellow, who rode for Lord Yamada, is not known," said Lord Nishida.

"I have heard so," I said.

"They came to the holding," said Lord Nishida, "pledging their swords to the house of Temmu. It seems their service to Lord Yamada was a deceit, that their hearts and loyalty were always with the house of Temmu, that they had labored secretly on its behalf, at great risk to themselves, in the very midst of the enemy."

"Of course," I said.

"They barely escaped the hand of Lord Temmu," said Lord Nishida.

"They had tarns," I said.

"Too," he said, "Lord Temmu has abandoned his interest in bones and shells."

"Daichi returned?" I said.

"We do not know his whereabouts," said Lord Nishida. "Lord Temmu desires to have him cast from the outer parapets, to the valley below."

I sipped my tea.

"I did not believe you, on the road to the palace of Yamada," he said.

"I thought you might not," I said.

"Your alleged masses of warriors and Ashigaru did not

exist," he said. "Those sighted were not uniformed, and were diversely armed. Banners were not in evidence. Why would forces of such potency not be more easily detected? Their ranging, and movements, were not those of armies, but of scouts or skirmishers. If Yamada had the forces you alleged at his disposal he would have done well to mass them, in formidable array, that we be disheartened. What cannot be seen may not be many, but few."

"They were peasants," I said.

"I thought so," said Lord Nishida. "We could have paved the road to the palace with their bodies."

"They would not have been committed in battle," I said. "Why did you not disabuse Lord Okimoto of his apprehensions?"

"I wished to see what you were up to," said Lord Nishida. "Conquest was within our grasp. What difference does it make whether the fist is closed on one day or another?"

"True," I said.

"It would have been well for the house of Temmu," he said, "had we retained you as a guest."

"But you failed to do so," I said.

"And thus," said he, "you made contact with the cavalry."

"Of course," I said.

"And were able to issue significant orders," he said.

"Yes," I said.

"And return, those orders transmitted," he said, "to issue your ultimatum."

"Forgive me," I said.

"It is just as well," he said. "Had we crushed Yamada and ended his house, it is not clear what might have been the consequences for the world."

"If any," I said.

"Yes," he said, "if any."

So two shogunates, as before, stood.

My thoughts drifted back to the grounds of the palace of Yamada. Kazumitsu, who had been a special officer to Lord Yamada, was now a loyal and honored daimyo, having succeeded to the authority, honors, lands, and goods of Lord Akio. Katsutoshi, now training his left hand to wield the companion sword, remained the captain of the shogun's guard.

Yasushi was promoted to high sword master, he who organizes and trains Ashigaru. The whereabouts of Arashi were not known, but it was rumored he, with a handful of armed fellows, haunted the towns, roads, and villages of the north. Relentlessly pursued, he could withdraw to the lands of Lord Yamada where, it seemed, he would be welcomed, and sheltered.

"Stay with me," Lord Yamada had said to Nodachi. "Rule by my side."

"Forgive me, honored father," said Nodachi. "But I am called by the shores of far seas, by lonely forests, by remote mountains. I will seek a cave. I must perfect my skills. I must meditate."

"You are mad, dear, misshapen brute," said Lord Yamada.

"The sanity of one is the madness of another," he said.

"You seek perfection?" said Lord Yamada.

"Of course," said Nodachi, bowing.

"Then you are a fool," said Lord Yamada. "The path to perfection is a path with no end."

"It is a path some will follow," said Nodachi.

"I will kill no more sons," said Lord Yamada. "I will have a hundred sons, a hundred swords at my side."

"I am a man of peace," said Nodachi.

"Are you not wedded to the sword?" asked Lord Yamada.

"There is no peace without the sword," said Nodachi.

He then bowed to his father, which bow was returned. He then turned about and took his leave. Neither the shogun nor any of his guards attempted to detain him.

"You intend to sail with the *River Dragon*," said Lord Nishida.

"Yes, Lord," I said. "Perhaps you will convey my farewells to Lord Temmu and Lord Okimoto."

"Lord Okimoto will doubtless compose a poem," said Lord Nishida. "He will then transcribe it onto a sheet of silk. His calligraphy is superb."

"I have heard so," I said.

"I shall miss you, Tarl Cabot, tarnsman," he said.

"And I you," I said.

"I have studied men much," said Lord Nishida, "and I do not understand them."

"Nor I," I said. "There is always love and honor, and greed and gold. Some ascend the steps of blood and paint the black dagger. Others grasp at sparkling pebbles and tiny disks of yellow metal. Others will die for a Home Stone."

"And which are you, Tarl Cabot, tarnsman?" he asked.

"I am unknown to myself," I said. "I am perhaps better known to others than to myself. Some are always wayfarers, strangers to themselves."

"The *River Dragon* sails tomorrow," said he.

"I know, my lord," I said.

There was much bustle on the wharf, I was jostled. A long string of stripped, neck-chained, back-braceleted slaves, mostly barbarians, but some Pani, was being boarded. Some mercenaries, intent on returning to the continent, were boarding, as well, packs on their back. Few, despite the protestations of recruiters, long ago on the continent, were returning richer than they came. Wealth can be earned by the sword, but blood and misery, weariness and cold, want and danger, are more common pay.

Yet men, still, will follow the way of the sword.

"Tal, Tarl Cabot, tarnsman," said Tajima.

"I had hoped you would see me off," I said. "How goes the cavalry?"

"Its beasts are healthy, its rounds are made, its weapons are sharpened," said Tajima.

"Two houses fear you," I said.

I had last seen Tajima at the camp of tarns, north of the holding of Lord Temmu, in his headquarters tent. He moved aside the lists of equipment and the maps on the small table, and clapped his hands, twice, briskly.

Nezumi hurried in, and knelt, head down, to await instructions.

"Stand, girl," he said, "and turn, twice, slowly, before us."

"Nice," I said.

She was no longer in the rough tunic of a field slave, but in the slight silk of a pleasure slave, brief, and yellow. Her hair was short, still, but well shaped and cut. Her body sparkled, for slaves are not free women. They must keep themselves clean, neat, and well-groomed, such that they will be attractive to men. Perhaps that is one reason free women hate them so.

Slaves, being owned, exist for their masters, and are to please them. She wore a light, flat, close-fitting collar, which closed and locked at the back of her neck.

Nezumi was indeed a lovely slave.

Men enjoy showing off their slaves, as they might any other belonging.

Tajima pointed to the ground, and she knelt, instantly, her head down.

We then paid her no more attention.

How careless she had been, I recalled, to have cast that beribboned missive from the outer parapet.

I supposed there were many ways of begging for the collar, some even unknown to the supplicant.

I recalled a conversation between them which I had overheard, at night, when camping in the open country, shortly after we had fled from that village in which we feared, and justifiably, we had been suspected.

"You saved my life," she had said.

"It is nothing," he had said.

"Still," she said.

"I wanted a girl for my collar," he said.

"I think there was more," she said.

"No," he said.

"Perhaps Master is less than candid," she said.

"Perhaps Nezumi wishes to be beaten," he said.

"There are many girls," she said. "No, I do not wish to be beaten."

"And most," he said, "are far more beautiful than Nezumi."

"Scarcely," she had said.

In this short debate, I had found myself siding with Nezumi. Many Pani women are quite beautiful, but I doubted that many were more beautiful than she, and certainly there would be few who would be far more beautiful. I am sure that Tajima had wanted her from the first moment he had seen her, when she was feigning the role of a contract woman in the quarters of Lord Nishida. It had not been suspected at that time that she was a spy for the house of Yamada, let alone that she might be one of his several daughters. She had frequently scorned and abused him as a poor warrior. How he must have dreamed of buying her contract! Now she had no more status than a tarsk, another beast which may be owned.

Tajima had regarded her, she kneeling at hand, head down, in the headquarters tent, in the camp of tarns.

"Look at me," he had said.

She had raised her head, instantly.

"Go to the kitchen tent," he said. "Go, cook our food."

"Yes, Master," she had said, rising, and hurrying to obey.

"Nezumi," he had called.

She had turned, in the opening of the tent.

He slapped a switch down, sharply, on the table, and Nezumi flinched, as though the blow had fallen on her smooth, bared skin.

"I trust we will be pleased," he said.

"Yes, Master!" she had cried, and hurried away.

"It is pleasant to own a woman," he said to me.

"What pleasure can compare to that of the mastery?" I said.

"Women are comfortable in the collar," he said.

"They belong in it," I said.

"They are grateful, and joyful, in the collar," he said, "owned and mastered."

"It does not matter," I said, "as they are slaves."

"True," he said.

"Where is Nezumi?" I asked, standing on the wharf, in the bustle, men moving about me, Pani and barbarians.

"I left her at the camp," he said, "chained by the neck to a post."

"You know she loves you," I said.

"What is the vulnerable, helpless love of a slave?" he asked.

"The deepest and most profound love that a woman can bear a man," I said.

"They cannot help themselves," he said. "They need masters. They have been bred for masters."

"I know a world where many never find their masters," I said.

"I recall such a world," said Tajima.

"I think you love Nezumi," I said.

"Do not joke," said Tajima. "She is a slave."

"I think you would die for her," I said.

"Quite possibly," said Tajima. "She is my property."

"I wish you well," I said, bowing.

"And I, you," said he, returning the bow.

He then withdrew, and I could see him no longer, for the many men, and even slaves, about.

Interestingly, I had never received the opportunity to give Aiko to Ichiro, my bannerman. It may be recalled that Haruki had ventured to the hiding place of Ichiro and the tarns, where Aiko was in attendance, and that they had then returned, by tarn, to the grounds of the palace. It was after that that Ichiro had waited for darkness, to retrieve me, if possible, from the camp of the house of Temmu, where I had presented myself to Lords Nishida and Okimoto, in the hope, first, of preventing the advance of the invasion force, and, secondly, of somehow managing to make contact with the cavalry. My ultimate goal, naturally enough, under the circumstances, was to bring the situation between the rival houses of Temmu and Yamada to the point where neither house could achieve, or plausibly claim, victory. In this way neither Priest-Kings nor Kurii could claim the benefits accruing to the outcome of a dark, portentous wager, one in which the stakes were, substantially, a world, and perhaps two.

So Aiko found herself on the palace grounds, brought by Ichiro and Haruki, while Lord Yamada, Nodachi, I, and some others, and the many peasants of Arashi, advanced to meet, and discomfit, the forces of Temmu on the north road. Once I had arranged the peasants, and set them about their diversions, and had arrested the progress of Lord Yamada, in such a way as to suggest he was fully ready for battle, but hoped to lure the invasion force farther south, perhaps deeper into a trap, I had contacted Lords Nishida and Okimoto under the pretense of warning them of imminent danger. Given the higher rank and the usual circumspection of Lord Okimoto, on which I had counted, I had managed to halt their march, at least temporarily, and purchase some days of truce, while messages were being exchanged between their road camp and the distant holding of the northern shogun. These days, and the availability of tarns, allowing an expedited communication, gave me the opportunity to marshal the cavalry in such a way that I would be justified in issuing my ultimatum to both houses, peace, or destruction. During these days Aiko came to the attention of Lord Yamada, who had returned to his palace, following the fortification of the road camp. He regarded her, naturally enough, given her beauty, as a possible wife. Indeed, without discounting the sometimes marvelous beauty of the daughters of peasants, whose sales tend to fill the ranks of contract women, Lord Yamada suspected, given not only her features and lines, but the obscurity of her antecedents, and her lack of family, that she may not have been originally of the peasantry. Inquiries were made of Eito, the rich peasant who had unclaimed her in the village, and it was learned she was a scion of the nobility, in this case of a fallen house, defeated in battle, and had been sold, with other children of the house, years ago. It was as a small child, perhaps three or four years old, that she had been purchased by Eito. Lord Yamada, of course, understood her as a slave, but not as an unclaimed slave. As she was given to assisting Haruki in the garden, Lord Yamada naturally assumed that Haruki, who was a free man, owned her. It seemed she bore some resemblance to one who had once been Lord Yamada's favorite wife, she who had been the daughter of Haruki, and the mother of, amongst others, Nodachi, whom Haruki had saved from the strangler's cord. She had died of poison in the women's quarters, for which crime Lord Yamada had chosen ten women by lot, and had them beheaded. As noted earlier, if she had been of high birth, all might have been slain. Ichiro, too, of course, as the matter had been concealed, did not know her as unclaimed, but also thought she must belong to Haruki. Further, he had become much enamored of her. As matters turned out, both Lord Yamada and Ichiro approached Haruki. I was present. Ichiro had no more than a handful of copper. Lord Yamada, obviously, even in the depleted state of his treasury, could offer much more. "I can take her, if I please," said Lord Yamada. "I am shogun." "But," said Haruki, "who then will tend your garden?" "Very well," said Lord Yamada, "I will offer you a golden chain. It is a hundred times her value." "Perhaps," said Haruki to Lord Yamada, "I will sell her to this young man, for his fine handful of copper." "Do you dare, young tarnsman," asked Lord Yamada, "bid against me?" "Yes, great lord," said Ichiro. "Forgive me!" "But perhaps," said Haruki, "she is not for sale." "Two golden chains!" said Lord Yamada. "And I will give you a dozen slaves to help you in the garden!" "But, great lord," said Haruki. "I do not own her." "Who owns her?" cried both Ichiro and Lord Yamada, neither pleased, at all. Haruki looked down at Aiko, who was kneeling, as she was a slave in the presence of free persons. "I claim you!" said Haruki to Aiko. "Now I own her," he said to Ichiro and Lord Yamada. Then he said to Aiko, "You are free!" "I do not understand," said Ichiro. "What are you doing?" said Lord Yamada. "Rise up," said Haruki to Aiko. He then pointed to the confused, trembling Aiko. "This is a free woman," he said. "This is madness," said Lord Yamada. "Not at all," said Haruki. "I could not give her to you without injuring my friend, Ichiro, and I cannot give her to Ichiro without displeasing my shogun. Thus, she is free." "I do not want to be free!" she wept, looking to Ichiro. "Be my wife," said Lord Yamada. "You will be high amongst my women." "And you?" asked Aiko of Ichiro. "Be the wife of a great shogun," said Ichiro. And then he turned away, sadly. He had gone only a few steps when Aiko ran after him, put herself in his path, threw herself to her knees, and cried out, face uplifted, tears run upon her cheeks. "Behold this girl!" she cried. "She is before you! She is a slave, and has always been a slave. She desires a master! The secret slave is now bared to the world, as would be her body if masters wished. She acknowledges that she is a slave, publicly, before witnesses! She now performs an act of submission!" And she then put her head down and covered his feet with kisses. "I did not know that you were worthless!" said Ichiro, angrily. "Yes, Master," she said. "I am worthless!" Then she looked up. "I am helpless now!" she said. "I am submitted, I am at your mercy. What will you do with me?" "What would you have me do?" he asked. "Accept me!" she begged. "Accept me!" "What is your name?" he asked. "I have no name," she said, "I am a slave." "You are not collared," he said. "Many women who are slaves are not collared," she said. "We will have you fitted with one," he said. "Slaves should be in their collars." "Yes, Master. Thank you, Master," she said. "I will call you 'Aiko'," he said. "You are Aiko." "Yes, Master," she said. "I am Aiko, Master!" "You are accepted," he said, "and claimed." She then collapsed at his feet, weeping, with joy.

"It seems, gardener *san,*" said Lord Yamada, "that I have lost."
"No, great shogun," said Haruki. "You could have interfered,
and did not. It is one of your greatest victories."
"Let us inspect the state of the blue climbers," said the shogun.
"They are doing nicely," said Haruki.

As you may suppose, Lord Temmu, with victory almost in his
grasp, was furious with the withdrawal, and return, of the small
invasion force sent south. Were not defenseless lands spread
out before him? Was not the very palace of his mortal enemy
empty and desolate? Had not the iron dragon itself flown on his
behalf? Then he found himself confronted by the ultimatum of
an upstart, a mere barbarian. He and Lord Yamada, for no clear
reason, were to keep within their ancestral borders and, under no
circumstances, to resume hostilities. If this simple arrangement
was not honored, fire was to rain from the sky. The peace was
to be kept by those who had the elusiveness and power to see
that it was kept. Naturally, threats were made, and bribes offered,
by both sides, but the barbarian, and certain others, high in the
cavalry, remained unshaken in their peculiar resolve.
"Both houses, of course," the barbarian informed them, "will
contribute to the upkeep, comfort, and welfare of the cavalry."
"Tribute!" cried Lord Temmu.
"Rather," said the barbarian, "a modest charge, to defray the
costs of maintaining the peace."
"You are bandits," said Lord Okimoto.
"Astride demon birds," suggested the barbarian, who, as you
might suppose, was I.
"We may seize you, and hold you as a hostage," said Lord
Temmu.
"I have considered that possibility in the orders issued to the
cavalry," I said. "The orders are explicit. In such a development,
the offending house is to be destroyed, and, if the matter is
unclear, both houses are to be destroyed."
"What of you?" asked Lord Okimoto.
"The orders are clear," I said, "and will be obeyed."
"We have a secret hold over you," said Lord Temmu.
"Were you to inform me of this hold," I said, "I fear it would
no longer be a secret."

"This is no joke," said Lord Okimoto.

"Speak," I said.

"This matter goes back, even to the northern forests, and before the setting forth of the ship of Tersites," said Lord Temmu.

"It was feared," said Lord Nishida, "that you might be reluctant to join our cause, and we had much need of a tarn cavalry, that required to balance the numerical superiority of the troops of Lord Yamada."

"I understand," I said.

"But you proved amenable," he said.

"Yes," I said.

"Why?" he asked.

"I am not sure," I said. "Perhaps I was curious, perhaps it suggested adventure, perhaps the daring of Thassa, the seeking of the World's End, and such, riches perhaps, perhaps the challenge of forming, equipping, training, and testing in battle a new form of tarn cavalry." I did not mention that, significant in my choice, was my respect for, and admiration of, Lord Nishida, who had commanded at Tarncamp. Lord Okimoto had commanded at Shipcamp, from whose wharf the ship of Tersites had taken the Alexandra downstream to Thassa.

Why does one trust one man and not another? Why would one follow one man, and not another? One does trust one man rather than another. One would follow one man, rather than another. But why is seldom clear. I did trust Lord Nishida. I would follow him, at least provisionally. Ahead lay vast, green, turbulent Thassa.

"So I organized and trained the cavalry," I said.

"And commanded it," said Lord Okimoto, "subject, of course, to the will of the shogun."

"Following my betrayal by the house of Temmu," I said, "which I trust has not been forgotten, the tarn cavalry became an independent arm, and so it remains."

"Unfortunately," said Lord Temmu.

"The hold, of course, remains," said Lord Okimoto.

"The secret hold?" I said.

"We were pleased, of course," said Lord Nishida, "that we needed not have recourse to such a mode of influence."

"I, too, then," I said, "must be pleased."

"You will surrender the tarn cavalry to the house of Temmu," said Lord Temmu. "You will relocate it to the grounds of the holding. Its former officers are to be relieved of their appointments. We will designate a new chain of command, one unequivocally loyal to our house."

"I differ, noble lord," I said.

"The hold remains, tarnsman," said Lord Okimoto.

"What hold?" I said.

"Unfortunately," said Lord Nishida, "the shogun now feels it is necessary to have recourse to such a regrettable mode of influence."

"I do not understand," I said.

"It has to do with a woman," said Lord Nishida.

I recalled that, long ago, near the edge of the northern forest, on the continent, shortly after I had been placed there by the ship of Peisistratus, a slaver, come from the steel world of Lord Arcesilaus, once that of Lord Agamemnon, the unwitting slave, Constantina, foolishly thinking she was a free woman, now the acknowledged, recognized, and explicit slave, Saru, had alluded to something of this nature, but, questioned, knew little of the matter. As the whole matter seemed tenuous and obscure, and doubtful, and nothing had come of it, I had dismissed it as false, even absurd, and, at best, as hearsay, founded on ungrounded rumor, if that.

"What woman?" I said.

"Perhaps you recall," said Lord Okimoto, "the straits of the former siege, when desolation and starvation prowled about our gates."

"Of course," I said.

"Slaves were bartered for as little as a *fukuro* of rice," he said.

"I recall that," I said.

"All but one," said Lord Okimoto.

"I wondered about that," I said. "I supposed her a favorite of the shogun."

"Perhaps you would care to meet her," said Lord Temmu.

"Certainly," I said.

"Ho, Cecily," I said, on the dock.

The former English girl, whom I had acquired on a steel

world, knelt amongst the throng. I feared she might be buffeted. The wharf was crowded. The pack on her back was secured by two straps across her body.

"You are ready to board," I said.

"Yes, Master," she said, happily, looking up.

"It is pleasant to have a woman on her knees before you," I said.

"It is pleasant for a woman to be on her knees, before her master," she said.

"You may go to my cabin," I said.

"How shall I greet you?" she asked.

"Naked," I said, "in my bunk, the switch held between your teeth."

"Yes, Master," she said, happily, and rose up, and, a moment later, I saw her ascend the gangplank to the high deck of the *River Dragon*. I saw, too, that the eyes of several fellows watched, as well. I was sure the luscious she-sleen was well aware of the eyes upon her. How excited and proud, and pleased, are slaves to be so regarded, to realize how their lineaments, more than hinted at in their brief garb, lure the eye and whet the appetites of manhood. How marvelous for a woman to be so desired! How can a woman be more a female than in a collar?

"Licinius Lysias," I said, "he of Turmus!"

"Tal, Commander," he said.

"You have chosen to return to the continent," I said.

"Yes, Commander," he said.

Licinius Lysias, long ago, in a training exercise at Tarncamp, from tarnback, had attempted the assassination of Lord Nishida. He had later figured in the attack on Tarncamp, after which, the attack successfully resisted, he had, in flight, taken refuge in a tharlarion stable, and held the slave, Saru, as a hostage. I had feigned, as though under duress, accommodating his request for a tarn, to abet his escape, with the hostage. By means of a drugged bota at the saddle and counting on the return of an unguided tarn to its cot, we had captured Licinius Lysias and rescued the slave. Learning that he was to be crucified, and as I disapproved of ugly deaths and he had not injured the slave, I had given him a chance for his life, freeing him to flee into the woods. He had been later recaptured. Perhaps wary of displeasing me, as I was important to the cavalry, he had been taken in chains aboard the ship of Tersites, where he was to be put to the oar in one of the great ship's nested galleys. Eventually he was freed of his chains and, during the traumas and exigencies of the ensuing months, particularly once the islands had been reached, and the need for armed men became more desperate, he had been allowed to serve with our mercenary contingents, rather as though he had been originally recruited in Brundisium. In this capacity, grateful and dedicated, he had served faithfully, and well.

"You should soon board," I said.

"I shall, shortly, Commander," said he. "My pack is already stowed. But there are vendors from the local villages, at the end of the wharf, and I wish to purchase small articles."

"Something by which to remember the World's End?" I asked.

"Ceramics," he said, "and tiny tokens of carved jade."

"I wish you well," I said.

"And I, you, Commander," he said.

I watched him make his way through the crowd toward the land end of the wharf, toward a cluster of townsmen, merchants, and peasants, each with their case or sack of goods.

I heard the second gong.

Water would be licking higher now on the pilings of the wharf.

Shortly after the third gong the mooring lines would be freed, retrieved, and the ship would cast off.

"This way," had said Lord Okimoto, leading me through one of the long corridors in the castle of Temmu, the central keep of the mountaintop holding.

He stopped before a large door, but one not much different from similar doors along the hallway.

It was, however, bolted shut, on the outside.

"I advise you, Tarl Cabot, tarnsman," said Lord Okimoto, ponderous in his long, colorful, swollen robes, "to accede to the polite request of Lord Temmu."

"The surrender of the tarn cavalry, its relocation, the replacement of its officers with his creatures, and such," I said.

"Yes," said Lord Okimoto.

"What is on the other side of the door?" I said.

"You shall see," he said.

He slid back the bolt.

"Do not bolt the door when I am within," I said.

"I will not," he said. "We have no wish to accept the consequences of detaining you."

"The orders issued to the cavalry are quite clear," I said.

"That is understood," he said.

He opened the door, and I entered. He then closed the door. I listened. The bolt was not moved.

The room was a typical Pani room, ample, airy, tasteful, and sparsely furnished, with a few mats, a low table, and a painted screen, suggesting marsh birds in flight. It was naturally lit, with a large panel open to the outside, leading to a terrace. One could not, however, reach the terrace from the room, as the opening was barred.

I was surprised.

"Forgive me, lady," I said. "A mistake has been made."

I had expected to find something different in this room. I had expected to find a slave, one not much different, if at all, from those who had been bartered for a *fukuro*, or so, of rice, during the miseries of the siege. Perhaps it would be a slave from Port Kar, or perhaps from Ko-ro-ba, where I had first donned the scarlet of the warrior, with whom I would be threatened, whose fate might be dire, unless I complied with the commands of Lord Temmu.

But this gave every appearance of being a free woman.

Moreover, she was not in the kimono and obi, and fitted with the comb and slippers, of a high Pani female, but might have been encountered in a salon of glorious Ar, on a boulevard in Turia, in a market in Argentum, at a song drama in Torcadino, at the races in Venna. She was garbed in the colorful robes of concealment common in the high cities, and gracefully veiled.

"You!" she said. Her hand reached up and clutched the veiling more closely about her features.

"I do not think I understand," I said. "It seems you know me."

She moved back, until her back was pressed against the bars which prevented one from reaching the terrace.

For some reason, she seemed frightened.

I trusted that she was not distressed.

I suppose that it is difficult for one unfamiliar with Gorean culture to appreciate the social status of the Gorean free woman, at least in the high cities. It is quite different from the status, such as it is, in which the women of, say, Earth, are commonly held. In a world where, in effect, all women are free, freedom does not mean very much, but, in a culture where not all women are free, it means a great deal. Indeed, I have sometimes suspected that the low status of the "free woman" on Earth, together with her common lack of veiling, the freedom with which she reveals her wrists, hands, ankles, and such, have led many Goreans to regard her as open slave stock, as opposed to, in the view of some, concealed slave stock, as in the case of the Gorean free woman. I think there is little doubt that the transition between a Gorean free woman and slavery is far more radical and cataclysmic than that between an Earth woman and slavery. On the other hand, the Gorean free woman is familiar with slaves, and may have owned some of her own, is wholly familiar with the condition, and such, whereas the Earth girl is commonly unfamiliar with such things. Accordingly, in contrast with the Gorean free woman, the Earth girl's understanding that she is going to be marked, collared, and sold is likely to take her very much unawares. The capture and enslavement of a Gorean free woman is usually regarded as a coup. Earth girls, on the other hand, are herded and handled much as the meaningless but lovely cattle they are taken to be.

"I think, high lady," I said, "I have been introduced into the wrong room. It seems rooms were changed, and my guide was not informed. I am in the wrong place. Forgive me. I shall withdraw."

"Who did you expect to find?" she asked.

"Forgive me, lady," I said. "I intend no insult, but I expected to find a slave."

"You do not recognize me?" she said.

"You are discreetly veiled," I said.

"You do not recognize my voice?" she said.

"It reminds me of one whose voice it cannot be," I said.

"And whose voice would that be?" she asked.

"It is not important," I said.

"I have been told to wait for you," she said.

"Then," I said, "I am somehow in the right room."

"I must wait for you," she said.

"As the door was bolted," I said, "it seems you had little choice in the matter."

"This room," she said, "is a cell."

"Are you under sentence?" I asked.

"Have you come to put me to your blade," she asked, "now, before you leave the room?"

"No," I said.

"I may yet live a time?" she said.

"Of course," I said.

"You have come to carry me away?" she said.

"No," I said. "You seem to know me, but I do not know you."

"You are Tarl Cabot," she said, "a tarnsman, the commander of the cavalry."

"I am Tarl Cabot," I said, "and a tarnsman. I no longer command the cavalry. The commander of the cavalry is now a Pani tarnsman, the warrior, Tajima." Both Torgus and Lysander had elected to return to the continent, with many other mercenaries, on the *River Dragon*.

"I am called 'Adraste'," she said.

"A lovely Cosian name," I said. "'Called'?" I asked.

"Yes," she said. "It is the name which has been put on me."

"I see," I said.

In that moment, the room changed.

Clouds must have sped from the sun, because the sunlight poured into the room, like fire, and cast the shadows of bars across the room.

I strode to her, and she pushed back, frightened, against the bars, and I bent down, and drew up the hem of her robes to the calf.

"You are not shod," I said.

"No," she said.

"A well-turned calf," I said, and dropped the hem of the robes, and backed away.

"Those ankles would look well, shackled," I said.

"They have been shackled, often enough," she said.

"How dare you don the garments of a free woman?" I said.

"I must dress as I am told," she said.

"Remove your veil," I said.

She tore it away.

"It cannot be!" I whispered.

"It is," she said, coldly.

"Replace your veil," I said. "And remove it properly, gracefully."

"Am I commanded?" she asked.

"Yes," I said.

"You dare to command me?" she asked.

"Do you wish to be whipped?" I asked.

"You could do that—to me?" she asked.

"I trust a command need not be repeated," I said.

She then replaced the veil, and, seductively, removed it.

"Shall I now remove my other garments?" she asked.

"No," I said.

"I am face-stripped before you," she said. "Perhaps that is sufficient."

"It will do for now," I said.

"You are hateful and weak," she said.

"I never betrayed a Home Stone," I said.

"Tarsk!" she exclaimed.

"Perhaps you are aware," I said, "that there is an enormous bounty on you, an enormous reward for your return to Ar, and the judgment of Marlenus, Ubar of Ubars."

"Ten thousand tarn disks," she said, "of gold, and of double weight."

"That is my understanding," I said.

Such wealth would buy fleets, armies, and cities.

"I suppose it is little enough," I said, "for the apprehension of an arch villainess, who conspired with dissident elements in the city to betray Ar to her enemies, and would then rule, as a puppet, a false Ubara, under the aegis of Cos and her allies."

"I was truly Ubara!" she said.

"Only on the sufferance of Myron, *polemarkos* of Temos, military governor of Ar."

"I ruled!" she cried.

"To the extent permitted by the spears of Cos, and her allies."

"I was muchly justified," she said. "By humiliation, by deed, and blood!"

"How so?" I said.

"I, the daughter of Marlenus," she said, "was captured by Rask of Treve, and kept for a time as his slave. He fell enamored, the fool, of a blond, worthless, barbarian chit, El-in-or, and gave me to a panther girl, Verna, by name, who took me to the northern forests, a slave. There I was eventually sold, and was purchased by Samos, of Port Kar. When I was returned by Samos to Ar I was sequestered by Marlenus."

"You had begged to be purchased," I said, "a slave's act, and thus you shamed Marlenus, and he confined you, in effect, to chambers in the Central Cylinder. When an accident befell him in the Voltai and he was thought dead, the conspirators recruited you and the dark work was begun. Later, Marlenus, whose accident had temporarily produced a loss of memory, returned to the city, recovered his memory, and the restoration was begun."

"I was innocent," she said.

"As an ost," I said.

"No!" she said.

"How is it that you are here?" I asked.

"I do not know," she said. "The city rose, the streets were filled with vengeful citizens, citadels and guard stations were stormed, men cried for blood, proscription lists were posted, hundreds of collaborators were caught and impaled. We tried to hold the Central Cylinder, but could not do so. Men climbed toward us, with brands of fire and blades of steel. Tarnsmen wheeled about. We would make our last stand on the roof of the Central Cylinder. Seremides, commander of the Taurentians, would try to buy his freedom, delivering me to the enemy, sacrificing me to the wrath of Marlenus. Then there was smoke, blasts of light, a vehicle which moved like a cloud of steel, or a steel bird without wings, and I lost consciousness. I awakened on a chain in a compound in the northern forests, in a place called Shipcamp. Across a broad river, when the gates of the compound were opened, I saw a mighty ship, on which, later, I and others, secured and hooded, were boarded. For the most part, I, and others, were confined below decks."

In her removal from the roof of the Central Cylinder, I saw the work, of course, of either Priest-Kings or Kurii, or both.

"I understand little, if anything, of this," she said.

"Much is obscure," I said, "but you were abducted that those of Lord Temmu might have some means to force me to their will."

"Because of your helpless love of me!" she laughed.

"That seems to be their thinking on the matter," I said.

"And now I am here," she said.

"As am I," I said.

"Once we were Companions," she said.

"No longer," I said. The Gorean Companionship terminates in a year, unless renewed.

"You deserted me!" she charged.

"It would seem so," I said. How could I speak to her of warring species, of Priest-Kings and Kurii, of fabulous weapons and technologies, of a fearful contest on which the fate of worlds might hang?

"You are a despicable tarsk," she said.

"I never betrayed a Home Stone," I said.

"Many men," she said, "have found me beautiful."

"You are beautiful," I said.

"And yet you fled from me," she said, angrily.

"It seems so," I said.

"You tired of me?" she said.

"One would be less likely to tire of you, than to cast you aside, as worthless," I said.

"I am the most beautiful woman on all Gor!" she said.

"Do not be absurd," I said. "There are thousands upon thousands of women on Gor as beautiful as you, or more beautiful, and mostly in collars."

"Hateful beast!" she snarled.

"Beware," I said.

"None are of the blood of Marlenus!" she cried.

"You were disowned," I said, "following your shaming of Marlenus, prior to your sequestration in the Central Cylinder."

"One cannot disown blood!" she said.

"True," I said.

"And I am of the blood of Marlenus!" she cried.

"Perhaps," I said.

"'Perhaps'?" she cried.

"I see little of Marlenus in you," I said.

"Beast!" she wept, and threw herself toward me, to strike me with her small fists, but I caught her wrists, and held them, she then helpless in my grasp. I regarded her. Fear came into her eyes. She knew that, as she was held, she might, if I wished, by a suitable pressure applied to those helpless, slender wrists, be forced to her knees before me.

I released her, and she retreated to the bars, and stood there, against them, her back to them. "Beast!" she said.

"You were brought to Port Kar after your purchasing in the northern forests by Samos of Port Kar," I said. "At that time, I was in Port Kar, returned there recently from the northern forests, crippled, confined to a chair, having been cut by a sword which bore a smear of poison on its blade. There, in the holding of Samos of Port Kar, your then master, you were brought before me, and you, in your impatience, pride, and anger, scorned, derided, and mocked me."

"Justly so," she said. "You were always of Earth, the world of slaves and fools! I had once thought you a man, but how wrong I was! Though I had twice tried to kill you, once in tarnflight over the great Spider Swamp south of Ar, and once in its vicinity, with a knife, you neither slew me nor put me to the collar and brand. How soft you were, how forgiving you were, contemptible weakling! How like those of Earth! Have they no claws, no fangs, no blood, no heart? How far you were from the proud, severe, proportioned ways of Gor! And in the camp of Mintar the Merchant, when I pathetically petitioned the iron, when I implored the release of my womanhood, and the mercy of bondage, when I sought your collar, when I begged that you would make me your slave, that I might be fulfilled and owned, that I might be wholly and uncompromisingly yours, as much as a boot or tarsk, you refused me! Oh, how much a man of Earth you were! A woman might kneel before you, needfully, begging to be your slave, and you, startled, taken aback, upset, confused, and embarrassed, reddened and sweating, knowing not what to do or how to respond, would hurry her to her feet, implicitly chiding her for her deepest needs, and deliver her to the woeful ice and exile of freedom! Men and women are not the same, oh, piteous scion of the smug, gray world, so vain of its pollutions and peculiar pathologies! So you will not accept us as we were bred to be? You will deny the woman to herself, as you would deny the man to himself! As you will then; so be it! How I detested, and do detest, your weakness, your futility, and vacillation! And I saw you then, in the hall of the holding of Samos of Port Kar, bent over, bundled in your blankets for warmth, weak, confined to that chair, scarcely able to move! I knew then how I might, with impunity, even from you, denounce you for the failure, the weakling and fool, you were! So I, to my delight, and in security, castigated and berated you, well and lengthily, as you so richly deserved."

"I have not forgotten," I said.

"And even then," she said, "when Samos would have put me to the lash, even had me cast bound to the urts in the canals of the city, you did nothing, but requested that Samos deliver me to the city of my Home Stone, Ar, and to my father, Marlenus, as a free woman!"

"He did so," I said.

"Yes!" she said. "But he did more, as well! He had seen to it that it was inscribed on my papers, certified with the seal of the slaver, that I had begged to be purchased. This appeared as an endorsement on my papers. Such things are of interest in some cases, to some masters."

"I would think so," I said, "as in the case of a Ubar's daughter."

"And then he, and two members of his crew, who had accompanied us to Ar, independently confirmed the matter."

"And you confessed the matter?" I said.

"Surely," she said. "How could I not? Naturally, of course, I proclaimed its justification!"

"Goreans admit no justification for that act," I said.

"Beast!" she said.

"And so," I said, "as you had shamed Marlenus, he saw to it that you would be kept from public view, that you would be hidden, that you would remain sequestered in the Central Cylinder."

"Yes!" she said, in rage.

"Until," I said, "Marlenus, on a hunting trip, disappeared somewhere in the Voltai range and traitors, emboldened by his absence, approached you."

"Perhaps," she said.

"I may not be as you remember me," I said.

"Men of Earth do not change," she said.

"The men of Earth and those of Gor," I said, "are of the same species. Goreans have an Earth origin, however remote in some cases. Culture is involved. Some cultures deny and suppress human nature; others, for whatever reason, accept it, and liberate it."

"The Pani," she said, "allegedly, in virtue of my presence, have some hold over you?"

"That is their view," I said.

"You are to comply with their wishes, or some lamentable fate is to be imposed on me?" she said.

"That is my understanding," I said.

I recalled the eel pool in the stadium, or theater, of Lord Yamada. I did not doubt but what some similar arrangement, or worse, would be at the disposal of Lord Temmu.

"Then I am safe," she said.

"How so?" I said.

"You will protect me," she said. "You will do as they wish."

"Why?" I asked.

"'Why'?" she asked.

"Yes," I said.

"That I might not be jeopardized, or put at risk!" she said.

"I see," I said.

"I am again important," she said, excitedly. "Once again I have power!"

"You are a slave," I said.

"I do not understand," she said.

"You are a slave," I said. "Is that so hard to understand?"

"I am Talena!" she said. "Daughter of Marlenus!"

"No," I said, "Talena was a free woman, disowned as the daughter of Marlenus. You are Adraste, a slave at the World's End."

"You must do as they say!"

"Why?" I asked.

"You are weak, complaisant," she said. "You are a man of Earth!"

"I shall withdraw," I said.

"We were Companions," she said. "We drank together the wine of Companionship!"

"The Companionship is done," I said, "years ago. It was never renewed. It is void. Too, it is not unusual that a woman who was once a Companion falls into bondage. Indeed, sometimes they come into the possession of their former Companions. You cannot expect a woman who has worn the collar to be accepted into the honor of Companionship. She has been spoiled for that. Too, only a fool frees a slave girl. Surely you know the saying. And, too, a woman who might be an indifferent, or poor, Companion, is often of much greater interest when she is chained to a slave ring, at the foot of a master's couch."

"You cannot abandon me!" she said.

"You are mistaken," I said.

"You cannot do that," she said. "You are a fool of Earth, as all the others of that smug, feeble orb! You have been nurtured into futility from the cradle! You are sweet, kind, sensitive, thoughtful, understanding, weak, stupid, and manipulable! Beware, lest I shed a tear, or reproach you for ambition, pride, vulgarity, bullying, or manhood!"

"I tremble," I said.

"Do so!" she said.

"Once, as you say, you thought you knew me, and were mistaken," I said. "Well, once I, as well, thought I knew you, and was mistaken. I learned of you in the hall of Samos of Port Kar, when I was half paralyzed. I learned of you in Ar, when you dishonored Marlenus, not in begging to be purchased in a far place, but in conspiring with other traitors to secure the throne of Ar, when you undermined and dissipated her military in the delta of the Vosk, when you opened the gates of the city to her enemies, when you had her walls razed, when you confiscated properties and looted treasuries, when you sat in judgment of your fellow citizens."

"I was justified in all I did!" she said.

"That is denied," I said, "by ten thousand tarn disks of gold, of double weight."

"Tarsk," she hissed.

"I leave," I said.

"You cannot!" she cried.

"I do," I said.

"You cannot," she insisted.

"Why?" I asked.

"You love me," she said.

"Love," I said, "for a slave?"

"For Talena, daughter of Marlenus!" she said.

"You are Adraste," I said, "a slave."

"Then for Adraste," she said, "a slave!"

"What fool could love a slave?" I asked.

"What man cannot?" she said.

"There are many slaves," I said.

"But only one such as I!" she said, triumphantly.

"Each slave is unique," I said, "and different and special in her collar."

"But they are all slaves!" she said.

"Yes," I said, "wholly, and completely."

"You love me!" she said.

"So I must do whatever Lord Temmu asks?" I said.

"Yes!" she said.

"But I will not," I said.

"I do not understand," she said, shaken.

"Do not fear," I said. "No dire fate will be imposed upon you by Lord Temmu as a consequence of my decision, lest the cavalry retaliate."

"You do love me!" she said.

"You are of little interest," I said. "But you are a vulnerable, helpless, owned beast. I would do as much for a tarsk, a verr, or kaiila."

"I hate you!" she screamed.

I then left the chamber.

Outside, I slid the bolt back into place, securing the door.

"Ho!" I called, on the crowded wharf, noting his approach. "The third gong will ring presently. It is time you arrived. Docksmen are already at the mooring cleats."

"Tal," said Pertinax, leading his string of three fair beasts, back-braceleted, strung on a tandem-collared leash. Each was clad in a brief, plain tunic. When he stopped, to greet me, each knelt, her head down. Pertinax trained them well. "It took a bit of time with the vendors at the wharf's end," he said, "to find a suitably attractive switch."

"It is a beauty," I said, examining the implement. It was about two feet Gorean long, supple, of medium width, with a loop at one end, which might go about a master's wrist. "It should keep good order amongst your beasts," I said.

"It will," he said.

"I see you have wasted little money on their garmenture," I said.

"I had a good buy on cheap cloth," he said.

"The tunics are rather brief, are they not?" I said.

"Not at all," he said. "I like them that way."

"It might scandalize free women," I said.

"Let them be scandalized," he said. "Perhaps one day they will be so garbed."

"You had best board," I said. "Time is short."

"*Kajirae*," said he, "raise your heads."

"All beauties," I said.

He held the switch to the lips of Jane, the former Lady Portia Lia Serisia, of Sun Gate Towers, of Ar, a scion of the Serisii, once a major banking power in Ar. It had been obliterated following the restoration of Marlenus, having collaborated with the occupation forces.

She tenderly and lovingly, and humbly, kissed and licked the switch for a few moments, and then looked up, adoringly, at her master, hoping that he would be pleased. I gathered from her position on the tandem leash that she was first girl.

Pertinax next held the switch to Kameko, his lovely Pani slave. From the ministrations, delicate, moist, and tender, she bestowed on the switch I gathered she was well satisfied with her collar, though perhaps she would have preferred to be the single slave of so strong and fine a master.

"What do you think of her?" asked Pertinax.

"She is coming along nicely," I said.

"Is she not beautiful?" said Pertinax.

"Yes," I said.

Her lips were slightly parted, and she dared not meet our eyes.

A free woman may look boldly into the eyes of a free man, why not, she is free, but a girl in her collar, aware of her collar, is not likely to do so.

But Kameko was pleased to be spoken of in such a way. What slave would not be pleased, to be found of interest by free men?

"She will be a delight on the continent," said Pertinax. "She will be exotic, and special. There are few Pani slaves there."

"You will be pleased to march her, in the promenades," I said.

"Of course," he said.

"On a leash of brightly colored leather?"

"Perhaps on a rope," he said.

"Clothed?" I said.

"I have not decided," he said.

"But see that she earns her slave gruel, by much labor in the furs," I said.

"The first duty of the slave is to please her master," said Pertinax.

"I see that you have a third slave," I said.

"The poorest of the lot," he said.

He then held the switch before blond-haired, blue-eyed Saru, formerly Miss Margaret Wentworth, of New York City, on the world, Earth. How far were those two now from the august halls of finance on a far world! She had been far above him, he on that world a worshipful clerk. Never, on that world, might he have hoped to aspire to such a woman. Now she was at his feet, braceleted, leashed, and scarcely garbed, as his slave. In her great financial institution, she had functioned as a solicitor of investment capital, a project in which she well utilized the assets of her intelligence, beauty, and meretricious, seductive skills, promising much and delivering nothing. Naive, gullible men, often of considerable means, strove to please her. Many clients and much wealth did she secure for her superiors. But then she, mercenary, greedy, and corrupt, was approached by agents of Gor. It seemed an easy fortune might be had from obscure employers. Apprised she should have a male colleague to aid in dissembling her true status and role on Gor, she had enlisted Gregory Smith, well aware, from small incidents, of his remote, hopeless, infatuation with her. So she had brought him with her to Gor as a subordinate and menial. As such, he had had to endure her myriad directives, her insufferable, unpleasant temperament, her insolence, her impatience and vanity, her contempt, and her frequent criticisms, disparagements, and insults. Unknown to herself, aside from her brief role in meeting a tarnsman on the shore of Thassa, at the edge of the forest, and seeing that he was brought to Tarncamp, she had been preselected, in virtue of a standing order, for a Gorean collar, and would be delivering herself, as well, to Tarncamp. Her complexion, hair color, and eye color would be rare in the islands. It was supposed, accordingly, that she might constitute a charming, agreeable gift for a shogun. While she, on Gor, had fallen to the mark and collar, her minion, Gregory White, had remained free. Engaged in manual labor, he had grown lean and powerful, quick and agile, fierce and severe; he had studied with Nodachi, the swordsman; he had learned the tarn, the lance and bow, and manhood; he had taken for himself the proud name, Pertinax.

Saru looked up from her knees at her master, Pertinax. For a moment I thought I detected a flash of resentment in her eyes. Her small wrists struggled against the metal which held them pinioned behind her back. There was a tiny sound of the linkage. "Do you wish to speak, slave?" inquired Pertinax. "No, Master," she whispered. The switch was before her face. "Do you beg to engage in submissive behaviors?" asked Pertinax, coldly. Fear came into her eyes. "Yes, Master," she said. She then reached her head forward and kissed, and then licked, submissively, the barrel of the switch. Then, interestingly, she shuddered, and then, more fervently, even desperately, pressed her lips, again and again, to the switch. It was as though something had suddenly changed within her, as though a barrier had fallen, as though a wall of ice had broken apart, and, melting, revealed a lush, arable, inviting terrain beyond, green in its grass and warm in its sun. She then, piteously, pressed her lips again to the switch. And then her small, soft tongue caressed it, twice. She looked up, again. "May I speak, Master?" she begged.

"Yes," he said, drawing back the switch.

"I always loved you," she said, "even on Earth, when I despised you, for your weakness. I dreamed of being your slave! Even in my contempt of you, I would take no other with me to this perilous, beautiful world! Now I kneel before you, braceleted, leashed, in your collar, your slave!"

"All of you," said Pertinax. "Rise up, keep your heads down."

"Yes, Master," they said, rising, heads down.

"I take it your gear is stowed," I said.

"Yes," said Pertinax, "yesterday, not long after yours."

"Good," I said. "I shall see you on board." I then looked to the large sleen, lying beside me. "Ramar," I said, "go with Pertinax."

"Are you not boarding now?" asked Pertinax.

"I want to feel the broad, solid planks of the wharf beneath my feet," I said. "We will be long enough at sea."

I watched Pertinax, with his leashed charges, ascend the gangplank. Ramar, with his limping gait, was close behind.

I heard a tiny sound, which I could not, in the instant, place.

"Beware!" cried a loud, startled voice.

Instinctively I dropped to one knee, and a body, dark, robed, hurtled over me, and I glimpsed a flash of metal. Before thinking, I leaped up, and, violently, as though treading on a serpent, thrust down with my boot at the back of the assailant's neck, and it snapped the vertebrae at the base of the skull. One does not long survive such a blow. In moments I turned over the inert, staring body. "Daichi," I said. "Who is Daichi?" said Licinius Lysias. "A reader of bones and shells," I said. "I do not understand," said Licinius Lysias. "It is a way of allegedly reading fortunes, discovering truths, and foretelling the future," I said. "Lord Temmu, at one time, took such things seriously. This man, Daichi, was his court reader of bones and shells." "I see," said Licinius Lysias. "You have saved my life," I said. "As you once spared mine," he said. We embraced, comrades in arms. Men had cleared a space about us. "Did you find your tokens, your mementos, your souvenirs of the World's End?" I asked Licinius Lysias. "I have some things," he said. "Here is another," I said, removing the small box of bones and shells, and its strap, from the body of Daichi. "Keep it," I said, "as a souvenir from the World's End." "Will not Lord Temmu object?" he asked. "No," I said, "he no longer has use for such things."

"This man has been recently sought," said a Pani guardsmen, armed with a glaive, as were two others behind him.

"He has been found," I said. "Inform Lord Temmu."

"He was to have been cast from the outer parapet," said one of the guardsmen.

"That will not now be necessary," I said.

"No," said the chief guardsman. "It will be done."

"As you will," I said.

The guardsman signified that two docksmen lift the body and remove it from the wharf.

"I do not understand," said a man. "How could Daichi dare to attack this man, publicly, on a crowded wharf?"

"Perhaps," said a fellow, "the bones and shells foretold success."

"It seems they were mistaken," said a man.

"It would not be the first time," I said.

At that moment the third gong rang out.

Some mercenaries rushed past me, hurrying to the gangplank.

"We must board!" said Licinius Lysias, gripping the small box.

"I shall join you, momentarily," I said.

The tiny sound I had heard, almost at the same moment as the shouted warning of Licinius Lysias, and the attack of Daichi, had been the movement of some of those tiny articles, bones and shells, loose in the box.

I looked about the wharf.

I must soon board.

The *River Dragon* loomed above me. Waters were now high on the wharf's palings, only a few horts below the planks.

I looked about, once more.

"Lord Nishida!" I said.

He bowed, which bow I returned.

Behind him were two Ashigaru, and, between them, in their keeping, was a woman, shamefully unveiled, but otherwise decorously clad in the many folds and colors of the robes of concealment. Her hands were behind her back, where, I supposed, they were bound, or braceleted.

"You have come to see me off," I said. "I had hoped you would."

"You waited," he said.

"Of course," I said.

"We have been well met, Tarl Cabot, tarnsman," he said. "We have shared much, in Tarncamp, in Shipcamp, aboard the great ship of Tersites, and here, in the islands, which you call the World's End."

"I am honored to have served with you," I said.

"And with Lord Temmu, and Lord Okimoto?" he said.

"There," I said, "perhaps somewhat less honored."

"We owe you much for the cavalry," he said, "and very little at present."

"I am sorry," I said. "But let the peace be kept."

"It will be," he said, "for a time."

"I think," I said, "that titanic forces have been balanced here, in the islands."

"Perhaps," he said, "on the far continent, in a clear sky, lightning broods."

"Not only larls and sleen are territorial," I said.

To be sure, here were territories beyond the ken of roaring larls and snarling sleen, territories which consisted of worlds.

"Here is the woman," he said, gesturing to the slave, "in virtue of which we were to command your loyalty and service."

"You had it without her," I said.

"For which we are grateful," he said.

"Lord Temmu," I said, "would doubtless have preferred to possess a relocated cavalry, staffed according to his will."

"Yes," said Lord Nishida, "but he more prefers the security and integrity of his holding and lands. There is little to be gained if the unpleasant death of a slave is followed by a rain of fire from the sky."

"I counted, in this matter," I said, "on the rationality of Lord Temmu, if not on his character or honor."

"In the circumstances," said Lord Nishida, "you understand that the slave is no longer of interest, or importance."

"Yes," I said.

"Accordingly," he said, "we abandon her here, on the wharf."

"As you will," I said.

The dark eyes of the slave, Adraste, flashed with fury. Her body seethed with rage.

"I wish you well, dear friend," said Lord Nishida.

"I wish you well, dear friend," I said.

We exchanged bows.

He then turned, and left, followed by the two Ashigaru.

"So I am abandoned," she said, "cast aside, discarded!"

"You are no longer of importance," I said.

"To no one?" she said.

"To no one," I said.

She shook her hands behind her back, angrily, and I heard the tiny sound of metal. So she was back braceleted.

"Your wrists are fastened," I said. "I would not struggle, if I were you. You are helpless, whether you realize it or not, whether you like it or not. If I were you, I would not risk marking your wrists. That might, to some degree, lower your price."

"Price!" she cried.

"Yes," I said, "price."

"I am beyond price!" she said.

"Only free women are beyond price," I said. "On the block, every woman has her price."

"You despicable tarsk!" she said.

"In the siege," I said, "most slaves, all but you, as I understand it, were bartered, most for a *fukuro* of rice, some for two."

"So?" she said, angrily.

"Had you not been of interest, politically," I said, "I wonder what you would have gone for."

"For ten thousand *fukuros* of rice!" she said.

"I would think, a single *fukuro*," I said.

"I am the daughter of a Ubar!" she cried.

"It is true," I said, "that that might raise the price of even a homely girl."

"Beast!" she said.

"But here," I said, "at the World's End, you are only another pretty slave, prettier than many, and not so pretty as others."

She looked away, angrily.

"You are helpless," I said. "Beware of marking your wrists."

"Tarsk!"

"The key to your bracelets, I take it," I said, "is on a string around your neck." This was common in such situations, the delivery of a braceleted slave to a new house, or master.

"Yes!" she said.

"The third gong has sounded," I said. "The ship will soon depart." I turned away.

"Wait!" she cried. "Tarl! Tarl!"

"Did you dare," I asked, not turning, "place the name of a free man, so, on your lips, those of a slave?"

"You cannot abandon me!" she said.

"Why not?" I asked, refusing to look upon her.

"You could leave me here, alone, braceleted, helpless, on a wharf, at the World's End?"

"Why not?" I asked.

"I am Talena, the daughter of Marlenus of Ar!" she cried.

I turned about, to face her.

"Once," I said, "then no longer."

Surely she understood she had been disowned, and was then no longer the daughter of the great Marlenus; surely she understood that she was now an item of livestock, of slave stock, and had no name but what masters might put on her, should they choose to name her.

To be sure, she was a beautiful object, a lovely article of merchandise. Similarly, there are beautiful kaiila, some with sleeker lines than others.

"You will not leave me here!"

"Why not?" I asked.

"Because I own you," she said. "You are mine. You are caught in the toils of my net!"

"I do not understand," I said.

"Love!" she said. "You love me! You are mine! You are helplessly in love with me!"

"No," I said.

"'No'?" she said.

"No," I said. "Once, perhaps, but no more. I know you now."

"Beast!" she hissed.

"As you wish," I said.

"Even so," she said, "you will not leave me here!"

"Why not?" I said.

"I am beautiful!" she said.

I surveyed the greenish cast in those flashing eyes, the olive skin, the loose, black hair, rich and abundant about her shoulders, the delicacy of her features, so deliciously and exquisitely feminine, so exciting, the hint of a marketable figure beneath those clumsy robes of concealment. It was hard to believe that something so lovely, and slavelike, could be of the blood of Marlenus of Ar. She might, on the block, I thought, bring as much as two silver tarsks, sold, of course, as a girl, only as a girl, as nothing but a girl, not as an item of perhaps political interest.

"Comely, surely," I said.

"Commander!" said a mariner, having descended the gangplank, which few now climbed, and pattered toward me, his sandals slapping on the warm, broad planks of the wharf. "We must cast off! Hurry! Hurry!"

"I am with you," I said, turning, to follow him.

"Wait! Wait!" she cried.

I continued on, striding away.

I heard the rustle of the cumbersome garments, and the sound of her small, bared feet, as she hurried behind me. As before, she had not been allowed sandals, or slippers. Dramatic was the contrast between the rich, abundant, colorful robes of concealment, suitable for a free woman of a high city on the continent, and her feet, as bared as those of a low slave.

"Wait, wait!" she wept.

I turned about, abruptly, impatiently.

She stopped, instantly.

"Do not abandon me!" she said. "Do not leave me here!"

She read my angry gaze, and knelt.

Was she not a slave?

It was pleasant to have her on her knees before me. What man does not want a beautiful woman on her knees before him?

Too, she was a slave.

Slaves are selected for their beauty.

What man does not desire to own a beautiful slave?

I then turned away, again.

"Wait, Master!" cried the voice, behind me, wildly, pleadingly. "Do not abandon Adraste! Do not leave Adraste behind! Please, wait, Master! Adraste dares not rise from her knees without permission! Adraste begs Master to take her with him."

I turned about, once more.

"Hurry!" urged the mariner.

She was on her knees, some feet behind, broken, shuddering, conquered, lips trembling. "Do not leave Adraste here!" she wept. "Take her with you! She begs your collar, your chains, whatever marking you would put on her! Do not refuse her, again. Once more she is prostrate before you, a piteous supplicant! Have her trained, have her taught the kisses and caresses of the slave, have her taught the lascivious dances of the slave, the movements of the slave! She is before you, begging to be yours, wholly and without compromise! Put her to your feet, despise her and abuse her, if you wish, as the worthless, meaningless slave she is!"

"Better to leave you here," I said, "to be put to what purposes might please the Pani."

"Love me!" she cried.

"Do not speak foolishly," I said. "You are a slave. One does not love slaves; one owns them, one lusts for them, one masters them, and teaches them their sex."

There is a Gorean saying that a woman learns her sex only in a collar.

"All women," she said, "desire to be lusted for, and mastered!"

"The slave exists," I said, "to please the master, wholly, and in every way."

"I know," she said.

"She is not her own," I said. "She is the master's."

"I want to be my master's," she said. "I want to be the object of his lust, of his unbridled and unequivocal lust!"

"Then you are a slave," I said.

"Yes!" she said. "I am a slave! Lust for me, own me, master me! Do you think I want the diffidence, the timidity, the respectful, shy, timorous handling endured by a free woman? I want a master! I have dreamed of a master! I long for a master!"

"Liar," I said.

"Please," she said. "It is true, Master! Do you not know this from as long ago as the tents of Mintar?"

"Clever she-sleen," I said.

"No!" she said.

"Perhaps," I said, "I will convey you to Ar, to the mercy of Marlenus, and that of the court torturers."

She regarded me wildly, miserably.

"Death by public torture can take a month," I said. "Doubtless thousands from Ar, and her environs, for a thousand pasangs about, will come to see you, to witness the fate of a traitor and false Ubara, to insult her, to jeer her, to mock and curse her, to spit upon her, to add their flaming twig or tiny splinter to her torments."

"No, no!" she wept.

"It will be holiday," I said.

"You would sell me for the ten thousand golden tarns of double weight!" she said.

"It would be more than I could get for you on the block," I said.

"Beast!" she wept.

"My needs are simple, and my means sufficient," I said. "I could scatter the wealth to multitudes in the street. It would be a splendid gesture, and would mean holiday, indeed."

"But you will not do so," she said.

"No," I said.

"Because you are a man of Earth," she said.

"No," I said, "because I have no wish to subject a helpless, vulnerable animal to so fearful a fate. It is ugly. It seems to me not fitting."

"An animal?" she said.

"Yes," I said.

"You see me as an animal?" she said.

"It is what you are," I said. Surely she knew that though not all animals were slaves, all slaves were animals.

I pointed to my feet.

She rose hurriedly to her feet, hurried to me, and knelt before me, her head down.

Her lips pressed against my sea boots, her wrists braceleted behind her, and I saw the moist imprints on the leather, again and again, and the moist streaks on them, from the caresses of her tongue.

"You are far from the throne of Ar," I said.

"Yes, Master," she said.

"Hurry, hurry, Commander!" cried the mariner.

I drew the slave forcibly to her feet, and thrust her, stumbling, into the keeping of the mariner.

"Bring her aboard," I said.

The slave cried out with joy.

"This woman is a high slave, is she not?" asked the mariner.

"No," I said. "She is a low slave, a common slave."

"What shall be done with her?"

"Once she is on board," I said, "remove her clothing,

completely, and then chain her below, with other low slaves, in the foulest of your slave holds."

"Yes, Commander!" said the mariner.

"You cannot have that done to me," she said. "You are a man of Earth!"

"I have learned Gor," I said. "I am of Gor."

"No!" she said.

"What is a man of Earth?" I asked.

"A pathetic weakling," she said, "shallow, manipulable, and eager to please, the puppet of a pathological, unnatural culture, a patriot of self-betrayal, one who prides himself on treason to his own blood, the creature of what he is told, one who will not think, one who will not raise his eyes to the stars, nor listen to the beating of his own heart."

"Perhaps it is not so," I said.

"There are no Goreans on Earth!" she said.

"You are mistaken," I said. "There are many. Indeed, in the heart of every male, there is a Gorean, even if only a secret, concealed Gorean. Do you think men are so willing to relinquish manhood, or so stupid as to submit like dumb animals to their impoverishment, belling, and slaughter? Even the mighty larl can be brought down by a swarm of squealing urts, but this does not prove the superiority of the urt to the larl, to the lonely, proud hunter, content in his mountain vastnesses, prowling about, alert and soft-footed, in remote wildernesses."

She looked behind herself, wildly, as the mariner, his hand on her upper right arm, half dragged her to the gangplank.

I thought of Cecily, waiting in my cabin. When she heard my footstep she would place the switch, crosswise, between her teeth, and await my entry.

One could grow fond of Cecily.

I would then gently remove the switch from between her teeth, and lay it aside.

To be sure, the slave, however much desired and cherished, grateful for the kindness of the master, that she will be kept, as she wishes, in helpless bondage, and joyful in her submission, is not to be allowed to forget that she is a slave, and only that. Accordingly the bindings, blindfoldings, gaggings, occasional strokes, and such, which remind her of her condition, that she is a female and owned, that she is a woman, and her master's slave. These things, for she is a slave, and desires to be a slave, confirms her bondage, and reassures her, that she is truly what she is, and desires to be, her master's slave.

I looked up to the rail of the *River Dragon*. Licinius Lysias was at the rail, looking down. He lifted the small box of bones and shells and shook it, and then pointed to the slave, being half dragged up the gangplank. "I see you, too, have a souvenir of the World's End," he said.

I waved to him, and hurried to the gangplank.

I had no sooner crossed it than the mariners drew it inboard.

The ropes were cast off from the mooring cleats by docksmen, and were being drawn aboard the *River Dragon* by mariners.

I saw the wharf, water risen almost to the planks, begin to slip to the side.

Looking up, I saw the battened sails being raised, and opened to the wind.

The slave, still in the grip of the mariner, had not yet been conducted below.

"What are you going to do with me?" she said.

"Sell you in Brundisium," I said.

"No!" she said.

"With other slaves," I said.

"No, no!" she said.

"If I were you," I said, "I would be reticent about revealing my antecedents, or former history."

"You cannot sell me!" she said.

"Do not fear," I said. "Given your veiling, and half-veiling, in your rare public appearances, few will know the former Ubara of Ar by sight. Further, I do not think it is likely that anyone is likely to recognize the former Ubara of Ar in one girl amongst others, vended one after another, in a cheap market in Brundisium."

"A cheap market?" she said.

"Yes," I said, "that pleases me. But, too, in such a market you would be less likely to be recognized."

"But low men," she said, "patronize such markets."

"Rejoice," I said, "in such a market you might prove a genuine bargain."

"Beast!" she said.

"Perhaps you would prefer the Curulean, in Ar," I said.

"But who will buy me?" she said.

"He who bids the highest," I said.

"In such markets," she said, "girls go for copper!"

"I know," I said.

"You are amused!" she said.

"Yes," I said.

"Tarsk!" she said.

"Doubtless, in time," I said, "you will have dozens of sales, dozens of collars, and dozens of masters."

"I hate you," she said.

I turned to the mariner in whose charge was the slave. "Strip her," I said, "and see that she is chained with other slaves, in the foulest of the slave holds."

"She is a low slave then, truly," said the mariner.

"Yes," I said, "a low slave, a very low slave."

The slave then, looking behind her, over her shoulder, her small wrists braceleted behind her, was dragged from my sight.

It occurred to me that she had been, from time to time, insufficiently respectful of a free man, but I effected nothing critical. She would soon learn slave deference, and her new lot in life.

I turned back to the rail. The wharf was slipping sway. I could hear the sails moving in the wind. I looked up from the wharf to the lofty holding of the shogun, Lord Temmu. Clouds were about the graceful roof of the castle. I saw a tarn aflight. I then turned my attention to the east, and the vast, swelling billows of Thassa, extending before me to the horizon.

I thought of astute, patient, brilliant Lord Nishida, of swaying, ponderous Lord Okimoto, poet, and master of calligraphy, and Lord Temmu, his narrow, covetous eyes to the south, and the dominions of Lord Yamada. Haruki would be tending his garden. I thought, too, of bold, young Tajima, so bright, and earnest, and of a slave, Nezumi. And I thought, too, of a short, thickly bodied, homely man, in whose hands a sword could sing, and part a grain of rice on a human forehead.

Thassa lay ahead, and, far off, the continent.

The World's End was now behind me.

About the Author

John Norman, born in Chicago, Illinois, in 1931, is the creator of the Gorean Saga, the longest running series of adventure novels in science fiction history. Starting in December 1966 with *Tarnsman of Gor*, the series was put on hold after its twenty-fifth installment, *Magicians of Gor*, in 1988, when DAW refused to publish its successor, *Witness of Gor*. After several unsuccessful attempts to find a trade publishing outlet, the series was brought back into print in 2001. Norman has also produced a separate, three installment science fiction series, the Telnarian Histories, plus two other fiction works (*Ghost Dance* and *Time Slave*), a nonfiction paperback (*Imaginative Sex*), and a collection of thirty short stories, entitled Norman *Invasions*. The *Totems of Abydos* was published in spring 2012.

All of Norman's work is available both in print and as ebooks. The Internet has proven to be a fertile ground for the imagination of Norman's ever-growing fan base, and at Gor Chronicles (www.gorchronicles.com), a website specially created for his tremendous fan following, one may read everything there is to know about this unique fictional culture.

Norman is married and has three children.